Praise for *Life Time*

"A welcome collection by a master of Eng
written."

—Kirkus

"Highly recommended; these powerful and serious stories span the career to date of a critically acclaimed, prize-winning author. . . . The themes in these pieces include political activism, race relations, love, family and relationships, remembrances of times past, the notion of home and being transplanted elsewhere, everyday life, and much more. . . . Gordimer's characters and situations are complex and multifaceted, and it is a testament to her literary skill that she can pack so much depth of meaning into each story."

—*Library Journal*

"For those new to Gordimer, *Life Times* is a marvelous introduction to her writing. For those who know her work, it is a worthy reminder of the enduring power of her art. . . . What ultimately makes Gordimer's stories matter is her extraordinary ability to get beneath our skin, forcing us to acknowledge our own uncomfortable fellowship with her humanly flawed characters."

—*BookPage*

"[Gordimer] is incredibly gifted at revealing the most subtle character details. . . . These stories offer a fascinating portrait of contemporary South Africa. What they reveal, above all, is a writer willing to face issues of cruelty, hypocrisy, and despair, and refusing to back down."

—*The Dallas Morning News*

"This Nobel Prize–winning South African writer is as vital and independent as she has ever been. Boundaries in her fiction and politics exist to be challenged. . . . In her work, as in her life, [Gordimer] recognizes all the compelling reasons for despair that there are in the world and refuses to be intimidated."

—*The Telegraph* (London)

"Daring . . . Gordimer's are stories of the human soul—regardless of the color of the skin it comes wrapped in. . . . [Her] writing is a humane intervention between the two factions of what seemed, at times, a hopelessly divided society. Her characters are messengers who could cross boundaries in the imagination that would have been forbidden in reality. . . . Thrilling."

—*The Independent* (London)

"[Albert] Camus's statement 'The moment when I am no longer more than a writer, I will cease to write' helps to explain the vitality of this extraordinary writer and the moral gaze she has cast—arch and rigorous—over literature and politics in the past sixty years."

—*The Guardian* (London)

ABOUT THE AUTHOR

Nadine Gordimer's fourteen novels include *The Conservationist*, joint winner of the Booker Prize, *Burger's Daughter*, *July's People*, *The Pickup*, *A Sport of Nature*, and *Get a Life*, all available from Penguin. Her nine collections of short stories include *Loot*, and, most recently, *Beethoven Was One-Sixteenth Black*, also available from Penguin. She has collected and edited *Telling Tales*, an anthology published in fourteen languages whose royalties go to HIV/AIDS organizations. In 1991 she was awarded the Nobel Prize in Literature. She lives in Johannesburg, South Africa.

LIFE TIMES

Stories

NADINE GORDIMER

PENGUIN BOOKS

PENGUIN BOOKS

Published by the Penguin Group
Penguin Group (USA) Inc., 375 Hudson Street, New York, New York 10014, U.S.A.
Penguin Group (Canada), 90 Eglinton Avenue East, Suite 700, Toronto,
Ontario, Canada M4P 2Y3 (a division of Pearson Penguin Canada Inc.)
Penguin Books Ltd, 80 Strand, London WC2R 0RL, England
Penguin Ireland, 25 St Stephen's Green, Dublin 2, Ireland (a division of Penguin Books Ltd)
Penguin Group (Australia), 250 Camberwell Road, Camberwell,
Victoria 3124, Australia (a division of Pearson Australia Group Pty Ltd)
Penguin Books India Pvt Ltd, 11 Community Centre, Panchsheel Park, New Delhi – 110 017, India
Penguin Group (NZ), 67 Apollo Drive, Rosedale, Auckland 0632,
New Zealand (a division of Pearson New Zealand Ltd)
Penguin Books (South Africa) (Pty) Ltd, 24 Sturdee Avenue,
Rosebank, Johannesburg 2196, South Africa

Penguin Books Ltd, Registered Offices:
80 Strand, London WC2R 0RL, England

First published in Great Britain by Bloomsbury Publishing 2010
First published in the United States of America by Farrar, Straus and Giroux 2010
Published in Penguin Books 2011

1 3 5 7 9 10 8 6 4 2

THE LIBRARY OF CONGRESS HAS CATALOGED THE HARDCOVER EDITION AS FOLLOWS:
Gordimer, Nadine.
Life times: stories, 1952–2007 / Nadine Gordimer. — 1st American ed.
p. cm.
ISBN 978-0-374-27053-7 (hc.)
ISBN 978-0-14-311983-8 (pbk.)
1. South Africa—Fiction. I. Title.
PR9369.3.G6L54 2010
823'914—dc22 2010023403

Printed in the United States of America

Reinhold Cassirer

12 March 1908–17 October 2001
1 March 1953–17 October 2001

Contents

A Soldier's Embrace

Something Out There

Jump

Loot

Beethoven Was One-Sixteenth Black

Stories Since 2007

The Soft Voice of the Serpent

The Soft Voice of the Serpent

He was only twenty-six and very healthy and he was soon strong enough to be wheeled out into the garden. Like everyone else, he had great and curious faith in the garden: 'Well, soon you'll be up and able to sit out in the garden,' they said, looking at him fervently, with little understanding tilts of the head. Yes, he would be out . . . in the garden. It was a big garden enclosed in old, dark, sleek, pungent firs, and he could sit deep beneath their tiered fringes, down in the shade, far away. There was the feeling that there, in the garden, he would come to an understanding; that it would come easier there. Perhaps there was something in this of the old Eden idea; the tender human adjusting himself to himself in the soothing impersonal presence of trees and grass and earth, before going out into the stare of the world.

The very first time it was so strange; his wife was wheeling him along the gravel path in the sun and the shade, and he felt exactly as he did when he was a little boy and he used to bend and hang, looking at the world upside down, through his ankles. Everything was vast and open, the sky, the wind blowing along through the swaying, trembling greens, the flowers shaking in vehement denial. Movement . . .

A first slight wind lifted again in the slack, furled sail of himself; he felt it belly gently, so gently he could just feel it, lifting inside him.

So she wheeled him along, pushing hard and not particularly well with her thin pretty arms – but he would not for anything complain of the way she did it or suggest that the nurse might do better, for he knew that would hurt her – and when they came to a spot that he liked, she put the brake on the chair and settled him there for the morning. That was the first time and now he sat there every day. He read a lot, but his attention was arrested sometimes, quite suddenly and compellingly, by the sunken place under the rug where his leg used to be. There was his one leg, and next to it, the rug flapped loose. Then looking, he felt his leg not there; he felt it go, slowly, from the toe to the thigh. He felt that he had no leg. After a few minutes he went back to his book. He never let the realisation quite reach him; he let himself realise it physically, but he never quite let it get at *him*. He felt it pressing up, coming, coming, dark, crushing, ready to burst – but he always turned away, just in time, back to his book. That was his system; that was the way he was going to do it. He would let it come near, irresistibly near, again and again, ready to catch him alone in the garden. And again and again he would turn it back, just in time. Slowly it would become a habit, with the reassuring strength of a habit. It would become such a habit never to get to the point of realising it, *that he would never realise it*. And one day he would find that he had achieved what he wanted: *he would feel as if he had always been like that*.

Then the danger would be over, for ever.

In a week or two he did not have to read all the time; he could let himself put down the book and look about him, watching the firs part silkily as a child's fine straight hair in the wind, watching the small birds tightroping the telephone wire, watching the fat old dove trotting after his refined patrician grey women, purring with lust. His wife came and sat beside him, doing her sewing, and sometimes they spoke, but often they sat for hours, a whole morning, her movements at work small and unobtrusive as the birds', he resting his head back and looking at a blur of sky through half-closed eyes. Now and then her eye, habitually looking inwards, would catch the signal of some little happening, some point of colour in the garden, and her laugh or exclamation drawing his attention to it would suddenly clear away the silence. At eleven o'clock she would get up and put down her sewing and go into the house to fetch their tea; crunching slowly away into the sun up the path, going easily, empowered by the sun rather than her own muscles. He watched her go, easily . . . He was healing. In the static quality of his gaze, in the relaxed feeling of his mouth, in the upward-lying palm of his hand, there was annealment . . .

One day a big locust whirred dryly past her head, and she jumped up with a cry, scattering her sewing things. He laughed at her as she bent about picking them up, shuddering. She went into the house to fetch the tea, and he began to read. But presently he put down the book and, yawning, noticed a reel of pink cotton that she had missed, lying in a rose bed.

He smiled, remembering her. And then he became conscious of a curious old-mannish little face, fixed upon him in a kind of hypnotic dread. There, absolutely stilled with fear beneath his glance, crouched a very big locust. What an amusing face the thing had! A lugubrious long face, that somehow suggested a bald head, and such a glum mouth. It looked like some little person out of a Disney cartoon. It moved slightly, still looking up fearfully at him. Strange body, encased in a sort of old-fashioned creaky armour. He had never realised before what ridiculous-looking insects locusts were! Well, naturally not; they occur to one collectively, as a pest – one doesn't go around looking at their faces.

The face was certainly curiously human and even expressive, but looking at the body, he decided that the body couldn't really be called a body at all. With the face, the creature's kinship with humans ended. The body was flimsy paper stretched over a frame of matchstick, like a small boy's home-made aeroplane. And those could not be thought of as legs – the great saw-toothed back ones were like the parts of an old crane, and the front ones like – like one of her hairpins, bent in two. At that moment the creature slowly lifted up one of the front legs, and passed it tremblingly over its head, stroking the left antenna down. Just as a man might take out a handkerchief and pass it over his brow.

He began to feel enormously interested in the creature, and leaned over in his chair to see it more closely. It sensed him and beneath its stiff, plated sides, he was surprised to see the pulsations of a heart. How fast it was breathing . . . He leaned away a little, to frighten it less.

Watching it carefully, and trying to keep himself effaced from its consciousness by not moving, he became aware of some struggle going on in the thing. It seemed to gather itself together in muscular concentration: this coordinated force then passed along its body in a kind of petering tremor, and ended in a stirring along the upward shaft of the great black legs. But the locust remained where it was. Several times this wave of effort currented through it and was spent, but the next time it ended surprisingly in a few hobbling, uneven steps, undercarriage – aeroplane-like again – trailing along the earth.

Then the creature lay, fallen on its side, antennae turned stretched out towards him. It groped with its hands, feeling for a hold on the soft ground, bending its elbows and straining. With a heave, it righted itself, and as it did so, he saw – leaning forward again – what was the trouble. It was the same trouble. His own trouble. The creature had lost one leg. Only the long upward shaft of its left leg remained, with a neat round aperture where, no doubt, the other half of the leg had been jointed in.

Now as he watched the locust gather itself again and again in that concentration of muscle, spend itself again and again in a message that was so puzzlingly never obeyed, he knew exactly what the creature felt. Of course he knew that feeling! That absolute certainty that the leg was there: one had only to lift it . . . The upward shaft of the locust's leg quivered, lifted; why then couldn't he walk? He tried again. The message came; it was going, through, the leg was lifting, now it was ready – now! . . . The shaft sagged in the air, with nothing, nothing to hold it up.

He laughed and shook his head: he *knew* . . . Good Lord, *exactly* like – he called out to the house – 'Come quickly! Come and see! You've got another patient!'

'What?' she shouted. 'I'm getting tea.'

'Come and look!' he called. 'Now!'

'. . . What is it?' she said, approaching the locust distastefully.

'Your locust!' he said. She jumped away with a little shriek.

'Don't worry – it can't move. It's as harmless as I am. You must have knocked its leg off when you hit out at it!' He was laughing at her.

'Oh, I didn't!' she said reproachfully. She loathed it but she loathed to hurt, even more. 'I never even touched it! All I hit was air . . . I couldn't possibly have hit it. Not its leg off.'

'All right then. It's another locust. But it's lost its leg, anyway. You should just see it . . . It doesn't know the leg isn't there. God, I know exactly how that feels . . . I've been watching it, and honestly, it's uncanny. I can see it feels just like I do!'

She smiled at him, sideways; she seemed suddenly pleased at something. Then, recalling herself, she came forward, bent double, hands upon her hips.

'Well, if it can't move . . .' she said, hanging over it.

'Don't be frightened,' he laughed. 'Touch it.'

'Ah, the poor thing,' she said, catching her breath in compassion. 'It can't walk.'

'Don't encourage it to self-pity,' he teased her.

She looked up and laughed. 'Oh you –' she parried, assuming a frown. The locust kept its solemn silly face turned to her. 'Shame, isn't he a funny old man,' she said. 'But what will happen to him?'

'I don't know,' he said, for being in the same boat absolved him from responsibility or pity. 'Maybe he'll grow another one. Lizards grow new tails, if they lose them.'

'Oh, *lizards*,' she said. '– but not these. I'm afraid the cat'll get him.'

'Get another little chair made for him and you can wheel him out here with me.'

'Yes,' she laughed. 'Only for him it would have to be a kind of little cart, with wheels.'

'Or maybe he could be taught to use crutches. I'm sure the farmers would like to know that he was being kept active.'

'The poor old thing,' she said, bending over the locust again. And reaching back somewhere into an inquisitive childhood she picked up a thin wand of twig and prodded the locust, very gently. 'Funny thing is, it's even the same leg, the left one.' She looked round at him and smiled.

'I know,' he nodded, laughing. 'The two of us . . .' And then he shook his head and, smiling, said it again: 'The two of us.'

She was laughing and just then she flicked the twig more sharply than she meant to and at the touch of it there was a sudden flurried papery whirr, and the locust flew away.

She stood there with the stick in her hand, half afraid of it again, and appealed, unnerved as a child, 'What happened? What happened?'

There was a moment of silence.

'Don't be a fool,' he said irritably.

They had forgotten that locusts can fly.

The Amateurs

They stumbled round the Polyclinic, humpy in the dark with their props and costumes. 'A drain!' someone shouted, 'Look out!' 'Drain ahead!' They were all talking at once.

The others waiting in the car stared out at them; the driver leaned over his window: 'All right?'

They gesticulated, called out together.

'– Can't hear. Is it OK?' shouted the driver.

Peering, chins lifted over bundles, they arrived back at the car again. 'There's nobody there. It's all locked up.'

'Are you sure it was the Polyclinic?'

'Well, it's very nice, I must say!'

They stood around the car, laughing in the pleasant little adventure of being lost together.

A thin native who had been watching them suspiciously from the dusty-red wash set afloat upon the night by the one street light, came over and mumbled, 'I take you . . . You want to go inside?' He looked over his shoulder to the location gates.

'Get in,' one young girl nudged the other towards the car. Suddenly they all got in, shut the doors.

'I take you,' said the boy again, his hands deep in his pockets.

At that moment a light wavered down the road from the gates, a bicycle swooped swallow-like upon the car, a fat police-boy in uniform shone a torch. 'You in any trouble there, sir?' he roared. His knobkerrie swung from his belt.

'No, but we've come to the wrong place—'

'You having any trouble?' insisted the police-boy. The other shrank away into the light. He stood hands in pockets, shoulders hunched, looking at the car from the street light.

'We're supposed to be giving a play – concert – tonight, and we were told it would be at the Polyclinic. Now there's nobody there,' the girl called impatiently from the back seat.

'Concert, sir? It's in the Hall, sir. Just follow me.'

Taken over by officialdom, they went through the gates, saluted and stared at, and up the rutted street past the Beer Hall, into the location. Only a beer-brazen face, blinking into the car lights as they passed, laughed and called out something half-heard.

Driving along the narrow, dark streets, they peered white-faced at the windows, wanting to see what it was like. But, curiously, it seemed that although they might want to see the location, the location didn't want to see them. The rows of low two-roomed houses with their homemade tin and packing-case lean-tos and beans growing up the chicken wire, throbbed only here and there with the faint pulse of a candle; no one was to be seen. Life seemed always to be in the next street, voices singing far off and shouts, but when the car turned the corner – again, there was nobody.

The bicycle wobbled to a stop in front of them. Here was the Hall, here were lights, looking out like sore eyes in the moted air, here were people, more part of the dark than the light, standing about in straggling curiosity. Two girls in flowered headscarves stood with their arms crossed leaning against the wall of the building; some men cupped their hands over an inch of cigarette and drew with the intensity of the stub-smoker.

The amateur company climbed shrilly out of their car. They nearly hadn't arrived at all! What a story to tell! Their laughter, their common purpose, their solidarity before the multifarious separateness of the audiences they faced, generated once again that excitement that so often seized them. What a story to tell!

Inside the Hall, the audience had been seated long ago. They sat in subdued rows, the women in neat flowered prints, the men collared-and-tied, heads of pens and pencils ranged sticking out over their jacket pockets. They were a specially selected audience of schoolteachers, who, with a sprinkling of social workers, two clerks from the administrative offices, and a young girl who had matriculated, were the educated of the rows and rows of hundreds and hundreds who lived and ate and slept and talked and loved and died in the houses outside. Those others had not been asked, and were not to be admitted because they would not understand.

The ones who had been asked waited as patiently as the children they taught in their turn. When would the concert begin?

In an atmosphere of brick-dust and bright tin shavings behind the stage, the actors and actresses struggled to dress and paint their faces in a newly built small room intended to be used for the cooking of meat at location dances. The bustle and sideburns of a late-Victorian English drawing room went on; a young woman whitened her hair with talcum powder and pinned a great hat like a feathery ship upon it. A fat young man sang, with practised nasal innuendo, the latest dance-tune while he adjusted his pince-nez and covered his cheerful head with a clerical hat.

'You're not bothering with make-up?' A man in a wasp-striped waistcoat came down from the stage.

A girl looked up from her bit of mirror, face of a wax doll.

'Your ordinary street make-up'll do – they don't know the difference,' he said.

'But of course I'm making-up,' said the girl, quite disstressed. She was melting black grease paint in a teaspoon over someone's cigarette lighter.

'No need to bother with moustaches and things,' the man said to the other men. 'They won't understand the period anyway. Don't bother.'

The girl went on putting blobs of liquid grease paint on her eyelashes, holding her breath.

'I think we should do it properly,' said the young woman, complaining.

'All right, all right.' He slapped her on the bustle. 'In that case you'd better stick a bit more cotton wool in your bosom – you're not nearly pouter-pigeon enough.'

'For God's sake, can't you open the door, somebody,' asked the girl. 'It's stifling.'

The door opened upon a concrete yard; puddles glittered, one small light burned over the entrance to a men's lavatory. The night air was the strong yellow smell of old urine. Men from the street slouched in and out, and a tall slim native, dressed in the universal long-hipped suit that in the true liberalism of petty gangsterdom knows no colour bar or national exclusiveness, leaned back on his long legs, tipped back his hat, and smiled on teeth pretty as a girl's.

'I'm going to close it again,' said the fat young man grimly.

'Oh, no one's going to eat you,' said the girl, picking up her parasol.

They all went backstage, clambered about, tested the rickety steps; heard the murmur of the audience like the sea beyond the curtain.

'You'll have to move that chair a bit,' the young woman was saying, 'I can't possibly get through that small space.'

'Not with that behind you won't,' the young man chuckled fatly. 'Now remember, if you play well, we'll put it across. If you act well enough, it doesn't matter whether the audience understands what you're saying or not.'

'Of course – look at French films.'

'It's not that. It's not the difficulty of the language so much as the situations . . . The manners of a Victorian drawing room – the whole social code – how can they be expected to understand . . .' – the girl's eyes looked out behind the doll's face.

They began to chaff one another with old jokes; the clothes they wore, the slips of the tongue that twisted their lines: the gaiety of working together set them teasing and laughing. They stood waiting behind the makeshift wings, made of screens. Cleared their throats; somebody belched.

They were ready.

When would the concert begin?

The curtain screeched back on its rusty rings; the stage opened on Oscar Wilde's *The Importance of Being Earnest*.

At first there was so much to *see*; the mouths of the audience parted with pleasure at the sight of the fine ladies and gentlemen dressed with such colour and variety; the women? – gasp at them; the men? – why, laugh at them, of course. But gradually the excitement of looking became acceptance, and they began to listen, and they began not to understand. Their faces remained alight, lifted to the stage, their attention was complete, but it was the attention of mystification. They watched the players as a child watches a drunken man, attracted by his babbling and his staggering, but innocent of the spectacle's cause or indications.

The players felt this complete attention, the appeal of a great blind eye staring up at their faces, and a change began to work in them. A kind of hysteria of effort gradually took hold of them, their gestures grew broader, the women threw great brilliant smiles like flowers out into the half-dark over the footlights, the men strutted and lifted their voices. Each frowning in asides at the hamming of the other, they all felt at the same time this bubble of queerly anxious, exciting devilment of over-emphasis bursting in themselves. The cerebral acid of Oscar Wilde's love scenes was splurged out by the oglings and winks of musical comedy, as surely as a custard pie might blot the thin face of a cynic. Under the four-syllable inanities, under the mannerisms and the posturing of the play, the bewitched amateurs knocked up a recognisable human situation. Or perhaps it was the audience that found it, looking so closely, so determined, picking up a look, a word, and making something for themselves out of it.

In an alien sophistication they found there was nothing *real* for them, so they made do with the situations that are traditionally laughable and are unreal for everyone – the strict dragon of a mother, the timid lover, the disdainful young girl. When a couple of stage lovers exited behind the screens that served for wings, someone remarked to his neighbour, very jocular: 'And what do they do behind there!' Quite a large portion of the hall heard it and laughed at this joke of their own.

'Poor Oscar!' whispered the young girl, behind her hand.

'Knew it wouldn't do,' hissed the striped waistcoat.

From her position at the side of the stage the young girl kept seeing the round, shining, rapt face of an elderly schoolteacher. His head strained up towards the stage, and a wonderful, broad, entire smile never left his face. He was asleep. She watched him anxiously out of the corner of her eye, and saw that every now and then the movement of his neighbour, an unintentional jolt, would wake him up: then the smile would fall, he would taste his mouth with his tongue, and a tremble of weariness troubled his guilt. The smile would open out again: he was asleep.

After the first act, the others, the people from outside who hadn't been asked, began to come into the hall. As if what had happened between the players and the audience inside had somehow become known, given itself away into the air, so that suddenly the others felt that *they* might as well be allowed in, too. They pushed past the laconic police-boys at the door, coming in in twos and threes, barefoot, bringing a child by the hand or a small hard bundle of a baby. They sat where they could, stolidly curious, and no one dared question their right of entry, now. The audience pretended not to see them. But they were, by very right of their insolence, more demanding and critical. During the second act, when the speeches were long, they talked and passed remarks amongst themselves; a baby was allowed to wail. The schoolteachers kept their eyes on the stage, laughed obediently, tittered appreciatively, clapped in unison.

There was something else in the hall, now; not only the actors and the audience groping for each other in the blind smile of the dark and the blind dazzle of the lights; there was something that lived, that continued uncaring, on its own. On a seat on the side the players could see someone in a cap who leaned forward, eating an orange. A fat girl hung with her arm round her friend, giggling into her ear. A foot in a pointed shoe waggled in the aisle; the people from outside sat irregular as they pleased; what was all the fuss about anyway? When something amused them, they laughed as long as they liked. The laughter of the schoolteachers died away: they knew that the players were being kept waiting.

But when the curtain jerked down on the last act, the whole hall met in a sweeping excitement of applause that seemed to feed itself and to shoot off fresh bursts as a rocket keeps showering again and again as its sparks die in the sky. Applause came from their hands like a song, each pair of palms taking strength and enthusiasm from the other. The players gasped, could not catch their breath: smiling, just managed to hold their heads above the applause. It filled the hall to the brim, then sank, sank. A young woman in a black velvet headscarf got up from the front row and came slowly up on to the stage, her hands clasped. She smiled faintly at the players, swallowed. Then her voice, the strange, high, minor-keyed voice of an African girl, went out across the hall.

'Mr Mount and his company, ladies and gentlemen' – she turned to the players – 'we have tried to tell you what you have done here, for us tonight' – she paused and looked at them all, with the pride of acceptance – 'we've tried to show you, just now, with our hands and our voices what we think of this wonderful thing you have brought to us here in Athalville Location.' Slowly, she swung back to the audience: a deep, growing chant of applause rose. 'From the bottom of our hearts, we thank you, all of us here who have had the opportunity to see you, and we hope in our hearts you will come to us again *many times*. This play tonight not only made us see what people can do, even in their spare time after work, if they *try*; it's made us feel that perhaps we could try and occupy our leisure in such a way, and learn, ourselves, and also give other people pleasure – the way everyone in this whole hall tonight' – her knee bent and arm outstretched, she passed her hand over the lifted heads – 'everyone here has been made *happy*.' A warm murmur was drawn from the audience; then complete silence. The girl took three strides to the centre of the stage. 'I ask you,' she cried out, and the players felt her voice like a shock, 'is this perhaps the answer to our juvenile delinquency here in Athalville? If our young boys and girls' – her hand pointed at a brown beardless face glazed with attention – 'had something like this to do in the evenings, would so many of them be at the police station? Would we be afraid to walk out in the street? Would our mothers be crying over their children? – Or would Athalville be a better place, and the mothers and fathers full of pride? Isn't this what we need?'

The amateurs were forgotten by themselves and each other, abandoned dolls, each was alone. No one exchanged a glance. And out in front stood the girl, her arm a sharp angle, her nostrils lifted. The splash of the footlights on her black cheek caught and made a sparkle out of a single tear.

Like the crash of a crumbling building, the wild shouts of the people fell upon the stage; as the curtain jerked across, the players recollected themselves, went slowly off.

The fat young man chuckled to himself in the back of the car. 'God, what we didn't do to that play!' he laughed.

'What'd you kiss me again for?' cried the young woman in surprise. '– I didn't know what was happening. We never had a kiss there, before – and all of a sudden' – she turned excitedly to the others – 'he takes hold of me and kisses me! I didn't know what was happening!'

'They liked it,' snorted the young man. '*One* thing they understood anyway!'

'Oh, I don't know—' said someone, and seemed about to speak.

But instead there was a falling away into silence.

The girl was plucking sullenly at the feathered hat, resting on her knee. 'We cheated them; we shouldn't have done it,' she said.

'But what could we *do*?' The young woman turned shrilly, her eyes open and hard, excitedly determined to get an answer: an answer somewhere, from someone.

But there was no answer.

'We didn't know what to do,' said the fat young man uncertainly, forgetting to be funny now, the way he lost himself when he couldn't remember his lines on the stage.

Six Feet of the Country

Six Feet of the Country

My wife and I are not real farmers – not even Lerice, really. We bought our place, ten miles out of Johannesburg on one of the main roads, to change something in ourselves, I suppose; you seem to rattle about so much within a marriage like ours. You long to hear nothing but a deep satisfying silence when you sound a marriage. The farm hasn't managed that for us, of course, but it has done other things, unexpected, illogical. Lerice, who I thought would retire there in Chekhovian sadness for a month or two, and then leave the place to the servants while she tried yet again to get a part she wanted and become the actress she would like to be, has sunk into the business of running the farm with all the serious intensity with which she once imbued the shadows in a playwright's mind. I should have given it up long ago if it had not been for her. Her hands, once small and plain and well kept – she was not the sort of actress who wears red paint and diamond rings – are hard as a dog's pads.

I, of course, am there only in the evenings and on weekends. I am a partner in a luxury travel agency, which is flourishing – needs to be, as I tell Lerice, in order to carry the farm. Still, though I know we can't afford it, and though the sweetish smell of the fowls Lerice breeds sickens me, so that I avoid going past their runs, the farm is beautiful in a way I had almost forgotten – especially on a Sunday morning when I get up and go out into the paddock and see not the palm trees and fishpond and imitation-stone bird bath of the suburbs but white ducks on the dam, the lucerne field brilliant as window dresser's grass, and the little, stocky, mean-eyed bull, lustful but bored, having his face tenderly licked by one of his ladies. Lerice comes out with her hair uncombed, in her hand a stick dripping with cattle dip. She will stand and look dreamily for a moment, the way she would pretend to look sometimes in those plays.

'They'll mate tomorrow,' she will say. 'This is their second day. Look how she loves him, my little Napoleon.'

So that when people come out to see us on Sunday afternoon, I am likely to hear myself saying as I pour out the drinks, 'When I drive back home from the city every day, past those rows of suburban houses, I wonder how the devil we ever did stand it . . . Would you care to look around?'

And there I am, taking some pretty girl and her young husband stumbling down to our river bank, the girl catching her stockings on the mealie-stooks and stepping over cow turds humming with jewel-green flies while she says, '. . . the *tensions* of the damned city. And you're near enough to get into town to a show, too! I think it's wonderful. Why, you've got it both ways!'

And for a moment I accept the triumph as if I *had* managed it – the impossibility that I've been trying for all my life – just as if the truth was that you could get it 'both ways', instead of finding yourself with not even one way or the other but a third, one you had not provided for at all.

But even in our saner moments, when I find Lerice's earthy enthusiasms just as irritating as I once found her histrionical ones, and she finds what she calls my 'jealousy' of her capacity for enthusiasm as big a proof of my inadequacy for her as a mate as ever it was, we do believe that we have at least honestly escaped those tensions peculiar to the city about which our visitors speak. When Johannesburg people speak of 'tension', they don't mean hurrying people in crowded streets, the struggle for money, or the general competitive character of city life. They mean the guns under the white men's pillows and the burglar bars on the white men's windows. They mean those strange moments on city pavements when a black man won't stand aside for a white man.

Out in the country, even ten miles out, life is better than that. In the country, there is a lingering remnant of the pre-transitional stage; our relationship with the blacks is almost feudal. Wrong, I suppose, obsolete, but more comfortable all around. We have no burglar bars, no gun. Lerice's farm boys have their wives and their piccanins living with them on the land. They brew their sour beer without the fear of police raids. In fact, we've always rather prided ourselves that the poor devils have nothing much to fear, being with us; Lerice even keeps an eye on their children, with all the competence of a woman who has never had a child of her own, and she certainly doctors them all – children and adults – like babies whenever they happen to be sick.

It was because of this that we were not particularly startled one night last winter when the boy Albert came knocking at our window long after we had gone to bed. I wasn't in our bed but sleeping in the little dressing-room-*cum*-linen-room next door, because Lerice had annoyed me and I didn't want to find myself softening towards her simply because of the sweet smell of the talcum powder on her flesh after her bath. She came and woke me up. 'Albert says one of the boys is very sick,' she said. 'I think you'd better go down and see. He wouldn't get us up at this hour for nothing.'

'What time is it?'

'What does it matter?' Lerice is maddeningly logical.

I got up awkwardly as she watched me – how is it I always feel a fool when I have deserted her bed? After all, I know from the way she never looks at me when she talks to me at breakfast the next day that she is hurt and humiliated at my not wanting her – and I went out, clumsy with sleep.

'Which of the boys is it?' I asked Albert as we followed the dance of my torch.

'He's too sick. Very sick, baas,' he said.

'But who? Franz?' I remembered Franz had had a bad cough for the past week.

Albert did not answer; he had given me the path, and was walking along beside me in the tall dead grass. When the light of the torch caught his face, I saw that he looked acutely embarrassed. 'What's this all about?' I said.

He lowered his head under the glance of the light. 'It's not me, baas. I don't know. Petrus he send me.'

Irritated, I hurried him along to the huts. And there, on Petrus's iron bedstead, with its brick stilts, was a young man, dead. On his forehead there was still a light, cold sweat; his body was warm. The boys stood around as they do in the kitchen when it is discovered that someone has broken a dish – uncooperative, silent. Somebody's wife hung about in the shadows, her hands wrung together under her apron.

I had not seen a dead man since the war. This was very different. I felt like the others – extraneous, useless. 'What was the matter?' I asked.

The woman patted at her chest and shook her head to indicate the painful impossibility of breathing.

He must have died of pneumonia.

I turned to Petrus. 'Who was this boy? What was he doing here?' The light of a candle on the floor showed that Petrus was weeping. He followed me out the door.

When we were outside, in the dark, I waited for him to speak. But he didn't. 'Now, come on, Petrus, you must tell me who this boy was. Was he a friend of yours?'

'He's my brother, baas. He came from Rhodesia to look for work.'

The story startled Lerice and me a little. The young boy had walked down from Rhodesia to look for work in Johannesburg, had caught a chill from sleeping out along the way, and had lain ill in his brother Petrus's hut since his arrival three days before. Our boys had been frightened to ask us for help for him because we had never been intended ever to know of his presence. Rhodesian natives are barred from entering the Union unless they have a permit; the young man was an illegal immigrant. No doubt our boys had managed the whole thing successfully several times before; a number of relatives must have walked the seven or eight hundred miles from poverty to the paradise of zoot suits, police raids and black slum townships that is their Egoli, City of Gold – the Bantu name for Johannesburg. It was merely a matter of getting such a man to lie low on our farm until a job could be found with someone who would be glad to take the risk of prosecution for employing an illegal immigrant in exchange for the services of someone as yet untainted by the city.

Well, this was one who would never get up again.

'You would think they would have felt they could tell *us*,' said Lerice next morning. 'Once the man was ill. You would have thought at least—' When she is getting intense over something, she has a way of standing in the middle of a room as people do when they are shortly to leave on a journey, looking searchingly about her at the most familiar objects as if she had never seen them before. I had noticed that in Petrus's presence in the kitchen, earlier, she had had the air of being almost offended with him, almost hurt.

In any case, I really haven't the time or inclination any more to go into everything in our life that I know Lerice, from those alarmed and pressing eyes of hers, would like us to go into. She is the kind of woman who doesn't mind if she looks plain, or odd; I don't suppose she would even care if she knew how strange she looks when her whole face is out of proportion with urgent uncertainty. I said, 'Now I'm the one who'll have to do all the dirty work, I suppose.'

She was still staring at me, trying me out with those eyes – wasting her time, if she only knew.

'I'll have to notify the health authorities,' I said calmly. 'They can't just cart him off and bury him. After all, we don't really know what he died of.'

She simply stood there, as if she had given up – simply ceased to see me at all.

I don't know when I've been so irritated. 'It might have been something contagious,' I said. 'God knows.' There was no answer.

I am not enamoured of holding conversations with myself. I went out to shout to one of the boys to open the garage and get the car ready for my morning drive to town.

As I had expected, it turned out to be quite a business. I had to notify the police as well as the health authorities, and answer a lot of tedious questions: how was it I was ignorant of the boy's presence? If I did not supervise my native quarters, how did I know that that sort of thing didn't go on all the time? Etcetera, etcetera. And when I flared up and told them that so long as my natives did their work, I didn't think it my right or concern to poke my nose into their private lives,

I got from the coarse, dull-witted police sergeant one of those looks that come not from any thinking process going on in the brain but from that faculty common to all who are possessed by the master-race theory – a look of insanely inane certainty. He grinned at me with a mixture of scorn and delight at my stupidity.

Then I had to explain to Petrus why the health authorities had to take away the body for a post-mortem – and, in fact, what a post-mortem was. When I telephoned the health department some days later to find out the result, I was told that the cause of death was, as we had thought, pneumonia, and that the body had been suitably disposed of. I went out to where Petrus was mixing a mash for the fowls and told him that it was all right, there would be no trouble; his brother had died from that pain in his chest. Petrus put down the paraffin tin and said, 'When can we go to fetch him, baas?'

'To fetch him?'

'Will the baas please ask them when we must come?'

I went back inside and called Lerice, all over the house. She came down the stairs from the spare bedrooms, and I said, '*Now* what am I going to do? When I told Petrus, he just asked calmly when they could go and fetch the body. They think they're going to bury him themselves.'

'Well, go back and tell him,' said Lerice. 'You must tell him. Why didn't you tell him then?'

When I found Petrus again, he looked up politely. 'Look, Petrus,' I said. 'You can't go to fetch your brother. They've done it already – they've *buried* him, you understand?'

'Where?' he said slowly, dully, as if he thought that perhaps he was getting this wrong.

'You see, he was a stranger. They knew he wasn't from here, and they didn't know he had some of his people here so they thought they must bury him.' It was difficult to make a pauper's grave sound like a privilege.

'Please, baas, the baas must ask them.' But he did not mean that he wanted to know the burial place. He simply ignored the incomprehensible machinery I told him had set to work on his dead brother; he wanted the brother back.

'But, Petrus,' I said, 'how can I? Your brother is buried already. I can't ask them now.'

'Oh, baas!' he said. He stood with his bran-smeared hands uncurled at his sides, one corner of his mouth twitching.

'Good God, Petrus, they won't listen to me! They can't, anyway. I'm sorry, but I can't do it. You understand?'

He just kept on looking at me, out of his knowledge that white men have everything, can do anything; if they don't, it is because they won't.

And then, at dinner, Lerice started. 'You could at least phone,' she said.

'Christ, what d'you think I am? Am I supposed to bring the dead back to life?'

But I could not exaggerate my way out of this ridiculous responsibility that had been thrust on me. 'Phone them up,' she went on. 'And at least you'll be able to tell him you've done it and they've explained that it's impossible.'

She disappeared somewhere into the kitchen quarters after coffee. A little later she came back to tell me, 'The old father's coming down from Rhodesia to be at the funeral. He's got a permit and he's already on his way.'

Unfortunately, it was not impossible to get the body back. The authorities said that it was somewhat irregular, but that since the hygiene conditions had been fulfilled, they could not refuse permission for exhumation. I found out that, with the undertaker's charges, it would cost twenty pounds. Ah, I thought, that settles it. On five pounds a month, Petrus won't have twenty pounds – and just as well, since it couldn't do the dead any good. Certainly I should not offer it to him myself. Twenty pounds – or anything else within reason, for that matter – I would have spent without grudging it on doctors or medicines that might have helped the boy when he was alive. Once he was dead, I had no intention of encouraging Petrus to throw away, on a gesture, more than he spent to clothe his whole family in a year.

When I told him, in the kitchen that night, he said, 'Twenty pounds?'

I said, 'Yes, that's right, twenty pounds.'

For a moment, I had the feeling, from the look on his face, that he was calculating. But when he spoke again I thought I must have imagined it. 'We must pay twenty pounds!' he said in the faraway voice in which a person speaks of something so unattainable that it does not bear thinking about.

'All right, Petrus,' I said, and went back to the living room.

The next morning before I went to town, Petrus asked to see me. 'Please, baas,' he said, awkwardly handing me a bundle of notes. They're so seldom on the giving rather than the receiving side, poor devils, that they don't really know how to hand money to a white man. There it was, the twenty pounds, in ones and halves, some creased and folded until they were soft as dirty rags, others smooth and fairly new – Franz's money, I suppose, and Albert's, and Dora the cook's, and Jacob the gardener's, and God knows who else's besides, from all the farms and smallholdings round about. I took it in irritation more than in astonishment, really – irritation at the waste, the uselessness of this sacrifice by people so poor. Just like the poor everywhere, I thought, who stint themselves the decencies of life in order to insure themselves the decencies of death. So incomprehensible to people like Lerice and me, who regard life as something to be spent extravagantly and, if we think about death at all, regard it as the final bankruptcy.

The servants don't work on Saturday afternoon anyway, so it was a good day for the funeral. Petrus and his father had borrowed our donkey cart to fetch the coffin from the city, where, Petrus told Lerice on their return, everything was 'nice' – the coffin waiting for them, already sealed up to save them from what must have been a rather unpleasant sight after two weeks' interment. (It had taken all that time for the authorities and the undertaker to make the final arrangements for moving the body.) All morning, the coffin lay in Petrus's hut, awaiting the trip to the little old burial ground, just outside the eastern boundary of our farm, that was a relic of the days when this was a real farming district rather than a fashionable rural estate. It was pure chance that I happened to be down there near the fence when the procession came past; once again Lerice had forgotten her promise to me and had made the house uninhabitable on a Saturday afternoon. I had come home and been infuriated to find her in a pair of filthy old slacks and with her hair uncombed since the night before, having all the varnish scraped off the living-room floor, if you please. So I had taken my No. 8 iron and gone off to practise my approach shots. In my annoyance, I had forgotten about the funeral, and was reminded only when I saw the procession coming up the path along the outside of the fence towards me; from where I was standing, you can see the graves quite clearly, and that day the sun glinted on bits of broken pottery, a lopsided homemade cross, and jam jars brown with rain water and dead flowers.

I felt a little awkward, and did not know whether to go on hitting my golf ball or stop at least until the whole gathering was decently past. The donkey cart creaks and screeches with every revolution of the wheels, and it came along in a slow, halting fashion somehow peculiarly suited to the two donkeys who drew it, their little potbellies rubbed and rough, their heads sunk between the shafts, and their ears flattened back with an air submissive and downcast; peculiarly suited, too, to the group of men and women who came along slowly behind. The patient ass. Watching, I thought, you can see now why the creature became a biblical symbol. Then the procession drew level with me and stopped, so I had to put down my club. The coffin was taken down off the cart – it was a shiny, yellow-varnished wood, like cheap furniture – and the donkeys twitched their ears against the flies. Petrus, Franz, Albert and the old father from Rhodesia hoisted it on their shoulders and the procession moved on, on foot. It was really a very awkward moment. I stood there rather foolishly at the fence, quite still, and slowly they filed past, not looking up, the four men bent beneath the shiny wooden box, and the straggling troop of mourners. All of them were servants or neighbours' servants whom I knew as casual, easygoing gossipers about our lands or kitchen. I heard the old man's breathing.

I had just bent to pick up my club again when there was a sort of jar in the flowing solemnity of their processional mood; I felt it at once, like a wave of heat along the air, or one of those sudden currents of cold catching at your legs in a placid stream. The old man's voice was muttering something; the people had stopped, confused, and they bumped into one another, some pressing to go on, others hissing them to be still. I could see that they were embarrassed, but they could not ignore the voice; it was much the way that the mumblings of a prophet, though not clear at first, arrest the mind. The corner of the coffin the old man carried was sagging at an angle; he seemed to be trying to get out from under the weight of it. Now Petrus expostulated with him.

The little boy who had been left to watch the donkeys dropped the reins and ran to see. I don't know why – unless it was for the same reason people crowd around someone who has fainted in a cinema – but I parted the wires of the fence and went through, after him.

Petrus lifted his eyes to me – to anybody – with distress and horror. The old man from Rhodesia had let go of the coffin entirely, and the three others, unable to support it on their own, had laid it on the ground, in the pathway. Already there was a film of dust lightly wavering up its shiny sides. I did not understand what the old man was saying; I hesitated to interfere. But now the whole seething group turned on my silence. The old man himself came over to me, with his hands outspread and shaking, and spoke directly to me, saying something that I could tell from the tone, without understanding the words, was shocking and extraordinary.

'What is it, Petrus? What's wrong?' I appealed.

Petrus threw up his hands, bowed his head in a series of hysterical shakes, then thrust his face up at me suddenly. 'He says, "My son was not so heavy."'

Silence. I could hear the old man breathing; he kept his mouth a little open, as old people do.

'My son was young and thin,' he said at last, in English.

Again silence. Then babble broke out. The old man thundered against everybody; his teeth were yellowed and few, and he had one of those fine, grizzled, sweeping moustaches that one doesn't often see nowadays, which must have been grown in emulation of early Empire builders. It seemed to frame all his utterances with a special validity, perhaps merely because it was the symbol of the traditional wisdom of age – an idea so fearfully rooted that it carries still something awesome beyond reason. He shocked them; they thought he was mad, but they had to listen to him. With his own hands he began to prise the lid off the coffin and three of the men came forward to help him. Then he sat down on the ground; very old, very weak, and unable to speak, he merely lifted a trembling hand towards what was there. He abdicated, he handed it over to them; he was no good any more.

They crowded round to look (and so did I), and now they forgot the nature of this surprise and the occasion of grief to which it belonged, and for a few minutes were carried up in the delightful astonishment of the surprise itself. They gasped and flared noisily with excitement. I even noticed the little boy who had held the donkeys jumping up and down, almost weeping with rage because the backs of the grown-ups crowded him out of his view.

In the coffin was someone no one had ever seen before: a heavily built, rather light-skinned native with a neatly stitched scar on his forehead – perhaps from a blow in a brawl that had also dealt him some other, slower-working injury, which had killed him.

I wrangled with the authorities for a week over that body. I had the feeling that they were shocked, in a laconic fashion, by their own mistake, but that in the confusion of their anonymous dead they were helpless to put it right. They said to me, 'We are trying to find out,' and 'We are still making inquiries.' It was as if at any moment they might conduct me into their mortuary and say, 'There! Lift up the sheets; look for him – your poultry boy's brother. There are so many black faces – surely one will do?'

And every evening when I got home, Petrus was waiting in the kitchen. 'Well, they're trying. They're still looking. The baas is seeing to it for you, Petrus,' I would tell him. 'God, half the time I should be in the office I'm driving around the back end of the town chasing after this affair,' I added aside, to Lerice, one night.

She and Petrus both kept their eyes turned on me as I spoke, and, oddly, for those moments they looked exactly alike, though it sounds impossible: my wife, with her high, white forehead and her attenuated Englishwoman's body, and the poultry boy, with his horny bare feet below khaki trousers tied at the knee with string and the peculiar rankness of his nervous sweat coming from his skin.

'What makes you so indignant, so determined about this now?' said Lerice suddenly.

I stared at her. 'It's a matter of principle. Why should they get away with a swindle? It's time these officials had a jolt from someone who'll bother to take the trouble.'

She said, 'Oh.' And as Petrus slowly opened the kitchen door to leave, sensing that the talk had gone beyond him, she turned away, too.

I continued to pass on assurances to Petrus every evening, but although what I said was the same and the voice in which I said it was the same, every evening it sounded weaker. At last, it became clear that we would never get Petrus's brother back, because nobody really knew where he was. Somewhere in a graveyard as uniform as a housing scheme, somewhere under a number that didn't belong to him, or in the medical school, perhaps, laboriously reduced to layers of muscle and strings of nerve? Goodness knows. He had no identity in this world anyway.

It was only then, and in a voice of shame, that Petrus asked me to try and get the money back.

'From the way he asks, you'd think he was robbing his dead brother,' I said to Lerice later. But as I've said, Lerice had got so intense about this business that she couldn't even appreciate a little ironic smile.

I tried to get the money; Lerice tried. We both telephoned and wrote and argued, but nothing came of it. It appeared that the main expense had been the undertaker, and after all he had done his job. So the whole thing was a complete waste, even more of a waste for the poor devils than I had thought it would be.

The old man from Rhodesia was about Lerice's father's size, so she gave him one of her father's old suits, and he went back home rather better off, for the winter, than he had come.

Face from Atlantis

Somehow it wasn't altogether a surprise when Waldeck Brand and his wife bumped into Carlitta at a theatre in New York in 1953. The Brands were six thousand miles away from their home in South Africa, and everywhere they had visited in England and Europe before they came to America they had met Waldeck's contemporaries from Heidelberg whom he hadn't seen for twenty years and never had expected to see ever again. It had seemed a miracle to Waldeck that all these people, who had had to leave Germany because they were liberals (like himself), or Jews, or both, not only had survived transplantation but had thrived, and not only had thrived but had managed to do so each in the manner and custom of the country which had given him sanctuary.

Of course, Waldeck Brand did not think it a miracle that *he* had survived and conformed to a pattern of life lived at the other end of the world to which he had belonged. (Perhaps it is true, after all, that no man can believe in the possibility of his own failure or death.) It seemed quite natural that the gay young man destined primarily for a good time and, secondly, for the inheritance of his wealthy father's publishing house in Berlin should have become a director of an important group of gold mines in southernmost Africa, a world away from medieval German university towns where he had marched at the head of the student socialist group, and the Swiss Alps where he had skied and shared his log cabin with a different free-thinking girl every winter, and the Kurfürstendamm where he had strolled with his friends, wearing elegant clothes specially ordered from England. Yet to him – and to his South African wife, who had been born and had spent the twenty-seven years of her life in Cape Town, looking out, often and often, over the sea which she had now crossed for the first time – it was a small miracle that his Heidelberg friend, Siggie Bentheim, was to be found at the foreign editor's desk of a famous right-of-centre newspaper in London, and another university friend, Stefan Rosovsky, now become Stefan Raines, was president of a public utility company in New York and had a finger or two dipped comfortably in oil, too. To Waldeck, Siggie was the leader of a Communist cell, an ugly little chap, best student in the Institut fur Sozialwissenschaften, whose tiny hands were dry-skinned and shrunken, as if political fervour had used up his blood like fuel. Stefan was the soulful-eyed Russian boy with the soft voice and the calm delivery of dry wit who tutored in economics and obviously was fitted for nothing but an academic career as an economist.

And to Eileen, Waldeck Brand's wife, both were people who lived, changeless, young, enviable, in a world that existed only in Waldeck's three green leather photograph albums. Siggie was the one who sat reading the *Arbeiterpolitik*, oblivious of the fact that a picture was being taken, in the photograph where a whole dim, underexposed room (Waldeck's at Heidelberg) was full of students. Eileen had been to a university in South Africa, but she had never seen students like that: such good-looking, happy, bold-eyed boys, such beautiful girls, smoking cigarettes in long holders and stretching out their legs in pointed-toed shoes beneath their short skirts. Someone was playing a guitar in that picture. But Siggie Bentheim (you could notice those hands, around the edges of the pages) read a paper.

Stefan was not in that picture, but in dozens of others. In particular, there was one taken in Budapest. A flashlight picture, taken in a night club. Stefan holds up a glass of champagne, resigned in his dinner suit, dignified in a silly paper cap. New Year in Budapest, before Hitler, before the war. Can you imagine it? Eileen was fascinated by those photograph albums and those faces. Since she had met and married Waldeck in 1952, she had spent many hours looking at the albums. When she did so, a great yawning envy opened through her whole body. She was young, and the people pictured in those albums were all, even if they were alive, over forty by now. But that did not matter; that did not count. That world of the photograph albums was not lost only by those who had outgrown it into middle age. It was *lost*. Gone. It did not belong to a new youth. It was not hers, although she was young. It was *no use* being young, now, in the forties and fifties. She thought of the green albums as the record of an Atlantis.

Waldeck had never been back to Europe since he came as a refugee to South Africa twenty years before. He had not kept up a regular correspondence with his scattered student friends, though one or two had written, at intervals of four or five years, and so for some, when Waldeck took his wife to Europe and America, he had the address-before-the-last, and for others the vaguest ideas of their whereabouts. Yet he found them all, or they found him. It was astonishing. The letters he wrote to old addresses were forwarded; the friends whom he saw knew where other friends lived, or at least what jobs they were doing, so that they could be traced that way, simply by a telephone call. In London there were dinner parties and plain drinking parties, and there they were – the faces from Atlantis, gathered together in a Strand pub. One of the women was a grandmother; most of the men were no longer married to women Waldeck remembered them marrying, and had shed their old political faiths along with their hair. But all were alive, and living variously, and in them was still the peculiar vigour that showed vividly in those faces, caught in the act of life long ago, in the photograph albums.

Once or twice in London, Waldeck had asked one old friend or another, 'What happened to Carlitta? Does anyone know where Carlitta is?'

Siggie Bentheim, eating Scotch salmon at Rules, like any other English journalist who can afford to, couldn't remember Carlitta. Who was she? Then Waldeck remembered that the year when everyone got to know Carlitta was the year that Siggie spent in Lausanne.

Another old friend remembered her very well. 'Carlitta! Not in England, at any rate. Carlitta!'

Someone else caught the name, and called across the table, 'Carlitta was in London, oh, before the war. She went to America thirteen or fourteen years ago.'

'Did she ever marry poor old Klaus Schultz? My God, he was mad about the girl!'

'Marry him! No-o-o! Carlitta wouldn't marry him.'

'Carlitta was a collector of scalps, all right,' said Waldeck, laughing.

'Well, do you wonder?' said the friend.

Eileen knew Carlitta well, in picture and anecdote. Eileen had a favourite among the photographs of her, too, just as she had the one of Stefan in Budapest on New Year's Eve. The photograph was taken in Austria, on one of Waldeck's skiing holidays. It was a clear print and the snow was blindingly white. In the middle of the whiteness stood a young girl, laughing away from the camera in the direction of something or someone outside the picture. Her little face, burnished by the sun, shone dark against the snow. There was a highlight on each firm, round cheekbone, accentuated in laughter. She was beautiful in the pictures of groups, too – in boats on the Neckar, in the gardens of the Schloss, in cafés and at student dances; even, once, at Deauville, even in the unbecoming bathing dress of the time. In none of the pictures did she face the camera. If, as in the ski picture, she was smiling, it was at someone in the group, and if she was not, her black pensive eyes, her beautiful little firm-fleshed face with the short chin, stared at the toes of her shoes, or at the smoke of her cigarette, arrested in its climbing arabesque by the click of the camera. The total impression of all these photographs of the young German girl was one of arrogance. She did not participate in the taking of a photograph; she was simply there, a thing of beauty which you could attempt to record if you wished.

One of the anecdotes about the girl was something that had happened on that skiing holiday. Carlitta and Klaus Schultz, Waldeck and one of his girls had gone together to the mountains. ('Oh, the luck of it!' Eileen had said to Waldeck at this point in his story, the first time he related it. 'You were eighteen? Nineteen?

And you were allowed to go off on your first love affair to the mountains. Can you imagine what would have happened if I had announced to my parents that I was going off on a holiday with a young lover? And in Austria, and skiing . . .' Poor Eileen, who had gone, every year, on a five-day cruise along the coast to stay at a 'family hotel' in Durban, accompanied by her parents and young brother and sister, or had been sent, in the winter vacation, with an uncle and cousins to hear the lions roar outside a dusty camp in the Kruger Park. She did not know which to envy Waldeck, Carlitta and Klaus most – the sexual freedom or the steep mountain snows.) Anyway, it was on the one really long and arduous climb of that delightful holiday that Carlitta, who for some hours had been less talkative than usual and had fallen back a little, sat down in the snow and refused to move. Waldeck had lagged behind the rest of the party to mend a broken strap on his rucksack, and so it was that he noticed her. When he asked her why she did not hurry on with him to catch up with the other members of the party, she said, perfectly calm, 'I want to sit here in the shade and rest. I'll wait here till you all come back.'

There was no shade. The party intended to sleep in a rest hut up the mountain, and would not pass that way again till next day. At first Waldeck laughed; Carlitta was famous for her gaiety and caprice. Then he saw that in addition to being perfectly calm, Carlitta was also perfectly serious. She was not joking, but suffering from some kind of peculiar hysteria. He begged and begged her to get up, but she would not. 'I am going to rest in the shade' was all she would answer.

The rest of the party was out of sight and he began to feel nervous. There was only one thing he could try. He went up kindly to the beautiful little girl and struck her sharply, twice, in the face. The small head swung violently this way, then that. Carlitta got up, dusted the snow from her trousers, and said to Waldeck, 'For God's sake, what are we waiting for? The others must be miles ahead.'

'And when Klaus heard what had happened,' Waldeck's story always ended, 'he could scarcely keep himself from crying, he was so angry that *he* had not been the one to revive Carlitta, and Carlitta saw his nose pinken and swell slightly with the effort of keeping back the tears, and she noted how very much he must be in love with her and how easy it would be to torment him.'

Wretched Klaus! He was the blond boy with the square jaw who always frowned and smiled directly into the camera. Eileen had a theory that young people didn't even fall in love like that any more. That, too, had gone down under the waves.

Waldeck and his young wife arrived in New York on a Tuesday. Stefan Raines came to take them out to dinner that very first night. Eileen, who had never seen him before in her life, was even more overjoyed than Waldeck to find that he had not changed. As soon as they came out of the elevator and saw him standing in the hotel lobby with a muffler hanging down untied on the lapels of his dark coat, they knew he had not changed. He wore the presidency of the public utility company, the wealth and the Fifth Avenue apartment just as he had worn the paper cap in the Budapest night club on New Year's Eve long ago. Stefan's American wife was not able to accompany them that night, so the three dined alone at the Pierre. After dinner Stefan wanted to know if he should drive them to Times Square and along Broadway or anywhere else they'd read about, but they told him that he was the only sight they wanted to see so soon after their arrival. They talked for two hours over dinner, Stefan asking and Waldeck answering eager questions about the old Heidelberg friends whom Waldeck and Eileen had seen in London. Stefan went to London sometimes, and he had seen one or two, but many whom he hadn't been able to find for years seemed to have appeared out of their hiding places for Waldeck. In fact, there were several old Berlin and Heidelberg friends living in New York whom Stefan had seen once, or not at all, but who, on the Brands' first day in New York, had already telephoned their hotel. 'We love Waldeck. Better than we love each other,' said Stefan to his friend's wife, his black eyes looking quietly out over the room, the corners of his mouth indenting in his serious smile that took a long time to open out, brightening his eyes as it did until they shone like the dark water beneath a lamplight on a Venetian canal where Eileen had stood with her husband a few weeks before.

Eileen seemed to feel her blood warm in the palms of her hands, as if some balm had been poured over them. No man in South Africa could say a thing like that! The right thing, the thing from the heart. You had to have the assurance of Europe, of an old world of civilised human relationships behind you before you could say, simply and truthfully, a thing like that.

It was the moment for the mood of the conversation to take a turn. Waldeck said curiously, suddenly remembering, 'And whatever became of Carlitta? Did you ever see Carlitta? Peter told me, in London, that she had come to live in America.'

'Now that's interesting that you should ask,' said Stefan. 'I've wondered about her, too. I saw her once, twelve – more – thirteen years back. When first she arrived in America. She was staying quite near the hotel where you're living now. I took her out to lunch – not very sumptuous; I was rather poor at the time – and I never saw her again. She was beautiful. You remember? She was always beautiful—' he crinkled his eyes to dark slits, as if to narrow down the aperture of memory upon her – 'even in a bad restaurant in New York, she was – well, the word my son would use is the best for her – she was terrific. Minute and terrific.'

'That's it. That's it.' Waldeck spoke around the cigar he held between his teeth, trying to draw up a light.

'We adored her,' said Stefan, shaking his head slowly at the wonder of it.

'So you too, Stefan, you too?' said Eileen with a laugh.

'Oh, none of us was in love with Carlitta. Only Klaus, and he was too stupid. He doesn't count. We only adored. We knew it was useless to fall in love with her. Neither she nor we believed any one of us was good enough for her.'

'So you don't think she's in New York?' asked Waldeck.

Stefan shook his head. 'I did hear, from someone who knew her sister, that she had married an American and gone to live in Ohio.' He stopped and chuckled congestedly. 'Carlitta in Ohio. I don't believe it . . . Well, we should move along from here now, you know. Sure there isn't *anywhere* you'd like to go before bedtime?'

The girl from South Africa remembered that one of the things she'd always wanted to do if ever she came to New York was to hear a really fat Negro woman singing torch songs, so Stefan took them to a place where the air-conditioning apparatus kept the fog of smoke and perfume and liquor fumes moving around the tables while an enormous yellow blubber of a woman accompanied her own voice, quakingly with her flesh and thunderously on the piano.

It was only two nights later that Eileen came out of the ladies' room to join her husband in a theatre foyer during the interval and found him embracing a woman in a brown coat. As Waldeck held the woman away from him, by the shoulders, as if to take a good look at her after he had kissed her, Eileen saw a small face with a wide grin and really enormous eyes. As Eileen approached she noticed a tall, sandy-haired man standing by indulgently. When she reached the three, Waldeck turned to her with the pent-up, excited air he always had when he had secretly bought her a present, and he held out his hand to draw her into the company. In the moment before he spoke, Eileen felt a stir of recognition at the sight of the woman's hair, smooth brown hair in which here and there a grey filament of a coarser texture showed, refusing to conform to the classic style, centre-parted and drawn back in a bun, in which the hair was worn.

'Do you know who this is?' said Waldeck almost weakly. 'It's Carlitta.'

Eileen was entitled to a second or two in which to be taken aback, to be speechless in the face of coincidence. In that moment, however, the coincidence did not even occur to her; she simply took in, in an intense perception outside of time, the woman before her – the brown coat open to show the collar of some nondescript silk caught together with a little brooch around the prominent tendons of the thin, creased neck; the flat, taut chest; the dowdy shoes with brown, punched-leather bows coming too high on the instep of what might have been elegant feet. And the head. Oh, that was the head she had seen before, all right; that was the head that, hair so sleek it looked like a satin turban, inclined with a mixture of coquetry, invitation, amusement and disdain towards a ridiculously long cigarette holder. That hair was brown, after all, and not the Spanish black of the photographs and imagination. And the face. Well, there is a stage in a woman's life when her face gets too thin or too fat. This face had reached that stage and become too thin. It was a prettily enough shaped face, with a drab, faded skin, as if it was exposed to but no longer joyously took colour from the sun. Towards the back of the jaw line, near the ears, the skin sagged sallowly. Under the rather thick, attractive brows the twin caves of the eyes were finely puckered and mauvish. In this faded, fading face (it was like an old painting of which you are conscious that it is being faded away by the very light by which you are enabled to look at it) the eyes had lost nothing; they shone on, greedily and tremendous, just as they had always been, in the snow, reflecting the Neckar, watching the smoke unfurl to the music of the guitar. They were round eyes with scarcely any white to them, like the beautiful eyes of Negro children, and the lashes, lower as well as upper, were black and thick. Their assertion in that face was rather awful.

The woman who Waldeck said was Carlitta took Eileen's hand. 'Isn't it fantastic? We're only up from Ohio this morning,' she said, smiling broadly. Her teeth were small, childishly square and still good. On her neglected face the lipstick was obviously a last-minute adornment.

'And this is Edgar,' Waldeck was saying, 'Edgar Hicks. Carlitta's husband.'

The tall, sandy-haired man shook Eileen's hand with as much flourish as a stage comedian. 'Glad to know you,' he said. Eileen saw that he wore hexagonal rimless glasses, and a clip across his tie spelled in pinkish synthetic gold 'E.J.H.'

'Carlitta Hicks—' Waldeck put out a hand and squeezed Carlitta's elbow. 'I can't believe it.'

'Sure is extraordinary,' said Mr Hicks. 'Carlitta here and I haven't been up to New York for more than three years.'

'*Ach*, no, darling,' said Carlitta, frowning and smiling quickly. She used her face so much, no wonder she had worn it out. 'Four at least. You remember, that last time was at Christmas.' She added to Waldeck, 'Once in a blue moon is enough for me. Our life . . .' She half lifted a worn hand, gave a little sudden intake of breath through her fine nostrils, as if to suggest that their life, whatever it was, was such that the pleasures of New York or anywhere else offered no rival enticement. She had still a slight German accent to soften the American pronunciation of her speech.

Everyone was incoherent. Waldeck kept saying excitedly, 'I haven't been out of South Africa since I arrived there twenty years ago. I'm in New York two days and I find Carlitta!'

There was time only to exchange the names of hotels and to promise to telephone tomorrow. Then the theatre bell interrupted. As they parted, Waldeck called back, 'Keep Sunday lunch free. Stefan's coming. We'll all be together . . .'

Carlitta's mouth pursed; her eyes opened wide in a pantomime 'Lovely' across the crowd.

'And yet I'm not really entirely surprised,' Waldeck whispered to his wife in the darkening theatre. 'It's been happening to us in one way or another all the time. What do you think of the husband? What about Mr Edgar Hicks from Ohio?' he added with a nudge.

In the dark, as the curtain rose, Eileen followed it with her eyes for a moment and then said, 'I shouldn't have known her. I don't think I should ever have known her.'

'But Carlitta hasn't changed at all!' said Waldeck.

Waldeck was on the telephone, talking to Stefan, immediately after breakfast next morning. Passing to and fro between the bedroom and the bathroom, Eileen could see him, his body hitched up on to the corner of the small desk, smiling excitedly at what must have been Stefan's quiet incredulity. 'But I tell you he actually is some sort of farmer in Ohio. Yes. Well, that's what I wanted to know. I can't really say – very tall and fairish and thin. Very American . . . Well, you know what I mean – a certain type of American, then. Slow, drawling way of speaking. Shakes your hand a long time. A weekend farmer, really. He's got some job with a firm that makes agricultural implements, in the nearby town. She said she runs pigs and chickens. Can you believe it? So is it all right about Sunday? I can imagine you are . . . *Ach*, the same old Carlitta.'

Sunday was a clear, sharp spring day in New York, exactly the temperature and brightness of a winter day in Johannesburg. Stefan rang up to say he would call for the Brands at about eleven, so that they could drive around a little before meeting Carlitta and her husband for luncheon.

'Will it be all right if I wear slacks?' asked Eileen. She always wore slacks on Sundays in Johannesburg.

'Certainly not,' said Stefan gravely. 'You cannot lunch in a restaurant in New York in slacks.'

Eileen put on a suit she had bought in London. She was filled with a childlike love and respect for Stefan; she would not have done the smallest thing to displease him or to prejudice his opinion of her. When he arrived to fetch the Brands he said, equally gravely, 'You look very well in that suit,' and led them to his car, where his wife, whom they had met in the course of the week, sat waiting.

His wife was perhaps an odd choice for Stefan, and then again perhaps she was not; she went along with the presidency, the wealth and the Fifth Avenue apartment, and left his inner balance unchanged. She was not so young as Eileen, but young, and a beauty. An American beauty, probably of Swedish or Norwegian stock. Hers was the style of blonde beauty in which the face is darker than the hair, which was not dyed but real. It was clean and shiny and almost silvery-fair, and she wore it as such women do, straight and loose. She wore black, and when she stood up you noticed that hers was the kind of tall figure that, although the shoulders are broad and the breasts full, tapers to too-narrow hips and too-thin legs. Her eyes were green and brilliant, and crinkled up, friendly, and on the wrist of one beautiful ungloved hand she wore a magnificent broad antique bracelet of emeralds and diamonds. Otherwise she was unadorned, without even a wedding ring. As she shifted along the seat of the car, a pleasant fragrance stirred from her, the sort of fragrance the expensive Fifth Avenue stores were then releasing into the foyers of their shops, to convince their customers of the arrival of the time to buy spring clothes. When she smiled and spoke, in a soft American voice without much to say, her teeth showed fresh as the milk teeth of a child.

Eileen thought how different were this woman and herself (with her large, Colonial, blue-eyed, suburban prettiness) from the sort of girls with whom Waldeck and Stefan had belonged in the world that was lost to them – girls of the twenties, restlessly independent, sensual and intellectual, citizens of the world with dramatic faces, girls such as Carlitta, inclining her dark Oriental head, had been.

The four drove through Central Park, rather threadbare after the snow and before the blossom. Then they went down to the East River, where the bridges hung like rainbows, glittering, soaring, rejoicing the heart in the sky above the water, where men have always expected to find their visions. They stopped the car at the United Nations building, and first walked along on the opposite side of the street, alongside the shabby, seedy shops, the better to see the great molten-looking façade of glass, like a river flowing upwards, on the administrative block. The glass calmly reflected the skyline, as a river reflects, murky green and metallic, the reeds. Then they crossed the street and wandered about a bit along the line of flagstaffs, with the building hanging above them. The Brands resolved to come back again another day and see the interior.

'So far, there's nothing to beat your bridges,' said Eileen. 'Nothing.'

They drove now uptown to an elegant, half-empty restaurant which had about it the air of recovering from Saturday night. There they sat drinking whisky while they waited.

'I don't know what we can do with the husband,' said Waldeck, shrugging and giggling.

'That's all right,' said Stefan. 'Alice will talk to him. Alice can get along with anybody.' His wife laughed good-naturedly.

'You know, he's *worthy* . . .' said Waldeck.

'I know,' said Stefan, comforting.

'Same old Carlitta, though,' said Waldeck, smiling reminiscently. 'You'll see.'

His wife Eileen looked at him. 'Oh, she's not,' she said, distressed. 'She's not. Oh, how can you say that to Stefan?' The girl from South Africa looked at the two men and the woman who sat with her, and around the panelled and flower-decorated room, and suddenly she felt a very long way from home.

Just at that moment, Carlitta and Mr Edgar Hicks came across the room towards them. Stefan got up and went forward with palms upturned to meet them; Waldeck rose from his seat; a confusion of greetings and introductions followed. Stefan kissed Carlitta on both cheeks gently. Edgar Hicks pumped his hand. In Edgar Hicks's other hand was the Palm Beach panama with the paisley band which he had removed from his head as he entered. The hovering attendant took it from him and took Carlitta's brown coat.

Carlitta wore the niggly-patterned silk dress that had shown its collar under the coat the night at the theatre, the same shoes, the same cracked beige kid gloves. But above the bun and level with the faded hairline, she had on what was obviously a brand new hat, a hat bought from one of the thousands of 'spring' hats displayed that week before Easter, a perky, mass-produced American hat of the kind which makes an American middle-class woman recognisable anywhere in the world. Its newness, its frivolous sense of its own emphemerality (it was so much in fashion that it would be old-fashioned once Easter was over) positively jeered at everything else Carlitta wore. Whether it was because she fancied the sun still painted her face the extraordinary rich glow that showed against the snow in the picture of herself laughing in Austria years ago, or whether there was some other reason, her face was again without make-up except for a rub of lipstick. Under the mixture of artificial light and daylight, faint darkening blotches, not freckles but something more akin to those liver marks elderly people get on the backs of their hands, showed on her temples and her jawline. But her eyes, of course, her eyes were large, dark, quick.

She and her husband consulted together over what they should eat, he suggesting slowly, she deciding quickly, and from then on she never stopped talking. She talked chiefly to her two friends

Waldeck and Stefan, who sat on either side of her. Edgar Hicks, after a few trying minutes with Eileen, who found it difficult to respond to any of his conversational gambits, discovered that Alice Raines rode horses and, like a swamp sucking in fast all around its victim, involved her in a long, one-sided argument about the merits of two different types of saddle. Edgar preferred the one type and simply assumed that Alice must be equally adamant about the superiority of the other. Although his voice was slow, it was unceasing and steady, almost impossible to interrupt.

Eileen did not mind the fact that she was not engaged in conversation. She was free to listen to and to watch Carlitta with Stefan and Waldeck. And now and then Carlitta, forking up her coleslaw expertly as any born American, looked over to Eileen with a remark or query – 'That's what *I* say, anyway,' or 'Wouldn't you think so?' Carlitta first told briefly about her stay in London when she left Germany, then about her coming to the United States, and her short time in New York. 'In the beginning, we stayed in that hotel near Grand Central. We behaved like tourists, not like people who have come to stay. We used to go to Coney Island and rowing on the lake in Central Park, and walking up and down Fifth Avenue – just as if we were going to go back to Germany in a few weeks.'

'Who's we?' asked Stefan. 'Your sister?'

'No, my sister was living in a small apartment near the river. Klaus,' she said, shrugging her worn shoulders with the careless, culpable gesture of an adolescent. Stefan nodded his head in confirmation towards Waldeck; of course, he remembered, Klaus had followed her or come with her to America. Poor Klaus.

'What happened to him?' asked Stefan.

'I don't know,' she said. 'He went to Mexico.'

Her audience of three could guess very well how it had been. When she had tired of Coney Island and the outside of Fifth Avenue shops and the rowing in Central Park, Klaus had found out once again that in the new world, as in the old, he had nothing more than amusement value for her.

'After three months—' Carlitta had not paused in her narrative – 'I went to stay with my sister and brother-in-law – she had been here some years already. But he got a job with a real-estate scheme, and they went to live on one of the firm's housing projects – you know, a little house, another little house next door, a swing for the kids, the same swing next door. I came back to New York on my own and I found a place in Greenwich Village.'

Ah, now, there was a setting in which one could imagine the Carlitta of the photographs, the beautiful, Oriental-looking German girl from Heidelberg, with the bold, promising eyes. And at the moment at which Eileen thought this, her ear caught the drawl of Edgar Hicks. '. . . now, our boy's the real independent type. Now, only the other day . . .' Edgar Hicks! Where had Edgar Hicks come in? She looked at him, carefully separating the flesh from the fine fringe of bone in his boiled trout, the knife held deliberately in his freckled hand.

'Did you live in Greenwich Village?' Eileen said to him suddenly.

He interrupted his description of his boy's seat in the saddle to turn and say, surprised, 'No, ma'am, I certainly didn't. I've never spent more than two consecutive weeks in New York in my life.' He thought Eileen's question merely a piece of tourist curiosity, and returned to Alice Raines, his boy and the saddle.

Carlitta had digressed into some reminiscence about Heidelberg days, but when she paused, laughing from Stefan to Waldeck with a faltering coquettishness that rose in her like a half-forgotten mannerism, Eileen said, 'Where did you and your husband meet?'

'In a train,' Carlitta said loudly and smiled, directed at her husband.

He took it up across the table. 'Baltimore and Ohio line,' he said, well rehearsed. There was the feeling that all the few things he had to say had been slowly thought out and slowly spoken many times before. 'I was sittin' in the diner havin' a beer with my dinner, and in comes this little person looking mighty proud and cute as you can make 'em . . .' So it went on, the usual story, and Edgar Hicks spared them no detail of the romantic convention. 'Took Carlitta down to see my folks the following month and we were married two weeks after that,' he concluded at last. He had expected to marry one of the local girls he'd been to school with; it was clear that Carlitta was the one and the ever-present adventure of his life. Now they had a boy who rode as naturally as an Indian and didn't watch television; he liked to raise his own chickens and have independent pocket money from the sale of eggs.

'Carlitta,' Stefan said, aside, 'how long were you in Greenwich Village?'

'Four years,' she said shortly, replying from some other part of her mind; her attention and animation were given to the comments with which she amplified her husband's description of their child's remarkable knowledge of country lore, his superiority over town-bred children.

Eileen overheard the low, flat reply. Four years! Four years about which Carlitta had said not a word, four years which somehow or other had brought her from the arrogant, beautiful, 'advanced' girl with whom Waldeck and Stefan could not fall in love because they and she agreed they were not good enough for her, to the girl who would accept Edgar Hicks a few weeks after a meeting on a train.

Carlitta felt the gaze of the girl from South Africa. A small patch of bright colour appeared on each of Carlitta's thin cheekbones. Perhaps it was the wine. Perhaps it was the wine, too, that made her voice rise, so that she began to talk of her life on the Ohio farm with a zest and insistence which made the whole table her audience. She told how she never went to town unless she had to; *never* more than once a month. How country people, like herself, discovered a new rhythm of life, something people who lived in towns had forgotten. How country people slept differently, tasted their food differently, had no nerves. 'I haven't a nerve in my body, any more. Absolutely placid,' she said, her sharp little gestures, her black eyes in the pinched face challenging a denial. 'Nothing ever happens but a change of season,' she said arrogantly to people for whom there were stock-market crashes, traffic jams, crowded exhibitions and cocktail parties. 'Birth and growth among the animals and the plants. Life. Not a cement substitute.' No one defended the city, but she went on as if someone had. 'I live as instinctively as one of our own animals. So does my child. I mean, for one thing, we don't have to worry about clothes.'

Eileen said rather foolishly, as if in reflex, 'Stefan said I couldn't wear slacks to a New York restaurant today.'

'Stefan was always a snob.' Carlitta's little head struck like a snake.

Eileen was taken aback; she laughed nervously, looking very young. Carlitta grinned wickedly under the hat whose straw caught the light concentrically, like a gramophone record. Stefan's wife smiled serenely and politely, as if this were a joke against her husband. She had taken off the jacket of her suit, and beneath it she wore a fine lavender-coloured sweater with a low, round neck. She had been resting her firm neck against her left hand, and now she took the hand away; hers was the kind of wonderful blood-mottled fair skin that dented white with the slightest pressure, filled up pink again the way the sea seeps up instantly through footprints in wet sand. She looked so healthy, so well cared for that she created a moment of repose around herself; everyone paused, resting his gaze upon her.

Then Carlitta's thin little sun-sallow neck twisted restlessly. 'I don't know how you stand it,' she said. 'I don't know how you can live in New York year after year.'

'We go away,' Stefan said soothingly. 'We go to Europe most summers, to Switzerland to my mother, or to Italy. Alice loves Italy.'

'Italy,' said Carlitta, suddenly turning over a piece of lobster on her plate as if she suspected that there must be something bad beneath it. 'Spain.'

'You remember how you went off to the Pyrenees?' Waldeck said to her. From his tone it was clear that this was quite a story, if Carlitta cared to tell it.

'You can't imagine how time flies on the farm,' said Carlitta. 'The years . . . just go. Sometimes, in summer, I simply walk out of the house and leave my work and go and lie down in the long grass. Then you can hear nothing, nothing at all.'

'Maybe the old cow chewing away under the pear tree,' said Edgar tenderly. Then with a chuckle that brought a change of tone: 'Carlitta takes a big part in community affairs, too, you know. She doesn't tell you that she's on the library committee in town, and last year she was lady president of the Parent-Teacher Association. Ran a bazaar made around three hundred dollars.' There was a pause. Nobody spoke. 'I'm an Elk myself,' he added. 'That's why we're going to Philadelphia Thursday. There's a convention on over there.'

Carlitta suddenly put down her fork with a gesture that impatiently terminated any current subject of conversation. (Eileen thought: she must always have managed conversation like that, long ago in smoky, noisy student rooms, jerking the talk determinedly the way she wanted it.) Her mind seemed to hark back to the subject of dress. 'Last year,' she said, 'we invited some city friends who were passing through town to a supper party. Now it just so happened that that afternoon I could see a storm banking up. I knew that if the storm came in the night it was goodbye to our hay. So I decided to make a hay-making party out of the supper. When those women came with their high-heeled fancy sandals and their gauzy frocks I put pitchforks into their hands and sent them out into the field to help get that hay in under cover. Of course I'd forgotten that they'd be bound to be rigged out in something ridiculous. You should have seen their faces!' Carlitta laughed gleefully. 'Should have seen their shoes!'

The young girl from South Africa felt suddenly angry. Amid the laughter, she said quietly, 'I think it was an awful thing to do. If I'd been a guest, I should flatly have refused.'

'Eileen!' said Waldeck mildly. But Carlitta pointedly excluded from her notice the girl from South Africa, whom Waldeck was apparently dragging around the world and giving a good time. Carlitta was sitting stiffly, her thin hands caught together, and she never took her eyes off Alice Raines's luxuriantly fleshed neck, as if it were some object of curiosity, quite independent of a human whole.

'If only they'd seen how idiotic they looked, stumbling about,' she said fiercely. Her eyes were extraordinarily dark, brimming with brightness. If her expression had not been one of malicious glee, Eileen would have said that there were tears in them.

* * *

After lunch, the Brands and the Raineses parted from the Hickses. Carlitta left the restaurant with Waldeck and Stefan on either arm, and that way she walked with them to the taxi stand at the end of the block, turning her small head from one to the other, tiny between them. 'I just couldn't keep her away from her two boyfriends today,' Edgar said indulgently, walking behind with Eileen and Alice. At this point the thin, middle-aged woman between the two men dropped their arms, bowed down, apparently with laughter at some joke, in the extravagant fashion of a young girl, and then caught them to her again.

Edgar and Carlitta got into a taxi, and the others went in Stefan's car back to his apartment. It was three o'clock in the afternoon, but Stefan brought in a bottle of champagne. The weak sunlight coming in the windows matched the wine. 'Carlitta,' said Stefan before he drank. 'Still "terrific". Beautiful.' Eileen Brand, sitting on a yellow sofa, felt vaguely unhappy, as if she had wandered into the wrong room, the wrong year. She even shook her head sadly, so slowly that no one noticed.

'I told you, same old Carlitta,' said Waldeck. There was a silence. 'And that husband,' Waldeck went on. 'The life they lead. So unlike Carlitta.'

'And because of that, so like her,' said Stefan. 'She always chose the perverse, the impossible. She obviously adores him. Just like Carlitta.'

Eileen Brand wanted to stand up and beg of the two men, for their own sake – no, to save her, Eileen, from shame (oh, how could she know her reasons!) – *see* she is changed; see Carlitta is old, faded, exists, as Carlitta, no more!

She had stood up without knowing it. 'What's the matter, Eileen?' Waldeck looked up. As she opened her mouth to tell him, to tell them both, a strange thing happened. It seemed that her whole mind turned over and showed her the truth. And the truth was much worse than what she had wanted to tell them. For they were right. Carlitta had not changed. They were right, but not in the way they thought. Carlitta had not changed *at all*, and that was why there was a sense of horror about meeting her; that was why she was totally unlike any one of the other friends they had met. Under that faded face, in that worn body, was the little German girl of the twenties, arrogant in a youth that did not exist, confidently disdainful in the possession of a beauty that was no longer there.

And what did *she* think of Ohio? Of good Edgar Hicks? Even of the boy who raised chickens and didn't look at television?

'Nothing,' said Eileen. 'I'd like a little more wine.'

It so happened that a day or two later, Stefan's business took him to Philadelphia. 'Don't forget Carlitta and her husband are staying at the Grand Park,' Waldeck said.

'Oh, I'll find them,' said Stefan.

But when he came back to New York and dined with his wife, Waldeck and Eileen the same night, he seemed entirely to have forgotten his expressed intention. 'I had a hell of a job dodging that Edgar Hicks,' he said, by the way. 'Wherever I went I seemed to bump into that Elk convention. They were everywhere. Every time I saw a panama hat with a paisley band I had to double on my tracks and go the other way. Once he nearly saw me. I just managed to squeeze into an elevator in time.'

And they all laughed, as if they had just managed it, too.

Which New Era Would That Be?

Jake Alexander, a big, fat coloured man, half Scottish, half African, was shaking a large pan of frying bacon on the gas stove in the back room of his Johannesburg printing shop when he became aware that someone was knocking on the door at the front of the shop. The sizzling fat and the voices of the five men in the back room with him almost blocked out sounds from without, and the knocking was of the steady kind that might have been going on for quite a few minutes. He lifted the pan off the flame with one hand and with the other made an impatient silencing gesture, directed at the bacon as well as the voices. Interpreting the movement as one of caution, the men hurriedly picked up the tumblers and cups in which they had been taking their end-of-the-day brandy at their ease, and tossed the last of it down. Little yellow Klaas, whose hair was like ginger-coloured wire wool, stacked the cups and glasses swiftly and hid them behind the dirty curtain that covered a row of shelves.

'Who's that?' yelled Jake, wiping his greasy hands down his pants.

There was a sharp and playful tattoo, followed by an English voice: 'Me – Alister. For heaven's sake, Jake!'

The fat man put the pan back on the flame and tramped through the dark shop, past the idle presses, to the door, and flung it open. 'Mr Halford!' he said. 'Well, good to see you. Come in, man. In the back there, you can't hear a thing.' A young Englishman with gentle eyes, a stern mouth and flat, colourless hair, which grew in an untidy, confused spiral from a double crown, stepped back to allow a young woman to enter ahead of him. Before he could introduce her, she held out her hand to Jake, smiling, and shook his firmly. 'Good evening. Jennifer Tetzel,' she said.

'Jennifer, this is Jake Alexander,' the young man managed to get in, over her shoulder.

The two had entered the building from the street through an archway lettered NEW ERA BUILDING. 'Which new era would that be?' the young woman had wondered aloud, brightly, while they were waiting in the dim hallway for the door to be opened, and Alister Halford had not known whether the reference was to the discovery of deep-level gold mining that had saved Johannesburg from the ephemeral fate of a mining camp in the nineties, or to the optimism after the settlement of labour troubles in the twenties, or to the recovery after the world went off the gold standard in the thirties – really, one had no idea of the age of these buildings in this run-down end of the town. Now, coming in out of the deserted hallway gloom, which smelled of dust and rotting wood – the smell of waiting – they were met by the live, cold tang of ink and the homely, lazy odour of bacon fat – the smell of acceptance. There was not much light in the deserted workshop. The host blundered to the wall and switched on a bright naked bulb, up in the ceiling. The three stood blinking at one another for a moment: a coloured man with the fat of the man of the world upon him, grossly dressed – not out of poverty but obviously because he liked it that way – in a rayon sports shirt that gaped and showed two hairy stomach rolls hiding his navel in a lipless grin, the pants of a good suit, misbuttoned and held up round the waist by a tie instead of a belt, and a pair of expensive sports shoes, worn without socks; a young Englishman in a worn greenish tweed suit with a neo-Edwardian cut to the waistcoat that labelled it a leftover from undergraduate days; a handsome white woman who, as the light fell upon her, was immediately recognisable to Jake Alexander.

He had never met her before, but he knew the type well – had seen it over and over again at meetings of the Congress of Democrats, and other organisations where progressive whites met progressive blacks. These were the white women who, Jake knew, persisted in regarding themselves as your equal. That was even worse, he thought, than the parsons who persisted in regarding *you* as *their* equal. The parsons had had ten years at school and seven years at a university and theological school; you had carried sacks of vegetables from the market to white people's cars from the time you were eight years old until you were apprenticed to a printer, and your first woman, like your mother, had been a servant, whom you had visited in a backyard room, and your first gulp of whisky, like many of your other pleasures, had been stolen while a white man was not looking. Yet the good parson insisted that your picture of life was exactly the same as his own: *you* felt as *he* did. But these women – oh, Christ! – these women felt as *you* did. They were sure of it. They thought they understood the humiliation of the pure-blooded black African walking the streets only by the permission of a pass written out by a white person, and the guilt and swagger of the coloured man light-faced enough to slink, fugitive from his own skin, into the preserves – the cinemas, bars, libraries that were marked EUROPEANS ONLY. Yes, breathless with stout sensitivity, they insisted on walking the whole teeter-totter of the colour line. There was no escaping their understanding. They even insisted on feeling the resentment *you* must feel at their identifying themselves with your feelings . . .

Here was the black hair of a determined woman (last year they wore it pulled tightly back into an oddly perched knot; this year it was cropped and curly as a lap dog's), the round, bony brow unpowdered in order to show off the tan, the red mouth, the unrouged cheeks, the big, lively, handsome eyes, dramatically painted, that would look into yours with such intelligent, eager honesty – eager to mirror what Jake Alexander, a big, fat slob of a coloured man interested in women, money, brandy and boxing, was feeling. Who the hell wants a woman to look at you honestly, anyway? What has all this to do with a *woman* – with what men and women have for each other in their eyes? She was wearing a wide black skirt, a white cotton blouse baring a good deal of her breasts, and earrings that seemed to have been made by a blacksmith out of bits of scrap iron. On her feet she had sandals whose narrow thongs wound between her toes, and the nails of the toes were painted plum colour. By contrast, her hands were neglected-looking – sallow, unmanicured – and on one thin finger there swivelled a huge gold seal ring. She was beautiful, he supposed with disgust.

He stood there, fat, greasy, and grinning at the two visitors so lingeringly that his grin looked insolent. Finally he asked, 'What brings you this end of town, Mr Halford? Sightseeing with the lady?'

The young Englishman gave Jake's arm a squeeze, where the short sleeve of the rayon shirt ended. 'Just thought I'd look you up, Jake,' he said, jolly.

'Come on in, come on in,' said Jake on a rising note, shambling ahead of them into the company of the back room. 'Here, what about a chair for the lady?' He swept a pile of handbills from the seat of a kitchen chair on to the dusty concrete floor, picked up the chair, and plonked it down again, in the middle of the group of men, who had risen awkwardly, like zoo bears to the hope of a bun, at the visitors' entrance. 'You know Maxie Ndube? And Temba?' Jake said, nodding at two of the men who surrounded him.

Alister Halford murmured with polite warmth his recognition of Maxie, a small, dainty-faced African in neat, businessman's dress, then said inquiringly and hesitantly to Temba, 'Have we? When?'

Temba was a coloured man – a mixture of the bloods of black slaves and white masters, blended long ago, in the days when the Cape of Good Hope was a port of refreshment for the Dutch East India Company. He was tall and pale, with a large Adam's apple, enormous black eyes, and the look of a musician in a jazz band; you could picture a trumpet lifted to the ceiling in those long yellow hands, that curved spine hunched forward to shield a low note. 'In Durban last year, Mr Halford, you remember?' he said eagerly. 'I'm sure we met – or perhaps I only saw you there.'

'Oh, at the Congress? Of course I remember you!' Halford apologised. 'You were in a delegation from the Cape?'

'Miss—?' Jake Alexander waved a hand between the young woman, Maxie and Temba.

'Jennifer. Jennifer Tetzel,' she said again clearly, thrusting out her hand. There was a confused moment when both men reached for it at once and then hesitated, each giving way to the other. Finally the handshaking was accomplished, and the young woman seated herself confidently on the chair.

Jake continued, offhand, 'Oh, and of course Billy Boy—' Alister signalled briefly to a black man with sad, bloodshot eyes, who stood awkwardly, back a few steps, against some rolls of paper – 'and Klaas and Albert.' Klaas and Albert had in their mixed blood some strain of the Bushman, which gave them a batrachian yellowness and toughness, like one of those toads that (prehistoric as the Bushman is) are mythically believed to have survived into modern times (hardly more fantastically than the Bushman himself has survived) by spending centuries shut up in an air bubble in a rock. Like Billy Boy, Klaas and Albert had backed away, and, as if abasement against the rolls of paper, the wall or the window were a greeting in itself, the two little coloured men and the big African only stared back at the masculine nods of Alister and the bright smile of the young woman.

'You up from the Cape for anything special now?' Alister said to Temba as he made a place for himself on a corner of a table that was littered with photographic blocks, bits of type, poster proofs, a bottle of souring milk, a bow tie, a pair of red braces and a number of empty Coca-Cola bottles.

'I've been living in Durban for a year. Just got the chance of a lift to Jo'burg,' said the gangling Temba.

Jake had set himself up easily, leaning against the front of the stove and facing Miss Jennifer Tetzel on her chair. He jerked his head towards Temba and said, 'Real banana boy.' Young white men brought up in the strong Anglo-Saxon tradition of the province of Natal are often referred to, and refer to themselves, as 'banana boys', even though fewer and fewer of them have any connection with the dwindling number of vast banana estates that once made their owners rich. Jake's broad face, where the bright pink cheeks of a Highland complexion – inherited, along with his name, from his Scottish father – showed oddly through his coarse, coffee-coloured skin, creased up in appreciation of his own joke. And Temba threw back his head and laughed, his Adam's apple bobbing, at the idea of himself as a cricket-playing white public-school boy.

'There's nothing like Cape Town, is there?' said the young woman to him, her head charmingly on one side, as if this conviction was something she and he shared.

'Miss Tetzel's up here to look us over. She's from Cape Town,' Alister explained.

She turned to Temba with her beauty, her strong provocativeness, full on, as it were. 'So we're neighbours?'

Jake rolled one foot comfortably over the other and a spluttering laugh pursed out the pink inner membrane of his lips.

'Where did you live?' she went on, to Temba.

'Cape Flats,' he said. Cape Flats is a desolate coloured slum in the bush outside Cape Town.

'Me, too,' said the girl, casually.

Temba said politely, 'You're kidding,' and then looked down uncomfortably at his hands, as if they had been guilty of some clumsy movement. He had not meant to sound so familiar; the words were not the right ones.

'I've been there nearly ten months,' she said.

'Well, some people've got queer tastes,' Jake remarked, laughing, to no one in particular, as if she were not there.

'How's that?' Temba was asking her shyly, respectfully.

She mentioned the name of a social rehabilitation scheme that was in operation in the slum. 'I'm assistant director of the thing at the moment. It's connected with the sort of work I do at the university, you see, so they've given me fifteen months' leave from my usual job.'

Maxie noticed with amusement the way she used the word 'job', as if she were a plumber's mate; he and his educated African friends – journalists and schoolteachers – were careful to talk only of their 'professions'. 'Good works,' he said, smiling quietly.

She planted her feet comfortably before her, wriggling on the hard chair, and said to Temba with mannish frankness, 'It's a ghastly place. How in God's name did you survive living there? I don't think I can last out more than another few months, and I've always got my flat in Cape Town to escape to on Sundays, and so on.'

While Temba smiled, turning his protruding eyes aside slowly, Jake looked straight at her and said, 'Then why do you, lady, why *do* you?'

'Oh, I don't know. Because I don't see why anyone else – any one of the people who live there – should have to, I suppose.' She laughed before anyone else could at the feebleness, the philanthropic uselessness of what she was saying. 'Guilt, what-have-you . . .'

Maxie shrugged, as if at the mention of some expensive illness, which he had never been able to afford and whose symptoms he could not imagine.

There was a moment of silence; the two coloured men and the big black man standing back against the wall watched anxiously, as if some sort of signal might be expected, possibly from Jake Alexander, their boss, the man who, like themselves, was not white, yet who owned his own business, and had a car, and money, and strange friends – sometimes even white people, such as these. The three of them were dressed in the ill-matched cast-off clothing that all humble workpeople who are not white wear in Johannesburg, and they had not lost the ability of primitives and children to stare, unembarrassed and unembarrassing.

Jake winked at Alister; it was one of his mannerisms – a bookie's wink, a stage comedian's wink. 'Well, how's it going, boy, how's it going?' he said. His turn of phrase was bar-room bonhomie; with luck, he *could* get into a bar, too. With a hat to cover his hair, and his coat collar well up, and only a bit of greasy pink cheek showing, he had slipped into the bars of the shabbier Johannesburg hotels with Alister many times and got away with it. Alister, on the other hand, had got away with the same sort of thing narrowly several times, too, when he had accompanied Jake to a shebeen in a coloured location, where it was illegal for a white man to be, as well as illegal for anyone at all to have a drink; twice Alister had escaped a raid by jumping out of a window. Alister had been in South Africa only eighteen months, as correspondent for a newspaper in England, and because he was only two or three years away from undergraduate escapades, such incidents seemed to give him a kind of nostalgic pleasure; he found them funny. Jake, for his part, had decided long ago (with the great help of the money he had made) that he would take the whole business of the colour bar as humorous. The combination of these two attitudes, stemming from such immeasurably different circumstances, had the effect of making their friendship less self-conscious than is usual between a white man and a coloured one.

'They tell me it's going to be a good thing on Saturday night?' said Alister, in the tone of questioning someone in the know. He was referring to a boxing match between two coloured heavyweights, one of whom was a protégé of Jake's.

Jake grinned deprecatingly, like a fond mother. 'Well, Pikkie's a good boy,' he said. 'I tell you, it'll be something to see.' He danced about a little on his clumsy toes, in pantomime of the way a boxer nimbles himself, and collapsed against the stove, his belly shaking with laughter at his breathlessness.

'Too much smoking, too many brandies, Jake,' said Alister.

'With me, it's too many women, boy.'

'We were just congratulating Jake,' said Maxie in his soft, precise voice, the indulgent, tongue-in-cheek tone of the protégé who is superior to his patron, for Maxie was one of Jake's boys, too – of a different kind. Though Jake had decided that for him being on the wrong side of a colour bar was ludicrous, he was as indulgent to those who took it seriously and politically, the way Maxie did, as he was to any up-and-coming youngster who, say, showed talent in the ring or wanted to go to America and become a singer. They could all make themselves free of Jake's pocket, and his printing shop, and his room with a radio in the lower end of the town, where the building had fallen below the standard of white people but was far superior to the kind of thing most coloureds and blacks were accustomed to.

'Congratulations on what?' the young white woman asked. She had a way of looking up around her, questioningly, from face to face, that came of long familiarity with being the centre of attention at parties.

'Yes, you can shake my hand, boy,' said Jake to Alister. 'I didn't see it, but these fellows tell me that my divorce went through. It's in the papers today.'

'Is that so? But from what I hear, you won't be a free man long,' Alister said teasingly.

Jake giggled, and pressed at one gold-filled tooth with a strong fingernail. 'You heard about the little parcel I'm expecting from Zululand?' he asked.

'Zululand?' said Alister. 'I thought your Lila came from Stellenbosch.'

Maxie and Temba laughed.

'Lila? *What* Lila?' said Jake with exaggerated innocence.

'You're behind the times,' said Maxie to Alister.

'You know I like them – well, sort of round,' said Jake. 'Don't care for the thin kind, in the long run.'

'But Lila had red hair!' Alister goaded him. He remembered the incongruously dyed, artificially straightened hair on a fine coloured girl whose nostrils dilated in the manner of certain fleshy water plants seeking prey.

Jennifer Tetzel got up and turned the gas off on the stove, behind Jake. 'That bacon'll be like charred string,' she said.

Jake did not move – merely looked at her lazily. 'This is not the way to talk with a lady around.' He grinned, unapologetic.

She smiled at him and sat down, shaking her earrings. 'Oh, I'm divorced myself. Are we keeping you people from your supper? Do go ahead and eat. Don't bother about us.'

Jake turned around, gave the shrunken rashers a mild shake, and put the pan aside. 'Hell, no,' he said. 'Any time. But—' turning to Alister – 'won't you have something to eat?' He looked about, helpless and unconcerned, as if to indicate an absence of plates and a general careless lack of equipment such as white women would be accustomed to use when they ate. Alister said quickly, no, he had promised to take Jennifer to Moorjee's.

Of course, Jake should have known; a woman like that would *want* to be taken to eat at an Indian place in Vrededorp, even though she was white, and free to eat at the best hotel in town. He felt suddenly, after all, the old gulf opening between himself and Alister: what did *they* see in such women – bristling, sharp, all-seeing, knowing women, who talked like men, who wanted to show all the time that, apart from sex, they were exactly the same as men? He looked at Jennifer and her clothes, and thought of the way a white woman could look: one of those big, soft, European women with curly yellow hair, with very high-heeled shoes that made them shake softly when they walked, with a strong scent, like hot flowers, coming up, it seemed, from their jutting breasts under the lace and pink and blue and all the other pretty things they wore – women with nothing resistant about them except, buried in white, boneless fingers, those red, pointed nails that scratched faintly at your palms.

'You should have been along with me at lunch today,' said Maxie to no one in particular. Or perhaps the soft voice, a vocal tiptoe, was aimed at Alister, who was familiar with Maxie's work as an organiser of African trade unions. The group in the room gave him their attention (Temba with the little encouraging grunt of one who has already heard the story), but Maxie paused a moment, smiling ruefully at what he was about to tell. Then he said, 'You know George Elson?' Alister nodded. The man was a white lawyer who had been arrested twice for his participation in anti-discrimination movements.

'Oh, George? I've worked with George often in Cape Town,' put in Jennifer.

'Well,' continued Maxie, 'George Elson and I went out to one of the industrial towns on the East Rand. We were interviewing the bosses, you see, not the men, and at the beginning it was all right, though once or twice the girls in the offices thought I was George's driver – "Your boy can wait outside".' He laughed, showing small, perfect teeth; everything about him was finely made – his straight-fingered dark hands, the curved African nostrils of his small nose, his little ears, which grew close to the sides of his delicate head. The others were silent, but the young woman laughed, too.

'We even got tea in one place,' Maxie went on. 'One of the girls came in with two cups and a tin mug. But old George took the mug.'

Jennifer Tetzel laughed again, knowingly.

'Then, just about lunchtime, we came to this place I wanted to tell you about. Nice chap, the manager. Never blinked an eye at me, called me Mister. And after we'd talked, he said to George, "Why not come home with me for lunch?" So of course George said, "Thanks, but I'm with my friend here." "Oh, that's OK," said the chap. "Bring him along." Well, we go along to this house, and the chap disappears into the kitchen, and then he comes back and we sit in the lounge and have a beer, and then the servant comes along and says lunch is ready. Just as we're walking into the dining room, the chap takes me by the arm and says, "I've had *your* lunch laid on a table on the stoep. You'll find it's all perfectly clean and nice, just what we're having ourselves."'

'Fantastic,' murmured Alister.

Maxie smiled and shrugged, looking around at them all. 'It's true.'

'After he'd asked you, and he'd sat having a drink with you?' Jennifer said closely, biting in her lower lip, as if this were a problem to be solved psychologically.

'Of course,' said Maxie.

Jake was shaking with laughter, like some obscene Silenus. There was no sound out of him, but saliva gleamed on his lips, and his belly, at the level of Jennifer Tetzel's eyes, was convulsed.

Temba said soberly, in the tone of one whose goodwill makes it difficult for him to believe in the unease of his situation, 'I certainly find it worse here than at the Cape. I can't remember, y'know, about buses. I keep getting put off European buses.'

Maxie pointed to Jake's heaving belly. 'Oh, I'll tell you a better one than that,' he said. 'Something that happened in the office one day. Now, the trouble with me is, apparently, I don't talk like a native.' This time everyone laughed, except Maxie himself, who, with the instinct of a good raconteur, kept a polite, modest, straight face.

'You know that's true,' interrupted the young white woman. 'You have none of the usual softening of the vowels of most Africans. And you haven't got an Afrikaans accent, as some Africans have, even if they get rid of the Bantu thing.'

'Anyway, I'd had to phone a certain firm several times,' Maxie went on, 'and I'd got to know the voice of the girl at the other end, and she'd got to know mine. As a matter of fact, she must have liked the sound of me, because she was getting very friendly. We fooled about a bit, exchanged first names, like a couple of kids – hers was Peggy – and she said, eventually, "Aren't you ever going to come to the office yourself?"' Maxie paused a moment, and his tongue flicked at the side of his mouth in a brief, nervous gesture. When he spoke again, his voice was flat, like the voice of a man who is telling a joke and suddenly thinks that perhaps it is not such a good one after all. 'So I told her I'd be in next day, about four. I walked in, sure enough, just as I said I would. She was a pretty girl, blonde, you know, with very tidy hair – I guessed she'd just combed it to be ready for me. She looked up and said "Yes?," holding out her hand for the messenger's book or parcel she thought I'd brought. I took her hand and shook it and said, "Well, here I am, on time – I'm Maxie – Maxie Ndube."'

'What'd she do?' asked Temba eagerly.

The interruption seemed to restore Maxie's confidence in his story. He shrugged gaily. 'She almost dropped my hand, and then she pumped it like a mad thing, and her neck and ears went so red I thought she'd burn up. Honestly, her ears were absolutely shining. She tried to pretend she'd known all along, but I could see she was terrified someone would come from the inner office and see her shaking hands with a native. So I took pity on her and went away. Didn't even stay for my appointment with her boss. When I went back to keep the postponed appointment the next week, we pretended we'd never met.'

Temba was slapping his knee. 'God, I'd have loved to see her face!' he said.

Jake wiped away a tear from his fat cheek – his eyes were light blue, and produced tears easily when he laughed – and said, 'That'll teach you not to talk swanky, man. Why can't you talk like the rest of us?'

'Oh, I'll watch out on the "missus" and "baas" stuff in future,' said Maxie.

Jennifer Tetzel cut into their laughter with her cool, practical voice. 'Poor little girl, she probably liked you awfully, Maxie, and was really disappointed. You mustn't be too harsh on her. It's hard to be punished for not being black.'

The moment was one of astonishment rather than irritation. Even Jake, who had been sure that there could be no possible situation between white and black he could not find amusing, only looked quickly from the young woman to Maxie, in a hiatus between anger, which he had given up long ago, and laughter, which suddenly failed him. On his face was admiration more than anything else – sheer, grudging admiration. This one was the best yet. This one was the coolest ever.

'Is it?' said Maxie to Jennifer, pulling in the corners of his mouth and regarding her from under slightly raised eyebrows. Jake watched. Oh, she'd have a hard time with Maxie. Maxie wouldn't give up his suffering-tempered blackness so easily. You hadn't much hope of knowing what Maxie was feeling at any given moment, because Maxie not only never let you know but made you guess wrong. But this one was the best yet.

She looked back at Maxie, opening her eyes very wide, twisting her sandalled foot on the swivel of its ankle, smiling. 'Really, I assure you it is.'

Maxie bowed to her politely, giving way with a falling gesture of his hand.

Alister had slid from his perch on the crowded table, and now, prodding Jake playfully in the paunch, he said, 'We have to get along.'

Jake scratched his ear and said again, 'Sure you won't have something to eat?'

Alister shook his head. 'We had hoped you'd offer us a drink, but—'

Jake wheezed with laughter, but this time was sincerely concerned. 'Well, to tell you the truth, when we heard the knocking, we just swallowed the last of the bottle off, in case it was someone it shouldn't be. I haven't a drop in the place till tomorrow. Sorry, chappie. Must apologise to you, lady, but we black men've got to drink in secret. If we'd've known it was you two . . .'

Maxie and Temba had risen. The two wizened coloured men, Klaas and Albert, and the sombre black Billy Boy shuffled helplessly, hanging about.

Alister said, 'Next time, Jake, next time. We'll give you fair warning and you can lay it on.'

Jennifer shook hands with Temba and Maxie, called 'Goodbye! Goodbye!' to the others, as if they were somehow out of earshot in that small room. From the door, she suddenly said to Maxie, 'I feel I must tell you. About that other story – your first one, about the lunch. I don't believe it. I'm sorry, but I honestly don't. It's too illogical to hold water.'

It was the final self-immolation by honest understanding. There was absolutely no limit to which that understanding would not go. Even if she could not believe Maxie, she must keep her determined good faith with him by confessing her disbelief. She would go to the length of calling him a liar to show by frankness how much she respected him – to insinuate, perhaps, that she was *with him*, even in the need to invent something about a white man that she, because she herself was white, could not believe. It was her last bid for Maxie.

The small, perfectly made man crossed his arms and smiled, watching her out. Maxie had no price.

Jake saw his guests out of the shop, and switched off the light after he had closed the door behind them. As he walked back through the dark, where his presses smelled metallic and cool, he heard, for a few moments, the clear voice of the white woman and the low, noncommittal English murmur of Alister, his friend, as they went out through the archway into the street.

He blinked a little as he came back to the light and the faces that confronted him in the back room. Klaas had taken the dirty glasses from behind the curtain and was holding them one by one under the tap in the sink. Billy Boy and Albert had come closer out of the shadows and were leaning their elbows on a roll of paper. Temba was sitting on the table, swinging his foot. Maxie had not moved, and stood just as he had, with his arms folded. No one spoke.

Jake began to whistle softly through the spaces between his front teeth, and he picked up the pan of bacon, looked at the twisted curls of meat, jellied now in cold white fat, and put it down again absently. He stood a moment, heavily, regarding them all, but no one responded. His eye encountered the chair that he had cleared for Jennifer Tetzel to sit on. Suddenly he kicked it, hard, so that it went flying on to its side. Then, rubbing his big hands together and bursting into loud whistling to accompany an impromptu series of dance steps, he said 'Now, boys!' and as they stirred, he plonked the pan down on the ring and turned the gas up till it roared beneath it.

The Smell of Death and Flowers

The party was an unusual one for Johannesburg. A young man called Derek Ross – out of sight behind the 'bar' at the moment – had white friends and black friends, Indian friends and friends of mixed blood, and sometimes he liked to invite them to his flat all at once. Most of them belonged to the minority that, through bohemianism, godliness, politics, or a particularly sharp sense of human dignity, did not care about the difference in one another's skins. But there were always one or two – white ones – who came, like tourists, to see the sight, and to show that they did not care, and one or two black or brown or Indian ones who found themselves paralysed by the very ease with which the white guests accepted them.

One of the several groups that huddled to talk, like people sheltering beneath a cliff, on divans and hard borrowed chairs in the shadow of the dancers, was dominated by a man in a grey suit, Malcolm Barker. 'Why not pay the fine and have done with it, then?' he was saying.

The two people to whom he was talking were silent a moment, so that the haphazard noisiness of the room and the organised wail of the gramophone suddenly burst in irrelevantly upon the conversation. The pretty brunette said, in her quick, officious voice, 'Well, it wouldn't be the same for Jessica Malherbe. It's not quite the same thing, you see . . .' Her stiff, mascaraed lashes flickered an appeal – for confirmation, and for sympathy because of the impossibility of explaining – at a man whose gingerish whiskers and flattened, low-set ears made him look like an angry tomcat.

'It's a matter of principle,' he said to Malcolm Barker.

'Oh, quite, I see,' Malcolm conceded. 'For someone like this Malherbe woman, paying the fine's one thing; sitting in prison for three weeks is another.'

The brunette rapidly crossed and then uncrossed her legs. 'It's not even quite that,' she said. 'Not the unpleasantness of being in prison. Not a sort of martyrdom on Jessica's part. Just the *principle.*' At that moment a black hand came out from the crush of dancers bumping round and pulled the woman to her feet; she went off, and as she danced she talked with staccato animation to her African partner, who kept his lids half lowered over his eyes while she followed his gentle shuffle. The ginger-whiskered man got up without a word and went swiftly through the dancers to the 'bar', a kitchen table covered with beer and gin bottles, at the other end of the small room.

'*Satyagraha*,' said Malcolm Barker, like the infidel pronouncing with satisfaction the holy word that the believers hesitate to defile.

A very large and plain African woman sitting next to him smiled at him hugely and eagerly out of shyness, not having the slightest idea what he had said.

He smiled back at her for a moment, as if to hypnotise the onrush of some frightening animal. Then, suddenly, he leaned over and asked in a special, loud, slow voice, 'What do you do? Are you a teacher?'

Before the woman could answer, Malcolm Barker's young sister-in-law, a girl who had been sitting silent, pink and cold as a porcelain figurine, on the window sill behind his back, leaned her hand for balance on his chair and said urgently, near his ear, 'Has Jessica Malherbe really been in prison?'

'Yes, in Port Elizabeth. And in Durban, they tell me. And now she's one of the civil-disobedience people – defiance campaign leaders who're going to walk into some native location forbidden to Europeans. Next Tuesday. So she'll land herself in prison again. For Christ's sake, Joyce, what are you drinking that stuff for? I've told you that punch is the cheapest muck possible—'

But the girl was not listening to him any longer. Balanced delicately on her rather full, long neck, her fragile-looking face with the eyes and the fine, short line of nose of a Marie Laurencin painting was looking across the room with the intensity peculiar to the blank-faced. Hers was an essentially two-dimensional prettiness: flat, dazzlingly pastel-coloured, as if the mask of make-up on the unlined skin *were* the face; if one had turned her around, one would scarcely have been surprised to discover canvas. All her life she had suffered from this impression she made of not being quite real.

'She *looks* so nice,' she said now, her eyes still fixed on some point near the door. 'I mean she uses good perfume, and everything. You can't imagine it.'

Her brother-in-law made as if to take the tumbler of alcohol out of the girl's hand, impatiently, the way one might take a pair of scissors from a child, but, without looking at him or at her hands, she changed the glass from one hand to the other, out of his reach. 'At least the brandy's in a bottle with a recognisable label,' he said peevishly. 'I don't know why you don't stick to that.'

'I wonder if she had to eat the same food as the others,' said the girl.

'You'll feel like death tomorrow morning,' he said, 'and Madeline'll blame me. You are an obstinate little devil.'

A tall, untidy young man, whose blond head outtopped all others like a tousled palm tree, approached with a slow, drunken smile and, with exaggerated courtesy, asked Joyce to dance. She unhurriedly drank down what was left in her glass, put the glass carefully on the window sill and went off with him, her narrow waist upright and correct in his long arm. Her brother-in-law followed her with his eyes, irritatedly, for a moment, then closed them suddenly, whether in boredom or in weariness one could not tell.

The young man was saying to the girl as they danced, 'You haven't left the side of your husband – or whatever he is – all night. What's the idea?'

'My brother-in-law,' she said. 'My sister couldn't come because the child's got a temperature.'

He squeezed her waist; it remained quite firm, like the crisp stem of a flower. 'Do I know your sister?' he asked. Every now and then his drunkenness came over him in a delightful swoon, so that his eyelids dropped heavily and he pretended that he was narrowing them shrewdly.

'Maybe. Madeline McCoy – Madeline Barker now. She's the painter. She's the one who started that arts-and-crafts school for Africans.'

'Oh, yes. Yes, I know,' he said. Suddenly, he swung her away from him with one hand, executed a few loose-limbed steps around her, lost her in a collision with another couple, caught her to him again, and, with an affectionate squeeze, brought her up short against the barrier of people who were packed tight as a rugby scrum around the kitchen table, where the drinks were. He pushed her through the crowd to the table.

'What d'you want, Roy, my boy?' said a little, very black-faced African, gleaming up at them.

'Barberton'll do for me.' The young man pressed a hand on the African's head, grinning.

'Ah, that stuff's no good. Sugar-water. Let me give you a dash of Pineapple. Just like mother makes.'

For a moment, the girl wondered if any of the bottles really did contain Pineapple or Barberton, two infamous brews invented by African natives living in the segregated slums that are called locations. Pineapple, she knew, was made out of the fermented fruit and was supposed to be extraordinarily intoxicating; she had once read a newspaper report of a shebeen raid in which the Barberton still contained a lopped-off human foot – whether for additional flavour or the spice of witchcraft, it was not known.

But she was reassured at once. 'Don't worry,' said a good-looking blonde, made up to look heavily suntanned, who was standing at the bar. 'No shebeen ever produced anything much more poisonous than this gin-punch thing of Derek's.' The host was attending to the needs of his guests at the bar, and she waved at him a glass containing the mixture that the girl had been drinking over at the window.

'Not gin. It's arak – lovely,' said Derek. 'What'll you have, Joyce?'

'Joyce,' said the gangling young man with whom she had been dancing. 'Joyce. That's a nice name for her. Now tell her mine.'

'Roy Wilson. But you seem to know each other quite adequately without names,' said Derek. 'This is Joyce McCoy, Roy – and, Joyce, these are Matt Shabalala, Brenda Shotley, Mahinder Singh, Martin Mathlongo.'

They smiled at the girl: the shiny-faced African, on a level with her shoulder; the blonde woman with the caked powder cracking on her cheeks; the handsome, scholarly-looking Indian with the high, bald dome; the ugly light-coloured man, just light enough for freckles to show thickly on his fleshy face.

She said to her host, 'I'll have the same again, Derek. Your punch.' And even before she had sipped the stuff, she felt a warmth expand and soften inside her, and she said the names over silently to herself

– Matt Sha-ba-lala, Martin Math-longo, Ma-hinder Singh. Out of the corner of her eye, as she stood there, she could just see Jessica Malherbe, a short, plump white woman in an elegant black frock, her hair glossy, like a bird's wing, as she turned her head under the light while she talked.

Then it happened, just when the girl was most ready for it, just when the time had come. The little African named Matt said, 'This is Miss Joyce McCoy – Eddie Ntwala,' and stood looking on with a smile while her hand went into the slim hand of a tall, light-skinned African with the tired, appraising, cynical eyes of a man who drinks too much in order to deaden the pain of his intelligence. She could tell from the way little Shabalala presented the man that he must be someone important and admired, a leader of some sort, whose every idiosyncrasy – the broken remains of handsome, smoke-darkened teeth when he smiled, the wrinkled tie hanging askew – bespoke to those who knew him his distinction in a thousand different situations. She smiled as if to say, 'Of course, Eddie Ntwala himself, I knew it,' and their hands parted and dropped.

The man did not seem to be looking at her – did not seem to be looking at the crowd or at Shabalala, either. There was a slight smile around his mouth, a public smile that would do for anybody. 'Dance?' he said, tapping her lightly on the shoulder. They turned to the floor together.

Eddie Ntwala danced well and unthinkingly, if without much variation. Joyce's right hand was in his left, his right hand on the concavity of her back, just as if – well, just as if he were anyone else. And it was the first time – the first time in all her twenty-two years. Her head came just to the point of his lapel, and she could smell the faint odour of cigarette smoke in the cloth. When he turned his head and her head was in the path of his breath, there was the familiar smell of wine or brandy breathed down upon her by men at dances. He looked, of course, apart from his eyes – eyes that she had seen in other faces and wondered if she would ever be old enough to understand – exactly like any errand 'boy' or house 'boy'. He had the same close-cut wool on his head, the same smooth brown skin, the same rather nice high cheekbones, the same broad-nostrilled small nose. Only, he had his arm around her and her hand in his and he was leading her through the conventional arabesques of polite dancing. She would not let herself formulate the words in her brain: I am dancing with a black man. But she allowed herself to question, with the careful detachment of scientific inquiry, quietly inside herself: 'Do I feel anything? What do I feel?' The man began to hum a snatch of the tune to which they were dancing, the way a person will do when he suddenly hears music out of some forgotten phase of his youth; while the hum reverberated through his chest, she slid her eyes almost painfully to the right, not moving her head, to see his very well-shaped hand – an almost feminine hand compared to the hands of most white men – dark brown against her own white one, the dark thumb and the pale one crossed, the dark fingers and the pale ones folded together. 'Is this exactly how I always dance?' she asked herself closely. 'Do I always hold my back exactly like this, do I relax just this much, hold myself in reserve to just this degree?'

She found she was dancing as she always danced.

I feel nothing, she thought. *I feel nothing.*

And all at once a relief, a mild elation, took possession of her, so that she could begin to talk to the man with whom she was dancing. In any case, she was not a girl who had much small talk; she knew that at least half the young men who, attracted by her exceptional prettiness, flocked to ask her to dance at parties never asked her again because they could not stand her vast minutes of silence. But now she said in her flat, small voice the few things she could say – remarks about the music and the pleasantness of the rainy night outside. He smiled at her with bored tolerance, plainly not listening to what she said. Then he said, as if to compensate for his inattention, 'You from England?'

She said, 'Yes. But I'm not English. I'm South African, but I've spent the last five years in England. I've only been back in South Africa since December. I used to know Derek when I was a little girl,' she added, feeling that she was obliged to explain her presence in what she suddenly felt was a group conscious of some distinction or privilege.

'England,' he said, smiling down past her rather than at her. 'Never been so happy anywhere.'

'London?' she said.

He nodded. 'Oh, I agree,' she said. 'I feel the same about it.'

'No, you don't, McCoy,' he said very slowly, smiling at her now. 'No, you don't.'

She was silenced at what instantly seemed her temerity.

He said, as they danced around again, 'The way you speak. Really English. Whites in SA can't speak that way.'

For a moment, one of the old, blank, impassively pretty-faced silences threatened to settle upon her, but the second glass of arak punch broke through it, and, almost animated, she answered lightly, 'Oh, I find I'm like a parrot. I pick up the accent of the people among whom I live in a matter of hours.'

He threw back his head and laughed, showing the gaps in his teeth. 'How will you speak tomorrow, McCoy?' he said, holding her back from him and shaking with laughter, his eyes swimming. 'Oh, how will you speak tomorrow, I wonder?'

She said, immensely daring, though it came out in her usual small, unassertive feminine voice, a voice gently toned for the utterance of banal pleasantries, 'Like you.'

'Let's have a drink,' he said, as if he had known her a long time – as if she were someone like Jessica Malherbe. And he took her back to the bar, leading her by the hand; she walked with her hand loosely swinging in his, just as she had done with young men at country-club dances. 'I promised to have one with Rajati,' he was saying. 'Where has he got to?'

'Is that the one I met?' said the girl. 'The one with the high, bald head?'

'An Indian?' he said. 'No, you mean Mahinder. This one's his cousin, Jessica Malherbe's husband.'

'She's married to an Indian?' The girl stopped dead in the middle of the dancers. 'Is she?' The idea went through her like a thrill. She felt startled as if by a sudden piece of good news about someone who was important to her. Jessica Malherbe – the name, the idea – seemed to have been circling about her life since before she left England. Even there, she had read about her in the papers: the daughter of a humble Afrikaner farmer, who had disowned her in the name of a stern Calvinist God for her anti-nationalism and her radical views; a girl from a back-veld farm – such a farm as Joyce herself could remember seeing from a car window as a child – who had worked in a factory and educated herself and been sent by her trade union to study labour problems all over the world; a girl who negotiated with ministers of state; who, Joyce had learned that evening, had gone to prison for her principles. Jessica Malherbe, who was almost the first person the girl had met when she came in to the party this evening, and who turned out to look like any well-groomed English woman you might see in a London restaurant, wearing a pearl necklace and smelling of expensive perfume. An Indian! It was the final gesture. Magnificent. A world toppled with it – Jessica Malherbe's father's world. An Indian!

'Old Rajati,' Ntwala was saying. But they could not find him. The girl thought of the handsome, scholarly-looking Indian with the domed head, and suddenly she remembered that once, in Durban, she had talked across the counter of a shop with an Indian boy. She had been down in the Indian quarter with her sister, and they had entered a shop to buy a piece of silk. She had been the spokeswoman, and she had murmured across the counter to the boy and he had said, in a voice as low and gentle as her own, no, he was sorry, that length of silk was for a sari, and could not be cut. The boy had very beautiful, unseeing eyes, and it was as if they spoke to each other in a dream. The shop was small and deep-set. It smelled strongly of incense, the smell of the village church in which her grandfather had lain in state before his funeral, the scent of her mother's garden on a summer night – the smell of death and flowers, compounded, as the incident itself came to be, of ugliness and beauty, of attraction and repulsion. For just after she and her sister had left the little shop, they had found themselves being followed by an unpleasant man, whose presence first made them uneasily hold tightly to their handbags but who later, when they entered a busy shop in an attempt to get rid of him, crowded up against them and made an obscene advance. He had had a vaguely Eurasian face, they believed, but they could not have said whether or not he was an Indian; in their disgust, he had scarcely seemed human to them at all.

She tried now, in the swarming noise of Derek's room, to hear again in her head the voice of the boy saying the words she remembered so exactly: 'No, I am sorry, that length of silk is for a sari, it cannot be cut.' But the tingle of the alcohol that she had been feeling in her hands for quite a long time became a kind of sizzling singing in her ears, like the sound of bubbles rising in aerated water, and all that she could convey to herself was the curious finality of the phrase: *can-not-be-cut*, *can-not-be-cut*.

She danced the next dance with Derek. 'You look sweet tonight, old thing,' he said, putting wet lips to her ear. 'Sweet.'

She said, 'Derek, which is Rajati?'

He let go her waist. 'Over there,' he said, but in an instant he clutched her again and was whirling her around and she saw only Mahinder Singh and Martin Mathlongo, the big, freckled coloured man, and the back of some man's dark neck with a businessman's thick roll of fat above the collar.

'Which?' she said, but this time he gestured towards a group in which there were white men only, and so she gave up.

The dance was cut short with a sudden wailing screech as someone lifted the needle of the gramophone in the middle of the record, and it appeared that a man was about to speak. It turned out that it was to be a song and not a speech, for Martin Mathlongo, little Shabalala, two coloured women and a huge African woman with cork-soled green shoes grouped themselves with their arms hanging about one another's necks. When the room had quietened down, they sang. They sang with extraordinary beauty, the men's voices deep and tender, the women's high and passionate. They sang in some Bantu language, and when the song was done, the girl asked Eddie Ntwala, next to whom she found herself standing, what they had been singing about. He said as simply as a peasant, as if he had never danced with her, exchanging sophisticated banter, 'It's about a young man who passes and sees a girl working in her father's field.'

Roy Wilson giggled and gave him a comradely punch on the arm. 'Eddie's never seen a field in his life. Born and bred in Apex Location.'

Then Martin Mathlongo, with his spotted bow tie under his big, loose-mouthed, strong face, suddenly stood forward and began to sing 'Ol' Man River'. There was something insulting, defiant, yet shamefully supplicating in the way he sang the melodramatic, servile words, the way he kneeled and put out his big hands with their upturned pinkish palms. The dark faces in the room watched him, grinning as if at the antics of a monkey. The white faces looked drunk and withdrawn.

Joyce McCoy saw that, for the first time since she had been introduced to her that evening, she was near Jessica Malherbe. The girl was feeling a strong distress at the sight of the coloured man singing the blackface song, and when she saw Jessica Malherbe, she put – with a look, as it were – all this burden at the woman's feet. She put it all upon her, as if *she* could make it right, for on the woman's broad, neatly made-up face there was neither the sullen embarrassment of the other white faces nor the leering self-laceration of the black.

The girl felt the way she usually felt when she was about to cry, but this time it was the prelude to something different. She made her way with difficulty, for her legs were the drunkest part of her, murmuring politely, 'Excuse me,' as she had been taught to do for twenty-two years, past all the people who stood, in their liquor daze, stolid as cows in a stream. She went up to the trade-union leader, the veteran of political imprisonment, the glossy-haired woman who used good perfume. 'Miss Malherbe,' she said, and her blank, exquisite face might have been requesting an invitation to a garden party. 'Please, Miss Malherbe, I want to go with you next week. I want to march into the location.'

Next day, when Joyce was sober, she still wanted to go. As her brother-in-law had predicted, she felt sick from Derek's punch, and every time she inclined her head, a great, heavy ball seemed to roll slowly from one side to the other inside her skull. The presence of this ball, which sometimes felt as if it were her brain itself, shrunken and hardened, rattling like a dried nut in its shell, made it difficult to concentrate, yet the thought that she would march into the location the following week was perfectly clear. As a matter of fact, it was almost obsessively clear.

She went to see Miss Malherbe at the headquarters of the Civil Disobedience Campaign, in order to say again what she had said the night before. Miss Malherbe did again just what *she* had done the night before – listened politely, was interested and sympathetic, thanked the girl, and then gently explained that the movement could not allow anyone but bona-fide members to take part in such actions. 'Then I'll become a member now,' said Joyce. She wore today a linen dress as pale as her own skin, and on the square of bare, matching flesh at her neck hung a little necklace of small pearls – the sort of necklace that is given to a girl child and added to, pearl by pearl, a new one on every birthday. Well, said Miss Malherbe, she could join the movement, by all means – and would not that be enough? Her support would be much appreciated. But no, Joyce wanted to *do* something; she wanted to march with the others into the location. And before she left the office, she was formally enrolled.

When she had been a member for two days, she went to the headquarters to see Jessica Malherbe again. This time, there were other people present; they smiled at her when she came in, as if they already had heard about her. Miss Malherbe explained to her the gravity of what she wanted to do. Did she realise that she might have to go to prison? Did she understand that it was the policy of the passive resisters to serve their prison sentences rather than to pay fines? Even if she did not mind for herself, what about her parents, her relatives? The girl said that she was over twenty-one; her only parent, her mother, was in England; she was responsible to no one.

She told her sister Madeline and her brother-in-law nothing. When Tuesday morning came, it was damp and cool. Joyce dressed with the consciousness of the performance of the ordinary that marks extraordinary days. Her stomach felt hollow; her hands were cold. She rode into town with her brother-in-law, and all the way his car popped the fallen jacaranda flowers, which were as thick on the street beneath the tyres as they were on the trees. After lunch, she took a tram to Fordsburg, a quarter where Indians and people of mixed blood, debarred from living anywhere better, lived alongside poor whites, and where, it had been decided, the defiers were to foregather. She had never been to this part of Johannesburg before, and she had the address of the house to which she was to go written in her tartan-silk-covered notebook in her minute, backward-sloping hand. She carried her white angora jacket over her arm and she had put on sensible flat sandals. I don't know why I keep thinking of this as if it were a lengthy expedition, requiring some sort of special equipment, she thought; actually it'll be all over in half an hour. Jessica Malherbe said we'd pay bail and be back in town by 4.30.

The girl sat in the tram and did not look at the other passengers, and they did not look at her, although the contrast between her and them was startling. They were thin, yellow-limbed children with enormous sooty eyes; bleary-eyed, shuffling men, whom degeneracy had enfeebled into an appearance of indeterminate old age; heavy women with swollen legs, who were carrying newspaper parcels; young, almost white factory girls whose dull, kinky hair was pinned up into a decent simulation of fashionable style, and on whose proud, pert faces rouge and lipstick had drawn a white girl's face. Sitting among them, Joyce looked – quite apart from the social difference apparent in her clothes – so different, so other, that there were only two possible things to think about her, and which one thought depended upon one's attitude: either she was a kind of fairy – ideal, exquisite, an Ariel among Calibans – or she was something too tender, something unfinished, and beautiful only in the way the skin of the unborn lamb, taken from the belly of the mother, is beautiful, because it is a thing as yet unready for this world.

She got off at the stop she had been told to and went slowly up the street, watching the numbers. It was difficult to find out how far she would have to walk, or even, for the first few minutes, whether she was walking in the right direction, because the numbers on the doorways were half-obliterated, or ill-painted, or sometimes missing entirely. As in most poor quarters, houses and stores were mixed, and, in fact, some houses were being used as business premises, and some stores had rooms above, in which, obviously, the storekeepers and their families lived. The street had a flower name, but there were no trees and no gardens. Most of the shops had Indian firm names amateurishly written on homemade wooden signboards or curlicued and flourished in signwriter's yellow and red across the lintel: Moonsammy Dadoo, Hardware, Ladies Smart Outfitting & General; K. P. Patel & Sons, Fruit Merchants; Vallabhir's Bargain Store. A shoemaker had enclosed the veranda of his small house as a workshop, and had hung outside a huge black tin shoe, of a style worn in the twenties.

The gutters smelled of rotting fruit. Thin *café-au-lait* children trailed smaller brothers and sisters; on the veranda of one of the little semi-detached houses a lean light-coloured man in shirt-sleeves was shouting, in Afrikaans, at a fat woman who sat on the steps. An Indian woman in a sari and high-heeled European shoes was knocking at the door of the other half of the house. Farther on, a very small house, almost eclipsed by the tentacles of voracious-looking creepers, bore a polished brass plate with the name and consulting hours of a well-known Indian doctor.

The street was quiet enough; it had the dead, listless air of all places where people are making some sort of living in a small way. And so Joyce started when a sudden shriek of drunken laughter came from behind a rusty corrugated-iron wall that seemed to enclose a yard. Outside the wall, someone was sitting on a patch of the tough, gritty grass that sometimes scrabbles a hold for itself on worn city pavements; as the girl passed, she saw that the person was one of the white women tramps whom she occasionally saw in the city crossing a street with the peculiar glassy purposefulness of the outcast.

She felt neither pity nor distaste at the sight. It was as if, dating from this day, her involvement in action against social injustice had purged her of sentimentality; she did not have to avert her gaze. She looked quite calmly at the woman's bare legs, which were tanned, with dirt and exposure, to the colour of leather. She felt only, in a detached way, a prim, angry sympathy for the young pale-brown girl who stood nursing a baby at the gate of the house just beyond, because she had to live next door to what was almost certainly a shebeen.

Then, ahead of her in the next block, she saw three cars parked outside a house and knew that that must be the place. She walked a little faster, but quite evenly, and when she reached it – no. 260, as she had been told – she found that it was a small house of purplish brick, with four steps leading from the pavement to the narrow veranda. A sword fern in a paraffin tin, painted green, stood on each side of the front door, which had been left ajar, as the front door sometimes is in a house where there is a party. She went up the steps firmly, over the dusty imprints of other feet, and, leaning into the doorway a little, knocked on the fancy glass panel of the upper part of the door. She found herself looking straight down a passage that had a worn flowered linoleum on the floor. The head of a small Indian girl – low forehead and great eyes – appeared in a curtained archway halfway down the passage and disappeared again instantly.

Joyce McCoy knocked again. She could hear voices, and, above all the others, the tone of protest in a woman's voice.

A bald white man with thick glasses crossed the passage with quick, nervous steps and did not, she thought, see her. But he might have, because, prompted perhaps by his entry into the room from which the voices came, the pretty brunette woman with the efficient manner, whom the girl remembered from the party, appeared suddenly with her hand outstretched, and said enthusiastically, 'Come *in*, my dear. Come inside. Such a racket in there! You could have been knocking all day.'

The girl saw that the woman wore flimsy sandals and no stockings, and that her toenails were painted like the toes of the languid girls in *Vogue*. The girl did not know why details such as these intrigued her so much, or seemed so remarkable. She smiled in greeting and followed the woman into the house.

Now she was really there; she heard her own footsteps taking her down the passage of a house in Fordsburg. There was a faintly spicy smell about the passage; on the wall she caught a glimpse of what appeared to be a photograph of an Indian girl in European bridal dress, the picture framed with fretted gold paper, like a cake frill. And then they were in a room where everyone smiled at her quickly but took no notice of her. Jessica Malherbe was there, in a blue linen suit, smoking a cigarette and saying something to the tall, tousle-headed Roy Wilson, who was writing down what she said. The bald man was talking low and earnestly to a slim woman who wore a man's wrist watch and had the hands of a man. The tiny African, Shabalala, wearing a pair of spectacles with thin tortoise-shell rims, was ticking a pencilled list. Three or four others, black and white, sat talking. The room was as brisk with chatter as a birds' cage.

Joyce lowered herself gingerly on to a dining-room chair whose legs were loose and swayed a little. And as she tried to conceal herself and sink into the composition of the room, she noticed a group sitting a little apart, near the windows, in the shadow of the heavy curtains, and, from the arresting sight of them, saw the whole room as it was beneath the overlay of people. The group was made up of an old Indian woman, and a slim Indian boy and another Indian child, who were obviously her grandchildren. The woman sat with her feet apart, so that her lap, under the voluminous swathings of her sari, was broad, and in one nostril a ruby twinkled. Her hands were little and beringed – a fat woman's hands. Her forehead was low beneath the coarse black hair and the line of tinsel along the sari, and she looked out through the company of white men and women, Indian men in business suits, Africans in clerkly neatness, as if she were deaf or could not see. Yet when Joyce saw her eyes move, as cold and as lacking in interest as the eyes of a tortoise, and her foot stir, asserting an inert force of life, like the twitch in a muscle of some supine creature on a mudbank, the girl knew it was not deafness or blindness that kept the woman oblivious of the company but simply the knowledge that this house, this room, was her place. She was here before the visitors came; she would not move for them; she would be here when they had gone. And the children clung with their grandmother, knowing that she was the kind who could never be banished to the kitchen or some other backwater.

From the assertion of this silent group the girl became aware of the whole room (*their* room), of its furnishings: the hideous 'suite' upholstered in imitation velvet with a stamped design of triangles and sickles; the yellow varnished table with the pink silk mat and the brass vase of paper roses; the easy chairs with circular apertures in the arms where coloured glass ashtrays were balanced; the crudely coloured photographs; the barbola vase; the green ruched-silk cushions; the standard lamp with more platforms for more coloured glass ashtrays; the gilded plaster dog that stood at the door. An Indian went over and said something to the old woman with the proprietary, apologetic, irritated air of a son who wishes his mother would keep out of the way; as he turned his head, the girl saw something familiar in the angle and recognised him as the man the back of whose neck she had seen when she was trying to identify Jessica Malherbe's husband at the party. Now he came over to her, a squat, pleasant man, with a great deal of that shiny black Indian hair making his head look too big for his body. He said, 'My congratulations. My wife, Jessica, tells me you have insisted on identifying yourself with today's defiance. Well, how do you feel about it?'

She smiled at him with great difficulty; she really did not know why it was so difficult. She said, 'I'm sorry. We didn't meet that night. Just your cousin – I believe it is? – Mr Singh.' He was such a remarkably commonplace-looking Indian, Jessica Malherbe's husband, but Jessica Malherbe's husband after all – the man with the roll of fat at the back of his neck.

She said, 'You don't resemble Mr Singh in the least,' feeling that it was herself she offended by the obvious thought behind the comparison, and not this fat, amiable middle-aged man, who needed only to be in his shirtsleeves to look like any well-to-do Indian merchant, or in a grubby white coat, and unshaven, to look like a fruit-and-vegetable hawker. He sat down beside her (she could see the head of the old woman just beyond his ear), and as he began to talk to her in his Cambridge-modulated voice, she began to notice something that she had not noticed before. It was curious, because surely it must have been there all the time; then again it might not have been – it might have been released by some movement of the group of the grandmother, the slender boy and the child, perhaps from their clothes – but quite suddenly she began to be aware of the odour of incense. Sweet and dry and smoky, like the odour of burning leaves – she began to smell it. Then she thought, it must be in the furniture, the curtains; the old woman burns it and it permeates the house and all the gewgaws from Birmingham, and Denver, Colorado, and American-occupied Japan. Then it did not remind her of burning leaves any longer. It was incense, strong and sweet. The smell of death and flowers. She remembered it with such immediacy that it came back literally, absolutely, the way a memory of words or vision never can.

'Are you all right, Miss McCoy?' said the kindly Indian, interrupting himself because he saw that she was not listening and that her pretty, pale, impassive face was so white and withdrawn that she looked as if she might faint.

She stood up with a start that was like an inarticulate apology and went quickly from the room. She ran down the passage and opened a door and closed it behind her, but the odour was there, too, stronger than ever, in somebody's bedroom, where a big double bed had an orange silk cover. She leant with her back against the door, breathing it in and trembling with fear and with the terrible desire to be safe: to be safe from one of the kindly women who would come, any moment now, to see what was wrong; to be safe from the gathering up of her own nerve to face the journey in the car to the location, and the faces of her companions, who were not afraid, and the walk up the location street.

The very conventions of the life which, she felt, had insulated her in softness against the sharp, joyful brush of real life in action came up to save her now. If she was afraid, she was also polite. She had been polite so long that the colourless formula of good manners, which had stifled so much spontaneity in her, could also serve to stifle fear.

It would be so *terribly rude* simply to run away out of the house, and go home, now.

That was the thought that saved her – the code of a well-brought-up child at a party – and it came to her again and again, slowing down her thudding heart, uncurling her clenched hands. *It would be terribly rude to run away now*. She knew with distress, somewhere at the back of her mind, that this was the wrong reason for staying, but it worked. Her manners had been with her longer and were stronger than her fear. Slowly the room ceased to sing so loudly about her, the bedspread stopped dancing up and down before her eyes, and she went slowly over to the mirror in the door of the wardrobe and straightened the belt of her dress, not meeting her own eyes. Then she opened the door and went down the passage and back again into the room where the others were gathered, and sat down in the chair she had left. It was only then that she noticed that the others were standing – had risen, ready to go.

'What about your jacket, my dear. Would you like to leave it?' the pretty brunette said, noticing her.

Jessica Malherbe was on her way to the door. She smiled at Joyce and said, 'I'd leave it, if I were you.'

'Yes, I think so, thank you.' She heard her own voice as if it were someone else's.

Outside, there was the mild confusion of deciding who should go with whom and in which car. The girl found herself in the back of the car in which Jessica Malherbe sat beside the driver. The slim, mannish woman got in; little Shabalala got in but was summoned to another car by an urgently waving hand. He got out again, and then came back and jumped in just as they were off. He was the only one who seemed excited. He sat forward, with his hands on his knees. Smiling widely at the girl, he said, 'Now we really are taking you for a ride, Miss McCoy.'

The cars drove through Fordsburg and skirted the city. Then they went out on one of the main roads that connect the gold-mining towns of the Witwatersrand with each other and with Johannesburg. They passed mine dumps, pale grey and yellow; clusters of neat, ugly houses, provided for white mineworkers;

patches of veld, where the rain of the night before glittered thinly in low places; a brickfield; a foundry; a little poultry farm. And then they turned in to a muddy road, along which they followed a native bus that swayed under its load of passengers, exhaust pipe sputtering black smoke, canvas flaps over the windows wildly agitated. The bus thundered ahead through the location gates, but the three cars stopped outside. Jessica Malherbe got out first, and stood, pushing back the cuticles of the nails of her left hand as she talked in a businesslike fashion to Roy Wilson. 'Of course, don't give the statement to the papers unless they ask for it. It would be more interesting to see *their* version first, and come along with our own afterwards. But they *may* ask—'

'There's a press car,' Shabalala said, hurrying up. 'There.'

'Looks like Brand, from the *Post*.'

'Can't be Dick Brand; he's transferred to Bloemfontein,' said the tall, mannish woman.

'Come here, Miss McCoy, you're the baby,' said Shabalala, straightening his tie and twitching his shoulders, in case there was going to be a photograph. Obediently, the girl moved to the front.

But the press photographer waved his flashbulb in protest. 'No, I want you walking.'

'Well, you better get us before we enter the gates or you'll find yourself arrested, too,' said Jessica Malherbe, unconcerned. 'Look at that,' she added to the mannish woman, lifting her foot to show the heel of her white shoe, muddy already.

Lagersdorp Location, which they were entering and which Joyce McCoy had never seen before, was much like all such places. A high barbed-wire fence – more a symbol than a means of confinement, since, except for the part near the gates, it had comfortable gaps in many places – enclosed almost a square mile of dreary little dwellings, to which the African population of the nearby town came home to sleep at night. There were mean houses and squalid tin shelters and, near the gates where the administrative offices were, one or two decent cottages, which had been built by the white housing authorities 'experimentally' and never duplicated; they were occupied by the favourite African clerks of the white location superintendent. There were very few shops, since every licence granted to a native shop in a location takes business away from the white stores in the town, and there were a great many churches, some built of mud and tin, some neo-Gothic and built of brick, representing a great many sects.

They began to walk, the seven men and women, towards the location gates. Jessica Malherbe and Roy Wilson were a little ahead, and the girl found herself between Shabalala and the bald white man with thick glasses. The flashbulb made its brief sensation, and the two or three picannins who were playing with tin hoops on the roadside looked up, astonished. A fat native woman selling oranges and roast mealies shouted speculatively to a passer-by in ragged trousers.

At the gateway, a fat black policeman sat on a soapbox and gossiped. He raised his hand to his cap as they passed. In Joyce McCoy, the numbness that had followed her nervous crisis began to be replaced by a calm embarrassment; as a child she had often wondered, seeing a circle of Salvation Army people playing a hymn out of tune on a street corner, how it would feel to stand there with them. Now she felt she knew. Little Shabalala ran a finger around the inside of his collar, and the girl thought, with a start of warmth, that he was feeling as she was; she did not know that he was thinking what he had promised himself he would not think about during this walk – that very likely the walk would cost him his job. People did not want to employ Africans who 'made trouble'. His wife, who was immensely proud of his education and his cleverness, had said nothing when she learnt that he was going – had only gone, with studied consciousness, about her cooking. But, after all, Shabalala, like the girl – though neither he nor she could know it – was also saved by convention. In his case, it was a bold convention – that he was an amusing little man. He said to her as they began to walk up the road, inside the gateway, 'Feel the bump?'

'I beg your pardon?' she said, polite and conspiratorial.

A group of ragged children, their eyes alight with the tenacious beggarliness associated with the East rather than with Africa, were jumping and running around the white members of the party, which they thought was some committee come to judge a competition for the cleanest house, or a baby show. 'Penny, missus, penny, penny, baas!' they whined. Shabalala growled something at them playfully in their own language before he answered, with his delightful grin, wide as a slice of melon. 'The bump over the colour bar.'

Apart from the children, who dropped away desultorily, like flying fish behind a boat, no one took much notice of the defiers. The African women, carrying on their heads food they had bought in town, or bundles of white people's washing, scarcely looked at them. African men on bicycles rode past, preoccupied. But when the party came up parallel with the administration offices – built of red brick, and, along with the experimental cottages at the gate and the clinic next door, the only buildings of European standard in the location – a middle-aged white man in a suit worn shiny on the seat and the elbows (his slightly stooping body seemed to carry the shape of his office chair and desk) came out and stopped Jessica Malherbe. Obediently, the whole group stopped; there was an air of quiet obstinacy about them. The man, who was the location superintendent himself, evidently knew Jessica Malherbe, and was awkward with the necessity of making this an official and not a personal encounter. 'You know that I must tell you it is prohibited for Europeans to enter Lagersdorp Location,' he said. The girl noticed that he carried his glasses in his left hand, dangling by one earpiece, as if he had been waiting for the arrival of the party and had jumped up from his desk nervously at last.

Jessica Malherbe smiled, and there was in her smile something of the easy, informal amusement with which Afrikaners discount pomposity. 'Mr Dougal, good afternoon. Yes, of course, we know you have to give us official warning. How far do you think we'll get?'

The man's face relaxed. He shrugged and said, 'They're waiting for you.'

And suddenly the girl, Joyce McCoy, felt this – the sense of something lying in wait for them. The neat, stereotyped faces of African clerks appeared at the windows of the administrative offices. As the party approached the clinic, the European doctor, in his white coat, looked out; two white nurses and an African nurse came out on to the veranda. And all the patient African women who were sitting about in the sun outside, suckling their babies and gossiping, sat silent while the party walked by – sat silent, and had in their eyes something of the look of the Indian grandmother, waiting at home in Fordsburg.

The party walked on up the street, and on either side, in the little houses, which had homemade verandas flanking the strip of worn, unpaved earth that was the pavement, or whose front doors opened straight out on to a foot or two of fenced garden, where hens ran and pumpkins had been put to ripen, doors were open, and men and women stood, their children gathered in around them, as if they sensed the approach of a storm. Yet the sun was hot on the heads of the party, walking slowly up the street. And they were silent, and the watchers were silent, or spoke to one another only in whispers, each bending his head to another's ear but keeping his eyes on the group passing up the street. Someone laughed, but it was only a drunk – a wizened little old man – returning from some shebeen. And ahead, at the corner of a crossroad, stood the police car, a black car, with the aerial from its radio-communication equipment a shining lash against all the shabbiness of the street. The rear doors opened and two heavy, smartly dressed policemen got out and slammed the doors behind them. They approached the party slowly, not hurrying themselves. When they drew abreast, one said, as if in reflex, 'Ah – good afternoon.' But the other cut in, in an emotionless official voice, 'You are all under arrest for illegal entry into Lagersdorp Location. If you'll just give us your names . . .'

Joyce stood waiting her turn, and her heart beat slowly and evenly. She thought again, as she had once before – how long ago was that party? – I feel *nothing*. It's all right. I feel *nothing*.

But as the policeman came to her, and she spelled out her name for him, she looked up and saw the faces of the African onlookers who stood nearest her. Two men, a small boy and a woman, dressed in ill-matched cast-offs of European clothing, which hung upon them without meaning, like coats spread on bushes, were looking at her. When she looked back, they met her gaze. And she felt, suddenly, not *nothing* but what they were feeling, at the sight of her, a white girl, taken – incomprehensibly, as they themselves were used to being taken – under the force of white men's wills, which dispensed and withdrew life, which imprisoned and set free, fed or starved, like God himself.

Not for Publication

Not for Publication

It is not generally known – and it is never mentioned in the official biographies – that the Prime Minister spent the first eleven years of his life, as soon as he could be trusted not to get under a car, leading his uncle about the streets. The uncle was not really blind, but nearly, and he was certainly mad. He walked with his right hand on the boy's left shoulder; they kept moving part of the day, but they also had a pitch on the cold side of the street, between the legless man near the post office who sold bootlaces and copper bracelets, and the one with the doll's hand growing out of one elbow, whose pitch was outside the YWCA. That was where Adelaide Graham-Grigg found the boy, and later he explained to her, 'If you sit in the sun they don't give you anything.'

Miss Graham-Grigg was not looking for Praise Basetse. She was in Johannesburg on one of her visits from a British Protectorate, seeing friends, pulling strings, and pursuing, on the side, her private study of following up the fate of those people of the tribe who had crossed the border and lost themselves, sometimes over several generations, in the city. As she felt down through the papers and letters in her bag to find a sixpence for the old man's hat, she heard him mumble something to the boy in the tribe's tongue – which was not in itself anything very significant in this city where many African languages could be heard. But these sounds formed in her ear as words: it was the language that she had learnt to understand a little. She asked, in English, using only the traditional form of address in the tribe's tongue, whether the old man was a tribesman? But he was mumbling the blessings that the clink of a coin started up like a kick to a worn and useless mechanism. The boy spoke to him, nudged him; he had already learnt in a rough way to be a businessman. Then the old man protested, no, no, he had come a long time from that tribe. A long, long time.

He was Johannesburg. She saw that he confused the question with some routine interrogation at the pass offices, where a man from another territory was always in danger of being endorsed out to some forgotten 'home'. She spoke to the boy, asking him if he came from the Protectorate. He shook his head terrifiedly; once before he had been ordered off the streets by a welfare organisation. 'But your father? Your mother?' Miss Graham-Grigg said, smiling. She discovered that the old man had come from the Protectorate, from the very village she had made her own, and that his children had passed on to their children enough of the language for them all to continue to speak it among themselves down to the second generation born in the alien city.

Now the pair were no longer beggars to be ousted from her conscience by a coin: they were members of the tribe. She found out what township they went to ground in after the day's begging, interviewed the family, established for them the old man's right to a pension in his adopted country, and, above all, did something for the boy. She never succeeded in finding out exactly who he was – she gathered he must have been the illegitimate child of one of the girls in the family, his parentage concealed so that she might go on with her schooling. Anyway, he was a descendant of the tribe, a displaced tribesman, and he could not be left to go on begging in the streets. That was as far as Miss Graham-Grigg's thoughts for him went, in the beginning. Nobody wanted him particularly, and she met with no opposition from the family when she proposed to take him back to the Protectorate and put him to school. He went with her just as he had gone through the streets of Johannesburg each day under the weight of the old man's hand.

The boy had never been to school before. He could not write, but Miss Graham-Grigg was astonished to discover that he could read quite fluently. Sitting beside her in her little car in the khaki shorts and shirt she had bought him, stripped of the protection of his smelly rags and scrubbed bare to her questions, he told her that he had learnt from the newspaper vendor whose pitch was on the corner; from the posters that changed several times a day, and then from the front pages of the newspapers and magazines spread there.

Good God, what had he not learnt on the street! Everything from his skin out unfamiliar to him, and even that smelling strangely different – this detachment, she realised, made the child talk as he could never have done when he was himself. Without differentiation, he related the commonplaces of his life; he had also learnt from the legless copper bracelet man how to make *dagga* cigarettes and smoke them for a nice feeling. She asked him what he thought he would have done when he got older, if he had had to keep on walking with his uncle, and he said that he had wanted to belong to one of the gangs of boys, some little older than himself, who were very good at making money. They got money from white people's pockets and handbags without them even knowing it, and if the police came they began to play their penny whistles and sing.

She said with a smile, 'Well, you can forget all about the street, now. You don't have to think about it ever again.'

And he said, 'Yes, med-dam' and she knew she had no idea what he was thinking – how could she? All she could offer were more unfamiliarities, the unfamiliarities of generalised encouragement, saying, 'And soon you will know how to write.'

She had noticed that he was hatefully ashamed of not being able to write. When he had had to admit it, the face that he turned open and victimised to her every time she spoke had the squinting grimace – teeth showing and a grown-up cut between the faint, child's eyebrows – of profound humiliation. Humiliation terrified Adelaide Graham-Grigg as the spectacle of savage anger terrifies others. That was one of the things she held against the missionaries: how they stressed Christ's submission to humiliation, and so had conditioned the people of Africa to humiliation by the white man.

Praise went to the secular school that Miss Graham-Grigg's committee of friends of the tribe in London had helped pay to set up in the village in opposition to the mission school. The sole qualified teacher was a young man who had received his training in South Africa and now had been brought back to serve his people; but it was a beginning. As Adelaide Graham-Grigg often said to the Chief, shining-eyed as any proud daughter, 'By the time independence comes we'll be free not only of the British Government, but of the church as well.' And he always giggled a little embarrassedly, although he knew her so well and was old enough to be her father, because her own father was both a former British MP and the son of a bishop.

It was true that everything was a beginning; that was the beauty of it – of the smooth mud houses, red earth, flies and heat that visitors from England wondered she could bear to live with for months on end, while their palaces and cathedrals and streets choked on a thousand years of used-up endeavour were an ending. Even Praise was a beginning; one day the tribe would be economically strong enough to gather its exiles home, and it would no longer be necessary for its sons to sell their labour over that border. But it soon became clear that Praise was also exceptional. The business of learning to read from newspaper headlines was not merely a piece of gutter-wit; it proved to have been the irrepressible urge of real intelligence. In six weeks the boy could write, and from the start he could spell perfectly, while boys of sixteen and eighteen never succeeded in mastering English orthography. His arithmetic was so good that he had to be taught with the Standard Three class instead of the beginners; he grasped at once what a map was; and in his spare time showed a remarkable aptitude for understanding the workings of various mechanisms, from water pumps to motorcycle engines. In eighteen months he had completed the Standard Five syllabus, only a year behind the average age of a city white child with all the background advantage of a literate home.

There was as yet no other child in the tribe's school who was ready for Standard Six. It was difficult to see what could be done, now, but send Praise back over the border to school. So Miss Graham-Grigg decided it would have to be Father Audry. There was nothing else for it. The only alternative was the mission school, those damned Jesuits who'd been sitting in the Protectorate since the days when the white imperialists were on the grab, taking the tribes under their 'protection' – and the children the boy would be in class with there wouldn't provide any sort of stimulation, either. So it would have to be Father Audry, and South Africa. He was a priest, too, an Anglican one, but his school was a place where at least, along with the pious pap, a black child could get an education as good as a white child's.

When Praise came out into the veld with the other boys his eyes screwed up, against the size: the land ran away all round, and there was no other side to be seen; only the sudden appearance of the sky, that was even bigger. The wind made him snuff like a dog. He stood helpless as the country men he had seen caught by changing traffic lights in the middle of a street. The bits of space between buildings came together, ballooned uninterruptedly over him, he was lost; but there were clouds as big as the buildings had been, and even though space was vaster than any city, it was peopled by birds. If you ran for ten minutes into the veld the village was gone; but down low on the ground thousands of ants knew their way between their hard mounds that stood up endlessly as the land.

He went to herd cattle with the other boys early in the mornings and after school. He taught them some gambling games they had never heard of. He told them about the city they had never seen. The money in the old man's hat seemed a lot to them, who had never got more than a few pennies when the mail train stopped for water at the halt five miles away; so the sum grew in his own estimation, too, and he exaggerated it a bit. In any case, he *was* forgetting about the city; in a way; not Miss Graham-Grigg's way, but in the manner of a child, who makes, like a wasp building with his own spittle, his private context within the circumstance of his surroundings, so that the space around him was reduced to the village, the pan where the cattle were taken to drink, the halt where the train went by; whatever particular patch of sand or rough grass astir with ants the boys rolled on, heads together, among the white egrets and the cattle. He learnt from the others what roots and leaves were good to chew, and how to set wire traps for spring-hares. Though Miss Graham-Grigg had said he need not, he went to church with the children on Sundays.

He did not live where she did, in one of the Chief's houses, but with the family of one of the other boys; but he was at her house often. She asked him to copy letters for her. She cut things out of the newspapers she got and gave them to him to read; they were about aeroplanes, and dams being built, and the way the people lived in other countries. 'Now you'll be able to tell the boys all about the Volta Dam, that is also in Africa – far from here – but still, in Africa,' she said, with that sudden smile that reddened her face. She had a gramophone and she played records for him. Not only music, but people reading out poems, so that he knew that the poems in the school reader were not just short lines of words, but more like songs. She gave him tea with plenty of sugar and she asked him to help her to learn the language of the tribe, to talk to her in it. He was not allowed to call her madam or missus, as he did the white women who had put money in the hat, but had to learn to say Miss Graham-Grigg.

Although he had never known any white women before except as high-heeled shoes passing quickly in the street, he did not think that all white women must be like her; in the light of what he had seen white people, in their cars, their wealth, their distance, to be, he understood nothing that she did. She looked like them, with her blue eyes, blonde hair and skin that was not one colour but many – brown where the sun burned it, red when she blushed – but she lived here in the Chief's houses, drove him in his car, and sometimes slept out in the fields with the women when they were harvesting kaffircorn far from the village. He did not know why she had brought him there, or why she should be kind to him. But he could not ask her, any more than he would have asked her why she went out and slept in the fields when she had a gramophone and a lovely gas lamp (he had been able to repair it for her) in her room. If when they were talking together, the talk came anywhere near the pitch outside the post office, she became slowly very red, and they went past it, either by falling silent or (on her part) talking and laughing rather fast.

That was why he was amazed the day she told him that he was going back to Johannesburg. As soon as she had said it she blushed darkly for it, her eyes pleading confusion: so it was really from her that the vision of the pitch outside the post office came again. But she was already speaking: '—to school. To a really good boarding school, Father Audry's school, about nine miles from town. You must get your chance at a good school, Praise. We really can't teach you properly any longer. Maybe you'll be the teacher here, yourself, one day. There'll be a high school and you'll be the headmaster.'

She succeeded in making him smile; but she looked sad, uncertain. He went on smiling because he couldn't tell her about the initiation school that he was about to begin with the other boys of his age group. Perhaps someone would tell her. The other women. Even the Chief. But you couldn't fool her with smiling.

'You'll be sorry to leave Tebedi and Joseph and the rest.'

He stood there, smiling.

'Praise, I don't think you understand about yourself – about your brain.' She gave a little sobbing giggle, prodded at her own head. 'You've got an awfully good one. More in there than other boys – you know? It's something special – it would be such a waste. Lots of people would like to be clever like you, but it's not easy, when you are the clever one—?'

He went on smiling. He did not want her face looking into his any more and so he fixed his eyes on her feet, white feet in sandals with the veins standing out over the ankles like the feet of Christ dangling above his head in the church.

Adelaide Graham-Grigg had met Father Audry before, of course. All those white people who do not accept the colour bar in Southern Africa seem to know each other, however different the bases of their rejection. She had sat with him on some committee or other in London a few years earlier, along with a couple of exiled white South African leftists and a black nationalist leader. Anyway, everyone knew him – from the newspapers if nowhere else: he had been warned, in a public speech by the Prime Minister of South Africa, Dr Verwoerd, that the interference of a churchman in political matters would not be tolerated. He continued to speak his mind, and (as the newspapers quoted him) 'to obey the commands of God before the dictates of the State'. He had close friends among African and Indian leaders, and it was said that he even got on well with certain ministers of the Dutch

Reformed Church, that, in fact, *he* was behind some of the dissidents who now and then questioned Divine Sanction for the colour bar – such was the presence of his restless, black-cassocked figure, stammering eloquence and jagged handsome face.

He had aged since she saw him last; he was less handsome. But he had still what he would have as long as he lived: the unconscious bearing of a natural prince among men that makes a celebrated actor, a political leader, a successful lover; an object of attraction and envy who, whatever his generosity of spirit, is careless of one cruelty for which other people will never forgive him – the distinction, the luck with which he was born.

He was tired and closed his eyes in a grimace straining at concentration when he talked to her, yet in spite of this she felt the dimness of the candle of her being within his radius. Everything was right, with him; nothing was quite right with her. She was only thirty-six but she had never looked any younger. Her eyes were the bright shy eyes of a young woman but her feet and hands with their ridged nails had the look of tension and suffering of extremities that would never caress: she saw it, he saw it, she knew in his presence that they were deprived for ever.

Her humiliation gave her force. She said, 'I must tell you we want him back in the tribe – I mean, there are terribly few with enough education even for administration. Within the next few years we'll desperately need more and more educated men . . . We shouldn't want him to be allowed to think of becoming a priest.'

Father Audry smiled at what he knew he was expected to come out with: that if the boy chose the way of the Lord, etc.

He said, 'What you want is someone who will turn out to be an able politician without challenging the tribal system.'

They both laughed, but, again, he had unconsciously taken the advantage of admitting their deeply divergent views; he believed the chiefs must go, while she, of course, saw no reason why Africans shouldn't develop their own tribal democracy instead of taking over the Western pattern.

'Well, he's a little young for us to be worrying about that now, don't you think . . . ?' He smiled. There were a great many papers on his desk and she had the sense of pressure of his preoccupation with other things. 'What about the Lemeribe Mission? What's the teaching like these days – I used to know Father Chalmon when he was there—'

'I wouldn't send him to those people,' she said spiritedly, implying that he knew her views on missionaries and their role in Africa. In this atmosphere of candour they discussed Praise's background. Father Audry suggested that the boy should be encouraged to resume relations with his family, once he was back within reach of Johannesburg.

'They're pretty awful.'

'It would be best for him to acknowledge what he was, if he is to accept what he is to become.' He got up with a swish of his black skirts and strode, stooping in the opened door, to call, 'Simon, bring the boy.' Miss Graham-Grigg was smiling excitedly towards the doorway, all the will to love pacing behind the bars of her glance.

Praise entered in the navy-blue shorts and white shirt of his new school uniform. The woman's kindness, the man's attention, got him in the eyes like the sun striking off the pan where the cattle had been taken to drink. Father Audry came from England, Miss Graham-Grigg had told him, like herself. That was what they were, these two white people who were not like any white people he had seen to be. What they were was being English. From far off; six thousand miles from here, as he knew from his geography book.

Praise did very well at the new school. He sang in the choir in the big church on Sundays; his body, that was to have been made a man's out in the bush, was hidden under the white robes. The boys smoked in the lavatories and once there was a girl who came and lay down for them in a storm-water ditch behind the workshops. He knew all about these things from before, on the streets and in the location where he had slept in one room with a whole family. But he did not tell the boys about the initiation. The women had not said anything to Miss Graham-Grigg. The Chief hadn't, either. Soon when Praise thought about it he realised that by now it must be over. Those boys must have come back from the bush. Miss

Graham-Grigg had said that after a year, when Christmas came, she would fetch him for the summer holidays. She did come and see him twice that first year, when she was down in Johannesburg, but he couldn't go back with her at Christmas because Father Audry had him in the Nativity play, and was giving him personal coaching in Latin and algebra. Father Audry didn't actually teach in the school at all – it was 'his' school simply because he had begun it, and it was run by the Order of which he was Father Provincial – but the reports of the boy's progress were so astonishing that, as he said to Miss Graham-Grigg, one felt one must give him all the mental stimulation one could.

'I begin to believe we may be able to sit him for his matric when he is just sixteen.' Father Audry made the pronouncement with the air of doing so at the risk of sounding ridiculous.

Miss Graham-Grigg always had her hair done when she got to Johannesburg, she was looking pretty and optimistic. 'D'you think he could do a Cambridge entrance? My committee in London would set up a scholarship, I'm sure – investment in a future Prime Minister for the Chief!'

When Praise was sent for, she said she hardly knew him; he hadn't grown much, but he looked so *grown-up*, with his long trousers and glasses. 'You really needn't wear them when you're not working,' said Father Audry. 'Well, I suppose if you take 'em on and off you keep leaving them about, eh?' They both stood back, smiling, letting the phenomenon embody in the boy.

Praise saw that she had never been reminded by anyone about the initiation. She began to give him news of his friends, Tebedi and Joseph and the others, but when he heard their names they seemed to belong to people he couldn't see in his mind.

Father Audry talked to him sometimes about what Father called his 'family', and when first he came to the school he had been told to write to them. It was a well-written, well-spelled letter in English, exactly the letter he presented as a school exercise when one was required in class. They didn't answer. Then Father Audry must have made private efforts to get in touch with them, because the old woman, a couple of children who had been babies when he left and one of his grown-up 'sisters' came to the school on a visiting day. They had to be pointed out to him among the other boys' visitors; he would not have known them, nor they him.

He said, 'Where's my uncle?' – because he would have known him at once; he had never grown out of the slight stoop of the left shoulder where the weight of the old man's hand had impressed the young bone. But the old man was dead.

Father Audry came up and put a long arm round the bent shoulder and another long arm round one of the small children and said from one to the other: 'Are you going to work hard and learn a lot like your brother?' and the small black child stared up into the nostrils filled with strong hair, the tufted eyebrows, the red mouth surrounded by the pale jowl dark-pored with beard beneath the skin, and then down, torn by fascination, to the string of beads that hung from the leather belt.

They did not come again, but Praise did not much miss visitors because he spent more and more time with Father Audry. When he was not actually being coached, he was set to work to prepare his lessons or do his reading in the Father's study, where he could concentrate as one could not hope to do up at the school. Father Audry taught him chess as a form of mental gymnastics, and was jubilant the first time Praise beat him. Praise went up to the house for a game nearly every evening after supper. He tried to teach the other boys but after the first ten minutes of explanation of moves, someone would bring out the cards or dice and they would all play one of the old games that were played in the streets and yards and locations. Johannesburg was only nine miles away; you could see the lights.

Father Audry rediscovered what Miss Graham-Grigg had found – that Praise listened attentively to music, serious music. One day Father Audry handed the boy the flute that had lain for years in its velvet-lined box that bore still the little silver nameplate: Rowland Audry. He watched while Praise gave the preliminary swaying wriggle and assumed the bent-kneed stance of all the urchin performers Father Audry had seen, and then tried to blow down it in the shy, fierce attack of penny whistle music. Father

Audry took it out of his hands. 'It's what you've just heard there.' Bach's unaccompanied flute sonata lay on the record player. Praise smiled and frowned, giving his glasses a lift with his nose – a habit he was developing. 'But you'll soon learn to play it the right way round,' said Father Audry, and with the lack of self-consciousness that comes from the habit of privilege, put the flute to his mouth and played what he remembered after ten years.

He taught Praise not only how to play the flute, but also the elements of musical composition, so that he should not simply play by ear, or simply listen with pleasure, but also understand what it was that he heard. The flute-playing was much more of a success with the boys than the chess had been, and on Saturday nights, when they sometimes made up concerts, he was allowed to take it to the hostel and play it for them. Once he played in a show for white people, in Johannesburg; but the boys could not come to that; he could only tell them about the big hall at the university, the jazz band, the African singers and dancers with their red lips and straightened hair, like white women.

The one thing that dissatisfied Father Audry was that the boy had not filled out and grown as much as one would have expected. He made it a rule that Praise must spend more time on physical exercise – the school couldn't afford a proper gymnasium, but there was some equipment outdoors. The trouble was that the boy had so little time; even with his exceptional ability, it was not going to be easy for a boy with his lack of background to matriculate at sixteen. Brother George, his form master, was certain he could be made to bring it off; there was a specially strong reason why everyone wanted him to do it since Father Audry had established that he would be eligible for an open scholarship that no black boy had ever won before – what a triumph that would be, for the boy, for the school, for all the African boys who were considered fit only for the inferior standard of 'Bantu education'! Perhaps some day this beggar-child from the streets of Johannesburg might even become the first black South African to be a Rhodes Scholar. This was what Father Audry jokingly referred to as Brother George's 'sin of pride'. But who knew? It was not inconceivable. So far as the boy's physique was concerned – what Brother George said was probably true: 'You can't feed up for those years in the streets.'

From the beginning of the first term of the year he was fifteen Praise had to be coached, pressed on, and to work as even he had never worked before. His teachers gave him tremendous support; he seemed borne along on it by either arm so that he never looked up from his books. To encourage him, Father Audry arranged for him to compete in certain inter-school scholastic contests that were really intended for the white Anglican schools – a spelling team, a debate, a quiz contest. He sat on the platform in the polished halls of huge white schools and gave his correct answers in the African-accented English that the boys who surrounded him knew only as the accent of servants and delivery men.

Brother George often asked him if he were tired. But he was not tired. He only wanted to be left with his books. The boys in the hostel seemed to know this; they never asked him to play cards any more, and even when they shared smokes together in the lavatory, they passed him his drag in silence. He specially did not want Father Audry to come in with a glass of hot milk. He would rest his cheek against the pages of the books, now and then, alone in the study; that was all. The damp stone smell of the books was all he needed. Where he had once had to force himself to return again and again to the pages of things he did not grasp, gazing in blankness at the print until meaning assembled itself, he now had to force himself when it was necessary to leave the swarming facts, outside which he no longer seemed to understand anything. Sometimes he could not work for minutes at a time because he was thinking that Father Audry would come in with the milk. When he did come, it was never actually so bad. But Praise couldn't look at his face. Once or twice when he had gone out again, Praise shed a few tears. He found himself praying, smiling with the tears and trembling, rubbing at the scalding water that ran down inside his nose and blotched on the books.

One Saturday afternoon when Father Audry had been entertaining guests at lunch he came into the study and suggested that the boy should get some fresh air – go out and join the football game for an hour or so. But Praise was struggling with geometry problems from the previous year's matriculation paper that, to Brother George's dismay, he had suddenly got all wrong that morning.

Father Audry could imagine what Brother George was thinking: was this an example of the phenomenon he had met with so often with African boys of a lesser calibre – the inability, through lack of an assumed cultural background, to perform a piece of work well known to them, once it was presented in a slightly different manner outside of their own textbooks? Nonsense, of course, in this case; everyone was over-anxious about the boy. Right from the start he'd shown that there was nothing mechanistic about his thought processes; he had a brain, not just a set of conditioned reflexes.

'Off you go. You'll manage better when you've taken a few knocks on the field.'

But desperation had settled on the boy's face like obstinacy. 'I must, I must,' he said, putting his palms down over the books.

'Good. Then let's see if we can tackle it together.'

The black skirt swishing past the shiny shoes brought a smell of cigars. Praise kept his eyes on the black beads; the leather belt they hung from creaked as the big figure sat down. Father Audry took the chair on the opposite side of the table and switched the exercise book round towards himself. He scrubbed at the thick eyebrows till they stood out tangled, drew the hand down over his great nose, and then screwed his eyes closed a moment, mouth strangely open and lips drawn back in a familiar grimace. There was a jump, like a single painful hiccup, in Praise's body. The Father was explaining the problem gently, in his offhand English voice.

He said, 'Praise? D'you follow' – the boy seemed sluggish, almost deaf, as if the voice reached him as the light of a star reaches the earth from something already dead.

Father Audry put out his fine hand, in question or compassion. But the boy leapt up dodging a blow. 'Sir – no. Sir – no.'

It was clearly hysteria; he had never addressed Father Audry as anything but 'Father'. It was some frightening retrogression, a reversion to the subconscious, a place of symbols and collective memory. He spoke for others, out of another time. Father Audry stood up but saw in alarm that by the boy's retreat he was made his pursuer, and he let him go, blundering in clumsy panic out of the room.

Brother George was sent to comfort the boy. In half an hour he was down on the football field, running and laughing. But Father Audry took some days to get over the incident. He kept thinking how when the boy had backed away he had almost gone after him. The ugliness of the instinct repelled him; who would have thought how, at the mercy of the instinct to prey, the fox, the wild dog long for the innocence of the gentle rabbit and the lamb. No one had shown fear of him ever before in his life. He had never given a thought to the people who were not like himself; those from whom others turn away. He felt at last a repugnant and resentful pity for them, the dripping-jawed hunters. He even thought that he would like to go into retreat for a few days, but it was inconvenient – he had so many obligations. Finally, the matter-of-factness of the boy, Praise, was the thing that restored normality. So far as the boy was concerned, one would have thought that nothing had happened. The next day he seemed to have forgotten all about it; a good thing. And so Father Audry's own inner disruption, denied by the boy's calm, sank away. He allowed the whole affair the one acknowledgement of writing to Miss Graham-Grigg – surely that was not making too much of it – to suggest that the boy was feeling the tension of his final great effort, and that a visit from her, etc.; but she was still away in England – some family troubles had kept her there for months, and in fact she had not been to see her protégé for more than a year.

Praise worked steadily on the last lap. Brother George and Father Audry watched him continuously. He was doing extremely well and seemed quite overcome with the weight of pride and pleasure when Father Audry presented him with a new black fountain pen: this was the pen with which he was to write the matriculation exam. On a Monday afternoon Father Audry, who had been in conference with the Bishop all morning, looked in on his study, where every afternoon the boy would be seen sitting at the table that had been moved in for him. But there was no one there. The books were on the table. A chute of sunlight landed on the seat of the chair. Praise was not found again. The school was searched; and then the police were informed; the boys questioned; there were special prayers said in the mornings and evenings. He had not taken anything with him except the fountain pen.

When everything had been done there was nothing but silence; nobody mentioned the boy's name. But Father Audry was conducting investigations on his own. Every now and then he would get an idea that would bring a sudden hopeful relief. He wrote to Adelaide Graham-Grigg '. . . what worries me – I believe the boy may have been on the verge of a nervous breakdown. I am hunting everywhere . . .'; was it possible that he might make his way to the Protectorate? She was acting as confidential secretary to the Chief, now, but she wrote to say that if the boy turned up she would try to make time to deal with the situation. Father Audry even sought out, at last, the 'family' – the people with whom Miss Graham-Grigg had discovered Praise living as a beggar. They had been moved to a new township and it took some time to trace them. He found No. 28b, Block E, in the appropriate ethnic group. He was accustomed to going in and out of African homes and he explained his visit to the old woman in matter-of-fact terms at once, since he knew how suspicious of questioning the people would be. There were no interior doors in these houses and a woman in the inner room who was dressing moved out of the visitor's line of vision as he sat down. She heard all that passed between Father Audry and the old woman and presently she came in with mild interest.

Out of a silence the old woman was saying 'My-my-my-my!' – shaking her head down into her bosom in a stylised expression of commiseration; they had not seen the boy. 'And he spoke so nice, everything was so nice in the school.' But they knew nothing about the boy, nothing at all.

The younger woman remarked, 'Maybe he's with those boys who sleep in the old empty cars there in town – you know? – there by the beer-hall?'

Through Time and Distance

They had been on the road together seven or eight years, Mondays to Fridays. They did the Free State one week, the northern and eastern Transvaal the next, Natal and Zululand a third. Now and then they did Bechuanaland and Southern Rhodesia and were gone for a month. They sat side by side, for thousands of miles and thousands of hours, the commercial traveller, Hirsch, and his boy. The boy was a youngster when Hirsch took him on, with one pair of grey flannels, a clean shirt and a nervous sniff; he said he'd been a lorry driver, and at least he didn't stink – 'When you're shut up with them in a car all day, believe me, you want to find a native who doesn't stink.' Now the boy wore, like Hirsch, the line of American-cut suits that Hirsch carried, and fancy socks, suede shoes and an anti-magnetic watch with a strap of thick gilt links, all bought wholesale. He had an ear of white handkerchief always showing in his breast pocket, though he still economically blew his nose in his fingers when they made a stop out in the veld.

He drove, and Hirsch sat beside him, peeling back the pages of paperbacks, jerking slowly in and out of sleep, or scribbling in his order books. They did not speak. When the car flourished to a stop outside the verandah of some country store, Hirsch got out without haste and went in ahead – he hated to 'make an impression like a hawker', coming into a store with his goods behind him. When he had exchanged greetings with the storekeeper and leant on the counter chatting for a minute or two, as if he had nothing to do but enjoy the dimness of the interior, he would stir with a good-humoured sigh: 'I'd better show you what I've got. It's a shame to drag such lovely stuff about in this dust. Phillip!' – his face loomed in the doorway a moment – 'get a move on there.'

So long as it was not raining, Phillip kept one elbow on the rolled-down window, the long forearm reaching up to where his slender hand, shaded like the coat of some rare animal from tea-rose pink on the palm to dark matt brown on the back, appeared to support the car's gleaming roof like a caryatid. The hand would withdraw, he would swing out of the car on to his feet, he would carry into the store the cardboard boxes, suitcases, and, if the store carried what Hirsch called 'high-class goods' as well, the special stand of men's suits hanging on a rail that was made to fit into the back of the car. Then he would saunter out into the street again, giving his tall shoulders a cat's pleasurable movement under fur – a movement that conveyed to him the excellent drape of his jacket. He would take cigarettes out of his pocket and lean, smoking, against the car's warm flank.

Sometimes he held court; like Hirsch, he had become well known on the regular routes. The country people were not exactly shy of him and his kind, but his clothes and his air of city knowhow imposed a certain admiring constraint on them, even if, as in the case of some of the older men and women, they disapproved of the city and the aping of the white man's ways. He was not above playing a game of *morabaraba*, an ancient African kind of draughts, with the blacks from the grain and feed store in a dorp on the Free State run. Hirsch was always a long time in the general store next door, and, meanwhile, Phillip pulled up the perfect creases of his trousers and squatted over the lines of the board drawn with a stone in the dust, ready to show them that you couldn't beat a chap who had got his training in the big lunch-hour games that are played every day outside the wholesale houses in Johannesburg. At one or two garages, where the petrol attendants in foam-rubber baseball caps given by Shell had picked up a lick of passing sophistication, he sometimes got a poker game. The first time his boss, Hirsch, discovered him at this (Phillip had overestimated the time Hirsch would spend over the quick hand of Klabberyas he was obliged to take, in the way of business, with a local storekeeper), Hirsch's anger at being kept waiting vanished in a kind of amused and grudging pride. 'You're a big fella, now, eh, Phillip? I've made a man of you. When you came to me you were a real piccanin. Now you've been around so much, you're taking the boys' money off them on the road. Did you win?'

'Ah, no, sir,' Phillip suddenly lied, with a grin.

'Ah-h-h, what's the matter with you? You didn't win?' For a moment Hirsch looked almost as if he were about to give him a few tips. After that, he always passed his worn packs of cards on to his boy.

And Phillip learned, as time went by, to say, 'I don't like the sound of the engine, boss. There's something loose there. I'm going to get underneath and have a look while I'm down at the garage taking petrol.'

It was true that Hirsch had taught his boy everything the boy knew, although the years of silence between them in the car had never been broken by conversation or an exchange of ideas. Hirsch was one of those pale, plump, freckled Jews, with pale blue eyes, a thick snub nose and the remains of curly blond hair that had begun to fall out before he was twenty. A number of his best stories depended for their denouement on the fact that somebody or other had not realised that he was a Jew. His pride in this belief that nobody would take him for one was not conventionally anti-Semitic, but based on the reasoning that it was a matter of pride, on the part of the Jewish people, that they could count him among them while he was fitted by nature with the distinguishing characteristics of a more privileged race. Another of his advantages was that he spoke Afrikaans as fluently and idiomatically as any Afrikaner. This, as his boy had heard him explain time and again to English-speaking people, was essential, because, low and ignorant as these back-veld Afrikaners were – hardly better than the natives, most of them – they knew that they had their government up there in power now, and they wouldn't buy a sixpenny line from you if you spoke the language of the rooineks – the red-neck English.

With the Jewish shopkeepers, he showed that he was quite at home, because, as Phillip, unpacking the sample range, had overheard him admit a thousand times, he was Jewish born and bred – why, his mother's brother was a rabbi – even though he knew he didn't look it for a minute. Many of these shops were husband-and-wife affairs, and Hirsch knew how to make himself pleasant to the wives as well. In his chaff with them, the phrases 'the old country' and 'my father, God rest his soul' were recurrent. There was also an earnest conversation that began: 'If you want to meet a character, I wish you could see my mother. What a spirit. She's seventy-five, she's got sugar and she's just been operated for cataract, but I'm telling you, there's more go in her than—'

Every now and then there would be a store with a daughter, as well: not very young, not very beautiful, a worry to the mother who stood with her hands folded under her apron, hoping the girl would slim down and make the best of herself, and to the father, who wasn't getting any younger and would like to see her settled. Hirsch had an opening for this subject, too, tested and tried. 'Not much life for a girl in a place like this, eh? It's a pity. But some of the town girls are such rubbish, perhaps it's better to marry some nice girl from the country. Such rubbish – the Jewish girls, too; oh, yes, they're just as bad as the rest these days. I wouldn't mind settling down with a decent girl who hasn't run around so much. If she's not so smart, if she doesn't get herself up like a film star, well, isn't it better?'

Phillip thought that his boss was married – in some places, at any rate, he talked about 'the wife' – but perhaps it was only that he had once been married, and, anyway, what was the difference when you were on the road? The fat, ugly white girl at the store went and hid herself among the biscuit tins, the mother, half daring to hope, became vivacious by proxy, and the father suddenly began to talk to the traveller intimately about business affairs.

Phillip found he could make the same kind of stir among country blacks. Hirsch had a permit to enter certain African reserves in his rounds, and there, in the humble little shops owned by Africans – shanties, with the inevitable man at work on a treadle sewing machine outside – he used his boy to do business with them in their own lingo. The boy wasn't half bad at it, either. He caught on so quick, he was often the one to suggest that a line that was unpopular in the white dorps could be got rid of in the reserves. He would palm off the stuff like a real showman.

'They can be glad to get anything, boss,' he said, with a grin. 'They can't take a bus to town and look in the shops.' In spite of his city clothes and his signet ring and all, the boy was exactly as simple as they were, underneath, and he got on with them like a house on fire. Many's the time some old woman or little kid came running up to the car when it was all packed to go on again and gave him a few eggs or a couple of roasted mealies in a bit of newspaper.

Early on in his job driving for Hirsch, Phillip had run into a calf; it did not stir on the deserted red-earth road between walls of mealie fields that creaked in a breeze. 'Go on,' said his boss, with the authority of one who knows what he is doing, who has learned in a hard school. 'Go on, it's dead, there's nothing to do.' The young man hesitated, appalled by the soft thump of the impact with which he had given his first death-dealing blow. 'Go on. There could have been a terrible accident. We could have turned over. These farmers should be prosecuted, the way they don't look after the cattle.'

Phillip reversed quickly, avoided the body in a wide curve and drove on. That was what made life on the road; whatever it was, soft touch or hard going, lie or truth, it was left behind. By the time you came by again in a month or two months, things had changed, forgotten and forgiven, and whatever you got yourself into this time, you had always the secret assurance that there would be another breathing space before you could be got at again.

Phillip had married after he had been travelling with Hirsch for a couple of years; the girl had had a baby by him earlier, but they had waited, as Africans sometimes do, until he could get a house for her before they actually got married. They had two more children, and he kept them pretty well – he wasn't too badly paid, and of course he could get things wholesale, like the stove for the house. But up Piet Retief way, on one of the routes they took every month, there was a girl he had been sleeping with regularly for years. She swept up the hair cuttings in the local barbershop, where Hirsch sometimes went for a trim if he hadn't had a chance over the weekend in Johannesburg. That was how Phillip had met her; he was waiting in the car for Hirsch one day, and the girl came out to sweep the step at the shop's entrance. 'Hi, *wena sisi*. I wish you would come and sweep my house for me,' he called out drowsily.

For a long time now she had worn a signet ring, nine carats, engraved with his first name and hers; Hirsch did not carry anything in the jewellery line, but of course Phillip, in the fraternity of the road, knew the boys of other travellers who did. She was a plump, hysterical little thing, with very large eyes that could accommodate unshed tears for minutes on end, and – something unusual for black women – a faint moustache outlining her top lip. She would have been a shrew to live with, but it was pleasant to see how she awaited him every month with coy, bridling passion. When she pressed him to settle the date when they might marry, he filched some minor item from the extensive women's range that Hirsch carried, and that kept her quiet until next time. Phillip did not consider this as stealing, but as part of the running expenses of the road to which he was entitled, and he was trustworthy with his boss's money or goods in all other circumstances.

In fact, if he had known it and if Hirsch had known it, his filching fell below the margin for dishonesty that Hirsch, in his reckoning of the running expenses of the road, allowed: 'They all steal, what's the good of worrying about it? You change one, you get a worse thief, that's all.' It was one of Hirsch's maxims in the philosophy of the road.

The morning they left on the Bechuanaland run, Hirsch looked up from the newspaper and said to his boy, 'You've got your passbook, eh?' There was the slightest emphasis on the 'you've', an emphasis confident rather than questioning. Hirsch was well aware that, although the blurred front-page picture before him showed black faces open-mouthed, black hands flung up triumphant around a bonfire of passbooks, Phillip was not the type to look for trouble.

'Yes, sir, I've got it,' said Phillip, overtaking, as the traffic lights changed, a row of cars driven by white men; he had driven so much and so well that there was a certain beauty in his performance – he might have been skiing, or jumping hurdles.

Hirsch went back to the paper; there was nothing in it but reports of this anti-pass campaign that the natives had started up.

He read them all with a deep distrust of the amorphous threat that he thought of as 'trouble', taking on any particular form. Trouble was always there, hanging over every human head, of course; it was only when it drew near, 'came down', that it took on a specific guise: illness, a drop in business, the blacks wanting to live like white men. Anyway, he himself had nothing to worry about: his boy knew his job, and he knew he must have his pass on him in case, in a routine demand in the streets of any of the villages they passed through, a policeman should ask him to show it.

Phillip was not worried, either. When the men in the location came to the door to urge him to destroy his pass, he was away on the road, and only his wife was at home to assure them that he had done so; when some policeman in a dorp stopped him to see it, there it was, in the inner pocket of the rayon lining of his jacket. And one day, when this campaign or another was successful, he would never need to carry it again.

At every call they made on that trip, people were eager for news of what was happening in Johannesburg. Old barefoot men in the dignity of battered hats came from the yards behind the stores, trembling with dread and wild hope. Was it true that so many people were burning their passes that the police couldn't arrest them all? Was it true that in such-and-such a location people had gone to the police station and left passes in a pile in front of the door? Was it the wild young men who called themselves Africanists who were doing this? Or did Congress want it, did the old Chief, Luthuli, call for it too?

'We are going to free you all of the pass,' Phillip found himself declaiming. Children, hanging about, gave the Congress raised-thumb salute. 'The white man won't bend our backs like yours, old man.' They could see for themselves how much he had already taken from the white man, wearing the same clothes as the white man, driving the white man's big car – an emissary from the knowledgeable, political world of the city, where black men were learning to be masters. Even Hirsch's cry, 'Phillip, get a move on there!', came as an insignificant interruption, a relic of the present almost become the past.

Over the border, in the British protectorate, Bechuanaland, the interest was just as high. Phillip found it remarkably easy to talk to the little groups of men who approached him in the luxurious dust that surrounded village buildings, the kitchen boys who gathered in country hotel yards where cats fought beside glittering mounds of empty beer bottles. 'We are going to see that this is the end of the pass. The struggle for freedom – the white man won't stand on our backs –'

It was a long, hot trip. Hirsch, pale and exhausted, dozed and twitched in his sleep between one dorp and the next. For the last few months he had been putting pills instead of sugar into his tea, and he no longer drank the endless bottles of lemonade and ginger beer that he had sent the boy to buy at every stop for as long as he could remember. There was a strange, sweetish smell that seemed to follow Hirsch around these days; it settled in the car on that long trip and was there even when Hirsch wasn't; but Phillip, who, like most travellers' boys, slept in the car at night, soon got used to it.

They went as far as Francistown, where, all day, while they were in and out of the long line of stores facing the railway station, a truckload of Herero women from further north in the Kalahari Desert sat beside the road in their Victorian dress, turbaned, unsmiling, stiff and voluminous, like a row of tea cosies. The travelling salesmen did not go on to Rhodesia. From Francistown they turned back for Johannesburg, with a stop overnight at Palapye Road, so that they could make a detour to Serowe, an African town of round mud houses, dark euphorbia hedges and tinkling goat bells, where the deposed chief and his English wife lived on a hill in a large house with many bathrooms, but there was no hotel. The hotel in Palapye Road was a fly-screened box on the railway station, and Hirsch spent a bad night amid the huffing and blowing of trains taking water and the bursts of stamping – a gigantic Spanish dance – of shunting trains.

They left for home early on Friday morning. By half-past five in the afternoon they were flying along towards the outskirts of Johannesburg, with the weary heat of the day blowing out of the windows in whiffs of high land and the sweat suddenly deliciously cool on their hands and foreheads. The row of suits on the rack behind them slid obediently down and up again with each rise and dip accomplished in the turn of the road. The usual landmarks, all in their places, passed unlooked at: straggling, small-enterprise factories, a brickfield, a chicken farm, the rose nursery with the toy Dutch windmill, various gatherings of low, patchy huts and sagging houses – small locations where the blacks who worked round about lived. At one point, the road closely skirted one of these places; the children would wave and shout from where they played in the dirt. Today, quite suddenly, a shower of stones came from them. For a moment Hirsch truly thought that he had become aware of a sudden summer hailstorm; he was always so totally enclosed by the car it would not have been unusual for him not to have noticed a storm rising. He put his hand on the handle that raised the window; instantly, a sharp grey chip pitted the fold of flesh between thumb and first finger.

'Drive on,' he yelled, putting the blood to his mouth. 'Drive on!' But his boy, Phillip, had at the same moment seen what they had blundered into. Fifty yards ahead a labouring green bus, its windows, under flapping canvas, crammed with black heads, had lurched to a stop. It appeared to burst as people jumped out at doors and windows; from the houses, a jagged rush of more people met them and spread around the bus over the road.

Phillip stopped the car so fiercely that Hirsch was nearly pitched through the windscreen. With a roar the car reversed, swinging off the road sideways on to the veld, and then swung wildly around on to the road again, facing where it had come from. The steering wheel spun in the ferocious, urgent skill of the pink-and-brown hands. Hirsch understood and anxiously trusted; at the feel of the car righting itself, a grin broke through in his boy's face.

But as Phillip's suede shoe was coming down on the accelerator, a black hand in a greasy, buttonless coat sleeve seized his arm through the window, and the car rocked with the weight of the bodies that flung and clung against it. When the engine stalled, there was quiet; the hand let go of Phillip's arm. The men and women around the car were murmuring to themselves, pausing for breath; their power and indecision gave Hirsch the strongest feeling he had ever had in his life, a sheer, pure cleavage of terror that, as he fell apart, exposed – tiny kernel, his only defence, his only hope, his only truth – the will to live. 'You talk to them,' he whispered, rapping it out, confidential, desperately confident. 'You tell them – one of their own people, what can they want with you? Make it right. Let them take the stuff. Anything, for God's sake. You understand me? Speak to them.'

'They can't want nothing with this car,' Phillip was saying loudly and in a superior tone. 'This car is not the government.'

But a woman's shrill demand came again and again, and apparently it was to have them out. 'Get out, come on, get out,' came threateningly, in English, at Hirsch's window, and at his boy's side a heated, fast-breathing exchange in their own language.

Phillip's voice was injured, protesting, and angry. 'What do you want to stop us for? We're going home from a week selling on the road. Any harm in that? I work for him, and I'm driving back to Jo'burg. Come on now, clear off. I'm a Congress man myself—'

A thin woman broke the hearing with a derisive sound like a shake of castanets at the back of her tongue. 'Congress! Everybody can say. Why you're working?'

And a man in a sweatshirt, with a knitted woollen cap on his head, shouted, 'Stay-at-home. Nobody but traitors work today. What are you driving the white man for?'

'I've just told you, man, I've been away a week in Bechuanaland. I must get home somehow, mustn't I? Finish this, man, let us get on, I tell you.'

They made Hirsch and his boy get out of the car, but Hirsch, watching and listening to the explosive vehemence between his boy and the crowd, clung to the edge of a desperate, icy confidence: the boy was explaining to them – one of their own people. They did not actually hold Hirsch, but they stood around him, men whose nostrils moved in and out as they breathed; big-breasted warriors from the washtub who looked at him, spoke together, and spat; even children, who filled up the spaces between the legs so that the stirring human press that surrounded him was solid and all alive. 'Tell them, can't you?' he kept appealing, encouragingly.

'Where's your pass?'

'His pass, his pass!' the women began to yell.

'Where's your pass?' the man who had caught Phillip through the car window screamed in his face.

And he yelled back, too quickly, 'I've burned it! It's burned! I've finished with the pass!'

The women began to pull at his clothes. The men might have let him go, but the women set upon his fine city clothes as if he were an effigy. They tore and poked and snatched, and there – perhaps they had not really been looking for it or expected it – at once, fell the passbook. One of them ran off with it through the crowd, yelling and holding it high and hitting herself on the breast with it. People began to fight over it, like a souvenir. 'Burn! Burn!' 'Kill him!'

Somebody gave Phillip a felling blow aimed for the back of his neck, but whoever it was was too short to reach the target and the blow caught him on the shoulder blade instead.

'O my God, tell them, tell them, your own people!' Hirsch was shouting angrily. With a perfect, hypnotising swiftness – the moment of survival, when the buck outleaps the arc of its own strength past the lion's jaws – his boy was in the car, and with a shuddering rush of power, shaking the men off as they came, crushing someone's foot as the tyres scudded madly, drove on.

'Come back!' Hirsch's voice, although he could not hear it, swelled so thick in his throat it almost choked him. 'Come back, I tell you!' Beside him and around him, the crowd ran. Their mouths were wide, and he did not know for whom they were clamouring – himself or the boy.

A Chip of Glass Ruby

When the duplicating machine was brought into the house, Bamjee said, 'Isn't it enough that you've got the Indians' troubles on your back?' Mrs Bamjee said, with a smile that showed the gap of a missing tooth but was confident all the same, 'What's the difference, Yusuf? – we've all got the same troubles.'

'Don't tell me that. We don't have to carry passes; let the natives protest against passes on their own, there are millions of them. Let them go ahead with it.'

The nine Bamjee and Pahad children were present at this exchange as they were always; in the small house that held them all there was no room for privacy for the discussion of matters they were too young to hear, and so they had never been too young to hear anything. Only their sister and half-sister, Girlie, was missing; she was the eldest, and married. The children looked expectantly, unalarmed and interested, at Bamjee, who had neither left the dining room nor settled down again to the task of rolling his own cigarettes, which had been interrupted by the arrival of the duplicator. He looked at the thing that had come hidden in a wash-basket and conveyed in a black man's taxi, and the children turned on it, too, their black eyes surrounded by thick lashes like those still, open flowers with hairy tentacles that close on whatever touches them.

'A fine thing to have on the dining-room table,' was all he said at last. They smelled the machine among them; a smell of cold black grease. He went out, heavily on tiptoe, in his troubled way.

'It's going to go nicely on the sideboard!' Mrs Bamjee was busy making a place by removing the two pink glass vases filled with plastic carnations and the hand-painted velvet runner with the picture of the Taj Mahal.

After supper she began to run off leaflets on the machine. The family lived in the dining room – the three other rooms in the house were full of beds – and they were all there. The older children shared a bottle of ink while they did their homework, and the two little ones pushed a couple of empty milk bottles in and out the legs of chairs. The three-year-old fell asleep and was carted away by one of the girls. They all drifted off to bed eventually; Bamjee himself went before the older children – he was a fruit and vegetable hawker and was up at half past four every morning to get to the market by five.

'Not long now,' said Mrs Bamjee. The older children looked up and smiled at him. He turned his back on her. She still wore the traditional clothing of a Muslim woman, and her body, which was scraggy and unimportant as a dress on a peg when it was not host to a child, was wrapped in the trailing rags of a cheap sari, and her thin black plait was greased. When she was a girl, in the Transvaal town where they lived still, her mother fixed a chip of glass ruby in her nostril; but she had abandoned that adornment as too old-style, even for her, long ago.

She was up until long after midnight, turning out leaflets. She did it as if she might have been pounding chillies.

Bamjee did not have to ask what the leaflets were. He had read the papers. All the past week Africans had been destroying their passes and then presenting themselves for arrest. Their leaders were jailed on charges of incitement, campaign offices were raided – someone must be helping the few minor leaders who were left to keep the campaign going without offices or equipment. What was it the leaflets would say – 'Don't go to work tomorrow', 'Day of Protest', 'Burn Your Pass for Freedom'? He didn't want to see.

He was used to coming home and finding his wife sitting at the dining-room table deep in discussion with strangers or people whose names were familiar by repute. Some were prominent Indians, like the lawyer, Dr Abdul Mohammed Khan, or the big businessman, Mr Moonsamy Patel, and he was flattered, in a suspicious way, to meet them in his house. As he came home from work next day he met Dr Khan coming out of the house, and Dr Khan – a highly educated man – said to him, 'A wonderful woman'. But Bamjee had never caught his wife out in any presumption; she behaved properly, as any Muslim woman should, and once her business with such gentlemen was over would never, for instance, have sat down to eat with them.

He found her now back in the kitchen, setting about the preparation of dinner and carrying on a conversation on several different wavelengths with the children. 'It's really a shame if you're tired of lentils, Jimmy, because that's what you're getting – Amina, hurry up, get a pot of water going – don't worry, I'll mend that in a minute, just bring the yellow cotton, and there's a needle in the cigarette box on the sideboard.'

'Was that Dr Khan leaving?' said Bamjee.

'Yes, there's going to be a stay-at-home on Monday. Desai's ill, and he's got to get the word around by himself. Bob Jali was up all last night printing leaflets, but he's gone to have a tooth out.' She had always treated Bamjee as if it were only a mannerism that made him appear uninterested in politics, the way some woman will persist in interpreting her husband's bad temper as an endearing gruffness hiding boundless goodwill, and she talked to him of these things just as she passed on to him neighbours' or family gossip.

'What for do you want to get mixed up with these killings and stonings and I don't know what? Congress should keep out of it. Isn't it enough with the Group Areas?'

She laughed. 'Now, Yusuf, you know you don't believe that. Look how you said the same thing when the Group Areas started in Natal. You said we should begin to worry when we get moved out of our own houses here in the Transvaal. And then your own mother lost her house in Noorddorp, and there you are; you saw that nobody's safe. Oh, Girlie was here this afternoon, she says Ismail's brother's engaged – that's nice, isn't it? His mother will be pleased; she was worried.'

'Why was she worried?' asked Jimmy, who was fifteen, and old enough to patronise his mother.

'Well, she wanted to see him settled. There's a party on Sunday week at Ismail's place – you'd better give me your suit to take to the cleaners tomorrow, Yusuf.'

One of the girls presented herself at once. 'I'll have nothing to wear, Ma.'

Mrs Bamjee scratched her sallow face. 'Perhaps Girlie will lend you her pink, eh? Run over to Girlie's place now and say I say will she lend it to you?'

The sound of commonplaces often does service as security, and Bamjee, going to sit in the armchair with the shiny armrests that was wedged between the dining table and the sideboard, lapsed into an unthinking doze that, like all times of dreamlike ordinariness during those weeks, was filled with uneasy jerks and starts back into reality. The next morning, as soon as he got to market, he heard that Dr Khan had been arrested. But that night Mrs Bamjee sat up making a new dress for her daughter; the sight disarmed Bamjee, reassured him again, against his will, so that the resentment he had been making ready all day faded into a morose and accusing silence. Heaven knew, of course, who came and went in the house during the day. Twice in that week of riots, raids and arrests he found black women in the house when he came home; plain ordinary native women in doeks, drinking tea. This was not a thing other Indian women would have in their homes, he thought bitterly; but then his wife was not like other people, in a way he could not put his finger on, except to say what it was not: not scandalous, not punishable, not rebellious. It was, like the attraction that had led him to marry her, Pahad's widow with five children, something he could not see clearly.

When the Special Branch knocked steadily on the door in the small hours of Tuesday morning he did not wake up, for his return to consciousness was always set in his mind to half past four, and that was more than an hour away. Mrs Bamjee got up herself, struggled into Jimmy's raincoat, which was hanging over a chair, and went to the front door. The clock on the wall – a wedding present when she married Pahad – showed three o'clock when she snapped on the light, and she knew at once who it was on the other side of the door. Although she was not surprised, her hands shook like a very old person's as she undid the locks and the complicated catch on the wire burglar-proofing. And then she opened the door and they were there – two coloured policemen in plain clothes. 'Zanip Bamjee?'

'Yes.'

As they talked, Bamjee woke up in the sudden terror of having overslept. Then he became conscious of men's voices. He heaved himself out of bed in the dark and went to the window, which, like the front door, was covered with a heavy mesh of thick wire against intruders from the dingy lane it looked upon. Bewildered, he appeared in the dining room, where the policemen were searching through a soapbox of papers beside the duplicating machine.

'Yusuf, it's for me,' Mrs Bamjee said.

At once, the snap of a trap, realisation came. He stood there in an old shirt before the two policemen, and the woman was going off to prison because of the natives. 'There you are!' he shouted, standing away from her. 'That's what you've got for it. Didn't I tell you? Didn't I? That's the end of it now. That's the finish. That's what it's come to.'

She listened with her head at the slightest tilt to one side, as if to ward off a blow, or in compassion.

Jimmy, Pahad's son, appeared at the door with a suitcase; two or three of the girls were behind him. 'Here, Ma, you take my green jersey.' 'I've found your clean blouse.' Bamjee had to keep moving out of their way as they helped their mother to make ready. It was like the preparation for one of the family festivals his wife made such a fuss over; wherever he put himself they bumped into him. Even the two policemen mumbled 'Excuse me,' and pushed past into the rest of the house to continue their search. They took with them a tome that Nehru had written in prison; it had been bought from a persevering travelling salesman and kept, for years, on the mantelpiece. 'Oh, don't take that, please,' Mrs Bamjee said suddenly, clinging to the arm of the man who had picked it up.

The man held it away from her.

'What does it matter, Ma?'

It was true that no one in the house had ever read it; but she said, 'It's for my children.'

'Ma, leave it.' Jimmy, who was squat and plump, looked like a merchant advising a client against a roll of silk she had set her heart on. She went into the bedroom and got dressed. When she came out in her old yellow sari with a brown coat over it, the faces of the children were behind her like faces on the platform at a railway station. They kissed her goodbye. The policemen did not hurry her, but she seemed to be in a hurry just the same.

'What am I going to do?' Bamjee accused them all.

The policemen looked away patiently.

'It'll be all right. Girlie will help. The big children can manage. And, Yusuf—' The children crowded in around her; two of the younger ones had awakened and appeared, asking shrill questions.

'Come on,' said the policemen.

'I want to speak to my husband.' She broke away and came back to him, and the movement of her sari hid them from the rest of the room for a moment. His face hardened in suspicious anticipation against the request to give some message to the next fool who would take up her pamphleteering until he, too, was arrested. 'On Sunday,' she said. 'Take them on Sunday.' He did not know what she was talking about. 'The engagement party,' she whispered, low and urgent. 'They shouldn't miss it. Ismail will be offended.'

They listened to the car drive away. Jimmy bolted and barred the front door, and then at once opened it again; he put on the raincoat that his mother had taken off. 'Going to tell Girlie,' he said.

The children went back to bed. Their father did not say a word to any of them; their talk, the crying of the younger ones and the argumentative voices of the older, went on in the bedrooms. He found himself alone; he felt the night all around him. And then he happened to meet the clock face and saw with a terrible sense of unfamiliarity that this was not the secret night but an hour he should have recognised: the time he always got up. He pulled on his trousers and his dirty white hawker's coat and wound his grey muffler up to the stubble on his chin and went to work.

The duplicating machine was gone from the sideboard. The policemen had taken it with them, along with the pamphlets and the conference reports and the stack of old newspapers that had collected on top of the wardrobe in the bedroom – not the thick dailies of the white men, but the thin, impermanent-looking papers that spoke up, sometimes interrupted by suppression or lack of money, for the rest. It was all gone. When he had married her and moved in with her and her five children, into what had been the Pahad and became the Bamjee house, he had not recognised the humble, harmless, and apparently useless routine tasks – the minutes of meetings being written up on the dining-room table at night, the government blue books that were read while the latest baby was suckled, the employment of the fingers of the older children in the fashioning of crinkle-paper Congress rosettes – as activity intended to move mountains. For years and years he had not noticed it, and now it was gone.

The house was quiet. The children kept to their lairs, crowded on the beds with the doors shut. He sat and looked at the sideboard, where the plastic carnations and the mat with the picture of the Taj Mahal were in place. For the first few weeks he never spoke of her. There was the feeling, in the house, that he had wept and raged at her, that boulders of reproach had thundered down upon her absence, and yet he had said not one word. He had not been to enquire where she was; Jimmy and Girlie had gone to Mohammed Ebrahim, the lawyer, and when he found out that their mother had been taken – when she was arrested, at least – to a prison in the next town, they had stood about outside the big prison door for hours while they waited to be told where she had been moved from there. At last they had discovered that she was fifty miles away, in Pretoria. Jimmy asked Bamjee for five shillings to help Girlie pay the train fare to Pretoria, once she had been interviewed by the police and had been given a permit to visit her mother; he put three two-shilling pieces on the table for Jimmy to pick up, and the boy, looking at him keenly, did not know whether the extra shilling meant anything, or whether it was merely that Bamjee had no change.

It was only when relations and neighbours came to the house that Bamjee would suddenly begin to talk. He had never been so expansive in his life as he was in the company of these visitors, many of them come on a polite call rather in the nature of a visit of condolence. 'Ah, yes, yes, you see how I am – you see what has been done to me. Nine children, and I am on the cart all day. I get home at seven or eight. What are you to do? What can people like us do?'

'Poor Mrs Bamjee. Such a kind lady.'

'Well, you see for yourself. They walk in here in the middle of the night and leave a houseful of children. I'm out on the cart all day, I've got a living to earn.' Standing about in his shirtsleeves, he became quite animated; he would call for the girls to bring fruit drinks for the visitors. When they were gone, it was as if he, who was orthodox if not devout and never drank liquor, had been drunk and abruptly sobered up; he looked dazed and could not have gone over in his mind what he had been saying. And as he cooled, the lump of resentment and wrongedness stopped his throat again.

Bamjee found one of the little boys the centre of a self-important group of championing brothers and sisters in the dining room one evening. 'They've been cruel to Ahmed.'

'What has he done?' said the father.

'Nothing! Nothing!' The little girl stood twisting her handkerchief excitedly.

An older one, thin as her mother, took over, silencing the others with a gesture of her skinny hand. 'They did it at school today. They made an example of him.'

'What is an example?' said Bamjee impatiently.

'The teacher made him come up and stand in front of the whole class, and he told them, "You see this boy? His mother's in jail because she likes the natives so much. She wants the Indians to be the same as natives."'

'It's terrible,' he said. His hands fell to his sides. 'Did she ever think of this?'

'That's why Ma's *there*,' said Jimmy, putting aside his comic and emptying out his schoolbooks upon the table. 'That's all the kid needs to know. Ma's there because things like this happen. Petersen's a coloured teacher, and it's his black blood that's brought him trouble all his life, I suppose. He hates anyone who says everybody's the same, because that takes away from him his bit of whiteness that's all he's got. What d'you expect? It's nothing to make too much fuss about.'

'Of course, you are fifteen and you know everything,' Bamjee mumbled at him.

'I don't say that. But I know Ma, anyway.' The boy laughed.

There was a hunger strike among the political prisoners, and Bamjee could not bring himself to ask Girlie if her mother was starving herself too. He would not ask; and yet he saw in the young woman's face the gradual weakening of her mother. When the strike had gone on for nearly a week one of the elder children burst into tears at the table and could not eat. Bamjee pushed his own plate away in rage.

Sometimes he spoke out loud to himself while he was driving the vegetable lorry. 'What for?' Again and again: 'What for?' She was not a modern woman who cut her hair and wore short skirts. He had married a good plain Muslim woman who bore children and stamped her own chillies. He had a sudden vision of her at the duplicating machine, that night just before she was taken away, and he felt himself maddened, baffled and hopeless. He had become the ghost of a victim, hanging about the scene of a crime whose motive he could not understand and had not had time to learn.

The hunger strike at the prison went into the second week. Alone in the rattling cab of his lorry, he said things that he heard as if spoken by someone else, and his heart burned in fierce agreement with them. 'For a crowd of natives who'll smash our shops and kill us in our houses when their time comes.' 'She will starve herself to death there.' 'She will die there.' 'Devils who will burn and kill us.' He fell into bed each night like a stone, and dragged himself up in the mornings as a beast of burden is beaten to its feet.

One of these mornings, Girlie appeared very early, while he was wolfing bread and strong tea – alternate sensations of dry solidity and stinging heat – at the kitchen table. Her real name was Fatima, of course, but she had adopted the silly modern name along with the clothes of the young factory girls among whom she worked. She was expecting her first baby in a week or two, and her small face, her cut and curled hair and the sooty arches drawn over her eyebrows did not seem to belong to her thrust-out body under a clean smock. She wore mauve lipstick and was smiling her cocky little white girl's smile, foolish and bold, not like an Indian girl's at all.

'What's the matter?' he said.

She smiled again. 'Don't you know? I told Bobby he must get me up in time this morning. I wanted to be sure I wouldn't miss you today.'

'I don't know what you're talking about.'

She came over and put her arm up around his unwilling neck and kissed the grey bristles at the side of his mouth. 'Many happy returns! Don't you know it's your birthday?'

'No,' he said. 'I didn't know, didn't think—' He broke the pause by swiftly picking up the bread and giving his attention desperately to eating and drinking. His mouth was busy, but his eyes looked at her, intensely black. She said nothing, but stood there with him. She would not speak, and at last he said, swallowing a piece of bread that tore at his throat as it went down, 'I don't remember these things.'

The girl nodded, the Woolworth baubles in her ears swinging. 'That's the first thing she told me when I saw her yesterday – don't forget it's Bajie's birthday tomorrow.'

He shrugged over it. 'It means a lot to children. But that's how she is. Whether it's one of the old cousins or the neighbour's grandmother, she always knows when the birthday is. What importance is my birthday, while she's sitting there in a prison? I don't understand how she can do the things she does when her mind is always full of woman's nonsense at the same time – that's what I don't understand with her.'

'Oh, but don't you see?' the girl said. 'It's because she doesn't want anybody to be left out. It's because she always remembers; remembers everything – people without somewhere to live, hungry kids, boys who can't get educated – remembers all the time. That's how Ma is.'

'Nobody else is like that.' It was half a complaint.

'No, nobody else,' said his stepdaughter.

She sat herself down at the table, resting her belly. He put his head in his hands. 'I'm getting old' – but he was overcome by something much more curious, by an answer. He knew why he had desired her, the ugly widow with five children; he knew what way it was in which she was not like others; it was there, like the fact of the belly that lay between him and her daughter.

Some Monday for Sure

My sister's husband, Josias, used to work on the railways but then he got this job where they make dynamite for the mines. He was the one who sits out on that little iron seat clamped to the back of the big red truck, with a red flag in his hand. The idea is that if you drive up too near the truck or look as if you're going to crash into it, he waves the flag to warn you off. You've seen those trucks often on the Main Reef Road between Johannesburg and the mining towns – they carry the stuff and have DANGER – EXPLOSIVES painted on them. The man sits there, with an iron chain looped across his little seat to keep him from being thrown into the road, and he clutches his flag like a kid with a balloon. That's how Josias was, too. Of course, if you didn't take any notice of the warning and went on and crashed into the truck, he would be the first to be blown to high heaven and hell, but he always just sits there, this chap, as if he has no idea when he was born or that he might not die on a bed an old man of eighty. As if the dust in his eyes and the racket of the truck are going to last for ever.

My sister knew she had a good man but she never said anything about being afraid of this job. She only grumbled in winter, when he was stuck out there in the cold and used to get a cough (she's a nurse), and on those times in summer when it rained all day and she said he would land up with rheumatism, crippled, and then who would give him work? The dynamite people? I don't think it ever came into her head that any day, every day, he could be blown up instead of coming home in the evening. Anyway, you wouldn't have thought so by the way she took it when he told us what it was he was going to have to do.

I was working down at a garage in town, that time, at the petrol pumps, and I was eating before he came in because I was on night shift. Emma had the water ready for him and he had a wash without saying much, as usual, but then he didn't speak when they sat down to eat, either, and when his fingers went into the mealie meal he seemed to forget what it was he was holding and not to be able to shape it into a mouthful. Emma must have thought he felt too dry to eat, because she got up and brought him a jam tin of the beer she had made for Saturday. He drank it and then sat back and looked from her to me, but she said, 'Why don't you eat?' and he began to, slowly. She said, 'What's the matter with you?' He got up and yawned and yawned, showing those brown chipped teeth that remind me of the big ape at the Johannesburg zoo that I saw once when I went with the school. He went into the other room of the house, where he and Emma slept, and he came back with his pipe. He filled it carefully, the way a poor man does; I saw, as soon as I went to work at the filling station, how the white men fill their pipes, stuffing the tobacco in, shoving the tin half-shut back into the glovebox of the car.

'I'm going down to Sela's place,' said Emma. 'I can go with Willie on his way to work if you don't want to come.'

'No. Not tonight. You stay here.' Josias always speaks like this, the short words of a schoolmaster or a boss-boy, but if you hear the way he says them, you know he is not really ordering you around at all, he is only asking you.

'No, I told her I'm coming,' Emma said, in the voice of a woman having her own way in a little thing.

'Tomorrow.' Josias began to yawn again, looking at us with wet eyes.

'Go to bed,' Emma said, 'I won't be late.'

'No, no, I want to . . .' he blew a sigh '—when he's gone, man—' he moved his pipe at me. 'I'll tell you later.'

Emma laughed. 'What can you tell that Willie can't hear—' I've lived with them ever since they were married. Emma always was the one who looked after me, even before, when I was a little kid. It was true that whatever happened to us happened to us together. He looked at me; I suppose he saw that I was a man, now: I was in my blue overalls with Shell on the pocket and everything.

He said, '. . . they want me to do something . . . a job with the truck.'

Josias used to turn out regularly to political meetings and he took part in a few protests before everything went underground, but he had never been more than one of the crowd. We had Mandela and the rest of the leaders, cut out of the paper, hanging on the wall, but he had never known, personally, any of them. Of course there were his friends Ndhlovu and Seb Masinde who said they had gone underground and who occasionally came late at night for a meal or slept in my bed for a few hours.

'They want to stop the truck on the road . . .'

'Stop it?' Emma was like somebody stepping into cold dark water; with every word that was said she went deeper. 'But how can you do it – when? Where will they do it?' She was wild, as if she must go out and prevent it all happening right then.

I felt that cold water of Emma's rising round the belly because Emma and I often had the same feelings, but I caught also, in Josias's not looking at me, a signal Emma couldn't know. Something in me jumped at it like catching a swinging rope. 'They want the stuff inside . . . ?'

Nobody said anything.

I said, 'What a lot of big bangs you could make with that, man,' and then shut up before Josias needed to tell me to.

'So what're you going to do?' Emma's mouth stayed open after she had spoken, the lips pulled back.

'They'll tell me everything. I just have to give them the best place on the road – that'll be the Free State road, the others're too busy . . . and . . . the time when we pass . . .'

'You'll be dead.' Emma's head was shuddering and her whole body shook; I've never seen anybody give up like that. He was dead already, she saw it with her eyes and she was kicking and screaming without knowing how to show it to him. She looked like she wanted to kill Josias herself, for being dead. 'That'll be the finish, for sure. He's got a gun, the white man in front, hasn't he, you told me. And the one with him? They'll kill you. You'll go to prison. They'll take you to Pretoria gaol and hang you by the rope . . . yes, he's got the gun, you told me, didn't you . . . many times you told me . . .'

'The others've got guns too. How d'you think they can hold us up? – they've got guns and they'll come all round him. It's all worked out—'

'The one in front will shoot you, I know it, don't tell me, I know what I say—' Emma went up and down and around till I thought she would push the walls down – they wouldn't have needed much pushing, in that house in Tembekile Location – and I was scared of her. I don't mean for what she would do to me if I got in her way, or to Josias, but for what might happen to her: something like taking a fit or screaming that none of us would be able to forget.

I don't think Josias was sure about doing the job before but he wanted to do it now. 'No shooting. Nobody will shoot me. Nobody will know that I know anything. Nobody will know I tell them anything. I'm held up just the same like the others! Same as the white man in front! Who can shoot me? They can shoot me for that?'

'Someone else can go, I don't want it, do you hear? You will stay at home, I will say you are sick . . . you will be killed, they will shoot you . . . Josias, I'm telling you, I don't want . . . I won't . . .'

I was waiting my chance to speak, all the time, and I felt Josias was waiting to talk to someone who had caught the signal. I said quickly, while she went on and on, 'But even on that road there are some cars?'

'Roadblocks,' he said, looking at the floor. 'They've got the signs, the ones you see when a road's being dug up, and there'll be some men with picks. After the truck goes through they'll block the road so that any other cars turn off on to the old road there by Kalmansdrif. The same thing on the other side, two miles on. There where the farm road goes down to Nek Halt.'

'Hell, man! Did you have to pick what part of the road?'

'I know it like this yard. Don't I?'

Emma stood there, between the two of us, while we discussed the whole business. We didn't have to worry about anyone hearing, not only because Emma kept the window wired up in that kitchen, but also because the yard the house was in was a real Tembekile Location one, full of babies yelling and people shouting, night and day, not to mention the transistors playing in the houses all round. Emma was looking at us all the time and out of the corner of my eye I could see her big front going up and down fast in the neck of her dress.

'. . . so they're going to tie you up as well as the others?'

He drew on his pipe to answer me.

We thought for a moment and then grinned at each other; it was the first time for Josias, that whole evening.

Emma began collecting the dishes under our noses. She dragged the tin bath of hot water from the stove and washed up. 'I said I'm taking my off on Wednesday. I suppose this is going to be next week.' Suddenly, yet talking as if carrying on where she let up, she was quite different.

'I don't know.'

'Well, I have to know because I suppose I must be at home.'

'What must you be at home for?' said Josias.

'If the police come I don't want them talking to *him*,' she said, looking at us both without wanting to see us.

'The police—' said Josias, and jerked his head to send them running, while I laughed, to show her.

'And I want to know what I must say.'

'What must you say? Why? They can get my statement from me when they find us tied up. In the night I'll be back here myself.'

'Oh yes,' she said, scraping the mealie meal he hadn't eaten back into the pot. She did everything as usual; she wanted to show us nothing was going to wait because of this big thing, she must wash the dishes and put ash on the fire. 'You'll be back, oh yes. Are you going to sit here all night, Willie? – Oh yes, you'll be back.'

And then, I think, for a moment Josias saw himself dead, too; he didn't answer when I took my cap and said so long, from the door.

I knew it must be a Monday. I notice that women quite often don't remember ordinary things like this, I don't know what they think about – for instance, Emma didn't catch on that it must be Monday, next Monday or the one after, some Monday for sure, because Monday was the day that we knew Josias went with the truck to the Free State Mines. It was Friday when he told us and all day Saturday I had a terrible feeling that it was going to be *that* Monday, and it would be all over before I could – what? I didn't know, man. I felt I must at least see where it was going to happen. Sunday I was off work and I took my bicycle and rode into town before there was even anybody in the streets and went to the big station and found that although there wasn't a train on Sundays that would take me all the way, I could get one that would take me about thirty miles. I had to pay to put the bike in the luggage van as well as for my ticket, but I'd got my wages on Friday. I got off at the nearest halt to Kalmansdrif and then I asked people along the road the best way. It was a long ride, more than two hours. I came out on the main road from the sand road just at the turn-off Josias had told me about. It was just like he said: a tin sign 'Kalmansdrif' pointing down the road I'd come from. And the nice blue tarred road, smooth, straight ahead: was I glad to get on to it! I hadn't taken much notice of the country so far, while I was sweating along, but from then on I woke up and saw everything. I've only got to think about it to see it again now. The veld is flat round about there, it was the end of winter, so the grass was dry. Quite far away and very far apart there was a hill and then another, sticking up in the middle of nothing, pink colour, and with its point cut off like the neck of a bottle. Ride and ride, these hills never got any nearer and there were none beside the road. It all looked empty but there were some people there. It's funny you don't notice them like you do in town. All our people, of course; there were barbed-wire fences, so it must have been white farmers' land, but they've got the water and their houses are far off the road and you can usually see them only by the big dark trees that hide them. Our people had mud houses and there would be three or four in the same place made hard by goats and people's feet. Often the huts were near a kind of crack in the ground, where the little kids played and where, I suppose, in summer, there was water. Even now the women were managing to do washing in some places. I saw children run to the road to jig about and stamp when cars passed, but the men and women took no interest in what was up there. It was funny to think that I was just like them, now, men and women who are always busy inside themselves with jobs, plans, thinking about how to get money or how to talk to someone about something important, instead of like the children, as I used to be only a few years ago, taking in each small thing around them as it happens.

Still, there were people living pretty near the road. What would they do if they saw the dynamite truck held up and a fight going on? (I couldn't think of it, then, in any other way except like I'd seen hold-ups in Westerns, although I've seen plenty of fighting, all my life, among the location gangs and drunks – I was ashamed not to be able to forget those kid-stuff Westerns at a time like this.) Would they go running away to the white farmer? Would somebody jump on a bike and go for the police? Or if there was no bike, what about a horse? – I saw someone riding a horse.

I rode slowly to the next turn-off, the one where a farm road goes down to Nek Halt. There it was, just like Josias said. Here was where the other roadblock would be. But when he spoke about it there was nothing in between! No people, no houses, no flat veld with hills on it! It had been just one of those things grown-ups see worked out in their heads: while all the time here it was, a real place where people had cooking fires, I could hear a herd boy yelling at a dirty bundle of sheep, a big bird I've never seen in town balanced on the barbed-wire fence right in front of me . . . I got off my bike and it flew away.

I sat a minute on the side of the road. I'd had a cold drink in an Indian shop in the dorp where I'd got off the train, but I was dry again inside my mouth, while plenty of water came out of my skin, I can tell you. I rode back down the road looking for the exact place I would choose if I were Josias. There was a stretch where there was only one kraal, with two houses, and that quite a way back from the road. Also there was a dip where the road went over a donga. Old stumps of trees and nothing but cows' business down there; men could hide. I got off again and had a good look round.

But I wondered about the people, up top. I don't know why it was, I wanted to know about those people just as though I was going to have to go and live with them, or something. I left the bike down in the donga and crossed the road behind a Cadillac going so fast the air smacked together after it, and I began to trek over the veld to the houses. I know that most of our people live like this, in the veld, but I'd never been into houses like that before. I was born in some location (I don't know which one, I must ask Emma one day) and Emma and I lived in Goughville Location with our grandmother. Our mother worked in town and she used to come and see us sometimes, but we never saw our father and Emma thinks that perhaps we didn't have the same father, because she remembers a man before I was born, and after I was born she didn't see him again. I don't really remember anyone, from when I was a little kid, except Emma. Emma dragging me along so fast my arm almost came off my body, because we had nearly been caught by the Indian while stealing peaches from his lorry: we did that every day.

We lived in one room with our grandmother but it was a tin house with a number and later on there was a street light at the corner. These houses I was coming to had a pattern all over them marked into the mud they were built of. There was a mound of dried cows' business, as tall as I was, stacked up in a pattern, too. And then the usual junk our people have, just like in the location: old tins, broken things collected in white people's rubbish heaps. The fowls ran sideways from my feet and two old men let their talking die away into a-has and e-hes as I came up. I greeted them the right way to greet old men and they nodded and went on e-he-ing and a-ha-ing to show that they had been greeted properly. One of them had very clean ragged trousers tied with string and sat on the ground, but the other, sitting on a bucket seat that must have been taken from some scrapyard car, was dressed in a way I've never seen – from the old days, I suppose. He wore a black suit with very wide trousers, laced boots, a stiff white collar and black tie and, on top of it all, a broken old hat. It was Sunday, of course, so I suppose he was all dressed up. I've heard that these people who work for farmers wear sacks most of the time. The old ones didn't ask me what I wanted there. They just peered at me with their eyes gone the colour of soapy water because they were so old. And I didn't know what to say because I hadn't thought what I was going to say, I'd just walked. Then a little kid slipped out of the dark doorway quick as a cockroach. I thought perhaps everyone else was out because it was Sunday but then a voice called from inside the other house, and when the child didn't answer, called again, and a woman came to the doorway.

I said my bicycle had a puncture and could I have some water.

She said something into the house and in a minute a girl, about fifteen she must've been, edged past her carrying a paraffin tin and went off to fetch water. Like all the girls that age, she never looked at you. Her body shook under an ugly old dress and she almost hobbled in her hurry to get away. Her head was tied up in a rag-doek right down to the eyes the way old-fashioned people do, otherwise she would have been quite pretty, like any other girl. When she had gone a little way the kid went pumping after her, panting, yelling, opening his skinny legs wide as scissors over stones and antheaps, and then he caught up with her and you could see that right away she was quite different, I knew how it was, she yelled at him, you heard her laugh as she chased him with the tin, whirled around from out of his clutching hands, struggled with him; they were together like Emma and I used to be when we got away from the old lady, and from the school, and everybody. And Emma was also one of our girls who have the big strong comfortable bodies of mothers even when they're still kids, maybe it comes from always lugging the smaller one round on their backs.

A man came out of the house behind the woman and was friendly. His hair had the dusty look of someone who's been sleeping off drink. In fact, he was still a bit heavy with it.

'You coming from Jo'burg?'

But I wasn't going to be caught out being careless at all, Josias could count on me for that.

'Vereeniging.'

He thought there was something funny there – nobody dresses like a Jo'burger, you could always spot us a mile off – but he was too full to follow it up.

He stood stretching his sticky eyelids open and then he fastened on me the way some people will do. 'Can't you get me work there where you are?'

'What kind of work?'

He waved a hand describing me. 'You got a good work.'

'S'all right.'

'Where you working now?'

'Garden boy.'

He tittered, 'Look like you work in town,' shook his head.

I was surprised to find the woman handing me a tin of beer, and I squatted on the ground to drink it. It's mad to say that a mud house can be pretty, but those patterns made in the mud looked nice. It must have been done with a sharp stone or stick when the mud was smooth and wet, the shapes of things like big leaves and moons filled in with lines that went all one way in this shape, another way in that, so that as you looked at the walls in the sun some shapes were dark and some were light, and if you moved the light ones went dark and the dark ones got light instead. The girl came back with the heavy tin of water on her head making her neck thick. I washed out the jam tin I'd had the beer in and filled it with water. When I thanked them, the old men stirred and a-ha-ed and e-he-ed again.

The man made as if to walk a bit with me, but I was lucky, he didn't go more than a few yards. 'No good,' he said. 'Every morning, five o'clock, and the pay . . . very small.'

How I would have hated to be him, a man already married and with big children, working all his life in the fields wearing sacks. When you think like this about someone he seems something you could never possibly be, as if it's his fault, and not just the chance of where he happened to be born. At the same time I had a crazy feeling I wanted to tell him something wonderful, something he'd never dreamt could happen, something he'd fall on his knees and thank me for. I wanted to say, 'Soon you'll be the farmer yourself and you'll have shoes like me and your girl will get water from your windmill. Because on Monday, or another Monday, the truck will stop down there and all the stuff will be taken away and they

– Josias, me; even you, yes – we'll win for ever.' But instead all I said was, 'Who did that on your house?' He didn't understand and I made a drawing in the air with my hand.

'The women,' he said, not interested.

Down in the donga I sat a while and then threw away the tin and rode off without looking up again to where the kraal was.

It wasn't that Monday. Emma and Josias go to bed very early and of course they were asleep by the time I got home late on Sunday night – Emma thought I'd been with the boys I used to go around with at weekends. But Josias got up at half past four every morning, then, because it was a long way from the location to where the dynamite factory was, and although I didn't usually even hear him making the fire in the kitchen which was also where I was sleeping, that morning I was awake the moment he got out of bed next door. When he came into the kitchen I was sitting up in my blankets and I whispered loudly – 'I went there yesterday. I saw the turn-off and everything. Down there by the donga, ay? Is that the place?'

He looked at me, a bit dazed. He nodded. Then, 'Wha'd'you mean you went there?'

'I could see that's the only good place. I went up to the houses, too, just to see . . . the people are all right. Not many. When it's not Sunday there may be nobody there but the old man – there were two, I think one was just a visitor. The man and the woman will be over in the fields somewhere, and that must be quite far, because you can't see the mealies from the road . . .' I could feel myself being listened to carefully, getting in with him (and if with him, with *them*) while I was talking, and I knew exactly what I was saying, absolutely clearly, just as I would know exactly what I was doing.

He began to question me; but like I was an older man or a clever one; he didn't know what to say. He drank his tea while I told him all about it. He was thinking. Just before he left he said, 'I shouldn't've told you.'

I ran after him, outside, into the yard. It was still dark. I blurted in the same whisper we'd been using, 'Not today, is it?' I couldn't see his face properly but I knew he didn't know whether to answer or not.

'Not today.' I was so happy I couldn't go to sleep again.

In the evening Josias managed to make some excuse to come out with me alone for a bit. He said, 'I told them you were a hundred per cent. It's just the same as if I know.'

'Of course, no difference. I just haven't had much of a chance to do anything . . .' I didn't carry on: '. . . because I was too young'; we didn't want to bring Emma into it. And anyway, no one but a real kid is too young any more. Look at the boys who are up for sabotage.

I said, 'Have they got them all?'

He hunched his shoulders.

'I mean, even the ones for the picks and spades . . . ?'

He wouldn't say anything, but I knew I could ask. 'Oh, *boetie*, man, even just to keep a look out, there on the road . . .'

I know he didn't want it but once they knew I knew, and that I'd been there and everything, they were keen to use me. At least that's what I think. I never went to any meetings or anything where it was planned, and beforehand I only met the two others who were with me at the turn-off in the end, and we were told exactly what we had to do by Seb Masinde. Of course, neither of us said a word to Emma. The Monday that we did it was three weeks later and I can tell you, although a lot's happened to me since then, I'll never forget the moment when we flagged the truck through with Josias sitting there on the back in his little seat. Josias! I wanted to laugh and shout there in the veld; I didn't feel scared – what was there to be scared of, he'd been sitting on a load of dynamite every day of his life for years now, so what's the odds. We had one of those tins of fire and a bucket of tar and the real 'Road Closed' signs from the PWD and everything went smooth at our end. It was at the Nek Halt end that the trouble started when one of these AA patrol bikes had to come along (Josias says it was something new, they'd never met a patrol on that road that time of day, before) and get suspicious about the block there. In the meantime the truck was stopped all right but someone was shot and Josias tried to get the gun from the white man up in front of the truck and there was a hell of a fight and they had to make a get-away with the stuff in a car and van back through our block, instead of taking over the truck and driving it to a hiding place to offload. More than half the stuff had to be left behind in the truck. Still, they got clean away with what they did get and it was never found by the police. Whenever I read in the papers here that something's been blown up back at home, I wonder if it's still one of our bangs. Two of our people got picked up right away and some more later and the whole thing was all over the papers with speeches by the Chief of Special Branch about a master plot and everything. But Josias got away OK. We three chaps at the roadblock just ran into the veld to where there were bikes hidden. We went to a place we'd been told in Rustenburg district for a week and then we were told to get over to Bechuanaland. It wasn't so bad; we had no money but around Rustenburg it was easy to pinch paw-paws and oranges off the farms . . . Oh, I sent a message to Emma that I was all right; and at that time it didn't seem true that I couldn't go home again.

But in Bechuanaland it was different. We had no money, and you don't find food on trees in that dry place. They said they would send us money; it didn't come. But Josias was there too, and we stuck together; people hid us and we kept going. Planes arrived and took away the big shots and the white refugees but although we were told we'd go too, it never came off. We had no money to pay for ourselves. There were plenty others like us, in the beginning. At last we just walked, right up Bechuanaland and through Northern Rhodesia to Mbeya, that's over the border in Tanganyika, where we were headed for. A long walk; took Josias and me months. We met up with a chap who'd been given a bit of money and from there sometimes we went by bus. No one asks questions when you're nobody special and you walk, like all the other African people themselves, or take the buses that the whites never use; it's only if you've got the money for cars or to arrive in an aeroplane that all these things happen that you read about: getting sent back over the border, refused permits and so on. So we got here, to Tanganyika at last, down to this town of Dar es Salaam where we'd been told we'd be going.

There's a refugee camp here and they give you a shilling or two a day until you get work. But it's out of town, for one thing, and we soon left there and found a room down in the native town. There are some nice buildings, of course, in the real town – nothing like Johannesburg or Durban, though – and that used to be the white town, the whites who are left still live there, but the Africans with big jobs in the government and so on live there too. Some of our leaders who are refugees like us live in these houses and have big cars; everyone knows they're important men, here, not like at home when if you're black you're just rubbish for the locations. The people down where we lived are very poor and it's hard to get work because they haven't got enough work for themselves, but I've got my standard seven and I managed to get a small job as a clerk. Josias never found steady work. But that didn't matter so much because the big thing was that Emma was able to come to join us after five months, and she and I earn the money. She's a nurse, you see, and Africanisation started in the hospitals and the government was short of nurses. So Emma got the chance to come up with a party of them sent for specially from South Africa and Rhodesia. We were very lucky because it's impossible for people to get their families up here. She came in a plane paid for by the government, and she and the other girls had their photograph taken for the newspaper as they got off at the airport. That day she came we took her to the beach, where everyone can bathe, no restrictions, and for a cool drink in one of the hotels (she'd never been in a hotel before), and we walked up and down the road along the bay where everyone walks and where you can see the ships coming in and going out so near that the men out there wave to you. Whenever we bumped into anyone else from home they would stop and ask her about home, and how everything was. Josias and I couldn't stop grinning to hear us all, in the middle of Dar, talking away in our language about the things we know. That day it was like it had happened already: the time when we are home again and everything is our way.

* * *

Well, that's nearly three years ago, since Emma came. Josias has been sent away now and there's only Emma and me. That was always the idea, to send us away for training. Some go to Ethiopia and some go to Algeria and all over the show and by the time they come back there won't be anything Verwoerd's men know in the way of handling guns and so on that they won't know better. That's for a start. I'm supposed to go too, but some of us have been waiting a long time. In the meantime I go to work and I walk about this place in the evenings and I buy myself a glass of beer in a bar when I've got money. Emma and I have still got the flat we had before Josias left and two nurses from the hospital pay us for the other bedroom. Emma still works at the hospital but I don't know how much longer. Most days now since Josias's gone she wants me to walk up to fetch her from the hospital when she comes off duty, and when I get under the trees on the drive I see her staring out looking for me as if I'll never turn up ever again. Every day it's like that. When I come up she smiles and looks like she used to for a minute but by the time we're ten yards on the road she's shaking and shaking her head until the tears come and saying over and over, 'A person can't stand it, a person can't stand it.' She said right from the beginning that the hospitals here are not like the hospitals at home, where the nurses have to know their job. She's got a whole ward in her charge and now she says they're worse and worse and she can't trust anyone to do anything for her. And the staff don't like having strangers working with them anyway. She tells me every day like she's telling me for the first time. Of course it's true that some of the people don't like us being here. You know how it is, people haven't got enough jobs to go round, themselves. But I don't take much notice; I'll be sent off one of these days and until then I've got to eat and that's that.

The flat is nice with a real bathroom and we are paying off the table and six chairs she liked so much, but when we walk in, her face is terrible. She keeps saying the place will never be straight. At home there was only a tap in the yard for all the houses but she never said it there. She doesn't sit down for more than a minute without getting up at once again, but you can't get her to go out, even on these evenings when it's so hot you can't breathe. I go down to the market to buy the food now, she says she can't stand it. When I asked what – because at the beginning she used to like the market, where you can pick a live fowl for yourself, quite cheap – she said those little rotten tomatoes they grow here, and the dirty people all shouting and she can't understand. She doesn't sleep, half the time, at night, either, and lately she wakes me up. It happened only last night. She was standing there in the dark and she said: 'I felt bad.'

I said, 'I'll make you some tea,' though what good could tea do.

'There must be something the matter with me,' she says. 'I must go to the doctor tomorrow.'

'Is it pains again, or what?'

She shakes her head slowly, over and over, and I know she's going to cry again. 'A place where there's no one. I get up and look out the window and it's just like I'm not awake. And every day, every day. I can't ever wake up and be out of it. I always see this town.'

Of course it's hard for her. I've picked up Swahili and I can get around all right; I mean I can always talk to anyone if I feel like it, but she hasn't learnt more than *ahsante* – she could've picked it up just as easily, but she *can't*, if you know what I mean. It's just a noise to her, like dogs barking or those black crows in the palm trees. When anyone does come here to see her – someone else from home, usually, or perhaps I bring the Rhodesian who works where I do, she only sits there and whatever anyone talks about she doesn't listen until she can sigh and say, 'Heavy, heavy. Yes, for a woman alone. No friends, nobody. For a woman alone, I can tell you.'

Last night I said to her, 'It would be worse if you were at home, you wouldn't have seen Josias or me for a long time.'

She said, 'Yes, it would be bad. Sela and everybody. And the old crowd at the hospital . . . but just the same, it would be bad. D'you remember how we used to go right into town on my Saturday off? The people – ay! Even when you were twelve you used to be scared you'd lose me.'

'I wasn't scared, you were the one was scared to get run over sometimes.' But in the location when we stole fruit and sweets from the shops, Emma could always grab me out of the way of trouble, Emma always saves me. The same Emma. And yet it's not the same. And what could I do for her?

I suppose she wants to be back there now. But still she wouldn't be the same. I don't often get the feeling she knows what I'm thinking about, any more, or that I know what she's thinking, but she said, 'You and he go off, you come back or perhaps you don't come back, you know what you must do. But for a woman? What shall I do there in my life? What shall I do here? What time is this for a woman?'

It's hard for her. Emma. She'll say all that often now, I know. She tells me everything so many times. Well, I don't mind it when I fetch her from the hospital and I don't mind going to the market. But straight after we've eaten, now, in the evenings, I let her go through it once and then I'm off. To walk in the streets when it gets a bit cooler in the dark. I don't know why it is but I'm thinking so bloody hard about getting out there in the streets that I push down my food as fast as I can without her noticing. I'm so keen to get going I feel queer, kind of tight and excited. Just until I can get out and not hear. I wouldn't even mind skipping the meal. In the streets in the evening everyone is out. On the grass along the bay the fat Indians in their white suits with their wives in those fancy coloured clothes. Men and their girls holding hands. Old watchmen like beggars, sleeping in the doorways of the shut shops. Up and down people walk, walk, just sliding one foot after the other because now and then, like somebody lifting a blanket, there's air from the sea. She should come out for a bit of air in the evening, man. It's an old, old place this, they say. Not the buildings, I mean; but the place. They say ships were coming here before even a place like London was a town. She thought the bay was so nice, that first day. The lights from the ships run all over the water and the palms show up a long time even after it gets dark. There's a smell I've smelled ever since we've been here – three years! I don't mean the smells in the native town; a special warm night smell. You can even smell it at three in the morning. I've smelled it when I was standing about with Emma, by the window; it's as hot in the middle of the night here as it is in the middle of the day at home – funny, when you look at the stars and the dark. Well, I'll be going off soon. It can't be long now. Now that Josias is gone. You've just got to wait your time; they haven't forgotten about you. Dar es Salaam. Dar. Sometimes I walk with another chap from home, he says some things, makes you laugh! He says the old watchmen who sleep in the doorways get their wives to come there with them. Well, I haven't seen it. He says we're definitely going with the next lot. Dar es Salaam. Dar. One day I suppose I'll remember it and tell my wife I stayed three years there, once. I walk and walk, along the bay, past the shops and hotels and the German church and the big bank, and through the mud streets between old shacks and stalls. It's dark there and full of other walking shapes as I go past light coming from the cracks in the walls, where the people are in their homes.

Friday's Footprint

Friday's Footprint

The hotel stood a hundred yards up from the bank of the river. On the lintel above the screen door at the entrance, small gilt letters read: J. P. CUNNINGHAM, LICENSED TO SELL MALT, WINE AND SPIRITUOUS LIQUORS; the initials had been painted in over others that had been painted out. Sitting in the office off the veranda, at the old, high, pigeonhole desk stuffed with papers, with the cardboard files stacked round her in record of twenty years, she turned her head now and then to the water. She did not see it, the sheeny, gnat-hazy surface of the tropical river; she rested her eyes a moment. And then she turned back to her invoices and accounts, or wrote out, in her large, strong hand, the lunch and dinner menus: Potage of Green Peas, Crumbed Chop and Sauter Potatoes – the language, to her an actual language, of hotel cooking, that was in fact the garbled remnant influence of the immigrant chef from Europe who had once stuck it out in the primitive kitchen for three months, on his way south to the scope and plush of a Johannesburg restaurant.

She spent most of the day in the office, all year. The only difference was that in winter she was comfortable, it was even cool enough for her to need to wear a cardigan, and in summer she had to sit with her legs spread under her skirt while the steady trickle of sweat crept down the inner sides of her thighs and collected behind her knees. When people came through the squealing screen door on to the hotel veranda, and hung about in the unmistakable way of new arrivals (this only happened in winter, of course; nobody came to that part of Central Africa in the summer, unless they were obliged to) she would sense rather than hear them, and she would make them wait a few minutes. Then she would get up from the desk slowly, grinding back her chair, pulling her dress down with one hand, and appear. She had never learnt the obsequious yet superior manner of a hotelkeeper's wife – the truth was that she was shy, and, being a heavy forty-year-old woman, she expressed this in lame brusqueness. Once the new guests had signed the register, she was quite likely to go back to her bookkeeping without having shown them to their rooms or called a boy to carry their luggage. If they ventured to disturb her again in her office, she would say, astonished, 'Hasn't someone fixed you up? My husband, or the housekeeper? Oh Lord—' And she would go through the dingy company of the grass chairs in the lounge, and through the ping-pong room that smelled strongly of red floor polish and cockroach repellent, to find help.

But usually people didn't mind their offhand reception. By the time they arrived at the river village they had travelled two days from the last village over desert and dried-out salt pans; they had slept out under the crushing silence of a night sky that ignored them and held no human sound other than their own small rustlings. They were inclined to emerge from their jeeps feeling unreal. The sight of Mrs Cunningham, in her flowered print dress, with a brooch on her big bosom, and her big, bright-skinned face looking clerically dazed beneath her thick permanent, was the known world, to them; Friday's footprint in the sand. And when she appeared in the bar, in the evening, they found out that she was quite nice, after all. She wore a ribbon in her large head of light curly hair, then, and like many fat women, she looked suddenly not young, but babyish. She did not drink – occasionally she would giggle experimentally over a glass of sweet sherry – and would sit reading a week-old Johannesburg paper that someone had brought up with him in his car.

A man served the drinks with light, spry movements that made everything he did seem like sleight of hand.

'Is that really Mrs Cunningham's *husband*?' newcomers would ask, when they had struck up acquaintance with the three permanent guests – the veterinary officer, the meteorological officer and the postmaster. The man behind the bar, who talked out of the curl of his upper lip, was small and slender and looked years younger than she did, although of course he was not – he was thirty-nine and only a year her junior. Outdoors, and in the daylight, his slenderness was the leanness of cured meat, his boy film-star face, with the satyr-shaped head of upstanding curly hair, the black, frown-framed eyes and forward-jutting mouth, was a monkey face, lined, watchful, always old.

Looking at him in the light of the bar, one of the permanent guests would explain, behind his glass, 'Her second husband, of course. Arthur Cunningham's dead. But this one's some sort of relative of her first husband, he's a Cunningham, too.'

Rita Cunningham did not always see nothing when she turned to look at the water. Sometimes (what times? she struggled to get herself to name – oh, times; when she had slept badly, or when – things – were not right) she saw the boat coming across the flooded river. She looked at the wide, shimmering, sluggish water where the water lilies floated shining in the sun and she began to see, always at the same point, approaching the middle of the river from the other bank, the boat moving slowly under its heavy load. It was their biggest boat; it was carrying eight sewing machines and a black-japanned iron double bedstead as well as the usual stores, and Arthur and three store boys were sitting on top of the cargo. As the boat reached the middle of the river, it turned over, men and cargo toppled, and the iron bed came down heavily on top of their flailing arms, their arms stuck through the bars as the bed sank, taking them down beneath it. That was all. There was a dazzle of sun on the water, where they had been; the water lilies were thickest there.

She had not been there when it happened. She had been in Johannesburg on that yearly holiday that they all looked forward to so much. She had been sitting in the best seats on the stand at the Wanderers' Ground, the third day running, watching the international cricket test between South Africa and the visiting New Zealand team. Three of her children were with her – the little boy had the autographs of all the men in both teams; and Johnny was there. Johnny Cunningham, her husband's stepbrother, who had worked with them at the hotel and the stores for the last few years, and who, as he did every year since he had begun to work for them, had driven her down to Johannesburg, so that she could have a longer holiday than the time her husband, Arthur, could spare away from his work. The arrangement was always that Arthur came down to Johannesburg after his wife had been there for two weeks, and then Johnny Cunningham drove himself back to the hotel alone, to take care of things there.

Ever since she was a girl, she had loved cricket. At home, up in the territory, she'd have the radio going in the hotel office while she worked, if there was a cricket commentary on, just as some people might like a little background music. She was happy, that day, high up in the stand in the shade. The grass was green, the figures of the players plaster-white. The sweet, short sound of the ball brought good-natured murmurs, roars of approval, dwindling growls of disappointment following it, from the crowd. There was the atmosphere of ease of people who are well enough off to take a day's holiday from the office and spend it drinking beer, idly watching a game, and getting a red, warm look, so that they appear more like a bed of easy-growing flowers than a crowd of human faces. Every now and then, a voice over the loudspeaker would announce some request or other – would the owner of car TJ 986339 please report to the ticket office at once; a lady's fob watch had been lost, and would anyone . . . et cetera; an urgent telegram, I repeat, an urgent telegram awaits Mr So-and-so . . . The voice was addicted to the phrase 'I repeat,' and there were mock groans here and there, among the crowd, every time the voice began to speak – she herself had exchanged a little shrug of amusement with someone in the row ahead who had turned in exasperation at the umpteenth 'I repeat' that day. And then, at exactly quarter past three in the afternoon, her own name was spoken by the voice. 'Will Mrs Rita Cunningham, of Olongwe, I repeat, Olongwe, please report to the main entrance immediately. This is an urgent message for Mrs Rita Cunningham. Will Mrs Cunningham please report . . .'

She turned to Johnny at once, surprised, pulling a face.

'I wouldn't know,' he said, giving a short, bored laugh. (He preferred a good fast rugby game any time, but Arthur, wanting to give him a treat, had said to his wife, 'Get a cricket ticket for Johnny too, take Johnny along one of the days.')

She said, smiling and confused, bridling, 'Somebody's making a silly ass of me, calling me out like this.'

'Awright,' he said, slapping down his box of cigarettes and getting up with the quickness of impatience, 'I'll go.'

She hesitated a moment; she had suddenly thought of her fourth child, the naughty one, Margie, who had been left playing at the house of the Johannesburg relatives with whom the Cunninghams were staying. 'Oh, I'd better go. I suppose it must be Margie; I wonder what she's gone and done to herself now, the little devil.'

Johnny sat down again. 'Please yourself.' And she got up and made her way up the stand. As soon as she got to the entrance she saw her sister Ruth's car drawn up right at the gates where no one was allowed to park, and before she had seen her sister and her brother-in-law standing there, turned towards her, a throb of dread beat up once, in her throat.

'What happened? Did she run in the street—' she cried, rushing up to them. The man and the woman stared at her as if they were afraid of her.

'Not Margie,' said the man. 'It's not Margie. Come into the car.'

And in the car, outside the cricket ground, still within sound of the plock of the ball and the voice of the crowd rising to it, they told her that a telegram had come saying that Arthur had been drowned that morning, bringing a boatload of goods over the flooded river.

She did not cry until she got all the way back to the hotel on the bank of the river. She left the children behind, with her sister (the two elder girls went to boarding school in Johannesburg, anyway), and Johnny Cunningham drove her home.

Once, in the middle of a silence as vast as the waste of sand they were grinding through, she said, 'Who would ever have dreamt it would happen to him. The things he'd done in his time, and never come to any harm.'

'Don't tell me,' Johnny agreed, his pipe between his teeth.

In Johannesburg they had all said to one another, 'It'll hit her when she gets back.' But although she had believed the fact of her husband's death when she was away from the village, in the unreality of the city – once she saw and smelled the village again, once she stepped into the hotel, it all seemed nonsense. Nothing was changed. It was all there, wasn't it? The wildebeest skins pegged out to tan, the old horns half buried in the sand, the plaster Johnny Walker on the counter in the bar; the river.

Two days later one of the store boys came over to the hotel with some cheques for her to sign, and, standing in the office doorway with his old hat in his hand, said to her in a hoarse low voice, as if he wanted no one, not even the dead, to overhear, 'He was a good man. Missus, he was a very good man. Oh, missus.'

She cried. While she wrote her name on the cheques and silently handed them back to the elderly black man, it came: strong pity for Arthur, who had been alive, as she was, and was now dead. When she was alone again she sat on at the desk staring at the spikes of invoices and the rubber stamps and the scratched and ink-stained wood, and she wept in pity for the pain of that strong, weathered man, filling his lungs with water with every breath under the weight of the iron bedstead. She wept at the cruel fact of death; perhaps that was not quite what her relatives in Johannesburg had meant when they had said that it would hit her when she got home – but she wept, anyway.

Slowly, in short bursts of confidence that stopped abruptly or tailed off in embarrassment, people began to talk to her about the drowning. This one spared her this detail, another told her it and spared her something else; so it was that she had put together, out of what she had been told, that silent, unreal, orderly picture, scarcely supplemented at all by imagination, since she had very little, that she sometimes saw rise on the river and sink out of sight again.

The facts were simple and horrible. Arthur Cunningham had been doing what he had done dozens of times before; what everyone in the village had done time and again, whenever the river was flooded and the bridge was down. The bridge was either down or under water almost every year, at the height of the rainy season, and when this happened the only way to reach the village was by boat. That December day there was a pack of stuff to get across the river – all the food for the hotel and the store goods, which had come up north by truck. Arthur Cunningham was the sort of man who got things done himself; that was the only way to get them done. He went back and forth with the boys four times, that morning, and they were making some headway. 'Come on, let's see if we c'n git things going,' he kept chivvying at the white assistants who were in charge of unloading the trucks, and were sweating with haste and the nervous exhaustion of working under his eye. 'I dunno, honestly, I've got my boat, I've got my team of boys, and what's happening? I'm waiting for you blokes. Don't tickle that stuff, there, man! For Christ's sake, get cracking. Get it on, get it on!'

The Africans took his manner – snarling, smiling, insulting in its assumption (true) that he could do everything his workers did, but in half the time and twice as well – better than the white men. They laughed and grumbled back at him, and groaned under his swearing and his taunts. When the boat was fully loaded for the fifth trip, he noticed the black-japanned double bed, in its component parts, but not assembled, propped against a crate. 'What about that thing?' he yelled. 'Don't keep leaving that behind for the next lot, you bloody fools. Get it on, get it on. That's a new bed for the Chief's new wife, that's an important order.' And he roared with laughter. He went up to a pimply little twenty-two-year-old clerk, whose thin hair, tangled with the rims of his glasses, expressed wild timidity. 'You shouldn't be too young to know how important a nice comfortable big bed is? You expect the old Chief to wait till tomorrow? How'd'you feel, if you were waiting for that beautiful bed for a beautiful new woman—' And while the young man peered at him, startled, Arthur Cunningham roared with laughter again.

'Mr Cunningham, the boat's full,' another white assistant called.

'Never mind, full! Put it on, man. I'm sick of seeing that bed lying here. Put it on!'

'I don't know how you'll get it over, it makes the whole load top-heavy.'

Arthur Cunningham walked up to his clerk. He was a man of middle height, with a chest and a belly, big, hard and resonant, like the body of a drum, and his thick hands and sandy-haired chest, that always showed in the open neck of his shirt, were blotched and wrinkled with resistance to and in tough protection against the sun. His face was red and he had even false teeth in a lipless mouth that was practical-looking rather than mean or unkind.

'Come on, Harris,' he said, as if he were taking charge of a child. 'Come on now, and no damn nonsense. Take hold here.' And he sent the man, tottering under the weight of the foot of the bed while he himself carried the head, down to the boat.

Rita had married him when she was twenty-three, and he was sixteen or seventeen years older than she was. He had looked almost exactly the same when she married him as he did the last time ever that she saw him, when he stood in the road with his hands on the sides of his belly and watched the car leave for Johannesburg. She was a virgin, she had never been in love, when she married him; he had met her on one of his trips down south, taken a fancy to her, and that was that. He always did whatever he liked and got whatever he wanted. Since she had never been made love to by a young man, she accepted his command of her in bed as the sum of love; his tastes in love-making, like everything else about him, were formed before she knew him, and he was as set in this way as he was in others. She never knew him, of course, because she had nothing of the deep need to possess his thoughts and plumb his feelings that comes of love.

He was as generous as his tongue was rough, which meant that his tongue took the edge off his generosity at least as often as his generosity took the sting out of his tongue. He had hunted and fished and traded all over Africa, and he had great contempt for travellers' tales. When safari parties stayed at his hotel, he criticised their weapons (What sort of contraption do you call that? I've shot round about fifty lion in my lifetime, without any telescopic sights, I can tell you), their camping equipment (I don't know what all this fuss is about water filters and what-not. I've drunk water that was so filthy I've had to lean over and draw it into my mouth through a bit of rag, and been none the worse for it), and their general helplessness. But he also found experienced native guides for these people, and lent them the things they had forgotten to buy down south. He was conscious of having made a number of enemies, thinly scattered in that sparsely populated territory, and was also conscious of his good standing, of the fact that everybody knew him, and of his ownership of the hotel, the two stores, and whatever power there was in the village.

His stepmother had been an enemy of his, in that far-off childhood that he had overcome long ago, but he had had no grudge against his young stepbrother, her son, who must have had his troubles, too, adopted into a house full of Cunninghams. Johnny'd been rolling around the world for ten years or so – America, Mexico, Australia – when he turned up in the territory one day, stony-broke and nowhere in particular to go. Arthur wasn't hard on him, though he chaffed him a bit, of course, and after the boy'd been loafing around the river and hotel for a month, Arthur suggested that he might give a hand in one of the stores. Johnny took the hint in good part – 'Got to stop being a bum sometime, I suppose,' he said, and turned out to be a surprisingly good worker. Soon he was helping at the hotel, too – where, of course, he was living, anyway. And soon he was one of the family, doing whatever there was to be done.

Yet he kept himself to himself. 'I've got a feeling he'll just walk out, when he feels like it, same as he came,' Rita said to Arthur, with some resentment. She had a strong sense of loyalty and was always watchful of any attempt to take advantage of her husband, who had in such careless abundance so many things that other men wanted.

'Oh for Pete's sake, Rita, he's a bit of a natural sourpuss, that's all. He lives his life and we live ours. There's nothing wrong with the way he works, and nothing else about old Johnny interests me.'

The thing was, in a community the size of the village, and in the close life of the little hotel, that life of Johnny Cunningham's was lived, if in inner isolation, outwardly under their noses. He ate at table with them, usually speaking only when he was spoken to. When, along with the Cunningham couple, he got drawn into a party of hotel guests, he sat drinking with great ease but seldom bothered to contribute anything to the talk, and would leave the company with an abrupt, sardonic-sounding 'Excuse me' whenever he pleased.

The only times he came 'out of his shell', as Rita used to put it to her husband, were on dance nights. He had arrived in the territory during the jive era, but his real triumphs on the floor came with the advent of rock 'n' roll. He learnt it from a film, originally – the lounge of the hotel was the local cinema, too, on Thursday nights – and he must have supplemented his self-teaching on the yearly holidays in Johannesburg. Anyway, he was expert, and on dance nights he would take up from her grass chair one of the five or six lumpy girls from the village, at whom he never looked, at any other time, let alone spoke to, and would transform her within the spell of his own rhythm. Sometimes he did this with women among the hotel guests, too; 'Look at old Johnny, giving it stick,' Arthur Cunningham would say, grinning, in the scornfully admiring tone of someone praising a performance that he wouldn't stoop to, himself. There was something about Johnny, his mouth slightly open, the glimpse of saliva gleaming on his teeth, his head thrown back and his eyes narrowed while his body snaked on stooping legs and nimble feet, that couldn't be ignored.

'Well, he seems to be happy that way,' Rita would say with a laugh, embarrassed for the man.

Sometimes Johnny slept with one of these women guests (there was no bed that withheld its secrets from the old German housekeeper, who, in turn, insisted on relating all she knew to Rita Cunningham). It was tacitly accepted that there was some sort of connection between the rock 'n' roll performance and the assignation; who would ever notice Johnny at any other time? But in between these infrequent one- or two-night affairs, he took no interest in women, and it seemed clear that marriage was something that never entered his head. Arthur paid him quite well, but he seemed neither to save nor to have any money. He bet (by radio, using the meteorological officer's broadcasting set) on all the big races in Cape Town, Durban and Johannesburg, and he had bought three cars, all equally unsuitable for road conditions up in the territory, and tinkered them to death in Arthur's workshop.

When he came back to the hotel with Rita Cunningham after Arthur was drowned, he went on with his work as usual. But after a week, all the great bulk of work, all the decisions that had been Arthur's, could not be ignored any longer by considerate employees hoping to spare the widow. She said to Johnny at lunch, in her schoolgirlish way, 'Can you come to the office afterwards? I mean, there're some things we must fix up—' When she came into the office he was already there, standing about like a workman, staring at the calendar on the wall.

'Who's going to see that the store orders don't overlap, now?' she said. 'We've got to make that somebody's job. And somebody'll have to take over the costing of perishable goods, too, not old Johnson, Arthur always said he didn't have a clue about it.'

Johnny scratched his ear and said, 'D'you want me to do it?'

They looked at each other for a moment, thinking it over. There was no sign on his face either of eagerness or reluctance.

'Well, if you could, Johnny, I think that's best . . .' And after a pause, she turned to something else. 'Who can we make responsible for the bar – the ordering and everything? D'you think we should try and get a man?'

He shrugged. 'If you like. You could advertise in Jo'burg, or p'raps in Rhodesia. You won't get anybody decent to come up here.'

'I know.' The distress of responsibility suddenly came upon her.

'You could try,' he said again.

'We'll get some old soak, I suppose, who can't keep a job anywhere else.'

'Sure,' he said with his sour smile.

'You don't think,' she said, 'I mean just for now – Couldn't we manage it between us? I mean you could serve, and perhaps the Allgood boy from the garage could come at weekends to give a hand, and then you and I could do the ordering?'

'Sure,' he said, rocking from his heels to his toes and back again, and looking out of the window, 'I can do it, if you want to try.'

She still could not believe that the wheels of these practical needs were carrying her along, and with her, the hotel and the two stores. 'Oh yes,' she said, distracted, 'I think it'll be OK, just for the time being, until I can . . .' She did not finish what she was saying because she did not know what it was for which the arrangement was to be a makeshift.

She took it for granted that she meant to sell the hotel and the two stores. Two of the children were at school in the south, already; the other two would have to follow when they had outgrown the village school, in a year or two. What was the point in her staying on, there, in a remote village, alone, two thousand miles from her children or her relatives?

She talked, and she believed she acted, for the first six months after Arthur was drowned, as if the sale of the hotel and stores was imminent and inevitable. She even wrote to an agent in Johannesburg and an old lawyer friend in Rhodesia, asking their advice about what sort of price she could expect to get for her property and her businesses – Arthur had left everything to her.

Johnny had taken over most of Arthur's work. She, in her turn, had taken over some of Johnny's. Johnny drove back to Johannesburg to fetch the two younger children home, and the hotel and the stores went on as usual. One evening when she was doing some work in the office after dinner, and giving half her attention to the talk of hotel matters with him, she added the usual proviso – 'It would do in the meantime.'

Johnny was hissing a tune through his teeth while he looked up the price of a certain brand of gin in a file of liquor wholesalers' invoices – he was sure he remembered Arthur had a cheaper way of buying it than he himself knew – and he stopped whistling but went on looking and said, 'What'll you do with yourself in Johannesburg, anyway, Rita? You'll have money and you won't need a job.'

She put down her pen and turned round, clutching at the straw of any comment on her position that would help her feel less adrift. 'Wha'd'you mean?'

'I suppose you'll buy a house somewhere near your sister and live there looking after the two little kids.'

'Oh, I don't know,' she parried, but faltering, 'I suppose I'd buy a house . . .'

'Well, what else could you do with yourself?'

He had made it all absolutely clear to her. It came over her with innocent dismay – she had not visualised it, thought about it, for herself: the house in a Johannesburg suburb, the two children at school in the mornings, the two children in bed after seven each night, her sister saying, you must come down to us just whenever you like.

She got up slowly and turned, leaning her rump against the ridge of the desk behind her, frowning, unable to speak.

'You've got something, here,' he said.

'But I always wanted to go. The summer – it's so hot. We always said, one day, when the children—' All her appeals to herself failed. She said, 'But a woman – it's silly – how can I carry on?'

He watched her with interest, but would not save her with an interruption. He smoked and held his half-smoked cigarette between thumb and first finger, turned inwards towards his palm. He laughed. 'You are carrying on,' he said. He made a pantomime gesture of magnificence, raising his eyebrows, waggling his head slowly and pulling down the corners of his mouth. 'All going strong. The whole caboodle. What you got to worry about?'

She found herself laughing, the way children laugh when they are teased out of tears.

In the next few weeks, a curious kind of pale happiness came over her. It was the happiness of relief from indecision, the happiness of confidence. She did not have to wonder if she could manage – she had been managing all the time! The confidence brought out something that had been in her all her life, dormant; she was capable, even a good businesswoman. She began to take a firm hand with the children, with the hotel servants, with the assistants at the stores. She even wrote a letter to the liquor wholesaler, demanding, on a certain brand of gin, the same special discount that her late husband had squeezed out of him.

When the lawyer friend from Rhodesia, who was in charge of Arthur's estate, came up to consult with her, she discussed with him the possibility of offering Johnny – not a partnership, no – but some sort of share, perhaps a fourth share in the hotel and the stores.

'The only thing is, will he stay?' she said.

'Why shouldn't he stay?' said the lawyer, indicating the sound opportunity that was going to be offered to the man.

'Oh, I don't know,' she said. 'I always used to say to Arthur, I had the feeling he was the sort of man who would walk off, one day, same as he came.'

In view of the steady work he had done – 'Oh, I must be fair,' Rita hastened to agree with the lawyer. 'He *has* worked terribly hard, he's been wonderful, since it happened' – the lawyer saw no cause for concern on this point; in any case the contract, when he drew it up, would be a watertight one and would protect her interests against any such contingency.

The lawyer went home to Rhodesia to draw up the contract that was never needed. In three months, she was married to Johnny. By the time the summer rainy season came round, and he was the one who was bringing the supplies across the river in the boat, this year, he was her husband and Arthur's initials were painted out and his were painted in, in their place, over the door.

To the meteorological officer, the veterinary officer and the postmaster – those permanent residents of the hotel who had known them both for years – and the people of the village, the marriage seemed quite sensible, really; a matter of convenience – though, of course, also rather funny – there were a number of jokes about it current in the village for a time. To her – well, it was not until after the marriage was an accomplished fact that she began to try to understand what it was, and what had brought it about.

At the end of that first winter after Arthur's death, Johnny had had an affair with one of the women in a safari party that was on its way home to the south. Rita knew about it, because, as usual, the housekeeper had told her. But on the day the party left (Rita knew which woman it was, a woman not young, but with a well-dieted and massaged slimness) Johnny came into the office after the two jeeps had left and plonked himself down in the old cane chair near the door. Rita turned her head at the creak of the cane, to ask him if he knew whether the cook had decided, for the lunch menu, on a substitute for the chops that had gone off, and his eyes, that had been closed in one of those moments of sleep that fall like a shutter on lively, enervated wakefulness, flew open. He yawned and grinned, and his one eye twitched, as if it winked at her, of itself. 'Boy, that's that,' he said.

It was the first time, in the seven years he had been at the hotel, that he had ever, even obliquely, made any sort of comment on the existence of his private life or the state of his feelings. She blushed, like a wave of illness. He must have seen the red coming up over the skin of her neck and her ears and her face. But, stonily, he didn't mind her embarrassment or feel any of his own. And so, suddenly, there was intimacy; it existed between them as if it had always been there, taken for granted. They were alone together. They had an existence together apart from the hotel and the stores, and the making of decisions about practical matters. He wouldn't have commented to her on his affair with a woman while Arthur was alive and she herself was a married woman. But now, well – it was in his careless face – she was simply a grown-up person, like any other, and she knew that babies weren't found under gooseberry bushes.

After that, whenever he came into the office, they were alone together. She felt him when she sat at her desk with her back to him; her arms tingled into gooseflesh and she seemed to feel a mocking eye (not his, she knew he was not looking at her) on a point exactly in the middle of the back of her neck. She did not know whether she had looked at him or not, before, but now she was aware of the effort of not looking at him, while he ate at table with her, or served in the bar, or simply ran, very lithe, across the sandy road.

And she began – it was an uncomfortable, shameful thing to her, something like the feeling she had had when she was adolescent – to be conscious of her big breasts. She would fold her arms across them when she stood talking to him. She hated them jutting from her underarm nearly to her waist, filling her dress, and, underneath, the hidden nipples that were brown as an old bitch's teats since the children were born. She wanted to hide her legs, too – so thick and strong, the solid-fleshed, mottled calves with their bristly blonde hairs, and the heavy bone of the ankles marked with bruises where, bare-legged, she constantly bumped them against her desk.

She said to him one morning, after a dance night at the hotel – it simply came out of her mouth – 'That Mrs Burns seems to have taken a fancy to you.'

He gave a long, curly-mouthed yawn. He was looking into space, absent; and then he came to himself, briskly; and he smiled slowly, right at her. 'Uh, that. Does she?'

She began to feel terribly nervous. 'I mean I–I – thought she had her eye on you. The way she was laughing when she danced with you.' She laughed, jeering a little.

'She's a silly cow, all right,' he said. And as he went out of the bar, where they were checking the empties together, he put his hand experimentally on her neck, and tweaked her earlobe. It was an ambiguous caress; she did not know whether he was amused by her or if – he meant it, as she put it to herself.

He did not sleep with her until they were married; but, of course, they were married soon. He moved into the big bedroom with her, then, but he kept on his old, dingy rondavel outside the main building, for his clothes and his fishing tackle and the odds and ends of motorcar accessories he kept lying about, and he usually took his siesta in there, in the summer. She lay on her bed alone in the afternoon dark behind the curtains that glowed red with the light and heat that beat upon them from outside, and she looked at his empty bed. She would stare at that place where he lay, where he actually slept, there in the room with her, not a foot away, every night. She had for him a hundred small feelings more tender than any she had ever known, and yet included in them was what she had felt at other rare moments in her life: when she had seen a bird, winged by a shot, fall out of flight formation over the river; when she had first seen one of her own children, ugly, and crying at being born. Sometimes, at the beginning, she would go over in her mind the times when he had made love to her; even at her desk, with the big ledgers open in front of her, and the sound of one of the boys rubbing the veranda floor outside, her mind would let fall the figures she was collating and the dreamy recapitulation of a night would move in. He did not make love to her very often, of course – not after the first few weeks. (He would always pinch her, or feel her arm, when he thought of it, though.) Weeks went by and it was only on dance nights, when usually she went to their room long before him, that he would come in, moving lightly, breathing whisky in the dark, and come over to her as if by appointment. Often she heard him sigh as he came in. He always went through the business of love-making in silence; but to her, in whom a thousand piercing cries were deafening without a sound, it was accepted as part of the extraordinary clamour of her own silence.

As the months went by, he made love to her less and less often, and she waited for him. In tremendous shyness and secrecy, she was always waiting for him. And, oddly, when he did come to her again, next day she would feel ashamed. She began to go over and over things that had happened in the past; it was as if the ability to recreate in her mind a night's love-making had given her a power of imagination she had never had before, and she would examine in recreation, detail by detail, scenes and conversations that were long over. She began always to have the sense of searching for something; searching slowly and carefully. That day at the cricket. A hundred times, she brought up for examination the way she had turned to look at Johnny, when the voice called her name; the way he had laughed, and said, 'Please yourself.' The silence between them in the car, driving back to the territory. The dance nights, long before that, when she had sat beside Arthur and watched Johnny dance. The times she had spoken distrustfully of him to Arthur. It began to seem to her that there was something of conspiracy about all these scenes. Guilt came slowly through them, a stain from deep down. She was beset by the impossibility of knowing – and then again she believed without a doubt – and then, once more, she absolved herself – was there *always* something between her and Johnny? Was it there, waiting, a gleaming eye in the dark, long before Arthur was drowned? All she could do was go over and over every shred of evidence of the past, again and again, reading now yes into it, now no.

She began to think about Arthur's drowning; she felt, crazily, that she and Johnny *knew* Arthur was drowning. They sat in the Wanderers' stand while they knew Arthur was drowning. While there, over there, right in front of the hotel, where she was looking, through the office window (not having to get up from the desk, simply turning her head), the boat with the eight sewing machines and the black-japanned double bed was coming over the water . . . The boat was turning over . . . The arms of the men (who was it who had taken care not to spare her that detail?) came through the iron bedhead, it took the men down with it – Arthur with his mouth suddenly stopped for ever with water.

She did not say one word to Johnny about all this. She would not have known how to put it into words, even to herself. It had no existence outside the terrifying freedom of her own mind, that she had stumbled down into by mistake, and that dwarfed the real world about her. Yet she changed, outwardly, protectively, to hide what only she knew was there – the shameful joy of loving. It was then that she started to talk about Johnny as 'he' and 'him', never referring to him by name, and to speak of him in the humorous, half-critical, half-nagging way of the wife who takes her husband for granted, no illusions and no nonsense about it. 'Have you seen my spouse around?' she would ask, or 'Where's that husband of mine?'

On dance nights, in the winter, he still astonished guests by his sudden emergence from taciturnity into rock'n' roll. The housekeeper no longer told any tales of his brief ventures into the beds where other men's women slept, and so, of course, Rita presumed there weren't any. For herself, she learnt to live with her guilt of loving, like some vague, chronic disorder. It was no good wrestling with it; she had come to understand that – for some reason she didn't understand – the fact, the plain fact that she had never committed the slightest disloyalty to Arthur all through their marriage, provided no cure of truth. She and Johnny never quarrelled, and if the hotel and the businesses didn't expand (Arthur was the one for making plans and money) at least they went on just as before. The summer heat, the winter cool, came and went again and again in the reassuring monotony that passes for security.

The torture of imagination died away in her almost entirely. She lost the power to create the past. Only the boat remained, sometimes rising up from her mind on the river through the commonplace of the day in the office, just as once her nights with Johnny had come between her and immediate reality.

One morning in the fourth winter of their marriage, they were sitting at table together in the hotel dining room, eating the leisurely and specially plentiful breakfast of a Sunday. The dining room was small and friendly; you could carry on a conversation from one table to the next. The meteorologist and the postmaster sat together at their table, a small one near the window, distinguished by the special sauce bottles and the bottles of vitamin pills and packet of crispbread that mark the table of the regular from that of the migrant guest in a hotel. The veterinary officer had gone off for a weekend's shooting. There were two tables of migrants in the room; one had the heads of three gloomy lion-hunters bent together in low discussion over their coffee, the other held a jolly party who had come all the way from Cape Town, and the leaders of which were a couple who had been in the territory and stayed at the hotel twice or three times before. They had received a bundle of newspapers by post from the south the day before, and they were making them do in place of Sunday papers. Johnny was fond of the magazine sections of newspapers; he liked the memoirs of famous sportsmen or ex-spies that were always to be found in them, and he liked to do the crossword. He had borrowed the magazine section of a Johannesburg paper from one of the party, and had done the crossword while he ate his bacon and fried liver and eggs. Now, while he drank a second or third cup of coffee, he found a psychological quiz, and got out his pencil again.

'He's like a kid doing his homework,' said Rita, sitting lazily in her chair, with her heavy legs apart and her shoulders rounded, smoking over her coffee. She spoke over her shoulder, to the people who had loaned the paper, and smiled and jerked her head in the direction of her husband.

'Isn't he busy this morning,' one of the women agreed.

'Hardly been able to eat a thing, he's been so hard at it,' said the man who had been at the hotel before. And, except for the lion-hunters, the whole dining room laughed.

'Just a minute,' Johnny said, lifting a finger but not looking up from his quiz. 'Just a minute – I got a set of questions to answer here. You're in this too, Rita. You got to answer, too, in this one.'

'Not me. You know I've got no brains. You don't get me doing one of those things on a Sunday morning.'

'Doesn't need brains,' he said, biting off the end of his sentence like a piece of thread. ' "How good a husband are you?" – there you are –'

'As if he needs a quiz to tell him that,' she said, at the Cape Town party, who at once began to laugh at the scepto-comical twist to her face. 'I'll answer that one, my boy.' And again they all laughed.

'Here's yours,' he said, feeling for his coffee cup behind the folded paper. '"How good a wife are you?"'

'Ah, that's easy,' she said, pretending to show off, 'I'll answer that one, too.'

'You go ahead,' he said, with a look to the others, chin back, mouth pursed down. 'Here you are. "Do you buy your husband's toilet accessories, or does he choose his own?"'

'Come again?' she said. 'What they mean, toilet accessories?'

'His soap, and his razor and things,' called a man from the other table. 'Violet hair-oil to put on his hair!'

Johnny ran a hand through his upstanding curls and shrank down in his seat.

Even the postmaster, who was rather shy, twitched a smile.

'No, but seriously,' said Rita, through the laughter, 'how can I choose a razor for a man? I ask you!'

'All they want to know is, do you or don't you,' said Johnny. 'Come on, now.'

'Well, if it's a razor, of course I don't,' Rita said, appealing to the room.

'Right! You don't. "No."' Johnny wrote.

'Hey – wait a minute, what about the soap? I do buy the soap. I buy the soap for every man in this hotel! Don't I get any credit for the soap—'

There were cries from the Cape Town table – 'Yes, that's not fair, Johnny, if she buys the soap.'

'She buys the soap for the whole bang shoot of us.'

Johnny put down the paper. 'Well, who's she supposed to be a good wife *to*, anyway!'

All ten questions for the wife were gone through in this manner, with interruptions, suggestions and laughter from the dining room in general. And then Johnny called for quiet while he answered his ten. He was urged to read them out, but he said no, he could tick off his yesses and nos straight off; if he didn't they'd all be sitting at breakfast until lunchtime. When he had done, he counted up his wife's score and his own, and turned to another page to see the verdict.

'Come on, let's have it,' called the man from the Cape Town table. 'The suspense is horrible.'

Johnny was already skimming through the column. 'You really want to hear it?' he said. 'Well, I'm warning you—'

'Oh, get on with it,' Rita said, with the possessive, irritated, yet placid air of a wife, scratching a drop of dried egg yolk off the print bosom of her dress.

'Well, here goes,' he said, in the tone of someone entering into the fun of the thing. '"There is clearly something gravely wrong with your marriage. You should see a doctor or better still, a psychiatrist"' – he paused for effect, and the laugh – '"and seek help, as soon as possible!"'

The man from Cape Town laughed till the tears ran into the creases at the corners of his eyes. Everyone else laughed and talked at once.

'If that isn't the limit!'

'This psychology stuff!'

'Have you ever—!'

'Is there anything they *don't* think of in the papers these days!'

'There it is, my dear,' said Johnny, folding the paper in mock solemnity, and pulling a funereal, yet careless face.

She laughed with him. She laughed looking down at her shaking body where the great cleft that ran between her breasts showed at the neck of her dress. She laughed and she heard, she alone heard, the catches and trips in her throat like the mad cries of some creature buried alive. The blood of a blush burned her whole body with agonising slowness. When the laughter had died down she got up and not looking at Johnny – for she knew how he looked, she knew that unembarrassed gaze – she said something appropriate and even funny, and with great skill went easily, comfortably sloppily, out of the dining room. She felt Johnny following behind her, as usual, but she did not fall back to have him keep up with her, and, as usual after breakfast, she heard him turn off, whistling, from the passage into the bar, where there was the aftermath of Saturday night to clear up.

She got to the office. At last she got to the office and sat down in her chair at the roll-top desk. The terrible blush of blood did not abate; it was as if something had burst inside her and was seeping up in a stain through all the layers of muscle and flesh and skin. She felt again, as she had before, a horrible awareness of her big breasts, her clumsy legs. She clenched her hand over the sharp point of a spike that held invoices and felt it press pain into her palm. Tears were burning hot on her face and her hands, the rolling lava of shame from that same source as the blush. And at last, Arthur! she called in a clenched, whimpering whisper, Arthur! grinding his name between her teeth, and she turned desperately to the water, to the middle of the river where the lilies were. She tried with all her being to conjure up once again out of the water *something*; the ghost of comfort, of support. But that boat, silent and unbidden, that she had so often seen before, would not come again.

The Bridegroom

He came into his road camp that afternoon for the last time. It was neater than any house would ever be; the sand raked smooth in the clearing, the water drums under the tarpaulin, the flaps of his tent closed against the heat. Thirty yards away a black woman knelt, pounding mealies, and two or three children, grey with Kalahari dust, played with a skinny dog. Their shrillness was no more than a bird's piping in the great spaces in which the camp was lost.

Inside his tent, something of the chill of the night before always remained, stale but cool, like the air of a church. There was his iron bed, with its clean pillowcase and big kaross. There was his table, his folding chair with the red canvas seat, and the chest in which his clothes were put away. Standing on the chest was the alarm clock that woke him at five every morning and the photograph of the seventeen-year-old girl from Francistown whom he was going to marry. They had been there a long time, the girl and the alarm clock; in the morning when he opened his eyes, in the afternoon when he came off the job. But now this was the last time. He was leaving for Francistown in the Roads Department ten-tonner, in the morning; when he came back, the next week, he would be married and he would have with him the girl, and the caravan which the department provided for married men. He had his eye on her as he sat down on the bed and took off his boots; the smiling girl was like one of those faces cut out of a magazine. He began to shed his working overalls, a rind of khaki stiff with dust that held his shape as he discarded it, and he called, easily and softly, '*Ou Piet, ek wag.*' But the bony black man with his eyebrows raised like a clown's, in effort, and his bare feet shuffling under the weight, was already at the tent with a tin bath in which hot water made a twanging tune as it slopped from side to side.

When he had washed and put on a clean khaki shirt and a pair of worn grey trousers, and streaked back his hair with sweet-smelling pomade, he stepped out of his tent just as the lid of the horizon closed on the bloody eye of the sun. It was winter and the sun set shortly after five; the grey sand turned a fading pink, the low thorn scrub gave out spreading stains of lilac shadow that presently all ran together; then the surface of the desert showed pocked and pored, for a minute or two, like the surface of the moon through a telescope, while the sky remained light over the darkened earth and the clean crystal pebble of the evening star shone. The campfires – his own and the black men's, over there – changed from near-invisible flickers of liquid colour to brilliant focuses of leaping tongues of light; it was dark. Every evening he sat like this through the short ceremony of the closing of the day, slowly filling his pipe, slowly easing his back round to the fire, yawning off the stiffness of his labour. Suddenly he gave a smothered giggle, to himself, of excitement. Her existence became real to him; he saw the face of the photograph, posed against a caravan door. He got up and began to pace about the camp, alert to promise. He kicked a log farther into the fire, he called an order to Piet, he walked up towards the tent and then changed his mind and strolled away again. In their own encampment at the edge of his, the road gang had taken up the exchange of laughing, talking, yelling and arguing that never failed them when their work was done. Black arms gestured under a thick foam of white soap, there was a gasp and splutter as a head broke the cold force of a bucketful of water, the gleaming bellies of iron cooking-pots were carried here and there in the talkative preparation of food. He did not understand much of what they were saying – he knew just enough Tswana to give them his orders, with help from Piet and one or two others who understood his own tongue, Afrikaans – but the sound of their voices belonged to this time of evening. One of the babies who always cried was keeping up a thin, ignored wail; the naked children were playing the chasing game that made the dog bark. He came back and sat down again at the fire, to finish his pipe.

After a certain interval (it was exact, though it was not timed by a watch, but by long habit that had established the appropriate lapse of time between his bath, his pipe and his food) he called out, in Afrikaans, 'Have you forgotten my dinner, man?'

From across the patch of distorted darkness where the light of the two fires did not meet, but flung wobbling shapes and opaque, overlapping radiances, came the hoarse, protesting laugh that was, better than the tribute to a new joke, the pleasure in constancy to an old one.

Then a few minutes later: 'Piet! I suppose you've burned everything, eh?'

'Baas?'

'Where's the food, man?'

In his own time the black man appeared with the folding table and an oil lamp. He went back and forth between the dark and light, bringing pots and dishes and food, and nagging with deep satisfaction, in a mixture of English and Afrikaans. 'You want *koeksusters*, so I make *koeksusters*. You ask me this morning. So I got to make the oil nice and hot, I got to get everything ready . . . It's a little bit slow. Yes, I know. But I can't get everything quick, quick. You hurry tonight, you don't want wait, then it's better you have *koeksusters* on Saturday, then I'm got time in the afternoon, I do it nice . . . Yes, I think next time it's better . . .'

Piet was a good cook. 'I've taught my boy how to make everything,' the young man always told people, back in Francistown. 'He can even make *koeksusters*,' he had told the girl's mother, in one of those silences of the woman's disapproval that it was so difficult to fill. He had had a hard time, trying to overcome the prejudice of the girl's parents against the sort of life he could offer her. He had managed to convince them that the life was not impossible, and they had given their consent to the marriage, but they still felt that the life was unsuitable, and his desire to please and reassure them had made him anxious to see it with their eyes and so forestall, by changes, their objections. The girl was a farm girl, and would not pine for town life, but, at the same time, he could not deny to her parents that living on a farm with her family around her, and neighbours only thirty or forty miles away, would be very different from living two hundred and twenty miles from a town or village, alone with him in a road camp 'surrounded by a gang of kaffirs all day', as her mother had said. He himself simply did not think at all about what the girl would do while he was out on the road; and as for the girl, until it was over, nothing could exist for her but the wedding, with her two little sisters in pink walking behind her, and her dress that she didn't recognise herself in, being made at the dressmaker's, and the cake that was ordered with a tiny china bride and groom in evening dress, on the top.

He looked at the scored table, and the rim of the open jam tin, and the salt cellar with a piece of brown paper tied neatly over the broken top, and said to Piet, 'You must do everything nice when the missus comes.'

'Baas?'

They looked at each other and it was not really necessary to say anything.

'You must make the table properly and do everything clean.'

'Always I make everything clean. Why you say now I must make clean—'

The young man bent his head over his food, dismissing him.

While he ate his mind went automatically over the changes that would have to be made for the girl. He was not used to visualising situations, but to dealing with what existed. It was like a lesson learned by rote; he knew the totality of what was needed, but if he found himself confronted by one of the component details, he foundered: he did not recognise it or know how to deal with it. The boys must keep out of the way. That was the main thing. Piet would have to come to the caravan quite a lot, to cook and clean. The boys – especially the boys who were responsible for the maintenance of the lorries and road-making equipment – were always coming with questions, what to do about this and that. They'd mess things up, otherwise. He spat out a piece of gristle he could not swallow; his mind went to something else. The women over there – they could do the washing for the girl. They were such a raw bunch of kaffirs, would they ever be able to do anything right? Twenty boys and about five of their women – you couldn't hide them under a thorn bush. They just mustn't hang around, that's all. They must just understand that they mustn't hang around. He looked round keenly through the shadow-puppets of the half-dark on the margin of his fire's light; the voices, companionably quieter, now, intermittent over food, the echoing *chut!* of wood being chopped, the thin film of a baby's wail through which all these sounded – they were on their own side. Yet he felt an odd, rankling suspicion.

His thoughts shuttled, as he ate, in a slow and painstaking way that he had never experienced before in his life – he was worrying. He sucked on a tooth; Piet, Piet, that kaffir talks such a hell of a lot. How's Piet going to stop talking, talking every time he comes near? If he talks to her . . . Man, it's sure he'll talk to her. He thought, in actual words, what he would say to Piet about this; the words were like those unsayable things that people write on walls for others to see in private moments, but that are never spoken in their mouths.

Piet brought coffee and *koeksusters* and the young man did not look at him.

But the *koeksusters* were delicious, crisp, sticky and sweet, and as he felt the familiar substance and taste on his tongue, alternating with the hot bite of the coffee, he at once became occupied with the pure happiness of eating as a child is fully occupied with a bag of sweets. *Koeksusters* never failed to give him this innocent, total pleasure. When first he had taken the job of overseer to the road gang, he had had strange, restless hours at night and on Sundays. It seemed that he was hungry. He ate but never felt satisfied. He walked about all the time, like a hungry creature. One Sunday he actually set out to walk (the Roads Department was very strict about the use of the ten-tonner for private purposes) the fourteen miles across the sand to the cattle-dipping post where the government cattle officer and his wife, Afrikaners like himself and the only other white people between the road camp and Francistown, lived in their corrugated-iron house. By a coincidence, they had decided to drive over and see him, that day, and they had met him a little less than halfway, when he was already slowed and dazed by heat. But shortly after that Piet had taken over the cooking of his meals and the care of his person, and Piet had even learned to make *koeksusters*, according to instructions given to the young man by the cattle officer's wife. The *koeksusters*, a childhood treat that he could indulge in whenever he liked, seemed to mark his settling down; the solitary camp became a personal way of life, with its own special arrangements and indulgences.

'*Ou Piet! Kêrel!* What did you do to the *koeksusters*, hey?' he called out joyously.

A shout came that meant 'Right away.' The black man appeared, drying his hands on a rag, with the diffident, kidding manner of someone who knows he has excelled himself.

'Whatsa matter with the *koeksusters*, man?'

Piet shrugged. 'You must tell me. I don't know what's matter.'

'Here, bring me some more, man.' The young man shoved the empty plate at him, with a grin. And as the other went off, laughing, the young man called, 'You must always make them like that, see?'

He liked to drink at celebrations, at weddings or Christmas, but he wasn't a man who drank his brandy every day. He would have two brandies on a Saturday afternoon, when the week's work was over, and for the rest of the time, the bottle that he brought from Francistown when he went to collect stores lay in the chest in his tent. But on this last night he got up from the fire on impulse and went over to the tent to fetch the bottle (one thing he didn't do, he didn't expect a kaffir to handle his drink for him; it was too much of a temptation to put in their way). He brought a glass with him, too, one of a set of six made of tinted imitation cut glass, and he poured himself a tot and stretched out his legs where he could feel the warmth of the fire through the soles of his boots. The nights were not cold, until the wind came up at two or three in the morning, but there was a clarifying chill to the air; now and then a figure came over from the black men's camp to put another log on the fire whose flames had dropped and become blue. The young man felt inside himself a similar low incandescence; he poured himself another brandy. The long yelping of the jackals prowled the sky without, like the wind about a house; there was no house, but the sounds beyond the light his fire tremblingly inflated into the dark

– that jumble of meaningless voices, crying babies, coughs and hawking – had built walls to enclose and a roof to shelter. He was exposed, turning naked to space on the sphere of the world as the speck that is a fly plastered on the window of an aeroplane, but he was not aware of it.

The lilt of various kinds of small music began and died in the dark; threads of notes, blown and plucked, that disappeared under the voices. Presently a huge man whose thick black body had strained apart every seam in his ragged pants and shirt loped silently into the light and dropped just within it, not too near the fire. His feet, intimately crossed, were cracked and weathered like driftwood. He held to his mouth a one-stringed instrument shaped like a lyre, made out of a half-moon of bent wood with a ribbon of dried palm leaf tied from tip to tip. His big lips rested gently on the strip and while he blew, his one hand, by controlling the vibration of the palm leaf, made of his breath a small, faint, perfect music. It was caught by the very limits of the capacity of the human ear; it was almost out of range. The first music men ever heard, when they began to stand upright among the rushes at the river, might have been like it. When it died away it was difficult to notice at what point it really had gone.

'Play that other one,' said the young man, in Tswana. Only the smoke from his pipe moved.

The pink-palmed hands settled down round the instrument. The thick, tender lips were wet once. The faint desolate voice spoke again, so lonely a music that it came to the player and listener as if they heard it inside themselves. This time the player took a short stick in his other hand and, while he blew, scratched it back and forth inside the curve of the lyre, where the notches cut there produced a dry, shaking, slithering sound, like the far-off movement of dancers' feet. There were two or three figures with more substance than the shadows, where the firelight merged with the darkness. They came and squatted. One of them had half a paraffin tin, with a wooden neck and other attachments of gut and wire. When the lyre-player paused, lowering his piece of stick and leaf slowly, in ebb, from his mouth, and wiping his lips on the back of his hand, the other began to play. It was a thrumming, repetitive, banjo tune. The young man's boot patted the sand in time to it and he took it up with hand-claps once or twice. A thin, yellowish man in an old hat pushed his way to the front past sarcastic remarks and twittings and sat on his haunches with a little clay bowl between his feet. Over its mouth there was a keyboard of metal tongues. After some exchange, he played it and the others sang low and nasally, bringing a few more strollers to the fire. The music came to an end, pleasantly, and started up again, like a breath drawn. In one of the intervals the young man said, 'Let's have a look at that contraption of yours, isn't it a new one?' and the man to whom he signalled did not understand what was being said to him but handed over his paraffin-tin mandolin with pride and also with amusement at his own handiwork.

The young man turned it over, twanged it once, grinning and shaking his head. Two bits of string and an old jam tin and they'll make a whole band, man. He'd heard them playing some crazy-looking things. The circle of faces watched him with pleasure; they laughed and lazily remarked to each other; it was a funny-looking thing, all right, but it worked. The owner took it back and played it, clowning a little. The audience laughed and joked appreciatively; they were sitting close in to the fire now, painted by it.

'Next week' – the young man raised his voice gaily – 'next week when I come back, I bring radio with me, plenty real music. All the big white bands play over it—'

Someone who had once worked in Johannesburg said, 'Satchmo,' and the others took it up, understanding that this was the word for what the white man was going to bring from town. Satchmo. Satch-mo. They tried it out, politely.

'Music, just like at a big white dance in town. Next week.' A friendly, appreciative silence fell, with them all resting back in the warmth of the fire and looking at him indulgently. A strange thing happened to him. He felt hot, over first his neck, then his ears and his face. It didn't matter, of course; by next week they would have forgotten. They wouldn't expect it. He shut down his mind on a picture of them, hanging round the caravan to listen, and him coming out on the steps to tell them—

He thought for a moment that he would give them the rest of the bottle of brandy. Hell, no, man, it was mad. If they got the taste for the stuff, they'd be pinching it all the time. He'd give Piet some sugar and yeast and things from the stores, for them to make beer tomorrow when he was gone. He put his hands deep in his pockets and stretched out to the fire with his head sunk on his chest. The lyre-player picked up his flimsy piece of wood again, and slowly what the young man was feeling inside himself seemed to find a voice; up into the night beyond the fire, it went, uncoiling from his breast and bringing ease. As if it had been made audible out of infinity and could be returned to infinity at any point, the lonely voice of the lyre went on and on. Nobody spoke, the barriers of tongues fell with silence. The whole dirty tide of worry and planning had gone out of the young man. The small, high moon, outshone by a spiky spread of cold stars, repeated the shape of the lyre. He sat for he was not aware how long, just as he had for so many other nights, with the stars at his head and the fire at his feet.

But at last the music stopped and time began again. There was tonight; there was tomorrow, when he was going to drive to Francistown. He stood up; the company fragmented. The lyre-player blew his nose into his fingers. Dusty feet took their accustomed weight. They went off to their tents and he went off to his. Faint plangencies followed them. The young man gave a loud, ugly, animal yawn, the sort of unashamed personal noise a man can make when he lives alone. He walked very slowly across the sand; it was dark but he knew the way more surely than with his eyes. 'Piet! Hey!' he bawled as he reached his tent. 'You get up early tomorrow, eh? And I don't want to hear the lorry won't start. You get it going and then you call me. D'you hear?'

He was lighting the oil lamp that Piet had left ready on the chest and as it came up softly it brought the whole interior of the tent with it: the chest, the bed, the clock and the coy smiling face of the seventeen-year-old girl. He sat down on the bed, sliding his palms through the silky fur of the kaross. He drew a breath and held it for a moment, looking round purposefully. And then he picked up the photograph, folded the cardboard support back flat to the frame, and put it in the chest with all his other things, ready for the journey.

Livingstone's Companions

Livingstone's Companions

In the House that afternoon the Minister of Foreign Affairs was giving his report on the President's visit to Ethiopia, Kenya and Tanzania. 'I would like to take a few minutes to convey to you the scene when we arrived at the airport,' he was saying, in English, and as he put the top sheet of his sheaf of notes under the last, settling down to it, Carl Church in the press gallery tensed and relaxed his thigh muscles – a gesture of resignation. 'It's hard to describe the enthusiasm that greeted the President everywhere he went. Everywhere crowds, enormous crowds. If those people who criticise the President's policies and cry neo-colonialism when he puts the peace and prosperity of our country first—'

There were no Opposition benches since the country was a one-party state, but the dissident faction within the party slumped, blank-faced, while a deep hum of encouragement came from two solid rows of the President's supporters seated just in front of Carl Church.

'. . . those who are so quick to say that our President's policies are out of line with the OAU could see how enthusiastically the President is received in fellow member states of the OAU, they would think before they shout, believe me. They would see it is they who are out of line, who fail to understand the problems of Pan-Africa, they who would like to see our crops rot in the fields, our people out of work, our development plans come to a full stop' – assent swarmed, the hum rose – 'and all for an empty gesture of fist-shaking' – the two close-packed rows were leaning forward delightedly; polished shoes drummed the floor – 'they know as well as you and I will not free the African peoples of the white-supremacy states south of our borders.'

The Foreign Minister turned to the limelight of approval. The President himself was not in the House; some members watched the clock (gift of the United States Senate) whose graceful copper hand moved with a hiccup as each minute passed. The Speaker in his long curly wig was propped askew against the tall back of his elaborate chair. His clerk, with the white pompadour, velvet bow and lacy jabot that were part of the investiture of sovereignty handed down from the British, was a perfect papier-mâché blackamoor from an eighteenth-century slave trader's drawing room. The House was panelled in local wood whose scent the sterile blast of the air-conditioning had not yet had time to evaporate entirely. Carl Church stayed on because of the coolness, the restful incense of new wood – the Foreign Minister's travelogue wasn't worth two lines of copy. Between the Minister and the President's claque the dialogue of banal statement and deep-chested response went on beamingly, obliviously.

'. . . can assure you . . . full confidence lies in . . .'

Suddenly the Speaker made an apologetic but firm gesture to attract the Minister's attention: 'Mr Minister, would it be convenient to adjourn at this point . . . ?'

The clique filed jovially out of the House. The Chamberlain came into the foyer carrying his belly before turned-out thighs, his fine African calves looking well in courtier's stockings, silver buckles flashing on his shoes. Waylaid on the stairs by another journalist, the Minister was refusing an interview with the greatest amiability, in the volume of voice he had used in the House, as if someone had forgotten to turn off the public address system.

With the feeling that he had dozed through a cinema matinée, Carl Church met the glare of the afternoon as a dull flash of pain above his right eye. His hired car was parked in the shade of the building – these were the little ways in which he made some attempt to look after himself: calculating the movement of the sun when in hot countries, making sure that the hotel bed wasn't damp, in cold ones. He drove downhill to the offices of the broadcasting station, where his paper had arranged telex facilities. In the prematurely senile building, unfinished and decaying after five years, the unevenness of the concrete floors underfoot increased his sensation of slowed reactions. He simply looked in to see if there was anything for him; the day before he had sent a long piece on the secessionist movement in the Southern Province and there just might be a word of commendation from the Africa desk. There *was* something: '100 YEARS ANNIVERSARY ROYAL GEOGRAPHICAL SOCIETY PARTY SENT SEARCH FOR LIVINGSTONE STOP YOU WELL PLACED RETRACE STEPS LIVINGSTONES LAST JOURNEY SUGGEST LAKES OR INTERIOR STOP THREE THOUSAND WORDS SPECIAL FEATURE 16TH STOP THANKS BARTRAM.'

He wanted to fling open bloody Bartram's bloody door – the words were in his mouth, overtaking each other. *Church is out there, he'll come up with the right sort of thing. Remember his 'Peacock Throne' piece?* Oh yes. He had been sent to Iran for the coronation of the Shahanshah, he was marked down to have to do these beautiful, wryly understated sidelights. Just as a means of self-expression, between running about after Under Ministers and party bosses and driving through the bush at a hundred in the shade to look at rice fields planned by the Chinese and self-help pig farms run by the Peace Corps, and officially non-existent guerrilla training camps for political refugees from neighbouring countries. He could put a call through to London. How squeakily impotent the voice wavering across the radio telephone. Or he could telex a blast; watch all the anticipated weariness, boredom and exasperation punching a domino pattern on clean white tape.

Slowly pressure subsided from his temples. He was left sulkily nursing the grievance: don't even realise the 'lakes and interior' are over the border! In the next country. Don't even know that. The car whined up the hill again (faulty differential this one had) to the office full of dead flies and posters of ski slopes where the airline agency girl sat. There was a Viscount the next day, a local Dakota the day after. 'I'll wait-list you. You're sure to get on. Just be at the airport half an hour early.'

He was there before anybody. Such a pretty black girl at the weigh-bay; she said with her soft, accented *English*, 'It looks good. You're top of the list, don't worry, sir.'

'I'm not worried, I assure you.' But it became a point of honour, like the obligation to try to win in some silly game – once you'd taken the trouble to get to the airport, you must succeed in getting away. He watched the passengers trailing or hurrying up with their luggage and – smug devils – presenting their tickets. He tried to catch the girl's eye now and then to see how it was going. She gave no sign, except, once, a beautiful airline smile, something she must have learnt in her six weeks' efficiency and deportment course. Girls were not beautiful, generally, in this part of Africa; the women of Vietnam had spoilt him for all other women, anyway. In the steps of Livingstone, or women of the world, by our special correspondent. But even in his mind, smart phrases like that were made up, a picture of himself saying them, Carl A. Church, the foreign correspondent in the air-conditioned bar (when asked what the American-style initial stood for, the story went that he had said to a bishop, 'Anti, Your Grace'). Under his absurdly tense attention for each arrival at the weigh-bay there was the dark slow movement of the balance of past and present that regulates the self-estimate by which one really manages to live. He was seeing again – perhaps for the first time since it happened, five? six? years ago – a road in Africa where the women were extremely beautiful. She was standing on the edge of the forest with a companion, breasts of brown silk, a water mark of sunlight lying along them. A maroon and blue *pagne* hid the rest of her. On a sudden splendid impulse he had stopped the car (that one had a worn clutch) and offered her money, but she refused. Why? The women of that country had been on sale to white men for a number of generations. She refused. Why me? Well, he accepted that when it came to women, whom he loved so well, his other passion – the desire to defend the rights of the individual of any colour or race – did not bear scrutiny.

Now a blonde was up at the weigh-bay for the second or third time; the black girl behind it was joined by an airline official in shirtsleeves. They consulted a list while the blonde went on talking. At last she turned away and, looking round the echoing hall with the important expression of someone with a complaint to confide, this time came and sat on the bench where he waited. Among her burdens was a picture in brown paper that had torn over the curlicues of the gilt frame. Her thin hands had rings thrust upon them like those velvet Cleopatra's needles in the jewellers'. She puts on everything she's got, when she travels; it's the safest way to carry it. And probably there's a pouch round her middle, containing the settlement from her last ex-husband. Carl Church had noticed the woman before, from some small sidetrack of his mind, even while she existed simply as one of the lucky ones with a seat on the plane. She was his vintage, that's why; the blonde page-boy broken into curling locks by the movement of her shoulders, the big red mouth, the high heels, the girlish floral beach-dress – on leaves during the war, girls his own age looked like that. But this one had been out in the sun for twenty years. Smiled at him; teeth still good. Ugly bright blue eyes, cheap china. She knew she still had beautiful legs, nervous ankles all hollows and tendons. Her dead hair tossed frowsily. He thought, tender to his own past: she's horrible.

'This's the second morning I've sat here cooling my heels.' Her bracelets shook, dramatising exasperation. 'The second day running. I only hope to God I'm on this time.'

He said, 'Where're you trying to get to?' But of course he knew before she answered. He waited a moment or two, and then strolled up to the weigh-bay. 'Still top of the list, I hope?' – in an undertone.

The airline man, standing beside the black beauty, answered brusquely, 'There's just the one lady before you, sir.'

He began to argue.

'We can't help it, sir. It's a compassionate, came through from the town office.'

He went back and sat down.

She said, 'You're going on the same plane?'

'Yes.' Not looking her way, the bitch, he watched with hope as boarding time approached and there were no new arrivals at the weigh-bay. She arranged and rearranged her complicated hand luggage; rivalry made them aware of one another. Two minutes to boarding time, the airline girl didn't want him to catch her eye, but he went over to her just the same. She said, cheerfully relieved of responsibility, 'Doesn't look as if anyone's going to get a seat. Everybody's turned up. We're just checking.'

He and the blonde lady were left behind. Hostility vanished as the others filed off down the Red Route. They burst into talk at once, grumbling about the airline organisation.

'Imagine, they've been expecting me for days.' She was defiantly gay.

'Dragging out here for nothing – I was assured I'd get a seat, no trouble at all.'

'Well, that's how people are these days – my God, if I ran my hotel like that. Simply relax, what else can you do? Thank heaven I've got a firm booking for tomorrow.'

A seat on tomorrow's plane, eh; he slid out of the conversation and went to look for the reservations counter. There was no need for strategy, after all; he got a firm booking, too. In the bus back to town, she patted the seat beside her. There were two kinds of fellow travellers, those who asked questions and those who talked about themselves. She took the bit of a long cigarette holder between her teeth and quoted her late husband, told how her daughter, 'a real little madam', at boarding school, got on like a house on fire with her new husband, said how life was what you put into it, as she always reminded her son; people asked how could one stand it, up there, miles away from everything, on the lake, but she painted, she was interested in interior decorating, she'd run the place ten years by herself, took some doing for a woman.

'On the lake?'

'Gough's Bay Hotel.' He saw from the stare of the blue eyes that it was famous – he should have known.

'Tell me, whereabout are the graves, the graves of Livingstone's companions?'

The eyes continued to stare at him, a corner of the red mouth drew in proprietorially, carelessly unimpressed. 'My graves. On my property. Two minutes from the hotel.'

He murmured surprise. 'I'd somehow imagined they were much further north.'

'And there's no risk of bilharzia *whatever*,' she added, apparently dispelling a rumour. 'You can water-ski, goggle-fish – people have a marvellous time.'

'Well, I may turn up someday.'

'My dear, I've never let people down in my life. We'd find a bed somewhere.'

He saw her at once, in another backless flowered dress, when he entered the departure lounge next morning. 'Here we go again' – distending her nostrils in mock resignation, turning down the red lips. He gave her his small-change smile and took care to lag behind when the passengers went across the runway. He sat in the tail of the plane, and opened the copy of Livingstone's last journals, bought that morning. 'Our sympathies are drawn out towards our humble hardy companions by a community of interests, and, it may be, of perils, which make us all friends.' The book rested on his thighs and he slept through the hour-and-a-half's journey. Livingstone had walked it, taking ten months and recording his position by the stars. This could be the lead for his story, he thought: waking up to the recognition of the habits of his mind like the same old face in the shaving mirror.

The capital of this country was hardly distinguishable from the one he had left. The new national bank with air-conditioning and rubber plants changed the perspective of the row of Indian stores. Behind the main street a native market stank of dried fish. He hired a car, borrowed a map from the hotel barman and set out for 'the interior' next day, distrusting – from long experience – both car and map. He had meant merely to look up a few places and easy references in the journals, but had begun to read and gone on half the night.

> A wife ran away, I asked how many he had; he told me twenty in all: I then thought he had nineteen too many. He answered with the usual reason, 'But who would cook for strangers if I had but one?' . . . It is with sorrow that I have to convey the sad intelligence that your brother died yesterday morning about ten o'clock . . . no remedy seemed to have much effect. On the 20th he was seriously ill but took soup several times, and drank claret and water with relish . . . A lion roars mightily. The fish-hawk utters his weird voice in

> the morning, as if he lifted up to a friend at a great distance, in a sort of falsetto key . . . The men engaged refuse to go to Matipa's, they have no honour . . . Public punishment to Chirango for stealing beads, fifteen cuts; diminished his load to 40 lbs . . . In four hours we came within sight of the lake, and saw plenty of elephants and other game.

How enjoyable it would have been to read the journals six thousand miles away, in autumn, at home, in London. As usual, once off the circuit that linked the capital with the two or three other small towns that existed, there were crossroads without signposts, and place names that turned out to be one general store, an African bar and a hand-operated petrol pump, unattended. He was not fool enough to forget to carry petrol, and he was good at knocking up the bar owners (asleep during the day). As if the opening of the beer refrigerator and the record player were inseparably linked – as a concept of hospitality if not mechanically – African jazz jog-trotted, clacked and drummed forth while he drank on a dirty veranda. Children dusty as chickens gathered. As he drove off the music stopped in mid-record.

By early afternoon he was lost. The map, sure enough, failed to indicate that the fly-speck named as Moambe was New Moambe, a completely different place in an entirely different direction from that of Old Moambe, where Livingstone had had a camp, and had talked with chiefs whose descendants were active in the present-day politics of their country (another lead). Before setting out, Carl Church had decided that all he was prepared to do was take a car, go to Moambe, take no more than two days over it, and write a piece using the journey as a peg for what he did know something about – this country's attempt to achieve a form of African socialism. That's what the paper would get, all they would get, except the expense account for the flight, car and beers. (The beers were jotted down as 'Lunch, Sundries, Gratuities, £3. 10.' No reason, from Bartram's perspective, why there shouldn't be a Livingstone Hilton in His Steps.) But when he found he had missed Moambe and past three in the afternoon was headed in the wrong direction, he turned the car savagely in the road and made for what he hoped would turn out to be the capital. All they would get would be the expense account. He stopped and asked the way of anyone he met, and no one spoke English. People smiled and instructed the foreigner volubly, with many gestures. He had the humiliation of finding himself twice back at the same crossroads where the same old man sat calmly with women who carried dried fish stiff as Chinese preserved ducks. He took another road, any road, and after a mile or two of hesitancy and obstinacy – turn back or go on? – thought he saw a signpost ahead. This time it was not a dead tree. A sagging wooden finger drooped down a turn-off: GOUGH'S BAY LAZITI PASS.

The lake.

He was more than a hundred miles from the capital. With a sense of astonishment at finding himself, he focused his existence, here and now, on the empty road, at a point on the map. He turned down to petrol, a bath, a drink – that much, at least, so assured that he did not have to think of it. But the lake was farther away than the casualness of the sign would indicate. The pass led the car whining and grinding in low gear round silent hillsides of white rock and wild fig trees leaning out into ravines. This way would be impassable in the rains; great stones scraped the oil sump as he disappeared into steep stream-beds, dry, the sand wrung into hanks where torrents had passed. He met no one, saw no hut. When he coughed, alone in the car he fancied this noise of his thrown back from the stony face of hill to hill like the bark of a solitary baboon. The sun went down. He thought: there was only one good moment the whole day; when I drank that beer on the veranda, and the children came up the steps to watch me and hear the music.

An old European image was lodged in his tiredness: the mirage, if the road ever ended, of some sort of southern resort village, coloured umbrellas, a street of white hotels beside water and boats. As the road unravelled from the pass into open bush, there came that moment when, if he had had a companion, they would have stopped talking. Two, three miles; the car rolled in past the ruins of an arcaded building to the barking of dogs, the horizontal streak of water behind the bush, outhouses and water tanks, a raw new house. A young man in bathing trunks with his back to the car stood on the portico steps, pushing a flipper off one foot with the toes of the other. As he hopped for balance he looked round. Blond wet curls licked the small head on the tall body, vividly empty blue eyes were the eyes of some nocturnal animal dragged out in daylight.

'Can you tell me where there's a hotel?'

Staring, on one leg: 'Yes, this's the hotel.'

Carl Church said, foolishly pleasant, 'There's no sign, you see.'

'Well, place's being redone.' He came, propping the flippers against the wall, walking on the outside edges of his feet over the remains of builders' rubble. 'Want any help with that?' But Carl Church had only his typewriter and the one suitcase. They struggled indoors together, the young man carrying flippers, two spearguns and goggles.

'Get anything?'

'Never came near the big ones.' His curls sprang and drops flowed from them. He dropped the goggles, then a wet gritty flipper knocked against Carl Church. 'Hell, I'm sorry.' He dumped his tackle on a desk in the passage, looked at Carl Church's case and portable, put gangling hands upon little hips and took a great breath: 'Where those boys are when you want one of them – that's the problem.'

'Look, I haven't booked,' said Church. 'I suppose you've got a room?'

'What's today?' Even his eyelashes were wet. The skin on the narrow cheekbones whitened as if over knuckles.

'Thursday.'

A great question was solved triumphantly, grimly. 'If it'd been Saturday, now – the weekends, I mean, not a chance.'

'I think I met someone on the plane—'

'Go on—' The face cocked in attention.

'She runs a hotel here . . . ?'

'Madam in person. D'you see who met her? My stepfather?' But Carl Church had not seen the airport blonde once they were through customs. 'That's Lady Jane all right. Of course she hasn't turned up here yet. So she's arrived, eh? Well thanks for the warning. Just a sec, you've got to sign,' and he pulled over a leather register, yelling, 'Zelide, where've you disappeared to—' as a girl with a bikini cutting into heavy red thighs appeared and said in the cosy, long-suffering voice of an English provincial, 'You're making it all wet, Dick – oh give here.'

They murmured in telegraphic intimacy. 'What about number 16?'

'I thought a chalet.'

'Well, I dunno, it's your job, my girl—'

She gave a parenthetic yell and a barefoot African came from the back somewhere to shoulder the luggage. The young man was dismantling his speargun, damp backside hitched up on the reception desk. The girl moved his paraphernalia patiently aside. 'W'd you like some tea in your room, sir?'

'Guess who was on the plane with him. Lady Godiva. So we'd better brace ourselves.'

'Dickie! Is she really?'

'In person.'

The girl led Carl Church out over a terrace into a garden where rondavels and cottages were dispersed. It was rapidly getting dark; only the lake shone. She had a shirt knotted under her breasts over the bikini, and when she shook her shaggy brown hair – turning on the light in an ugly little outhouse that smelled of cement – a round, boiled face smiled at him. 'These chalets are brand new. We might have to move you Saturday, but jist as well enjoy yourself in the meantime.'

'I'll be leaving in the morning.'

Her cheeks were so sunburned they looked as if they would bleed when she smiled. 'Oh what a shame. Aren't you even going to have a go at spear-fishing?'

'Well, no; I haven't brought any equipment or anything.'

He might have been a child who had no bucket and spade; 'Oh not to worry, Dick's got all the gear. You come out with us in the morning, after breakfast – OK?'

'Fine,' he said, knowing he would be gone.

The sheets of one bed witnessed the love-making of previous occupants; they had not used the other. Carl Church stumbled around in the dark looking for the ablution block – across a yard, but the light switch did not work in the bathroom. He was about to trudge over to the main house to ask for a lamp when he was arrested by the lake, as by the white of an eye in a face hidden by darkness. At least there was a towel. He took it and went down in his pants, feeling his way through shrubs, rough grass, over turned-up earth, touched by warm breaths of scent, startled by squawks from lumps that resolved into fowls, to the lake. It held still a skin of light from the day that had flown upward. He entered it slowly; it seemed to drink him in, ankles, knees, thighs, sex, waist, breast. It was cool as the inside of a mouth. Suddenly hundreds of tiny fish leapt out all round him, bright new tin in the warm, dark, heavy air.

'. . . I enclose a lock of his hair; I had his papers sealed up soon after his decease and will endeavour to transmit them all to you exactly as he left them.'

Carl Church endured the mosquitoes and the night heat only by clinging to the knowledge, through his tattered sleep, that soon it would be morning and he would be gone. But in the morning there was the lake. He got up at five to pee. He saw now how the lake stretched to the horizon from the open arms of the bay. Two bush-woolly islands glided on its surface; it was the colour of pearls. He opened his stale mouth wide and drew in a full breath, half sigh, half gasp. Again he went down to the water and, without bothering whether there was anybody about, took off his pyjama shorts and swam. Cool. Impersonally cool, at this time. The laved mosquito bites stung pleasurably. When he looked down upon the water while in it, it was no longer nacre, but pellucid, a pale and tender green. His feet were gleaming tendrils. A squat spotted fish hung near his legs, mouthing. He didn't move, either. Then he did what he had done when he was seven or eight years old, he made a cage of his hands and pounced – but the element reduced him to slow motion, everything, fish, legs, glassy solidity, wriggled and flowed away and slowly undulated into place again. The fish returned. On a dead tree behind bird-splattered rocks ellipsed by the water at this end of the beach, a fish-eagle lifted its head between hunched white shoulders and cried out; a long whistling answer came across the lake as another flew in. He swam around the rocks through schools of fingerlings as close as gnats, and hauled himself up within ten feet of the eagles. They carried the remoteness of the upper air with them in the long-sighted gaze of their hooded eyes; nothing could approach its vantage; he did not exist for them, while the gaze took in the expanse of the lake and the smallest indication of life rising to its surface. He came back to the beach and walked with a towel round his middle as far as a baobab tree where a black man with an ivory bangle on either wrist was mending nets, but then he noticed a blue bubble on the verge – it was an infant afloat on some plastic beast, its mother in attendance – and turned away, up to the hotel.

He left his packed suitcase on the bed and had breakfast. The dining room was a veranda under sagging grass matting; now, in the morning, he could see the lake, of course, while he ate. He was feeling for change to leave for the waiter when the girl padded in, dressed in her bikini, and shook cornflakes into a plate. 'Oh hello, sir. Early bird you are.' He imagined her lying down at night just as she was, ready to begin again at once the ritual of alternately dipping and burning her seared flesh. They chatted. She had been in Africa only three months, out from Liverpool in answer to an advertisement – receptionist/secretary, hotel in beautiful surroundings.

'More of a holiday than a job,' he said.

'Don't make me laugh' – but she did. 'We were on the go until half past one, night before last, making the changeover in the bar. You see the bar used to be here—' she lifted her spoon at the wall, where he now saw mildew-traced shapes beneath a mural in which a girl in a bosom-laced peasant outfit appeared to have given birth, through one ear, Rabelaisian fashion, to a bunch of grapes. He had noticed the old Chianti bottles, by lamplight, at dinner the night before, but not the mural. 'Dickie's got his ideas, and then she's artistic, you see.' The young man was coming up the steps of the veranda that moment, stamping his sandy feet at the cat, yelling towards the kitchen, blue eyes open as the fish's had been staring at Carl Church through the water. He wore his catch like a kilt, hooked all round the belt of his trunks.

'I been thinking about those damn trees,' he said.

'Oh my heavens. How many's still there?'

'*There* all right, but nothing but blasted firewood. Wait till she sees the holes, just where she had them dug.'

The girl was delighted by the fish: 'Oh pretty!'

But he slapped her hands and her distractibility away. 'Some people ought to have their heads read,' he said to Carl Church. 'If you can tell me why I had to come back here, well, I'd be grateful. I had my own combo, down in Rhodesia.' He removed the fish from his narrow middle and sat on a chair turned away from her table.

'Why don't we get the boys to stick 'em in, today? They could've died after being planted out, after all, ay?'

He seemed too gloomy to hear her. Drops from his wet curls fell on his shoulders. She bent towards him kindly, wheedlingly, meat of her thighs and breasts pressing together. 'If we put two boys on it, they'd have them in by lunchtime? Dickie? And if it'll make her happy? Dickie?'

'I've got ideas of my own. But when Madam's here you can forget it, just forget it. No sooner start something – just get started, that's all – she chucks it up and wants something different again.' His gaze wavered once or twice to the wall where the bar had been. Carl Church asked what the fish were. He didn't answer, and the girl encouraged, 'Perch. Aren't they, Dickie? Yes, perch. You'll have them for your lunch. Lovely eating.'

'Oh what the hell. Let's go. You ready?' he said to Church. The girl jumped up and he hooked an arm round her neck, feeling in her rough hair.

'Course he's ready. The black flippers'll fit him – the stuff's in the bar,' she said humouringly.

'But I haven't even got a pair of trunks.'

'Who cares? I can tell you I'm just-not-going-to-worry-a-damn. Here Zelide, I nearly lost it this morning.' He removed a dark stone set in Christmas-cracker baroque from his rock-scratched hand, nervous-boned as his mother's ankles, and tossed it for the girl to catch.

'Come, I've got the trunks,' she said, and led Carl Church to the bar by way of the reception desk, stopping to wrap the ring in a pink tissue and pop it in the cash box.

The thought of going to the lake once more was irresistible. His bag was packed; an hour or two wouldn't make any difference. He had been skin-diving before, in Sardinia, and did not expect the bed of the lake to compare with the Mediterranean, but if the architecture of undersea was missing, the fish one could get at were much bigger than he had ever caught in the Mediterranean. The young man disappeared for minutes and rose again between Carl Church and the girl, his Gothic Christ's body sucked in below the nave of ribs, his goggles leaving weals like duelling scars on his white cheekbones. Water ran from the tarnished curls over the bright eyeballs without seeming to make him blink. He brought up fish deftly and methodically and the girl swam back to shore with them, happy as a retrieving dog.

Neither she nor Carl Church caught much themselves. And then Church went off on his own, swimming slowly with the borrowed trunks inflating above the surface like a striped Portuguese man-of-war, and far out, when he was not paying attention but looking back at the skimpy white buildings, the flowering shrubs and even the giant baobab razed by distance and the optical illusion of the heavy waterline, at eye-level, about to black them out, he heard a fish-eagle scream just overhead; looked up, looked down, and there below him saw three fish at different levels, a mobile swaying in the water. This time he managed the gun without thinking; he had speared the biggest.

The girl was as impartially overjoyed as she was when the young man had a good catch. They went up the beach, laughing, explaining, a water-intoxicated progress. The accidental bump of her thick sandy thigh against his was exactly the tactile sensation of contact with the sandy body of the fish, colliding with him as he carried it. The young man was squatting on the beach, now, his long back arched over his knees. He was haranguing, in an African language, the old fisherman with the ivory bracelets who was still at work on the nets. There were dramatic pauses, accusatory rises of tone, hard jerks of laughter, in the monologue. The old man said nothing. He was an Arabised African from far up the lake somewhere in East Africa, and wore an old towel turban as well as the ivory; every now and then he wrinkled back his lips on tooth-stumps. Three or four long black dugouts had come in during the morning and were beached; black men sat motionless in what small shade they could find. The baby on his blue swan still floated under his mother's surveillance – she turned a visor of sunglasses and hat. It was twelve o'clock; Carl Church merely felt amused at himself – how different the measure of time when you were absorbed in something you didn't earn a living by. 'Those must weigh a pound apiece,' he said idly, of the ivory manacles shifting on the net-mender's wrists.

'D'you want one?' the young man offered. (*My graves*, the woman had said, *on my property*.) 'I'll get him to sell it to you. Take it for your wife.'

But Carl Church had no wife at present, and no desire for loot; he preferred everything to stay as it was, in its place, at noon by the lake. Twenty thousand slaves a year had passed this way, up the water. Slavers, missionaries, colonial servants – all had brought something and taken something away. He would have a beer and go, changing nothing, claiming nothing. He plodded to the hotel a little ahead of the couple, who were mumbling over hotel matters and pausing now and then to fondle each other. As his bare soles encountered the smoothness of the terrace steps he heard the sweet, loud, reasonable feminine voice, saw one of the houseboy-waiters racing across in his dirty jacket – and quickly turned away to get to his room unnoticed. But with a perfect instinct for preventing escape, she was at once out upon the dining-room veranda, all crude blues and yellows – hair, eyes, flowered dress, a beringed hand holding the cigarette away exploratively. Immediately, her son passed Church in a swift, damp tremor.

'Well, God, look at my best girl – mm-MHH . . . madam in person.' He lifted her off her feet and she landed swirling giddily on the high heels in the best tradition of the Fred Astaire films she and Carl Church had been brought up on. Her laugh seemed to go over her whole body.

'Well?'

'And so, my girl?'

They rocked together. 'You been behaving yourself in the big city?'

'Dickie – for Pete's sake – he's like a spaniel –' calling Carl Church to witness.

A warm baby-smell beside him (damp crevices and cold cream) was the presence of the girl. 'Oh Mrs Palmer, we were so worried you'd got lost or something.'

'My dear. My you're looking well—' The two vacant, inescapable blue stares took in the bikini, the luxuriously inflamed skin, as if the son's gaze were directed by the mother's. Mrs Palmer and the girl kissed but Mrs Palmer's eyes moved like a lighthouse beam over the wall where the bar was gone, catching Carl Church in his borrowed swimming trunks. 'Wha'd'you think of my place?' she asked. 'How d'you like it here, eh? Not that I know it myself, after two months . . .' Hands on hips, she looked at the peasant girl and the mildewed outlines as if she were at an exhibition.

She faced sharply round and her son kissed her on the mouth: 'We're dying for a beer, that's what. We've been out since breakfast. Zelide, the boy—'

'Yes, he *knows* he's on duty on the veranda today – just a minute, I'll get it—'

Mrs Palmer was smiling at the girl wisely. 'My dear, once you start doing their jobs for them . . .'

'Shadrach!' The son made a megaphone of his hands, shaking his silver identification bracelet out of the way. The girl stood, eagerly bewildered.

'Oh it's nothing. Only a minute—' and bolted.

'Where is the bar, now, Dickie?' said his mother as a matter of deep, polite interest.

'I must get some clothes on and return your trunks,' Carl Church was saying.

'Oh, it makes a world of difference. You'll see. You can move in that bar. Don't you think so?' The young man gave the impression that he was confirming a remark of Church's rather than merely expressing his own opinion. Carl Church, to withdraw, said, 'Well, I don't know what it was like before.'

She claimed him now. 'It was here, in the open, of course, people loved it. A taverna atmosphere. Dickie's never been overseas.'

'Really *move*. And you've got those big doors.'

She drew Church into the complicity of a smile for grown-ups, then remarked, as if for her part the whole matter were calmly accepted, settled, 'I presume it's the games room?'

Her son said to Church, sharing the craziness of women, 'There never was a games room, it was the lounge, can you see a lot of old birds sitting around in armchairs in a place like this?'

'The lounge that was going to be redecorated as a games room,' she said. She smiled at her son.

The girl came back, walking flat-footed under a tray's weight up steps that led by way of a half-built terrace to the new bar. As Carl Church went to help her she breathed, 'What a performance.'

Mrs Palmer drew on her cigarette and contemplated the steps: 'Imagine the breakages.'

The four of them were together round beer bottles. Church sat helplessly in his borrowed trunks that crawled against his body as they dried, drinking pint after pint and aware of his warmth, the heat of the air, and all their voices rising steadily. He said, 'I must get going,' but the waiter had called them to lunch three times; the best way to break up the party was to allow oneself to be forced to table. The three of them ate in their bathing costumes while madam took the head, bracelets colliding on her arms.

He made an effort to get precise instructions about the best and quickest route back to the capital, and was told expertly by her, 'There's no plane out until Monday, nine-fifteen, I suppose you know that.'

'I have no reason whatever to doubt your knowledge of plane schedules,' he said, and realised from the turn of phrase that he must be slightly drunk, on heat and the water as much as beer.

She knew the game so well that you had only to finger a counter unintentionally for her to take you on. 'I told you I never let anyone down.' She blew a smokescreen; appeared through it. 'Where've they put you?'

'Oh, he's in one of the chalets, Mrs Palmer,' the girl said. 'Till tomorrow, anyway.'

'Well, there you are, relax,' she said. 'If the worst comes to the worst, there's a room in my cottage.' Her gaze was out over the lake, a tilting, blind brightness with black dugouts appearing like sunspots, but she said, 'How're my jacarandas coming along? Someone was telling me there's no reason why they shouldn't do, Dickie. The boys must make a decent trench round each one and let it *fill up* with water once a week, *right* up, d'you see?'

'The effect of travel on a man whose heart is in the right place is that the mind is made more self-reliant; it becomes more confident of its own resources – there is greater presence of mind. The body is soon well-knit; the muscles of the limbs grow hard as a board . . . the countenance is bronzed and there is no dyspepsia.'

Carl Church slept through the afternoon. He woke to the feeling of helplessness he had at lunch. But no chagrin. This sort of hiatus had opened up in the middle of a tour many times – lost days in a blizzard on Gander airport, a week in quarantine at Aden. This time he had the journals instead of a Gideon Bible. 'Nothing fell from his lips as last words to survivors. We buried him today by a large baobab tree.' There was no point in going back to the capital if he couldn't get out of the place till Monday. His mind was closed to the possibility of trying for Moambe, again; that was another small rule for self-preservation: if something goes wrong, write it off. He thought, it's all right here; the dirty, ugly room had as much relevance to 'spoiling' the eagles and the lake as he had had to the eagles when he climbed close. On his way down to the lake again he saw a little group – mother, son, receptionist – standing round the graveside of one of the holes for trees. Dickie was still in his bathing trunks.

Church had the goggles and the flippers and the speargun, and he swam out towards the woolly islands – they were unattainably far – and fish were dim dead leaves in the water below him. The angle of the late afternoon sun left the underwater deserted, filled with motes of vegetable matter and sand caught by oblique rays of light. Milky brilliance surrounded him, his hands went out as if to feel for walls; there was the apprehension, down there, despite the opacity and tepidity, of night and cold. He shot up to the surface and felt the day on his eyelids. Lying on the sand, he heard the eagles cry now behind him on the headland, where trees held boulders in their claws, now over the lake. A pair of piebald kingfishers squabbled, a whirling disk, in midair, and plummeted again and again. Butterflies with the same black and white markings went slowly out over the water. The Arabised fisherman was still working at his nets.

Some weekend visitors arrived from the hotel, shading their eyes against the sheen of the lake; soon they stood in it like statues broken off at the waist. Voices flew out across the water after the butterflies. As the sun drowned, a dhow climbed out of its dazzle and dipped steadily towards the beach. It picked up the fisherman and his nets, sending a tiny boat ashore. The dhow lay beating slowly, like an exhausted bird. The visitors ran together to watch as they would have for a rescue, a monster – any sign from the lake.

Carl Church had been lying with his hand slack on the sand as on a warm body; he got up and walked past the people, past the baobab, as far along the beach as it went before turning into an outwork of oozy reeds. He pushed his feet into his shoes and went up inland, through the thorn bushes. As soon as he turned his back on it, the lake did not exist; unlike the sea that spread and sucked in your ears even when your eyes were closed. A total silence. Livingstone could have come upon the lake quite suddenly, and just as easily have missed it. The mosquitoes and gnats rose with the going down of the sun. Swatted on Church's face, they stuck in sweat. The air over the lake was free, but the heat of day cobwebbed the bush. 'We then hoped that his youth and unimpaired constitution would carry him through . . . but about six o'clock in the evening his mind began to wander and continued to. His bodily powers continued gradually to sink till the period mentioned when he quietly expired . . . there he rests in sure and certain hope of a glorious Resurrection.' He thought he might have a look at the graves, the graves of Livingstone's companions, but the description of how to find them given him that morning by the young man and the girl was that of people who know a place so well they cannot imagine anyone being unable to walk straight to it. A small path, they said, just off the road. He found himself instead among ruined arcades whose whiteness intensified as the landscape darkened. It was an odd ruin: a solid complex of buildings, apparently not in bad repair, had been pulled down. It was the sort of demolition one saw in a fast-growing city, where a larger structure would be begun at once where the not-old one had been. The bush was all around; as far as the Congo, as far as the latitude where the forests began. A conical anthill had risen to the height of the arcades, where a room behind them must have been. A huge moon sheeny as the lake came up and a powdery blue heat held in absolute stillness. Carl Church thought of the graves. It was difficult to breathe; it must have been hell to die here, in this unbearable weight of beauty not shared with the known world, licked in the face by the furred tongue of this heat.

Round the terrace and hotel the ground was pitted by the stakes of high heels; they sounded over the floors where everyone else went barefoot. The shriek and scatter of chickens opened before a constant coming and going of houseboys and the ragged work gang whose activities sent up the regular grunt of axe thudding into stumps and the crunch of spade gritting into earth. The tree-holes had been filled in. Dickie was seen in his bathing trunks but did not appear on the beach. Zelide wore a towelling chemise over her bikini, and when the guests were at lunch, went from table to table bending to talk softly with her rough hair hiding her face. Carl Church saw that the broken skin on her nose and cheeks was repaired with white cream. She said confidentially, 'I just wanted to tell you there'll be a sort of beach party tonight, being Saturday. Mrs Palmer likes to have a fire on the beach, and some snacks – you know. Of course, we'll all eat here first. You're welcome.'

He said, 'How about my room?'

Her voice sank to a chatty whisper, 'Oh it'll be all right, one crowd's cancelled.'

Going to the bar for cigarettes, he heard mother and son in there. 'Wait, wait, all that's worked out. I'mn'a cover the whole thing with big blow-ups of the top groups, the Stones and the Shadows and such-like.'

'Oh grow up, Dickie my darling, you want it to look like a teen-ager's bedroom?'

Church went quietly away, remembering there might be a packet of cigarettes in the car, but bumped into Dickie a few minutes later, in the yard. Dickie had his skin-diving stuff and was obviously on his way to the lake. 'I get into shit for moving the bar without telling the licensing people over in town, and then she says let's have the bar counter down on the beach tonight – all in the same breath, that's *nothing* to her. At least when my stepfather's here he knows just how to put the brake on.'

'Where is he?'

'I don't know, something about some property of hers, in town. He's got to see about it. But he's always got business all over, for her. I had my own band, you know, we've even toured Rhodesia. I'm a solo artist, really. Guitar. I compose my own stuff. I mean, what I play's original, you see. Night club engagements and such-like.'

'That's a tough life compared with this,' Church said, glancing at the speargun.

'Oh, this's all right. If you learn how to do it well, y'know? I've trained myself. You've got to concentrate. Like with my guitar. I have to go away and be *undisturbed*, you understand – right away. Sometimes the mood comes, sometimes it doesn't. Sometimes I compose all night. I got to be left *in peace*.' He was fingering a new thick silver chain on his wrist. 'Lady Jane, of course. God knows what it cost. She spends a fortune on presents. You sh'd see what my sister gets when she's home. And what she gave my stepfather – I mean before, when they weren't married yet. He must have ten pairs of cuff-links, gold, I don't know what.' He sat down under the weight of his mother's generosity.

Zelide appeared among the empty gas containers and beer crates outside the kitchen. 'Oh, Dickie, you've had no lunch. I don't think he ever tastes a thing he catches.'

Dickie squeezed her thigh and said coldly, 'S'best time, now. People don't know it. Between now and about half past three.'

There had always been something more than a family resemblance about that face; at last it fell into place in Church's mind. Stiff blond curls, skull ominously present in the eye sockets, shiny cheekbones furred with white hairs, blue-red lips, and those eyes that seemed to have no eyelids, to turn away from nothing and take in nothing: the face of the homosexual boy in the Berlin twenties, the perfect, impure master-race face of a George Grosz drawing.

'Oh Dickie, I wish you'd eat something. And he's got to play tonight.' They watched him lope off lightly down the garden. Her hair and the sun obscured her. 'They're both artistic, you see, that's the trouble. What a performance.'

'Are you sorry you came?'

'Oh no. The weather's so lovely, I mean, isn't it?'

It was becoming a habit to open Livingstone's Journals at random before falling stunned-asleep. 'Now that I am on the point of starting another trip into Africa I feel quite exhilarated: when one travels with the specific object in view of ameliorating the condition of the natives every act becomes ennobled.' The afternoon heat made him think of women, this time, and he gave up his siesta because he believed that daydreams of this kind were not so much adolescent as – worse – a sign of approaching age. He was getting – too far along, for pauses like this; for time out. If he were not preoccupied with doing the next thing, he did not know what to do. His mind turned to death, the graves that his body would not take the trouble to visit. His body turned to women; his body was unchanged. It took him down to the lake, heavy and vigorous, reddened by the sun under the black hairs shining on his belly.

The sun was high in a splendid afternoon. In half an hour he missed three fish and began to feel challenged. Whenever he dived deeper than fifteen or eighteen feet his ears ached much more than they ever had in the sea. Out of training, of course. And the flippers and goggles lent by the hotel really did not fit properly. The goggles leaked at every dive, and he had to surface quickly, water in his nostrils. He began to let himself float aimlessly, not diving any longer, circling around the enormous boulders with their steep polished flanks like petrified tree trunks. He was aware, as he had been often when skin-diving, of how active his brain became in this world of silence; ideas and images interlocking in his mind while his body was leisurely moving, enjoying at once the burning sun on his exposed shoulders and the cooling water on his shrunken penis – good after too many solitary nights filled with erotic dreams.

Then he saw the fish, deep down, twenty feet maybe, a yellowish nonchalant shape which seemed to pasture in a small forest of short dead reeds. He took a noble breath, dived with all the power and swiftness he could summon from his body, and shot. The miracle happened again. The nonchalant shape became a frenzied spot of light, reflecting the rays of the sun in a series of flashes through the pale blue water as it swivelled in agony round the spear. It was – this moment – the only miracle Church knew; no wonder Africans used to believe that the hunter's magic worked when the arrow found the prey.

He swam up quickly, his eyes on the fish hooked at the end of the spear, feeling the tension of its weight while he was hauling it and the line between spear and gun straightened. Eight pounds, ten, perhaps. Even Dickie with his silver amulets and bracelets couldn't do better. He reached the surface, hurriedly lifted the goggles to rid them of water, and dived again: the fish was still continuing its spiralling fight. He saw now that he had not transfixed it; only the point of the spear had penetrated the body. He began carefully to pull the line towards him; the spear was in his hand when, with a slow motion, the fish unhooked itself before his eyes.

In its desperate, thwarted leaps it had unscrewed the point and twirled loose. This had happened once before, in the Mediterranean, and since then Church had taken care to tighten the spear-head from time to time while fishing. Today he had forgotten. Disappointment swelled in him. Breathlessness threatened to burst him like a bubble. He had to surface, abandoning the gun in order to free both arms. The fish disappeared round a boulder with the point of the harpoon protruding from its open belly amid flimsy pinkish ribbons of entrails; the gun was floating at mid distance between the surface and the bed of the lake, anchored to the spear sunk in dead reeds.

Yet the splendour of the afternoon remained. He lay and smoked and drank beer brought by a waiter who roamed the sand, flicking a napkin. Church had forgotten what had gone wrong, to bring him to this destination. He was *here*; as he was not often fully present in the places and situations in which he found himself. It was some sort of answer to the emptiness he had felt on the bed. Was this how the first travellers had borne it, each day detached from the last and the next, taking each night that night's bearing by the stars?

Madam – Lady Jane in person – had sent down a boy to pick up bottle tops and cigarette stubs from the water's edge. She had high standards. (She had said so in the bar last night. 'The trouble is, *they'll* never be any different, they just don't know how to look after anything.') This was the enlightenment the discoverers had brought the black man in the baggage he portered for them on his head. This one was singing to himself as he worked. If the plans that were being made in the capital got the backing of the World Bank and the UN Development Fund and all the rest of it, his life would change. Whatever happened to him, he would lose the standard that had been set by people who maintained it by using him to pick up their dirt. Church thought of the ruin – he'd forgotten to ask what it was. Lady Jane's prefabricated concrete blocks and terrazzo would fall down more easily.

He had had a shirt washed and although he was sweating under the light bulb when he put it on for dinner, he seemed to have accustomed himself to the heat, now. He was also very sunburned. The lady with the small child sat with a jolly party of Germans in brown sandals – apparently from a Lutheran Mission nearby – and there was a group of men down from the capital on a bachelor binge of skin-diving and drinking who were aware of being the life of the place. They caught out at Zelide, her thick feet pressed into smart shoes, her hair lifted on top of her head, her eyes made up to twice their size. She bore her transformation bravely, smiling.

'You are coming down to the beach, arnch you?' She went, concerned, from table to table. Mrs Palmer's heels announced her with the authority of a Spanish dancer. She had on a strapless blue dress and silver sandals, and carried a little gilt bag like an outsize cigarette box. She joined the missionary party: '*Wie geht's*, Father, have you been missing me?' Dickie didn't appear. Through the frangipani, the fire on the beach was already sending up scrolls of flame.

Church knew he would be asked to join one group or another and out of a kind of shame of anticipated boredom (last night there had been one of those beer-serious conversations about the possibility of the end of the world: 'They say the one thing'll survive an atomic explosion is the ant. The ant's got something special in its body, y'see') he went into the empty bar after dinner. The little black barman was almost inaudible, in order to disguise his lack of English. There was an array of fancy bottles set up on the shelves but most of them seemed to belong to Mrs Palmer's store of objets d'art: 'Is finish'.' Church had to content himself with a brandy from South Africa. He asked whether a dusty packet of cigarillos was for sale, and the barman's hand went from object to object on display before the correct one was identified. Church was smoking and throwing darts as if they were stones, when Dickie came in. Dickie wore a dinner jacket; his lapels were blue satin, his trousers braided, his shirt tucked and frilled; his hands emerged from ruffles and the little finger of the left one rubbed and turned the baroque ring on the finger beside it. He hung in the doorway a moment like a tall, fancy doll; his mother might have put him on a piano.

Church said, 'My God, you're grand,' and Dickie looked down at himself for a second, without interest, as one acknowledges one's familiar working garb. The little barman seemed flattened by Dickie's gaze.

'Join me?'

Dickie gave a boastful, hard-wrung smile. 'No thanks. I think I've had enough already.' He had the look his mother had had, when Church asked her where her hotel was. 'I've been drinking all afternoon. Ever since a phone call.'

'Well you don't look it,' said Church. But it was the wrong tone to take up.

Dickie played a tattoo on the bar with the ringed hand, staring at it. 'There was a phone call from Bulawayo, and a certain story was repeated to me. Somebody's made it their business to spread a story.'

'That's upsetting.'

'It may mean the loss of a future wife, that's what. My fiancée in Bulawayo. Somebody *took the trouble* to tell her there's a certain young lady in the hotel here with me. Somebody had nothing better to do than make trouble. But that young lady is my mother's secretary-receptionist, see? She works here, she's *employed*, just like me. Just like I'm the manager.'

From country to country, bar to bar, Church was used to accepting people's own versions of their situations, quite independently of the facts. He and Dickie contemplated the vision of Dickie fondling Zelide in the garden as evidence of the correctness of his relations with the secretary-receptionist. 'Couldn't you explain?'

'Usually if I'm, you know, depressed and that, I play my guitar. But I've just been strumming. No, I don't think I'll have any more tonight, I'm full enough already. The whole afternoon.'

'Why don't you go to Bulawayo?'

Dickie picked up the darts and began to throw them, at an angle, from where he sat at the bar; while he spoke he scored three bull's-eyes. 'Huh, I think I'll clear out altogether. Here I earn fifty quid a month, eh? I can earn twenty pounds a night – *a night* – with a personal appearance. I've got a whole bundle of my own compositions and one day, boy! – there's got to be one that hits the top. One day it's got to happen. All my stuff is copyright, you see. Nobody's gonna cut a disc of my stuff without my permission. I see to that. Oh I could play you a dozen numbers I'm working on, they're mostly sad, you know – the folk type of thing, that's where the money is now. What's a lousy fifty quid a month?'

'I meant a quick visit, to put things straight.'

'Ah, somebody's mucked up my life, all right' – he caught Church's eye as if to say, you want to see it again? – and once again planted three darts dead-centre. 'I'll play you some of my compositions if you like. Don't expect too much of my voice, though, because as I say I've been drinking all afternoon. I've got no intention whatever of playing for them down there. An artist thrown in, fifty quid a month, they can think again.' He ducked under the doorway and was gone. He returned at once with a guitar and bent over it professionally, making adjustments. Then he braced his long leg against the bar rail, tossed back his skull of blond curls, began a mournful lay – broke off: 'I'm full of pots, you know, my voice' – and started again, high and thin, at the back of his nose.

It was a song about a bride, and riding away, and tears you cannot hide away. Carl Church held his palm round the brandy glass to conceal that it was empty and looked down into it. The barman had not moved from his stance with both hands before him on the bar and the bright light above him beating sweat out of his forehead and nose like an answer exacted under interrogation. When the stanza about death and last breath was reached, Dickie said, 'It's a funny thing, me nearly losing my engagement ring this morning, eh? I might have known something' – paused – and thrummed once, twice. Then he began the song over again.

Carl Church signalled for the brandy bottle. But suddenly Mrs Palmer was there, a queen to whom no door may be closed. 'Oh show a bit of spunk! Everyone's asking for you. I tell him, everyone has to take a few cracks in life, am I right?'

'Well, of course.'

'Come on then, don't encourage him to feel sorry for himself. My God, if I'd sat down and cried every time.'

Dickie went on playing and whispering the words to himself.

'Can't you do something with him?'

'Let's go and join the others, Dickie,' Church said; he drank off the second brandy.

'One thing I've never done is let people down,' Mrs Palmer was saying. 'But these kids've got no sense of responsibility. What'd happen without me I don't know.'

Dickie spoke. 'Well you can have it. You can have the fifty pounds a month and the car. The lot.'

'Oh yes, they'd look fine without me, I can tell you. I would have given everything I've built up over to him, that was the idea, once he was married. But they know everything at once, you know, you can't teach them anything.'

'Come on Dickie, what the hell – just for an hour.'

They jostled him down to the fire-licked faces on the beach. A gramophone was playing and people were dancing barefoot. There were not enough women and men in shorts were drinking and clowning. Dickie was given beer; he made cryptic remarks that nobody listened to. Somebody stopped the gramophone with a screech and Dickie was tugged this way and that in a clamour to have him play the guitar. But the dancers put the record back again. The older men among the bachelors opposed the rhythm of the dancers with a war dance of their own: Hi-zoom-a-zoom-ba, zoom-zoom-zoom. Zelide kept breaking away from her partners to offer a plate of tiny burnt sausages like bird-droppings. HI-ZOOM-A-ZOOM-BA – ZOOM-ZOOM-ZOOM. Light fanned from the fire showed the dancers as figures behind gauze, but where Church was marooned, near the streaming flames, faces were gleaming, gouged with grotesque shadow. Lady Jane had a bottle of gin for the two of them. The heat of the fire seemed to consume the other heat, of the night, so that the spirit going down his gullet snuffed out on the way in a burning evaporation. HI-ZOOM-A-ZOOM-BA. At some point he was dancing with her, and she put a frangipani flower in his ear. Now Dickie, sitting drunk on a box with his long legs at an angle like a beetle's, wanted to play the guitar but nobody would listen. Church could make out from the shapes Dickie's mouth made that he was singing the song about the bride and riding away, but the roar of the bachelors drowned it: Hold him down, you Zulu warrior, hold him DOWN, you Zulu chief-chief-ief. Every now and then a slight movement through the lake sent a soft, black glittering glance in reflection of the fire. The lake was not ten feet away but as time went by Church had the impression that it would not be possible for him to walk down, through the barrier of jigging firelight and figures, and let it cover his ankles, his hands. He said to her, topping up the two glasses where they had made a place in the sand, 'Was there another hotel?'

'There's been talk, but no one else's ever had the initiative, when it comes to the push.'

'But whose was that rather nice building, in the bush?'

'Not *my* idea of a hotel. My husband built it in forty-nine. Started it in forty-nine, finished it fifty-two or -three. Dickie was still a kiddie.'

'But what happened? It looks as if it's been deliberately pulled down.'

CHIEF-UH-IEF-UH-IEF-IEF-IEF. The chorus was a chanting grunt.

'It was what?'

She was saying, '. . . died, I couldn't even give it away. I always told him, it's no good putting up a bloody palace of a place, you haven't got the class of person who appreciates it. Too big, far too big. No atmosphere, whatever you tried to do with it. People like to feel cosy and free and easy.'

He said, 'I liked that colonnaded veranda, it must have been rather beautiful,' but she was yanked away to dance with one of the bachelors.

Zelide wandered about anxiously: 'You quite happy?'

He took her to dance; she was putting a good face on it. He said, 'Don't worry about them, they're tough. Look at those eyes.'

'If there was somewhere to go,' she said. 'It's not like a town, not like at home, you know – you can just disappear. Oh there she is, for God's sake—'

He said to Mrs Palmer, 'That veranda, before you bulldozed it—' but she took no notice and attacked him at once: 'Where's Dickie? I don't see Dickie.'

'I don't know where the hell Dickie is.'

Clinging to his arm she dragged him through the drinkers, the dancers, the bachelors, round the shadowy human lumps beyond the light that started away from each other, making him give a snuffling laugh because they were like the chickens that first day. She raced him stumbling up the dark terraces to Dickie's cottage, but it was overpoweringly empty with the young man's smell of musky leather and wet wool. She was alarmed as an animal who finds the lair deserted. 'I tell you, he'll do something to himself.' Ten yards from the bungalows and the main house, the bush was the black end of the world; they walked out into it and stood helplessly. A torch was a pale, blunt, broken stump of light. 'He'll do away with himself,' she panted.

Church was afraid her breathing would turn to hysterics; 'Come on, now, come on,' he coaxed her back to the lights burning in the empty hotel. She went, but steered towards quarters he had not noticed or visited. There were lamps in pink shades. Photographs of her in the kind of dress she was wearing that night, smiling over the head of an infant Dickie. A flowered sofa they sat down on, and a little table with filigree boxes and a lighter shaped like Aladdin's lamp and gilt-covered matchbooks with *Dorothy* stamped across the corner.

'Take some,' she said, and began putting them in his pockets, both outer pockets of his jacket and the inner breast pocket. 'Take some, I've got hundreds.' She dropped her head against him and let the blonde curls muffle her face: 'Like his father did,' she said. 'I know it. I tell you I know it.'

'He's passed out somewhere, that's all.' She smelled of Chanel No. 5, the only perfume he could identify, because he had bought it on the black market for various girls in Cairo during the war. Where she leant on him her breasts were warmer than the rest of her.

'I tell you I know he'll do something to himself sooner or later. It runs in families, I know it.'

'Don't worry. It's all right.' He thought: an act of charity. It was terribly dark outside; the whole night was cupped round the small flickering of flames and figures, figures like flames, reaching upwards in flame, snatched by the dark, on the beach. He knew the lake was there; neither heard nor seen, quite black. The lake. The lake. He felt, inevitably, something resembling desire, but it was more like a desire for the cool mouth of waters that would close over ankles, knees, thighs, sex. He was drunk and not very capable, and felt he would never get there, to the lake. The lake became an unslakable thirst, the night-thirst, the early-morning thirst that cannot stir a hand for the surcease of water.

When he awoke sometime in his chalet, it was because consciousness moved towards a sound that he could identify even before he was awake. Dickie was playing the guitar behind closed doors somewhere, playing again and again the song of the bride and the riding away.

Zelide wore her bikini, drawing up the bill for him in the morning. The demarcation lines at shoulder-straps and thighs had become scarlet weals; the sun was eating into her, poor cheerful adventuring immigrant. She had been taken up by the bachelors and was about to go out with them in their boat. 'Maybe we'll bump into each other again,' she said.

And of course they might; handed around the world from country to country, minor characters who crop up. There was an air of convalescence about the hotel. On the terrace, empty bottles were coated with ants; down at the beach, boys were burying the ashes of the bonfire and their feet scuffed over the shapes – like resting-places flattened in grass by cattle – where couples had been secreted by the night. He saw Mrs Palmer in a large sunhat, waving her tough brown arms about in command over a gang who, resting on their implements, accepted her as they did sun, flies and rain. Two big black pairs of sunglasses – his and hers – flashed back and forth blindly as they stood, with Zelide, amid the building rubble in the garden.

'Don't forget to look us up if ever you're out this way.'

'One never knows.'

'With journalists, my God, no, you could find yourself at the North Pole! We'll always find a bed for you. Has Dickie said goodbye?'

'Say goodbye to him for me, will you?'

She put out her jingling, gold-flashing hand and he saw (as if it had been a new line on his own face) the fine, shiny tan of her forearm wrinkle with the movement. 'Happy landings,' she said.

Zelide watched him drive off. 'You've not forgotten anything? You'd be surprised at people. I don't know what to do with the stuff, half the time.' She smiled and her stomach bulged over the bikini; she had the sort of pioneering spirit, the instincts of self-preservation appropriate to her time and kind.

Past the fowls, water tanks and outhouses, the hot silent arcades of the demolished hotel, the car rocked and swayed over the track. Suddenly he saw the path, the path he had missed the other day, to the graves of Livingstone's companions. It was just where Dickie and Zelide had said. He was beyond it by the time he understood this, but all at once it seemed absurd not even to have gone to have a look, after three days. He stopped the car and walked back. He took the narrow path that was snagged with thorn bushes and led up the hill between trees too low and meagre of foliage to give shade. The earth was picked clean by the dry season. Flies settled at once upon his shoulders. He was annoyed by the sound of his own lack of breath; and then there, where the slope of the hill came up short against a steep rise, the gravestones stood with their backs to rock. The five neat headstones of the monuments commission were surmounted each by an iron cross on a circle. The names, and the dates of birth and death – the deaths all in the last quarter of the nineteenth century – were engraved on the granite. A yard or two away, but in line with the rest, was another gravestone. Carl Church moved over to read the inscription: In Memory of Richard Alastair Macnab, Beloved Husband of Dorothy and Father of Richard and Heather, died 1957. They all looked back, these dead companions, to the lake, the lake that Carl Church (turning to face as they did, now) had had silent behind him all the way up; the lake that, from here, was seen to stretch much farther than one could tell, down there on the shore or at the hotel: stretching still – even from up here – as far as one could see, flat and shining; a long way up Africa.

Why Haven't You Written?

His problem was hardening metal; finding a way to make it bore, grind, stutter through auriferous and other mineral-bearing rock without itself being blunted. The first time he spoke to the Professor's wife, sitting on his left, she said how impossible that sounded, like seeking perpetual motion or eternal life – nothing could bear down against resistance without being worn away in the process? He had smiled and they had agreed with dinner-table good humour that she was translating into abstract terms what was simply a matter for metallurgy.

They did not speak now. He did not see her face. All the way to the airport it was pressed against his coat-muffled arm and he could look down only on the nest of hair that was the top of her head. He asked the taxi driver to close the window because a finger of cold air was lifting those short, overlaid crescents of light hair. At the airport he stood by while she queued to weigh in and present her ticket. He had the usual impulse to buy, find something for her at the last minute, and as usual there was nothing she wanted that he could give her. The first call came and they sat on with his arm round her. She dared not open her mouth; misery stopped her throat like vomit: he knew. At the second call, they rose. He embraced her clumsily in his coat, they said the usual reassurances to each other, she passed through the barrier and then came back in a crazy zigzag like a mouse threatened by a broom, to clutch his hand another time. Ashamed, half-dropping her things, she always did that, an unconscious effort to make no contact definitively the last.

And that was that. She was gone. It was as it always was; the joking, swaggering joy of arrival carried with it this reverse side; in their opposition and inevitability they were identical. He was used to it, he should be used to it, he should be used to never getting used to it because it happened again and again. The mining group in London for whom he was consultant tungsten carbide metallurgist sent him to Australia, Peru, and – again and again – the United States. In seven or eight visits he had been in New York for only two days and spent a weekend, once, in Chicago, but he was familiar with the middle-sized, Middle West, middle-everything towns (as he described them at home to friends in London) like the one he was left alone in now, where he lived in local motels and did his work among mining men and accepted the standard hospitality of good business relations. He was on first-name terms with his mining colleagues and their wives in these places and at Christmas would receive cards addressed to his wife and him as Willa and Duggie, although, of course, the Middle Westerners had never met her. Even if his wife could have left the children and the Group had been prepared to pay her fare, there wasn't much to be seen in the sort of places in America his work took him to.

In them, it was rare to meet anyone outside the mining community. The Professor's wife on his left at dinner that night was there because she was somebody's sister-in-law. Next day, when he recognised her standing beside him at the counter of a drugstore she explained that she was on a visit to do some research in the local university library for her husband, Professor Malcolm, of the Department of Political Science in the university of another Middle Western town not far away. And it was this small service she was able to carry out for the Professor that had made everything possible. Without it, perhaps the meetings at dinner and in the drugstore would have been the only times, the beginning and the end: the end before the beginning. As it was, again and again the Professor's wife met the English metallurgist in towns of Middle Western America, he come all the way from London to harden metal, she come not so far from home to search libraries for material for her husband's thesis.

It was snowing while a taxi took him back along the road from the airport to the town. It seemed to be snowing up from the ground, flinging softly at the windscreen, rather than falling. To have gone on driving into the snow that didn't reach him but blocked out the sight of all that was around him – but there was a dinner, there was a report he ought to write before the dinner. He actually ground his teeth like a bad-tempered child – always these faces to smile at, these reports to sit over, these letters to write. Even when she was with him, he had to leave her in the room while he went to friendly golf games and jolly dinners with engineers who knew how much *they* missed a bit of home life when they had to be away from the wife and youngsters. Even when there were no dinner parties he had to write reports late at night in the room where she lay in bed and fell asleep, waiting for him. And always the proprietorial, affectionately reproachful letters from home: '. . . nothing from you . . . For goodness' sake, a line to your mother . . . It would cheer up poor little mumpy Ann no end if she got a postcard . . . nothing for ten days, now; darling, can't help getting worried when you don't . . .'

Gone: and no time, no peace to prepare for what was waiting to be realised in that motel room. He could not go back to that room right away. Drive on with the huge silent handfuls of snow coming at him, and the windscreen wipers running a screeching fingernail to and fro over glass: he gave the driver an address far out of the way, then when they had almost reached it said he had changed his mind and (to hell with the report) went straight to the dinner although it was much too early. 'For heaven's sakes! Of *course* not. Fix yourself a drink, Duggie, you know where it all is by now . . .' The hostess was busy in the kitchen, a fat beautiful little girl in leotards and dancing pumps came no farther than the doorway and watched him, finger up her nose.

They always drank a lot in these oil-fired igloos, down in the den where the bar was, with its collection of European souvenirs or home-painted Mexican mural, up in the sitting room round the colour TV after dinner, exchanging professional jokes and anecdotes. They found Duggie in great form: that dry English sense of humour. At midnight he was dropped between the hedges of dirty ice shovelled on either side of the motel entrance. He stood outside the particular door, he fitted the key and the door swung open on an absolute assurance – the dark, centrally-heated smell of Kim

Malcolm and Crispin Douglas together, his desert boots, her hair lacquer, zest of orange peel, cigarette smoke in cloth, medicated nasal spray, salami, newspapers. For a moment he didn't turn on the light. Then it sprang from under his finger and stripped the room: gone; empty, ransacked. He sat down in his coat. What had he done the last time? People went out and got drunk or took a pill and believed in the healing sanity of morning. He had drunk enough and he never took pills. Last time he had left when she did, been in some other place when she was in some other place.

She had put the cover on the typewriter and there was a dustless square where the file with material for Professor Malcolm's thesis used to be. He took his notes for his report out of the briefcase and rolled a sheet of paper into the typewriter. Then he sat there a long time, hands on the machine, hearing his own breathing whistling slightly through his blocked left nostril. His heart was driven hard by the final hospitable brandy. He began to type in his usual heavy and jerky way, all power in two forefingers.

In the morning – in the morning nothing could efface the hopeless ugliness of that town. They laughed at it and made jokes about the glorious places he took her to. She had said, if we could stay with each other for good, but only on condition that we lived in this town? She had made up the scene: a winter day five years later, with each insisting it was the other's turn to go out in the freezing slush to buy drink and each hurling at the other the reproach – it's because of *you* I got myself stuck here. She was the one who pulled the curtain aside on those streets of shabby snow every morning, on the vacant lots with their clapboard screens, on the grey office blocks with lights going on through the damp-laden smog as people began the day's work, and it was she who insisted – be fair – that there was a quarter of an hour or so, about five in the evening, when the place had its moment; a sort of Arctic spectrum, the fire off a diamond, was reflected from the sunset on the polluted frozen river upon the glass faces of office blocks, and the evening star was caught hazily in the industrial pall.

In the morning frozen snot hung from the roofs of wooden houses. A company car drove him to his first appointment. Figures in the street with arms like teddy bears, the elbow joints stiffened by layers of clothing. A dog burning a patch of urine through the snow. In the cafeteria at lunch (it was agreed that it was crazy, from the point of view of everyone's waistline, to lay on an executive lunch for him every day) he walked past Lily cups of tuna fish salad and bowls of Jell-O, discussing percussive rock drilling and the heat treatment of steel. Some drills were behaving in an inexplicable manner and he was driven out to the mine to see for himself. A graveyard all the way, tombstones of houses and barns under snow. Sheeted trees. White mounds and ridges whose purpose could only be identified through excavation, like those archaeological mounds, rubbish heaps of a vanished culture silted over by successive ones. He did not know why the tungsten carbide-tipped drills were not fulfilling their promised performance; he would have to work on it. He lied to one generous colleague that he had been invited to dinner with another and he walked about the iron-hard streets of the downtown area (the freeze had crusted the slush, the crust was being tamped down by the pressure of feet) with his scarf over his mouth, and at last ended up at the steak house where they used to go. Because he was alone the two waitresses talked to each other near him as if he were not there. Each table had a small glass box which was a selector for the jukebox; one night she had insisted that they ought to hear a record that had been the subject of controversy in the newspapers because it was supposed to include, along with the music, the non-verbal cries associated with love-making, and they had laughed so much at the groans and sighs that the bloody slabs of meat on the wooden boards got cold before they ate them. Although he thought it senseless to fill himself up with drink he did finish the whole bottle of wine they used to manage between them. And every night, making the excuse that he wanted to 'work on' the problem of the drill, pleading tiredness, lying about an invitation he didn't have, he went from brutal cold into fusty heat and out to brutal cold again, sitting in bars and going to the steak house or the Chinese restaurant and then back to bars again, until the final confrontation with cold was only half-felt on his stiff hot face and he trudged back along planes of freezing wind to the motel room or sat behind a silent taxi driver, sour to have to be out on such nights, as he had sat coming home alone from the airport with the snow flinging itself short of his face.

The freeze continued. The TV weatherman gabbling cheerily before his map showed the sweep of great snowstorms over whole arcs of this enormous country. On the airport she had left from, planes were grounded for days. The few trains there were, ran late. In addition, there was a postal strike and no letters, nothing from England, but also nothing from her, and no hope of a phone call, either, because she had flown straight to join the Professor at his mother's home in Florida, and she could neither telephone from the house nor hope to get out to do so from elsewhere at night, when he was in the motel room; they dared not risk a call to the Company during the day. He moved between the room – whose silence, broken only by Walter Cronkite and the weatherman, filled with his own thoughts as if it were some monstrous projection, a cartoon balloon, issuing from his mind – he moved between that room and the Japanese-architect-designed headquarters of the Company, which existed beneath blizzard and postal strike as an extraordinary bunker with contemplative indoor pools, raked-stone covered courtyards, cheerful rows of Jell-O and tuna fish salad. He woke in the dark mornings to hear the snow plough grinding along the streets. Men struck with picks into the rock of ice that covered the sidewalks a foot solid. The paper said all post offices were deep in drifts of accumulated mail, and sealed the mouths of all mail boxes. England did not exist and Florida – was there really anyone in Florida? It was a place where, the weatherman said, the temperature was in the high seventies, and humid. She had forgotten a sheet of notes that must have come loose from the file, and the big yellow fake sponge (it was what she had been buying when they found themselves together in the drugstore of that other Middle Western town) that she now always brought along. She would be missing the sponge, in Florida, but there was no way to get it to her. He kept the sponge and the sheet of paper on the empty dressing table. Overnight, every night, more snow fell. Like a nail he was driven deeper and deeper into isolation.

He came from dinner with the Chief Mining Engineer and his party at the country club (the Chief Mining Engineer always took his wife out to eat on Saturday nights) and was possessed by such a dread of the room that he told the taxi driver to take him to the big chain hotel, that had seventeen floors and a bar on top. It was full of parties like the one he had just left; he was the only solitary. Others did not look outside, but fiddling with a plastic cocktail stirrer in the shape of a tiny sword he saw through the walls of glass against which the blue-dark pressed that they were surrounded by steppes of desolation out there beyond the feebly lit limits of the town. Wolves might survive where effluvia from paper mills had made fish swell up and float, and birds choked on their crops filled with pesticide-tainted seeds. He carried the howl somewhere inside him. It was as close as that slight whistling from the blocked sinus in his left nostril. When the bar shut he went down with those chattering others in an elevator that cast them all back into the street.

The smell in the motel room had not changed through his being alone there. He felt so awake, so ready to tackle something, some work or difficulty, that he took another drink, a big swallow of neat whisky, and, that night, wrote a letter to Willa. I'm not coming back, he said. I have gone so far away that it would be stupid to waste it – I mean the stage I've reached. Of course I am sorry that you have been such a good wife, that you will always be such a good wife and nothing can change you. Because so long as I accept that you are a good wife, how can I find the guts to do it? I can go on being the same thing – your opposite number, the good husband, hoping for a better position and more money for us all, coming on these bloody dreary trips every winter (why don't they ever send me in good weather). But it's through subjecting myself to all this, putting up with what we think of as these partings for the sake of my work, that I have come to understand that they are not partings at all. They are nothing like partings. Do you understand?

It went on for two more pages. When he had finished he put it in an airmail envelope, stamped it, went out again – he had not taken off his coat or scarf – and walked through the ringing of his own footsteps in the terrible cold to where he remembered there was a mail box. Like all the others, the mouth was sealed over by some kind of gummed tape, very strong stuff reinforced by a linen backing. He slit it with a piece of broken bottle he found in the gutter, and pushed the letter in. When he got back to the room he still had the bit of glass in his hand. He fell asleep in his coat but must have woken later and undressed because in the morning he found himself in bed and in pyjamas.

He did not know how drunk he had been that night when he did it. Not so drunk that he was not well aware of the chaos of the postal strike; everyone had been agreeing at the country club that most of the mail piled up at the GPO could never be expected to reach its destination. Not so drunk that he had not counted on the fact that the letter would never get to England. Why, he had broken into the mail box, and the boxes were not being cleared. Just drunk enough to take what seemed to him the thousand-to-one chance the letter might get there. Suppose the army were to be called in to break the strike, as they had been in New York? Yet, for several days, it did not seem to him that *that* letter would ever be dispatched and delivered – that sort of final solution just didn't come off.

Then the joke went round the Company headquarters that mail was moving again: the Company had received, duly delivered, one envelope – a handbill announcing a sale (already over) at a local department store. Some wit from the administration department put it up in the cafeteria. He suddenly saw the letter, a single piece of mail, arriving at the house in London. He thought of writing – no, sending a cable – now that communications were open again, instructing that the letter was to be destroyed unopened.

She would never open a letter if asked not to, of course. She would put it on the bedside table at his side of the bed and wait for a private night-time explanation, out of the hearing of the children. But suppose the letter had been lost, buried under the drifts of thousands, mis-sorted, mis-dispatched – what would be made of a mystifying cable about a letter that had never come? The snow was melting, the streets glistened and his clothes were marked with the spray of dirty water thrown up by passing cars. He had impulses

– sober ones – to write and tell the Professor's wife, but when she unexpectedly did manage to telephone, the relief of pleasure at her voice back in the room so wrung him that he said nothing, and decided to say nothing in letters to her either; why disturb and upset her in this particularly disturbing and upsetting way.

He received a letter from London a fortnight old. There must have been later ones that hadn't turned up. He began to reason that if the letter did arrive in London, he might just manage to get there before it. And then? It was unlikely that he would be able to intercept it. But he actually began to hint to the colleagues at the Company that he would like to leave by the end of the week, be home in England for the weekend, after all, after six weeks' absence. The problem of the drill's optimum performance couldn't be solved in a day, anyway; he would have to go into the whole business back at the research laboratory in London. The Chief Mining Engineer said what a darned shame he had no leave now, before the greens were dry enough for the first eighteen holes of the year.

He forced himself not to think about the letter or at least to think about it as little as possible for the remaining days. Sometimes the idea of it came to him as a wild hope, like the sound of her voice suddenly in the room, from Florida. Sometimes it was a dry anxiety: what a childish, idiotic thing to have done, how insane to risk throwing everything away when, as the Professor's wife often said, nobody was being hurt: Professor Malcolm, the children, Willa – none of them. Resentment flowed into him like unreasonable strength – *I am being hurt!* Not so drunk, after all, not so drunk. Yet, of course, he was afraid of Willa, ranged there with two pretty children and a third with glasses blacked out over one eye to cure a squint. What could you do with that unreasonable, life-saving strength? – Against that little family group? And, back again to the thought of the Professor's wife, his being afraid disgusted him. He spoke to her once more before he left, and said, Why do we have to come last? Why do we count least? She accepted such remarks as part of the ragged mental state of parting, not as significant of any particular development. He put the phone down on her voice for the last time for this time.

He took the plane from Chicago late on Friday afternoon and by midnight was in early morning London. No school on Saturdays and Willa was there with the children at Heathrow. Airports, airports. In some times and places, for some men, it was the battlefield or the bullring, the courtroom or the church; for him it was airports. In that architectural mode of cheap glamour suited only to bathos his strongest experiences came; despair could not be distinguished from indigestion induced by time change, dread produced the same drawn face as muscle cramp; private joy exhibited euphoria that looked no different from that induced by individual bottles of Moët et Chandon. These were the only places where he ever wanted to weep, and no places could have been more ridiculous for this to happen to him.

Willa had a new haircut and the children were overcome with embarrassment by the eternal ten yards he had to walk towards them, and then flung themselves excitedly at him. Willa hugged his arm and pressed her cheek against that coatsleeve a moment; her mouth tasted of the toothpaste that they always used at home. The last phone call – only nine hours ago, that's all it was – receded into a depth, a distance, a silence as impossible to reach down through as the drifts of snow and piled-up letters . . . No letter, of course; he saw that at once. His wife cooked a special lunch and in the afternoon, when the children had gone off to the cinema with friends, he did what he must, he went to bed with her.

They talked a lot about the postal strike and how awful it had been. Nothing for days, more than two weeks! His mother had been maddening, telephoning every day, as if the whole thing were a conspiracy of the wife to keep the mother out of touch with her son. Crazy! And her letters – had he really got only one? She must have written at least four times; knowing that letters might not arrive only made one want to write more, wasn't it perverse? Why hadn't he phoned? Not that she really wanted him to, it was so expensive . . . by the way, it turned out that the youngest child had knock knees, he would have to have remedial treatment. Well, that was what he had thought – such an extravagance, and he couldn't believe, every day, that a letter might not come. She said, once: It must have been quite a nice feeling, sometimes, free of everything and everyone for a change – peaceful without us, eh? And he pulled down his mouth and said, Some freedom, snowed under in a motel in that godforsaken town. But the mining group was so pleased with his work that he was given a bonus, and that pleased her, that made her feel it was worth it, worth even the time he had had to himself.

He watched for the postman; sometimes woke up at night in a state of alarm. He even arranged, that first week, to work at home until about midday – getting his reports into shape. But there was nothing. For the second week, when he was keeping normal office hours, he read her face every evening when he came home; again, nothing. Heaven knows how she interpreted the way he looked at her: he would catch her full in the eyes, by mistake, now and then, and she would have a special slow smile, colouring up to her scrubbed little earlobes, the sort of smile you get from a girl who catches you looking at her across a bar. He was so appalled by that smile that he came home with a bunch of flowers. She embraced him and stood there holding the flowers behind his waist, rocking gently back and forth with him as they had done years ago. He thought – wildly again – how she was still pretty, quite young, no reason why she shouldn't marry again.

His anxiety for the letter slowly began to be replaced by confidence: it would not come. It was hopeless – safe – that letter would never come. Perhaps he had been very drunk after all, perhaps the mail box was a permanently disused one, or the letter hadn't really gone through the slot but fallen into the snow, the words melting and wavering while the ink ran with the thaw and the thin sheets of paper turned to pulp. He was safe. It was a good thing he had never told the Professor's wife. He took the children to the Motor Show, he got good seats for Willa, his mother and himself for the new *Troilus and Cressida* production at the Aldwych, and he wrote a long letter to Professor Malcolm's wife telling her about the performance and how much he would have loved to see it with her. Then he felt terribly depressed, as he often did lately now that he had stopped worrying about the letter and should have been feeling better, and there was nowhere to go for privacy, in depression, except the lavatory, where Willa provided the colour supplements of the Sunday papers for reading matter.

One morning just over a month after her husband had returned from the Middle West, Willa picked up the post from the floor as she brought the youngest home from school and saw a letter in her husband's handwriting. It had been date-stamped and re-date-stamped and was apparently about six weeks old. There is always something a bit flat about opening a letter from someone who has in the meantime long arrived and filled in, with anecdote and his presence, the time of absence when it was written. She vaguely saw herself producing it that evening as a kind of addendum to their forgotten emotions about the strike; by such small shared diversions did they keep their marriage close. But after she had given the little one his lunch she found a patch of sun for herself and opened the letter after all. In that chilly spring air, unaccustomed warmth seemed suddenly to become aural, sang in her ears at the pitch of cicadas, and she stopped reading. She looked out into the small garden amazedly, accusingly, as if to challenge a hoax. But there was no one to answer for it. She read the letter through. And again. She kept on reading it and it produced almost a sexual excitement in her, as a frank and erotic love letter might. She could have been looking through a keyhole at him lying on another woman. She took it to some other part of the garden, as the cat often carried the bloody and mangled mess of its prey from place to place, and read it again. It was a perfectly calm and reasonable and factual letter saying that he would not return, but she saw that it was indeed a love letter, a love letter about someone else, a love letter such as he had never written to her. She put it back in the creased and stained envelope and tore it up, and then she went out the gate and wandered down to the bus stop, where there was a lamp-post bin, and dropped the bits of paper into its square mouth among the used tickets.

Open House

Frances Taver was on the secret circuit for people who wanted to find out the truth about South Africa. These visiting journalists, politicians and churchmen all had an itinerary arranged for them by their consular representatives and overseas information services, or were steered around by a 'foundation' of South African business interests eager to improve the country's image, or even carted about to the model black townships, universities and beerhalls by the South African State Information service itself. But all had, carefully hidden among the most private of private papers (the nervous ones went so far as to keep it in code), the short list that would really take the lid off the place: the people one must see. A few were names that had got into the newspapers of the world as particularly vigorous opponents or victims of apartheid; a writer or two, a newspaper editor or an outspoken bishop. Others were known only within the country itself, and were known about by foreign visitors only through people like themselves who had carried the short list before. Most of the names on it were white names – which was rather frustrating, when one was after the real thing; but it was said in London and New York that there *were* still ways of getting to meet Africans, provided you could get hold of the right white people.

Frances Taver was one of them. Had been for years. From the forties when she had been a trade union organiser and run a mixed union of garment workers while this was legally possible, in the fifties, after her marriage, when she was manager of a black-and-white theatre group before that was disbanded by new legislation, to the early sixties, when she hid friends on the run from the police – Africans who were members of the newly banned political organisations – before the claims of that sort of friendship had to be weighed against the risk of the long spells of detention without trial introduced to betray it.

Frances Taver had few friends left now, and she was always slightly embarrassed when she heard an eager American or English voice over the telephone, announcing an arrival, a too-brief stay (of course), and the inevitable fond message of greetings to be conveyed from so-and-so – whoever it was who happened to have supplied the short list. A few years ago it had been fun and easy to make these visitors an excuse for a gathering that quite likely would turn into a party. The visitor would have a high old time learning to dance the *kwela* with black girls; he would sit fascinated, trying to keep sober enough to take it all in, listening to the fluent and fervent harangue of African, white and Indian politicals, drinking and arguing together in a paradox of personal freedom that, curiously, he couldn't remember finding where there were *no* laws against the mixing of races. And no one enjoyed his fascination more than the objects of it themselves; Frances Taver and her friends were amused, in those days, in a friendly way, to knock the 'right' ideas slightly askew. In those days: that was how she thought of it; it seemed very long ago. She saw the faces, sometimes, a flash in an absence filled with newspaper accounts of trials, hearsay about activities in exile, chance remarks from someone who knew someone else who had talked over the fence with one who was under house arrest. Another, an African friend banned for his activities with the African National Congress, who had gone 'underground', came to see her at long intervals, in the afternoons when he could be sure the house would be empty. Although she was still youngish, she had come to think of 'those days' as her youth; and he was a vision strayed from it.

The voice on the telephone, this time, was American – soft, cautious – no doubt the man thought the line was tapped. Robert Greenman Ceretti, from Washington; while they were talking, she remembered that this was the political columnist who had somehow been connected with the Kennedy administration. Hadn't he written a book about the Bay of Pigs? Anyway, she had certainly seen him quoted.

'And how are the Brauns – I haven't heard for ages—' She made the usual enquiries about the well-being of the mutual acquaintance whose greetings he brought, and he made the usual speech about how much he was hoping he'd be able to meet her? She was about to say, as always, come to dinner, but an absurd recoil within her, a moment of dull panic, almost, made her settle for an invitation to drop in for a drink two days later. 'If I can be of any help to you, in the meantime?' she had to add; he sounded modest and intelligent.

'Well, I do appreciate it. I'll look forward to Wednesday.'

At the last minute she invited a few white friends to meet him, a doctor and his wife who ran a tuberculosis hospital in an African reserve, and a young journalist who had been to America on a leadership exchange programme. But she knew what the foreign visitor wanted of her and she had an absurd – again, that was the word – compulsion to put him in the position where, alas, he could ask it. He was a small, cosy, red-headed man with a chipmunk smile, and she liked him. She drove him back to his hotel after the other guests had left, and they chatted about the articles he was going to write and the people he was seeing – had he been able to interview any important Nationalists, for example? Well, not yet, but he hoped to have something lined up for the following week, in Pretoria. Another thing he was worried about (here it came), he'd hardly been able to exchange a word with any black man except the one who cleaned his room at the hotel.

She heard her voice saying casually, 'Well, perhaps I might be able to help you, there,' and he took it up at once, gravely, gratefully, sincerely, smiling at her – 'I hoped you just might. If I could only get to talk with a few ordinary, articulate people. I mean, I think I've been put pretty much in the picture by the courageous white people I've been lucky enough to meet – people like you and your husband – but I'd like to know a little at first hand about what Africans themselves are thinking. If you could fix it, it'd be wonderful.'

Now it was done, at once she withdrew, from herself rather than him. 'I don't know. People don't want to talk any more. If they're doing anything, it's not something that can be talked about. Those that are left. Black and white. The ones you ought to see are shut away.'

They were sitting in the car, outside the hotel. She could see in his encouraging, admiring, intent face how he had been told that she, if anyone, could introduce him to black people, hers, if anyone's, was the house to meet them.

There was a twinge of vanity: 'I'll let you know. I'll ring you, then, Bob.' Of course they were already on first-name terms; lonely affinity overleapt acquaintance in South Africa when like-minded whites met.

'You don't have to say more than when and where. I didn't like to talk, that first day, over the phone,' he said.

They always had fantasies of danger. 'What can happen to you?' she said. Her smile was not altogether pleasant. They always protested, too, that their fear was not for themselves, it was on your behalf, etc. 'You've got your passport. You don't live here.'

She did not see Jason Madela from one month's end to the next but when she telephoned him at the building where she remembered him once having had an office on the fringe of the white town, he accepted the invitation to lunch just as if he had been one of the intimates who used to drop in any time. And then there was Edgar, Edgar Xixo the attorney, successor to her old friend Samson Dumile's practice; one could always get him. And after that? She could have asked Jason to bring someone along, perhaps one of the boxing promoters or gamblers it amused him to produce where the drinks were free – but that would have been too obvious, even for the blind eye that she and Jason Madela were able to turn to the nature of the invitation. In the end she invited little Spuds Buthelezi, the reporter. What did it matter? He was black, anyway. There was no getting out of the whole business, now.

She set herself to cook a good lunch, just as good as she had ever cooked, and she put out the drinks and the ice in the shelter of the glassed-in end of the big veranda, so that the small company should not feel lost. Her fading hair had been dyed to something approximating its original blonde and then streaked with grey, the day before, and she felt the appearance to be pleasingly artificial; she wore a bright, thick linen dress that showed off sunburned shoulders like the knobs of well-polished furniture, and she was aware that her blue eyes were striking in contrast with her tough brown face. She felt Robert Greenman Ceretti's eyes on her, a moment, as he stood in the sunny doorway; yes, she was also a woman, queening it alone among men at lunch.

'You mix the martinis, there's a dear,' she said. 'It's such a treat to have a real American one.' And while he bent about over bottles with the neatness of a small man, she was in and out of the veranda, shepherding the arrival of the other guests.

'This is Bob – Bob Ceretti, here on a visit from the States – Edgar Xixo.'

'Jason, this is Bob Ceretti, the man who has the ear of presidents—'

Laughter and protests mingled with the handing round of the drinks. Jason Madela, going to fat around the nape but still handsome in a frowning, Clark Gable way, stood about, glass in hand, as if in the habit acquired at cocktail parties. With his air of being distracted from more important things by irresistibly amusing asides, he was correcting a matter of terminology for Robert Ceretti – 'No, no, but you must understand that in the townships, a "situation" is a different thing entirely – well, *I'm* a situation, f'rinstance—'

He cocked his smile, for confirmation, to Xixo, whose eyes turned from one face to another in obedient glee – 'Oh, you're the *muti* man!'

'No, wait, but I'm trying to give Bob an obvious example' – more laughter, all round – '– a man who wears a suit every day, like a white man. Who goes to the office and prefers to talk English.'

'You think it derives from the use of the word as a genteelism for "job"? Would you say? You know – the Situations Vacant column in the newspapers?' The visitor sat forward on the edge of his chair, smiling up closely. 'But what's this "*muti*" you mentioned, now – maybe I ought to have been taking notes instead of shaking Frances's martini pitcher.'

'He's a medicine man,' Xixo was explaining, while Jason laughed – 'Oh for God's sake!' and tossed off the rest of his gin, and Frances went forward to bring the late arrival, Spuds Buthelezi, in his lattice-knit gold shirt and pale blue jeans, into the circle. When the American had exchanged names and had Spuds by the hand, he said, 'And what's Spuds, then?'

The young man had a dough-shaped, light-coloured face with tiny features stuck in it in a perpetual expression of suspicious surprise. The martinis had turned up the volume of voices that met him. 'I'll have a beer,' he said to Frances; and they laughed again.

Jason Madela rescued him, a giant flicking a fly from a glass of water. 'He's one of the eggheads,' he said. 'That's another category altogether.'

'Didn't you used to be one yourself, Jason?' Frances pretended a reproof: Jason Madela would want a way of letting Ceretti know that although he was a successful businessman in the townships, he was also a man with a university degree.

'Don't let's talk about my youthful misdemeanours, my dear Frances,' he said, with the accepted light touch of a man hiding a wound. 'I thought the men were supposed to be doing the work around here – I can cope with that,' and he helped her chip apart the ice cubes that had welded together as they melted. 'Get your servant to bring us a little hot water, that'll do it easily—'

'Oh I'm really falling down on the job!' Ceretti was listening carefully, putting in a low 'Go on' or 'You mean?' to keep the flow of Xixo's long explanation of problems over a travel document, and he looked up at Frances and Jason Madela offering a fresh round of drinks.

'You go ahead and talk, that's the idea,' Frances said.

He gave her the trusting grin of some intelligent small pet. 'Well, you two are a great combination behind the bar. Real teamwork of long association, I guess.'

'How long is it?' Frances asked, drily but gaily, meaning how many years had she and Jason Madela been acquaintances, and, playfully making as if to anticipate a blow, he said, 'Must be ten years and you were a grown-up girl even then' – although both knew that they had seen each other only across various rooms perhaps a dozen times in five years, and got into conversation perhaps half as often.

At lunch Edgar Xixo was still fully launched on the story of his difficulties in travelling back and forth to one of the former British Protectorates, now small, newly independent states surrounded by South African territory. It wasn't, he explained, as if he were asking for a passport: it was just a travel document he wanted, that's all, just a piece of paper from the Bantu Affairs Department that would allow him to go to Lesotho on business and come back.

'Now have I got this straight – you'd been there sometime?' Ceretti hung over the wisp of steam rising from his soup like a seer over a crystal ball.

'Yes, yes, you see, I had a travel document—'

'But these things are good for one exit and re-entry only.' Jason dispatched it with the good-humoured impatience of the quick-witted. 'We blacks aren't supposed to want to go wandering about the place. Tell them you want to take a holiday in Lourenço Marques – they'll laugh in your face. If they don't kick you downstairs. Oppenheimer and Charlie Engelhard can go off in their yachts to the South of France, but Jason Madela?'

He got the laugh he wanted, and, on the side, the style of his reference to rich and important white industrialists as decent enough fellows, if one happened to know them, suggested that *he* might. Perhaps he did, for all Frances Taver knew; Jason would be just the kind of man the white establishment would find if they should happen to decide they ought to make a token gesture of being in touch with the African masses. He was curiously reassuring to white people; his dark suits, white shirts, urbane conversation and sense of humour, all indistinguishable from their own and apparently snatched out of thin air, made it possible for them to forget the unpleasant facts of the life imposed on him and his kind. How tactful, how clever he was, too. She, just as well as any millionaire, would have done to illustrate his point; she was culpable: white, and free to go where she pleased. The flattery of being spared passed invisibly from her to him, like a promissory note beneath the table.

Edgar Xixo had even been summoned to The Greys, Special Branch headquarters, for questioning, he said – 'And I've never belonged to any political organisation, they know there've never been any charges against me. I don't know any political refugees in Lesotho, I don't want to *see* anybody – I have to go up and down simply because of business, I've got this agency selling equipment to the people at the diamond diggings, it could be a good thing if . . .'

'A little palm-grease, maybe,' said Jason Madela, taking some salad.

Xixo appealed to them all, dismayed. 'But if you offer it to the wrong one, that's the . . . ? In my position, an attorney!'

'Instinct,' said Madela. 'One can't learn it.'

'Tell me,' Ceretti signalled an appreciative refusal of a second helping of duck, while turning from his hostess to Madela. 'Would you say that bribery plays a big part in daily relations between Africans and officials? I don't mean the political police, of course – the white administration? Is that your experience?'

Madela sipped his wine and then turned the bottle so that he could read the label, saying meanwhile, 'Oh not what you'd call graft, not by your standards. Small stuff. When I ran a transport business I used to make use of it. Licences for the drivers and so on. You get some of these young Afrikaner clerks, they don't earn much and they don't mind who they pick up a few bob from. They can be quite reasonable. I was thinking there might be someone up at the Bantu Affairs offices. But you have to have a feeling for the right man' – he put down the bottle and smiled at Frances Taver – 'Thank heaven I'm out of it, now. Unless I should decide to submit some of my concoctions to the Bureau of Standards, eh?' and she laughed.

'Jason has broken the white monopoly of the hair-straightener and blood-purifier business,' Frances said gracefully, 'and the nice thing about him is that he has no illusions about his products.'

'But plenty of confidence,' he said. 'I'm looking into the possibilities of exporting my pills for men, to the States. I think the time's just ripe for American Negroes to feel they can buy back a bit of old Africa in a bottle, eh?'

Xixo picked about his leg of duck as if his problem itself were laid cold before them on the table. 'I mean, I've said again and again, show me anything on my record—'

The young journalist, Spuds Buthelezi, said in his heavy way, 'It might be because you took over Samson Dumile's show.'

Every time a new name was mentioned the corners of Ceretti's eyes flickered narrow in attention.

'Well, that's the whole thing!' Xixo complained to Ceretti. 'The fellow I was working for, Dumile, was mixed up in a political trial and he got six years – I took over the bona fide clients, that's all, my office isn't in the same building, nothing to do with it – but that's the whole thing!'

Frances suddenly thought of Sam Dumile, in this room of hers, three – two? – years ago, describing a police raid on his house the night before and roaring with laughter as he told how his little daughter said to the policeman, 'My father gets very cross if you play with his papers.'

Jason picked up the wine bottle, making to pass it round – 'Yes, please do, please do – what happened to the children?' she said.

Jason knew whose she meant; made a polite attempt. 'Where are Sam's kids?'

But Edgar Xixo was nodding in satisfied confirmation as Ceretti said, 'It's a pretty awful story. My God. Seems you can never hope to be in the clear, no matter how careful you are. My God.'

Jason remarked, aside, 'They must be around somewhere with relatives. He's got a sister in Bloemfontein.'

The dessert was a compound of fresh mangoes and cream, an invention of the house: 'Mangoes Frances' said the American. 'This is one of the African experiences I'd recommend.' But Jason Madela told them he was allergic to mangoes and began on the cheese which was standing by. Another bottle of wine was opened to go with the cheese and there was laughter – which Robert Ceretti immediately turned on himself – when it emerged out of the cross-talk that Spuds Buthelezi thought Ceretti had something to do with an American foundation. In the sympathetic atmosphere of food, drink and sunshine marbled with cigarette smoke, the others listened as if they had not heard it all before while Buthelezi, reluctant to waste the speech he had primed himself with, pressed Ceretti with his claim to a study grant that would enable him to finish his play. They heard him again outlining the plot and inspiration of the play – 'right out of township life' as he always said, blinking with finality, convinced that this was the only necessary qualification for successful authorship. He had patiently put together and taken apart, many times, in his play, ingredients faithfully lifted from the work of African writers who got published, and he was himself African: what else could be needed but someone to take it up?

Foundation or no foundation, Robert Ceretti showed great interest. 'Do you know the play at all, Frances? I mean,' (he turned back to the round, wine-open face of the young man) 'is it far enough along to show to anybody?'

And she said, finding herself smiling encouragingly, 'Oh yes – an early draft, he's worked on it a lot since then, haven't you – and there's been a reading . . . ?'

'I'll certainly get it to you,' Buthelezi said, writing down the name of Ceretti's hotel.

They moved back to the veranda for the coffee and brandy. It was well after three o'clock by the time they stood about, making their goodbyes. Ceretti's face was gleaming. 'Jason Madela's offered to drop me back in town, so don't you worry, Frances. I was just saying, people in America'll find it difficult to believe it was possible for me to have a lunch like this, here. It's been so very pleasant – pleasant indeed. We all had a good time. He was telling me that a few years ago a gathering like this would be quite common, but now there aren't many white people who would want to risk asking Africans and there aren't many Africans who would risk coming. I certainly enjoyed myself . . . I hope we haven't put you out, lingering so long . . . it's been a wonderful opportunity . . .' Frances saw them to the garden gate, talking and laughing; last remarks and goodbyes were called from under the trees of the suburban street.

When she came back alone the quiet veranda rang tense with vanished voices, like a bell tower after the hour has struck. She gave the cat the milk left over from coffee. Someone had left a half-empty packet of cigarettes; who was it who broke matches into little tents? As she carried the tray into the deserted kitchen, she saw a note written on the back of a bill taken from the spike. HOPE YOUR PARTY WENT WELL.

It was not signed, and was written with the kitchen ballpoint which hung on a string. But she knew who had written it; the vision from the past had come and gone again.

The servants Amos and Bettie had rooms behind a granadilla vine at the bottom of the yard. She called, and asked Bettie whether anyone had asked for her? No, no one at all.

He must have heard the voices in the quiet of the afternoon, or perhaps simply seen the cars outside, and gone away. She wondered if he knew who was there. Had he gone away out of consideration for her safety? They never spoke of it, of course, but he must know that the risks she took were carefully calculated, very carefully calculated. There was no way of disguising that from someone like *him*. Then she saw him smiling to himself at the sight of the collection of guests: Jason Madela, Edgar Xixo and Spuds Buthelezi – Spuds Buthelezi, as well. But probably she was wrong, and he would have come out among them without those feelings of reproach or contempt that she read into the idea of his gait, his face. HOPE YOUR PARTY WENT WELL. He may have meant just that.

Frances Taver knew Robert Ceretti was leaving soon, but she wasn't quite sure when. Every day she thought, I'll phone and say goodbye. Yet she had already taken leave of him, that afternoon of the lunch. Just telephone and say goodbye. On the Friday morning, when she was sure he would be gone, she rang up the hotel, and there it was, the soft, cautious American voice. The first few moments were awkward; he protested his pleasure at hearing from her, she kept repeating, 'I thought you'd be gone . . .' Then she said, 'I just wanted to say – about that lunch. You mustn't be taken in—'

He was saying, 'I've been so indebted to you, Frances, really you've been great.'

'—not phonies, no, that's not what I mean, on the contrary, they're very real, you understand?'

'Oh, your big good-looking friend, he's been marvellous. Saturday night we were out on the town, you know.' He was proud of the adventure but didn't want to use the word '*shebeen*' over the telephone.

She said, 'You must understand. Because the corruption's real. Even they've become what they are because things are the way they are. Being phony is being corrupted by the situation . . . and that's real enough. We're made out of *that*.'

He thought maybe he was finding it difficult to follow her over the telephone, and seized upon the word: 'Yes, the "situation" – he was able to slip me into what I gather is one of the livelier places.'

Frances Taver said, 'I don't want you to be taken in—'

The urgency of her voice stopped his mouth, was communicated to him even if what she said was not.

'—by anyone,' the woman was saying.

He understood, indeed, that something complicated was wrong, but he knew, too, that he wouldn't be there long enough to find out, that perhaps you needed to live and die there, to find out. All she heard over the telephone was the voice assuring her, 'Everyone's been marvellous . . . really marvellous. I just hope I can get back here some day – that is, if they ever let me in again . . .'

A Meeting in Space

Every morning he was sent to the baker and the French children slid out of dark walls like the village cats and walked in his footsteps. He couldn't understand what they said to each other, but he thought he understood their laughter: he was a stranger. He looked forward to the half-fearful, disdainful feeling their presence at his back gave him, and as he left the house expected at each alley, hole and doorway the start of dread with which he would see them. They didn't follow him into the baker's shop. Perhaps the baker wouldn't have them – they looked poor, and the boy knew, from the piccanins at home, that poor kids steal. He had never been into a bakery at home in South Africa; the baker-boy, a black man who rode a tricycle with a rattling bin on the front, came through the yard holding the loaves out of the way of the barking dogs, and put two white and one brown on the kitchen table. It was the same with fruit and vegetables; at home the old Indian, Vallabhbhai, stopped his greengrocer's lorry at the back gate, and his piccanin carried into the kitchen whatever you bought.

But here, the family said, part of the fun was doing your own shopping in the little shops that were hidden away by the switch-back of narrow streets. They made him repeat over and over again the words for asking for bread, in French, but once in the baker's shop he never said them, only pointed at the loaf he wanted and held out his hand with money in it. He felt that he was someone else, a dumb man perhaps. After a few days, if he were given change he would point again, this time at a bun with a glazing of jam. He had established himself as a customer. The woman who served chattered at him, smiled with her head on one side while she picked the money out of his palm; but he gave no sign of response.

There was another child who sometimes turned up with the usual group. He would hail them loudly, from across a street, in their own language, and stalk along with them for a bit, talking away, but he looked different. The boy thought it was just because this one was richer. Although he wore the usual canvas shoes and cotton shorts, he was hung about with all sorts of equipment – a camera and two other leather cases. He began to appear in the bakery each morning. He stood right near, as if the dumb person were also invisible, and peering up experiencedly under a thick, shiny fringe of brown hair, looked along the cakes on top of the counter while apparently discussing them in a joking, familiar way with the woman. He also appeared unexpectedly in other places, without the group. Once he was leaning against the damp archway to the tunnel that smelled like a school lavatory – it was the quick way from the upper level of streets to the lower. Another time he came out of the door of the streaky-pink-painted house with the

Ali Baba pots, as if he must have been watching at the window. Then he was balancing along the top of the wall that overlooked the pitch where in the afternoons the baker and other men played a bowling game with a heavy ball. Suddenly, he was outside the gate of the villa that the family were living in; he squatted on the doorstep of the house opposite, doing something to the inside of his camera. He spoke: 'You English?'

'Yes – not really – no. I mean, I speak English, but I come from South Africa.'

'Africa? You come from *Africa*? That's a heck of a way!'

'Fifteen hours or so. We came in a jet. We actually took a little longer because, you see, something went wrong with the one engine and we had to wait three hours in the middle of the night in Kano. Boy, was it hot, and there was a live camel wandering around.' The anecdote cut itself off abruptly; the family often said long-winded stories were a bore.

'I've had some pretty interesting experiences myself. My parents are travelling round the world and I'm going with them. Most of the time. I'll go back home to school for a while in the Fall. Africa. Fantastic. We may get out there sometime. D'you know anything about these darned Polaroids? It's stuck. I've got a couple of pictures of you I must show you. I take candid shots. All over the place. I've got another camera, a Minox, but I mostly use this one here because it develops the prints right in the box and you can give them to people right off. It's good for a laugh. I've got some pretty interesting pictures, too.'

'Where was I – in the street?'

'Oh I'm taking shots all the time. All over the place.'

'What's the other case?'

'Tape recorder. I'll get you on tape, too. I tape people at Zizi's Bar and in the *Place*, they don't know I'm doing it, I've got this minute little mike, you see. It's fantastic.'

'And what's in here?'

The aerial was pulled out like a silver wand. 'My transistor, of course, my beloved transistor. D'you know what I just heard? – "Help!" Are the Beatles popular down in Africa?'

'We saw them in London – live. My brother and sister and me. She bought the record of "Help!" but we haven't got anything to play it on, here.'

'Good God, some guys get all the breaks! You *saw* them. You notice how I've grown my hair? Say, look, I can bring down my portable player and your sister can hear her record.'

'What time can you come?'

'Any time you say. I'm easy. I've got to go for this darned French lesson now, and I *have* to be in at noon so that old Madame Blanche can give me my lunch before she quits, but I'll be around indefinitely after that.'

'Straight after lunch. About two. I'll wait for you here. Could you bring the pictures, as well – of me?'

Clive came racing through the tiny courtyard and charged the flyscreen door, letting it bang behind him. 'Hey! There's a boy who can speak English! He just talked to me! He's a real Amur-r-rican – just wait till you hear him. And you should see what he's got, a Polaroid camera – he's taken some pictures of me and I didn't even know him – and he's got a tiny little tape recorder, you can get people on it when they don't know – and the smallest transistor I've ever seen.'

His mother said, 'So you've found a pal. Thank goodness.' She was cutting up green peppers for salad, and she offered him a slice on the point of her knife, but he didn't see it.

'He's going round the world, but he goes back to America to school sometimes.'

'Oh, where? Does he come from New York?'

'I don't know, he said something about Fall, I think that's where the school is. The Fall, he said.'

'That's not a place, silly – it's what they call autumn.'

The shower was in a kind of cupboard in the kitchen-dining room, and its sliding door was shaken in the frame, from inside. The impatient occupant got it to jerk open: she was his sister. 'You've found what?' The enormous expectancy with which she had invested this holiday, for herself, opened her shining face under its plastic mob-cap.

'We can hear the record, Jen, he's bringing his player. He's from America.'

'How old?'

'Same as me. About.'

She pulled off the cap and her straight hair fell down, covering her head to the shoulders and her face to her eyelashes. 'Fine,' she said soberly.

His father sat reading *Nice-Matin* on one of the dining-table chairs, which was dressed, like a person, in a yellow skirt and a cover that fitted over its hard back. He had – unsuccessfully – put out a friendly foot to trip up the boy as he burst in, and now felt he ought to make another gesture of interest. As if to claim that he had been listening to every word, he said, 'What's your friend's name?'

'Oh, I don't know. He's American, he's the boy with the three leather cases—'

'Yes, all right—'

'You'll see him this afternoon. He's got a Beatle cut.' This last was addressed to the young girl, who turned, halfway up the stone stairs with a train of wet footprints behind her.

But of course Jenny, who was old enough to introduce people as adults do, at once asked the American boy who he was. She got a very full reply. 'Well, I'm usually called Matt, but that's short for my second name, really – my real names are Nicholas Matthew Rootes Keller.'

'Junior?' she teased, 'The Third?'

'No, why should I be? My father's name is Donald Rootes Keller. I'm named for my grandfather on my mother's side. She has one hell of a big family. Her brothers won five decorations between them, in the war. I mean, three in the war against the Germans, and two in the Korean War. My youngest uncle, that's Rod, he's got a hole in his back – it's where the ribs were – you can put your hand in. My hand, I mean' – he made a fist with a small, thin, tanned hand – 'not an adult person's. How much more would you say my hand had t'grow, I mean – would you say half as much again, as much as that? – to be a full-size, man's hand—' He measured it against Clive's; the two ten-year-old fists matched eagerly.

'Yours and Clive's put together – one full-size, king-size, man-size paw. Clip the coupon now. Enclose only one box-top or reasonable facsimile.'

But the elder brother's baiting went ignored or misunderstood by the two small boys. Clive might react with a faint grin of embarrassed pleasure and reflected glory at the reference to the magazine ad culture with which his friend was associated by his brother Mark. Matt went on talking in the innocence of one whose background is still as naturally accepted as once his mother's lap was.

He came to the villa often after that afternoon when the new Beatle record was heard for the first time on his player. The young people had nothing to do but wait while the parents slept after lunch (the *place*, where Jenny liked to stroll, in the evenings, inviting mute glances from boys who couldn't speak her language, was dull at that time of day) and they listened to the record again and again in the courtyard summerhouse that had been a pigsty before the peasant cottage became a villa. When the record palled, Matt taped their voices – 'Say something African!' – and Mark made up a jumble of the one or two Zulu words he knew, with cheerleaders' cries, words of abuse and phrases from familiar road signs, in Afrikaans. '*Sakabona! Voetsak hambakahle hou links malingi mushle – Vrystaat!*'

The brothers and sister rocked their rickety chairs back ecstatically on two legs when the record was played, but Matt listened with eyes narrowed and tongue turned up to touch his teeth, like an ornithologist who is bringing back alive the song of rare birds. 'Boy, thanks. Fantastic. That'll go into the documentary I'm going to make. Partly with my father's movie camera, I hope, and partly with my candid stills. I'm working on the script now. It's in the family, you see.' He had already explained that his father was writing a book (several books, one about each country they visited, in fact) and his mother was helping. 'They keep to a strict schedule. They start work around noon and carry on until about one a.m. That's why I've got to be out of the house very early in the morning and I'm not supposed to come back in till they wake up for lunch. And that's why I've got to keep out of the house in the afternoons, too; they got to have peace *and* quiet. For sleep *and* for work.'

Jenny said, 'Did you see his shorts – that Madras stuff you read about? The colours run when it's washed. I wish you could buy it here.'

'That's a marvellous transistor, Dad.' Mark sat with his big bare feet flat on the courtyard flagstones and his head hung back in the sun – as if he didn't live in it all the year round, at home; but this was France he basked in, not sunlight.

'W-e-ll, they spoil their children terribly. Here's a perfect example. A fifty-pound camera's a toy. What's there left for them to want when they grow up.'

Clive would have liked them to talk about Matt all the time. He said, 'They've got a Maserati at home in America, at least, they did have, they've sold it now they're going round the world.'

The mother said, 'Poor little devil, shut out in the streets with all that rubbish strung around his neck.'

'Ho, rubbish, I'm sure!' said Clive, shrugging and turning up his palms exaggeratedly. 'Of course, hundreds of dollars of equipment are worth nothing, you know, nothing at all.'

'And how much is one dollar, may I ask, mister?' Jenny had learned by heart, on the plane, the conversion tables supplied by the travel agency.

'I don't know how much it is in our money – I'm talking about America—'

'You're not to go down out of the village with him, Clive, ay, only in the village,' his father said every day.

He didn't go out of the village with the family, either. He didn't go to see the museum at Antibes or the potteries at Vallauris or even the palace, casino and aquarium at Monte Carlo. The ancient hill village inside its walls, whose disorder of streets had been as confusing as the dates and monuments of Europe's overlaid and overlapping past, became the intimate map of their domain – his and Matt's. The alley cats shared it but the people, talking their unintelligible tongue, provided a babble beneath which, while performed openly in the streets, his activities with Matt acquired secrecy: as they went about, they were hidden even more than by the usual self-preoccupation of adults. They moved from morning till night with intense purpose; you had to be quick around corners, you mustn't be seen crossing the street, you must appear as if from nowhere among the late afternoon crowd in the *place* and move among them quite unobtrusively. One of the things they were compelled to do was to get from the church – very old, with chicken wire where the stained glass must have been, and a faint mosaic, like a flaking transfer – to under the school windows without attracting the attention of the children. This had to be done in the morning, when school was in session; it was just one of the stone houses, really, without playgrounds: the dragging chorus of voices coming from it reminded him of the schools for black children at home. At other times the village children tailed them, jeering and mimicking, or in obstinate silence, impossible to shake off. There were fights and soon he learnt to make with his fingers effective insulting signs he didn't understand, and to shout his one word of French, their bad word – *merde*!

And Matt talked all the time. His low, confidential English lifted to the cheerful rising cadence of French as his voice bounced out to greet people and rebounded from the close walls back to the privacy of English and their head-lowered conclave again. Yet even when his voice had dropped to a whisper, his round dark eyes, slightly depressed at the outer corners by the beginning of an intelligent frown above his dainty nose, moved, parenthetically alert, over everyone within orbit. He greeted people he had never seen before just as he greeted local inhabitants. He would stop beside a couple of sightseers or a plumber lifting a manhole and converse animatedly. To his companion standing by, his French sounded much more French than when the village children spoke it. Matt shrugged his shoulders and thrust out his lower lip while he talked, and if some of the people he accosted were uncomfortable or astonished at being addressed volubly, for no particular reason, by someone they didn't know, he asked them questions (Clive could hear they were questions) in the jolly tone of voice that grown-ups use to kid children out of their shyness.

Sometimes one of the inhabitants, sitting outside his or her doorway on a hard chair, would walk inside and close the door when Matt called out conversationally. 'The people in this town are really psychotic, I can tell you,' he would say with enthusiasm, dropping back to English. 'I know them all, every one of them, and I'm not kidding.' The old women in wrinkled black stockings, long aprons and wide black hats who sat on the *place* stringing beans for Chez Riane, the open-air restaurant, turned walnut-meat faces and hissed toothlessly like geese when Matt approached. Riane ('She topped the popularity poll in Paris, can you believe it? It was just about the time of the Flood, my father says'), a woman the size of a prize fighter who bore to the displayed posters of herself the kinship of a petrified trunk to a twig in new leaf, growled something at Matt from the corner of her vivid mouth. 'I've got some great pictures of *her*. Of course, she's a bit *passé*.'

They got chased when Matt took a picture of a man and a girl kissing down in the parking area below the chateau. Clive carried his box camera about with him, now, but he only took pictures of the cats. Matt promised that Clive would get a shot of the dwarf – a real man, not in a circus – who turned the spit in the restaurant that served lamb cooked the special way they did it here, but, as Matt said, Clive didn't have the temperament for a great photographer. He was embarrassed, ashamed and frightened when the dwarf's enormous head with its Spanish dancer's sideburns reddened with a temper too big for him. But Matt had caught him on the Polaroid; they went off to sit in someone's doorway hung with strips of coloured plastic to keep out flies, and had a look. There was the dwarf's head, held up waggling on his little body like the head of a finger-puppet. 'Fantastic.' Matt was not boastful but professional in his satisfaction. 'I didn't have a good one of him before, just my luck, we hadn't been here a week when he went crazy and was taken off to some hospital. He's only just come back into circulation, it's a good thing you didn't miss him. You might've gone back to Africa and not seen him.'

* * *

The family, who had admired the boy's Madras shorts or his transistor radio, enjoyed the use of his elegant little record player, or welcomed a friend for Clive, began to find him too talkative, too often present, and too much on the streets. Clive was told that he *must* come along with the family on some of their outings. They drove twenty miles to eat some fish made into soup. They took up a whole afternoon looking at pictures.

'What time'll we be back?' he would rush in from the street to ask.

'I don't know – sometime in the afternoon.'

'Can't we be back by two?'

'Why on earth should we tie ourselves down to a time? We're on holiday.' He would rush back to the street to relay the unsatisfactory information.

When the family came home, the slim little figure with its trappings would be ready to wave at them from the bottom of their street. Once in the dark they made him out under the street light that streaked and flattened his face and that of the village halfwit and his dog; he looked up from conversation as if he had been waiting for a train that would come in on time. Another day there was a message laid out in the courtyard with matches end-to-end: WILL SEE YOU LATER MATT.

'What's the matter with those people, they don't even take the child down to the beach for a swim,' said the mother.

Clive heard, but was not interested. He had never been in the pink house with the Ali Baba pots. Matt emerged like one of the cats, and he usually had money. They found a place that sold bubblegum and occasionally they had pancakes – Clive didn't know that that was what they were going to be when Matt said he was going to buy some *crêpes* and what kind of jam did Clive like? Matt paid; there was his documentary film, and he was also writing a book – 'There's a lot of money in kids' books actually written by a kid,' he explained to the family. It was a spy story – 'Really exotic.' He expected to do well out of it, and he might sell some of his candid shots to *Time* and *Life* as well.

But one particularly lovely morning Clive's mother said as if she couldn't prevent herself, perhaps Matt would like to come with the family to the airport? The boys could watch the jets land while the grown-ups had business with the reservation office.

'Order yourselves a lemonade if you want it,' said the father; he meant that he would pay when he came back. They drank a lemonade-and-ice-cream each and then Matt said he'd like a black coffee to wash it down, so they ordered two coffees, and the father was annoyed when he got the bill – coffee was nothing at home, but in France they seemed to charge you for the glass of water you got with it.

'I can drink five or six coffees a day, it doesn't bother my liver,' Matt told everyone. And in Nice, afterwards, trailing round the Place Masséna behind Jenny, who wanted to buy a polo shirt like the ones all the French girls were wearing, the boys were not even allowed to go and look at the fountain alone, in case they got lost. Matt's voice fell to a whisper in Clive's ear but Clive hardly heard and did not answer: here, Matt was just an appendage of the family, like any other little boy.

It was Saturday and when they drove home up the steep road (the halfwit and his dog sat at the newly installed traffic light and Matt, finding his voice, called out of the window a greeting in French) the village was already beginning to choke with weekend visitors.

Directly lunch was down the boys raced to meet beneath the plaque that commemorated the birth in this street of Xavier Duval, Resistance fighter, killed on 20 October 1944. Clive was there first and, faithfully carrying out the technique and example of his friend, delightedly managed to take a candid shot of Matt before Matt realised that he was observed. It was one of the best afternoons they'd had.

'Saturdays are always good,' said Matt. 'All these psychotic people around. Just keep your eyes open, brother. I wrote Chapter Fourteen of my book at lunch. Oh, it was on a tray in my room – they were out until about four this morning and they didn't get up. It's set in this airport, you see – remember how you could just see my mouth moving and you couldn't hear a thing in the racket with that jet taking off? – well, someone gets murdered right there drinking coffee and no one hears the scream.'

They were walking through the car park, running their hands over the nacre-sleek hoods of sports models, and half-attentive to a poodle fight near the *pétanque* pitch and a human one that seemed about to break out at the busy entrance to the men's lavatories that tunnelled under the *place*. 'Ah, I've got enough shots of delinquents to last me,' Matt said. In accord they went on past the old girl in flowered trousers who was weeping over her unharmed, struggling poodle, and up the steps to the *place*, where most of the local inhabitants and all the visitors, whose cars jammed the park and stopped up the narrow streets, were let loose together, herded by Arab music coming from the boutique run by the French Algerians, on the chateau side, and the recorded voice, passionately hoarse, of Riane in her prime, from the direction of Chez Riane. The dwarf was there, talking between set teeth to a beautiful blonde American as if he were about to tear her apart with them; her friends were ready to die laughing, but looked kindly in order not to show it. The old women with their big black hats and apron-covered stomachs took up space on the benches. There were more poodles and an Italian greyhound like a piece of wire jewellery. Women who loved each other sat at the little tables outside Riane's, men who loved each other sat in identical mauve jeans and pink shirts, smoking, outside Zizi's Bar. Men and women in beach clothes held hands, looking into the doorways of the little shops and bars, and pulling each other along as the dogs pulled along their owners on fancy leashes. At the *Crêperie*, later, Matt pointed out Clive's family, probably eating their favourite liqueur pancakes, but Clive jerked him away.

They watched *pétanque* for a while; the butcher, a local champion, was playing to the gallery, all right. He was pink and wore a tourist's fishnet vest through which wisps of reddish chest-hair twined like a creeper. A man with a long black cape and a huge cat's-whisker moustache caused quite a stir. 'My God, I've been trying to get him for weeks—' Matt ducked, Clive quickly following, and they zigzagged off through the *pétanque* spectators. The man had somehow managed to drive a small English sports car right up on to the *place*; it was forbidden, but although the part-time policeman who got into uniform for Saturday afternoons was shouting at him, the man couldn't be forced to take it down again because whatever gap it had found its way through was closed by a fresh influx of people. 'He's a painter,' Matt said. 'He lives above the shoemaker's, you know that little hole. He doesn't ever come out except Saturdays and Sundays. I've got to get a couple of good shots of him. He looks to me the type that gets famous. Really psychotic, eh?' The painter had with him a lovely, haughty girl dressed like Sherlock Holmes in a man's tweeds and deerstalker. 'The car must be hers,' said Matt. 'He hasn't made it, yet; but I can wait.' He used up almost a whole film: 'With a modern artist, you want a few new angles.'

Matt was particularly talkative, even going right into Zizi's Bar to say hello to her husband, Emile. The family were still sitting at the *Crêperie*; the father signed to Clive to come over and at first he took no notice. Then he stalked up between the tables. 'Yes?'

'Don't you want some money?'

Before he could answer, Matt began jerking a thumb frantically. He ran. His father's voice barred him: 'Clive!'

But Matt had come flying: 'Over there – a woman's just fainted or died or something. We got to go—'

'What *for*?' said the mother.

'God almighty,' said Jenny.

He was gone with Matt. They fought and wriggled their way into the space that had been cleared, near the steps, round a heavy woman lying on the ground. Her clothes were twisted; her mouth bubbled. People argued and darted irresistibly out of the crowd to do things to her; those who wanted to try and lift her up were pulled away by those who thought she ought to be left. Someone took off her shoes. Someone ran for water from Chez Riane but the woman couldn't drink it. One day the boys had found a workman in his blue outfit and cement-crusted boots lying snoring near the old pump outside the Bar Tabac, where the men drank. Matt got him, too; you could always use a shot like that for a dead body, if the worst came to the worst. But this was the best ever. Matt finished up what was left of the film with the painter on it and had time to put in a new one, while the woman still lay there, and behind the noise of the crowd and the music the see-saw hoot of the ambulance could be heard, coming up the road to the village walls from the port below. The ambulance couldn't get on to the *place*, but the men in their uniforms carried a stretcher over people's heads and then lifted the woman aboard. Her face was purplish as cold hands on a winter morning and her legs stuck out. The boys were part of the entourage that followed her to the ambulance, Matt progressing with sweeping hops, on bended knee, like a Russian dancer, in order to get the supine body in focus at an upward angle.

When it was all over, they went back to the *Crêperie* to relate the sensational story to the family; but they had not been even interested enough to stay, and had gone home to the villa. 'It'll be really *something* for you to show them down in Africa!' said Matt. He was using his Minox that afternoon, and he promised that when the films were developed, he would have copies made for Clive. 'Darn it, we'll have to wait until my parents take the films to Nice – you can't get them developed up here. And they only go in on Wednesdays.'

'But I'll be gone by then,' said Clive suddenly.

'Gone? Back to Africa?' All the distance fell between them as they stood head-to-head jostled by the people in the village street, all the distance of the centuries when the continent was a blank outline on the maps, as well as the distance of miles. 'You mean you'll be back in *Africa*?'

Clive's box camera went into his cupboard along with the other souvenirs of Europe that seemed to have shed their evocation when they were unpacked amid the fresh, powerful familiarity of home. He boasted a little, the first day of the new term at school, about the places he had been to; but within a few weeks, when cities and palaces that he had seen for himself were spoken of in history or geography classes, he did not mention that he had visited them and, in fact, the textbook illustrations and descriptions did not seem to be those of anything he knew. One day he searched for his camera to take to a sports meeting, and found an exposed film in it. When it was developed, there were the pictures of the cats. He turned them this way up and that, to make out the thin, feral shapes on cobblestones and the disappearing blurs round the blackness of archways. There was also the picture of the American boy, Matt, a slim boy with knees made big out of focus, looking – at once suspicious and bright – from under his uncut hair.

The family crowded round to see, smiling, filled with pangs for what the holiday was and was not, while it lasted.

'The *Time-Life* man himself!'

'Poor old Matt – what was his other name?'

'You ought to send it to him,' said the mother. 'You've got the address? Aren't you going to keep in touch?'

But there was no address. The boy Matt had no street, house, house in a street, room in a house like the one they were in. 'America,' Clive said, 'he's in America.'

Rain-Queen

We were living in the Congo at the time; I was nineteen. It must have been my twentieth birthday we had at the Au Relais, with the Gattis, M. Niewenhuys and my father's site manager. My father was building a road from Elisabethville to Tshombe's residence, a road for processions and motorcades. It's Lubumbashi now, and Tshombe's dead in exile. But at that time there was plenty of money around and my father was brought from South Africa with a free hand to recruit engineers from anywhere he liked; the Gattis were Italian, and then there was a young Swede. I didn't want to leave Johannesburg because of my boyfriend, Alan, but my mother didn't like the idea of leaving me behind, because of him. She said to me, 'Quite honestly, I think it's putting too much temptation in a young girl's way. I'd have no one to blame but myself.' I was very young for my age, then, and I gave in.

There wasn't much for me to do in E'ville. I was taken up by some young Belgian married women who were only a few years older than I was. I had coffee with them in town in the mornings, and played with their babies. My mother begged them to speak French to me; she didn't want the six months there to be a complete waste. One of them taught me how to make a chocolate mousse, and I made myself a dress under the supervision of another; we giggled together as I had done a few years before with the girls at school.

Everyone turned up at the Au Relais in the evenings and in the afternoons when it had cooled off a bit we played squash – the younger ones in our crowd, I mean. I used to play every day with the Swede and Marco Gatti. They came straight from the site. Eleanora Gatti was one of those Mediterranean women who not only belong to a different sex, but seem to be a species entirely different from the male. You could never imagine her running or even bending to pick something up; her white bosom in square-necked dresses, her soft hands with rings and jewel-lidded watch, her pile of dark hair tinted a strange tarnished marmalade colour that showed up the pallor of her skin – all was arranged like a still life. The Swede wasn't married.

After the game Marco Gatti used to put a towel round his neck tennis-star fashion and his dark face was gilded with sweat. The Swede went red and blotchy. When Marco panted it was a grin, showing white teeth and one that was repaired with gold. It seemed to me that all adults were flawed in some way; it set them apart. Marco used to give me a lift home and often came in to have a drink with my father and discuss problems about the road. When he was outlining a difficulty he had a habit of smiling and putting a hand inside his shirt to scratch his breast. In the open neck of his shirt some sort of amulet on a chain rested on the dark hair between his strong pectoral muscles. My father said proudly, 'He may look like a tenor at the opera, but he knows how to get things done.'

I had never been to the opera; it wasn't my generation. But when Marco began to kiss me every afternoon on the way home, and then to come in to talk to my father over beer as usual, I put it down to the foreignness in him.

I said, 'It seems so funny to walk into the room where Daddy is.'

Marco said, 'My poor little girl, you can't help it if you are pretty, can you?'

It rains every afternoon there, at that time of year. A sudden wind would buffet the heat aside, flattening paper against fences in the dust. Fifteen minutes later – you could have timed it by the clock – the rain came down so hard and noisy we could scarcely see out of the windscreen and had to talk as loudly as if we were in an echoing hall. The rain usually lasted only about an hour. One afternoon we went to the site instead of to my parents' house – to the caravan that was meant to be occupied by one of the engineers but never had been, because everyone lived in town. Marco shouted against the downpour, 'You know what the Congolese say? "When the rain comes, quickly find a girl to take home with you until it's over."' The caravan was just like a little flat, with everything you needed. Marco showed me – there was even a bath. Marco wasn't tall (at home the girls all agreed we couldn't look at any boy under six foot) but he had the fine, strong legs of a sportsman, covered with straight black hairs, and he stroked my leg with his hard yet furry one. That was a caress we wouldn't have thought of, either. I had an inkling we really didn't know anything.

The next afternoon Marco seemed to be taking the way directly home, and I said in agony, 'Aren't we going to the caravan?' It was out, before I could think.

'Oh my poor darling, were you disappointed?' He laughed and stopped the car there and then and kissed me deep in both ears as well as the mouth. 'All right, the caravan.'

We went there every weekday afternoon – he didn't work on Saturdays, and the wives came along to the squash club. Soon the old Congolese watchman used to trot over from the labourers' camp to greet us when he saw the car draw up at the caravan; he knew I was my father's daughter. Marco chatted with him for a few minutes, and every few days gave him a tip. At the beginning, I used to stand by as if waiting to be told what to do next, but Marco had what I came to realise must be adult confidence. 'Don't look so worried. He's a nice old man. He's my friend.'

Marco taught me how to make love, in the caravan, and everything that I had thought of as 'life' was put away, as I had at other times folded the doll's clothes, packed the Monopoly set and the sample collection, and given them to the servant. I stopped writing to my girl friends; it took me weeks to get down to replying to Alan's regular letters, and yet when I did so it was with a kind of professional pride that I turned out a letter of the most skilful ambiguity – should it be taken as a love letter, or should it not? I felt it would be beyond his powers – powers of experience – to decide. I alternately pitied him and underwent an intense tingling of betrayal – actually cringing away from myself in the flesh. Before my parents and in the company of friends, Marco's absolutely unchanged behaviour mesmerised me: I acted as if nothing had happened because for him it was really as if nothing had happened. He was not pretending to be natural with my father and mother – he *was* natural. And the same applied to our behaviour in the presence of his wife. After the first time he made love to me I had looked forward with terror and panic to the moment when I should have to see Eleanora again; when she might squeeze my hand or even kiss me on the cheek as she sometimes did in her affectionate, feminine way. But when I walked into our house that Sunday and met her perfume and then all at once saw her beside my mother talking about her family in Genoa, with Marco, my father and another couple sitting there – I moved through the whirling impression without falter.

Someone said, 'Ah here she is at last, our Jillie!'

And my mother was saying (I had been riding with the Swede), 'I don't know how she keeps up with Per, they were out dancing until three o'clock this morning—' and Marco, who was twenty-nine (1 December, Sagittarius, domicile of Jupiter), was saying, 'What it is to be young, eh?', and my father said, 'What time did you finally get to bed, after last night, anyway, Marco—' and Eleanora, sitting back with her plump smooth knees crossed, tugged my hand gently so that we should exchange a woman's kiss on the cheek.

I took in the smell of Eleanora's skin, felt the brush of her hair on my nose; and it was done, for ever. We sat talking about some shoes her sister-in-law had sent from Milan. It was something I could never have imagined: Marco and I, as we really were, didn't exist here; there was no embarrassment. The Gattis, as always on Sunday mornings, were straight from eleven o'clock Mass at the Catholic cathedral, and smartly dressed.

As in most of these African places there was a shortage of white women in Katanga and my mother felt much happier to see me spending my time with the young married people than she would have been to see me taken up by the mercenaries who came in and out of E'ville that summer. 'They're experienced men,' she said – as opposed to boys and married men, 'and of course they're out for what they can get. They've got nothing to lose; next week they're in another province, or they've left the country. I don't blame them. I believe a girl has to know what the world's like, and if she is fool enough to get involved with that crowd, she must take the consequences.' She seemed to have forgotten that she had not wanted to leave me in Johannesburg in the company of Alan. 'She's got a nice boy at home, a decent boy who respects her. I'd far rather see her just enjoying herself generally, with you young couples, while we're here.' And there was always Per, the Swede, to even out the numbers; she knew he wasn't 'exactly Jillie's dream of love'. I suppose that made him safe, too. If I was no one's partner in our circle, I was a love object, handed round them all, to whom it was taken for granted that the homage of a flirtatious attitude was paid. Perhaps this was supposed to represent my compensation: if not the desired of any individual, then recognised as desirable by them all.

'Oh of course, you prefair to dance with Jeelie,' Mireille, one of the young Belgians, would say to her husband, pretending offence. He and I were quite an act, at the Au Relais, with our cha-cha. Then he would whisper to her in their own language, and she would giggle and punch his arm.

Marco and I were as famous a combination on the squash court as Mireille's husband and I were on the dance floor. This was the only place, if anyone had had the eyes for it, where our love-making showed. As the weeks went by and the love-making got better and better, our game got better and better. The response Marco taught me to the sound of spilling grain the rain made on the caravan roof held good between us on the squash court. Sometimes the wives and spectators broke into spontaneous applause; I was following Marco's sweat-oiled excited face, anticipating his muscular reactions in play as in bed. And when he had beaten me (narrowly) or we had beaten the other pair, he would hunch my shoulders together within his arm, laughing, praising me in Italian to the others, staggering about with me, and he would say to me in English, 'Aren't you a clever girl, eh?'; only he and I knew that that was what he said to me at other times. I loved that glinting flaw in his smile, now. It was Marco, like all the other things I knew about him: the girl cousin he had been in love with when he used to spend holidays with her family in the Abruzzi mountains; the way he would have planned Tshombe's road if he'd been in charge – 'But I like your father, you understand? – it's good to work with your father, you know?'; the baby cream from Italy he used for the prickly heat round his waist.

The innocence of the grown-ups fascinated me. They engaged in play-play, while I had given it up; I began to feel arrogant among them. It was pleasant. I felt arrogant – or rather tolerantly patronising – towards the faraway Alan, too. I said to Marco, 'I wonder what he'd do if he knew' – about me; the caravan with the dotted curtains, the happy watchman, the tips, the breath of the earth rising from the wetted dust. Marco said wisely that Alan would be terribly upset.

'And if Eleanora knew?'

Marco gave me his open, knowing, assured smile, at the same time putting the palm of his hand to my cheek in tender parenthesis. 'She wouldn't be pleased. But in the case of a man—' For a moment he was Eleanora, quite unconsciously he mimicked the sighing resignation of Eleanora, receiving the news (seated, as usual), aware all the time that men were like that.

Other people who were rumoured or known to have had lovers occupied my mind with a special interest. I chattered on the subject, '. . . when this girl's husband found out, he just walked out of the house without any money or anything and no one could find him for weeks,' and Marco took it up as one does what goes without saying: 'Well of course. If I think of Eleanora with someone – I mean – I would become mad.'

I went on with my second-hand story, enjoying the telling of all its twists and complications, and he laughed, following it with the affectionate attention with which he lit everything I said and did, and getting up to find the bottle of Chianti, wipe out a glass and fill it for himself. He always had wine in the caravan. I didn't drink any but I used to have the metallic taste of it in my mouth from his.

In the car that afternoon he had said maybe there'd be a nice surprise for me, and I remembered this and we lay and wrangled teasingly about it. The usual sort of thing: 'You're learning to be a real little nag, my darling, a little nag, eh?'

'I'm not going to let go until you tell me.'

'I think I'll have to give you a little smack on the bottom, eh, just like this, eh?'

The surprise was a plan. He and my father might be going to the Kasai to advise on some difficulties that had cropped up for a construction firm there. It should be quite easy for me to persuade my father that I'd like to accompany him, and then if Marco could manage to leave Eleanora behind, it would be almost as good as if he and I were to take a trip alone together.

'You will have your own room?' Marco asked.

I laughed. 'D'you think I'd be put in with Daddy?' Perhaps in Italy a girl wouldn't be allowed to have her own hotel room.

Now Marco was turning his attention to the next point: 'Eleanora gets sick from the car, anyway – she won't want to come on bad roads, and you can get stuck, God knows what. No, it's quite all right, I will tell her it's no pleasure for her.' At the prospect of being in each other's company for whole days and perhaps nights we couldn't stop smiling, chattering and kissing, not with passion but delight. My tongue was loosened as if I *had* been drinking wine.

* * *

Marco spoke good English.

The foreign turns of phrase he did have were familiar to me. He did not use the word 'mad' in the sense of angry. 'I would become mad': he meant exactly that, although the phrase was not one that we English-speaking people would use. I thought about it that night, alone, at home; and other nights. Out of his mind, he meant. If Eleanora slept with another man, Marco would be insane with jealousy. He said so to me because he was a really honest person, not like the other grown-ups – just as he said, 'I like your father, eh? I don't like some of the things he does with the road, but he is a good man, you know?' Marco was in love with me; I was his treasure, his joy, some beautiful words in Italian. It was true; he was very, very happy with me. I could see that. I did not know that people could be so happy; Alan did not know. I was sure that if I hadn't met Marco I should never have known. When we were in the caravan together I would watch him all the time, even when we were dozing I watched out of slit eyes the movement of his slim nostril with its tuft of black hair, as he breathed, and the curve of his sunburned ear through which capillary-patterned light showed. Oh Marco, Eleanora's husband, was beautiful as he slept. But he wasn't asleep. I liked to press my feet on his as if his were pedals and when I did this the corner of his mouth smiled and he said something with the flex of a muscle somewhere in his body. He even spoke aloud at times: my name. But I didn't know if he knew he had spoken it. Then he would lie with his eyes open a long time, but not looking at me, because he didn't need to: I was there. Then he would get up, light a cigarette, and say to me, 'I was in a dream . . . oh, I don't know . . . it's another world.'

It was a moment of awkwardness for me because I was entering the world from my childhood and could not conceive that, as adults did – as he did – I should ever need to find surcease and joy elsewhere, in another world. He escaped, with me. I entered, with him. The understanding of this I knew would come about for me as the transfiguration of the gold tooth from a flaw into a characteristic had come. I still did not know everything.

I saw Eleanora nearly every day. She was very fond of me; she was the sort of woman who, at home, would have kept attendant younger sisters round her to compensate for the children she did not have. I never felt guilty towards her. Yet, before, I should have thought how awful one would feel, taking the closeness and caresses that belonged, by law, to another woman. I was irritated at the stupidity of what Eleanora said; the stupidity of her not knowing. How idiotic that she should tell me that Marco had worked late on the site again last night, he was so conscientious, etc. – wasn't I with him, while she made her famous veal scaloppini and they got overcooked? And she was a nuisance to us. 'I'll have to go – I must take poor Eleanora to a film tonight. She hasn't been anywhere for weeks.' 'It's the last day for parcels to Italy, tomorrow – she likes me to pack them with her, the Christmas parcels, you know how Eleanora is about these things.' Then her aunt came out from Italy and there were lunches and dinners to which only Italian-speaking people were invited because the signora couldn't speak English. I remember going there one Sunday – sent by my mother with a contribution of her special ice cream. They were all sitting round in the heat on the veranda, the women in one group with the children crawling over them, and Marco with the men in another, his tie loose at the neck of his shirt (Eleanora had made him put on a suit), gesturing with a toothpick, talking and throwing cigar butts into Eleanora's flower-trough of snake cactus.

And yet that evening in the caravan he said again, 'Oh good God, I don't want to wake up . . . I was in a dream.' He had appeared out of the dark at our meeting-place, barefoot in espadrilles and tight thin jeans, like a beautiful fisherman.

I had never been to Europe. Marco said, 'I want to drive with you through Piemonte, and take you to the village where my father came from. We'll climb up to the walls from the church and when you get to the top – only then – I'll turn you round and you'll see Monte Bianco far away. You've heard nightingales, eh – never heard them? We'll listen to them in the pear orchard, it's my uncle's place, there.'

I was getting older every day. I said, 'What about Eleanora?' It was the nearest I could get to what I always wanted to ask him: 'Would you still become mad?'

Would you still become mad?

And now?

And now – two months, a week, six weeks later?

Now would you still become mad?

'Eleanora will spend some time in Pisa after we go back to Italy, with her mother and the aunts,' he was saying.

Yes, I knew why, too; knew from my mother that Eleanora was going to Pisa because there was an old family doctor there who was sure, despite everything the doctors in Milan and Rome had said, that poor Eleanora might still one day have a child.

I said, 'How would you feel if Alan came here?'

But Marco looked at me with such sensual confidence of understanding that we laughed.

I began to plan a love affair for Eleanora. I chose Per as victim not only because he was the only presentable unattached man in our circle, but also because I had the feeling that it might just be possible to attract her to a man younger than herself, whom she could mother. And Per, with no woman at all (except the pretty Congolese prostitutes good for an hour in the rain, I suppose) could consider himself lucky if he succeeded with Eleanora. I studied her afresh. Soft white gooseflesh above her stocking-tops, breasts that rose when she sighed – that sort of woman. But Eleanora did not even seem to understand that Per was being put in her way (at our house, at the Au Relais) and Per seemed equally unaware of or uninterested in his opportunities.

And so there was never any way to ask my question. Marco and I continued to lie making love in the caravan while the roof made buckling noises as it contracted after the heat of the day, and the rain. Tshombe fled and returned; there were soldiers in the square before the post office, and all sorts of difficulties arose over the building of the road. Marco was determined, excitable, harassed and energetic – he sprawled on the bed in the caravan at the end of the day like a runner who has just breasted the tape. My father was nervous and didn't know whether to finish the road. Eleanora was nervous and wanted to go back to Italy. We made love and when Marco opened his eyes to consciousness of the road, my father, Eleanora, he said, 'Oh for God's sake, *why* . . . it's like a dream . . .'

I became nervous too. I goaded my mother: 'The Gattis are a bore. That female *Buddha*.'

I developed a dread that Eleanora would come to me with her sighs and her soft-squeezing hand and say, 'It always happens with Marco, little Jillie, you mustn't worry. I know all about it.'

And Marco and I continued to lie together in that state of pleasure in which nothing exists but the two who make it. Neither roads, nor mercenary wars, nor marriage, nor the claims and suffering of other people entered that tender, sensual dream from which Marco, although so regretfully, always returned.

What I dreaded Eleanora might say to me was never said, either. Instead my mother told me one day in the tone of portentous emotion with which older women relive such things, that Eleanora, darling Eleanora, was expecting a child. After six years. Without having to go to Pisa to see the family doctor there. Yes, Eleanora had conceived during the rainy season in E'ville, while Marco and I made love every afternoon in the caravan, and the Congolese found themselves a girl for the duration of a shower.

It's years ago, now.

Poor Marco, sitting in Milan or Genoa at Sunday lunch, toothpick in his fingers, Eleanora's children crawling about, Eleanora's brothers and sisters and uncles and aunts around him. But I have never woken up from that dream. In the seven years I've been married I've had – how many lovers? Only I know. A lot – if you count the very brief holiday episodes as well.

It *is* another world, that dream, where no wind blows colder than the warm breath of two who are mouth to mouth.

A Soldier's Embrace

Town and Country Lovers

One

Dr Franz-Josef von Leinsdorf is a geologist absorbed in his work; wrapped up in it, as the saying goes – year after year the experience of this work enfolds him, swaddling him away from the landscapes, the cities and the people, wherever he lives: Peru, New Zealand, the United States. He's always been like that, his mother could confirm from their native Austria. There, even as a handsome small boy he presented only his profile to her: turned away to his bits of rock and stone. His few relaxations have not changed much since then. An occasional skiing trip, listening to music, reading poetry – Rainer Maria Rilke once stayed in his grandmother's hunting lodge in the forests of Styria and the boy was introduced to Rilke's poems while very young.

Layer upon layer, country after country, wherever his work takes him – and now he has been almost seven years in Africa. First the Côte d'Ivoire, and for the past five years, South Africa. The shortage of skilled manpower brought about his recruitment here. He has no interest in the politics of the countries he works in. His private preoccupation-within-the-preoccupation of his work has been research into underground watercourses, but the mining company that employs him in a senior though not executive capacity is interested only in mineral discovery. So he is much out in the field – which is the veld, here – seeking new gold, copper, platinum and uranium deposits. When he is at home – on this particular job, in this particular country, this city – he lives in a two-roomed flat in a suburban block with a landscaped garden, and does his shopping at a supermarket conveniently across the street. He is not married – yet. That is how his colleagues, and the typists and secretaries at the mining company's head office, would define his situation. Both men and women would describe him as a good-looking man, in a foreign way, with the lower half of the face dark and middle-aged (his mouth is thin and curving, and no matter how close-shaven his beard shows like fine shot embedded in the skin round mouth and chin) and the upper half contradictorily young, with deep-set eyes (some would say grey, some black), thick eyelashes and brows. A tangled gaze: through which concentration and gleaming thoughtfulness perhaps appear as fire and languor. It is this that the women in the office mean when they remark he's not unattractive. Although the gaze seems to promise, he has never invited any one of them to go out with him. There is the general assumption he probably has a girl who's been picked for him, he's bespoken by one of his own kind, back home in Europe where he comes from. Many of these well-educated Europeans have no intention of becoming permanent immigrants; neither the remnant of white colonial life nor idealistic involvement with Black Africa appeals to them.

One advantage, at least, of living in underdeveloped or half-developed countries is that flats are serviced. All Dr von Leinsdorf has to do for himself is buy his own supplies and cook an evening meal if he doesn't want to go to a restaurant. It is simply a matter of dropping in to the supermarket on his way from his car to his flat after work in the afternoon. He wheels a trolley up and down the shelves, and his simple needs are presented to him in the form of tins, packages, plastic-wrapped meat, cheeses, fruit and vegetables, tubes, bottles . . . At the cashiers' counters where customers must converge and queue there are racks of small items uncategorised, for last-minute purchase. Here, as the coloured girl cashier punches the adding machine, he picks up cigarettes and perhaps a packet of salted nuts or a bar of nougat. Or razor blades, when he remembers he's running short. One evening in winter he saw that the card-board display was empty of the brand of blades he preferred, and he drew the cashier's attention to this. These young coloured girls are usually pretty unhelpful, taking money and punching their machines in a manner that asserts with the time-serving obstinacy of the half-literate the limit of any responsibility towards customers, but this one ran an alert glance over the selection of razor blades, apologised that she was not allowed to leave her post, and said she would see that the stock was replenished 'next time'. A day or two later she recognised him, gravely, as he took his turn before her counter – 'I ahssed them, but it's out of stock. You can't get it. I did ahss about it.' He said this didn't matter. 'When it comes in, I can keep a few packets for you.' He thanked her.

He was away with the prospectors the whole of the next week. He arrived back in town just before nightfall on Friday, and was on his way from car to flat with his arms full of briefcase, suitcase and canvas bags when someone stopped him by standing timidly in his path. He was about to dodge round unseeingly on the crowded pavement but she spoke. 'We got the blades in now. I didn't see you in the shop this week, but I kept some for when you come. So . . .'

He recognised her. He had never seen her standing before, and she was wearing a coat. She was rather small and finely made, for one of them. The coat was skimpy but no big backside jutted. The cold brought an apricot-graining of warm colour to her cheekbones, beneath which a very small face was quite delicately hollowed, and the skin was smooth, the subdued satiny colour of certain yellow wood. That crepey hair, but worn drawn back flat and in a little knot pushed into one of the cheap wool chignons that (he recognised also) hung in the miscellany of small goods along with the razor blades, at the supermarket. He said thanks, he was in a hurry, he'd only just got back from a trip – shifting the burdens he carried, to demonstrate. 'Oh shame.' She acknowledged his load. 'But if you want I can run in and get it for you quickly. If you want.'

He saw at once it was perfectly clear that all the girl meant was that she would go back to the supermarket, buy the blades and bring the packet to him there where he stood, on the pavement. And it seemed that it was this certainty that made him say, in the kindly tone of assumption used for an obliging underling, 'I live just across there – Atlantis – that apartment building. Could you drop them by, for me – number seven hundred and eighteen, seventh floor—'

She had not before been inside one of these big flat buildings near where she worked. She lived a bus- and train-ride away to the west of the city, but this side of the black townships, in a township for people her tint. There was a pool with ferns, not plastic, and even a little waterfall pumped electrically over rocks, in the entrance of the building Atlantis; she didn't wait for the lift marked GOODS but took the one meant for whites and a white woman with one of those sausage-dogs on a lead got in with her but did not pay her any attention. The corridors leading to the flats were nicely glassed-in, not draughty.

He wondered if he should give her a twenty-cent piece for her trouble – ten cents would be right for a black; but she said, 'Oh no – please, here—' standing outside his open door and awkwardly pushing back at his hand the change from the money he'd given her for the razor blades. She was smiling, for the first time, in the dignity of refusing a tip. It was difficult to know how to treat these people, in this country; to know what they expected. In spite of her embarrassing refusal of the coin, she stood there, completely unassuming, fists thrust down the pockets of her cheap coat against the cold she'd come in from, rather pretty thin legs neatly aligned, knee to knee, ankle to ankle.

'Would you like a cup of coffee or something?'

He couldn't very well take her into his study-cum-living room and offer her a drink. She followed him to his kitchen, but at the sight of her pulling out the single chair to drink her cup of coffee at the kitchen table, he said, 'No – bring it in here—' and led the way into the big room where, among his books and his papers, his files of scientific correspondence (and the cigar boxes of stamps from the envelopes) his racks of records, his specimens of minerals and rocks, he lived alone.

It was no trouble to her; she saved him the trips to the supermarket and brought him his groceries two or three times a week. All he had to do was to leave a list and the key under the doormat, and she would come up in her lunch hour to collect them, returning to put his supplies in the flat after work. Sometimes he was home and sometimes not. He bought a box of chocolates and left it, with a note, for her to find; and that was acceptable, apparently, as a gratuity.

Her eyes went over everything in the flat although her body tried to conceal its sense of being out of place by remaining as still as possible, holding its contours in the chair offered her as a stranger's coat is set aside and remains exactly as left until the owner takes it up to go. 'You collect?'

'Well, these are specimens – connected with my work.'

'My brother used to collect. Miniatures. With brandy and whisky and that, in them. From all over. Different countries.'

The second time she watched him grinding coffee for the cup he had offered her she said, 'You always do that? Always when you make coffee?'

'But of course. Is it no good, for you? Do I make it too strong?'

'Oh it's just I'm not used to it. We buy it ready – you know, it's in a bottle, you just add a bit to the milk or water.'

He laughed, instructive: 'That's not coffee, that's a synthetic flavouring. In my country we drink only real coffee, fresh, from the beans – you smell how good it is as it's being ground?'

She was stopped by the caretaker and asked what she wanted in the building? Heavy with the bona fides of groceries clutched to her body, she said she was working at number 718, on the seventh floor. The caretaker did not tell her not to use the whites' lift; after all, she was not black; her family was very light-skinned.

There was the item 'grey button for trousers' on one of his shopping lists. She said as she unpacked the supermarket carrier 'Give me the pants, so long, then,' and sat on his sofa that was always gritty with fragments of pipe tobacco, sewing in and out through the four holes of the button with firm, fluent movements of the right hand, gestures supplying the articulacy missing from her talk. She had a little yokel's, peasant's (he thought of it) gap between her two front teeth when she smiled that he didn't much like, but, face ellipsed to three-quarter angle, eyes cast down in concentration with soft lips almost closed, this didn't matter.

He said, watching her sew, 'You're a good girl'; and touched her.

* * *

She remade the bed every late afternoon when they left it and she dressed again before she went home. After a week there was a day when late afternoon became evening, and they were still in the bed.

'Can't you stay the night?'

'My mother,' she said.

'Phone her. Make an excuse.' He was a foreigner. He had been in the country five years, but he didn't understand that people don't usually have telephones in their houses, where she lived. She got up to dress. He didn't want that tender body to go out in the night cold and kept hindering her with the interruption of his hands; saying nothing. Before she put on her coat, when the body had already disappeared, he spoke. 'But you must make some arrangement.'

'Oh my mother!' Her face opened to fear and vacancy he could not read.

He was not entirely convinced the woman would think of her daughter as some pure and unsullied virgin . . . 'Why?'

The girl said, 'S'e'll be scared. S'e'll be scared we get caught.'

'Don't tell her anything. Say I'm employing you.' In this country he was working in now there were generally rooms on the roofs of flat buildings for tenants' servants.

She said: 'That's what I told the caretaker.'

She ground fresh coffee beans every time he wanted a cup while he was working at night. She never attempted to cook anything until she had watched in silence while he did it the way he liked, and she learned to reproduce exactly the simple dishes he preferred. She handled his pieces of rock and stone, at first admiring the colours – 'It'd make a beautiful ring or a necklace, ay.' Then he showed her the striations, the formation of each piece, and explained what each was, and how, in the long life of the earth, it had been formed. He named the mineral it yielded, and what that was used for. He worked at his papers, writing, writing, every night, so it did not matter that they could not go out together to public places. On Sundays she got into his car in the basement garage and they drove to the country and picnicked away up in the Magaliesberg, where there was no one. He read or poked about among the rocks; they climbed together, to the mountain pools. He taught her to swim. She had never seen the sea. She squealed and shrieked in the water, showing the gap between her teeth, as – it crossed his mind – she must do when among her own people. Occasionally he had to go out to dinner at the houses of colleagues from the mining company; she sewed and listened to the radio in the flat and he found her in the bed, warm and already asleep, by the time he came in. He made his way into her body without speaking; she made him welcome without a word.

Once he put on evening dress for a dinner at his country's consulate; watching him brush one or two fallen hairs from the shoulders of the dark jacket that sat so well on him, she saw a huge room, all chandeliers and people dancing some dance from a costume film – stately, hand-to-hand. She supposed he was going to fetch, in her place in the car, a partner for the evening. They never kissed when either left the flat; he said, suddenly, kindly, pausing as he picked up cigarettes and keys, 'Don't be lonely.' And added, 'Wouldn't you like to visit your family sometimes, when I have to go out?'

He had told her he was going home to his mother in the forests and mountains of his country near the Italian border (he showed her on the map) after Christmas. She had not told him how her mother, not knowing there was any other variety, assumed he was a medical doctor, so she had talked to her about the doctor's children and the doctor's wife who was a very kind lady, glad to have someone who could help out in the surgery as well as the flat.

She remarked wonderingly on his ability to work until midnight or later, after a day at work. She was so tired when she came home from her cash register at the supermarket that once dinner was eaten she could scarcely keep awake. He explained in a way she could understand that while the work she did was repetitive, undemanding of any real response from her intelligence, requiring little mental or physical effort and therefore unrewarding, his work was his greatest interest, it taxed his mental capacities to their limit, exercised all his concentration, and rewarded him constantly as much with the excitement of a problem presented as with the satisfaction of a problem solved.

He said later, putting away his papers, speaking out of a silence: 'Have you done other kinds of work?'

She said, 'I was in a clothing factory before. Sportbeau shirts; you know? But the pay's better in the shop.'

Of course. Being a conscientious newspaper reader in every country he lived in, he was aware that it was only recently that the retail consumer trade in this one had been allowed to employ coloureds as shop assistants; even punching a cash register represented advancement. With the continuing shortage of semi-skilled whites a girl like this might be able to edge a little farther into the white-collar category. He began to teach her to type. He was aware that her English was poor, even though, as a foreigner, in his ears her pronunciation did not offend, nor categorise her as it would in those of someone of his education whose mother tongue was English. He corrected her grammatical mistakes but missed the less obvious ones because of his own sometimes exotic English usage – she continued to use the singular pronoun 'it' when what was required was the plural 'they'. Because he was a foreigner (although so clever, as she saw) she was less inhibited than she might have been by the words she knew she misspelled in her typing. While she sat at the typewriter she thought how one day she would type notes for him, as well as making coffee the way he liked it, and taking him inside her body without saying anything, and sitting (even if only through the empty streets of quiet Sundays) beside him in his car, like a wife.

On a summer night near Christmas – he had already bought and hidden a slightly showy but nevertheless good watch he thought she would like – there was a knocking at the door that brought her out of the bathroom and him to his feet, at his work-table. No one ever came to the flat at night; he had no friends intimate enough to drop in without warning. The summons was an imperious banging that did not pause and clearly would not stop until the door was opened.

She stood in the open bathroom doorway gazing at him across the passage into the living room; her bare feet and shoulders were free of a big bath-towel. She said nothing, did not even whisper. The flat seemed to shake with the strong unhurried blows.

He made as if to go to the door, at last, but now she ran and clutched him by both arms. She shook her head wildly; her lips drew back but her teeth were clenched, she didn't speak. She pulled him into the bedroom, snatched some clothes from the clean laundry laid out on the bed and got into the wall cupboard, thrusting the key at his hand. Although his arms and calves felt weakly cold he was horrified, distastefully embarrassed at the sight of her pressed back crouching there under his suits and coat; it was horrible and ridiculous. *Come out!* he whispered.

No!

Come out!

She hissed: *Where? Where can I go?*

Never mind! Get out of there!

He put out his hand to grasp her. At bay, she said with all the force of her terrible whisper, baring the gap in her teeth: *I'll throw myself out the window.*

She forced the key into his hand like the handle of a knife. He closed the door on her face and drove the key home in the lock, then dropped it among coins in his trouser pocket.

He unslotted the chain that was looped across the flat door. He turned the serrated knob of the Yale lock. The three policemen, two in plain clothes, stood there without impatience although they had been banging on the door for several minutes. The big dark one with an elaborate moustache held out in a hand wearing a plaited gilt ring some sort of identity card.

Dr von Leinsdorf said quietly, the blood coming strangely back to legs and arms, 'What is it?'

The sergeant told him they knew there was a coloured girl in the flat. They had had information; 'I been watching this flat three months, I know.'

'I am alone here.' Dr von Leinsdorf did not raise his voice.

'I know, I know who is here. Come—' And the sergeant and his two assistants went into the living room, the kitchen, the bathroom (the sergeant picked up a bottle of after-shave cologne, seemed to study the French label) and the bedroom. The assistants removed the clean laundry that was laid upon the bed and then turned back the bedding, carrying the sheets over to be examined by the sergeant under the lamp. They talked to one another in Afrikaans, which the Doctor did not understand.

The sergeant himself looked under the bed, and lifted the long curtains at the window. The wall cupboard was of the kind that has no knobs; he saw that it was locked and began to ask in Afrikaans, then politely changed to English, 'Give us the key.'

Dr von Leinsdorf said, 'I'm sorry, I left it at my office – I always lock and take my keys with me in the mornings.'

'It's no good, man, you better give me the key.'

He smiled a little, reasonably. 'It's on my office desk.'

The assistants produced a screwdriver and he watched while they inserted it where the cupboard doors met, gave it quick, firm but not forceful leverage. He heard the lock give.

She had been naked, it was true, when they knocked. But now she was wearing a long-sleeved T-shirt with an appliquéd butterfly motif on one breast, and a pair of jeans. Her feet were still bare; she had managed, by feel, in the dark, to get into some of the clothing she had snatched from the bed, but she had no shoes. She had perhaps been weeping behind the cupboard door (her cheeks looked stained) but now her face was sullen and she was breathing heavily, her diaphragm contracting and expanding exaggeratedly and her breasts pushing against the cloth. It made her appear angry; it might simply have been that she was half-suffocated in the cupboard and needed oxygen. She did not look at Dr von Leinsdorf. She would not reply to the sergeant's questions.

They were taken to the police station where they were at once separated and in turn led for examination by the district surgeon. The man's underwear was taken away and examined, as the sheets had been, for signs of his seed. When the girl was undressed, it was discovered that beneath her jeans she was wearing a pair of men's briefs with his name on the neatly sewn laundry tag; in her haste, she had taken the wrong garment to her hiding-place.

Now she cried, standing there before the district surgeon in a man's underwear.

He courteously pretended not to notice. He handed briefs, jeans and T-shirt round the door, and motioned her to lie on a white-sheeted high table where he placed her legs apart, resting in stirrups, and put into her where the other had made his way so warmly a cold hard instrument that expanded wider and wider. Her thighs and knees trembled uncontrollably while the doctor looked into her and touched her deep inside with more hard instruments, carrying wafers of gauze.

When she came out of the examining room back to the charge office, Dr von Leinsdorf was not there; they must have taken him somewhere else. She spent what was left of the night in a cell, as he must be doing; but early in the morning she was released and taken home to her mother's house in the coloured township by a white man who explained he was the clerk of the lawyer who had been engaged for her by Dr von Leinsdorf. Dr von Leinsdorf, the clerk said, had also been bailed out that morning. He did not say when, or if she would see him again.

A statement made by the girl to the police was handed in to court when she and the man appeared to meet charges of contravening the Immorality Act in a Johannesburg flat on the night of — December, 19—. *I lived with the white man in his flat. He had intercourse with me sometimes. He gave me tablets to take to prevent me becoming pregnant.*

Interviewed by the Sunday papers, the girl said, 'I'm sorry for the sadness brought to my mother.' She said she was one of nine children of a female laundry worker. She had left school in Standard Three because there was no money at home for gym clothes or a school blazer. She had worked as a machinist in a factory and a cashier in a supermarket. Dr von Leinsdorf taught her to type his notes.

Dr Franz-Josef von Leinsdorf, described as the grandson of a baroness, a cultured man engaged in international mineralogical research, said he accepted social distinctions between people but didn't think they should be legally imposed. 'Even in my own country it's difficult for a person from a higher class to marry one from a lower class.'

The two accused gave no evidence. They did not greet or speak to each other in court. The Defence argued that the sergeant's evidence that they had been living together as man and wife was hearsay. (The woman with the dachshund, the caretaker?) The magistrate acquitted them because the state failed to prove carnal intercourse had taken place on the night of — December, 19—.

The girl's mother was quoted, with photograph, in the Sunday papers: 'I won't let my daughter work as a servant for a white man again.'

Two

The farm children play together when they are small; but once the white children go away to school they soon don't play together any more, even in the holidays. Although most of the black children get some sort of schooling, they drop every year further behind the grades passed by the white children; the childish vocabulary, the child's exploration of the adventurous possibilities of dam, koppies, mealie lands and veld – there comes a time when the white children have surpassed these with the vocabulary of boarding school and the possibilities of inter-school sports matches and the kind of adventures seen at the cinema. This usefully coincides with the age of twelve or thirteen; so that by the time early adolescence is reached, the black children are making, along with the bodily changes common to all, an easy transition to adult forms of address, beginning to call their old playmates missus and baasie – little master.

The trouble was Paulus Eysendyck did not seem to realise that Thebedi was now simply one of the crowd of farm children down at the kraal, recognisable in his sisters' old clothes. The first Christmas holidays after he had gone to boarding school he brought home for Thebedi a painted box he had made in his woodwork class. He had to give it to her secretly because he had nothing for the other children at the kraal. And she gave him, before he went back to school, a bracelet she had made of thin brass wire and the grey-and-white beans of the castor-oil crop his father cultivated. (When they used to play together, she was the one who had taught Paulus how to make clay oxen for their toy spans.) There was a craze, even in the *platteland* towns like the one where he was at school, for boys to wear elephant-hair and other bracelets beside their watch-straps; his was admired, friends asked him to get similar ones for them. He said the natives made them on his father's farm and he would try.

When he was fifteen, six feet tall, and tramping round at school dances with the girls from the 'sister' school in the same town; when he had learnt how to tease and flirt and fondle quite intimately these girls who were the daughters of prosperous farmers like his father; when he had even met one who, at a wedding he had attended with his parents on a nearby farm, had let him do with her in a locked storeroom what people did when they made love – when he was as far from his childhood as all this, he still brought home from a shop in town a red plastic belt and gilt hoop earrings for the black girl, Thebedi. She told her father the missus had given these to her as a reward for some work she had done – it was true she sometimes was called to help out in the farmhouse. She told the girls in the kraal that she had a sweetheart nobody knew about, far away, away on another farm, and they giggled, and teased, and admired her. There was a boy in the kraal called Njabulo who said he wished he could have bought her a belt and earrings.

When the farmer's son was home for the holidays she wandered far from the kraal and her companions. He went for walks alone. They had not arranged this; it was an urge each followed independently. He knew it was she, from a long way off. She knew that his dog would not bark at her. Down at the dried-up river bed where five or six years ago the children had caught a leguaan one great day – a creature that combined ideally the size and ferocious aspect of the crocodile with the harmlessness of the lizard – they squatted side by side on the earth bank. He told her traveller's tales: about school, about the punishments at school, particularly, exaggerating both their nature and his indifference to them. He told her about the town of Middleburg, which she had never seen. She had nothing to tell but she prompted with many questions, like any good listener. While he talked he twisted and tugged at the roots of white stinkwood and Cape willow trees that looped out of the eroded earth around them. It had always been a good spot for children's games, down there hidden by the mesh of old, ant-eaten trees held in place by vigorous ones, wild asparagus bushing up between the trunks, and here and there prickly pear cactus sunken-skinned and bristly, like an old man's face, keeping alive sapless until the next rainy season. She punctured the dry hide of a prickly pear again and again with a sharp stick while she listened. She laughed a lot at what he told her, sometimes dropping her face on her knees, sharing amusement with the cool shady earth beneath her bare feet. She put on her pair of shoes – white sandals, thickly Blanco-ed against the farm dust – when he was on the farm, but these were taken off and laid aside, at the river bed.

One summer afternoon when there was water flowing there and it was very hot she waded in as they used to do when they were children, her dress bunched modestly and tucked into the legs of her pants. The schoolgirls he went swimming with at dams or pools on neighbouring farms wore bikinis but the sight of their dazzling bellies and thighs in the sunlight had never made him feel what he felt now, when the girl came up the bank and sat beside him, the drops of water beading off her dark legs the only points of light in the earth-smelling, deep shade. They were not afraid of one another, they had known one another always; he did with her what he had done that time in the storeroom at the wedding, and this time it was so lovely, so lovely, he was surprised . . . and she was surprised by it, too – he could see in her dark face that was part of the shade, with her big dark eyes, shiny as soft water, watching him attentively: as she had when they used to huddle over their teams of mud oxen, as she had when he told her about detention weekends at school.

They went to the river bed often through those summer holidays. They met just before the light went, as it does quite quickly, and each returned home with the dark – she to her mother's hut, he to the farmhouse – in time for the evening meal. He did not tell her about school or town any more. She did not ask questions any longer. He told her, each time, when they would meet again. Once or twice it was very early in the morning; the lowing of the cows being driven to graze came to them where they lay, dividing them with unspoken recognition of the sound read in their two pairs of eyes, opening so close to each other.

He was a popular boy at school. He was in the second, then the first soccer team. The head girl of the 'sister' school was said to have a crush on him; he didn't particularly like her, but there was a pretty blonde who put up her long hair into a kind of doughnut with a black ribbon round it, whom he took to see films when the schoolboys and girls had a free Saturday afternoon. He had been driving tractors and other farm vehicles since he was ten years old, and as soon as he was eighteen he got a driver's licence and in the holidays, this last year of his school life, he took neighbours' daughters to dances and to the drive-in cinema that had just opened twenty kilometres from the farm. His sisters were married, by then; his parents often left him in charge of the farm over the weekend while they visited the young wives and grandchildren.

When Thebedi saw the farmer and his wife drive away on a Saturday afternoon, the boot of their Mercedes filled with fresh-killed poultry and vegetables from the garden that it was part of her father's work to tend, she knew that she must come not to the river bed but up to the house. The house was an old one, thick-walled, dark against the heat. The kitchen was its lively thoroughfare, with servants, food supplies, begging cats and dogs, pots boiling over, washing being damped for ironing, and the big deep freeze the missus had ordered from town, bearing a crocheted mat and a vase of plastic irises. But the dining room with the bulging-legged heavy table was shut up in its rich, old smell of soup and tomato sauce. The sitting-room curtains were drawn and the TV set silent. The door of the parents' bedroom was locked and the empty rooms where the girls had slept had sheets of plastic spread over the beds. It was in one of these that she and the farmer's son stayed together whole nights – almost: she had to get away before the house servants, who knew her, came in at dawn. There was a risk someone would discover her or traces of her presence if he took her to his own bedroom, although she had looked into it many times when she was helping out in the house and knew well, there, the row of silver cups he had won at school.

When she was eighteen and the farmer's son nineteen and working with his father on the farm before entering a veterinary college, the young man Njabulo asked her father for her. Njabulo's parents met with hers and the money he was to pay in place of the cows it is customary to give a prospective bride's parents was settled upon. He had no cows to offer; he was a labourer on the Eysendyck farm, like her father. A bright youngster; old Eysendyck had taught him bricklaying and was using him for odd jobs in construction, around the place. She did not tell the farmer's son that her parents had arranged for her to marry. She did not tell him, either, before he left for his first term at the veterinary college, that she thought she was going to have a baby. Two months after her marriage to Njabulo, she gave birth to a daughter. There was no disgrace in that; among her people it is customary for a young man to make sure, before marriage, that the chosen girl is not barren, and Njabulo had made love to her then. But the infant was very light and did not quickly grow darker as most African babies do. Already at birth there was on its head a quantity of straight, fine floss, like that which carries the seeds of certain weeds in the veld. The unfocused eyes it opened were grey flecked with yellow. Njabulo was the matt, opaque coffee-grounds colour that has always been called black; the colour of Thebedi's legs on which beaded water looked oyster-shell blue, the same colour as Thebedi's face, where the black eyes, with their interested gaze and clear whites, were so dominant.

Njabulo made no complaint. Out of his farm labourer's earnings he bought from the Indian store a cellophane-windowed pack containing a pink plastic bath, six napkins, a card of safety pins, a knitted jacket, cap and bootees, a dress, and a tin of Johnson's Baby Powder, for Thebedi's baby.

When it was two weeks old Paulus Eysendyck arrived home from the veterinary college for the holidays. He drank a glass of fresh, still-warm milk in the childhood familiarity of his mother's kitchen and heard her discussing with the old house-servant where they could get a reliable substitute to help out now that the girl Thebedi had had a baby. For the first time since he was a small boy he came right into the kraal. It was eleven o'clock in the morning. The men were at work in the lands. He looked about him, urgently; the women turned away, each not wanting to be the one approached to point out where Thebedi lived. Thebedi appeared, coming slowly from the hut Njabulo had built in white man's style, with a tin chimney and a proper window with glass panes set in straight as walls made of unfired bricks would allow. She greeted him with hands brought together and a token movement representing the respectful bob with which she was accustomed to acknowledge she was in the presence of his father or mother. He lowered his head under the doorway of her home and went in. He said, 'I want to see. Show me.'

She had taken the bundle off her back before she came out into the light to face him. She moved between the iron bedstead made up with Njabulo's checked blankets and the small wooden table where the pink plastic bath stood among food and kitchen pots, and picked up the bundle from the snugly blanketed grocer's box where it lay. The infant was asleep; she revealed the closed, pale, plump tiny face, with a bubble of spit at the corner of the mouth, the spidery pink hands stirring. She took off the woollen cap and the straight fine hair flew up after it in static electricity, showing gilded strands here and there. He said nothing. She was watching him as she had done when they were little, and the gang of children had trodden down a crop in their games or transgressed in some other way for which he, as the farmer's son, the white one among them, must intercede with the farmer. She disturbed the sleeping face by scratching or tickling gently at a cheek with one finger, and slowly the eyes opened, saw nothing, were still asleep, and then, awake, no longer narrowed, looked out at them, grey with yellowish flecks, his own hazel eyes.

He struggled for a moment with a grimace of tears, anger and self-pity. She could not put out her hand to him. He said, 'You haven't been near the house with it?'

She shook her head.

'Never?'

Again she shook her head.

'Don't take it out. Stay inside. Can't you take it away somewhere. You must give it to someone—'

She moved to the door with him.

He said, 'I'll see what I will do. I don't know.' And then he said: 'I feel like killing myself.'

Her eyes began to glow, to thicken with tears. For a moment there was the feeling between them that used to come when they were alone down at the river bed.

He walked out.

Two days later, when his mother and father had left the farm for the day, he appeared again. The women were away on the lands, weeding, as they were employed to do as casual labour in summer; only the very old remained, propped up on the ground outside the huts in the flies and the sun. Thebedi did not ask him in. The child had not been well; it had diarrhoea. He asked where its food was. She said, 'The milk comes from me.' He went into Njabulo's house, where the child lay; she did not follow but stayed outside the door and watched without seeing an old crone who had lost her mind, talking to herself, talking to the fowls who ignored her.

She thought she heard small grunts from the hut, the kind of infant grunt that indicates a full stomach, a deep sleep. After a time, long or short she did not know, he came out and walked away with plodding stride (his father's gait) out of sight, towards his father's house.

The baby was not fed during the night and although she kept telling Njabulo it was sleeping, he saw for himself in the morning that it was dead. He comforted her with words and caresses. She did not cry but simply sat, staring at the door. Her hands were cold as dead chickens' feet to his touch.

Njabulo buried the little baby where farm workers were buried, in the place in the veld the farmer had given them. Some of the mounds had been left to weather away unmarked, others were covered with stones and a few had fallen wooden crosses. He was going to make a cross but before it was finished the police came and dug up the grave and took away the dead baby: someone – one of the other labourers? their women? – had reported that the baby was almost white, that, strong and healthy, it had died suddenly after a visit by the farmer's son. Pathological tests on the infant corpse showed intestinal damage not always consistent with death by natural causes.

Thebedi went for the first time to the country town where Paulus had been to school, to give evidence at the preparatory examination into the charge of murder brought against him. She cried hysterically in the witness box, saying yes, yes (the gilt hoop earrings swung in her ears), she saw the accused pouring liquid into the baby's mouth. She said he had threatened to shoot her if she told anyone.

More than a year went by before, in that same town, the case was brought to trial. She came to court with a newborn baby on her back. She wore gilt hoop earrings; she was calm; she said she had not seen what the white man did in the house.

Paulus Eysendyck said he had visited the hut but had not poisoned the child.

The Defence did not contest that there had been a love relationship between the accused and the girl, or that intercourse had taken place, but submitted there was no proof that the child was the accused's.

The judge told the accused there was strong suspicion against him but not enough proof that he had committed the crime. The court could not accept the girl's evidence because it was clear she had committed perjury either at this trial or at the preparatory examination. There was the suggestion in the mind of the court that she might be an accomplice in the crime; but, again, insufficient proof.

The judge commended the honourable behaviour of the husband (sitting in court in a brown-and-yellow-quartered golf cap bought for Sundays) who had not rejected his wife and had 'even provided clothes for the unfortunate infant out of his slender means'.

The verdict on the accused was 'not guilty'.

The young white man refused to accept the congratulations of press and public and left the court with his mother's raincoat shielding his face from photographers. His father said to the press, 'I will try and carry on as best I can to hold up my head in the district.'

Interviewed by the Sunday papers, who spelled her name in a variety of ways, the black girl, speaking in her own language, was quoted beneath her photograph: 'It was a thing of our childhood, we don't see each other any more.'

A Soldier's Embrace

The day the ceasefire was signed she was caught in a crowd. Peasant boys from Europe who had made up the colonial army and freedom fighters whose column had marched into town were staggering about together outside the barracks, not three blocks from her house in whose rooms, for ten years, she had heard the blurred parade-ground bellow of colonial troops being trained to kill and be killed.

The men weren't drunk. They linked and swayed across the street; because all that had come to a stop, everything *had* to come to a stop: they surrounded cars, bicycles, vans, nannies with children, women with loaves of bread or basins of mangoes on their heads, a road gang with picks and shovels, a Coca-Cola truck, an old man with a barrow who bought bottles and bones. They were grinning and laughing in amazement. That it could be: there they were, bumping into each other's bodies in joy, looking into each other's rough faces, all eyes crescent-shaped, brimming greeting. The words were in languages not mutually comprehensible, but the cries were new, a whooping and crowing all understood. She was bumped and jostled and she let go, stopped trying to move in any self-determined direction. There were two soldiers in front of her, blocking her off by their clumsy embrace (how do you do it, how do you do what you've never done before) and the embrace opened like a door and took her in – a pink hand with bitten nails grasping her right arm, a black hand with a big-dialled watch and thong bracelet pulling at her left elbow. Their three heads collided gaily, musk of sweat and tang of strong sweet soap clapped a mask to her nose and mouth. They all gasped with delicious shock. They were saying things to each other. She put up an arm round each neck, the rough pile of an army haircut on one side, the soft negro hair on the other, and kissed them both on the cheek. The embrace broke. The crowd wove her away behind backs, arms, jogging heads; she was returned to and took up the will of her direction again – she was walking home from the post office, where she had just sent a telegram to relatives abroad: ALL CALM DON'T WORRY.

The lawyer came back early from his offices because the courts were not sitting although the official celebration holiday was not until next day. He described to his wife the rally before the Town Hall, which he had watched from the office-building balcony. One of the guerrilla leaders (not the most important; he on whose head the biggest price had been laid would not venture so soon and deep into the territory so newly won) had spoken for two hours from the balcony of the Town Hall. 'Brilliant. Their jaws dropped. Brilliant. They've never heard anything on that level: precise, reasoned – none of them would ever have believed it possible, out of the bush. You should have seen de Poorteer's face. He'd like to be able to get up and open his mouth like that. And be listened to like that . . .' The Governor's handicap did not even bring the sympathy accorded to a stammer; he paused and gulped between words. The blacks had always used a portmanteau name for him that meant the-crane-who-is-trying-to-swallow-the-bullfrog.

One of the members of the black underground organisation that could now come out in brass-band support of the freedom fighters had recognised the lawyer across from the official balcony and given him the freedom fighters' salute. The lawyer joked about it, miming, full of pride. 'You should have been there – should have seen him, up there in the official party. I told you – really – you ought to have come to town with me this morning.'

'And what did you do?' She wanted to assemble all details.

'Oh I gave the salute in return, chaps in the street saluted *me* . . . everybody was doing it. *It was marvellous*. And the police standing by; just to think, last month – only last week – you'd have been arrested.'

'Like thumbing your nose at them,' she said, smiling.

'Did anything go on around here?'

'Muchanga was afraid to go out all day. He wouldn't even run up to the post office for me!' Their servant had come to them many years ago, from service in the house of her father, a colonial official in the Treasury.

'But there was no excitement?'

She told him: 'The soldiers and some freedom fighters mingled outside the barracks. I got caught for a minute or two. They were dancing about; you couldn't get through. All very good-natured. – Oh, I sent the cable.'

An accolade, one side a white cheek, the other a black. The white one she kissed on the left cheek, the black one on the right cheek, as if these were two sides of one face.

That vision, version, was like a poster; the sort of thing that was soon peeling off dirty shopfronts and bus shelters while the months of wrangling talks preliminary to the takeover by the black government went by.

To begin with, the cheek was not white but pale or rather sallow, the poor boy's pallor of winter in Europe (that draft must have only just arrived and not yet seen service) with homesick pimples sliced off by the discipline of an army razor. And the cheek was not black but opaque peat-dark, waxed with sweat round the plump contours of the nostril. As if she could return to the moment again, she saw what she had not consciously noted: there had been a narrow pink strip in the darkness near the ear, the sort of tender stripe of healed flesh revealed when a scab is nicked off a little before it is ripe. The scab must have come away that morning: the young man picked at it in the troop carrier or truck (whatever it was the freedom fighters had; the colony had been told for years that they were supplied by the Chinese and Russians indiscriminately) on the way to enter the capital in triumph.

According to newspaper reports, the day would have ended for the two young soldiers in drunkenness and whoring. She was, apparently, not yet too old to belong to the soldier's embrace of all that a landmine in the bush might have exploded for ever. That was one version of the incident. Another: the opportunity taken by a woman not young enough to be clasped in the arms of the one who (same newspaper, while the war was on, expressing the fears of the colonists for their women) would be expected to rape her.

She considered this version.

She had not kissed on the mouth, she had not sought anonymous lips and tongues in the licence of festival. Yet she had kissed. Watching herself again, she knew that. She had – God knows why – kissed them on either cheek, his left, his right. It was deliberate, if a swift impulse: she had distinctly made the move.

She did not tell what happened not because her husband would suspect licence in her, but because he would see her – born and brought up in the country as the daughter of an enlightened white colonial official, married to a white liberal lawyer well known for his defence of blacks in political trials – as giving free expression to liberal principles.

She had not told, she did not know what had happened.

She thought of a time long ago when a school camp had gone to the sea and immediately on arrival everyone had run down to the beach from the train, tripping and tearing over sand dunes of wild fig, aghast with ecstatic shock at the meeting with the water.

De Poorteer was recalled and the lawyer remarked to one of their black friends, 'The crane has choked on the bullfrog. I hear that's what they're saying in the Quarter.'

The priest who came from the black slum that had always been known simply by that anonymous term did not respond with any sort of glee. His reserve implied it was easy to celebrate; there were people who 'shouted freedom too loud all of a sudden'.

The lawyer and his wife understood: Father Mulumbua was one who had shouted freedom when it was dangerous to do so, and gone to prison several times for it, while certain people, now on the Interim Council set up to run the country until the new government took over, had kept silent. He named a few, but reluctantly. Enough to confirm their own suspicions – men who perhaps had made some deal with the colonial power to place its interests first, no matter what sort of government might emerge from the new constitution? Yet when the couple plunged into discussion their friend left them talking to each other while he drank his beer and gazed, frowning as if at a headache or because the sunset light hurt his eyes behind his spectacles, round her huge-leaved tropical plants that bowered the terrace in cool humidity.

They had always been rather proud of their friendship with him, this man in a cassock who wore a clenched fist carved of local ebony as well as a silver cross round his neck. His black face was habitually stern – a high seriousness balanced by sudden splurting laughter when they used to tease him over the fist – but never inattentively ill at ease.

'What was the matter?' She answered herself; 'I had the feeling he didn't want to come here.' She was using a paper handkerchief dipped in gin to wipe greenfly off the back of a pale new leaf that had shaken itself from its folds like a cut-out paper lantern.

'Good lord, he's been here hundreds of times.'

'Before, yes.'

What things were they saying?

With the shouting in the street and the swaying of the crowd, the sweet powerful presence that confused the senses so that sound, sight, stink (sweat, cheap soap) ran into one tremendous sensation, she could not make out words that came so easily.

Not even what she herself must have said.

A few wealthy white men who had been boastful in their support of the colonial war and knew they would be marked down by the blacks as arch exploiters, left at once. Good riddance, as the lawyer and his wife remarked. Many ordinary white people who had lived contentedly, without questioning its actions, under the colonial government, now expressed an enthusiastic intention to help build a nation, as the newspapers put it. The lawyer's wife's neighbourhood butcher was one. 'I don't mind blacks.' He was expansive with her, in his shop that he had occupied for twelve years on a licence available only to white people. 'Makes no difference to me who you are so long as you're honest.' Next to a chart showing a beast mapped according to the cuts of meat it provided, he had hung a picture of the most important leader of the freedom fighters, expected to be first President. People like the butcher turned out with their babies clutching pennants when the leader drove through the town from the airport.

There were incidents (newspaper euphemism again) in the Quarter. It was to be expected. Political factions, tribally based, who had not fought the war, wanted to share power with the freedom fighters' party. Muchanga no longer went down to the Quarter on his day off. His friends came to see him and sat privately on their hunkers near the garden compost heap. The ugly mansions of the rich who had fled stood empty on the bluff above the sea, but it was said they would make money out of them yet – they would be bought as ambassadorial residences when independence came, and with it many black and yellow diplomats. Zealots who claimed they belonged to the party burned shops and houses of the poorer whites who lived, as the lawyer said, 'in the inevitable echelon of colonial society', closest to the Quarter. A house in the lawyer's street was noticed by his wife to be accommodating what was certainly one of those families, in the outhouses; green nylon curtains had appeared at the garage window, she reported. The suburb was pleasantly overgrown and well-to-do; no one rich, just white professional people and professors from the university. The barracks was empty now, except for an old man with a stump and a police uniform stripped of insignia, a friend of Muchanga, it turned out, who sat on a beer crate at the gates. He had lost his job as night watchman when one of the rich people went away, and was glad to have work.

The street had been perfectly quiet; except for that first day.

* * *

The fingernails she sometimes still saw clearly were bitten down until embedded in a thin line of dirt all round, in the pink blunt fingers. The thumb and thick fingertips were turned back coarsely even while grasping her. Such hands had never been allowed to take possession. They were permanently raw, so young, from unloading coal, digging potatoes from the frozen northern hemisphere, washing hotel dishes. He had not been killed, and now that day of the ceasefire was over he would be delivered back across the sea to the docks, the stony farm, the scullery of the grand hotel. He would have to do anything he could get. There was unemployment in Europe where he had returned, the army didn't need all the young men any more.

A great friend of the lawyer and his wife, Chipande, was coming home from exile. They heard over the radio he was expected, accompanying the future President as confidential secretary, and they waited to hear from him.

The lawyer put up his feet on the empty chair where the priest had sat, shifting it to a comfortable position by hooking his toes, free in sandals, through the slats. 'Imagine, Chipande!' Chipande had been almost a protégé – but they didn't like the term, it smacked of patronage. Tall, cocky, casual Chipande, a boy from the slummiest part of the Quarter, was recommended by the White Fathers' Mission (was it by Father Mulumbua himself? – the lawyer thought so, his wife was not sure they remembered correctly). A bright kid who wanted to be articled to a lawyer. That was asking a lot, in those days – nine years ago. He never finished his apprenticeship because while he and his employer were soon close friends, and the kid picked up political theories from the books in the house he made free of, he became so involved in politics that he had to skip the country one jump ahead of a detention order signed by the crane-who-was-trying-to-swallow-the-bullfrog.

After two weeks, the lawyer phoned the offices the guerrilla-movement-become-party had set up openly in the town but apparently Chipande had an office in the former colonial secretariat. There he had a secretary of his own; he wasn't easy to reach.

The lawyer left a message. The lawyer and his wife saw from the newspaper pictures he hadn't changed much: he had a beard and had adopted the Muslim cap favoured by political circles in exile on the East Coast.

He did come to the house eventually. He had the distracted, insistent friendliness of one who has no time to re-establish intimacy; it must be taken as read. And it must not be displayed. When he remarked on a shortage of accommodation for exiles now become officials, and the lawyer said the house was far too big for two people, he was welcome to move in and regard a self-contained part of it as his private living quarters, he did not answer but went on talking generalities.

The lawyer's wife mentioned Father Mulumbua, whom they had not seen since just after the ceasefire. The lawyer added, 'There's obviously some sort of big struggle going on, he's fighting for his political life there in the Quarter.'

'Again,' she said, drawing them into a reminder of what had only just become their past.

But Chipande was restlessly following with his gaze the movements of old Muchanga, dragging the hose from plant to plant, careless of the spray; 'You remember who this is, Muchanga?' she had said when the visitor arrived, yet although the old man had given, in their own language, the sort of respectful greeting even an elder gives a young man whose clothes and bearing denote rank and authority, he was not in any way overwhelmed nor enthusiastic – perhaps he secretly supported one of the rival factions?

The lawyer spoke of the latest whites to leave the country – people who had got themselves quickly involved in the sort of currency swindle that draws more outrage than any other kind of crime, in a new state fearing the flight of capital: 'Let them go, let them go. Good riddance.' And he turned to talk of other things – there were so many more important questions to occupy the attention of the three old friends.

But Chipande couldn't stay. Chipande could not stay for supper; his beautiful long velvety black hands with their pale lining (as she thought of the palms) hung impatiently between his knees while he sat forward in the chair, explaining, adamant against persuasion. He should not have been there, even now; he had official business waiting, sometimes he drafted correspondence until one or two in the morning. The lawyer remarked how there hadn't been a proper chance to talk; he wanted to discuss those fellows in the Interim Council Mulumbua was so warily distrustful of – what did Chipande know?

Chipande, already on his feet, said something dismissing and very slightly disparaging, not about the Council members but of Mulumbua – a reference to his connection with the Jesuit missionaries as an influence that 'comes through'. 'But I must make a note to see him sometime.'

It seemed that even black men who presented a threat to the party could be discussed only among black men themselves, now. Chipande put an arm round each of his friends as for the brief official moment of a photograph, left them; he who used to sprawl on the couch arguing half the night before dossing down in the lawyer's pyjamas. 'As soon as I'm settled I'll contact you. You'll be around, ay?'

'Oh we'll be around.' The lawyer laughed, referring, for his part, to those who were no longer. 'Glad to see you're not driving a Mercedes!' he called with reassured affection at the sight of Chipande getting into a modest car. How many times, in the old days, had they agreed on the necessity for African leaders to live simply when they came to power!

On the terrace to which he turned back, Muchanga was doing something extraordinary – wetting a dirty rag with Gilbey's. It was supposed to be his day off, anyway; why was he messing about with the plants when one wanted peace to talk undisturbed?

'Is those thing again, those thing is killing the leaves.'

'For heaven's sake, he could use methylated for that! Any kind of alcohol will do! Why don't you get him some?'

There were shortages of one kind and another in the country, and gin happened to be something in short supply.

Whatever the hand had done in the bush had not coarsened it. It, too, was suede-black, and elegant. The pale lining was hidden against her own skin where the hand grasped her left elbow. Strangely, black does not show toil – she remarked this as one remarks the quality of a fabric. The hand was not as long but as distinguished by beauty as Chipande's. The watch a fine piece of equipment for a fighter. There was something next to it, in fact looped over the strap by the angle of the wrist as the hand grasped. A bit of thong with a few beads knotted where it was joined as a bracelet. Or amulet. Their babies wore such things; often their first and only garment. Grandmothers or mothers attached it as protection. It had worked; he was alive at ceasefire. Some had been too deep in the bush to know, and had been killed after the fighting was over. He had pumped his head wildly and laughingly at whatever it was she – they – had been babbling.

The lawyer had more free time than he'd ever remembered. So many of his clients had left; he was deputed to collect their rents and pay their taxes for them, in the hope that their property wasn't going to be confiscated – there had been alarmist rumours among such people since the day of the ceasefire. But without the rich whites there was little litigation over possessions, whether in the form of the children of dissolved marriages or the houses and cars claimed by divorced wives. The Africans had their own ways of resolving such redistribution of goods. And a gathering of elders under a tree was sufficient to settle a dispute over boundaries or argue for and against the guilt of a woman accused of adultery. He had had a message, in a roundabout way, that he might be asked to be consultant on constitutional law to the party, but nothing seemed to come of it. He took home with him the proposals for the draft constitution he had managed to get hold of. He spent whole afternoons in his study making notes for counter- or improved proposals he thought he would send to Chipande or one of the other people he knew in high positions: every time he glanced up, there through his open windows was Muchanga's little company at the bottom of the garden. Once, when he saw they had straggled off, he wandered down himself to clear his head (he got drowsy, as he never did when he used to work twelve hours a day at the office). They ate dried shrimps, from the market: that's what they were doing! The ground was full of bitten-off heads and black eyes on stalks.

His wife smiled. 'They bring them. Muchanga won't go near the market since the riot.'

'It's ridiculous. Who's going to harm him?'

There was even a suggestion that the lawyer might apply for a professorship at the university. The chair of the Faculty of Law was vacant, since the students had demanded the expulsion of certain professors engaged during the colonial regime – in particular of the fuddy-duddy (good riddance) who had gathered dust in the Law chair, and the quite decent young man (pity about him) who had had Political Science. But what professor of Political Science could expect to survive both a colonial regime and the revolutionary regime that defeated it? The lawyer and his wife decided that since he might still be appointed in some consultative capacity to the new government it would be better to keep out of the university context, where the students were shouting for Africanisation, and even an appointee with his credentials as a fighter of legal battles for blacks against the colonial regime in the past might not escape their ire.

Newspapers sent by friends from over the border gave statistics for the number of what they termed 'refugees' who were entering the neighbouring country. The papers from outside also featured sensationally the inevitable mistakes and misunderstandings, in a new administration, that led to several foreign businessmen being held for investigation by the new regime. For the last fifteen years of colonial rule, Gulf had been drilling for oil in the territory, and just as inevitably it was certain that all sorts of questionable people, from the point of view of the regime's determination not to be exploited preferentially, below the open market for the highest bidder in ideological as well as economic terms, would try to gain concessions.

His wife said, 'The butcher's gone.'

He was home, reading at his desk; he could spend the day more usefully there than at the office, most of the time. She had left after breakfast with her fisherman's basket that she liked to use for shopping, she wasn't away twenty minutes. 'You mean the shop's closed?' There was nothing in the basket. She must have turned and come straight home.

'Gone. It's empty. He's cleared out over the weekend.'

She sat down suddenly on the edge of the desk; and after a moment of silence, both laughed shortly, a strange, secret, complicit laugh.

'Why, do you think?'

'Can't say. He certainly charged, if you wanted a decent cut. But meat's so hard to get, now; I thought it was worth it – justified.'

The lawyer raised his eyebrows and pulled down his mouth: 'Exactly.' They understood; the man probably knew he was marked to run into trouble for profiteering – he must have been paying through the nose for his supplies on the black market, anyway, didn't have much choice.

Shops were being looted by the unemployed and loafers (there had always been a lot of unemployed hanging around for the pickings of the town) who felt the new regime should entitle them to take what they dared not before. Radio and television shops were the most favoured objective for gangs who adopted the freedom fighters' slogans. Transistor radios were the portable luxuries of street life; the new regime issued solemn warnings, over those same radios, that looting and violence would be firmly dealt with but it was difficult for the police to be everywhere at once. Sometimes their actions became street battles, since the struggle with the looters changed character as supporters of the party's rival political factions joined in with the thieves against the police. It was necessary to be ready to reverse direction, quickly turning down a side street in detour if one encountered such disturbances while driving around town. There were bodies sometimes; both husband and wife had been fortunate enough not to see any close up, so far. A company of the freedom fighters' army was brought down from the north and installed in the barracks to supplement the police force; they patrolled the Quarter, mainly. Muchanga's friend kept his job as gatekeeper although there were armed sentries on guard: the lawyer's wife found that a light touch to mention in letters to relatives in Europe.

'Where'll you go now?'

She slid off the desk and picked up her basket. 'Supermarket, I suppose. Or turn vegetarian.' He knew that she left the room quickly, smiling, because she didn't want him to suggest Muchanga ought to be sent to look for fish in the markets along the wharf in the Quarter. Muchanga was being allowed to indulge in all manner of eccentric refusals; for no reason, unless out of some curious sentiment about her father?

She avoided walking past the barracks because of the machine guns the young sentries had in place of rifles. Rifles pointed into the air but machine guns pointed to the street at the level of different parts of people's bodies, short and tall, the backsides of babies slung on mothers' backs, the round heads of children, her fisherman's basket – she knew she was getting like the others: what she felt was afraid. She wondered what the butcher and his wife had said to each other. Because he was at least one whom she had known. He had sold the meat she had bought that these women and their babies passing her in the street didn't have the money to buy.

It was something quite unexpected and outside their own efforts that decided it. A friend over the border telephoned and offered a place in a lawyers' firm of highest repute there, and some prestige in the world at large, since the team had defended individuals fighting for freedom of the press and militant churchmen upholding freedom of conscience on political issues. A telephone call; as simple as that. The friend said (and the lawyer did not repeat this even to his wife) they would be proud to have a man of his courage and convictions in the firm. He could be satisfied he would be able to uphold the liberal principles everyone knew he had always stood for; there were many whites, in that country still ruled by a white minority, who deplored the injustices under which their black population suffered, etc., and believed you couldn't ignore the need for peaceful change, etc.

His offices presented no problem; something called Africa Seabeds (Formosan Chinese who had gained a concession to ship seaweed and dried shrimps in exchange for rice) took over the lease and the typists. The senior clerks and the current articled clerk (the lawyer had always given a chance to young blacks, long before other people had come round to it – it wasn't only the secretary to the President who owed his start to him) he managed to get employed by the new Trades Union Council; he still knew a few blacks who remembered the times he had acted for black workers in disputes with the colonial government. The house would just have to stand empty, for the time being. It wasn't imposing enough to attract an embassy but maybe it would do for a Chargé d'Affaires – it was left in the hands of a half-caste letting agent who was likely to stay put: only whites were allowed in, at the country over the border. Getting money out was going to be much more difficult than disposing of the house. The lawyer would have to keep coming back, so long as this remained practicable, hoping to find a loophole in exchange control regulations.

She was deputed to engage the movers. In their innocence, they had thought it as easy as that! Every large vehicle, let alone a pantechnicon, was commandeered for months ahead. She had no choice but to grease a palm, although it went against her principles, it was condoning a practice they believed a young black state must stamp out before corruption took hold. He would take his entire legal library, for a start; that was the most important possession, to him. Neither was particularly attached to furniture. She did not know what there was she felt she really could not do without. Except the plants. And that was out of the question. She could not even mention it. She did not want to leave her towering plants, mostly natives of South America and not Africa, she supposed, whose aerial tubes pushed along the terrace brick erect tips extending hourly in the growth of the rainy season, whose great leaves turned shields to the spatter of Muchanga's hose glancing off in a shower of harmless arrows, whose two-hand-span trunks were smooth and grooved in one sculptural sweep down their length, or carved by the drop of each dead leaf-stem with concave medallions marking the place and building a pattern at once bold and exquisite. Such things would not travel; they were too big to give away.

The evening she was beginning to pack the books, the telephone rang in the study. Chipande – and he called her by her name, urgently, commandingly – 'What is this all about? Is it true, what I hear? Let me just talk to him—'

'Our friend,' she said, making a long arm, receiver at the end of it, towards her husband.

'But you can't leave!' Chipande shouted down the phone. '*You* can't go! I'm coming round. *Now.*'

She went on packing the legal books while Chipande and her husband were shut up together in the living room.

'He cried. You know, he actually cried.' Her husband stood in the doorway, alone.

'I know – that's what I've always liked so much about them, whatever they do. They feel.'

The lawyer made a face: there it is, it happened; hard to believe.

'Rushing in here, after nearly a year! I said, but we haven't seen you, all this time . . . he took no notice. Suddenly he starts pressing me to take the university job, raising all sorts of objections, why not this . . . that. And then he really wept, for a moment.'

They got on with packing books like builder and mate deftly handling and catching bricks.

And the morning they were to leave it was all done; twenty-one years of life in that house gone quite easily into one pantechnicon. They were quiet with each other, perhaps out of apprehension of the tedious search of their possessions that would take place at the border; it was said that if you struck over-conscientious or officious freedom fighter patrols they would even make you unload a piano, a refrigerator or washing machine. She had bought Muchanga a hawker's licence, a hand-cart, and stocks of small commodities. Now that many small shops owned by white shopkeepers had disappeared, there was an opportunity for humble itinerant black traders. Muchanga had lost his fear of the town. He was proud of what she had done for him and she knew he saw himself as a rich merchant; this was the only sort of freedom he understood, after so many years as a servant. But she also knew, and the lawyer sitting beside her in the car knew she knew, that the shortages of the goods

Muchanga could sell from his cart, the sugar and soap and matches and pomade and sunglasses, would soon put him out of business. He promised to come back to the house and look after the plants every week; and he stood waving, as he had done every year when they set off on holiday. She did not know what to call out to him as they drove away. The right words would not come again; whatever they were, she left them behind.

For Dear Life

Swaying along in the howdah of her belly I make procession up steep streets. The drumming of her heart exalts me; I do not know the multitudes. With my thumb-hookah I pass among them unseen and unseeing behind the dancing scarlet brocades of her blood. From time to time I am lurched to rest. Habituation to the motion causes me to move: as if the hidden presence raps testy impatience. They place their hands to read a sign from where there is no cognition of their existence.

A wall-eyed twenty-five-year-old Arab with a knitted cap jumps back into the trench in a cheerful bound. Others clamber stockily, with the dazed open mouth of labourers and the scowl of sweat. Their work clothes are cast-off pinstripe pants brought in rumpled bundles from Tunis and Algiers. Closely modelled to their heads and growing low, straight across their foreheads, their kind of hair is a foreign head-gear by which they see themselves known even if they do not speak their soft, guttural, prophet's tongue. One has gold in his mouth, the family fortune crammed into crooked teeth. Another is emaciated as a beggar or wise man, big feet in earth-sculpted boots the only horizontal as his arms fly up with the pick. Eyes starred like clowns' with floury dust look up from the ditch just at the level where the distortion of the female body lifts a tent of skirt to show the female thighs. She's a young one. Mending roads and laying sewage pipes through the French resort over more than a year, they have seen her walking with the man who wanted her, in pursuit, hunting her even while he and she walked side by side, with his gilt-buckled waist, his handbag manacled to his wrist, his snakeskin-snug shirt showing sportsman shoulders, his satyr's curly red hair, thin on top, creeping down the back of his neck and breast-bone, glinting after her along with his eyes and smile.

Like the other women in this country, she was not for them. She did not nod at them then and the mouth parted now as she's approaching is not the beginning of the greeting she has for the postman or any village crone. She's simply panting under her eight-month burden: in there, another foreman, overseer, *patron* like the one who will come by any minute to make sure they are not idling.

Here – feel it?

Concentrate on the drained cappuccino cups spittled with chocolate-flecked foam. The boom of the juke box someone's set in motion seems to be preventing . . . as if it were a matter of hearing, through the palm!

Give me your hand—

A small-change clink as silver bracelets on the older woman's wrist move with volition surrendered.

There. *There*. Lower down, that's it – now you *must* be able to.

But was it not always something impossible to detect from outside . . . So long ago: tapping, plucking (yes, that was much more the way it was) – plucking at one's flesh from within as fingers fidget pleating cloth. If I were the one, now, you were inside, I should feel you. You would be unmistakable. You would be unlike the children he had or the children I had. You are a girl because he had no girl. His daughter with his stiff-legged walk (heron-legs, I used to say) and my bottom (bobtail, he used to say) and his oval nails and fine white skin behind the ears. You can crack your knee and ankle joints. Tea leaves tinsel the grey of your irises. Like him, like me. You have our face; when we used to see ourselves as a couple in the mirror of a lift that was carrying us clandestinely.

* * *

The doctor says they suck their thumbs in the womb. Sucks its thumb!

As if the doctor were a colleague the young husband confirms with a nod, gazing assessingly at the majestic mound that rises out of the level of water in the bath. Like many people without a profession he has a magazine-article amateur's claim to knowledge in many.

My boy's been shown what life is all about from when he wasn't more than an infant in arms. No sweets, look at the state my teeth are in. You'll finish school whatever happens. That's all very fine, earning enough to buy yourself a third-hand Porsche 'C' '59 at nineteen but at thirty-four you find yourself selling TV sets on commission, during a recession. No running around the summer streets, twelve years old and ought to be asleep at night. No chasing girls, catching them, squeezing their little breasts on the dark porch of the old church before it was pulled down. Steer clear of married women who keep you in bed, spoilt bitches, while their husbands get on in the world and buy the Panther Westwinds de Ville, modelled after the Bugatti Royal, best car ever made, Onassis had one, and Purdey guns, gold cigarette lighters, camera equipment, boats with every comfort (bar, sauna) – you could even live on board, for instance if you couldn't get a rent-controlled flat. Great lover, but the silk shirts and real kid boots from Italy don't last long when you're hanging around bars looking for work and all you get offered is the dirty jobs the Arabs are here to do. No smoking, either; bad enough that your mother and I mess up our lungs, 20 per cent reduction of life expectancy, they say. You'll have more sense or I'll know why. You'll be lucky. Women love red hair, a well-known sign of virility. You'll fly first class with free champagne. You'll fill in forms: 'Company Director'. *You'll do as I say*. If you aren't given Coca-Cola to taste, you won't miss it.

Feel – my belly's so hard. I'm like a rock.

She does not know the name, but she is thinking of a geode halved, in a shop window; a cave of crystals, a star cracked open. In there, curved as a bean, the wonder of her body blindly gazes.

* * *

How long to go?

It is an old woman's form of greeting. Her stiff dog stands with his front paws on the kitchen window and watches the heads below that come into view and pass. He lifts his nose slightly, as at a recollection, when a boy clatters from the baker's to the hotel with a headdress of loaves. Beside the dog the crone looks down at a dome under which sandalled feet show, like the cardboard feet of one of those anthropomorphic balloon toys, and above which a bright, smooth face smiles up at her with the kindly patronage of the young.

It can't be long: for her. Every day, when she and the dog manage to get as far as the front step to sit down in a series of very slow movements in the sun at noon, you can count the breaths left.

He will stand behind a desk in his Immigration Officer's uniform and stamp how long they can stay and when they must go. He will drive up in his big car that rises and sinks on its soft springs in the dust as a bird settles upon water, and not bother to get out, giving orders through the window to the one among them who understands the language a little better than the others.

No one will know who you are; not even you.

Only we, who are forgetting each other, will know who you never were.

Even possibilities pass.

I don't cry and I don't bleed.

My daughter wanted for nothing. I bought a Hammond organ on instalments because she's so musical. (Since she was a little thing.) She could have gone to a good convent although we're not religious. Right, she wanted a car, I got her a car and she drove around without a licence: I warned her. The boys were crazy for her; her mother talked to her. She looked like eighteen at fourteen with that figure and that beautiful curly red hair. You don't see anything like it, usually it all comes out of a bottle. I won't have her making herself cheap. She could go to study at the university or take up beauty culture. There's money in that. If anyone lays a finger on her—

The emaciated ditch-digger weeps sometimes as he digs. It is on Mondays that the sight occurs among them, when he is suffering from the drink their religion forbids. His brother has committed suicide in Marseilles knowing the sickness of the genitals he had was punishment for offending Allah by going with a white whore.

It is summer round the empty house in the fields the family left two generations ago. They can't go back, except to picnic like tourists who bring their cheese and wine and ashamed little caches of toilet paper on to anyone's property. There's no electricity and there's water only in a well. They spray the old vines once a year, and once a year come for the grapes. Cows from neighbouring farms stare from the grass with their calves.

I lean in the solid shadow of the mother's body, against her flanks.

To those who have already lived, an empty house is unimaginable. They build it only out of what has been placed by the hands of man: from the bricks that enclose space to the rugs put down and curtains drawn there, once – how can there be *nobody*? The ornamental wooden valance that is breaking away from the eaves is the blows of the grandfather who nailed it. The Virgin with a cake-doily gilt lace halo under glass is the bedroom faith of a grandmother. An old newspaper is the eyes of one who read it.

When I vacate this first place I'll leave behind the place that was all places. I'll leave behind nothing. There will be *nothing* – for I'm taking all with me, I'm taking it on . . . all, all, everything. In my swollen sex, obscene for my size, in my newly pressed-into-shape cranium containing the seed pearls of my brain cells, in my minute hands creased as bank notes or immigration papers. Head down, shoving, driven, meeting violence with violence, casting myself out like Jonah from the heaving host whale, bursting lungs that haven't breathed yet, swimming for dear life . . .

I don't see them covering their eyes in secret, I don't hear them wailing: it will all be gone through again!

Behind me, the torn membranes of my moorings.

Hauled from the deep where there is no light for sight I find eyes. The ancient Mediterranean sun smithereens against me like a joyous glass dashed to the ground.

Ta mère fit un pet foireux et tu naquis de sa colique.

I begin again.

Oral History

There's always been one house like a white man's house in the village of Dilolo. Built of brick with a roof that bounced signals from the sun. You could see it through the mopane trees as you did the flash of paraffin tins the women carried on their heads, bringing water from the river. The rest of the village was built of river mud, grey, shaped by the hollows of hands, with reed thatch and poles of mopane from which the leaves had been ripped like fish scales.

It was the chief's house. Some chiefs have a car as well but this was not an important chief, the clan is too small for that, and he had the usual stipend from the government. If they had given him a car he would have had no use for it. There is no road: the army patrol Land Rovers come upon the people's cattle, startled as buck, in the mopane scrub. The village has been there a long time. The chief's grandfather was the clan's grandfathers' chief, and his name is the same as that of the chief who waved his warriors to down assegais and took the first Bible from a Scottish Mission Board white man. *Seek and ye shall find*, the missionaries said.

The villagers in those parts don't look up, any more, when the sting-shaped army planes fly over twice a day. Only fish-eagles are disturbed, take off, screaming, keen swerving heads lifting into their invaded domain of sky. The men who have been away to work on the mines can read, but there are no newspapers. The people hear over the radio the government's count of how many army trucks have been blown up, how many white soldiers are going to be buried with *full military honours* – something that is apparently white people's way with their dead.

The chief had a radio, and he could read. He read to the headmen the letter from the government saying that anyone hiding or giving food and water to those who were fighting against the government's army would be put in prison. He read another letter from the government saying that to protect the village from these men who went over the border and came back with guns to kill people and burn huts, anybody who walked in the bush after dark would be shot. Some of the young men who, going courting or drinking to the next village, might have been in danger, were no longer at home in their fathers' care anyway. The young go away: once it was to the mines, now – the radio said – it was over the border to learn how to fight. Sons walked out of the clearing of mud huts; past the chief's house; past the children playing with the models of police patrol Land Rovers made out of twisted wire. The children called out, 'Where are you going?' The young men didn't answer and they hadn't come back.

There was a church of mopane and mud with a mopane flagpole to fly a white flag when somebody died; the funeral service was more or less the same protestant one the missionaries brought from Scotland and it was combined with older rituals to entrust the newly dead to the ancestors. Ululating women with whitened faces sent them on their way to the missionaries' last judgement. The children were baptised with names chosen by portent in consultation between the mother and an old man who read immutable fate in the fall of small bones cast like dice from a horn cup. On all occasions and most Saturday nights there was a beer-drink, which the chief attended. An upright chair from his house was brought out for him although everyone else squatted comfortably on the sand, and he was offered the first taste from an old decorated gourd dipper (other people drank from baked-bean or pilchard tins) – it is the way of people of the village.

It is also the way of the tribe to which the clan belongs and the subcontinent to which the tribe belongs, from Matadi in the west to Mombasa in the east, from Entebbe in the north to Empangeni in the south, that everyone is welcome at a beer-drink. No traveller or passer-by, poling down the river in his pirogue, leaving the snake-skin trail of his bicycle wheels through the sand, betraying his approach – if the dogs are sleeping by the cooking fires and the children have left their homemade highways – only by the brittle fragmentation of the dead leaves as he comes unseen through miles of mopane, is a presence to be questioned. Everyone for a long way round on both sides of the border near Dilolo has a black skin, speaks the same language and shares the custom of hospitality. Before the government started to shoot people at night to stop more young men leaving when no one was awake to ask, 'Where are you going?' people thought nothing of walking ten miles from one village to another for a beer-drink.

But unfamiliar faces have become unusual. If the firelight caught such a face, it backed into darkness. No one remarked the face. Not even the smallest child who never took its eyes off it, crouching down among the knees of men with soft, little boy's lips held in wonderingly over teeth as if an invisible grown-up hand were clamped there. The young girls giggled and flirted from the background, as usual. The older men didn't ask for news of relatives or friends outside the village. The chief seemed not to see one face or faces in distinction from any other. His eyes came to rest instead on some of the older men. He gazed and they felt it.

Coming out of the back door of his brick house with its polished concrete steps, early in the morning, he hailed one of them. The man was passing with his hobbling cows and steadily bleating goats; stopped, with the turn of one who will continue on his way in a moment almost without breaking step. But the summons was for him. The chief wore a frayed collarless shirt and old trousers, like the man, but he was never barefoot. In the hand with a big steel watch on the wrist, he carried his thick-framed spectacles, and drew down his nose between the fingers of the other hand; he had the authoritative body of a man who still has his sexual powers but his eyes flickered against the light of the sun and secreted flecks of matter like cold cream at the corners. After the greetings usual between a chief and one of his headmen together with whom, from the retreat in the mopane forest where they lay together in the same age group recovering from circumcision, he had long ago emerged a man, the chief said, 'When is your son coming back?'

'I have no news.'

'Did he sign for the mines?'

'No.'

'He's gone to the tobacco farms?'

'He didn't tell us.'

'Gone away to find work and doesn't tell his mother? What sort of child is that? Didn't you teach him?'

The goats were tonguing three hunchback bushes that were all that was left of a hedge round the chief's house. The man took out a round tin dented with child's toothmarks and taking care not to spill any snuff, dosed himself. He gestured at the beasts, for permission: 'They're eating up your house . . .' He made a move towards the necessity to drive them on.

'There is nothing left there to eat.' The chief ignored his hedge, planted by his oldest wife who had been to school at the mission up the river. He stood among the goats as if he would ask more questions. Then he turned and went back to his yard, dismissing himself. The other man watched. It seemed he might call after; but instead drove his animals with the familiar cries, this time unnecessarily loud and frequent.

Often an army patrol Land Rover came to the village. No one could predict when this would be because it was not possible to count the days in between and be sure that so many would elapse before it returned, as could be done in the case of a tax collector or cattle-dipping officer. But it could be heard minutes away, crashing through the mopane like a frightened animal, and dust hung marking the direction from which it was coming. The children ran to tell. The women went from hut to hut. One of the chief's wives would enjoy the importance of bearing the news: 'The government is coming to see you.'

He would be out of his house when the Land Rover stopped and a black soldier (murmuring towards the chief the required respectful greeting in their own language) jumped out and opened the door for the white soldier. The white soldier had learnt the names of all the local chiefs. He gave greetings with white men's brusqueness: 'Everything all right?'

And the chief repeated to him: 'Everything is all right.'

'No one been bothering you in this village?'

'No one is troubling us.'

But the white soldier signalled to his black men and they went through every hut busy as wives when they are cleaning, turning over bedding, thrusting gun-butts into the pile of ash and rubbish where the chickens searched, even looking in, their eyes dazzled by darkness, to the hut where one of the old women who had gone crazy had to be kept most of the time. The white soldier stood beside the Land Rover waiting for them. He told the chief of things that were happening not far from the village; not far at all. The road that passed five kilometres away had been blown up. 'Someone plants landmines in the road and as soon as we repair it they put them there again. Those people come from across the river and they pass this way. They wreck our vehicles and kill people.'

The heads gathered round weaved as if at the sight of bodies laid there horrifyingly before them.

'They will kill you, too – burn your huts, all of you – if you let them stay with you.'

A woman turned her face away: 'Aïe-aïe-aïe-aïe.'

His forefinger half-circled his audience. 'I'm telling you. You'll see what they do.'

The chief's latest wife, taken only the year before and of the age group of his elder grandchildren, had not come out to listen to the white man. But she heard from others what he had said, and fiercely smoothing her legs with grease, demanded of the chief, 'Why does he want us to die, that white man!'

Her husband, who had just been a passionately shuddering lover, became at once one of the important old with whom she did not count and could not argue. 'You talk about things you don't know. Don't speak for the sake of making a noise.'

To punish him, she picked up the strong, young girl's baby she had borne him and went out of the room where she slept with him on the big bed that had come down the river by barge, before the army's machine guns were pointing at the other bank.

He appeared at his mother's hut. There, the middle-aged man on whom the villagers depended, to whom the government looked when it wanted taxes paid and culling orders carried out, became a son – the ageless category, no matter from which age group to another he passed in the progression of her life and his. The old woman was at her toilet. The great weight of her body settled around her where she sat on a reed mat outside the door. He pushed a stool under himself. Set out was a small mirror with a pink plastic frame and stand, in which he caught sight of his face, screwed up. A large black comb; a little carved box inlaid with red lucky beans she had always had, he used to beg to be allowed to play with it fifty years ago. He waited, not so much out of respect as in the bond of indifference to all outside their mutual contact that reasserts itself when lions and their kin lie against one another.

She cocked a glance, swinging the empty loops of her stretched ear lobes. He did not say what he had come for.

She had chosen a tiny bone spoon from the box and was poking with trembling care up each round hole of distended nostril. She cleaned the crust of dried snot and dust from her delicate instrument and flicked the dirt in the direction away from him.

She said: 'Do you know where your sons are?'

'Yes, I know where my sons are. You have seen three of them here today. Two are in school at the mission. The baby – he's with the mother.' A slight smile, to which the old woman did not respond. Her preferences among the sons had no connection with sexual pride.

'Good. You can be glad of all that. But don't ask other people about theirs.'

As often when people who share the same blood share the same thought, for a moment mother and son looked exactly alike, he old-womanish, she mannish.

'If the ones we know are missing, there are not always empty places,' he said.

She stirred consideringly in her bulk. Leaned back to regard him: 'It used to be that all children were our own children. All sons our sons. *Old-fashion*, these people here' – the hard English word rolled out of their language like a pebble, and came to rest where aimed, at his feet.

It was spring: the mopane leaves turn, drying up and dying, spattering the sand with blood and rust – a battlefield, it must have looked, from the patrol planes. In August there is no rain to come for two months yet. Nothing grows but the flies hatch. The heat rises daily and the nights hold it, without a stir, till morning. On these nights the radio voice carried so clearly it could be heard from the chief's house all through the village. Many were being captured in the bush and killed by the army – *seek and destroy* was what the white men said now – and many in the army were being set upon in the bush or blown up in their trucks and buried with full military honours. This was expected to continue until October because the men in the bush knew that it was their last chance before the rains came and chained their feet in mud.

On these hot nights when people cannot sleep anyway, beer-drinks last until very late. People drink more; the women know this, and brew more. There is a fire but no one sits close round it.

Without a moon the dark is thick with heat; when the moon is full the dark shimmers thinly in a hot mirage off the river. Black faces are blue, there are watermarks along noses and biceps. The chief sat on his chair and wore shoes and socks in spite of the heat; those drinking nearest him could smell the suffering of his feet. The planes of jaw and lips he noticed in moonlight molten over them, moonlight pouring moths broken from white cases on the mopane and mosquitoes rising from the river, pouring glory like the light in the religious pictures people got at the mission – he had seen those faces about lately in the audacity of day, as well. An ox had been killed and there was the scent of meat sizzling in the village (just look at the behaviour of the dogs, they knew) although there was no marriage or other festival that called for someone to slaughter one of his beasts. When the chief allowed himself, at least, to meet the eyes of a stranger, the whites that had been showing at an oblique angle disappeared and he took rather than saw the full gaze of the seeing eye: the pupils with their defiance, their belief, their claim, hold, on him. He let it happen only once. For the rest, he saw their arrogant lifted jaws to each other and warrior smiles to the girls, as they drank. The children were drawn to them, fighting one another silently for places close up. Towards midnight – his watch had its own glowing galaxy – he left his chair and did not come back from the shadows where men went to urinate. Often at beer-drinks the chief would go home while others were still drinking.

He went to his brick house whose roof shone almost bright as day. He did not go to the room where his new wife and sixth son would be sleeping in the big bed, but simply took from the kitchen, where it was kept when not in use, a bicycle belonging to one of his hangers-on, relative or retainer. He wheeled it away from the huts in the clearing, his village and grandfather's village that disappeared so quickly behind him in the mopane, and began to ride through the sand. He was not afraid he would meet a patrol and be shot; alone at night in the sand forest, the forested desert he had known before and would know beyond his span of life, he didn't believe in the power of a roving band of government men to end that life. The going was heavy but he had mastered when young the art of riding on this, the only terrain he knew, and the ability came back. In an hour he arrived at the army post, called out who he was to the sentry with a machine gun, and had to wait, like a beggar rather than a chief, to be allowed to approach and be searched. There were black soldiers on duty but they woke the white man. It was the one who knew his name, his clan, his village, the way these modern white men were taught. He seemed to know at once why the chief had come; frowning in concentration to grasp details, his mouth was open in a smile and the point of his tongue curled touching at back teeth the way a man will verify facts one by one on his fingers. 'How many?'

'Six or ten or – but sometimes it's only, say, three or one . . . I don't know. One is here, he's gone; they come again.'

'They take food, they sleep, and off. Yes. They make the people give them what they want, that's it, eh? And you know who it is who hides them – who shows them where to sleep – of course you know.'

The chief sat on one of the chairs in that place, the army's place, and the white soldier was standing. 'Who is it—' the chief was having difficulty in saying what he wanted in English, he had the feeling it was not coming out as he had meant nor being understood as he had expected. 'I can't know who is it' – a hand moved restlessly, he held a breath and released it – 'in the village there's many, plenty people. If it's this one or this one—' He stopped, shaking his head with a reminder to the white man of his authority, which the white soldier was quick to placate.

'Of course. Never mind. They frighten the people; the people can't say no. They kill people who say no, eh; cut their ears off, you know that? Tear away their lips. Don't you see the pictures in the papers?'

'We never saw it. I heard the government say on the radio.'

'They're still drinking . . . How long – an hour ago?'

The white soldier checked with a look the other men, whose stance had changed to that of bodies ready to break into movement: grab weapons, run, fling themselves at the Land Rovers guarded in the dark outside. He picked up the telephone receiver but blocked the mouthpiece as if it were someone about to make an objection. 'Chief, I'll be with you in a moment. Take him to the duty room and make coffee. Just wait—' he leant his full reach towards a drawer in a cabinet on the left of the desk and, scrabbling to get it open, took out a half-full bottle of brandy. Behind the chief's back he gestured the bottle towards the chief, and a black soldier jumped obediently to take it.

The chief went to a cousin's house in a village the other side of the army post later that night. He said he had been to a beer-drink and could not ride home because of the white men's curfew.

The white soldier had instructed that he should not be in his own village when the arrests were made so that he could not be connected with these and would not be in danger of having his ears cut off for taking heed of what the government wanted of him, or having his lips mutilated for what he had told.

His cousin gave him blankets. He slept in a hut with her father. The deaf old man was aware neither that he had come nor was leaving so early that last night's moon, the size of the bicycle's reflector, was still shiny in the sky. The bicycle rode up on spring-hares without disturbing them, in the forest; there was a stink of jackal-fouling still sharp on the dew. Smoke already marked his village; early cooking fires were lit. Then he saw that the smoke, the black particles spindling at his face, were not from cooking fires. Instead of going faster as he pumped his feet against the weight of sand the bicycle seemed to slow along with his mind, to find in each revolution of its wheels the countersurge: to stop; not go on. But there was no way not to reach what he found. The planes only children bothered to look up at any longer had come in the night and dropped something terrible and alive that no one could have read or heard about enough to be sufficiently afraid of. He saw first a bloody kaross, a dog caught on the roots of an upturned tree. The earth under the village seemed to have burst open and flung away what it carried: the huts, pots, gourds, blankets, the tin trunks, alarm clocks, curtain-booth photographs, bicycles, radios and shoes brought back from the mines, the bright cloths young wives wound on their heads, the pretty pictures of white lambs and pink children at the knees of the golden-haired Christ the Scottish Mission Board first brought long ago – all five generations of the clan's life that had been chronicled by each succeeding generation in episodes told to the next. The huts had staved in like broken anthills. Within earth walls baked and streaked by fire the thatch and roof-poles were ash. He bellowed and stumbled from hut to hut, nothing answered frenzy, not even a chicken rose from under his feet. The walls of his house still stood. It was gutted and the roof had buckled. A black stiff creature lay roasted on its chain in the yard. In one of the huts he saw a human shape transformed the same way, a thing of stiff tar daubed on a recognisable framework. It was the hut where the mad woman lived; when those who had survived fled, they had forgotten her.

The chief's mother and his youngest wife were not among them. But the baby boy lived, and will grow up in the care of the older wives. No one can say what it was the white soldier said over the telephone to his commanding officer, and if the commanding officer had told him what was going to be done, or whether the white soldier knew, as a matter of procedure laid down in his military training for this kind of war, what would be done. The chief hanged himself in the mopane. The police or the army (much the same these days, people confuse them) found the bicycle beneath his dangling shoes. So the family hanger-on still rides it; it would have been lost if it had been safe in the kitchen when the raid came. No one knows where the chief found a rope, in the ruins of his village.

The people are beginning to go back. The dead are properly buried in ancestral places in the mopane forest. The women are to be seen carrying tins and grain panniers of mud up from the river. In talkative bands they squat and smear, raising the huts again. They bring sheaves of reeds exceeding their own height, balanced like the cross-stroke of a majuscular T on their heads. The men's voices sound through the mopane as they choose and fell trees for the roof supports.

A white flag on a mopane pole hangs outside the house whose white walls, built like a white man's, stand from before this time.

A Lion on the Freeway

Open up!
    Open up!
What hammered on the door of sleep?
Who's that?

*   *   *

Anyone who lives within a mile of the zoo hears lions on summer nights. A tourist could be fooled. Africa already; at last; even though he went to bed in yet another metropole.

Just before light, when it's supposed to be darkest, the body's at its lowest ebb and in the hospital on the hill old people die – the night opens, a black hole between stars, and from it comes a deep panting. Very distant and at once very close, right in the ear, for the sound of breath is always intimate. It grows and grows, deeper, faster, more rasping, until a great groan, a rising groan lifts out of the curved bars of the cage and hangs above the whole city—

And then drops back, sinks away, becomes panting again.

Wait for it; it will fall so quiet, hardly more than a faint roughness snagging the air in the ear's chambers. Just when it seems to have sunk between strophe and antistrophe, a breath is taken and it gasps once; pauses, sustaining the night as a singer holds a note. And begins once more. The panting reaches up up up down down down to that awe-ful groan—

Open up!
  Open up!
  Open your legs.

In the geriatric wards where lights are burning they take the tubes out of noses and the saline-drip needles out of arms and draw the sheets to cover faces. I pull the sheet over my head. I can smell my own breath caught there. It's very late; it's much too early to be awake. Sometimes the rubber tyres of the milk truck rolled over our sleep. You turned . . .

Roar is not the word. Children learn not to hear for themselves, doing exercises in the selection of verbs at primary school: 'Complete these sentences: The cat . . . s The dog . . . s The lion . . . s.' Whoever decided that had never listened to the real thing. The verb is onomatopoeically incorrect just as the heraldic beasts drawn by thirteenth- and fourteenth-century engravers at second hand from the observations of early explorers are anatomically wrong. Roar is not the word for the sound of great chaps sucking in and out the small hours.

The zoo lions do not utter during the day. They yawn; wait for their ready-slaughtered kill to be tossed at them; keep their unused claws sheathed in huge harmless pads on which top-heavy, untidy heads rest (the visualised lion is always a maned male), gazing through lid-slats with what zoo visitors think of in sentimental prurience as yearning.

Or once we were near the Baltic and the leviathan hooted from the night fog at sea. But would I dare to open my mouth now? Could I trust my breath to be sweet, these stale nights?

It's only on warm summer nights that the lions are restless. What they're seeing when they gaze during the day is nothing, their eyes are open but they don't see us – you can tell that when the lens of the pupil suddenly shutters at the close swoop of one of the popcorn-begging pigeons through the bars of the cage. Otherwise the eye remains blank, registering nothing. The lions were born in the zoo (for a few brief weeks the cubs are on show to the public, children may hold them in their arms). They know nothing but the zoo; they are not expressing our yearnings. It's only on certain nights that their muscles flex and they begin to pant, their flanks heave as if they had been running through the dark night while other creatures shrank from their path, their jaws hang tense and wet as saliva flows as if in response to a scent of prey, at last they heave up their too-big heads, heavy, heavy heads, and out it comes. Out over the suburbs. A dreadful straining of the bowels to deliver itself: a groan that hangs above the houses in a low-lying cloud of smog and anguish.

O Jack, O Jack, O Jack, oh – I heard it once through a hotel wall. Was alone and listened. Covers drawn over my head and knees drawn up to my fists. Eyes strained wide open. Sleep again! – my command. *Sleep again*.

* * *

It must be because of the new freeway that they are not heard so often lately. It passes its five-lane lasso close by, drawing in the valley between the zoo and the houses on the ridge. There is traffic there very late, too early. Trucks. Tankers, getting a start before daylight. The rising spray of rubber spinning friction on tarmac is part of the quality of city silence; after a time you don't hear much beyond it. But sometimes – perhaps it's because of a breeze. Even on a still summer night there must be some sort of breeze opening up towards morning. Not enough to stir the curtains, a current of air has brought, small, clear and distant, right into the ear, the sound of panting.

Or perhaps the neat whisky after dinner. The rule is don't drink after dinner. A metabolic switch trips in the brain: open up.

Who's that?

A truck of potatoes going through traffic lights quaked us sixteen flights up.

Slack with sleep, I was impaled in the early hours. You grew like a tree and lifted the pavements; everything rose, cracked and split free.

Who's that?

Or something read in the paper . . . Yes. Last night – this night – in the City Late, front page, there were the black strikers in the streets, dockers with sticks and knobkerries. A thick prancing black centipede with thousands of waving legs advancing. The panting grows louder, it could be in the garden or under the window; there comes that pause, that slump of breath. Wait for it: waiting for it. Prance, advance, over the carefully tended please keep off the grass. They went all through a city not far from this one, their steps are so rhythmical, waving sticks (no spears any more, no guns yet); they can cover any distance, in time. Shops and houses closed against them while they passed. And the cry that came from them as they approached – that groan straining, the rut of freedom bending the bars of the cage, he's delivered himself of it, it's as close as if he's out on the freeway now, bewildered, finding his way, turning his splendid head at last to claim what he's never seen, the country where he's king.

Something Out There

At the Rendezvous of Victory

A young black boy used to brave the dogs in white men's suburbs to deliver telegrams; Sinclair 'General Giant' Zwedu has those bite scars on his legs to this day.

So goes the opening paragraph of a 'profile' copyrighted by a British Sunday paper, reprinted by reciprocal agreement with papers in New York and Washington, syndicated as far as Australia and translated in both *Le Monde* and *Neue Züricher Zeitung*.

But like everything else he was to read about himself, it was not quite like that. No. Ever since he was a kid he loved dogs, and those dogs who chased the bicycle – he just used to whistle in his way at them, and they would stand there wagging their long tails and feeling silly. The scars on his legs were from wounds received when the white commando almost captured him, blew up one of his hideouts in the bush. But he understood why the journalist had decided to paint the wounds over as dog bites – it made a kind of novel opening to the story, and it showed at once that the journalist wasn't on the side of the whites. It was true that he who became Sinclair 'General Giant' Zwedu was born in the blacks' compound on a white man's sugar farm in the hottest and most backward part of the country, and that, after only a few years at a school where children drew their sums in the dust, he was the post office messenger in the farmers' town. It was in that two-street town, with the whites' Central Hotel, Main Road Garage, Buyrite Stores, Snooker Club and railhead, that he first heard the voice of the brother who was to become Prime Minister and President, a voice from a big trumpet on the top of a shabby van. It summoned him (there were others, but they didn't become anybody) to a meeting in the Catholic Mission Hall in Goodwill Township – which was what the white farmers called the black shanty town outside their own. And it was here, in Goodwill Township, that the young post office messenger took away the local Boy Scout troop organised by but segregated from the white Boy Scout troop in the farmers' town, and transformed the scouts into the Youth Group of the National Independence Party. Yes – he told them – you will be prepared. The party will teach you how to make a fire the government can't put out.

It was he who, when the leaders of the party were detained for the first time, was imprisoned with the future Prime Minister and became one of his chief lieutenants. He, in fact, who in jail made up defiance songs that soon were being sung at mass meetings, who imitated the warders, made pregnant one of the women prisoners who polished the cell floors (though no one believed her when she proudly displayed the child as his, he would have known *that* was true), and finally, when he was sent to another prison in order to remove his invigorating influence from fellow political detainees, overpowered three warders and escaped across the border.

It was this exploit that earned him the title 'General Giant' as prophets, saints, rogues and heroes receive theirs: named by the anonymous talk of ordinary people. He did not come back until he had wintered in the unimaginable cold of countries that offer refuge and military training, gone to rich desert cities to ask for money from the descendants of people who had sold Africans as slaves, and to the island where sugar-cane workers, as his mother and father had been, were now powerful enough to supply arms. He was with the first band of men who had left home with empty hands, on bare feet, and came back with AKM assault rifles, heat-guided missiles and limpet mines.

The future Prime Minister was imprisoned again and again and finally fled the country and established the party's leadership in exile. When Sinclair 'General Giant' met him in London or Algiers, the future Prime Minister wore a dark suit whose close weave was midnight blue in the light. He himself wore a bush outfit that originally had been put together by men who lived less like men than prides of lion, tick-ridden, thirsty, waiting in thickets of thorn. As these men increased in numbers and boldness, and he rose in command of them, the outfit elaborated into a combat uniform befitting his style, title and achievement. At the beginning of the war, he had led a ragged hit-and-run group; after four years and the deaths of many, which emphasised his giant indestructibility, his men controlled a third of the country and he was the man the white army wanted most to capture.

Before the future Prime Minister talked to the Organization of African Unity or United Nations he had now to send for and consult with his commander-in-chief of the liberation army, Sinclair 'General Giant' Zwedu. General Giant came from the bush in his Czech jeep, in a series of tiny planes from secret airstrips, and at last would board a scheduled jet liner among oil and mineral men who thought they were sitting beside just another dolled-up black official from some unheard-of state whose possibilities they might have to look into sometime. When the consultation in the foreign capital was over, General Giant did not fidget long in the patter of official cocktail parties, but would disappear to find for himself whatever that particular capital could offer to meet his high capacities – for leading men to fight without fear, exciting people to caper, shout with pleasure, drink and argue; for touching women. After a night in a bar and a bed with girls (he never had to pay professionals, always found well-off, respectable women, black or white, whose need for delights simply matched his own) he would take a plane back to Africa. He never wanted to linger. He never envied his brother, the future Prime Minister, his flat in London and the invitations to country houses to discuss the future of the country. He went back imperatively as birds migrate to Africa to mate and assure the survival of their kind, journeying thousands of miles, just as he flew and drove deeper and deeper into where he belonged until he reached again his headquarters – that the white commandos often claimed to have destroyed but could not be destroyed because his headquarters were the bush itself.

The war would not have been won without General Giant. At the Peace Conference he took no part in the deliberations but was there at his brother's, the future Prime Minister's side: a deterrent weapon, a threat to the defeated white government of what would happen if peace were not made. Now and then he cleared his throat of a constriction of boredom; the white delegates were alarmed as if he had roared.

Constitutional talks went on for many weeks; there was a ceasefire, of course. He wanted to go back – to his headquarters – home – but one of the conditions of the ceasefire had been that he should be withdrawn 'from the field' as the official term, coined in wars fought over poppy meadows, phrased it. He wandered about London. He went to nightclubs and was invited to join parties of Arabs who, he found, had no idea where the country he had fought for, and won for his people, was; this time he really did roar – with laughter. He walked through Soho but couldn't understand why anyone would like to watch couples making the movements of love-making on the cinema screen instead of doing it themselves. He came upon the Natural History Museum in South Kensington and was entranced by the life that existed anterior to his own unthinking familiarity with ancient nature hiding the squat limpet mines, the iron clutches of offensive and defensive hand grenades, the angular AKMs, metal blue with heat. He sent postcards of mammoths and gasteropods to his children, who were still where they had been with his wife all through the war – in the black location of the capital of his home country. Since she was his wife, she had been under police surveillance, and detained several times, but had survived by saying she and her husband were separated. Which was true, in a way; a man leading a guerrilla war has no family, he must forget about meals cooked for him by a woman, nights in a bed with two places hollowed by their bodies and the snuffle of a baby close by. He made love to a black singer from Jamaica, not young, whose style was a red-head wig rather than fashionable rigid pigtails. She composed a song about his bravery in the war in a country she imagined but had never seen, and sang it at a victory rally where all the brothers in exile as well as the white sympathisers with their cause, applauded her. In her flat she had a case of special Scotch whisky, twelve years old, sent by an admirer. She said – sang to him – Let's not let it get any older. As she worked only at night, they spent whole days indoors making love when the weather was bad – the big man, General Giant, was like a poor stray cat, in the cold rain: he would walk on the balls of shoe soles, shaking each foot as he lifted it out of the wet.

He was waiting for the OK, as he said to his brother, the future Prime Minister, to go back to their country and take up his position as commander-in-chief of the new state's Defence Force. His title would become an official rank, the highest, like that of army chiefs in Britain and the United States – General Zwedu.

His brother turned solemn, dark in his mind; couldn't be followed there. He said the future of the army was a tremendous problem at present under discussion. The two armies, black and white, who had fought each other, would have to be made one. What the discussions were also about remained in the dark: the defeated white government, the European powers by whom the new black state was promised loans for reconstruction, had insisted that Sinclair 'General Giant' Zwedu be relieved of all military authority. His personality was too strong and too strongly associated with the triumph of the freedom fighter army for him to be anything but a divisive reminder of the past, in the new, regular army. Let him stand for parliament in the first peacetime election, his legend would guarantee that he win the seat. Then the Prime Minister could find him some safe portfolio.

What portfolio? What? This was in the future Prime Minister's mind when General Giant couldn't follow him. 'What he knows how to do is defend our country, that he fought for', the future Prime Minister said to the trusted advisers, British lawyers and African experts from American universities. And while he was saying it, the others knew he did not want, could not have his brother Sinclair 'General Giant' Zwedu, that master of the wilderness, breaking the confinement of peacetime barracks.

He left him in Europe on some hastily invented mission until the independence celebrations. Then he brought him home to the old colonial capital that was now theirs, and at the airport wept with triumph and anguish in his arms, while schoolchildren sang. He gave him a portfolio – Sport and Recreation; harmless.

General Giant looked at his big hands as if the appointment were an actual object, held there. What was he supposed to do with it?

The great lungs that pumped his organ-voice failed; he spoke flatly, kindly, almost pityingly to his brother, the Prime Minister.

Now they both wore dark blue suits. At first, he appeared prominently at the Prime Minister's side as a tacit recompense, to show the people that he was still acknowledged by the Prime Minister as a co-founder of the nation, and its popular hero. He had played football on a patch of bare earth between wattle-branch goal posts on the sugar farm, as a child, and as a youth on a stretch of waste ground near the Catholic Mission Hall; as a man he had been at war, without time for games. In the first few months he rather enjoyed attending important matches in his official capacity, watching from a special box and later seeing himself sitting there, on a TV newsreel. It was a Sunday, a holiday amusement; the holiday went on too long. There was not much obligation to make speeches, in his cabinet post, but because his was a name known over the world, his place reserved in the mountain stronghold Valhalla of guerrilla wars, journalists went to him for statements on all kinds of issues. Besides, he was splendid copy, talkative, honest, indiscreet and emotional. Again and again, he embarrassed his government by giving an outrageous opinion, that contradicted government policy, on problems that were none of his business. The party caucus reprimanded him again and again. He responded by seldom turning up at caucus meetings. The caucus members said that Zwedu (it was time his 'title' was dropped) thought too much of himself and had taken offence. Again, he knew that what was assumed was not quite true. He was bored with the caucus. He wanted to yawn all the time, he said, like a hippopotamus with its huge jaws open in the sun, half-asleep, in the thick brown water of the river near his last headquarters. The Prime Minister laughed at this, and they drank together with arms round one another – as they did in the old days in the Youth Group. The Prime Minister told him – 'But seriously, sport and recreation are very important in building up our nation. For the next budget, I'll see that there's a bigger grant to your department, you'll be able to plan. You know how to inspire young men . . . I'm told a local team has adapted one of the freedom songs you made up, they sang it on TV.'

The Minister of Sport and Recreation sent his deputy to officiate at sports meetings these days and he didn't hear his war song become a football fans' chant. The Jamaican singer had arrived on an engagement at the Hilton that had just opened conference rooms, bars, a casino and nightclub on a site above the town where the old colonial prison used to be (the new prison was on the site of the former Peace Corps camp). He was there in the nightclub every night, drinking the brand of Scotch she had had in her London flat, tilting his head while she sang. The hotel staff pointed him out to overseas visitors – Sinclair 'General Giant' Zwedu, the General Giap, the Che Guevara of a terrible war there'd been in this country. The tourists had spent the day, taken by private plane, viewing game in what the travel brochure described as the country's magnificent game park but – the famous freedom fighter could have told them – wasn't quite that; was in fact his territory, his headquarters. Sometimes he danced with one of the women, their white teeth contrasting with shiny sunburned skin almost as if they had been black. Once there was some sort of a row; he danced too many times with a woman who appeared to be enjoying this intimately, and her husband objected. The 'convivial minister' had laughed, taken the man by the scruff of his white linen jacket and dropped him back in his chair, a local journalist reported, but the government-owned local press did not print his story or picture. An overseas journalist interviewed 'General Giant' on the pretext of the incident, and got from him (the minister was indeed convivial, entertaining the journalist to excellent whisky in the house he had rented for the Jamaican singer) some opinions on matters far removed from nightclub scandal.

When questions were asked in parliament about an article in an American weekly on the country's international alliances, 'General Giant' stood up and, again, gave expression to convictions the local press could not print. He said that the defence of the country might have been put in the hands of neo-colonialists who had been the country's enemies during the war – and he was powerless to do anything about that. But he would take the law into his own hands to protect the National Independence Party's principles of a people's democracy (he used the old name, on this occasion, although it had been shortened to National Party). Hadn't he fought, hadn't the brothers spilled their blood to get rid of the old laws and the old bosses, that made them *nothing?* Hadn't they fought for new laws under which they would be men? He would shed blood rather than see the party betrayed in the name of so-called rational alliances and national unity.

International advisers to the government thought the speech, if inflammatory, so confused it might best be ignored. Members of the cabinet and Members of Parliament wanted the Prime Minister to get rid of him. General Giant Zwedu? How? Where to? Extreme anger was always expressed by the Prime Minister in the form of extreme sorrow. He was angry with both his cabinet members and his comrade, without whom they would never have been sitting in the House of Assembly. He sent for Zwedu. (He must accept that name now; he simply refused to accommodate himself to anything, he illogically wouldn't even drop the 'Sinclair' though *that* was the name of the white sugar farmer his parents had worked for, and nobody kept those slave names any more.)

Zwedu: so at ease and handsome in his cabinet minister's suit (it was not the old blue, but a pinstripe flannel the Jamaican singer had ordered at his request, and brought from London), one could not believe wild and dangerous words could come out of his mouth. He looked good enough for a diplomatic post somewhere . . . Unthinkable. The Prime Minister, full of sorrow and silences, told him he must stop drinking. He must stop giving interviews. There was no mention of the Ministry; the Prime Minister did not tell his brother he would not give in to pressure to take that away from him, the cabinet post he had never wanted but that was all there was to offer. He would not take it away – at least not until this could be done decently under cover of a cabinet reshuffle. The Prime Minister had to say to his brother, you mustn't let me down. What he wanted to say was: What have I done to you?

There was a crop failure and trouble with the unions on the coal mines; by the time the cabinet reshuffle came the press hardly noticed that a Minister of Sport and Recreation had been replaced. Mr Sinclair Zwedu was not given an alternative portfolio, but he was referred to as a former minister when his name was added to the boards of multinational industrial firms instructed by their principals to Africanise. He could be counted upon not to appear at those meetings, either. His director's fees paid for cases of whisky, but sometimes went to his wife, to whom he had never returned, and the teenage children with whom he would suddenly appear in the best stores of the town, buying whatever they silently pointed at. His old friends blamed the Jamaican woman, not the Prime Minister, for his disappearance from public life. She went back to England – her reasons were sexual and honest, she realised she was too old for him – but his way of life did not recover; could not recover the war, the third of the country's territory that had been his domain when the white government had lost control to him and the black government did not yet exist.

The country is open to political and trade missions from both East and West, now, instead of these being confined to allies of the old white government. The airport has been extended. The new departure lounge is a sculpture gallery with reclining figures among potted plants, wearily waiting for connections to places whose directions criss-cross the colonial North–South compass of communication. A former Chief-of-Staff of the white army, who, since the black government came to power, has been retained as chief military adviser to the Defence Ministry, recently spent some hours in the lounge waiting for a plane that was to take him on a government mission to Europe. He was joined by a journalist booked on the same flight home to London, after a rather disappointing return visit to the country. Well, he remarked to the military man as they drank vodka and tonic together, who wants to read about rice-growing schemes instead of seek-and-destroy raids? This was a graceful reference to the ex-Chief-of-Staff's successes with that strategy at the beginning of the war, a reference safe in the cosy no man's land of a departure lounge, out of earshot of the new black security officials alert to any hint of encouragement of an old-guard white coup.

A musical gong preceded announcements of the new estimated departure time of the delayed British Airways plane. A swami found sweets somewhere in his saffron robes and went among the travellers handing out comfits with a message of peace and love. Businessmen used the opportunity to write reports on brief-cases opened on their knees. Black children were spores attached to maternal skirts. White children ran back and forth to the bar counter, buying potato crisps and peanuts. The journalist insisted on another round of drinks.

Every now and then the departure of some other flight was called and the display of groups and single figures would change; some would leave, while a fresh surge would be let in through the emigration barriers and settle in a new composition. Those who were still waiting for delayed planes became part of the permanent collection, so to speak; they included a Canadian evangelical party who read their gospels with the absorption other people gave to paperback thrillers, a very old black woman dry as the fish in her woven carrier, and a prosperous black couple, elegantly dressed. The ex-Chief-of-Staff and his companion were sitting not far behind these two, who flirted and caressed, like whites – it was quite unusual to see those people behaving that way in public. Both the white men noticed this although they were able to observe only the back of the man's head and the profile of the girl, pretty, painted, shameless as she licked his tiny black ear and lazily tickled, with long fingers on the stilts of purple nails, the roll of his neck.

The ex-Chief-of-Staff made no remark, was not interested – what did one *not* see, in the country, now that they had taken over. The journalist was the man who had written a profile, just after the war: *a young black boy used to brave the dogs in white men's suburbs* . . . Suddenly he leant forward, staring at the back of the black man's head. 'That's General Giant! I know those ears!' He got up and went over to the bar, turning casually at the counter to examine the couple from the front. He bought two more vodka and tonics, swiftly was back to his companion, the ice chuntering in the glasses. 'It's him. I thought so. I used to know him well. Him, all right. Fat! Wearing suede shoes. And the tart . . . where'd he find her!'

The ex-Chief-of-Staff's uniform, his thick wad of campaign ribbons over the chest and cap thrust down to his fine eyebrows, seemed to defend him against the heat rather than make him suffer, but the journalist felt confused and stifled as the vodka came out distilled once again in sweat and he did not know whether he should or should not simply walk up to 'General Giant' (no secretaries or security men to get past, now) and ask for an interview. Would anyone want to read it? Could he sell it anywhere? A distraction that made it difficult for him to make up his mind was the public address system nagging that the two passengers holding up flight something-or-other were requested to board the aircraft immediately. No one stirred. 'General Giant' (no mistaking him) simply signalled, a big hand snapping in the air, when he wanted fresh drinks for himself and his girl, and the barman hopped to it, although the bar was self-service. Before the journalist could come to a decision an air hostess ran in with the swish of stockings chafing thigh past thigh and stopped angrily, looking down at the black couple. The journalist could not hear what was said, but she stood firm while the couple took their time getting up, the girl letting her arm slide languidly off the man; laughing, arranging their hand luggage on each other's shoulders.

Where was he *taking* her?

The girl put one high-heeled sandal down in front of the other, as a model negotiates a catwalk. Sinclair 'General Giant' Zwedu followed her backside the way a man follows a paid woman, with no thought of her in his closed, shiny face, and the ex-Chief-of-Staff and the journalist did not know whether he recognised them, even saw them, as he passed without haste, letting the plane wait for him.

Letter from His Father

My dear son,

You wrote me a letter you never sent.

It wasn't for me – it was for the whole world to read. (You and your instructions that everything should be burned. Hah!) You were never open and frank with me – that's one of the complaints you say I was always making against you. You write it in the letter you didn't want me to read; so what does *that* sound like, eh? But I've read the letter now, I've read it anyway, I've read everything, although you said I put your books on the night-table and never touched them. You know how it is, here where I am: not something that can be explained to anyone who isn't here – they used to talk about secrets going to the grave, but the funny thing is there are no secrets here at all. If there was something you wanted to know, you should have known, if it doesn't let you lie quiet, then you can *have knowledge of it*, from here. Yes, you gave me that much credit, you said I was a true Kafka in 'strength . . . eloquence, endurance, a certain way of doing things on a grand scale' and I've not been content just to rot. In that way, I'm still the man I was, the go-getter. Restless. Restless. Taking whatever opportunity I can. There isn't anything, now, you can regard as hidden from me. Whether you say I left it unread on the night-table or whether you weren't man enough, even at the age of thirty-six, to show me a letter that was supposed to be for me.

I write to you after we are both dead. Whereas you don't stir. There won't be any response from you, I know that. You began that letter by saying you were afraid of me – and then you were afraid to let me read it. And now you've escaped altogether. Because without the Kafka will-power you can't reach out from nothing and nowhere. I was going to call it a desert, but where's the sand, where're the camels, where's the sun – I'm still *mensch* enough to crack a joke – you see? Oh excuse me, I forgot – you didn't like my jokes, my fooling around with kids. My poor boy, unfortunately you had no life in you, in all those books and diaries and letters (the ones you posted, to strangers, to women) you said it a hundred times before you put the words in my mouth, in your literary way, in that letter: you yourself were 'unfit for life'. So death comes, how would you say, quite naturally to you. It's not like that for a man of vigour like I was, I can tell you, and so here I am writing, talking . . . I don't know if there is a word for what this is. Anyway, it's *Hermann Kafka*. I've outlived you here, same as in Prague.

That is what you really accuse me of, you know, for sixty or so pages (I notice the length of that letter varies a bit from language to language, of course it's been translated into everything – I don't know what – Hottentot and Icelandic, Chinese, although you wrote it 'for me' in German). I *outlived* you, not for seven years, as an old sick man, after you died, but while you were young and alive. Clear as daylight, from the examples you give of being afraid of me, from the time you were a little boy: you were not afraid, you were envious. At first, when I took you swimming and you say you felt yourself a nothing, puny and weak beside my big, strong, naked body in the change-house – all right, you also say you were proud of such a father, a father with a fine physique . . . And may I remind you that father was taking the trouble and time, the few hours he could get away from the business, to try and make something of that *nebich*, develop his muscles, put some flesh on those poor little bones so he would grow up sturdy? But even before your barmitzvah the normal pride every boy has in his father changed to jealousy, with you. You couldn't be like me, so you decided I wasn't good enough for you: coarse, loud-mouthed, ate 'like a pig' (your very words), cut my fingernails at table, cleaned my ears with a toothpick. Oh yes, you can't hide anything from me, now, I've read it all, all the thousands and thousands of words you've used to shame your own family, your own father, before the whole world. And with your gift for words you turn everything inside out and prove, like a circus magician, it's love, the piece of dirty paper's a beautiful silk flag, you *loved your father too much*, and so – what? *You* tell me. You couldn't be like him? You wanted to be like *him*? The *ghasa*, the shouter, the gobbler? Yes, my son, these 'insignificant details' you write down and quickly dismiss – these details hurt. Eternally. After all, you've become immortal through writing, as you insist you did, only about me, 'everything was about you, father'; a hundred years after your birth, the Czech Jew, son of Hermann and Julie Kafka, is supposed to be one of the greatest writers who ever lived. Your work will be read as long as there are people to read it. That's what they say everywhere, even the Germans who burned your sisters and my grandchildren in incinerators. Some say you were also some kind of prophet (God knows what you were thinking, shut away in your room while the rest of the family was having a game of cards in the evening); after you died, some countries built camps where the things you made up for that story 'In The Penal Colony' were practised, and ever since then there have been countries in different parts of the world where the devil's work that came into your mind is still carried out – I don't want to think about it.

You were not blessed to bring any happiness to this world with your genius, my son. Not at home, either. Well, we had to accept what God gave. Do you ever stop to think whether it wasn't a sorrow for me (never mind – for once – how you felt) that your two brothers, who might have grown up to bring your mother and me joy, died as babies? And you sitting there at meals always with a pale, miserable, glum face, not a word to say for yourself, picking at your food . . . You haven't forgotten that I used to hold up the newspaper so as not to have to see that. You bear a grudge. You've told everybody. But you don't think about what there was in a father's heart. From the beginning. I had to hide it behind a newspaper – anything. For your sake.

Because you were never like any other child. You admit it: however we had tried to bring you up, you say you would have become a 'weakly, timid, hesitant person'. What small boy doesn't enjoy a bit of a rough-house with his father? But writing at thirty-six years old, you can only remember being frightened when I chased you, in fun, round the table, and your mother, joining in, would snatch you up out of my way while you shrieked. For God's sake, what's so terrible about that? I should have such memories of my childhood! I know you never liked to hear about it, it bored you, you don't spare me the written information that it 'wore grooves in your brain', but when *I* was seven years old I had to push my father's barrow from village to village, with open sores on my legs in winter. Nobody gave me delicacies to mess about on my plate; we were glad when we got potatoes. You make a show of me, mimicking how I used to say these things. But wasn't I right when I told you and your sisters – provided for by me, living like fighting-cocks because I stood in the business twelve hours a day – what did you know of such things? What did anyone know, what I suffered as a child? And then it's a sin if I wanted to give my own son a little pleasure I never had.

And that other business you *schlepped* up out of the past – the night I'm supposed to have shut you out on the *pavlatche*. Because of you the whole world knows the Czech word for the kind of balcony we had in Prague! Yes, the whole world knows that story, too. I am famous, too. You made me famous as the father who frightened his child once and for all: for life. Thank you very much. I want to tell you that I don't even remember that incident. I'm not saying it didn't happen, although you always had an imagination such as nobody ever had before or since, eh? But it could only have been the last resort your mother and I turned to – you know that your mother spoilt you, *over-protected* they would call it, now. You couldn't possibly remember how naughty you were at night, what a little tyrant you were, how you thought of every excuse to keep us sleepless. It was all right for you, you could nap during the day, a small child. But I had my business, I had to earn the living, I needed some rest. Pieces of bread, a particular toy you fancied, make wee-wee, another blanket on, a blanket taken off, drinks of water – there was no end to your tricks and whining. I suppose I couldn't stand it any longer. I feared to do you some harm. (You admit I never beat you, only scared you a little by taking off my braces in preparation to use them on you.) So I put you out of harm's way. That night. Just for a few minutes. It couldn't have been more than a minute. As if your mother would have let you catch cold! God forbid! And you've held it against me all your life. I'm sorry, I have to say it again, that old expression of mine that irritated you so much: I wish I had your worries.

Everything that went wrong for you is my fault. You write it down for sixty pages or so and at the same time you say to me 'I believe you are entirely blameless in the matter of our estrangement.' I was a 'true Kafka', you took after your mother's, the Löwy side, etc. – all you inherited from me, according to you, were your bad traits, without having the benefit of my vitality. I was 'too strong' for you. You could not help it; I could not help it. So? All you wanted was *for me to admit that*, and we could have lived in peace. You were judge, you were jury, you were accused; you sentenced yourself, first. 'At my desk, that is my place. My head in my hands – that is my attitude.' (And that's what your poor mother and I had to look at, that was our pride and joy, our only surviving son!) But I was accused, too; you were judge, you were jury in my case, too. Right? By what right? Fancy goods – you despised the family business that fed us all, that paid for your education. What concern was it of yours, the way I treated the shop assistants? You only took an interest so you could judge, judge. It was a mistake to have let you study law. You did nothing with your qualification, your expensive education that I slaved and ruined my health for. Nothing but sentence me. – Now what did I want to say? Oh yes. Look what you wanted me to admit, under the great writer's beautiful words. If something goes wrong, somebody must be to blame, eh? We were not straw dolls, pulled about from above on strings. One of *us* must be to blame. And don't tell me you think it could be you. The stronger is always to blame, isn't that so? I'm not a deep thinker like you, only a dealer in retail fancy goods, but isn't that a law of life? 'The effect you had on me was the effect you could not help having.' You think I'll believe you're paying me a compliment, forgiving me, when you hand me the worst insult any father could receive? If it's what I am that's to blame, then I'm to blame, to the last drop of my heart's blood and whatever this is that's survived my body, for what *I am*, for being alive and begetting a son! You! Is that it? Because of you *I* should never have lived at all!

You always had a fine genius (never mind your literary one) for working me up. And you knew it was bad for my heart condition. Now, what does it matter . . . but, as God's my witness, you aggravate me . . . you make me . . .

Well.

All I know is that I am to blame for ever. You've seen to that. It's written, and not alone by you. There are plenty of people writing books about Kafka, Franz Kafka. I'm even blamed for the name

I handed down, our family name. *Kavka* is Czech for jackdaw, so that's maybe the reason for your animal obsession. *Dafke*! Insect, ape, dog, mouse, stag, what didn't you imagine yourself. They say the beetle story is a great masterpiece, thanks to me – I'm the one who treated you like an inferior species, gave you the inspiration . . . You wake up as a bug, you give a lecture as an ape. Do any of these wonderful scholars think what this meant to me, having a son who didn't have enough self-respect to feel himself a man?

You have such a craze for animals, but may I remind you, when you were staying with Ottla at Zürau you wouldn't even undress in front of a cat she'd brought in to get rid of the mice . . .

Yet you imagined a dragon coming into your room. It said (an educated dragon, *noch*): 'Drawn hitherto by your longing . . . I offer myself to you.' Your longing, Franz: ugh, for monsters, for perversion. You describe a person (yourself, of course) in some crazy fantasy of living with a horse. Just listen to you, '. . . for a year I lived together with a horse in such ways as, say, a man would live with a girl whom he respects, but by whom he is rejected.' You even gave the horse a girl's name, Eleanor. I ask you, is that the kind of story made up by a normal young man? Is it decent that people should read such things, long after you are gone? But it's published, everything is published.

And worst of all, what about the animal in the synagogue. Some sort of rat, weasel, a marten you call it. You tell how it ran all over during prayers, running along the lattice of the women's section and even climbing down to the curtain in front of the Ark of the Covenant. A *schande*, an animal running about during divine service. Even if it's only a story – only you would imagine it. No respect.

You go on for several pages (in that secret letter) about my use of vulgar Yiddish expressions, about my 'insignificant scrap of Judaism', which was 'purely social' and so meant we couldn't 'find each other in Judaism' if in nothing else. This, from you! When you were a youngster and I had to drag you to the Yom Kippur services once a year you were sitting there making up stories about unclean animals approaching the Ark, the most holy object of the Jewish faith. Once you were grown up, you went exactly once to the Altneu synagogue. The people who write books about you say it must have been to please me. I'd be surprised. When you suddenly discovered you were a Jew, after all, of course your Judaism was highly intellectual, nothing in common with the Jewish customs I was taught to observe in my father's *shtetl*, pushing the barrow at the age of seven. Your Judaism was learnt at the Yiddish Theatre. That's a *nice* crowd! Those dirty-living travelling players you took up with at the Savoy Café. Your friend the actor Jizchak Löwy. No relation to your mother's family, thank God. I wouldn't let such a man even meet her. You had the disrespect to bring him into your parents' home, and I saw it was my duty to speak to him in such a way that he wouldn't ever dare to come back again. (Hah! I used to look down from the window and watch him, hanging around in the cold, outside the building, waiting for you.) And the Tschissik woman, that *nafke*, one of his actresses – I've found out you thought you were in love with her, a married woman (if you can call the way those people live a marriage). Apart from Fräulein Bauer you never fancied anything but a low type of woman. I say it again as I did then: if you lie down with dogs, you get up with fleas. You lost your temper (yes, you, this time), you flew into a rage at your father when he told you that. And when I reminded you of my heart condition, you put yourself in the right again, as usual, you said (I remember like it was yesterday) 'I make great efforts to restrain myself.' But now I've read your diaries, the dead don't need to creep into your bedroom and read them behind your back (which you accused your mother and me of doing), I've read what you wrote afterwards, that you sensed in me, your father, 'as always at such moments of extremity, the existence of a wisdom which I can no more than scent'. So you *knew*, while you were defying me, you knew I was right!

The fact is that you were anti-Semitic, Franz. You were never interested in what was happening to your own people. The hooligans' attacks on Jews in the streets, on houses and shops, that took place while you were growing up – I don't see a word about them in your diaries, your notebooks. You were only *imagining* Jews.

Imagining them tortured in places like your Penal Colony, maybe. I don't want to think about what that means.

Right, towards the end you studied Hebrew, you and your sister Ottla had some wild dream about going to Palestine. You, hardly able to breathe by then, digging potatoes on a kibbutz! The latest book about you says you were in revolt against the 'shopkeeper mentality' of your father's class of Jew; but it was the shopkeeper father, the buttons and buckles, braid, ribbons, ornamental combs, press studs, hooks and eyes, bootlaces, photo frames, shoe horns, novelties and notions that earned the bread for you to dream by. You were anti-Semitic, Franz; if such a thing is possible as for a Jew to cut himself in half. (For you, I suppose, anything is possible.) You told Ottla that to marry that goy Josef Davis was better than marrying ten Jews. When your great friend Brod wrote a book called *The Jewesses* you wrote there were too many of them in it. You saw them like lizards. (Animals again, low animals.) 'However happy we are to watch a single lizard on a footpath in Italy, we would be horrified to see hundreds of them crawling over each other in a pickle jar.' From where did you get such ideas? Not from your home, that I know.

And look how Jewish you are, in spite of the way you despised us – Jews, your Jewish family! You answer questions with questions. I've discovered that's your style, your famous literary style: your Jewishness. Did you or did you not write the following story, playlet, wha'd'you-call-it, your friend Brod kept every scribble and you knew he wouldn't burn even a scrap. 'Once at a spiritualist seance a new spirit announced its presence, and the following conversation with it took place. The spirit: Excuse me. The spokesman: Who are you? The spirit: Excuse me. The spokesman: What do you want? The spirit: To go away. The spokesman: But you've only just come. The spirit: It's a mistake. The spokesman: No, it isn't a mistake. You've come and you'll stay. The spirit: I've just begun to feel ill. The spokesman: Badly? The spirit: Badly? The spokesman: Physically? The spirit: Physically? The spokesman: You answer with questions. That will not do. We have ways of punishing you, so I advise you to answer, for then we shall soon dismiss you. The spirit: Soon? The spokesman: Soon. The spirit: In one minute? The spokesman: Don't go on in this miserable way . . .'

Questions without answers. Riddles. You wrote 'It is always only in contradiction that I can live. But this doubtless applies to everyone; for living, one dies, dying, one lives.' Speak for yourself! So who did you think you were when that whim took you – their prophet, Jesus Christ? What did you *want*? The *goyishe* heavenly hereafter? What did you mean when a lost man, far from his native country, says to someone he meets 'I am in your hands' and the other says, 'No. You are free and that is why you are lost'? What's the sense in writing about a woman 'I lie in wait for her in order not to meet her'? There's only one of your riddles I think I understand, and then only because for forty-two years, God help me, I had to deal with you myself. 'A cage went in search of a bird.' That's you. The cage, not the bird. I don't know why. Maybe it will come to me. As I say, if a person wants to, he can know everything, here.

All that talk about going away. You called your home (more riddles) 'My prison – my fortress'. You grumbled – in print, everything ended up in print, my son – that your room was only a passage, a thoroughfare between the living room and your parents' bedroom. You complained you had to write in pencil because we took away your ink to stop you writing. It was for your own good, your health – already you were a grown man, a qualified lawyer, but you know you couldn't look after yourself. Scribbling away half the night, you'd have been too tired to work properly in the mornings, you'd have lost your position at the Assicurazioni Generali (or was it by then the Arbeiter-Unfall-Versicherungs-Anstalt für das Königreich Böhmen, my memory doesn't get any better, here). And I wasn't made of money. I couldn't go on supporting everybody for ever.

You've published every petty disagreement in the family. It was a terrible thing, according to you, we didn't want you to go out in bad weather, your poor mother wanted you to wrap up. You with your delicate health, always sickly – you didn't inherit my constitution, it was only a lifetime of hard work, the business, the family worries that got me, in the end! You recorded that you couldn't go for a walk without your parents making a fuss, but at twenty-eight you were still living at home. Going away. My poor boy. You could hardly get yourself to the next room. You shut yourself up when people came to visit. Always crawling off to bed, sleeping in the day (oh yes, you couldn't sleep at night, not like anybody else), sleeping your life away. You invented *Amerika* instead of having the guts to emigrate, get up off the bed, pack up and go there, make a new life! Even that girl you jilted twice managed it. Did you know Felice is still alive somewhere, there now, in America? She's an old, old woman with great-grandchildren. They didn't get her into the death camps those highly educated people say you knew about before they happened. America you never went to, Spain you dreamt about . . . your Uncle Alfred was going to find you jobs there, in Madeira, the Azores . . . God knows where else. Grandson of a ritual slaughterer, a *schochet*, that was why you couldn't bear to eat meat, they say, and that made you weak and undecided. So that was my fault, too, because my poor father had to earn a living. When your mother was away from the flat, you'd have starved yourself to death if it hadn't been for me. And what was the result? You resented so much what I provided for you, you went and had your stomach pumped out! Like someone who's been poisoned! And you didn't forget to write it down, either: 'My feeling is that disgusting things will come out.'

Whatever I did for you was *dreck*. You felt 'despised, condemned, beaten down' by me. But you despised *me*; the only difference, I wasn't so easy to beat down, eh? How many times did you try to leave home, and you couldn't go? It's all there in your diaries, in the books they write about you. What about that other masterpiece of yours, 'The Judgement'. A father and son quarrelling, and then the son goes and drowns himself, saying 'Dear parents, I have always loved you, all the same.' The wonderful discovery about that story, you might like to hear, it proves Hermann Kafka most likely didn't want his son to grow up and be a man, any more than his son wanted to manage without his parents' protection. The *meshuggener* who wrote that, may he get rich on it! I wouldn't wish it on him to try living with you, that's all, the way we had to. When your hunchback friend secretly showed your mother a complaining letter of yours, to get you out of your duty of going to the asbestos factory to help your own sister's husband, Brod kept back one thing you wrote. But now it's all published, all, all, all the terrible things you thought about your own flesh and blood. 'I hate them all': father, mother, sisters.

You couldn't do without us – without me. You only moved away from us when you were nearly thirty-two, a time when every *man* has a wife and children already, a home of his own.

You were always dependent on someone. Your friend Brod, poor devil. If it hadn't been for the little hunchback, who would know of your existence today? Between the incinerators that finished your sisters and the fire you wanted to burn up your manuscripts, nothing would be left. The kind of men you invented, the Gestapo, confiscated whatever papers of yours there were in Berlin, and no trace of them has ever been found, even by the great Kafka experts who stick their noses into everything. You said you loved Max Brod more than yourself. I can see that. You liked the idea he had of you, that you knew wasn't yourself (you see, sometimes I'm not so *grob*, uneducated, knowing nothing but fancy goods, maybe I got from you some 'insights'). Certainly, I wouldn't recognise my own son the way Brod described you: 'the aura Kafka gave out of extraordinary strength, something I've never encountered elsewhere, even in meetings with great and famous men . . . the infallible solidity of his insights never tolerated a single lacuna, nor did he ever speak an insignificant word . . . He was life-affirming, ironically tolerant towards the idiocies of the world, and therefore full of sad humour.'

I must say, your mother who put up with your faddiness when she came back from a day standing in the business, your sisters who acted in your plays to please you, your father who worked his heart out for his family – we never got the benefit of your tolerance. Your sisters (except Ottla, the one you admit you were a bad influence on, encouraging her to leave the shop and work on a farm like a peasant, to starve herself with you on rabbit-food, to marry that goy) were giggling idiots, so far as you were concerned. Your mother never felt the comfort of her son's strength. You never gave us anything to laugh at, sad or otherwise. And you hardly spoke to me at all, even an insignificant word. Whose fault was it you were that person you describe 'strolling about on the island in the pool, where there are neither books nor bridges, hearing the music, but not being heard.' You wouldn't cross a road, never mind a bridge, to pass the time of day, to be pleasant to other people, you shut yourself in your room and stuffed your ears with Oropax against the music of life, yes, the sounds of cooking, people coming and going (what were we supposed to do, pass through closed doors?), even the singing of the pet canaries annoyed you, laughter, the occasional family tiff, the bed squeaking where normal married people made love.

What I've just said may surprise. That last bit, I mean. But since I died in 1931 I know the world has changed a lot. People, even fathers and sons, are talking about things that shouldn't be talked about. People aren't ashamed to read anything, even private diaries, even letters. There's no shame, anywhere. With that, too, you were ahead of your time, Franz. You were not ashamed to write in your diary, which your friend Brod would publish – you must have known he would publish everything, make a living out of us – things that have led one of the famous Kafka scholars to *study* the noises in our family flat in Prague. Writing about me: 'It would have been out of character for Hermann Kafka to restrain any noises he felt like making during coupling; it would have been out of character for Kafka, who was ultra-sensitive to noise and had grown up with these noises, to mention the suffering they caused him.'

You left behind you for everyone to read that the sight of your parents' pyjamas and nightdress on the bed disgusted you. Let me also speak freely like everyone else. You were made in that bed. That disgusts me: your disgust over a place that should have been holy to you, a place to hold in the highest respect. Yet you are the one who complained about my coarseness when I suggested you ought to find yourself a woman – buy one, hire one – rather than try to prove yourself a man at last, at thirty-six, by marrying some Prague Jewish tart who shook her tits in a thin blouse. Yes, I'm speaking of that Julie Wohryzek, the shoemaker's daughter, your second fiancée. You even had the insolence to throw the remark in my face, in that letter you didn't send, but I've read it anyway, I've read everything now, although you said I put 'In The Penal Colony' on the bedside table and never mentioned it again.

I have to talk about another matter we didn't discuss, father and son, while we were both alive – all right, it was my fault, maybe you're right, as I've said, times were different . . . Women. I must bring this up because – my poor boy – marriage was 'the greatest terror' of your life. You write that. You say your attempts to explain why you couldn't marry – on these depends the 'success' of the whole letter you didn't send. According to you, marrying, founding a family was 'the utmost a human being can succeed in doing at all'. Yet you couldn't marry. How is any ordinary human being to understand that? You wrote more than a quarter of a million words to Felice Bauer, but you couldn't be a husband to her. You put your parents through the farce of travelling all the way to Berlin for an engagement party (there's the photograph you had taken, the happy couple, in the books they write about you, by the way). The engagement was broken, was on again, off again. Can you wonder? Anyone who goes into a bookshop or library can read what you wrote to your fiancée when your sister Elli gave birth to our first granddaughter. You felt nothing but nastiness, envy against your brother-in-law because 'I'll never have a child.' No, not with the Bauer girl, not in a decent marriage, like anybody else's son; but I've found out you had a child, Brod says so, by a woman, Grete Bloch, who was supposed to be the Bauer girl's best friend, who even acted as matchmaker between you! What do you say to that? Maybe it's news to you. I don't know. (That's how irresponsible you were.) They say she went away. Perhaps she never told you.

As for the next one you tried to marry, the one you make such a song and dance over because of my remark about Prague Jewesses and the blouse, etc. – for once you came to your senses, and you called off the wedding only two days before it was supposed to take place. Not that I could have influenced you. Since when did you take into consideration what your parents thought? When you told me you wanted to marry the shoemaker's daughter – naturally I was upset. At least the Bauer girl came from a nice family. What I said about the blouse just came out, I'm human, after all. But I was frank with you, man to man. You weren't a youngster any more. A man doesn't have to marry a nothing who will go with anybody.

I saw what that marriage was about, my poor son. You wanted a woman. Nobody understood that better than I did, believe me, I was normal man enough, eh! There were places in Prague where one could get a woman. (I suppose whatever's happened, there still are, always will be.) I tried to help you; I offered to go along with you myself. I said it in front of your mother, who – yes, as you write you were so shocked to see, was in agreement with me. We wanted so much to help you, even your own mother would go so far as that.

But in that letter you didn't think I'd ever see, you accuse me of humiliating you and I don't know what else. You wanted to marry a tart, but you were insulted at the idea of buying one?

Writing that letter only a few days after you yourself called off your second try at getting married, aged thirty-six, you find that your father, as a man of the world, not only showed 'contempt' for you on that occasion, but that when he had spoken to you as a broad-minded father when you were a youngster, he had given you information that set off the whole ridiculous business of your never being able to marry, ever. Already, twenty years before the Julie Wohryzek row, with 'a few frank words' (as you put it) your father made you incapable of taking a wife and pushed you down 'into the filth as if it were my destiny'. You remember some walk with your mother and me on the Josefsplatz when you showed curiosity about, well, men's feelings and women, and I was open and honest with you and told you I could give you advice about where to go so that these things could be done quite safely, without bringing home any disease. You were sixteen years old, physically a man, not a child, eh? Wasn't it time to talk about such things?

Shall I tell you what *I* remember? Once you picked a quarrel with your mother and me because we hadn't educated you sexually – your words. Now you complain because I tried to guide you in these matters. I did – I didn't. Make up your mind. Have it your own way. Whatever I did, you believed it was *because of what I did* that you couldn't bring yourself to marry. When you thought you wanted the Bauer girl, didn't I give in, to please you? Although you were in no financial position to marry, although I had to give your two married sisters financial help, although I had worries enough, a sick man, you'd caused me enough trouble by persuading me to invest in a *mechulah* asbestos factory? Didn't I give in? And when the girl came to Prague to meet your parents and sisters, you wrote, 'My family likes her almost more than I'd like it to.' So it went as far as that: you couldn't like anything we liked, was that why you couldn't marry her?

A long time ago, a long way . . . ah, it all moves away, it's getting faint . . . But I haven't finished. Wait.

You say you wrote your letter because you wanted to explain why you couldn't marry. I'm writing this letter because you tried to write it for me. *You would take even that away from your father.* You answered your own letter, before I could. You made what you imagine as my reply part of the letter you wrote me. To save me the trouble . . . Brilliant, like they say. With your great gifts as a famous writer, you express it all better than I could. You are there, quickly, with an answer, before I can be. You take the words out of my mouth: while you are accusing yourself, in my name, of being 'too clever, obsequious, parasitic and insincere' in blaming your life on me, you are – yet again, one last time! – finally being too clever, obsequious, parasitic and insincere in the trick of stealing your father's chance to defend himself. A genius. What is left to say about you if – how well you know yourself, my boy, it's terrible – you call yourself the kind of vermin that doesn't only sting, but at the same time sucks blood to keep itself alive? And even that isn't the end of the twisting, the cheating. You then confess that this whole 'correction', 'rejoinder', as you, an expensively educated man, call it, 'does not originate' in your father but in you yourself, Franz Kafka. So you see, here's the proof, something *I* know you, with all your brains, can't know *for me*: you say you always wrote about me, it was all about me, your father; but it was all about you. The beetle. The bug that lay on its back waving its legs in the air and couldn't get up to go and see America or the Great Wall of China. You, you, self, self. And in your letter, after you have defended me against yourself, when you finally make the confession – right again, in the right again, always – you take the last word, in proof of your saintliness I could know nothing about, never understand, a businessman, a shopkeeper. That is your 'truth' about us you hoped might be able to 'make our living and our dying easier'.

The way you ended up, Franz. The last woman you found yourself. It wasn't our wish, God knows. Living with that Eastern Jewess, and in sin. We sent you money; that was all we could do. If we'd come to see you, if we'd swallowed our pride, meeting that woman, our presence would only have made you worse. It's there in everything you've written, everything they write about you: everything connected with us made you depressed and ill. We knew she was giving you the wrong food, cooking like a gypsy on a spirit stove. She kept you in an unheated hovel in Berlin . . . may God forgive me (Brod has told the world), I had to turn my back on her at your funeral.

Franz . . . When you received copies of your book 'In The Penal Colony' from Kurt Wolff Verlag that time . . . You gave me one and I said 'Put it on the night-table.' You say I never mentioned it again. Well, don't you understand – I'm not a literary man. I'm telling you now. I read a little bit, a page or two at a time. If you had seen that book, there was a pencil mark every two, three pages, so I would know next time where I left off. It wasn't like the books I knew – I hadn't much time for reading, working like a slave since I was a small boy, I wasn't like you, I couldn't shut myself up in a room with books, when I was young. I would have starved. But you know that. Can't you understand that I was – yes – not too proud – ashamed to let you know I didn't find it easy to understand your kind of writing, it was all strange to me.

Hah! I know I'm no intellectual, but I knew how to live!

Just a moment . . . give me time . . . there's a fading . . . Yes – can you imagine how we felt when Ottla told us you had tuberculosis? Oh how could you bring it over your heart to remind me I once said, in a temper, to a useless assistant coughing all over the shop (you should have had to deal with those lazy *goyim*), he ought to die, the sick dog. Did I know you would get tuberculosis, too? It wasn't our fault your lungs rotted. I tried to expand your chest when you were little, teaching you to swim; you should never have moved out of your own home, the care of your parents, to that rat-hole in the Schönbornpalais. And the hovel in Berlin . . . We had some good times, didn't we? Franz? When we had beer and sausages after the swimming lessons? At least you remembered the beer and sausages, when you were dying.

One more thing. It chokes me, I have to say it. I know you'll never answer. You once wrote 'Speech is possible only where one wants to lie.' You were too *ultra-sensitive* to speak to us, Franz. You kept silence, with the truth: those playing a game of cards, turning in bed on the other side of the wall – it was the sound of live people you didn't like. Your revenge, that you were too cowardly to take in life, you've taken here. We can't lie peacefully in our graves; dug up, unwrapped from our shrouds by your fame. To desecrate your parents' grave as well as their bed, aren't you ashamed? Aren't you ashamed – now? Well, what's the use of quarrelling. We lie together in the same grave – you, your mother and I. We've ended up as we always should have been, united. Rest in peace, my son. I wish you had let me.

Your father,
Hermann Kafka

Something Out There

Stanley Dobrow, using the Canonball Sureshot, one of three cameras he was given for his barmitzvah, photographed it. He did. *I promise you*, he said – as children adjure integrity by pledging to the future something that has already happened. His friends Hilton and Sharon also saw it: Stanley jacked himself from the pool, ran through the house leaving wet footprints all the way up the new stair carpet, and fetched the Canonball Sureshot.

The thrashing together of two tree tops – that was all that came out.

When other people claimed to have seen it – or another one like it: there were reports from other suburbs, quite far away – and someone's beautiful Persian tabby and someone else's fourteen-year-old dachshund were found mauled and dead, Stanley's father believed him and phoned a newspaper to report his son's witness. *Predator At Large In Plush Suburbs* was the headline tried out by a university graduate newly hired as a sub-editor; the chief sub thought 'predator' an upstage word for a mass-circulation Sunday paper and substituted 'wild animal', adding a question mark at the end of the line. The report claimed a thirteen-year-old schoolboy had been the first to see the creature, and had attempted to photograph it. Stanley's name, which had lost a syllable when his great-grandfather Leib Dobrowsky landed from Lithuania in 1920, was misspelt as 'Dobrov'. His mother carefully corrected this in the cuttings she sent to her mother-in-law, a cousin abroad, and to the collateral family who had given the camera. People telephoned: I believe your Stan was in the paper! *What* was it he saw?

A vet said the teeth-marks on the dead pets, Mrs Sheena McLeod's 'Natasha' and the Bezuidenhout family's beloved 'Fritzie', were consistent with the type of bite given by a wild cat. Less than a hundred years ago, *viverra civetta* must have been a common species in the koppies around the city; nature sometimes came back, forgot time and survived eight-lane freeways, returning to ancestral haunts. He recalled the suicidal swim of two elephants who struck out making for ancient mating grounds across Lake Kariba, beneath which 5,000 square kilometres of their old ruminants' pathways were drowned in a man-made sea. A former pet-shop owner wrote to *Readers' Views* with the opinion that the animal almost certainly was a vervet monkey, an escaped pet. Those who had seen it insisted it was a larger species, though most likely of the ape family. Stanley Dobrow and his two friends described the face reflected between trees, beside them on the surface of the swimming pool: dark face with 'far-back' eyes – whether what broke the image was Stanley's scramble from the water or the advance of the caterpillar device that crawled about the pool sucking up dirt, they never agreed.

Whatever it was, it made a nice change from the usual sort of news, these days. Nothing but strikes, exchanges of insults between factions of what used to be a power to be relied upon, disputes over boundaries that had been supposed to divide peace and prosperity between all, rioting students, farmers dissatisfied with low prices, consumers paying more for bread and mealie meal, more insults – these coming in the form of boycotts and censures from abroad, beyond the fished-out territorial waters. It was said the local fishing industry was ruined by poaching Russians (same old bad news).

Now this event that was causing excitement over in the Johannesburg suburbs: that was the kind of item there used to be – before the papers started calling blacks 'Mr' and publishing the terrible things communists taught them to say about the white man. Those good old stories of giant pumpkins and – Mrs Naas Klopper remembered it so well – when she was a little child, that lion that lived with a little fox terrier in its cage at the Jo'burg zoo; this monkey or whatever it was gave you something to wonder about again, talk about; it had something to do with your own life, it could happen to you (imagine! what a scare, to see a thing like that, some creature jumping out in your own yard), not like all that other stuff, that happened somewhere else, somewhere you'd never seen and never would, the United Nations there in New York, or the blacks' places – Soweto.

Mrs Naas Klopper (she always called herself, although her name was Hester) read in *Die Transvaaler* about the creature in the Johannesburg suburbs while waiting for the rice to boil in time for lunch. She sat in the split-level lounge of what she was always quietly aware of as her 'lovely home' Naas had built according to her artistic ideas when first he began to make money out of his agency for the sale of farmland and agricultural plots, fifteen years ago. Set on several acres outside a satellite country town where Klopper's Eiendoms Beperk flourished, the house had all the features of prosperous suburban houses in Johannesburg or Pretoria. The rice was boiling in an all-electric kitchen with eye-level microwave oven and cabinet deep-freezer. The bedrooms were en suite, with pot plants in the respectively pink and green bathrooms. The living room in which she sat on a nylon-velvet covered sofa had pastel plastic Venetian blinds as well as net curtains and matching nylon velvet drapes, and the twelve chairs in the dining area were covered with needlepoint worked in a design of shepherdesses and courtiers by Mrs Naas Klopper herself; the dried-flower-and-shell pictures were also her work, she had crocheted the tasselled slings by which plants were suspended above the cane furniture on the glassed sun-porch, and it was on a trip to the Victoria Falls, when Rhodesia was still Rhodesia, that she had bought the hammered copper plaques. The TV set was behind a carved console door. Stools set around the mini bar again bore the original touch – they were covered not exactly with modish zebra skin, but with the skins of impala which Naas himself had shot. Outside, there was a palette-shaped swimming pool like the one in which Stanley and friends, forty kilometres away in Johannesburg, had seen the face.

Yet although the lovely home was every brick as good as any modern lovely home in the city, it had something of the enclosing gloom of the farmhouse in which Naas had spent his childhood. He never brought that childhood to the light of reminiscence or reflection because he had put all behind him; he was on the other side of the divide history had opened between the farmer and the trader, the past when the Boers were a rural people and the *uitlanders* ran commerce, and the present, when the Afrikaners governed an industrialised state and had become entrepreneurs, stockbrokers, beer millionaires – all the synonyms for traders. When he began to plan the walls to house his wife's artistic ideas, a conception of dimness, long gaunt passages by which he had been contained at his Ma's place, and his Ouma's, loomed its proportions around the ideas. He met Mrs Naas now in the dark bare passage that led to the kitchen, on her way to drain the rice. They never used the front door, except for visitors; it seemed there were visitors: 'Ag, Hester, can you quickly make some coffee or tea?'

'I'm just getting lunch! It's all ready.'

There was something unnatural, assumed, about him that she had long associated with him 'doing business'. He did not have time to doff the manner for her, as a man will throw down his hat as he comes into the kitchen from his car in the yard. 'All right. Who is it, then?'

'Some people about the Kleynhans place. They're in the car, so long. A young couple. Unlock the front door.'

'Why'd you say tea?'

'They speak English.'

A good businessman thinks of everything; his wife smiled. And a good home-maker is always prepared. Her arched step in high-heeled shoes went to slide the bolt on the Spanish-style hand-carved door; while her husband flushed the lavatory and went out again through the kitchen, she took down her cake tins filled with rusks and home-made glazed biscuits to suit all tastes, English and other. The kettle was on and the cups set out on a cross-stitched traycloth before she sensed a press of bodies through the front entrance. She kept no servant in the house – had the gardener's wife in to clean three times a week, and the washwoman worked outside in the laundry – and could always feel at once, even if no sound were made, when the pine aerosol-fresh space in her lovely home was displaced by any body other than her own.

Naas's voice, speaking English the way we Afrikaners do (she thought of it), making it a softer, kinder language than it is, was the one she could make out, coming from the lounge. When he paused, perhaps they were merely smiling in the gap; were shy.

A young man got up to take the tray from her the moment she appeared; yes, silent, clumsy, polite – nicely brought up. The introductions were a bit confused, Naas didn't seem sure he had the name right, and she, Mrs Naas, had to say in *her* English, comfortable and friendly – turning to the young woman: 'What was your name, again?'

And the young man answered for his wife. 'She's Anna.'

Mrs Naas laughed. 'Yes, Anna, that's a good Afrikaans name, too, you know. But the other name?'

'I'm Charles Rosser.' He was looking anxiously for a place to set down the tray. Mrs Naas guided him to one of her coffee tables, moving a vase of flowers.

'Now is it with milk and sugar, Mrs Rosser? I've got lemon here, too, our own lemons from the garden.'

The young woman didn't expect to be waited on: really well brought up people. She was already there, standing to help serve the men; tall, my, and how thin! You could see her hip bones through her crinkly cotton skirt, one of those Indian skirts all the girls go around in nowadays. She wore glasses. A long thin nose spoilt her face, otherwise quite nice-looking, nothing on it but a bit of blue on the eyelids, and the forehead tugged tight by flat blonde hair twisted into a knob.

'It's tiring work all right, looking for accommodation.' (Naas knew all the estate agent's words, in English, he hardly ever was caught out saying 'house' when a more professional term existed.) 'Thirsty work.'

The young man checked the long draught he was taking from his cup. He smiled to Mrs Naas. 'This is very welcome.'

'Oh, only a pleasure. I know when I go to town to shop – I can tell you, I come home and I'm finished! That's why we built out here, you know; I said to my husband, it's going to be nothing but more cars, cars, and more motorbikes—'

'And she's talking of fifteen years ago! Now it's a madhouse, Friday and Saturday, all the Bantu buses coming into town from the location, the papers and beer cans thrown everywhere—' (Naas offered rusks and biscuits again) that's why you're wise to look for somewhere a bit out – not far out, mind you, the wife needs to be able to come in to go to the supermarket and that, you don't want to feel *cut off*—'

'I must say, I never feel cut off!' his wife enjoyed supporting him. 'I've got my peace and quiet, and there's always something to do with my hands.'

Naas spoke as if he had not already told her: 'We're going to look over the Kleynhans place.'

'Oh, I thought you've come from there!'

'We going now-now. I just thought, why pass by the house, let's at least have a cup of tea . . .'

'Is there anybody there?'

'Just the boy who looks after the garden and so on.'

When they spoke English together it seemed to them to come out like the dialogue from a television series. And the young couple sat mute, as the Klopper grandchildren did before the console when they came to spend a night.

'Can I fill up?' Standing beside her with his cup the young man reminded her not of Dawie who had Naas's brown eyes, didn't take after her side of the family at all, but of Herman, her sister Miemie's son. The same glistening, young blond beard, so manly it seemed growing like a plant while you looked at it. The short pink nose. Even the lips, pink and sun-cracked as a kid's.

'Come on! Have some more biscuits – please help yourself . . . And Mrs Rosser? – *please* – there's another whole tin in the kitchen . . . I forget there's no children in the house any more, I bake too much every time.'

She was shy, that girl; at last a smile out of her.

'Thanks, I'll have a rusk.'

'Well I'm glad you enjoy my rusks, an old, old family recipe. Oh you'll like the Kleynhans place. I always liked it, didn't I, Naas – I often say to my husband, that's the kind of place we ought to have. I've got a lovely home here, of course I wouldn't really change it, but it's so big, now, too big for two people. A lot of work; I do it all myself, I don't want anyone in my place, I don't want all that business of having to lock up my sugar and tea – no, I'll rather do everything myself. I can't stand to feel one of them there at my back all the time.'

'But there's nothing to be afraid of in this area.' Naas did not look at her but corrected her drift at a touch of the invisible signals of long familiarity.

'Oh no, this's a safe place to live. I'm alone all day, only the dog in the yard, and she's so old now – did she even wake up and come round the front when you came? – ag, poor old Ounooi! It's safe here, not like the *other* side of the town, near the location. You can't even keep your garden hose there, even the fence around your house – they'll come and take everything. But this side . . . no one will worry you.'

Perhaps the young man was not quite reassured. 'How far away would the nearest neighbours be?'

'No, not far. There's Reynecke about three or four kilometres, the other side of the koppie – there's a nice little koppie, a bit of real veld, you know, on the southern border of the property.'

'And the other sides? Facing the house?' The young man looked over to his wife, whose feet were together under her long skirt, cup neatly balanced on her lap, and eyes on cup, inattentive; then he smiled to Mr and Mrs Naas. 'We don't want to live in the country and at the same time be disturbed by neighbours' noise.'

Naas laughed and put a hand on each knee, thrusting his head forward amiably; over the years he had developed gestures that marked each stage in the conclusion of a land deal, as each clause goes to comprise a contract.

'You won't hear nothing but the birds.'

On a Thursday afternoon Doctors Milton Caro, pathologist, Grahame Fraser-Smith, maxillo-facial surgeon, Arthur Methus, gynaecologist and Dolf van Gelder, orthopaedic surgeon, had an encounter on Houghton Golf Course. Doctors Caro, Fraser-Smith, Methus and van Gelder are all distinguished specialists in their fields, with degrees from universities abroad as well as at home, and they are not available to the sick at all hours and on all days, like any general practitioner. In fact, since so many of the younger medical specialists have emigrated to take up appointments in safer countries – America, Canada, Australia – patients sometimes have the embarrassment of having recovered spontaneously before arriving for appointments that have to be booked a minimum of three months ahead. Others may have died; in which case, the ruling by the Medical Association that appointments not kept will be charged for, is waived.

The doctors do not consult on Thursday afternoons. The foursome, long-standing members of the Houghton Club, has an almost equally long-standing arrangement to tee off at 2 p.m. (Caro and van Gelder also take long walks together, carrying stout sticks, on Sunday mornings. Van Gelder would like to make jogging a punishable offence, like drunken driving. He sees too many cases of attributable Achilles tendonitis, of chondromalacia patellae caused by repetitive gliding of the patella over the femur, and, of course, of chronic strain of the ligaments, particularly in flat-footed patients.) On this particular afternoon Fraser-Smith and van Gelder were a strong partnership, and Methus was letting Caro down rather badly. It is this phenomenon of an erratic handicap that provides the pleasure mutually generated by the company. The style of their communication is banter; without error, there would be nothing to banter about. This Thursday the supreme opportunity arose because it was not Methus, in his ham-handed phase, who sent a ball way off into a grove of trees, but Fraser-Smith, who on the previous hole had scored an eagle. Van Gelder groaned, Fraser-Smith cursed himself in an amazement that heightened Caro's and Methus's mock glee. And then Caro, who had marked where the ball fell into shade, went good-naturedly with Fraser-Smith, who was short-sighted, over to the trees. Fraser-Smith, still cursing amiably, moved into the grove where Caro directed.

'Which side of the bush? Here? I'll never find the sodding thing.' At Guy's Hospital thirty years before he had picked up the panache of British cuss-words he never allowed himself to forget.

Caro, despite the Mayo Clinic and distinguished participation at international congresses on forensic medicine, called back in the gruff, slow homeliness of a Jewish country storekeeper's son whose early schooling was in Afrikaans. 'Ag, man, d'you want me to come and bleddy well hit it for you? It must be just on the left there, man!'

Exactly where the two men were gazing, someone – something that must have been crouching – rose, a shape broken by the shapes of trees; there was an instant when they, it, were aware of one another. And then whoever or whatever it was was gone, in a soft crashing confusion among branches and bushes. Caro shouted – ridiculously, he was the first to admit – 'Hey! Hey!'

'Well,' (they were embellishing their story at the clubhouse) 'I thought he'd pinched old Grahame's ball, and I wanted to say thanks very much, because Methus and I, we were playing like a pair of clowns, we needed some monkey-business to help us out . . .'

Fraser-Smith was sure the creature had gone up a tree, although when the foursome went to look where he thought it had climbed, there was nothing. Methus said if it hadn't been for all the newspaper tales they'd been reading, none of them would have got the mad idea it was anything but a man – one of the black out-of-works, the *dronkies* who have their drinking sessions in there; wasn't it true they were a problem for the groundsmen, no fence seemed to keep them and their litter out? There were the usual empty beer cans under the tree where Fraser-Smith said he . . . 'Anyway, the papers talked about a monkey, and we all saw – this was something big . . . a black, that's all, and he got a scare . . . you know, how you can't make out a black face in shadow, among leaves.'

Caro spoke aside: 'A black having a crap, exactly . . .'

But van Gelder was certain. No one had seen, in the moment the being had looked at the foursome, and the foursome had looked at it, a face, distinct garments, limbs. Van Gelder had observed the gait, and in gait van Gelder read bones. 'It was not a monkey. It was not a man. That was a baboon.'

The couple didn't have much to say for themselves, that day while Naas Klopper was showing them over the Kleynhans place. In his experience this was a bad sign. Clients who took an instant liking to a property always thought they were being shrewd by concealing their keenness to buy under voluble fault-picking calculated to bring down the price. They would pounce on disadvantages in every feature of aspect and construction. This meant the deed of sale was as good as signed. Those who said nothing were the ones who had taken an instant dislike to a property, or – as if they could read his mind, because, hell man, he was an old hand at the game, he never let slip a thing – uncannily understood at once that it was a bad buy. When people trailed around in silence behind him he filled that silence entirely by himself, every step and second of it, slapping with the flat of a hand the pump of whose specifications, volume of water per hour, etcetera, he spared no detail, opening stuck cupboard doors and scratching a white-ridged thumbnail down painted walls to the accompaniment of patter about storage space and spotless condition; and all the time he was wanting just to turn round and herd right out the front door people who were wasting his time.

But this girl didn't have the averted face of the wives who had made up their minds they wouldn't let their husbands buy. Naas knows what interests the ladies. They don't notice if guttering is rotted or electrical wiring is old and unsafe. What they care about is fitted kitchen units and whether the new suite will look right in what will be the lounge. When he pointed out the glassed-in stoep that would make a nice room for sewing and that, or a kiddies' playroom (but I don't suppose you've got any youngsters? – not yet, ay) she stood looking over it obediently through her big round glasses as if taking instructions. And the lounge, a bit original (two small rooms of the old farmhouse from the twenties knocked into one) with half the ceiling patterned pressed lead and the other 'modernised' with pine strips and an ox-wagon wheel adapted as a chandelier – she smiled, showing beautiful teeth, and nodded slowly all round the room, turning on her heel.

Same thing outside, with the husband. He was interested in the outhouses, of course. Nice double shed, could garage two cars – full of junk, naturally, when a place's been empty, only a boy in charge – Kleynhans's old boy, and his hundred-and-one hangers-on, wife, children, whatnot . . . 'But we'll get that all cleaned up for you, no problem.' Naas shouted for the boy, but the outhouse where he'd been allowed to live was closed, an old padlock on the door. 'He's gone off somewhere. Never here whenever I come, that's how he looks after the place. Well – I wanted to show you the room but I suppose it doesn't matter, the usual boy's room . . . p'raps you won't want to have anybody, like Mrs Klopper, you'll rather do for yourselves? Specially as you from overseas, ay . . .'

The young husband asked how big the room was, and whether, since the shed was open, there was no other closed storage room.

'Oh, like I said, just the usual boy's room, not *very* small, no. But you can easy brick in the shed if you want, I can send you good boys for building, it won't cost a lot. And there's those houses for pigs, at one time Kleynhans was keeping pigs. Clean them up – no problem. But man, I'm sure if you been doing a bit of farming in England you good with your hands, ay? You used to repairs and that? Of course. And here it doesn't cost much to get someone in to help . . . You know' (he cocked his head coyly) 'you and your wife, you don't sound like the English from England usually speak . . . ? You sound more like the English here.'

The wife looked at the husband and this time she was the one to answer at once, for him. 'Well, no. Because, you see – we're really Australian. Australians speak English quite a lot like South Africans.'

The husband added, 'We've been *living* in England, that's all.'

'Well, I thought so. I thought, well, if they English, it's from some part where I never heard the people speak!' Naas felt, in a blush of confidence, he was getting on well with this couple. 'Australian, that's good. A good country. A lot like ours. Only without our problems, ay.' (Naas allowed himself to pause and shake his head, exclaim, although it was a rule never to talk politics with clients.) 'There's a lot of exchange between sheep farmers in Australia and here in South Africa. Last year I think it was, my brother-in-law had some Australian farmers come to see him at his place in the Karoo – that's our best sheep country. He even ordered a ram from them. Six thousand Australian dollars! A lot of money, ay? Oh but what an animal. You should see – bee-yeu-tiful.'

In the house, neither husband nor wife remarked that the porcelain lid of the lavatory cistern was broken, and Naas generously drew their attention to it himself. 'I'll get you a new one cheap. Jewish chappies I know who run plumbing supplies, they'll always do me a favour. Anything you want in that line, you just tell me.'

In the garden, finally (Naas never let clients linger in a garden before entering a house on a property that had been empty a long time – a neglected garden puts people off), he sensed a heightened interest alerting the young couple. They walked round the walls of the house, shading their eyes to look at the view from all sides, while Naas tried to prop up a fallen arch of the wire pergola left from the days when Mrs Kleynhans was still alive. To tell the truth the view wasn't much. Apart from the koppie behind the house, just bare veld with black, burned patches, now, before the rains. Old Kleynhans liked to live isolated on this dreary bit of land, the last years he hadn't even let out the hundred acres of his plot to the Portuguese vegetable farmers, as he used to. As for the garden – nothing left, the blacks had broken the fruit trees for firewood, a plaster Snow White had fallen into the dry fishpond. It was difficult to find some feature of interest or beauty to comment on as he stood beside the couple after their round of the house, looking across the veld. He pointed. 'Those things over there, way over there. That's the cooling towers of the power station.' They followed his arm politely.

Of course, he should have suspected something. Unlikely that you could at last get rid of the Kleynhans place so easily. When they were back in town in Klopper's Eiendoms Beperk and Juffrou Jansens had brought the necessary documents into his office, it turned out that they wanted to rent the place for six months, with the option of purchase. They didn't want to buy outright. He knew it must be because they didn't have the money, but they wouldn't admit that. The husband brushed aside suggestions that a bond could be arranged on a very small deposit, Naas Klopper was an expert in these matters.

'You see, my wife is expecting a child, we want to be in the country for a while. But we're not sure if we're going to settle . . .'

Naas became warmly fatherly. 'But if you starting a family, that's the time to settle! You can run chickens there, man, start up the pigs again. Or hire out the land for someone else to work. In six months' time, who knows what's going to happen to land prices? Now it's rock bottom, man. I'll get you a ninety-per-cent bond.'

The girl looked impatient; it must have been embarrassment.

'She – my wife – she's had several miscarriages. A lot depends on that . . . if this time there's a child, we can make up our minds whether we want to farm here or not. If something goes wrong again . . . she might want to go back.'

'To Australia.' The girl spoke without looking at the men.

The Kleynhans place had been on Klopper's Eiendoms Beperk's books for nearly three years. And it seemed true what the husband said, they had money. They paid six months' rent in advance. So there was nothing to lose, so far as Mathilda Beukes, née Kleynhans, who had inherited the place, was concerned. Naas took their cheque. They didn't even want the place cleaned up before they moved in; energetic youngsters, they'd do it themselves. He gave them one last piece of advice, along with the keys. 'Don't keep on Kleynhans's old boy, he'll come to you with a long story, but I've told him before, he'll have to get off the place when someone moves in. He's no good.'

The couple agreed at once. In fact, the husband made their first and only request. 'Would you see to it, then, that he leaves by the end of the week? We want him to be gone before we arrive.'

'No-o-o problem. And listen, if you want a boy, I can get you one. My garden boy knows he can't send me *skelms*.' The young wife had been stroking, again and again, with one finger, the silver-furred petal of a protea in an arrangement of dried Cape flowers Naas had had on his desk almost as long as the Kleynhans place had been on his books. 'You love flowers, ay? I can see it! Here – take these with you. Please; have it. Mrs Klopper makes the arrangements herself.'

A baboon; unlikely.

Although the medical profession tacitly disapproves of gratuitous publicity among its members (as if an orthopaedic surgeon of the eminence of Dolf van Gelder needs to attract patients!) and Dr van Gelder refused an interview with a fat Sunday paper, the paper put together its story anyway. The journalist went to the head of the Department of Anthropology at the Medical School, and snipped out of a long disquisition recorded there on tape a popular account, translated into mass-circulation vocabulary, of the differences in the skeletal conformation and articulation in man, ape and baboon. The old girls yellowing along with the cuttings in the newspaper group's research library dug up one of those charts that show the evolutionary phases of anthropoid to hominid, with man an identikit compilation of his past and present. As there was no photograph of whatever the doctors had seen, the paper made do with the chart, blacking out the human genitalia, but leaving the anthropoids'. It was, after all, a family paper. WILL YOU KNOW HIM WHEN YOU MEET HIM? Families read that the ape-like creature which was 'terrorising the Northern Suburbs was not, in the expert opinion of the Professor of Anthropology, likely to be a baboon, whatever conclusions his respected colleague, orthopaedic surgeon and osteologist Dr Dolf van Gelder, had drawn from the bone conformation indicated by its stance or gait.

The Johannesburg zoo stated once again that no member of the ape family was missing, including any specimen of the genus *anthropopithecus*, which is most likely to be mistaken for man. There are regular checks of all inmates and of security precautions. The SPCA warned the public that whether a baboon or not, a member of the ape family is a danger to cats and dogs, and people should keep their pets indoors at night.

Since the paper was not a daily, a whole week had to go by before the result of the strange stirring in the fecund mud of association that causes people to write to newspapers about secret preoccupations set off by the subject of an article, could be read by them in print. 'Only Man Is Vile' (Rondebosch) wrote that since a coronary attack some years ago he had been advised to keep a pet to lessen cardiac anxiety. His marmoset, a Golden Lion tamarin from South America, had the run of the house 'including two cats and a Schipperke' and was like a mother to them. He could only urge other cardiac sufferers to ignore warnings about the dangers of pets. 'Had Enough' (Roosevelt Park) invited the ape, baboon, monkey, etc. to come and kill her neighbour's dog, who barked all night and was responsible for her daughter's anorexia nervosa. Howard C. Butterfield III had 'enjoyed your lovely country' until he and his wife were mugged only ten yards from the Moulin Rouge Hotel in Hillbrow, Johannesburg. He'd like to avail himself of the hospitality of 'your fine paper' to tell the black man who slapped his wife before snatching her purse that he had broken her dental bridgework, causing pain and inconvenience on what was to have been the holiday of a lifetime, and that he was no better than any uncivilised ape at large.

Mrs Naas Klopper made a detour on her way to visit her sister Miemie in Pretoria. She had her own car, of course, a ladies' car Naas provided for her, smaller than his Mercedes, a pretty green Toyota. She hadn't seen the Kleynhans place for, oh, four or five years – before the old man died. A shock. It *was* a mess; she felt sorry for that young couple . . . really.

She and her sister dressed up for each other, showing off new clothes as they had done when they were girls; the clean soles of her new ankle-strap shoes gritted against the stony drive as she planted the high heels well apart, for balance, and leant into the back of the car to take out her house-warming present.

The girl appeared in the garden, from the backyard. She must have heard the approach of a car.

Mrs Naas Klopper was coming towards her through weeds, insteps arched like proud fists under an intricacy of narrow yellow straps, the *bombé* of breasts flashing gold chains on blue polka dots that crowded together to form a border at the hem of the dress. The girl's recognition of the face, seen only once before, was oddly strengthened, like a touched-up photograph, by make-up the original hadn't been wearing: teeth brightly circled by red lips, blinking blue eyes shuttered with matching lids. Carried before the bosom was a large round biscuit drum flashing tinny colours.

Mrs Naas saw that she'd interrupted the girl in the middle of some dirty task – of course, settling in. The dull hair was broken free of the knot, on one side. Hooked behind an ear, it stuck to the sweaty neck. The breasts (Mrs Naas couldn't help noticing; why don't these young girls wear bras these days) were squashed by a shrunken T-shirt and the feet were in split *takkies*. The only evidence of femininity to which Mrs Naas's grooming could respond (as owners of the same make of vehicle, one humble, one a luxury model, passing on the highway silently acknowledge one another with a flick of headlights) was the Indian dingly-danglys the girl wore in her ears, answering the big fake pearls sitting on Mrs Naas's plump lobes.

'I'm not going to come in. I know how it is . . . This is just some of my buttermilk rusks you liked.'

The girl was looking at the tin, now in her hands, at the painted face of a smiling blonde child with a puppy and a bunch of roses, looking back at her. She said something, in her shy way, about Mrs Naas being generous.

'Ag, it's nothing. I was baking for myself, and I always take to my sister in Pretoria. You know, in our family we say, it's not the things you buy with money that counts, it's what you put your heart into when you make something. Even if it's only a rusk, ay? Is everything going all right?'

'Oh yes. We're fine, thank you.'

Mrs Naas tried to keep the weight on the balls of her feet; she could feel the spindle heels of her new shoes sinking into the weeds, that kind of green stain would never come off. 'Moving in! Don't tell me! I say to Naas, whatever happens, we have to stay in this house until I die. A person can never move all the stuff we've collected.'

What a shy girl she was. Mrs Naas had always heard Australians were friendly, like Afrikaners. The girl hardly smiled, her thick eyebrows moved in some kind of inhibition or agitation.

'We haven't got too much, luckily.'

'Has everything arrived now?'

'Oh . . . I think just about. Still a few packing cases to open.'

Mrs Naas was agreeing, shifting her heels unobtrusively. 'Unpacking is nothing, it's finding where to put things, ay. Ag, but it's a nice roomy old house—'

A black man came round from the yard, as the lady of the house had, but he didn't come nearer, only stood a moment, hammer in hand; wanting some further instructions from the missus, probably, and then seeing she was with another white person, knowing he mustn't interrupt.

'So at least you've got someone to help. That's good. I hope you didn't take a boy off the streets, my dear? There are some terrible loafers coming to the back door for work, criminals – my! – you must be careful, you know.'

The girl looked very solemn, impressed. 'No, we wouldn't do that.'

'Did someone find him for you?'

'No – well, not someone here. Friends in town. He had references.' She stopped a moment, and looked at Mrs Naas. 'So it's all right, I think. I'm sure. Thank you.'

She walked with Mrs Naas back to the car, hugging the biscuit tin.

'Well, there's plenty to keep him busy in this garden. Shame . . . the pergola was so pretty. But the grapes will climb again, you'll see, if you get all the rubbish cleared away. But don't *you* start digging and that . . . be careful of yourself. Have you been feeling all right?' And Mrs Naas put her left hand, with its diamond thrust up on a stalagmite of gold (her old engagement ring remodelled since Naas's prosperity by a Jew jeweller who gave him a good deal), on her own stomach, rounded only by good eating.

The girl looked puzzled. Then she forgot, at last, that shyness of hers and laughed, laughed and shook her head.

'No morning sickness?'

'No, no. I'm fine. Not sick at all.'

Mrs Naas saw that the girl, expecting in a strange country, must be comforted to have a talk with a motherly woman. Mrs Naas's body, which had housed Dawie, Andries, Aletta and Klein Dolfie, expanded against the tight clothes from which it would never burgeon irresistibly again, as the girl's would soon. 'I'll tell you something. This's the best time of your life. The first baby. That's something you'll never know again, never.' She drove off before the girl could see the tears that came to her eyes.

The girl went round back into the yard with her tall stalk, flat-footed in the old *takkies*.

The black man's gaze was fixed where she must reappear. He still held the hammer; uselessly. 'Is it all right?'

'Of course it's all right.'

'What's she want?'

'Didn't want anything. She brought us a present – this.' Her palm came down over the grin of the child on the tin drum.

He looked at the tin, cautious to see it for what it was.

'Biscuits. *Rusks.* The *vrou* of the agent who let this place to us. Charles and I had to have tea with her the first day we were here.'

'That's what she came for?'

'*Yes*. That's all. Don't you give something – take food when new neighbours move in?' As she heard herself saying it, she remembered that whatever the custom was among blacks – and God knows, they were the most hospitable if the poorest of people – he hadn't lived anywhere that could be called 'at home' for years, and his 'neighbours' had been fellow refugees in camps and military training centres. She gave him her big, culpable smile to apologise for her bourgeois naivety; it still surfaced from time to time, and it was best to admit so, openly. 'Nothing to get worried about. I don't mean they're really neighbours . . .' She made an arc with her chin and long neck, from side to side, sweeping the isolation of the house and yard within the veld.

The black man implied no suggestion that the white couple did not know their job, no criticism of the choice of place. Hardly! It could not have been better situated. 'Is she going to keep turning up, hey . . . What'll she think? I shouldn't have come into the garden.'

'No, no, Vusi. She won't think anything. It was OK she saw you. She just naturally assumes there'll be a black working away somewhere in the yard.'

'And Eddie?'

She placed the biscuit tin on the kennel, with its rusty chain to which no dog was attached.

'OK, two blacks. After all, this is a farming plot, isn't it? There's building going on. Where is he?'

'He went into the house as soon as I came back and told him . . .'

She was levering, with her fingernails, under the lid of the tin. 'Can you do this? My fingers aren't strong enough.'

The black man found the hammer in his hand, put it down and grasped the tin, his small brown nose wrinkling with effort. The lid flew off with a twang and went bowling down the yard, the girl laughing after it. It looped back towards the man and he leant gracefully and caught it up, laughing.

'What is this *boere* food, anyway?'

'Try it. They're good.'

They crunched rusks together in the sun, the black man's attention turning contemplatively, mind running ahead to what was not yet there, to the shed (big enough for two cars) before which the raw vigour of new bricks, cement and tools was dumped against the stagnation and decay of the yard.

The girl chewed energetically, wanting to free her mouth to speak. 'We'll have to get used to the idea people may turn up, for some reason or another. We'll just have to be prepared. So long as they don't find us in the house . . . it'll be all right.'

The black man no longer saw what was constructed in his mind; he saw the rusty chain, he leant again with that same straight-backed, sideways movement with which he had caught the lid, and jingled the links. 'Maybe we should get a dog, man. To warn.'

'That's an idea.' Then her face bunched unattractively, a yes-but. 'What do we do with it afterwards?'

He smiled at her indulgently; at things she still didn't understand, even though she chose to be here, in this place, with Eddie and with him.

The white couple had known two black men would be coming but not exactly when or how. Charles must have believed they would come at night, that would be the likeliest because the safest; the first three nights in the house he dragged the mattress off her bed into the kitchen, and his into the 'lounge', on which the front door opened directly, so that he or she would hear the men wherever they sought entry. Charles had great difficulty in sleeping with one eye open; he could stay awake until very late, but once his head was on a pillow sleep buried him deep within the hot, curly beard. She dozed off where she was – meetings, cinemas, parties, even driving – after around half past ten, but she could give her subconscious instructions, before going to bed, to wake her at any awaited signal of sound or movement. She set her inner alarm at hair-trigger, those three nights. An owl sent her swiftly to Charles; it might be a man imitating the call. She responded to a belch from the sink drain, skittering in the roof (mice?), even the faint thread of a cat's mew, that might have been in a dream, since she could not catch it again once it had awakened her.

But they came at two o'clock on the fourth afternoon. A small sagging van of the kind used by the petty entrepreneurs in firewood and junk commerce, *dagga*-running, livestock and human transport between black communities on either side of the borders with Swaziland, Lesotho or Botswana, backed down to the gate it had overshot. There were women and children with blankets covering their mouths against the dust, in the open rear. A young man jumped from the cab and dragged aside the sagging, silvery wire-and-scroll gate, with its plate 'Plot 185 Koppiesdrif'. Charles was out the front door and reversing the initiative at once: he it was who came to the man. His green eyes, at twenty-eight, already were narrowed by the plump fold of the lower lid that marks joviality – whether cruelly shrewd or good-natured – in middle age. The young black man was chewing gum. He did not interrupt the rhythms of his jaw: 'Charles.'

The couple had not been told what the men would look like. The man identified himself by the procedure (questions and specific answers) Charles had been taught to expect. Charles asked whether they wouldn't drive round to the yard. The other understood at once; it was more natural for blacks to conduct any business with a white man at his back door. Charles himself was staging the arrival in keeping with the unremarkable deliveries of building material that already had been made to the new occupiers of the plot. He walked ahead of the van, businesslike. In the yard another young man got out of the cab, and, with the first, from among the women swung down two zippered carry-alls and a crammed paper carrier. That was all.

The women and children, like sheep dazed by their last journey to the abattoir, moved only when the van drove off again, jolting them.

Charles and the girl had not been told the names or identity of the pair they expected. They exchanged only first names – Eddie was the one who had opened the gate, Vusi the one who had sat beside the unknown driver and got down in the yard. The girl introduced herself as 'Joy'. One of the men asked if there was something to eat. The white couple at once got in one another's way, suddenly unrehearsed now that the reality had begun, exchanging terse instructions in the kitchen, jostling one another to find sugar, a knife to slice tomatoes, a frying pan for the sausages which she forgot to prick. It seemed there was no special attitude, social formula of ease, created by a situation so far removed from the normal pattern of human concourse; so it was just the old, inappropriate one of stilted hospitality to unexpected guests that had to do, although these were not guests, the white couple were not hosts, and the arrival was according to plan. When sleeping arrangements came up, the men assumed the white couple were sleeping together and put their own things in the second bedroom. It was small and dark, unfurnished except for two new mattresses on the floor separated by an old trunk with a reading lamp standing on it, but there was no question of the other two favouring themselves with a better room; this one faced on the yard, no one would see blacks moving around at night in the bedroom of a white man's house.

The two zippered carry-alls, cheap copies of the hand luggage of jet-flight holidaymakers, held a change of jeans, a couple of shirts printed with bright leisure symbols of the Caribbean, a few books, and – in Eddie's – a mock-suede jacket with Indian fringes, Wild West style. As soon as they all knew each other well enough, he was teased about it, and had his quick riposte. 'But I'm not going to be extinct.' The strong paper carrier was one of those imprinted with a pop star's face black kids shake for sale on the street corners of Johannesburg. What came out of it, the white couple saw, was as ordinary as the loaves of bread and cardboard litres of *mageu* such bags usually carry; a transistor-tape player, Vusi's spare pair of sneakers, a pink towel and a plastic briefcase emptied of papers. Charles was to provide everything they might need. He himself had been provided with a combi. He went to the appointed places, at appointed times, to pick up what was necessary.

The combi had housewifely curtains across the windows – a practical adornment popular with farming families, whose children may sleep away a journey. It was impossible to tell, when Charles drove off or came back, whether there was anything inside it. On one of his return trips, he drew up at the level crossing and found himself beside Naas Klopper and Mrs Naas in the Mercedes. A train shuttered past like a camera gone berserk, lens opening and closing, with each flying segment of rolling stock, on flashes of the veld behind it. The optical explosion invigorated Charles. He waved and grinned at the estate agent and his wife.

They had used all three Holiday Inns in the vicinity. They had even driven out to cheap motels, which were safer, since local people of their class would be unlikely to be encountered there, but the time spent on the road cut into the afternoons which were all they had together. Besides, he felt the beds were dirty – a superficial papering of laundered sheets overlaid the sordidness that was other people's sex. He told her he could not bear to bring her to such rooms.

She did not care where she was, so long as she was with him and there was a bed. She said so, which was probably a mistake; but she wanted, with him, no cunning female strategy of being desired more than desiring: 'You are my first and last lover.' She was not hurt when he did not trade – at least – that there had not been anything like it before, for him, if he could not commit himself about what might come after. He was uneasy at the total, totted-up weight of precious privilege, finally, in his hands. He worried about security – her security. What would happen to her if her husband found out and divorced her? She didn't give this a thought; only worried, in her sense of responsibility for his career, what would happen if his wife found out and made a scandal.

His wife was away in Europe, the house was empty. A large house with a pan-handle drive, tunnelled through trees, the house itself in a lair of trees. But you are never alone in this country.

They are always there; the house-boy, the garden-boy mowing the lawn. They see everything; you can only do, in the end, what it is all right for them to see and remember. Impossible to take this newly beloved woman home where he longed to make love to her in his own bed. Even if by some pretext he managed to get rid of them, give them all a day off at once. They changed the sheets and brushed the carpets; a tender stain, a single hair of unfamiliar colour – impossible. So in the end even his room, his own bed, in a house where he paid for everything – nothing is your own, once you are married.

Ah, what recklessness the postponement of gratification produces, when it does not produce sublimation. (Could Freud have known that!) He had come back to the parking lot from the reception desk of a suburban hotel, his very legs and arms drawn together stiffly in shock; as he was about to enquire about bed and breakfast (they always asked for this, paid in advance, and disappeared at the end of an afternoon) he had seen a business acquaintance and a journalist to whom he was well known, coming straight towards him out of the hotel restaurant, loosening their ties against the high temperature. She drove off with him at once, but where to? There was nowhere. Yet never had they reached such painful tension of arousal, not touching or speaking as she drove. In the heat wave that afternoon she took a road to the old mine dumps. There, hidden from the freeway by Pharaonic pyramids of sand from which gold had been extracted by the cyanide process, she took off the wisp of nylon and lace between her legs, unzipped his beautiful Italian linen trousers, and, covering their bodies by the drop of her skirt, sat him into her. In their fine clothes, they were joined like two butterflies in the heat of a summer garden. When they slackened, had done, and he set himself to rights, he was appalled to see her, her lips swollen, her cheekbones fiery, the hair in front of her ears ringlets of sweat. In a car! The car her husband had given her, only a month before, new, to please her, because he had become aware, without knowing why, he couldn't please her any more. She, too, had nothing that was her own; her husband paid for everything that was hers. She said only one thing to him: 'When I was a little girl, I was always asking to be allowed to go and slide down the mine dumps. They promised to take me, they never did. I always think of that when I see mine dumps.'

But today she had thought of something else. He made up his mind he would have to take into his confidence a friend (himself suspected of running affairs from time to time) who had a cottage, at present untenanted, on one of his properties. There, among the deserted stables of an old riding school, mature lovers could let their urgencies of sex, confessional friendship and sweet clandestine companionship take their course in peace and dignity. The bed had been occupied only by people of their own kind. There was a refrigerator; ice and whisky. Sometimes she arrived with a rose and put it in a glass beside the bed. He couldn't remember when last he read a poem, since leaving school; or would again. She brought an old book with her maiden name on the flyleaf and read Pablo Neruda to him. Afterwards they fell asleep, and then woke to make love once more before losing each other safely in the rush-hour traffic back to town. (After the encounter at the hotel, they had decided it was best to travel separately.)

They were secure in that cottage – for as long as they would need security. Sometimes he would find the opportunity to remark: we are not children. I know, she would agree. He could be reassured she accepted that love could only have its span and must end without tears. One late afternoon they were lying timelessly, although they had less than half an hour left (it was the way to deal with an association absolutely restricted to the hours between three and six), naked, quiet, her hand languidly comforting his lolling penis, when they heard a scratching at the ox-eye window above the bedhead. He sat up. Jumped up, standing on the bed. She rolled over on to her face. There was the sound of something, feet, a body, landing on earth, scuffling, slap of branches. A spray of the old bougainvillaea that climbed the roof snapped back against the window. The window was empty.

He gently freed her face from the pillow. 'It's all right.'

She lay there looking at him. 'She's hired someone to follow you.'

'Don't be silly.'

'I know it. Did you see? A white man?'

He began to dress.

'Don't go out, my darling. For God's sake! Wait for him to go away.'

He sat on the side of the bed, in shirt and trousers. They listened for the sound of a car leaving. They knew why they had not heard it arrive; they had been making love.

Still no sound of a car.

'He must have walked through the bushes, all the way from the road.'

Her lover was deeply silent and thoughtful; as if this that had happened to them were something to which there was a way out, a solution!

'Somehow climbed up the bougainvillaea.' She began to shiver.

'It could have been a cat, you know, gone wild. Trying to get in. There are always cats around stables.'

'Oh no, oh no.' She pulled the bedclothes up to the level of her armpits, spoke with difficulty. 'I heard him laugh. A horrible little coughing laugh. That's why I put my face in the pillow.' Her cheeks flattened, a desperate expressionlessness.

He stroked her hand, denying, denying that someone could have been laughing at them, that they could ever be something to laugh at.

After a safe interval she dressed and they went outside. The bougainvillaea would give foothold up to the small window, but was cruelly thorny. She began to be able to believe that what she had heard was some sort of suppressed exclamation of pain – and serve the bastard right. Then they searched the ground for shoe prints but found nothing. The red earth crumbled with worm-shredded leaves would have packed down under the soles of shoes, but, as he pointed out to her, might not show the print of bare feet. Would some dirty Peeping Tom of a private detective take off his shoes and tear his clothes in the cause of his disgusting profession? She a little behind him – but she wouldn't let him go alone – they walked in every direction away from the cottage, and through the deserted stables where there were obvious hiding-places. But there was no one, one could feel there was no one, and on the paved paths over which rains had washed sand, no footprints but their own. On the way to their cars, they passed the granadilla vine they had remarked to one another on their way in, that had spread its glossy coat-of-mail over weakening shrubs and was baubled with unripe fruit. Now the ground was scattered with green eggs of granadillas, bitten into and then half-eaten or thrown away. He and she broke from one another, gathering them, examining them. Only a hungry fruit-eating animal would plunder so indiscriminately. He was the first to give spoken credence. 'I didn't want to tell you, but I thought I heard something, too. Not a laugh, a sort of bark or cough.'

Suddenly she had him by the waist, her head against his chest, they were laughing and giddy together. 'Poor monkey. Poor, poor old lonely monkey. Well, he's lucky; he can rest assured we won't tell anyone where to find him.'

When she was in her car, he lingered at her face, as always, turned to him through the window. There was curiosity mingled with tenderness in his. 'You don't mind a monkey watching us making love?'

She looked back at him with the honesty that she industriously shored up against illusions of any kind, preparing herself for – some day – their last afternoon. 'No, I don't mind. I don't mind at all.'

While Charles drove about the country fetching what was needed – sometimes away several days, covering long distances – Vusi and Eddie bricked up the fourth wall of the shed. The girl insisted on helping although she knew nothing about the type of work. 'Just show me.' That was her humble yet obstinate plea. She learnt how to mix cement in a puddle of the right consistency. Her long skinny arms with the blue vein running down the inside of the elbows were stronger than they looked; she steadied timber for the door-frame. The only thing was, she didn't seem to want to cook. They would rather have had her cook better meals for them than help with what they could have managed for themselves. She seemed to expect everyone in the house to prepare his own meals when he might feel hungry. The white man, Charles, did so, or cooked with her; this must be some special arrangement decided between them, a black woman would always cook every night for her lover, indeed for all the men in the house. She went to town once a week, when the combi was available, to buy food, but the kind of thing she bought was not what they wanted, what they felt like eating for these few weeks when they were sure there would be food available. Yoghurt, cheese, brown rice, nuts and fruit – the fruit was nice (Vusi had not seen apricots for so long, he ate a whole bagful at a sitting) but the frozen pork sausages she brought for them (she and Charles were vegetarian) weren't real meat. Eddie didn't want to complain but Vusi insisted, talking in their room at night, it was their right. 'That's what she's here for, isn't it, what they're both here for. We each do our job.' He asked her next day. 'Joy, man, bring some meat from town, man, not sausages.'

Eddie was emboldened, frowned agreement, but giggling. 'And some mealie-meal. Not always rice.'

'Oh Charles and I like mealie-pap too. But I thought you'd be insulted, you'd think I bought it specially for you.'

They all laughed with her, at her. As Vusi remarked once when the black men talked in the privacy of their own language, 'Joy' was a funny kind of cell-name for that girl, without flesh or flirtatiousness for any man to enjoy. Yet she was the one who came out bluntly with things that detached the four of them from their separate, unknown existences behind them and the separate existences that would be taken up ahead, and made a life of their own together, in this house and yard.

It took Charles, Vusi and Eddie to hang an articulated metal garage door in the entrance of the converted shed. It thundered smoothly down and was secured by a heavy padlock to a ring embedded in Joy's cement. There was the pleasure to be expected of any structure of brick and mortar successfully completed; a satisfaction in itself, no matter what mere stage of means to an end it might represent. They stood about, looking at it. Charles put his arm on the girl's shoulder, and she put out an arm on Vusi's.

Eddie raised and lowered the door again, for them.

'It reminds me of my grandfather's big old roll-top desk.'

Eddie looked up at the girl, from their handiwork. 'Desk like that? I never saw one. What did your grandfather do?'

'He was a magistrate. Sent people to jail.' She smiled.

'Hell, Joy, man!' Either it was a marvel that the girl's progenitor should have been a magistrate, or a marvel that a magistrate should have had her for a granddaughter.

One thing she never forgot to bring from town was beer. All four drank a lot of beer; the bottom shelf of the refrigerator was neatly stocked with cans. Charles went and fetched some and they sat in the yard before the shining door, slowly drinking. Vusi picked up tidily the tagged metal rings that snapped off the cans when they were opened.

Until the garage door was in place the necessities Charles brought in the combi had had to be stored in the house. Over the weeks the bedroom empty except for two mattresses and a trunk with a lamp was slowly furnished behind drawn curtains and a locked door whose key was kept in a place known only to Vusi – though, as Charles said to Joy, what sense in that? If anyone came they would kick in any locked door.

At night Eddie and Vusi lay low on their mattresses in a perspective that enclosed them with boxes and packing cases like a skyline of children's piled blocks. Eddie slept quickly but Vusi, with his shaved head with the tiny, gristly ears placed at exactly the level of the cheekbones that stretched his face and formed the widest plane of the whole skull, lay longing to smoke. Yet the craving was just another appetite, some petty recurrence, assuaged a thousand times and easily to be so again with something bought across a corner shop counter. Around him in the dark, a horizon darker than the dark held the cold forms in which the old, real, terrible needs of his life, his father's life and his father's father's life were now so strangely realised. He had sat at school farting the gases of an empty stomach, he had seen fathers, uncles, brothers, come home without work from days-long queues, he had watched, too young to understand, the tin and board that had been the shack he was born in, carted away by government demolishers. His bare feet had been shod in shoes worn to the shape of a white child's feet. He had sniffed glue to see a rosy future. He had taken a diploma by correspondence to better himself. He had spoken nobody's name under interrogation. He had left a girl and baby without hope of being able to show himself to them again. You could not eat the AKM assault rifles that Charles had brought in golf bags, you could not dig a road or turn a lathe with the limpet mines, could not shoe and clothe feet and body with the offensive and defensive hand grenades, could not use the AKM bayonets to compete with the white man's education, or to thrust a way out of solitary confinement in maximum security, and the wooden boxes that held hundreds of rounds of ammunition would not make even a squatter's shack for the girl and child. But all these hungers found their shape, distorted, forged as no one could conceive they ever should have to be, in the objects packed around him. These were made not for life; for death. He and Eddie lay there protected by it as they had never been by life.

During the day, he instructed Eddie in the correct use and maintenance of their necessities. He was the more experienced; he had been operational like this before. He checked detonators and timing devices, and the state of the ammunition. Necessities obtained the way these were were not always complete and in good order. He and Charles discussed the mechanisms and merits of various makes and classes of necessities; Charles had done his South African army service and understood such things.

Once the garage door like a grandfather's roll-top desk was installed, they were able to move everything into the shed. They did so at night, without talking and without light. There had been rain, by then. A bullfrog that had waited a whole season underground came up that night and accompanied the silent activity with his retching bellow.

A chimpanzee, some insist.

Just a large monkey, say others.

It was seen again in the suburb of wooded gardens where Stanley Dobrow took the only photograph so far obtained. If you could call that image of clashed branches a likeness of anything.

Every household in the fine suburb had several black servants – trusted cooks who were allowed to invite their grandchildren to spend their holidays in the backyard, faithful gardeners from whom the family watchdog was inseparable, a shifting population of pretty young housemaids whose long red nails and pertness not only asserted the indignity of being undiscovered or out-of-work fashion models but kept hoisted a cocky guerrilla pride against servitude to whites: there are many forms of resistance not recognised in orthodox revolutionary strategy. One of these girls said the beast slipped out of her room one night, just as she was crossing the yard from the kitchen. She had dropped her dinner, carried in one enamel dish covered with another to keep it hot. The cook, twenty-one years with the white family, told the lady of the house more likely it was one of the girl's boyfriends who had been to her room to 'check out' if there was another boyfriend there with her. Why hadn't she screamed?

The girl left without notice, anyway, first blazing out at the cook and the old gardener that if they didn't mind living 'like chickens in a *hok*', stuck away in a shit yard where anyone could come in over the wall and steal your things, murder you, while the whites had a burglar siren that went off if you breathed on their windows – if they were happy to yesbaas and yesmissus, with that horrible thing loose, baboons could bite off your whole hand – she wasn't. Couldn't they see the whites always ran away and hid and left us to be hurt?

And she didn't even have the respect not to bring up what had happened to the cook's brother, although the cook was still wearing the mourning band on the sleeve of the pastel-coloured overalls she spent her life in. He had been a watchman at a block of flats, sitting all night in the underground garage to guard the tenants' cars. He had an army surplus overcoat provided to keep him warm and a knobkerrie to defend himself with. But the thieves had a revolver and shot him in the stomach while the owners of the cars went on sleeping, stacked twelve storeys high over his dead body.

Other servants round about reported signs of something out there. It was common talk where they gathered, to hear from the

Chinese runner what symbol had come up in their daily gamble on the numbers game, in a lane between two of 'their' houses – after ten or twenty years, living just across the yard from the big house, there develops such a thing as a deferred sense of property, just as there can be deferred pain felt in a part of the human body other than that of its source. Since no one actually saw whoever or whatever was watching them – timid or threatening? – rumour began to go round that it was what (to reduce any power of malediction it might possess) they called – not in their own language with its rich vocabulary recognising the supernatural, but adopting the childish Afrikaans word – a spook.

An urban haunter, a factory or kitchen ghost. Powerless like themselves, long migrated from the remotest possibility of being a spirit of the ancestors just as they themselves, that kind of inner attention broken by the batter and scream of commuter trains, the jumping of mine drills and the harangue of pop music, were far from the possibility of any oracle making itself heard to them. A heavy drinker reminded how, two Christmases ago, on the koppie behind 'your' house (he indicated the Dobrow cook, Sophie) a man must have lost his footing coming over the rocks from the shebeen there, and was found dead on Boxing Day. They said that one came from Transkei. Someone like that had woken up now, without his body, and was trying to find his way back to the hostel where his worker's contract, thumbprint affixed, had long ago run out. That was all.

Eddie wanted Charles to hire a TV set.

'But Charlie, he just laughs, man, he doesn't do anything about it.' Eddie complained to him through remarks addressed to the others. And they laughed, too.

It was the time when what there was to be done was wait. Charles brought the Sunday papers. He had finished reading a leader that tried to find a moral lesson for both victim and perpetrator in one of the small massacres of an undeclared and unending war. His whole face, beard – like the head of a disgruntled lion resting on its paws – was slumped between two fists. 'You want to watch cabinet ministers preaching lies? Homeland chiefs getting twenty-one-gun salutes? Better go and weed your mealies if you're bored, man.' A small patch of these, evidently planted by the man who had looked after the Kleynhans place while it was unoccupied, had begun to grow silky in the sun, since the rain, and Eddie monitored their progress as though he and Vusi, Charles and Joy would be harvesting the cobs months ahead.

The girl sat on the floor under the ox-wagon wheel chandelier with its pink shades like carnival hats askew, sucking a strand of her hair as she read. Vusi had the single armchair and Eddie and Charles the sofa, whose snot-green plaid Joy could not tolerate, even here, and kept covered with a length of African cotton patterned with indigo cowrie shells: every time she entered this room, a reminder that one really had one's sense of being (but could not, absolutely not, now) among beautiful, loved objects of familiar use. The four exchanged sheets of newspaper restlessly, searching for the world around them with which they had no connection. The Prime Minister had made another of his speeches of reconciliation; each except Charles read in silence the threats of which it was composed. Charles spoke through lips distorted by the pressure of his fists under his fleshy face, one of those grotesque mouths of ancient Mediterranean cultures from which sibylline utterances are supposed to well.

> This government will not stand by and see the peace of mind of its peoples destroyed. It will not see the security of your homes, of your children asleep in their beds, threatened by those who lurk, outside law and order, ready to strike in the dark. It will not see the food snatched from your children's mouths by those who seek the economic destruction of our country through boycotts in the so-called United Nations and violence at home. I say to countries on our borders to whom we have been and shall continue to be good neighbours: we shall not hesitate to strike with all our might at those who harbour terrorists . . .

When they heard this rhetoric on the radio, they were accustomed to smile as people will when they must realise that those being referred to as monsters are the human beings drinking a glass of water, cutting a hangnail, writing a letter, in the same room; are themselves. Sometimes they would restore their sense of reality by derision (all of them) or one of them (Vusi or Charles) would reply to thin air with the other rhetoric, of rebellion; but the closer time drew them to act, the less need there was for platform language.

'Scared. Afraid.'

Vusi dropped single words, as if to see what rings of meaning others would feel ripple from them.

The girl looked up, not knowing if this was a question and if anyone was expected to answer it.

Eddie sniffed with a twist of the nose and cocked his head indifferently, parrying the words towards the public office, occupied by interchangeable faces, that had made the speech.

The moment passed, and with it perhaps some passing test Vusi had put them to – and himself. He had opened a hand on the extreme danger hidden in this boring, fly-buzzing Sunday 'living room'; in that instant they had all looked at it; and their silence said, calm: I know.

The allusion swerved away from themselves. Vusi was still speaking. 'Can't give any other reason why he should have them in his power, so he's got to scare them into it. Scare. That's all they've got left. What else is in that speech? After three hundred and fifty years. After how many governments? Spook people.'

It was a proposition that had comforted, spurred, lulled or inspired over many years. 'So?' Charles's beard jutted. 'That goes to show the power of fear, not the collapse of power.'

'Exactly. Otherwise we wouldn't need to be here.' Joy's reference to this house, their presence and purpose, sounded innocently vulgar: to be there was to have gone beyond discussion of why; to be freed of words.

Eddie gave hers a different, general application. 'If whites could have been cured of being scared of blacks, that would have solved everything?' He was laughing at the old liberal theory.

Charles swallowed a rough crumb of impulse to tell Eddie he didn't need Eddie to give him a lesson on class and economics.

'Hell, man . . . Just that there's no point in telling ourselves they're finished, they're running down.'

Joy heard in Charles's nervous asperity the fear of faltering he guarded against in others because it was in himself. There should be no love affairs between people doing this kind of – thing – (she still could not think of it as she wished to, as work to be done). She did not, now, want to be known by him as *she* knew *him*; there should be some conscious mental process available by which such knowledge would be withdrawn.

'Don't worry. If they're running down, it's because they know who's after them.' Eddie, talking big, seemed to become again the kid he must have been in street-gang rivalries that unknowingly rehearsed, for his generation of blacks, the awful adventure that was coming to them.

'They were finished when they took the first slave.' Knowledge of Vusi was barred somewhere between his murmured commonplaces and that face of his. He was not looking at any of them, now; but Joy had said once to Charles, in a lapse to referents of an esoteric culture she carefully avoided because these distanced him and her from Vusi and Eddie, that if Vusi were to be painted, the portrait would be one of those, like Velázquez' Philip IV, whose eyes would meet yours no matter from what angle the painting were to be seen.

Vusi and Eddie had not been on student tours to the Prado. Vusi's voice was matter-of-fact, hoarse. 'It doesn't matter how many times we have to sit here like this. They can't stop us because we can't stop. Never. Every time, when I'm waiting, I know I'm coming nearer.'

Eddie crackled back a page to frame something. 'Opening of Koeberg's going to be delayed by months and months, it says, ay Vusi?'

'Ja, I saw.'

Charles and Joy did not know if Vusi was one of those who had attacked the nuclear reactor installation at the Cape before it was ready to operate, earlier in the year. A classic mission; that was the phrase. A strategic target successfully hit; serious material damage, no deaths, no blood shed. This terrifying task produces its outstanding practitioners, like any other. They did not know if Eddie knew something about Vusi they didn't, had been told some night in the dark of the back room, while the two men lay there alone on their mattresses. Eddie's remark might indicate he did know; or that he was fascinatedly curious and thought Vusi might be coaxed, without realising it, into saying something revealing. But Vusi didn't understand flattery.

Eddie gave up. 'What's this committee of Cape Town whites who want it shut down?'

Charles took the paper from him. 'Koeberg's only thirty kilometres from Cape Town. A bicycle ride, man. Imagine what could happen once it's producing. But d'you see the way the story's handled? They write about "security" as if the place's a jeweller's shop that might be burgled, not a target we've already hit once.'

Joy read at an angle over his shoulder, an ugly strain on the tendons of her neck. 'Nobody wants to go to jail.'

Charles gave the sweet smile of his most critical mood, for the benefit of Vusi and Eddie. 'Ah well, but there are ways and ways, ay? A journalist learns to say what he wants without appearing to. But these fellows sit with the book of rules under their backsides . . . well, what'm I talking about – you need wits to outwit.'

'What makes you think they even want to?'

'Because it's their job! Let's leave convictions out of it!'

'No, she's right, man. If you work on these papers, you're just part of the system.' Eddie kept as souvenirs the catch-all terms from his Soweto days.

'To be fair' (for which ideal the girl hankered so seriously that she would not hesitate to contradict herself) 'there are some who want to . . . A few who've lost their jobs.'

'Someone reads this, what can he know afterwards?' A sheet went sailing from Vusi's hand to join those already spread about the floor. 'You must call in an interpreter, like in court, to know what's going on.'

'Like in court? *Jwaleka tsekisong?*' Eddie went zestfully into an act. A long burst in Sesotho; then in English: 'He can't remember a thing, My Lord.' Another lengthy Sesotho sentence, with the cadence, glares and head-shakings of vehement denial: 'He says yes, My Lord.' A rigmarole of obvious agreement: 'He says no, My Lord.' The pantomime of the bewildered, garrulous black witness, the white Afrikaner prosecutor fond of long English words and not much surer of their meaning than the witness or the bored black interpreter:

> I put it to you that you claim convenable amnesia.
>
> He says he doesn't know that Amnesia woman.
>
> I put it to you it's inconceivable you don't remember whether you were present on the night of the crime.
>
> He says he never made a child with that woman, My Lord.

Out of their amusement at his nonsense there was a rise of animation, change of key to talk of what or was not to be understood between the lines of reportage and guards of commentary; in this – the events of their world, which moved beneath the events of the world the newspapers reflected – the real intimacy latent in their strangeness to one another, their apparent ill-assortment, discovered itself. There was sudden happiness – yes, unlike any private happiness left behind, independent of circumstance, because all four had left behind, too, the 'normal' fears, repugnancies, prejudices, reservations that 'circumstance' as they had known it – what colour they were, what that colour had meant where they lived – had been for them. Nothing but a surge of intermittent current: but the knowledge that it would well up again made it possible to live with the irritations and inadequacies they chafed against one another now, waiting. Charles said it for them, grinning suddenly after an argument one day: 'Getting in one another's hair, here – it's a form of freedom, ay?'

Apart from politics, there wasn't much to engage, in Charles's Sunday papers. One printed for blacks reported the usual slum murders perpetrated with unorthodox weapons to hand; a soccer club scandal, and deaths at a wedding after drinking tainted home-brew. The whites' papers, of which Charles had brought several, and in two languages, had a financial crash, a millionaire's divorce settlement, a piece about that monkey no one could catch, which had stolen a maid's dinner.

Sunday torpor settled on the four. Charles slept with his beard-ringed mouth bubbling slightly, as Naas Klopper was sleeping ten kilometres away in his split-level lounge. Eddie wandered out to the yard, took off his shirt and sat on the back step in the sun, smoking, drinking a Coke and listening to a reggae tape as any young labourer would spend his lunch hour on the pavement outside whites' shops.

On a radio panel 'Talking of Nature' an SPCA official took the opportunity to condemn the cruelty of throwing out pet monkeys to fend for themselves when they outgrow the dimensions of a suitable domestic pet. Mariella Chapman heard him while preparing plums for jam according to the recipe given by her new mother-in-law over the weekend. Mariella and her husband had gone to visit his parents on the farm for the first time since their marriage five months ago, and had come home with a supermarket bag of fresh-picked plums and a leg of venison. Marais (his given name was his mother's maiden name) hung the leg before he went on duty early on Monday at John Vorster Square; he had to put up a hook in the kitchen window because their modern house didn't have a back stoep like the old house at home.

At police headquarters Sergeant Chapman (an English stoker in the 1880s jumped ship, married an Afrikaans girl and left the name scratched on a Boer family tree) took over the 7 a.m. shift of interrogation of one of the people held in detention there. It was a nice-enough-looking place to be stationed, right in town. The blue spandrel panels and glimpses of potted plants in the façade it presented to the passing city freeway could have been those of an apartment block; the cells in which these people were kept were within the core of the building.

It was tiring work, you need a lot of concentration, watching the faces of these politicals, never mind just getting something out of their mouths. He kept his hands off them. Unless, of course, expressly instructed by his superiors to do certain things necessary to make some of them talk. When they got out – particularly the white ones, with their clever lawyer friends and plenty money coming from the churches and the communists overseas – they often brought court cases against the state, you could find yourself standing there accused of assault, they tried to blacken your name in front of your wife, your mother and dad, who knew only your kindness and caresses. He wanted promotion, but he didn't want that. He did his duty. He did what he was told. And if it ever came to court – oh boy, I'm telling you, *jong* – all was on the Major's instructions, he could swear on the Bible to that.

No wonder most of them talked in the end. It was hard enough to do a number of shifts with them during the day or night, with breaks in between for a cup of coffee, something to eat, and best of all, a walk outside in the street; whereas most of them, like this tough nut he was handling with the Major now, were questioned by a roster of personnel twenty-four, thirty-six hours non-stop. And, as the Major had taught, even when these people were given coffee, a cigarette, allowed to sit down, they knew they were being watched and had to watch themselves all the time, for what they might let slip. It was one of the elementary lessons of this work that the gratification of a draw of smoke into the lungs might suddenly succeed in breaking the stoniest will and breaching trained revolutionary hostility towards and contempt for interrogators. (The Major was a very clever, highly educated and well-read man – you had to have someone like that for the class of detainee that was coming in these days, they'd just run rings round someone who'd only got his matric.) The Major said it didn't even matter if you got to feel sorry for them – the Major knew about this, although you always hid it; 'a bond of sympathy' was the first real step on the way to extracting a confession. Well, Sergeant Chapman didn't have any such feelings today. Inside his uniform his body was filled with the sap of sun and fresh air; the sight of the sleepless, unshaven man standing there, dazed and smelly (they sweated even if they shivered, under interrogation) made him sick (the Major warned that occasional revulsion was natural, but unproductive).

Why couldn't these people live like any normal person? A man with this one's brains and university degrees, English-speaking and whatnot, could become a big shot in business instead of a trade unionist letting a bunch of blacks strike and get him in trouble. When you interrogated a detainee, you had to familiarise yourself with all the details supplied by informers for his file; this one had a well-off father, a doctor wife, twin babies, an affair with a pretty student (admittedly, he had met her through her research connected with unions) and his parents-in-law's cottage at one of the best places for fishing on the coast, for his holidays. What more does a white man want? With a black man, all right, he wants what he can't have, and that can make a man sit eating his heart out in jail half his life. But how good to walk, on Saturday, to the dam where you used to swim as a kid, to be greeted (these people who incite blacks against us should just have seen) by the farm boys at the kraal with laughter and pleasure at your acquisition of a wife; to go out with your father to shoot jackals at sunset. There's something wrong with all these people who become enemies of their own country: this private theory was really the only aspect of his work – for security reasons – he talked about to his girl, who, of course (he sometimes smiled to forget), was now his wife. Something wrong with them. They're enemies because they can't enjoy their lives the way a normal white person in South Africa does.

He could get a cold drink or coffee and a snack in the canteen at John Vorster but in the early evening when he knew he'd have to stay late, maybe all night, to work on this man with the Major, he'd had just about enough of the place. He took his break where he and his mates liked to go, the Chinese takeaway and restaurant just down the street.

It had no name up and was entered through an old shopfront. There was the high sizzle of frying and the full volume of TV programmes, and the Chinese and his wife moved about very softly. Early in the day when there was no television transmission, a small radio diffused cheerful commercials at the same volume above their pale faces from whose blunt features and flat eyes expression seemed worn away as a cake of soap loses definition in daily use. They belonged to the ancient guild of those harmless itinerant providers, of all nationalities, who wheel their barrows close to the sinister scenes of life – the bombed towns, the refugee encampments, the fallen cities – providing soup or rum indiscriminately to victims in rags or invaders in tanks, so long as these can pay the modest charge. Convenient to concentration camps there were such quiet couples, minding their own business, selling coffee and schnapps to refresh jackbooted men off duty. Perhaps the Chinese and his wife felt protected by John Vorster Square and whatever they did not want to know happened there; perhaps they felt threatened by its proximity; both reasons to know nothing. Their restaurant had few ethnic pretensions of the usual kind – no velveteen dragons or wind chimes – but they had put up a shelf on the wall where the large colour television set was placed like a miniature cinema screen, at awkward eye level for diners. In front of the TV they kept an area clear of tables and had ranged a dozen chairs for the use of policemen. The policemen were not expected to buy a meal, and for the price of a packet of chips and a cold drink could relax from their duties, so nearby. Although they were not supposed to take alcohol before resuming these, and the Chinese couple did not have a licence to sell it, beer was silently produced for those who, the couple knew without having to be asked aloud, wanted it. The young policemen, joking and kidding as they commented on the programmes they were watching, created a friendly enclave in the place. Diners who had nothing much to say to one another felt at least part of some animation. Family treats for children and grandmothers were popular there, because the food was cheap; children, always fascinated by the thrill and fear sensed in anything military or otherwise authoritarian, ate their grey chicken soup while watching the policemen.

Sergeant Chapman found a few mates occupying the chairs. He joined them. The hot weather left the brand of their profession where their caps, now lying under their chairs, had pressed on their foreheads. Their private smog of cigarette smoke mingled with frying fumes wavered towards the TV screen; he was in time for the last ten minutes of an episode in a powdered-wig French historical romance, dubbed in Afrikaans. It ended with a duel, swords gnashing like knives and forks. 'Hey, man, look at that!'

'But they not really fighting, themselves. The actors. They have special experts dressed up like them.'

'OK, I don't say it's the actors; but it's helluva good, just the same, ay. To be able to do it so fast and not hurt each other.'

Then came the Prime Minister, speaking with his special effects (a tooled leather prop desk, and velvet ceremonial drape as backdrop) on reconciliation and total onslaught. Conversations started up among the young policemen while he was projected overhead and the dinner customers chewed with respectful attention. Two plainclothes men in their casual-smart bar-lounge outfits came in to buy takeaways, evidently pleased with themselves, and did not even seem to notice that their volubility was making it difficult for people to follow the PM's voice.

Sergeant Chapman took the opportunity to phone Mariella, although she knew he would be home late, if at all tonight. He still had these impulses to talk to her about nothing, over the phone, the way you can ten times a day with your girl. The telephone was not available to ordinary customers but the policemen knew they could use it. Its sticky handpiece and the privacy of the noise that surrounded him as he dialled were familiar. But Mariella did not answer with her soft voice of flirtation. She was terribly excited. He didn't know whether she was laughing or crying. When she went into the kitchen just now to get herself some bread and cheese (she wasn't going to bother with supper if he didn't come) the venison was gone from the window. Gone! Just like that. She went outside to see if it'd fallen from the hook – but no.

'No, of course, man, I put that hook in fast.'

'But still, it could have fallen – no, but anyway, the hook's still there. So I saw the meat must've been pinched. I ran to the street and then I rushed round the yard—'

'You shouldn't do that when I'm not there, they'll knife you if you try to catch them. I've told you, Mariella, stay in the house at night, don't open to anyone.'

But she was 'so cross, so excited' she fetched the torch and took the dog by the collar and looked everywhere.

'That's mad, man. I told you not to. Somebody could be tricking you to get you out of the house.'

'No wait, there was nobody, Marais, nobody was there, it was all right.'

'Well you were just lucky he'd already got away, I'm telling you, Mariella, you make me worry. There must be blacks hanging around the neighbourhood who know I'm often away late—'

'No, listen, just wait till you hear – Buller pulled away from me and jumped over the fence into the lane, you know, there by the veggie patch, and he was barking and scratching. So I climbed over and there it was on the ground – only it wasn't the meat and everything, it was just the bone. All the meat was torn off it! You'll see, you'll see the places where big teeth pulled away! It must have been that baboon, that monkey thing, no dog could reach so high! And there was an item on the radio about it only this morning! You'll see, only a bone's left.' And now she began to giggle intimately. 'Your poor Pa. He'll be mad with you for hanging it like that. We'll have to pretend we ate it, hay? Anyway, you'll be pleased to know my jam's OK. It set and everything . . . What should I do . . . send for the police? If it could be you that comes, I'll be already making the bed warm . . .'

Although she sounded so lovable he had to be serious and make her promise to keep all the windows locked. Apes were clever, they had hands like humans. It might even manage to lift a lever and get in, now that it had become so full of cheek. He came striding back to his mates with a swagger of sensation, a tale to tell. 'You know that escaped monkey? Came to our place and swiped the Blesbok leg we brought from the farm yesterday! True as God! I hung it in the window this morning!'

'Ag, man, Chapman. Your stories. Some black took it. Hanging it in the window! Wha'd'you think you were doing, man?'

'No way, *boet*. It was that bloody thing, all right. She's just told me: she found the bone there in the lane where it et it. Even a black's not going to tear raw meat with his teeth.'

That one was a toughie, all right – the detainee. When Sergeant Chapman took over again, the bloke was so groggy – like a loser after ten rounds – but he wouldn't talk, he wouldn't talk. At about ten o'clock he passed out and even the Major agreed to call it a day until six in the morning. Sergeant Chapman told him about the venison. The Major thought it a great joke but at the same time suggested the Sergeant's young wife ought to learn how to handle a firearm. Next time it might be more than a monkey out there in the yard. Sergeant Chapman ought to know the situation.

There had to be some sign that the plot was being cultivated. That was what black men were for; so Eddie hoed the mealie patch. Vusi kept to the house. He sat in his armchair and read a thick paperback whose pages, top and bottom, were splayed and puffed by exposure to climatic changes or by much thumbing. *Africa Undermined: A History of the Mining Companies and the Underdevelopment of Africa*: sometimes he would borrow a ballpoint from Joy, mark a passage. If he began to yawn and sigh this was a prelude to his suddenly getting up and disappearing into the back room. She would hear him tinkering there, the clink of small tools; she supposed it was to do with what was locked in the shed. She filled several hours a day with *Teach Yourself Portuguese*, but didn't have her cassettes with her, here, as a guide to pronunciation, so had to concentrate on the grammar. Vusi could have helped her with German – but Portuguese!

'How long were you there?' He had trained in East Germany. That much she knew about him.

'Two years and three months. We didn't learn from books. You just have to begin to talk, man, you have to make people understand you when you want something, that's the best way. But what d'you want to learn Portuguese for?'

'Mozambique. Charles and I thought of going there. To live.' She pulled her hair back down behind the arms of her glasses. 'I might go, anyway. Teach for a while.'

'What do you teach?'

She made an awkward face. 'I haven't much, yet. But I can teach history. The new education system there; I'd like to be involved . . .

in something like that. One day.' The two words passed to him as a token that she was not deserting.

'Ja. You'd like it. It's going to be a good place. And Charlie, he's learning too?'

'He was. But not now.'

Vusi picked up her book and tried out a phrase or two, smiled at his poor effort.

'You *do* speak Portuguese.'

'Some words . . . I was only there a couple of months, everyone talks English to you.' He managed, with an accent better than hers, a few more phrases, as if for his and her amusement.

He sat in his chair again, waiting, his face as he himself would never see it, not in any photograph or mirror. He was possessed by an expression far from anyone's reach, so deep in the past of himself, a sorrow he did not consciously feel there in the watergleam of his black eyes hidden in the ancient cave of skull, in the tenuousness of life in the fine gills of the nostrils, the extraordinary unconscious settling of the grooved lips – lips that, when he was unaware of himself, not using them to shape the half-articulate communication of a poorly educated black man's English, held in their form what has never been, might still be spoken.

Now when he did speak, on the conscious level of their being in the room together, it seemed to her he did not know who he was; she had to make the quick adjustment to his working perception of himself. 'You not really married?'

She looked at his mystery, while he showed simple curiosity.

'No. Not really anything.'

He understood – was meant to understand? – she doesn't sleep with Charlie. If so, it was a confidence that licensed questions. 'What's the idea?'

'Well. There's no other room for me, is there.'

He arched his head back against the chair, expelled a breath towards the ceiling with its pine-knots and pressed lead curlicues all four of them, at times, took tally of obsessively.

'We came to a sort of stop. About five months ago, after nearly six years. But we'd already accepted to do this, while we were still together, so we couldn't let that make any difference.'

'Hell, you're a funny kind of woman.'

It was said with detached admiration. She laughed. 'You know better than I do what matters.'

'Sure. Still—'

'It's *because* I'm a woman you say *still*—'

He saw she jealously took his admiration as some sort of discrimination within commitment. He shied away. There came out of that mouth of his a careless response a city black man picks up as the idiom of whites in the streets. 'That's one I can't handle.'

He escaped her, taking up *Africa Undermined* aimlessly and putting it down again on his way out of the room.

Charles returned from his daily run; part of the routine he had constructed for himself to support the waiting. His rump in satiny blue-and-red shorts rose and fell before motorists who overtook him and often waved in approval of his healthy employment of time. Eddie would have liked to come along (oh how long – five years – ago, as a seventeen-year-old in Soweto he had run in training, had ambitions as an amateur flyweight) but a black-and-white couple would have been conspicuous. Panting like a happy dog, shaggy with warm odours, Charles was brought up short, in the room, as when one enters where some event is just over; but all that he was sensing, without identifying this, was that he had been talked about in his absence.

Although once she would have made a peg with fingers on her nose and so sent him off to shower, she did not now have the rights over his body to tell him he stank of good sweat; just smiled quickly and went on with her future tenses. He meant to go and get dressed but the need to know everything his colleagues knew, to follow their minds wherever they went, that would have made him a natural chairman of the board if he had grown up responding differently to propitious 'circumstances', led him to have a look at what chapter Vusi had reached in his book, and then, although he himself had read the book, to begin reading, again, wherever the other man had made his mark in ballpoint blue.

Not suddenly – there must have been the too-soft impression before first Charles, then Joy became conscious of it – there was a voice never heard before, in the house where no one but the four of them ever entered, now. It was unexpected as the feeble cry of something newborn.

Vusi came into the room with an instrument from which he was producing a voice. He passed Charles and stood before Joy, playing a muffled, sweet, half-mumbled 'Georgia On My Mind' – yes, that was it, identified as a bird-call can be made out as phonetic syllables humans translate into words. From those lips rippling and contracting round a mouthpiece, beneath his fingers pressing crude buttons, the song was issuing from an instrument strangely recognisable, absurd and delightful. Every now and then he drew a gulp of breath, like a swimmer. He played on, the voice gaining power, sometimes stammering (the peculiar buttons got stuck), occasionally squealing, but achieving the gentle, wah-wah sonority, rocket rise to high note and steady gliding fall out of hearing that belong to one instrument alone.

While what they had to do was wait, Vusi made a saxophone.

It was for this that he had collected the tabbed rings off beer cans. The curved neck was perhaps the easiest. It was made of articulated sections hammered from jam tins. Some of the more intricate parts must have required a thicker material. There might be a few cartridge cases transformed in the keyboard. He had worked on the saxophone shut up in the shed with the necessities stored there, as well as away down at the pigsties, where it was tried out without anyone else being able to hear it.

The white couple marvelled over the thing. An extraordinary artefact, as well as a musical instrument. Having played it to the girl that first time it was ever played for others, Vusi was unmoved by praise because no one would see what they were really looking at, as laymen enthuse over something that can't be grasped through their secular appreciation.

He didn't know Charles was reminded of the ingenuity of objects displayed in the concentration camps of Europe, now museums.

These were made by the inmates out of nothing, effigies of the beautiful possibilities of a life to be lived.

The municipal art gallery owns a sacred monkey. A charming image, an Indian statuette copied by a Viennese artist in glazed ceramic, green as if carved out of deep water. It lives in a cupboard behind glass. The gallery is poorly endowed with the art of the African continent on which it stands, and has no example of the dog-faced ape of ancient Egyptian mythology, Cynocephalus, often depicted attendant upon the god Thoth, which she has seen in museums abroad and has been amused to recognise as the two-thousand-year-old spitting image of a baboon species still numerous in South Africa.

A set of pan pipes sticking up out of the bathwater: toes. A face reflected in the snout of the shiny tap bulged into a merry gourd with a Halloween mouth. She can look at that but she doesn't want to see the distortion of her lower torso which is reflected if she leans her head, in its plastic mob cap, against the back of the bath. Her legs become gangling and bowed, joined by huge feet at one end and a curved perspective that leads back to a hairy creature, crouched. There is nothing beyond this voracious pudenda; it has swallowed the body and head behind it. She lies in the bath for relaxation. Nobody's told her she's dying, but they're being brought down all around her, as a lion moves into a herd, tearing into the flesh of his victims. A breast off here; a piece of lung there; a bladder cut down to size. She lies on her back and palpates her breasts dutifully. There are ribs, but no lumps. The nipples don't rise; that's good, she doesn't like the masturbatory aspect of what doctors advise you to do to yourself, as a precaution, in order to stay alive. These breasts don't recognise her hands; they've known only male ones. Her hands don't make them remember those.

Despite the fun-palace image in the tap, her real thighs still have that firm classical roundness. They don't pile like half-set junket round the knees when she's standing. Not yet.

The delicately engraved imprint of autumn leaves – a few varicosed patches – is more or less covered by a tan.

However she lies, her stomach rises like the Leviathan.

It was always there, waiting, flattened between the hip bones, for its years to come! She doesn't take it too hard. These fantasies are the consequence of waking so early, and there's a simple scientific explanation for that: reduced hormonal activity means you need less sleep. She nods her head in sage comprehension when this is explained to her; what it really means is you sleep eight hours after love-making. She feels them, other people, sleeping this sleep in other rooms. It's true that as you get older you suddenly know what happened in childhood. She understands quite differently, now, the family joke she used to be told about how she crawled over to her mother's bed at dawn, lifted her sleeping eyelid and spat in her eye. Oh lovers, I envy you the sleep, not the love-making, but nobody would believe me. I am told to disbelieve myself. 'It's something a doctor can't really let himself prescribe . . . but you need to stop thinking you're not interesting to men any longer.'

Old stock; hers. She goes over it again, toes, thighs, twat (yes, put down the great notion it had of itself, temple of pleasure), nice breasts. The face can be left out of it, thank God, you can't verify your own face by looking down on it in the bath, wiggling it, spouting its flesh out of the water and scuttling it to sink to the belly button again. This is not a bath with mirrors, far nicer, it has a glass wall that looks on a tiny courtyard no bigger than an airshaft where shade-loving plants and ferns grow, ingeniously and economically watered, in time of drought, by the outlet from the bath. They flourish in water favoured by this flesh as the Shi-ites buy grace in the form of bathwater used by the Aga Khan. She ought to contemplate the plants instead. She feels she doesn't want to, she doesn't want to be distracted from what she has to see, but she forces herself – she must stop watching herself, and this makes her feel someone's watching her, there's a gaze forming outside her awareness of self, it exists for a moment between the greenery.

Looking at the woman in the bath. Seeing what she sees.

She thought of it as having struck her, first, as the head of antiquity, the Egyptian basalt rigidity, twice removed – as animal and attribute of a god – from man, but with a gleam of close golden brown eyes like a human's.

No. A *real* baboon, Peeping Tom at large in the suburbs.

She had to think of it as that. If not (soaking herself groggy, seeing things), it would have to be her own visitation; a man.

Eddie came upon some droppings not far from the back of the shed. They looked human, to him. All four went to the spot to have a look. The Kleynhans place was so isolated, except for the passage of life on the road, to which it offered no reason to pause. They had felt themselves safe from intruders.

The hard twist of excreta was plaited with fur and sinew: Charles picked it up in his bare hand. 'See that? It had rabbit for supper. A jackal.'

Joy gave a shivery laugh, although there was no prowling man to fear. 'So close to the house?'

Vusi was disbelieving. 'Nothing to eat there.' The converted shed with its roll-down metal door was just behind them.

'Well, they pad around, sniff around. I suppose this place's still got a whiff of chickens and pigs. It's quite common even now, you get the odd jackal roaming fairly near to towns.'

'Are you sure? How can you know it's jackal, Charlie?'

Charles waggled the dung under Eddie's nose.

'Hey, man!' Eddie backed off, laughing nervously.

Vusi was a tester of statements rather than curious. 'Can you tell all kinds of animals' business?'

'Of course. First there's the shape and size, that's easy, ay, anyone can tell an elephant's from a bird's—' They laughed, but Charles was matter-of-fact, as someone who no longer works in a factory will pick up a tool and use it with the same automative skill learnt on an assembly line. 'But even if the stuff is broken up, you can say accurately which animal by examining food content. The bushmen – the San, Khoikhoi – they've practised it for centuries, part of their hunting skills.'

'Is that what they taught you at Scouts, man?'

'No. Not Scouts exactly.'

'So where'd you pick it up?' Eddie rallied the others. 'A Number Two expert! He's clever, old Charlie. We're lucky to have a chap like him, ay!'

Joy was listening politely, half-smiling, to Charles retelling, laconically self-censored, what had been the confidences of their early intimacy.

'Once upon a time I was a game ranger, believe it or not.' That was one of the things he had tried in order to avoid others: not to have to go into metal and corrugated paper packaging in which his father and uncles held 40 per cent of the shares, not to take up (well, all right, if you're not cut out for business) an opening in a quasi-governmental fuel research unit – without, for a long time, knowing that there was no way out for him, neither the detachment of science nor the consolations of nature. Born what he was, where he was, knowing what he knew, outrage would have burned down to shame if he had thought his generation had any right left to something in the careers guide.

'You're kidding. Where?'

'Oh, around. An ignoramus with a B.Sc. Honours, but the Shangaan rangers educated me.'

'Oh, Kruger Park, you mean. They work there. That place.' Vusi's jerk of the head cut off his words like an appalled flick of fingers. Once, he had come in through that vast wilderness of protected species; an endangered one on his way to become operational. Fear came back to him as a layer of cold liquid under the scalp. All that showed was that his small stiff ears pulled slightly against his skull.

Charles wiped his palm on his pants and clasped hands behind his head, easing his neck, his matronly pectorals flexing to keep in trim while waiting. 'One day I'd like to apply the methodology to humans – a class *anal*ysis.' (He enjoyed their laughter.) 'The sewage from a white suburb and the sewage from a squatters' camp – you couldn't find a better way of measuring the level of sustenance afforded by different income levels, even the snobbery imposed by different occupations and aspirations. A black street-sweeper who scoffed half a loaf and a Bantu beer for lunch, a white executive who's digested oysters and a bottle of Fleur du Cap, – show me what you shit, man, and I'll tell you who you are.'

That afternoon a black man did appear in the yard. He was not a prowler, although he probably had been watching them, the Kleynhans place, since they'd moved in. He would have known from where this could be managed delicately, without disturbing them or being seen.

He was a middle-aged farm labourer dressed in his church clothes so that the master and the missus wouldn't chase him away as a *skelm*. But he needn't have worried, because the master and the missus never appeared from the house. He found the two men who worked there at Baas Kleynhans's place now, as he had done, farm boys. He had come to see how his mealies were getting along. Yes. Yes . . . There was a long pause, in which the corollary to that remark would have time to be understood: he had been circling round the Kleynhans place, round this moment, to come to the point – an agreement whereby he could claim his mealie crop when it was ready for harvest. These other two, his brothers (he spoke to them in Sesotho and they answered in that language, but when he asked where they were from they said Natal) were welcome to eat what they liked, he was only worried about the white farmer. Could they claim the patch as the usual bit of ground for pumpkins and mealies farmers allowed their blacks? He would come and weed the mealies himself very early in the morning, before the baas got up, he wouldn't bring his brothers any trouble.

But the young men were good young men. They wouldn't hear of *baba* doing that. The one in jeans and a shirt with pictures all over it (farm boys dressed just the same as youngsters from town, these days) said he was looking after the mealies, don't worry. Gazing round his old home yard, the man admired the new garage with the nice door that had been made out of the shed and asked why this new white man hadn't ploughed? What were they going to plant? And what was his (Vusi's) work, if this white man wasn't going to have any pigs or chickens? They explained that farming hadn't really begun yet. First they'd built the garage, and Vusi – Vusi had been working inside. Helping the farmer fix things up. Painting the house. Ah yes, Baas Kleynhans was sick a long time before he died, there was no one to look after the house nicely.

The three black men talked together in the yard for more than an hour. They drifted towards a couple of boxes that still stood there, from Charles's deliveries, and sat on them, facing one another, gesticulating and smoking, sometimes breaking the little knot with a high exclamation or a piece of mimicry, laughter. When the man took off his felt hat a lump at the centre of his dusty hairline was polished by the sun. The white couple got a look at them from the bathroom window. It was an opaque glass hatch that opened under layers of dead creeper. What was happening in the yard could have been seen and heard more clearly from the kitchen windows, but the white couple also would have been visible, there, and they could not understand what was being said, anyway.

At first they felt only anxiety. Then they began to feel like eavesdroppers, spies: those who have no commune, those on the outside. The slow accretion of past weeks that was the four of them – a containing: a shell, a habitation – was broken. Eddie and Vusi were out there, yet it was Charles and Joy who were alone. They had no way of knowing what it was they were witnessing.

The man wobbled away on an old bicycle, calling the dying fall of farewells that go back and forth between country blacks. Both the pair in the house and the pair outside waited, just as they were, for about ten minutes. Vusi was silent but Charles and Joy (still in the bathroom, with its snivelling tap) could hear the continuing murmur of Eddie in monologue.

They all met in the kitchen. The girl looked ridiculously breathless, to the two coming in from the yard, as if she had been climbing.

'He used to work for the man who owned this place before. He wants his mealies.'

Charles's emotions, like his blood, flushed near the surface. He was testy when anxious; now, impatient with Vusi. 'It took the whole afternoon to say that! Christ, we've been going crazy. You seemed to know the man. We thought – God knows what – that you were having to give explanations, that you were cornered – I don't know? And what could we do? You seemed to be *enjoying* yourselves, for Christ' sake . . .'

As anxiety found release his tone drained of accusation; he ended up excited, half-laughing, rolling tendrils of bright beard between thumb and finger. Like a fragment of food, at table, a shred of leaf from the dead creeper round the bathroom window clung to the hairs.

Eddie went to the fridge and took out beer. 'We should have given him something to drink, but I couldn't come into the white baas's kitchen and just take. He must've wondered why we didn't have any in his old room, man; I was scared he'd ask to go in there, and see no beds, nothing. I was already thinking could I say we had girlfriends somewhere, where we sleep. But he knows everybody for miles around this place.'

They discussed the man and decided there was nothing they could do except hope he would not come back too shortly. Soon it would not matter any more if he did.

Joy did not look at Charles but directed a remark at him: 'If we have to stay much longer I'll have to start wearing a pillow. When I met our friend the estate agent's wife at the chemist's last week she had a good look at me. "You don't show yet, do you, dear?"'

'Oh my God. You'd better stop going to town.'

She did not complain. Her hair was put up in an odd knot on the side of her head – she was a woman, after all, she played about with her appearance, waiting. The way of doing her hair was very unattractive; on the side from which it was pulled over, the bone behind her ear was prominent and her skull looked flattened. 'And what was that Cyclops eye on his forehead?'

Eddie winced, puzzled. 'That what?'

'Some lump I could see in the sun, quite big and shiny.'

Charles tossed the remark absently at her, no one was interested. 'A cyst, I suppose. I didn't notice.'

'Like a bulging eye in the middle of his head. Or one of Moses's horns growing.'

Vusi had no need of ring-tabs any longer – he dropped his in his emptied beer can and gave it a shake, sounding a rattle for attention. 'Kleynhans paid him fifteen rands a month. He worked for him for twelve years. When Kleynhans died, the daughter told the agent Klopper he could stay on without pay in that room in the yard until the place was sold. His son works at the brick-field and lives with his wife and kids with those other squatters near there. They've been chased off twice but they built their shack again. Since we came, the old man's living with them. No job. No permission to look for work in town. Nowhere to go.'

'Yes.' Charles dragged all five fingers again and again through his beard. 'Yes.'

A habitation of resolve, secreted by their presence among one another, contained them again, the four of them: waiting. They were quiet, not subdued; strongly alive. There was no need to talk. After a while Vusi fetched his saxophone and it spoke, gently. There was a summer storm coming up, first the single finger of a tree's branch paddling thick air, then the land expelling great breaths in gusts, common brown birds flinging themselves wildly, a raw, fresh-cut scent of rain falling somewhere else. So beautiful, the temperament of the earth. Waiting, they saw the rain, dangling over the pale spools that were the power station towers.

Ms Dot Lamb, chairperson of the Residents' Association of the suburb where, if an outlaw can be said to have taken up residence, this one seemed to have a base, since it kept returning there, requested an interview with the town councillor whom the residents had voted into office to protect their property and interests. The promise given by him produced no result – as if to show how little it felt itself threatened by the councillor, the creature 'cleaned up' as a resident put it, an entire bed of artichokes cultivated from imported seed for table use as an elegant first course. Ms Lamb called a meeting of the Association. She was a woman who got things done; the residents were people who wanted things done for them, without having to take the trouble themselves. It was she who had rallied them to contest the plan to build a home for spastic children among their houses. She had won (for them) the battle to stop toilets for blacks being built at the blacks' suburban bus terminus, making a strong case that this convenience, far from promoting public decency, would merely encourage the number of blacks who gathered to drink among the natural flora of the koppies that was such a treasured feature of the suburb. Now these koppies were being used by an escaped ape as well. Was it for this that ratepayers had been notified of increases in property taxes envisaged for the coming year? Valuable pets, loved companions of children, had been killed. People feared to leave small children to play in their own gardens.

The residents authorised Ms Lamb to take further steps. She wanted no more shilly-shallying with the so-called proper channels. She went straight to the local police station, kicked up a fuss, and actually got the superintendent to send two armed white policemen and a couple of black ones to mount a search along the ridge of koppies behind some of the finest homes in the suburb. They rounded up several illicit liquor sellers and arrested fifteen men without passes, but did not find what they had been instructed to.

The SPCA protested that an animal should not be hunted and shot by the police, like a criminal. Zoo officials offered to try and dart it. If, as a number of people insisted, it was an ape, it would find a safe home in the new ape-house, where at 3 p.m. every day the inmates perform a tea party for the amusement of children of all races.

Eddie went to the road and thumbed a lift in the African way, flagging a whole arm from waist level as if directing a motor race. He was wearing his Wild West jacket. Vusi and Charles were still asleep – some people can pass the time, waiting, by sleeping more – but Joy saw him go. Her hands tingled with anguish, as if she were going to be sick. She did not wake the others and did not know if she was doing what was right. She did not know whether, when they woke up, she would pretend she had not seen Eddie.

Eddie got a lift with a black man in a firm's panel van. They talked about soccer. He did not ask to be let down at the local dorp where Joy and Mrs Naas Klopper shopped. He went all the way – to Johannesburg.

Eddie had nothing to leave at the entrance to a supermarket where you were asked to deposit your briefcase or carrier bag in return for a numbered disc. He did not uncouple a trolley from the train against the wall, or pick up a plastic basket. He walked the lanes as if at a vast exhibition, passing arsenals of canned fruit, yellow mosaics of pickles in jars, flat, round and oval cans of pilchards, sardines, anchovies, mussels in brine and tuna in cottonseed oil, bottles of sauces, aerosol cans of chocolate topping, bins of coffee beans, packets of rice and lentils, sacks of mealie-meal and sugar, pausing now and then, as if to read the name of the artist: *Genuine Papadums*, *Poivre Vert de Madagascar* – and then passing on to pet and poultry foods, detergents, packaged meat like cross-sections of viscera under a microscope, pots, Irish Coffee glasses, can openers, electric pizza-makers, saws, chisels, light bulbs, roundabout stands of women's pantyhose, and greeting cards humorous, religious or sentimental. White women pushed small children or small dogs in the upper rack of trolleys. Black people turned over the packages of stewing meat. Other blacks, employees, wielded punches that printed prices on stocks they were replenishing. The piped music was interrupted by chimes and a voice regularly welcoming him (in his capacity as a shopper) and announcing today's specials. At the record and tape bar he spent half an hour turning over the decks of bright neat tapes the way others did meat packs. There were no facilities for listening to tapes or records, but he knew all the groups and individuals recorded, and their familiar music sealed within. A supermarket wouldn't have anything that hadn't been reissued in cheap mass pressings – you'd need a record shop for really good, new stuff. Going through these was just looking up what hadn't changed.

He queued at one of the exits holding a set of transistor batteries and a snuffbox-sized tin of ointment he hadn't seen since his mother used to put it on his sores as a kid. A *mama* ahead of him, turning to speak Setswana, at home here in this city in her slippers, outsize tweed skirt and nylon headscarf from some street-vendor's selection, assumed his support, as one of her own, in an argument over change with the aloof almost-white cashier. From the stand beside him he took, as a tourist picks up a last postcard, one of the pairs of sunglasses hooked there.

In the streets there were thousands like him. He crossed at traffic lights and walked pavements among them. Young ones loping in loose gangs of three or four, out of work or out of school, going nowhere. When you are that age, the city, where there is nothing for you, draws you from the townships, to which you always have to go back. Others, his own age, carrying their employers' mail and packages to the post office, daringly shaving their motorbikes past traffic, delivering medicines and film, legal documents, orders of hamburgers. Older ones in those top brass peaked caps and military tunics with which white people strangely choose to dress the humblest of their employees – doormen and commissionaires – like their military heroes. The city was blacker than he remembered it. Down the west end of Jeppe and Bree Streets, the same long bus queues making an accompanying line of fruit skins and Coke cans in the gutters, the same Portuguese eating-house selling pap and stew, the same taxi drivers using Diagonal Street as the backyard where they groomed their vehicles like proud racehorse owners, the same women crowded round the alley exit of the poultry wholesaler's to buy sloppy pails of chicken guts. But in the white part of the city, where there were no street stalls but banks and insurance company blocks, landscaped malls, caterpillars of people being carried from level to level – into what used to be the white centre of the city, his own kind seemed to have flowed. It was Saturday and there were light-coloureds, painters and carpenters of the building trade, dressed in pastel safari shorts and jackets, straw hats with paisley bands, like the Afrikaners who grandfathered them. Black kids of respectable families had dazzling white socks halfway up their small legs. Lovely black girls tilted the balance of their backsides to counter the angle of the high-heeled sandals it was apparently fashionable this year to wear with jeans; the nails of their crooked toes and beautiful hands signalled deep red as they approached and passed him. All would have to go back to the places for blacks, when they had spent their money; but there was no white centre to the city any more (he had forgotten, in five years, that this was so, or it had happened in those five years). They came in and surged all over it, it lived off them and for them. The male office-cleaners, tiny, bare-chested figures looking down, in the wind and dust blown from the mine dumps, from the tops of skyscrapers where they washed their clothes and drank beer, must be able to see their own people far below, flowing all round the company headquarters of the white race.

He spent a long time looking in windows filled with pocket calculators of all sizes and kinds, video equipment, cameras and the latest in walkabout tape players, which, as watches once had been, were being reduced to smaller and smaller format. Inside a shop he had this marvellous precision of workmanship demonstrated to him by a young Portuguese who probably had fled to this country from black rule in Mozambique just about the same time as Eddie had fled from his home, here in Johannesburg, eluding the political police from the handsome building with touches of blue paint, John Vorster Square, a few blocks from the shop in which he was now trying on headphones. 'S'wonderful, 'ey? You don't 'ardly feel them, they so light.' The young Portuguese was willing to show every feature of each shape, size and model. When Eddie left without 'making up his mind', he gave Eddie a card with a name written large and curly below the shop's printed title – *Manuel*. 'H'ask for me, I'll look after you.'

In an outfitter's Eddie was shown a range of casual trousers by an Indian employed there. 'This's what all the young chaps are wearing, man. Bright colours. What are you? Twenty-eight?' He sized up Eddie's waist with a frisker's glance. He admired Eddie's jacket: that certainly wasn't locally made! When Eddie didn't see anything he liked, he was reassured: 'Just look in next week, say, after Tuesday. We getting fabulous new stuff all the time. Whenever you passing . . .'

He roamed again towards the west end, to the queues from which he could catch a bus to get him part of his way back. He bought a carton of curried chicken and ate as he went along. Outside a white men's bar a black girl singled him out with a sidling look, and approached. He smiled and walked on: no thanks, *sisi*. With the prostitute's eye for the stranger in town, she was the only one in the city to recognise him: someone set apart in the crowd of his own kind from which he appeared indistinguishable.

Stanley Dobrow entered his photograph for the 'Picture of The Year' competition held by a morning paper.

Old Grahame Fraser-Smith – the 'old' was an epithet of comradeliness on the part of his colleagues, he was only forty-eight – got the idea in his head that although short-sighted, he had seen into the eyes of the creature. In the operating theatre, during those intervals between putting together broken faces with a human skill and ingenuity more miraculous than God's making of a woman out of a man's rib, he told the story differently, now. It seemed to him that as he bent down for the golf ball, he saw the creature bend first, just as he was doing, but farther off. And they looked at each other. You know how arresting eyes can be? It was hardly necessary to point this out where everyone around him was reduced to eyes above masks. No, true, he couldn't describe the body, certainly not the gait, as van Gelder insisted he could. Yet the eyes – you know how it is sometimes, in a room full of people, you see really only one person, you look into that pair of eyes and it's as if you are face to face, alone, with that person? It was like suddenly meeting someone seen many times on a photograph; or someone he'd been told about as a child; or someone people had been telling one another about for generations. He stopped there. He didn't want the assisting surgeons, anaesthetist, nurses, the medical students who came to watch the beauty of his work (about which he was genuinely modest) to reduce that encounter to something fanciful, and therefore funny. But if van Gelder was a bone man, so was he, a Hamlet who had contemplated and reconstructed with his own hands the living maxillo-facial structure of a thousand Yoricks. To himself he secretly continued: he had looked back into a consciousness from which part of his own came. There were claims from within oneself that could materialise only in these unsought ways, in apparently trivial or fortuitous happenings that could be felt but not understood. He thought of the experience as some sort of slip in the engagement of the cogs of time.

* * *

Eddie was there before dark.

Vusi and Charles were playing chess and Joy was burning rubbish in the front garden. So she was first to see him come as she was first to know he had gone. She had a broken branch and went on poking at whatever was burning until he had to pass her on his way up to the house. She put up a folded hand with her usual effacing gesture, smiling, not aware that she smeared the cobweb of flying ashes that had settled on her forehead. 'Hello.'

If she wouldn't ask any questions, he would.

Eddie stopped. 'What's that for?'

She was better-looking with the waves of flame melting the narrow definitions of her face, colouring and rounding it. 'A rat came into the bathroom. They're breeding in that pile of junk we threw out of the shed. I had to lug everything round here.'

He nodded. He had been away, but at once was together with her, with the others, again, in the knowledge that no fire could be made near what was behind the new garage door.

He went on to the house.

They must have heard him talking to Joy. They must have decided to talk it out calmly, but Charles struggled up from under his own self-control, the chessmen rolled over the floor. 'Are you bloody mad?' He was gone from the room.

Vusi did not seem to see Charles; opened his mouth dryly and closed it again.

Eddie dribbled one of the chessmen with the toe of his running shoe. He went out to the kitchen, and came back with a beer. Charles was there, gathering up the chessmen.

The release of gas from the beer can as he pierced it was like an opening exclamation from Eddie. 'Well, nothing happened. I went to town, I'm back.'

Vusi was silent, withholding his attention.

Charles had his big body safely chained down on a stool. 'I'm sorry. But it's clear you know what you did, what risk you took for us all.'

'There's nothing to worry about. *Nothing happened.*' Eddie spoke to Vusi. He had to reach Vusi. It was Vusi to whom they were all responsible, even in collective responsibility; Vusi, not Charles, to whom Joy had had to say she had seen Eddie take a lift, on the road, early in the morning. 'I didn't go to see anyone. You can believe that.'

Vusi gave a slow blink to dismiss any suggestion of mistrust. Eddie's presence was acknowledged. 'That's not the question, man. You could have been picked up.'

'Well, I wasn't.'

Joy came in and saw they were not quarrelling; it was no more possible for them to dare quarrel than for her to have made her bonfire near the shed. Discipline was the molecular pattern that attracted them back to their particular association. If Eddie had been picked up, even if he had not been recognised as a banned exile who had infiltrated, and had got away with being jailed as an ordinary pass-offender (the papers he had been provided with described him as a farm labourer and did not permit him to look for work in an urban area), the pattern would have been distorted. Vusi could not function without Eddie, Eddie and Vusi without Charles and Joy, Charles and Joy without Eddie and Vusi. The entity reconstituted itself irresistibly, there among the sofa covered with the conch-design cloth, the armchair that had become Vusi's, the fake ox-wagon wheel with its fly-haloed pink hats; there was no sending it flying apart, from within, by attacking (with the sort of open reproaches any ordinary relationship would withstand) the component – Eddie – that was once more in place, at the Kleynhans place.

The white pair later heard Vusi talking for a long time in his and Eddie's language in the second bedroom. Each made a mental translation, according to what they themselves would have been saying to Eddie, of what Vusi would be saying in the low cadence that seemed to vibrate the thin walls of the house like some swarm settled under the tin roof. Charles was giving him the hell he couldn't, aloud; above all, how could the kid Eddie risk *Vusi*, Vusi who had been operational before, who knew his job, who was needed to stay alive and had managed to survive four times the near certainty of imprisonment and death his job carried. Joy was asking why: if Eddie really knew why he was here – the reasons of his own life, of the lives of all his people for generations – then how could he have an impulse to drop back into the meek or loud-mouth compliance of the streets, still under that same magisterial authority of someone's long-dead white grandfather? Poor Eddie. It could only be because he had not understood properly why he had to be here and nowhere else; not taking advantage of slowly evolving opportunities to advance himself in the black business community, or to avail himself, at newly established technikons for blacks, of what, after all, were necessary skills for the service of his people, or to join the elite of black doctors allowed to practise only in black areas or black lawyers barred from taking chambers in white areas where the courts were. She could testify, in herself. She would not have been here if she had not found her own re-education, after the school where she had sung for God to save white South Africa. Without that re-education she would not have come to know for herself, for certain, that she could not now be bearing classified children (white) while living in a white suburb like that of the house with a view where she had grown up. She could not be anywhere but on the Kleynhans plot with a view of the power station.

That evening there was the rather prim atmosphere in the house that surrounds someone who has been drunk and now has slept it off. Eddie appeared, sobered of his single repetition, *Nothing happened*. Vusi must have told him that if he couldn't stand the Kleynhans place any longer, that was all right, because from tomorrow the three men would be out every night from midnight until just before dawn. It had been Charles's turn to cook (they had solved the problem of which sex was suited to the kitchen by having a roster) and, in spite of what sort of day it had been, he had made a mutton stew. Eddie loved mutton; but of course it had not been made with a treat for him in mind.

After they had eaten, the men went out into the yard. The moon was not yet risen. The light from the kitchen window touched shallowly the zinc glint of the garage door as it rolled up sufficiently for them to duck in. It rattled down behind them. Eddie didn't think it was working smoothly enough. 'Better get us some oil, Charlie, or it's soon going to rust.' Charles raised eyebrows, opened nostrils, swallowed a yawn, a man without tenure. While they were checking the heavy picks, the spades and black plastic sheeting Charles had laid in ready for the end of waiting, Joy didn't mind doing the washing-up on her own for once. If there was something practical to plan, the men liked to do it behind the outhouse door, where they were in tactile reach of the means by which what they were discussing was to be realised.

They were gone a long time. She took a beer from the fridge with her to the living room and turned on Eddie's tape player, which was always beside his end of the sofa as a pipe smoker will have his paraphernalia handy on a chair-arm. After she had told Vusi about seeing Eddie hitch a lift, she had made it possible for herself to keep out of everyone's way, all day. In order not to be with Vusi and Charles, not to sit around with them in that same room, or to be in the bedroom which was, after all, Charles's room as well, she had dragged cardboard boxes, rags, old bones, torn Afrikaans newspapers the black man who used to live in the yard had collected, to the front garden and made her bonfire among the broken poles of the pergola. Now she felt the comfort of being together with them once more – all three of them, Vusi, Charles and Eddie, although they were not in the room with her. The music was whatever Eddie had left in the player; a tape with a strong beat. All on her own, she began to dance, smiling to herself as if to others dancing towards and away from her. She worked off her sandals without pausing, and danced on the nap of the ugly rug Charles had bought along with the job-lot 'suite' to make a show to the Naas Kloppers of the district that the house was meant really to be lived in. Rhythm tossed her head and the knot of hair loosened and slowly unravelled, then swung from shoulder to shoulder. She threw her glasses on to Vusi's chair. At night, moths circled in place of flies above the lop-sided pink shades, falling singed; her bare feet trod one now and then. Her small breasts rose and fell against her chest like a necklace; she swooped and shook, swayed and softly sang.

Vusi's dreaming face, that had so little to do with the temporal level of his thoughts and actions, took the wash of crude 60-watt light from the chandelier, suddenly in the doorway. The face appeared to her as a wave of phosphorescence in the dark wake of the house around her movements might reveal a head from a submerged statue. Eddie and woolly Charles came up behind him.

She had no breath left, her mouth was open in a panting smile. 'Come on.' It could only be Eddie she summoned.

She went on dancing.

Eddie was standing there.

Slowly, Eddie began to stir to life, first from the hips, then with this-way-and-that slither and stub of the feet, then with the pelvis, the buttocks, the elbows, the knees, and as his whole body and head revived, moved to her.

Eddie and Joy were dancing.

Charles could dance only when drunk; a performing bear, round and round; sometimes some girl's teddy bear. He stretched out on the sofa, occupying Eddie's end as well, and smiled at them encouragingly. He might have been a father happily embarrassed to see a neglected daughter coming out of herself.

Before the tape ended Vusi fetched his saxophone. That voice that was strangely his own entered the room ahead of him, playing along with the beat, speaking to them all, one last time.

When signs were not noted for a week or so in a suburb where the fugitive had been active, residents there at once lost interest in having it trapped. So long as it attacked other people's cats and dogs, frightened other people's maids – that was other people's affair. Indignation and complaints shifted from suburb to suburb, from the affluent to the salaried man. The creature was no snob; or no respecter of persons, whichever way you cared to look at it. The policeman's venison in a lower-income-group housing estate, a pedigree Shih Tzu carried away when let out for its late-night leg-lift in an Inanda rose garden – each served equally as means of survival. And the creature never went beyond the bounds of white Johannesburg. Like the contract labourers who had to leave their families to find work where work was, like the unemployed who were endorsed out to where there was no work and somehow kept getting back in through the barbed strands of Influx Control; like all those who are the uncounted doubling of census figures for Soweto and Tembisa and Natalspruit and Alexandra townships, it was canny about where it was possible somehow to exist off the pickings of plenty. And if charity does not move those who have everything to spare, fear will. All the residents of the suburbs wanted was for the animal to be confined in its appropriate place, that's all, zoo or even circus. They were prepared to pay for this to be done. (But the owner of the largest circus that travels the country said it was unlikely an ape that had learnt to fend for itself in a hostile environment would be ever again psychologically amenable to training.)

Almost two months had passed since a thirteen-year-old schoolboy had been the first to sight the creature while playing with friends in the family swimming pool. Arriving as a result of somebody's lack of vigilance, it seemed to some people the menace might be trapped for ever in refuge among them, as an eel may fall by hazard into a well on its migratory nocturnal wriggle towards a suitable environment and survive for many years, growing enormous, down out of reach. It was inevitable that when it was worth a line or two in the papers, now, the creature was facetiously dubbed King Kong, and sometimes even King Kong of the mink-and-manure belt, although it had been seen only once, and then first by a horse, causing the horse to bolt with owner-rider, in the country estate area of the far Northern Suburbs. Former wife of the chairman of a public relations company, the rider was known to her friends as quite a gal, and typically she wheeled the horse and rode after the thing through a eucalyptus plantation, but never caught up or caught more than a glimpse of something dark. Anyway, that was no King Kong; what she'd chased was about the size of the average dwarf.

In the opinion of a zoologist, a monkey, baboon or ape may survive on the koppies round about Johannesburg, in summer, yes. But when the Highveld winter comes . . . *Simiadae* suffer from the common cold, die of pneumonia, like people – just like people.

* * *

One day, they disappeared.

The back bedroom was empty and nobody slept on the mattresses or read *Africa Undermined* by the light of the goose-neck lamp between them. Joy tugged the badly hung curtains across the windows and closed the door quietly as she went out. She could have moved in there, now, but didn't. She and Charles kept each other company, lying in the dark in the front bedroom and thinking in silence about Vusi and Eddie. He said to her once: 'One thing – you and I have been closer to those two than we'll ever be to anyone else in our lives, I don't care who that might be.'

It might be the lovers they once were, the lovers to come; wife, husband, children.

Once or twice in the following nights Charles went to Vusi and Eddie in the small hours. 'They say I shouldn't, any more. It's right; there's danger that might lead someone to them.' Only then did he add the conclusion – his conclusion and hers – to what he had said in the dark. 'And most likely we'll never see them again.'

There was not much to tidy up. It was just a careful routine matter of making sure there was nothing by which anyone could be identified. Neither to have it lying about nor in one's possession or on one's person: he stopped her from folding up her conch-printed cloth, now familiarly wrinkled from its use on the sofa. 'Well, I'll just let it stay where it is, then.'

'No you won't. Haven't you got some kind of dress or something of that stuff? Your preggy outfit? You've been seen wearing the same material.'

During the last few weeks, she had taken the precaution of making herself a loose shirt to disguise her lack of belly when she went shopping and might meet Mrs Naas Klopper. So there was another bonfire, this time down at what had once been the Kleynhans piggery. The cloth burned in patches; pieces, eaten into shapes by the flames, kept escaping destruction. Again, Joy had a branch with which to poke them back into the furnace heart of the fire. It served her right for carrying unnecessary possessions with her into a situation too different, from anything known, to be imagined in advance.

'But if you can't go to them any more, will they have enough food to last out?' And she, in what she thought of as her stupidity, her left-over dilettantism of austerity, not realising you eat while you can, had started off by buying them cheap sausages!

Charles was tearing apart the spines of a few books, with marginal notes in Vusi's handwriting, they had left behind. Feeding a fire with books was something he could not have believed he would ever do.

He stopped, with the peculiar weight of helplessness big men are subject to, when they must hold back. 'Eddie says he'll manage.'

She looked, in alarm.

'Vusi has his mind on only one thing. I don't think he cares whether he eats or not, now.'

The cotton cloth gave off the smell of its dye as it smouldered – the natural dye made from the indigo berry, she had been told like any tourist when she bought it in the other African country where she had received her new surname and passport on her way back to where she had been born. Now Eddie and Vusi, who were not known to her then, even under those names, were somewhere she had never seen. Charles had tried to describe it; she marvelled that it could have been adapted and wondered if it could possibly be maintained long enough. Charles explained that Vusi and Eddie would have to wait until the day, the hour, in which the exact coincidence of their preparedness, contingency arrangements, and the gap in the routine Vusi had studied, arrived. Vusi had this charted in his head as precisely as an analemma on a sundial.

Charles and Joy could sit on the front stoep, now, in the evenings, like any other plot owners taking the air. They sat drinking beer and she tried to visualise for herself where she had never seen, gazing way off, as to a horizon of mountains, at the only feature of the Kleynhans place view, the towers of the power station whose curved planes signalled after-light back to the sunken sun, and above whose height toy puffs of smoke were congealed by distance.

And then the man came on his bicycle to see how his mealies were doing. Charles and Joy were helping themselves to bread and coffee, in the kitchen, at seven in the morning; even Charles had not slept well. They saw him cautiously wheel the bicycle behind the shed, and then appear, sticking his neck out, withdrawing it, sticking it out, like a nervous rooster. He went up to the door of his old room and called softly, in his language. They watched him.

'Oh Christ.'

'I'll go.' Joy slept in an outsize T-shirt; she put her Indian skirt over it and went out into the yard with the right amount of white madam manner, not enough to be too repugnant to her, not too little to seem normal to the former Kleynhans labourer.

'Yes? Do you want something?'

Mild as her presence was, it clamped him by the leg; caught there, he took off his hat and greeted her in Afrikaans. '*Môre missus, môre missus*.'

She changed to Afrikaans, too. 'What it is you want here?'

He shook his head reassuringly, he wanted nothing from the missus, he asked nothing, only where was her boy? He wanted, please, to speak to her boy.

She was like all white missuses, she knew very well whom he meant but she suspected him, they always suspect a strange black man at the door. And she refused to understand because she knew he had something he wasn't telling – like his mealie patch he'd left on what was now her property. 'What boy? Which boy d'you mean? What's his name?'

No, missus, he didn't know the name – those two boys that work for the baas on the farm, now. Could he please see those boys? They were (in an inspiration, they had suddenly become) his wife's cousins.

Now the white missus smiled sympathetically. 'Oh those. No, they don't work here any more. They've gone. My husband has finished with the building, he didn't need them any longer.'

Gone?

He knew it was no use asking where. When black people leave a white man's place, they've gone, that's all; it's not the white man's business to know where they'll find work next. Then he had another sudden idea, and again he saw in her face she knew it as soon as he did. 'Does the baas need a boy for the farm? Me, I'm old Baas Kleynhans's boy, I'm work here before, long time.'

She was smiling refusal while he pleaded. 'No, no, I'm sorry. We don't need anyone. My husband's got someone coming – next month, yes, from another farm, his brother's farm—'

They knew exactly how to lie to each other, standing in the yard in which she was the newcomer and he the old inhabitant.

She said it again: she was sorry . . . And this gave him the courage of an opening.

'When I'm here before – after Oubaas Kleynhans he's die, I'm look after this place. Those mealies' (he pointed behind him) 'I'm plant them. And then the other baas he say I must go. Now those boy – your boy – I'm tell them it's my mealies and they say they can ask you, I can come for those mealies.'

'Oh the mealie patch? No, I don't know anything about that. But there are no mealies yet—' Both her hands turned palm up in smiling patronage.

'Not now. But when the mealies they're coming ready, that boy he's say he going ask you—'

'You can have the mealies.'

He grinned with nervous disbelief at the ease of his success. 'The baas he won't chase me?'

She must be one of those young white women who tell their men what they must do. She was sure: 'The baas won't chase you.'

'When the missus and the baas like to eat some of those mealies, when they coming still green, the missus must take.'

'Yes, thank you.' And then, the usual phrase from white people, who are always in a hurry to get things over, who don't seem to know or take any pleasure in the lingering disengagement that politely concludes a discussion: 'All right, then, eh?' And she was gone, back into the kitchen, while, since he hadn't been chased away, he took this as the permission he hadn't asked for – to go through the white people's property to look at his mealies.

Charles and Joy kept checking on whether the bicycle was still there, behind the shed. Half an hour later it was gone, and so must he be, although they had missed witnessing him ride away.

Charles heated up the coffee. He had not appeared before the man; the man would not be able to describe the baas, only the missus and the two boys who had worked for them. Joy blew on her cup. 'I really think he's harmless.'

But that was exactly what made him suspect – his humble pretext for having kept an eye on them for weeks, now, his innocent reason for trying to find out where Eddie and Vusi were: perfect opportunities for someone in plainclothes to have picked up a poor farm labourer out of work and offered him a few rands simply in return for telling what and whom he saw on a farm where nothing was growing but his trespassing patch of mealies.

'And if I had chased him away?'

'That'd've been much worse. For Pete's sake!'

Once approved, she had natural grounds for pointing out her forethought. 'I told him someone else was coming to work for us, but only next month. To hold him off and at the same time make the set-up not seem too unnatural.'

Charles opened his hands stiffly, doubtingly, and then made fists of them under his bearded jaw again. 'Next month.' That part of the proposition was good enough. The day after you have left a country it will be as remote, as a physical environment in which you may be apprehended, as it will be in a year. Next month would be no more able to reach them than the time, months ahead, when the mealies would be ready for eating. 'But now he'll be hanging around. He'll be arriving every day with his hoe and whatnot. He may bring friends with him.'

'So it would have been better if you'd gone out and played the heavy baas scene.'

'I've told you, you couldn't have done anything else.'

The occasional lapses of confidence in herself, that had roused his tenderness when they were lovers, now irritated Charles. You had no business to have gone this far, to be the back-up for Vusi and Eddie – all that meant – if you were still at the stage of allowing yourself self-doubt. But they were alone; no Vusi, no Eddie, and there they had to stay until Charles, on one of his outings in the combi, learnt that arrangements were ready for them to get away, as arrangements, at the beginning, had brought them successfully to Klopper's Eiendoms Beperk to look for a place in this area. They had only each other, even if it was in an awareness very different from that of the lovers they had been. They had lost the scent of one another's skin; but the house held them together, this place which they had occupied, not lived in, as in old wars soldiers occupied trenches and stuck up pictures of girls there. Neither said to the other what both felt while going matter-of-factly through this stage of what had been undertaken: some days, a desolate desire to get away from the house, the shed with the shiny roll-down door, the veld where except for the mealie patch, khakiweed filled in the pattern of rows where beans and potatoes had once grown; some hours, a sense of attachment to the room under the ox-wagon wheel chandelier and the curlicues of the pressed lead ceiling where the four of them had spent time that could never be recorded in the annals of ordinary life; to the outhouse they had bricked up together, and even to an aspect neither of them would ever have of any landscape again – the presence of the towers of the power station, away over the veld. This sense of attachment was so strong there seemed, while it lasted, no other reality anywhere to be found.

The ape family is not exactly omnivorous. Like the human animal, it is able to adapt its eating habits to changes of environment. If the creature had been a pet, or kept in any other form of captivity normal for a creature whose needs must be subordinate to the dominant human species, the diet supplied to it would have been fruit, vegetables and some cereal, probably stale bread. It also would have developed, as creatures do in mournful compensation for what they cannot tell those who keep them caged or secured by a chain to a perch, yearnings transformed into addiction to certain tidbits. Although members of the ape family are generally vegetarian in their wild state, in times of drought, for example, they will eat anything their agility and the strength of their hands equip them to catch; and in captivity this atavistic (so to speak) memory can be seen to rouse from quiet masturbation a perfectly well-fed blue-bottomed baboon in the Johannesburg zoo, whose prehensile bolt of lightning strikes down any pigeon who flies through the cage on the lookout for crumbs – he tears it apart instantly. The instinct must have been what returned to the fugitive when, in early weeks on the run, it killed or maimed dogs and cats. This surely was a period of great fear. Humans are the source of the terror of capture; a dog or cat is an intermediary who represents the lesser risk. To kill a suburban dog or cat is to destroy the enemy's envoy as well as to eat.

But after a while the creature changed its tastes. Or became more confident? Sergeant Abel van Niekerk and Constables Gqueka, Mcunu and Manaka had not been able to catch it. It had feasted on venison.

Now it lived by raiding dustbins; if not carelessly bold, then desperate. It still frequented the affluent suburbs where first seen, although now and then a sortie into the working-class white suburbs was again reported. Most likely it was from that class of home it had escaped (though no one was admitting any responsibility) because along with racing pigeons, rabbits, etc., an ape is a lower-income-group pet, conferring a distinction (that man who goes around with his tame monkey) on people who haven't much hope of attaining it as a company director or television personality.

A left-wing writer, taking up a sense of unfortunate duty to speak out on such paradoxes, wrote a stinging article noting sentimentality over a homeless animal, while – she gave precise figures – hundreds of thousands of black people had no adequate housing and were bulldozed out of the shelters they made for themselves. Some people of conservative views had a different attitude which nevertheless also expressed irritation with animal lovers and conservationists, who were more concerned about the welfare of a bloody ape than the peace and security one paid through the nose for in a high-class suburb well isolated from the other nuisances – white working-class, black, Indian or coloured townships. The monkey or whatever it was was in self-imposed exile. If it had been content to stay chained in a yard or caged in a zoo, its proper station in life, it wouldn't have had to live the life of an outlaw. If one might presume to do so without making oneself absurd by speaking in such terms of something less than human – well, serve the damn thing right.

* * *

Charles had found the cave. He had searched the veld within three or four kilometres of the power station, carrying a mining geologist's hammer and bag as the perfectly ordinary answer to anyone who might wonder what he was doing.

And he had found it. They called it 'the cave', right from the first night he took them there to see if it would do, but it wasn't a cave at all. It was the end of a rocky outcrop that sloped away underground into the grassland of the Highveld, sticking up unobtrusively from it like part of the steep deck of a wreck that is all that remains visible of a huge submerged liner of the past. Some growth had huddled round for the shelter of the lion-coloured rocks in winter, and the moisture condensed there in summer. In daylight, they saw the covering of leathery, rigid, black-green leaves, with a rusty sheen of hairs where the backs curled; to Charles, whose taxonomic habit would always assert itself, no matter how irrelevantly, wild plum in a favourite quartzite and shale habitat. Another muscular rope of a tree with dark thick leaves had split a great rock vertically but held it together; the rock fig. All this tough foliage, exposed to heat and frost without the protective interventions of cultivation, more natural than any garden growth, looked exactly like its antithesis – the indestructible synthetic leaves of artificial plants under neon lights. Hidden by it was a kind of shallow dugout which Charles thought to have been made by cattle (who will easily form a depression with the weight and shape of their bodies) at some time when this stretch of veld had been farmed. But when, those nights between midnight and dawn, he and Vusi and Eddie had used their picks to dig a pit, they had fallen through into what was (Charles saw) unmistakably an old stope. There were rough-dressed eucalyptus planks holding up the earth that sifted down on their heads as they tunnelled on a bit. Eddie found a tin teaspoon, its thickness doubled by rust. Vusi's pick broke an old liquor bottle; there was a trade name cast in relief by the mould in which the bottle had been made: *Hatherley Distillery*.

Charles had never heard of it: must be a very old bottle. 'Ja . . . So somebody worked a claim here, once . . . Long ago. I'd say round about ninety years. They came running from all over the world, and worked these little claims.'

'White men.' Eddie confirmed what went without saying.

'Yes. Oh yes – Germans and Frenchmen and Americans and Australians. As well as Englishmen. After the discovery of gold they poured into the Transvaal. Digging under every stone, sifting gravel in every river bed. But in the end only the financiers with capital to buy machinery for deep-level mining had a chance to get rich, eh.'

Eddie, by the hooded light of one of those lamps truck drivers set up when their vehicles break down on a freeway, patted the dust out of his thick pad of hair. 'D'you think there's still gold in this stuff?'

'Not in commercially viable quantities.' Charles wore a mock-shrewd face. 'Looks more like iron ore, to me, anyway . . .'

'Man, I never thought this thing would end up landing me working in the mines.'

Vusi stopped digging and grinned slowly, over Eddie's charm, gave an applauding click of the tongue.

As their brothers had for generations carried coal and sacks of potatoes, they unloaded and stowed in the pit they had dug the AKM assault rifles and bayonets, the grey limpet mines with detonators and timing devices, the defensive and offensive hand grenades. The pit was lined and covered with plastic sheeting and covered again with earth, grasses and small shrubs uprooted in the dark. The shelter for the two men was far less elaborately constructed. The stope was there; with Charles they hitched a sheet of plastic overhead to hold the loose earth and put down a couple of blankets off the mattresses in the back bedroom, some tins of food and packs of cigarettes. The entrance to the stope, already concealed on all but one side by the rocks, was covered with branches cut from the single freestanding tree that grew among them. (With another part of his mind, Charles identified, while hacking away at it, the Transvaal elm or white stinkwood, which would have grown much taller near water.)

They could not make fires. But before Vusi decided that his night visits should cease, Charles brought them a very small camper gas-ring, which was safe to use well back in the stope and during the day only, when any light from its tiny crown of blue flame would be absorbed in the light of the sun. That light had never seemed so total and shadowless, to them. It laid their silent rocks open like a sacrificial altar to a high hot sky from which even the faintest gauze of cloud was burned away. It surrounded them with a clarity in which they were the only things concealed, the only things it couldn't get at. At first they could not come out at all into the sun's Colossus eye, a fly's a million times faceted, that revealed the minutely striated smoothness of one tube of grass, the combination of colours that made up a flake of verdigris on a stone, the bronze collar on the carapace of a beetle working through a cake of cow dung. Then they found a narrow cleft where, one at a time, they could lie hidden and get some air through the overhang of coarse dusty leaves. Impossible for anyone straying past to see a human figure in there. If cows had used the shallow dugout to rest in, herdsmen, the boy children or old men who couldn't earn money in the cities, must have rested here, too. Both Vusi and Eddie had grown up in the black locations of industrial cities and had never spent days whose passing was marked only by the movement of cattle over the veld and the movement of the sun over the cattle. Eddie lay, in his turn, on the shelf among the rocks, in this – crazy – peace: *now*. What a time to feel such a thing; how was it possible that it still existed, with what was waiting, and buried, there in the pit.

Vusi used that peace to go over behind wide open eyes (again unable to smoke, this time because the trail would hang as marker above the deserted rocks) every detail of what he had learnt from his contacts, planned on that basis, and planned again to provide for any hitch that might upset the timing of the first plan. He knew from experience that nothing ever goes quite according to any plan. The wire that should be cut like a hair by an AKM bayonet turns out to be a brick wall, the watchtower that should be vacant for two minutes between the departure of one security guard and the arrival of the next is not vacant because the first guard has lingered to blow his nose in his fingers. Vusi's concentration matched the peace. A lizard ran softly over his foot as if over a dead body dumped among the rocks.

They played cards in their cave. They slept a lot. They had bursts of discussion; indiscriminately, about trivial matters – whether athletes lived longer than other people, whether you could stop smoking by having a Chinaman stick needles in your ear – and about segments of experience that somehow were not integrated into any continuity that is what is meant by 'a life'. Vusi told, as if something dreamt, how in Russia in summer when it was stuffily hot he had lain on the ground, like this, lain on some grass in a park and felt the terrible cold of the winter, still iron down in the earth; and Eddie was reminded of a sudden friendship with a guy in exile from the Cameroons he'd got to know in Algeria, for two weeks they'd argued over political groupings in Africa – and now it was a long time since he'd thought of the conclusions they'd been excited over. The silence would come back, broken by some floating reflection from Eddie ('It's true . . . they say in these very cold countries the earth stays frozen deep down'); and then holding once more.

After Charles, a white man and conspicuous, couldn't come to them, Eddie went at night across the veld all the way to the main road to take water from the backyard tap of an Indian store. He went there during the late afternoon and bought sugar and cigarettes, returning when it was safe, after dark. Vusi could have done without both, but said nothing to stop him. Since he had taken the liberty of wandering about the city that time, it was as if Eddie assumed it was accepted he had a charmed life. Anyway, smelling of earth and unwashed clothes, now, he was only one of the farm labourers who crowded the store for matches and mealie-meal, soap and sugar, and were given a few cheap sweets in lieu of small change. He brought back with him chewing-gum, *samoosas*, and some magazines published by whites for blacks – smiling black girls opened their legs on the covers. Vusi did not pass time with magazines and did not miss the books he had carried with him, hidden, across frontiers. He needed nothing. If the girl, Joy, could have seen him she would have seen that he had become one with that face of his.

Eddie amused himself, opening with a thumbnail some tiny white ovoid beads he found in a crevice of warm rock. Out of them the two men saw come transparent but perfect miniatures of the adult lizard. Their tender damp membrane could scarcely contain the pulse of life, but under the men's eyes they slid away to begin to live.

Mrs Lily Scholtz was hanging on the line the lilac nylon capes the clients of 'Chez Lily', her hairdressing salon, are given to wear, and which she brings home to pop into the washing machine every Sunday. Her husband, Bokkie, former mining shift-boss turned car salesman, was helping their neighbour with the vehicle he is building for drag racing. Mrs Scholtz heard the dustbin lid clang and thought her cat, named after a TV series Mrs Scholtz hadn't missed an episode of, some years back, was in there again. The dustbin is kept between the garage and the maid's room where Bokkie Scholtz does carpentry – his hobby; Patience Ngulungu doesn't live in, but comes to work from Naledi Township weekdays only. Mrs Scholtz found the lid off the bin but no sign of Dallas. As she bent to replace the lid, something landed on her back and bit her just below the right shoulder. Out of nowhere – as she was to relate many times. First thing she knew, there was this terrible pain, as if her arm were torn off – but it wasn't; without even realising that she did it, she had swung back with that same arm, holding the metal lid, at what had bitten her, just as you swat wildly at a bee. She did not hit anything; when she turned round there it was – she saw a big grey monkey already up on the roof of the garage. It was gibbering and she was screaming, Bokkie, Bokkie.

Mr Bokkie Scholtz said his blood ran cold. You know what Johannesburg is like these days. They are everywhere, loafers, illegals, robbers, murderers, the pass laws are a joke, you can't keep them out of white areas. He was over the wall from his neighbour's place and took the jump into his own yard, God knows how he didn't break a leg. And there she was with blood running down and a big grey baboon on the roof. (His wife refers to all these creatures as monkeys.) The thing was chattering, its lips curled back to show long fangs – that's what it'd sunk into her shoulder, teeth about an inch and a half long – can you imagine? He just wanted to get his wife safely out of the way, that's all. He pushed her into the kitchen and ran for his shotgun. When he got back to the yard, it was still on the roof (must have shinned up by the drainpipe, and to come down that way would have brought it right to Bokkie Scholtz's feet). He fired, but was in such a state, you can imagine – hands shaking – missed the head and got the bastard in the arm – funny thing, almost the same place it had bitten Lily. And then, would you believe it, one arm hanging useless, it ran round to the other side of the garage roof and took a leap – ten feet it must be – right over to that big old tree they call a Tree of Heaven, in the neighbour's garden on the other side. Of course he raced next door and he and the neighbours were after it, but it got away, from tree to tree (their legs are like another pair of arms), up that steep little street that leads to the koppies of Kensington Ridge, and he never had the chance of another shot at it.

The Bokkie Scholtzs' house is burglar-proofed, has fine wires on windows and doors which activate an alarm that goes hysterical, with noises like those science fiction films have taught come from outer space, whenever Dallas tries to get in through a fanlight. They have a half-breed Rottweiler who was asleep, apparently, on the front stoep, when the attack came. It just shows you – whatever you do, you can't call yourself safe.

On a Saturday night towards 2 a.m. there was an extensive power failure over the Witwatersrand area of the Transvaal. A number of parties were brought to an end in rowdy darkness. Two women and three men were trapped in an elevator on their way up to a night-club. There was a knifing in a discotheque stampede. A hospital had to switch over to emergency generators. Most people were in bed asleep and did not know about the failure until next morning, when they went to switch on a kettle. But clocks working off household mains marked an hour exactly: 1.36 a.m.

The early morning news mentioned the failure. The cause remained to be established. Alternative sources of power would soon be linked to restore electricity to affected suburbs in Johannesburg and peripheral areas. The midday news reported sabotage was not suspected. On television in the evening, no mention, but the radio announced from official sources that in the early hours of Sunday morning several limpet mines had struck a power station causing severe damage. There was no information about loss of life.

The newspapers, prohibited by Section 4 of the Protection of Information Act of 1982 and Section 29 of the Internal Security Act of 1982 from publishing anything they might learn about the extent of the damage, how and by whom it was caused, and not permitted to take photographs at the scene itself, titillated circulation with human interest stories (Bouncing Baby Boy Delivered by Candlelight) and, keeping the balance of a fine semantic nuance above the level where words break the law, recalled the number, nature and relative successes of similar acts of urban sabotage in the current year as compared with those of the two preceding years. It was all analysed academically, the way military strategists fight past wars on paper. There were maps with arrows indicating point of infiltration of saboteurs from neighbouring states, and broken lines in heavy type culminating in black stars: the conjectured route taken from point of entry to target. Sometimes the route by which the saboteurs probably made their escape, afterwards, was marked. Others had been caught, killed while security forces were giving chase, or put on trial. The sentence of death by hanging was passed and executed, in one or two cases.

The Prime Minister had been scheduled to make a major speech in a farming constituency where a by-election was to be held. Instead of having to counter dissatisfaction with his agricultural policy, he was able to call upon support from all sections of the community to meet the threat from beyond our borders that was always ready to strike at our country. He did not need to, nor did he mention this latest attack on its vitals, which had happened only three days before the speech; his face, composed somewhere between a funeral and a *stryddag*, was enough to put complaints about beef and maize prices to shame.

The release of official statements lags behind what people in the know come to know. A good journalist must have his contacts in both the regular police force and the security police. A manhunt was on, routine roadblocks and a close watch on all airports and border posts were being maintained: there was to be no further information supplied to the public while important leads were being followed. The important leads – everyone knew what those were. Another routine in such cases: a number of people, mostly blacks, had been detained even more promptly than normal power supplies could be restored, and were under interrogation, day after day, night after night, during which a name extorted by an agony of fear and solitude, and if that didn't bring results, by the infliction of physical pain, might or might not be that of someone who would attempt to blow up a power station. John Vorster Square and its suburban and rural annexes were working at optimum capacity. But Sergeant Marais Chapman had been taken off interrogation duty and sent with a couple of black security men to question people within a cordon of the area in which the towers of the power station were the veld landmark. One of the good journalists knew, without being able to publish a word in the meantime (the story was on file) that the police had been to the Indian at the store, who did not recognise any of the photographs they showed him, and that they had visited all plots and farms, questioning black labourers. It was in the course of these visits that they found an empty house, a deserted yard, at Plot 185 Koppiesdrif, where an old man with some story about being there to weed his mealie patch told them this was Baas Kleynhans's place but the oubaas was dead and the boys that worked there now, they had gone away two weeks ago, and the white people who were living in the house, last week he saw the missus but now this time when he came to weed his mealies, they were gone, too. The old man gave the name of the baas who looked after the farm now Baas Kleynhans was dead. So Naas Klopper – out of nowhere! – found the police sitting in Klopper's Eiendoms Beperk, waiting to ask what he could tell them about the Kleynhans place.

The journalist interviewed him shortly after. He wanted to talk to Klopper's wife, as well, because Klopper let slip that the white couple had 'taken us for a ride', they'd even had (the refreshment grew in proportion to the deception) a meal at the house – his wife had felt sorry for the girl, who was pregnant. But Mrs Naas did not want to give an interview to the English press; they would always twist in a nasty way something innocent that Afrikaners said. She did, however, talk to a nice young man from one of the Afrikaans papers, serving him coffee and those very same buttermilk rusks she'd baked and taken along to the young couple just after they'd moved in. She described again, as she had to the police, what the black looked like who had come from the yard, for a moment, with a tool or something (she couldn't quite remember) in his hand. Just like any other black – young, wearing jeans that were a bit smart, yes, for a farm boy. He hadn't said anything. The white girl hadn't spoken to him. But she was flustered when Mrs Naas – out of kindness, that's all, the girl said she was a foreigner – remarked she hoped the boy wasn't some loafer who'd come to the back door. Rosser their name was. They seemed such polite young people. Whenever she got to that point in her story, Mrs Naas was stopped by a long quavering sigh, as if somebody had caught her by the throat. She and whomever she was telling the tale to would look at one another in silence a moment; the journalist was not excepted. Something alien was burning slowly, like a stick of incense fuming in this room, Mrs Naas's split-level lounge, which had been so lovingly constructed, the slasto fireplace chosen stone by stone by Naas himself, the beasts whose skins covered the bar-stools shot by him, the tapestry made stitch by stitch by Mrs Naas in security against the rural poverty of the past and in certainty that these objects and artefacts were what civilisation is.

Mrs Naas – being a woman, being artistic – notices things more than a man does, Naas Klopper advised the police. It was Mrs Naas's description of the girl and the young man that they took back to compare with their files and photographs at John Vorster, and to use in the interrogations that, if they couldn't always wring words from the obdurate (and sometimes you couldn't get a sound out of these people, no matter what you did to them) might reveal an involuntary change of expression that made it worthwhile to press on for recognition, names, evidence of collusion. So it was the police had in their files, the journalist had in his article (biding its time for a Sunday front page), a description of the wanted white couple as a blond bearded man in his twenties and a young pregnant woman. The journalist had no description of any blacks who had taken part in the sabotage attack, although it was known that the actual job was done by blacks. It was the involvement of whites that was the newsworthy angle; one white revolutionary was worth twenty blacks.

If it was detrimental to state security to allow publication of any details about the saboteurs, it was useful to use certain details of the attack to impress upon the public evidence of what threatened them. Let State Information pick up the saboteurs' weapons and hold these at citizens' heads: that's the way to shut any big mouths asking awkward questions about why they had come to be threatened – everyone'd be quick enough to agree, then, they must give the Prime Minister, to save their skins, anything he demanded. A photograph of a cache of arms was released to all newspapers; AKM assault rifles, limpet mines with detonators and timing devices of the type it had been established had blown up part of the power station, defensive and offensive hand grenades with detonators, several hundred rounds of ammunition. Some Dragonov sniper rifles, actually from a different, earlier cache, were thrown in for added effect, as a piece of greenery gives the final touch to a floral arrangement. The sites on which these arms were discovered were not shown, but it was stated that some had been buried in the veld at a hideout among bushes where the saboteurs appeared to have lived prior to the attack, and some had been stored in the garage of a house on a plot. The 'reinforced' outhouse was thought to be an arsenal on which more than one group of saboteurs had drawn. A biscuit tin displayed in a corner of the photograph contained ammunition. When Mrs Naas Klopper saw it she gave a cry of recognition. There was the child with the puppy and the roses; her own biscuit tin, in which she had made the offering of rusks.

A baboon has been found dead in a lane.

The stench of decay led some children to it while they were roller skating. Its right arm was shattered and its fur tarred with blackened blood. Now somebody got a photograph of it, before the Baca municipal street-cleaners' gang were persuaded by a fifty-cent *bonsella* to take the carcass away on Monday morning.

Nobody wants to publish the photograph. The dead baboon was found the Sunday an attempt was made to blow up the power station. The sabotage attack filled the newspapers and has given people other preoccupations; after all, some of the suburbs the creature had made uneasy were without electricity for eighteen hours.

It has been identified as a young, full-grown, male Chacma baboon. Only a baboon, after all; not an orang-outan, not a chimpanzee – just a native species.

The Kleynhans Place has now been photographed by newspapermen for papers published in English, Afrikaans and Zulu for specific readerships, black, white and in-between, and for the international press. It has acquired a capital 'P' to distinguish its ominous status as a proper noun, the name of a threat within the midst of the community of law and order. If the Kleynhans Place can exist, undetected, a farming plot like any other on the books of Klopper's Eiendoms Beperk, what is left of the old, secure life?

Investigating the Kleynhans Place attack the police found two mattresses on the floor in the house, as well as two beds; old newspapers going back many weeks to that story about a monkey seen by some kids while they were swimming. Nothing there to work on. The only thing the white couple seemed to have forgotten was a home-made musical instrument, a sort of saxophone. (That was not ranged along with the exhibit of arms in the photograph released by the Security Chief to the press.) The Security Branch has searched its files for a political suspect known to have been a former musician. It is obvious the instrument was made by a black – a certain naive ingenuity, the kind of thing blacks manage to put together out of bits of junk in a mine compound or while serving long prison sentences. Contact with the Prisons Department in charge of Robben Island has brought the information that similar objects are sometimes made by the long-term politicals held there. This particular piece of work incorporated tin rings from beer cans (plenty of those found in the kitchen) and cartridges that match those in the cache of live ammunition.

Quite early on in their investigations the police released the information that one of the four people – two whites and two blacks – it has been established were responsible for the Kleynhans Place attack, was apprehended on the Swaziland border and killed in a shoot-out with the police. No policeman was injured in this incident. A guard at the power station lost two fingers but no other personnel were injured by the explosion, and there was no loss of life among personnel or public. The old man who had visited the Kleynhans Place to watch the progress of his mealie patch was brought to the police mortuary to look at the corpse of the dead black man. The face was in a state to be recognised although there wasn't much left of the body. He identified the face as that of one of the farm boys who had worked for the white missus he had seen on the Kleynhans Place; this old man was therefore the key link in the investigation, proving beyond doubt that the white couple had set up house for the purpose of providing cover and a safe place for all four to plan the attack, and to store the weapons and ammunition required. (Mr Naas Klopper has testified that an open shed had been audaciously turned into a magazine with a steel door.) The two black men posed as farm labourers until a few days before the attack, when they moved to an old, abandoned mine-working near the power station. Blankets, the remains of fast-food packets, marked their occupation out there in the veld.

Nobody knows who the saboteurs, alive or dead, really are. There are names, yes – as the investigation has proceeded, as the interrogations at John Vorster yield results, there have been names. On the wrist of the dead man there was a cheap chain bracelet with a small plaque, engraved 'Gende', and it has been established that this was one of the names of a man known as 'Eddie', 'Maxwell' or 'David Koza'. He had been among thousands detained in the riots of '76, as a schoolboy. He had left the country uncounted, when released; no one knew when he had gone and no one knows when he came back.

The white pair were not married. There is no such couple as Mr and Mrs Charles Rosser, who sat there shyly in Mrs Naas's lovely home. The Afrikaans first name, 'Anna', was not the girl's name. A Mr and Mrs Watson, living quietly in Port Elizabeth, who haven't seen her for years – she changed 'out of all recognition' through political views they couldn't tolerate – named her twenty-nine years ago 'for joy' at the birth of a little daughter. So far as they are aware she has never been to Australia. 'Charles' was christened Winston Derocher – one of those sentimental slips these politicals make, eh, coming as close as to call himself 'Rosser', when he must have known informants in England would supply John Vorster with a file on him!

The second black man, the survivor, has been identified as Zachariah Makakune, also know as Sidney Tluli. He is believed to have infiltrated from exile several times, and to have been responsible for other acts of sabotage, none of which involved loss of life, before the Kleynhans Place attack. But his luck must run out some day; he will kill or be killed. It was hoped that he had died in one of the South African Defence Force's attacks over the borders on African National Congress men given asylum in neighbouring countries, but it was discovered that the Defence Force was misinformed; he had moved house, and it was new tenants, a building worker and his family, citizens of that country who had never been beyond its borders, who had been machine-gunned in their beds in his place.

So nobody really knows who he was, the one who died after the Kleynhans Place attack, nor whom they believed themselves to be, the three who survived and disappeared. Nobody really knows which names mark the identity each has accepted within himself. And even this is not known fully to himself: all that brought him to this pass; this place, this time, this identity he feels. 'Charles', sometime lover of Joy, 'Charlie', brother of 'Vusi' and 'Eddie' – Winston Derocher, given his father's hero's name as first name, does not know that his distant French ancestor, de Rocher, founding a family too confused by the linguistic and cultural exchanges of treks and intermarriage to keep records, was a missionary who, like himself, lived by assertion of brotherhood – another kind – outside the narrow community of his skin. 'Vusi' does not know that the rotgut liquor bottle he found with the trade name *Hatherley Distillery* came from *Die Eerste Fabriek*, approved by President Paul Kruger, the prototype factory on the veld where 'Vusi's' own great-grandfather worked for the little money that was to become the customary level of wages for blacks, when the mining camp was proclaimed a town, a city, a great industrial complex.

Dr Grahame Fraser-Smith, looking back in fancy into the eyes of hominid evolution on a golf course, was ignorant of a more recent stage that had gone into his making. He doesn't know he is descended, only three human generations back, from a housemaid, Maisie McCulloch, who was imported by a mining magnate to empty the slops in a late Victorian colonial mansion now declared a national monument, and who left this position to be taken over by blacks, herself opening a brothel for all races in Jeppe Street.

No one has ever found out who let the baboon loose.

The sacred member of the ape family, the work of art in the municipal art gallery, has both a known and a hidden provenance. It is authenticated as an eighteenth-century European copy of a seventh-century statue from Māllapuram, India. The old lady who donated it had migrated to South Africa to escape racial persecution in Europe. She was not aware of the rarity of her gift, and thought she was making a display of generous patronage of the arts without sacrificing anything valuable in the private cache of European culture she had saved, along with her own life, from destruction.

The mine-working where Eddie and Vusi hid, that Charles identified as belonging to the turn of the nineteenth century, is in fact far, far older. It goes back further than anything in conventional or alternative history, or even oral tradition, back to the human presences who people anthropology and archaeology, to the hands that shaped the objects or fired the charcoal which may be subjected to carbon tests. No one knows that with the brief occupation of Vusi and Eddie, and the terrible tools that were all they had to work with, a circle was closed; because before the gold-rush prospectors of the 1890s, centuries before time was measured, here, in such units, there was an ancient mine-working out there, and metals precious to men were discovered, dug and smelted, for themselves, by black men.

Jump

Once Upon a Time

Someone has written to ask me to contribute to an anthology of stories for children. I reply that I don't write children's stories; and he writes back that at a recent congress/book fair/seminar a certain novelist said every writer ought to write at least one story for children. I think of sending a postcard saying I don't accept that I 'ought' to write anything.

And then last night I woke up – or rather was wakened without knowing what had roused me.

A voice in the echo chamber of the subconscious?

A sound.

A creaking of the kind made by the weight carried by one foot after another along a wooden floor. I listened. I felt the apertures of my ears distend with concentration. Again: the creaking. I was waiting for it; waiting to hear if it indicated that feet were moving from room to room, coming up the passage – to my door. I have no burglar bars, no gun under the pillow, but I have the same fears as people who do take these precautions, and my window panes are thin as rime, could shatter like a wineglass. A woman was murdered (how do they put it) in broad daylight in a house two blocks away, last year, and the fierce dogs who guarded an old widower and his collection of antique clocks were strangled before he was knifed by a casual labourer he had dismissed without pay.

I was staring at the door, making it out in my mind rather than seeing it, in the dark. I lay quite still – a victim already – but the arrhythmia of my heart was fleeing, knocking this way and that against its body-cage. How finely tuned the senses are, just out of rest, sleep! I could never listen intently as that in the distractions of the day; I was reading every faintest sound, identifying and classifying its possible threat.

But I learnt that I was to be neither threatened nor spared. There was no human weight pressing on the boards, the creaking was a buckling, an epicentre of stress. I was in it. The house that surrounds me while I sleep is built on undermined ground; far beneath my bed, the floor, the house's foundations, the stopes and passages of gold mines have hollowed the rock, and when some face trembles, detaches and falls, three thousand feet below, the whole house shifts slightly, bringing uneasy strain to the balance and counterbalance of brick, cement, wood and glass that hold it as a structure around me. The misbeats of my heart tailed off like the last muffled flourishes on one of the wooden xylophones made by the Chopi and Tsonga migrant miners who might have been down there, under me in the earth at that moment. The stope where the fall was could have been disused, dripping water from its ruptured veins; or men might now be interred there in the most profound of tombs.

I couldn't find a position in which my mind would let go of my body – release me to sleep again. So I began to tell myself a story; a bedtime story.

In a house, in a suburb, in a city, there were a man and his wife who loved each other very much and were living happily ever after. They had a little boy, and they loved him very much. They had a cat and a dog that the little boy loved very much. They had a car and a caravan trailer for holidays, and a swimming pool which was fenced so that the little boy and his playmates would not fall in and drown. They had a housemaid who was absolutely trustworthy and an itinerant gardener who was highly recommended by the neighbours. For when they began to live happily ever after they were warned, by that wise old witch, the husband's mother, not to take on anyone off the street. They were inscribed in a medical benefit society, their pet dog was licensed, they were insured against fire, flood damage and theft, and subscribed to the local Neighbourhood Watch, which supplied them with a plaque for their gates lettered YOU HAVE BEEN WARNED over the silhouette of a would-be intruder. He was masked; it could not be said if he was black or white, and therefore proved the property owner was no racist.

It was not possible to insure the house, the swimming pool or the car against riot damage. There were riots, but these were outside the city, where people of another colour were quartered. These people were not allowed into the suburb except as reliable housemaids and gardeners, so there was nothing to fear, the husband told the wife. Yet she was afraid that some day such people might come up the street and tear off the plaque YOU HAVE BEEN WARNED and open the gates and stream in . . . Nonsense, my dear, said the husband, there are police and soldiers and tear gas and guns to keep them away. But to please her – for he loved her very much and buses were being burned, cars stoned, and schoolchildren shot by the police in those quarters out of sight and hearing of the suburb – he had electronically controlled gates fitted. Anyone who pulled off the sign YOU HAVE BEEN WARNED and tried to open the gates would have to announce his intentions by pressing a button and speaking into a receiver relayed to the house. The little boy was fascinated by the device and used it as a walkie-talkie in cops and robbers play with his small friends.

The riots were suppressed, but there were many burglaries in the suburb and somebody's trusted housemaid was tied up and shut in a cupboard by thieves while she was in charge of her employers' house. The trusted housemaid of the man and wife and little boy was so upset by this misfortune befalling a friend left, as she herself often was, with responsibility for the possessions of the man and his wife and the little boy that she implored her employers to have burglar bars attached to the doors and windows of the house and an alarm system installed. The wife said, She is right, let us take heed of her advice. So from every window and door in the house where they were living happily ever after they now saw the trees and sky through bars, and when the little boy's pet cat tried to climb in by the fanlight to keep him company in his little bed at night, as it customarily had done, it set off the alarm keening through the house.

The alarm was often answered – it seemed – by other burglar alarms, in other houses, that had been triggered by pet cats or nibbling mice. The alarms called to one another across the gardens in shrills and bleats and wails that everyone soon became accustomed to, so that the din roused the inhabitants of the suburb no more than the croak of frogs and musical grating of cicadas' legs. Under cover of the electronic harpies' discourse intruders sawed the iron bars and broke into homes, taking away hi-fi equipment, television sets, cassette players, cameras and radios, jewellery and clothing, and sometimes were hungry enough to devour everything in the refrigerator or paused audaciously to drink the whisky in the cabinets or patio bars. Insurance companies paid no compensation for single malt, a loss made keener by the property owner's knowledge that the thieves wouldn't even have been able to appreciate what it was they were drinking.

Then the time came when many of the people who were not trusted housemaids and gardeners hung about the suburb because they were unemployed. Some importuned for a job: weeding or painting a roof; anything, baas, madam. But the man and his wife remembered the warning about taking on anyone off the street. Some drank liquor and fouled the street with discarded bottles. Some begged, waiting for the man or his wife to drive the car out of the electronically operated gates. They sat about with their feet in the gutters, under the jacaranda trees that made a green tunnel of the street – for it was a beautiful suburb, spoilt only by their presence – and sometimes they fell asleep lying right before the gates in the midday sun. The wife could never see anyone go hungry. She sent the trusted housemaid out with bread and tea, but the trusted housemaid said these were loafers and *tsotsis*, who would come and tie her up and shut her in a cupboard. The husband said, She's right. Take heed of her advice. You only encourage them with your bread and tea. They are looking for their chance . . . And he brought the little boy's tricycle from the garden into the house every night, because if the house was surely secure, once locked and with the alarm set, someone might still be able to climb over the wall or the electronically closed gates into the garden.

You are right, said the wife, then the wall should be higher. And the wise old witch, the husband's mother, paid for the extra bricks as her Christmas present to her son and his wife – the little boy got a spaceman outfit and a book of fairy tales.

But every week there were more reports of intrusion: in broad daylight and the dead of night, in the early hours of the morning, and even in the lovely summer twilight – a certain family was at dinner while the bedrooms were being ransacked upstairs. The man and his wife, talking of the latest armed robbery in the suburb, were distracted by the sight of the little boy's pet cat effortlessly arriving over the seven-foot wall, descending first with a rapid bracing of extended forepaws down on the sheer vertical surface, and then a graceful launch, landing with swishing tail within the property. The whitewashed wall was marked with the cat's comings and goings; and on the street side of the wall there were larger red-earth smudges that could have been made by the kind of broken running shoes, seen on the feet of unemployed loiterers, that had no innocent destination.

When the man and wife and little boy took the pet dog for its walk round the neighbourhood streets they no longer paused to admire this show of roses or that perfect lawn; these were hidden behind an array of different varieties of security fences, walls and devices. The man, wife, little boy and dog passed a remarkable choice: there was the low-cost option of pieces of broken glass embedded in cement along the top of walls, there were iron grilles ending in lance-points, there were attempts at reconciling the aesthetics of prison architecture with the Spanish Villa style (spikes painted pink) and with the plaster urns of neo-classical façades (twelve-inch pikes finned like zigzags of lightning and painted pure white). Some walls had a small board affixed, giving the name and telephone number of the firm responsible for the installation of the devices. While the little boy and the pet dog raced ahead, the husband and wife found themselves comparing the possible effectiveness of each style against its appearance; and after several weeks when they paused before this barricade or that without needing to speak, both came out with the conclusion that only one was worth considering. It was the ugliest but the most honest in its suggestion of the pure concentration-camp style, no frills, all evident efficacy. Placed the length of walls, it consisted of a continuous coil of stiff and shining metal serrated into jagged blades, so that there would be no way of climbing over it and no way through its tunnel without getting entangled in its fangs. There would be no way out, only a struggle getting bloodier and bloodier, a deeper and sharper hooking and tearing of flesh. The wife shuddered to look at it. You're right, said the husband, anyone would think twice . . . And they took heed of the advice on a small board fixed to the wall:

Consult DRAGON'S TEETH
The People For Total Security.

Next day a gang of workmen came and stretched the razor-bladed coils all round the walls of the house where the husband and wife and little boy and pet dog and cat were living happily ever after. The sunlight flashed and slashed, off the serrations, the cornice of razor thorns encircled the home, shining. The husband said, Never mind. It will weather. The wife said, You're wrong. They guarantee it's rust-proof. And she waited until the little boy had run off to play before she said, I hope the cat will take heed . . . The husband said, Don't worry, my dear, cats always look before they leap. And it was true that from that day on the cat slept in the little boy's bed and kept to the garden, never risking a try at breaching security.

One evening, the mother read the little boy to sleep with a fairy story from the book the wise old witch had given him at Christmas. Next day he pretended to be the Prince who braves the terrible thicket of thorns to enter the palace and kiss the Sleeping Beauty back to life: he dragged a ladder to the wall, the shining coiled tunnel was just wide enough for his little body to creep in, and with the first fixing of its razor-teeth in his knees and hands and head he screamed and struggled deeper into its tangle. The trusted housemaid and the itinerant gardener, whose 'day' it was, came running, the first to see and to scream with him, and the itinerant gardener tore his hands trying to get at the little boy. Then the man and his wife burst wildly into the garden and for some reason (the cat, probably) the alarm set up wailing against the screams while the bleeding mass of the little boy was hacked out of the security coil with saws, wire-cutters, choppers, and they carried it – the man, the wife, the hysterical trusted housemaid and the weeping gardener – into the house.

The Moment Before the Gun Went Off

Marais Van der Vyver shot one of his farm labourers, dead. An accident, there are accidents with guns every day of the week – children playing a fatal game with a father's revolver in the cities where guns are domestic objects, nowadays, hunting mishaps like this one, in the country – but these won't be reported all over the world. Van der Vyver knows his will be. He knows that the story of the Afrikaner farmer – regional party leader and commandant of the local security commando – shooting a black man who worked for him will fit exactly *their* version of South Africa, it's made for them. They'll be able to use it in their boycott and divestment campaigns, it'll be another piece of evidence in their truth about the country. The papers at home will quote the story as it has appeared in the overseas press, and in the back-and-forth he and the black man will become those crudely drawn figures on anti-apartheid banners, units in statistics of white brutality against the blacks quoted at the United Nations – he, whom they will gleefully be able to call 'a leading member' of the ruling party.

People in the farming community understand how he must feel. Bad enough to have killed a man, without helping the party's, the government's, the country's enemies, as well. They see the truth of that. They know, reading the Sunday papers, that when Van der Vyver is quoted saying he is 'terribly shocked', he will 'look after the wife and children', none of those Americans and English, and none of those people at home who want to destroy the white man's power will believe him. And how they will sneer when he even says of the farm boy (according to one paper, if you can trust any of those reporters), 'He was my friend, I always took him hunting with me.' Those city and overseas people don't know it's true: farmers usually have one particular black boy they like to take along with them in the lands; you could call it a kind of friend, yes, friends are not only your own white people, like yourself, you take into your house, pray with in church and work with on the party committee. But how can those others know that? They don't want to know it. They think all blacks are like the big-mouth agitators in town. And Van der Vyver's face, in the photographs, strangely opened by distress – everyone in the district remembers Marais Van der Vyver as a little boy who would go away and hide himself if he caught you smiling at him, and everyone knows him now as a man who hides any change of expression round his mouth behind a thick, soft moustache, and in his eyes by always looking at some object in hand, leaf of a crop fingered, pen or stone picked up, while concentrating on what he is saying, or while listening to you. It just goes to show what shock can do; when you look at the newspaper photographs you feel like apologising, as if you had stared in on some room where you should not be.

There will be an inquiry; there had better be, to stop the assumption of yet another case of brutality against farm workers, although there's nothing in doubt – an accident, and all the facts fully admitted by Van der Vyver. He made a statement when he arrived at the police station with the dead man in his bakkie. Captain Beetge knows him well, of course; he gave him brandy. He was shaking, this big, calm, clever son of Willem Van der Vyver, who inherited the old man's best farm. The black was stone dead, nothing to be done for him. Beetge will not tell anyone that after the brandy Van der Vyver wept. He sobbed, snot running on to his hands, like a dirty kid. The Captain was ashamed, for him, and walked out to give him a chance to recover himself.

Marais Van der Vyver left his house at three in the afternoon to cull a buck from the family of kudu he protects in the bush areas of his farm. He is interested in wildlife and sees it as the farmers' sacred duty to raise game as well as cattle. As usual, he called at his shed workshop to pick up Lucas, a twenty-year-old farmhand who had shown mechanical aptitude and whom Van der Vyver himself had taught to maintain tractors and other farm machinery. He hooted, and Lucas followed the familiar routine, jumping on to the back of the truck. He liked to travel standing up there, spotting game before his employer did. He would lean forward, braced against the cab below him.

Van der Vyver had a rifle and .300 ammunition beside him in the cab. The rifle was one of his father's, because his own was at the gunsmith's in town. Since his father died (Beetge's sergeant wrote 'passed on') no one had used the rifle and so when he took it from a cupboard he was sure it was not loaded. His father had never allowed a loaded gun in the house; he himself had been taught since childhood never to ride with a loaded weapon in a vehicle. But this gun was loaded. On a dirt track, Lucas thumped his fist on the cab roof three times to signal: look left. Having seen the white-ripple-marked flank of a kudu, and its fine horns raking through disguising bush, Van der Vyver drove rather fast over a pothole. The jolt fired the rifle. Upright, it was pointing straight through the cab roof at the head of Lucas. The bullet pierced the roof and entered Lucas's brain by way of his throat.

That is the statement of what happened. Although a man of such standing in the district, Van der Vyver had to go through the ritual of swearing that it was the truth. It has gone on record, and will be there in the archive of the local police station as long as Van der Vyver lives, and beyond that, through the lives of his children, Magnus, Helena and Karel – unless things in the country get worse, the example of black mobs in the towns spreads to the rural areas and the place is burned down as many urban police stations have been. Because nothing the government can do will appease the agitators and the whites who encourage them. Nothing satisfies them, in the cities: blacks can sit and drink in white hotels, now, the Immorality Act has gone, blacks can sleep with whites . . . It's not even a crime any more.

Van der Vyver has a high barbed security fence round his farmhouse and garden which his wife, Alida, thinks spoils completely the effect of her artificial stream with its tree-ferns beneath the jacarandas. There is an aerial soaring like a flagpole in the back yard. All his vehicles, including the truck in which the black man died, have aerials that swing their whips when the driver hits a pothole: they are part of the security system the farmers in the district maintain, each farm in touch with every other by radio, twenty-four hours out of twenty-four. It has already happened that infiltrators from over the border have mined remote farm roads, killing white farmers and their families out on their own property for a Sunday picnic. The pothole could have set off a landmine, and Van der Vyver might have died with his farm boy. When neighbours use the communications system to call up and say they are sorry about 'that business' with one of Van der Vyver's boys, there goes unsaid: it could have been worse.

It is obvious from the quality and fittings of the coffin that the farmer has provided money for the funeral. And an elaborate funeral means a great deal to blacks; look how they will deprive themselves of the little they have, in their lifetime, keeping up payments to a burial society so they won't go in boxwood to an unmarked grave. The young wife is pregnant (of course) and another little one, wearing red shoes several sizes too large, leans under her jutting belly. He is too young to understand what has happened, what he is witnessing that day, but neither whines nor plays about; he is solemn without knowing why. Blacks expose small children to everything, they don't protect them from the sight of fear and pain the way whites do theirs. It is the young wife who rolls her head and cries like a child, sobbing on the breast of this relative and that.

All present work for Van der Vyver or are the families of those who work; and in the weeding and harvest seasons, the women and children work for him, too, carried – wrapped in their blankets, on a truck, singing – at sunrise to the fields. The dead man's mother is a woman who can't be more than in her late thirties (they start bearing children at puberty) but she is heavily mature in a black dress between her own parents, who were already working for old Van der Vyver when Marais, like their daughter, was a child. The parents hold her as if she were a prisoner or a crazy woman to be restrained. But she says nothing, does nothing. She does not look up; she does not look at Van der Vyver, whose gun went off in the truck, she stares at the grave. Nothing will make her look up; there need be no fear that she will look up; at him. His wife, Alida, is beside him. To show the proper respect, as for any white funeral, she is wearing the navy blue and cream hat she wears to church this summer. She is always supportive, although he doesn't seem to notice it; this coldness and reserve – his mother says he didn't mix well as a child – she accepts for herself but regrets that it has prevented him from being nominated, as he should be, to stand as the party's parliamentary candidate for the district. He does not let her clothing, or that of anyone else gathered closely, make contact with him. He, too, stares at the grave. The dead man's mother and he stare at the grave in communication like that between the black man outside and the white man inside the cab the moment before the gun went off.

The moment before the gun went off was a moment of high excitement shared through the roof of the cab, as the bullet was to pass, between the young black man outside and the white farmer inside the vehicle. There were such moments, without explanation, between them, although often around the farm the farmer would pass the young man without returning a greeting, as if he did not recognise him. When the bullet went off what Van der Vyver saw was the kudu stumble in fright at the report and gallop away. Then he heard the thud behind him, and past the window saw the young man fall out of the vehicle. He was sure he had leapt up and toppled – in fright, like the buck. The farmer was almost laughing with relief, ready to tease, as he opened his door, it did not seem possible that a bullet passing through the roof could have done harm.

The young man did not laugh with him at his own fright. The farmer carried him in his arms, to the truck. He was sure, sure he could not be dead. But the young black man's blood was all over the farmer's clothes, soaking against his flesh as he drove.

How will they ever know, when they file newspaper clippings, evidence, proof, when they look at the photographs and see his face – guilty! guilty! they are right! – how will they know, when the police stations burn with all the evidence of what has happened now, and what the law made a crime in the past. How could they know that *they do not know*. Anything. The young black callously shot through the negligence of the white man was not the farmer's boy; he was his son.

The Ultimate Safari

The African Adventure Lives On . . . You can do it!
The ultimate safari or expedition
with leaders who know Africa.

—TRAVEL ADVERTISEMENT,
Observer, LONDON, 27/11/88

That night our mother went to the shop and she didn't come back. Ever. What happened? I don't know. My father also had gone away one day and never come back; but he was fighting in the war. We were in the war, too, but we were children, we were like our grandmother and grandfather, we didn't have guns. The people my father was fighting – the bandits, they are called by our government – ran all over the place and we ran away from them like chickens chased by dogs. We didn't know where to go. Our mother went to the shop because someone said you could get some oil for cooking. We were happy because we hadn't tasted oil for a long time; perhaps she got the oil and someone knocked her down in the dark and took that oil from her. Perhaps she met the bandits. If you meet them, they will kill you. Twice they came to our village and we ran and hid in the bush and when they'd gone we came back and found they had taken everything; but the third time they came back there was nothing to take, no oil, no food, so they burned the thatch and the roofs of our houses fell in. My mother found some pieces of tin and we put those up over part of the house. We were waiting there for her that night she never came back.

We were frightened to go out, even to do our business, because the bandits did come. Not into our house – without a roof it must have looked as if there was no one in it, everything gone – but all through the village. We heard people screaming and running. We were afraid even to run, without our mother to tell us where. I am the middle one, the girl, and my little brother clung against my stomach with his arms round my neck and his legs round my waist like a baby monkey to its mother. All night my first-born brother kept in his hand a broken piece of wood from one of our burnt house-poles. It was to save himself if the bandits found him.

We stayed there all day. Waiting for her. I don't know what day it was; there was no school, no church any more in our village, so you didn't know whether it was a Sunday or a Monday.

When the sun was going down, our grandmother and grandfather came. Someone from our village had told them we children were alone, our mother had not come back. I say 'grandmother' before 'grandfather' because it's like that: our grandmother is big and strong, not yet old, and our grandfather is small, you don't know where he is, in his loose trousers, he smiles but he hasn't heard what you're saying, and his hair looks as if he's left it full of soap suds. Our grandmother took us – me, the baby, my first-born brother, our grandfather – back to her house and we were all afraid (except the baby, asleep on our grandmother's back) of meeting the bandits on the way. We waited a long time at our grandmother's place. Perhaps it was a month. We were hungry. Our mother never came. While we were waiting for her to fetch us our grandmother had no food for us, no food for our grandfather and herself. A woman with milk in her breasts gave us some for my little brother, although at our house he used to eat porridge, same as we did. Our grandmother took us to look for wild spinach but everyone else in her village did the same and there wasn't a leaf left.

Our grandfather, walking a little behind some young men, went to look for our mother but didn't find her. Our grandmother cried with other women and I sang the hymns with them. They brought a little food – some beans – but after two days there was nothing again. Our grandfather used to have three sheep and a cow and a vegetable garden but the bandits had long ago taken the sheep and the cow, because they were hungry, too; and when planting time came our grandfather had no seed to plant.

So they decided – our grandmother did; our grandfather made little noises and rocked from side to side, but she took no notice – we would go away. We children were pleased. We wanted to go away from where our mother wasn't and where we were hungry. We wanted to go where there were no bandits and there was food. We were glad to think there must be such a place; away.

Our grandmother gave her church clothes to someone in exchange for some dried mealies and she boiled them and tied them in a rag. We took them with us when we went and she thought we would get water from the rivers but we didn't come to any river and we got so thirsty we had to turn back. Not all the way to our grandparents' place but to a village where there was a pump. She opened the basket where she carried some clothes and the mealies and she sold her shoes to buy a big plastic container for water. I said, *Gogo*, how will you go to church now even without shoes, but she said we had a long journey and too much to carry. At that village we met other people who were also going away. We joined them because they seemed to know where that was better than we did.

To get there we had to go through the Kruger Park. We knew about the Kruger Park. A kind of whole country of animals – elephants, lions, jackals, hyenas, hippos, crocodiles, all kinds of animals. We had some of them in our own country, before the war (our grandfather remembers; we children weren't born yet) but the bandits kill the elephants and sell their tusks, and the bandits and our soldiers have eaten all the buck. There was a man in our village without legs – a crocodile took them off, in our river; but all the same our country is a country of people, not animals. We knew about the Kruger Park because some of our men used to leave home to work there in the places where white people come to stay and look at the animals.

So we started to go away again. There were women and other children like me who had to carry the small ones on their backs when the women got tired. A man led us into the Kruger Park; are we there yet, are we there yet, I kept asking our grandmother. Not yet, the man said, when she asked him for me. He told us we had to take a long way to get round the fence, which he explained would kill you, roast off your skin the moment you touched it, like the wires high up on poles that give electric light in our towns. I've seen that sign of a head without eyes or skin or hair on an iron box at the mission hospital we used to have before it was blown up.

When I asked the next time, they said we'd been walking in the Kruger Park for an hour. But it looked just like the bush we'd been walking through all day, and we hadn't seen any animals except the monkeys and birds which live around us at home, and a tortoise that, of course, couldn't get away from us. My first-born brother and the other boys brought it to the man so it could be killed and we could cook and eat it. He let it go because he told us we could not make a fire; all the time we were in the park we must not make a fire because the smoke would show we were there. Police, wardens, would come and send us back where we came from. He said we must move like animals among the animals, away from the roads, away from the white people's camps. And at that moment I heard – I'm sure I was the first to hear – cracking branches and the sound of something parting grasses and I almost squealed because I thought it was the police, wardens – the people he was telling us to look out for – who had found us already. And it was an elephant, and another elephant, and more elephants, big blots of dark moved wherever you looked between the trees. They were curling their trunks round the red leaves of the mopane trees and stuffing them into their mouths. The babies leant against their mothers. The almost grown-up ones wrestled like my first-born brother with his friends – only they used trunks instead of arms. I was so interested I forgot to be afraid. The man said we should just stand still and be quiet while the elephants passed. They passed very slowly because elephants are too big to need to run from anyone.

The buck ran from us. They jumped so high they seemed to fly. The warthogs stopped dead, when they heard us, and swerved off the way a boy in our village used to zigzag on the bicycle his father had brought back from the mines. We followed the animals to where they drank. When they had gone, we went to their waterholes. We were never thirsty without finding water, but the animals ate, ate all the time. Whenever you saw them they were eating, grass, trees, roots. And there was nothing for us. The mealies were finished. The only food we could eat was what the baboons ate, dry little figs full of ants that grow along the branches of the trees at the rivers. It was hard to be like the animals.

When it was very hot during the day we would find lions lying asleep. They were the colour of the grass and we didn't see them at first but the man did, and he led us back and a long way round where they slept. I wanted to lie down like the lions. My little brother was getting thin but he was very heavy. When our grandmother looked for me, to put him on my back, I tried not to see. My first-born brother stopped talking; and when we rested he had to be shaken to get up again, as if he was just like our grandfather, he couldn't hear. I saw flies crawling on our grandmother's face and she didn't brush them off; I was frightened. I picked a palm leaf and chased them.

We walked at night as well as by day. We could see the fires where the white people were cooking in the camps and we could smell the smoke and the meat. We watched the hyenas with their backs that slope as if they're ashamed, slipping through the bush after the smell. If one turned its head, you saw it had big brown shining eyes like our own, when we looked at each other in the dark. The wind brought voices in our own language from the compounds where the people who work in the camps live. A woman among us wanted to go to them at night and ask them to help us. They can give us the food from the dustbins, she said, she started wailing and our grandmother had to grab her and put a hand over her mouth. The man who led us had told us that we must keep out of the way of our people who worked at the Kruger Park; if they helped us they would lose their work. If they saw us, all they could do was pretend we were not there; they had seen only animals.

Sometimes we stopped to sleep for a little while at night. We slept close together. I don't know which night it was – because we were walking, walking, any time, all the time – we heard the lions very near. Not groaning loudly the way they did far off. Panting, like we do when we run, but it's a different kind of panting: you can hear they're not running, they're waiting, somewhere near. We all rolled closer together, on top of each other, the ones on the edge fighting to get into the middle. I was squashed against a woman who smelled bad because she was afraid but I was glad to hold tight on to her. I prayed to God to make the lions take someone on the edge and go. I shut my eyes not to see the tree from which a lion might jump right into the middle of us, where I was. The man who led us jumped up instead, and beat on the tree with a dead branch. He had taught us never to make a sound but he shouted. He shouted at the lions like a drunk man shouting at nobody, in our village. The lions went away. We heard them groaning, shouting back at him from far off.

We were tired, so tired. My first-born brother and the man had to lift our grandfather from stone to stone where we found places to cross the rivers. Our grandmother is strong but her feet were bleeding. We could not carry the basket on our heads any longer, we couldn't carry anything except my little brother. We left our things under a bush. As long as our bodies get there, our grandmother said. Then we ate some wild fruit we didn't know from home and our stomachs ran. We were in the grass called elephant grass because it is nearly as tall as an elephant, that day we had those pains, and our grandfather couldn't just get down in front of people like my little brother, he went off into the grass to be on his own. We had to keep up, the man who led us always kept telling us, we must catch up, but we asked him to wait for our grandfather.

So everyone waited for our grandfather to catch up. But he didn't. It was the middle of the day; insects were singing in our ears and we couldn't hear him moving through the grass. We couldn't see him because the grass was so high and he was so small. But he must have been somewhere there inside his loose trousers and his shirt that was torn and our grandmother couldn't sew because she had no cotton. We knew he couldn't have gone far because he was weak and slow. We all went to look for him, but in groups, so we too wouldn't be hidden from each other in that grass. It got into our eyes and noses; we called him softly but the noise of the insects must have filled the little space left for hearing in his ears. We looked and looked but we couldn't find him. We stayed in that long grass all night. In my sleep I found him curled round in a place he had tramped down for himself, like the places we'd seen where the buck hide their babies.

When I woke up he still wasn't anywhere. So we looked again, and by now there were paths we'd made by going through the grass many times, it would be easy for him to find us if we couldn't find him. All that day we just sat and waited. Everything is very quiet when the sun is on your head, inside your head, even if you lie, like the animals, under the trees. I lay on my back and saw those ugly birds with hooked beaks and plucked necks flying round and round above us. We had passed them often where they were feeding on the bones of dead animals, nothing was ever left there for us to eat. Round and round, high up and then lower down and then high again. I saw their necks poking to this side and that. Flying round and round. I saw our grandmother, who sat up all the time with my little brother on her lap, was seeing them, too.

In the afternoon the man who led us came to our grandmother and told her the other people must move on. He said, If their children don't eat soon they will die.

Our grandmother said nothing.

I'll bring you water before we go, he told her.

Our grandmother looked at us, me, my first-born brother, and my little brother on her lap. We watched the other people getting up to leave. I didn't believe the grass would be empty, all around us, where they had been. That we would be alone in this place, the Kruger Park, the police or the animals would find us. Tears came out of my eyes and nose on to my hands but our grandmother took no notice. She got up, with her feet apart the way she puts them when she is going to lift firewood, at home in our village, she swung my little brother on to her back, tied him in her cloth – the top of her dress was torn and her big breasts were showing but there was nothing in them for him. She said, Come.

So we left the place with the long grass. Left behind. We went with the others and the man who led us. We started to go away, again.

There's a very big tent, bigger than a church or a school, tied down to the ground. I didn't understand that was what it would be, when we got there, away. I saw a thing like that the time our mother took us to the town because she heard our soldiers were there and she wanted to ask them if they knew where our father was. In that tent, people were praying and singing. This one is blue and white like that one but it's not for praying and singing, we live in it with other people who've come from our country. Sister from the clinic says we're two hundred without counting the babies, and we have new babies, some were born on the way through the Kruger Park.

Inside, even when the sun is bright it's dark and there's a kind of whole village in there. Instead of houses each family has a little place closed off with sacks or cardboard from boxes – whatever we can find – to show the other families it's yours and they shouldn't come in even though there's no door and no windows and no thatch, so that if you're standing up and you're not a small child you can see into everybody's house. Some people have even made paint from ground rocks and drawn designs on the sacks.

Of course, there really is a roof – the tent is the roof, far, high up. It's like a sky. It's like a mountain and we're inside it; through the cracks paths of dust lead down, so thick you think you could climb them. The tent keeps off the rain overhead but the water comes in at the sides and in the little streets between our places – you can only move along them one person at a time – the small kids like my little brother play in the mud. You have to step over them. My little brother doesn't play. Our grandmother takes him to the clinic when the doctor comes on Mondays. Sister says there's something wrong with his head, she thinks it's because we didn't have enough food at home. Because of the war. Because our father wasn't there. And then because he was so hungry in the Kruger Park. He likes just to lie about on our grandmother all day, on her lap or against her somewhere, and he looks at us and looks at us. He wants to ask something but you can see he can't. If I tickle him he may just smile. The clinic gives us special powder to make into porridge for him and perhaps one day he'll be all right.

When we arrived we were like him – my first-born brother and I. I can hardly remember. The people who live in the village near the tent took us to the clinic, it's where you have to sign that you've come – away, through the Kruger Park. We sat on the grass and everything was muddled. One sister was pretty with her hair straightened and beautiful high-heeled shoes and she brought us the special powder. She said we must mix it with water and drink it slowly. We tore the packets open with our teeth and licked it all up, it stuck round my mouth and I sucked it from my lips and fingers. Some other children who had walked with us vomited. But I only felt everything in my belly moving, the stuff going down and around like a snake, and hiccups hurt me. Another sister called us to stand in line on the verandah of the clinic but we couldn't. We sat all over the place there, falling against each other; the sisters helped each of us up by the arm and then stuck a needle in it. Other needles drew our blood into tiny bottles. This was against sickness, but I didn't understand, every time my eyes dropped closed I thought I was walking, the grass was long, I saw the elephants, I didn't know we were away.

But our grandmother was still strong, she could still stand up, she knows how to write and she signed for us. Our grandmother got us this place in the tent against one of the sides, it's the best kind of place there because although the rain comes in, we can lift the flap when the weather is good and then the sun shines on us, the smells in the tent go out. Our grandmother knows a woman here who showed her where there is good grass for sleeping mats, and our grandmother made some for us. Once every month the food truck comes to the clinic. Our grandmother takes along one of the cards she signed and when it has been punched we get a sack of mealie-meal. There are wheelbarrows to take it back to the tent; my first-born brother does this for her and then he and the other boys have races, steering the empty wheelbarrows back to the clinic. Sometimes he's lucky and a man who's bought beer in the village gives him money to deliver it – though that's not allowed, you're supposed to take that wheelbarrow straight back to the sisters. He buys a cold drink and shares it with me if I catch him. On another day, every month, the church leaves a pile of old clothes in the clinic yard. Our grandmother has another card to get punched, and then we can choose something: I have two dresses, two pants and a jersey, so I can go to school.

The people in the village have let us join their school. I was surprised to find they speak our language; our grandmother told me, That's why they allow us to stay on their land. Long ago, in the time of our fathers, there was no fence that kills you, there was no Kruger Park between them and us, we were the same people under our own king, right from our village we left to this place we've come to.

Now that we've been in the tent so long – I have turned eleven and my little brother is nearly three although he is so small, only his head is big, he's not come right in it yet – some people have dug up the bare ground around the tent and planted beans and mealies and cabbage. The old men weave branches to put up fences round their gardens. No one is allowed to look for work in the towns but some of the women have found work in the village and can buy things. Our grandmother, because she's still strong, finds work where people are building houses – in this village the people build nice houses with bricks and cement, not mud like we used to have at our home. Our grandmother carries bricks for these people and fetches baskets of stones on her head. And so she has money to buy sugar and tea and milk and soap. The store gave her a calendar she has hung up on our flap of the tent. I am clever at school and she collected advertising paper people throw away outside the store and covered my schoolbooks with it. She makes my first-born brother and me do our homework every afternoon before it gets dark because there is no room except to lie down, close together, just as we did in the Kruger Park, in our place in the tent, and candles are expensive. Our grandmother hasn't been able to buy herself a pair of shoes for church yet, but she has bought black school shoes and polish to clean them with for my first-born brother and me. Every morning, when people are getting up in the tent, the babies are crying, people are pushing each other at the taps outside and some children are already pulling the crusts of porridge off the pots we ate from last night, my first-born brother and I clean our shoes. Our grandmother makes us sit on our mats with our legs straight out so she can look carefully at our shoes to make sure we have done it properly. No other children in the tent have real school shoes. When we three look at them it's as if we are in a real house again, with no war, no away.

Some white people came to take photographs of our people living in the tent – they said they were making a film, I've never seen what that is though I know about it. A white woman squeezed into our space and asked our grandmother questions which were told to us in our language by someone who understands the white woman's.

How long have you been living like this?

She means here? our grandmother said. In this tent, two years and one month.

And what do you hope for the future?

Nothing. I'm here.

But for your children?

I want them to learn so that they can get good jobs and money.

Do you hope to go back to Mozambique – to your own country?

I will not go back.

But when the war is over – you won't be allowed to stay here? Don't you want to go home?

I didn't think our grandmother wanted to speak again. I didn't think she was going to answer the white woman. The white woman put her head on one side and smiled at us.

Our grandmother looked away from her and spoke – There is nothing. No home.

Why does our grandmother say that? Why? I'll go back. I'll go back through that Kruger Park. After the war, if there are no bandits any more, our mother may be waiting for us. And maybe when we left our grandfather, he was only left behind, he found his way somehow, slowly, through the Kruger Park, and he'll be there. They'll be home, and I'll remember them.

A Find

To hell with them.

A man who had bad luck with women decided to live alone for a while. He was twice married for love. He cleared the house of whatever his devoted second wife had somehow missed out when she left with the favourite possessions they had collected together – paintings, rare glass, even the best wines lifted from the cellar. He threw away books on whose flyleaf the first wife had lovingly written her new name as a bride. Then he went on holiday without taking some woman along. For the first time he could remember; but those tarts and tramps with whom he had believed himself to be in love had turned out unfaithful as the honest wives who had vowed to cherish him for ever.

He went alone to a resort where the rocks flung up the sea in ragged fans, the tide sizzled and sucked in the pools. There was no sand. On stones like boiled sweets, striped and flecked and veined, people – women – lay on salt-faded mattresses and caressed themselves with scented oils. Their hair was piled up and caught in elastic garlands of artificial flowers, that year, or dripped – as they came out of the water with crystal beads studding glossy limbs – from gilt clasps that flashed back and forth to the hoops looped in their ears. Their breasts were bared. They wore inverted triangles of luminescent cloth over the pubis, secured by a string that went up through the divide of the buttocks to meet two strings coming round from over the belly and hip-bones. In his line of vision, as they walked away down to the sea they appeared totally naked; when they came up out of the sea, gasping with pleasure, coming towards his line of vision, their breasts danced, drooped as the women bent, laughing, for towels and combs and the anointing oil. The bodies of some were patterned like tie-dyed fabric: strips and patches white or red where garments had covered bits of them from the fiery immersion of sun. The nipples of others were raw as strawberries, it could be observed that they could scarcely bear to touch them with balm. There were men, but he didn't see men. When he closed his eyes and listened to the sea he could smell the women – the oil.

He swam a great deal. Far out in the calm bay between windsurfers crucified against their gaudy sails, closer in shore where the surf trampled his head under hordes of white waters. A shoal of young mothers carried their infants about in the shallows. Denting its softness, naked against their mothers' flesh the children clung, so lately separated from it that they still seemed part of those female bodies in which they had been planted by males like himself. He lay on the stones to dry. He liked the hard nudging of the stones, fidgeting till he adjusted his bones to them, wriggling them into depressions until his contours were contained rather than resisted. He slept. He woke to see their shaven legs passing his head – women. Drops shaken from their wet hair fell on his warm shoulders. Sometimes he found himself swimming underwater beneath them, his tough-skinned body grazing past like a shark.

As men do at the shore when they are alone, he flung stones at the sea, remembering – regaining – the art of making them skim and skip across the water. Lying face down out of reach of the last rills, he sifted handfuls of sea-polished stones and, close up, began to see them as adults cease to see: the way a child will look and look at a flower, a leaf – a stone, following its alluvial stripes, its fragments of mysterious colour, its buried sprinklings of mica, feeling (he did) its egg- or lozenge-shape smoothed by the sea's oiled caressing hand.

Not all the stones were really stones. There were flattish amber ovals the gem-cutter ocean had buffed out of broken beer bottles. There were cabochons of blue and green glass (some other drowned bottle) that could have passed for aquamarines and emeralds. Children collected them in hats or buckets. And one afternoon among these treasures mixed with bits of Styrofoam discarded from cargo ships and other plastic jetsam that is cast, refloated and cast again, on shores all round the world, he found in the stones with which he was occupying his hand like a monk telling his beads, a real treasure. Among the pebbles of coloured glass was a diamond and sapphire ring. It was not on the surface of the stony beach, so evidently had not been dropped there that day by one of the women. Some darling, some rich man's treasure (or ensconced wife), diving off a yacht, out there, wearing her jewels while she fashionably jettisoned other coverings, must have felt one of the rings slipped from her finger by the water. Or didn't feel it, noticed the loss only when back on deck, rushed to find the insurance policy, while the sea drew the ring deeper and deeper down; and then, tiring of it over days, years, slowly pushed and washed it up to dump on land. It was a beautiful ring. The sapphire a large oblong surrounded by round diamonds with a baguette-cut diamond, set horizontally on either side of this brilliant mound, bridging it to an engraved circle.

Although it had been dug up from a good six inches down by his random fingering, he looked around as if the owner were sure to be standing over him.

But they were oiling themselves, they were towelling their infants, they were plucking their eyebrows in the reflection of tiny mirrors, they were sitting cross-legged with their breasts lolling above the squat tables where the waiter from the restaurant had placed their salads and bottles of white wine. He took the ring up to the restaurant; perhaps someone had reported a loss. The patronne drew back. She might have been being offered stolen goods by a fence. It's valuable. Take it to the police.

Suspicion arouses alertness; perhaps, in this foreign place, there was some cause to be suspicious. Even of the police. If no one claimed the ring, some local would pocket it. So what was the difference – he put it into his own pocket, or rather into the shoulder-bag that held his money, his credit cards, his car keys and sunglasses. And he went back to the beach and lay down again, on the stones, among the women. To think.

He put an advertisement in the local paper. *Ring found on Blue Horizon Beach, Tuesday 1st*, and the telephone and room number at his hotel. The patronne was right; there were many calls. A few from men, claiming their wives, mothers, girlfriends had, indeed, lost a ring on that beach. When he asked them to describe the ring, they took a chance: a diamond ring. But they could only prevaricate when pressed for more details. If a woman's voice was the wheedling, ingratiating one (even weepy, some of them) recognisable as that of some middle-aged con-woman, he cut off the call the moment she tried to describe her lost ring. But if the voice was attractive and sometimes clearly young, soft, even hesitant in its lying boldness, he asked the owner to come to his hotel to identify the ring.

Describe it.

He seated them comfortably before his open balcony with the light from the sea interrogating their faces. Only one convinced him she really had lost a ring; she described it in detail and went away, sorry to have troubled him. Others – some quite charming or even extremely pretty, dressed to seduce – would have settled for something else come of the visit, if they could not get away with their invented descriptions of a ring. They seemed to calculate that a ring is a ring; if it's valuable, it must have diamonds, and one or two were ingenious enough to say, yes, there were other precious stones with it, but it was an heirloom (grandmother, aunt) and they didn't really know the names of the stones.

But the colour? The shape?

They left as if affronted; or they giggled guiltily, they'd come just for a dare, a bit of fun. And they were quite difficult to get rid of politely.

Then there was one with a voice unlike that of any of the other callers, the controlled voice of a singer or an actress, maybe, expressing diffidence. I have given up hope. Of finding it . . . my ring. She had seen the advertisement and thought, no, no, it's no use. But if there were a million-to-one chance . . . He asked her to come to the hotel.

She was certainly forty, a born beauty with great, still, grey-green eyes and no help needed except to keep her hair peacock-black. It grew from a peak like a beak high on her round forehead and was drawn up to a coil on her crown, glossy as smoothed feathers. There was no sign of a fold where her breasts met, firmly spaced in the neck of a dress black as her hair. Her hands were made for rings; she spread long thumbs and fingers, turned palms out: And then it was gone, I saw a gleam a moment in the water—

Describe it.

She gazed straight at him, turned her head to direct those eyes away, and began to speak. Very elaborate, she said, platinum and gold . . . you know, it's difficult to be precise about an object you've worn so long you don't notice it any more. A large diamond . . . several. And emeralds, and red stones . . . rubies, but I think they had fallen out before . . .

He went to the drawer in the hotel desk-cum-dressing table and from under folders describing restaurants, cable TV programmes and room service available, he took an envelope. Here's your ring, he said.

Her eyes did not change. He held it out to her.

Her hand wafted slowly towards him as if under water. She took the ring from him and began to put it on the middle finger of her right hand. It would not fit but she corrected the movement with swift conjuring and it slid home over the third finger.

He took her out to dinner and the subject was not referred to. Ever again. She became his third wife. They live together with no more unsaid, between them, than any other couple.

Loot

Loot

Once upon our time, there was an earthquake: but this one is the most powerful ever recorded since the invention of the Richter scale made it possible for us to measure apocalyptic warnings.

It tipped a continental shelf. These tremblings often cause floods; this colossus did the reverse, drew back the ocean as a vast breath taken. The most secret level of our world lay revealed: the sea-bedded – wrecked ships, façades of houses, ballroom candelabra, toilet bowl, pirate chest, TV screen, mail coach, aircraft fuselage, cannon, marble torso, Kalashnikov, metal carapace of a tourist bus-load, baptismal font, automatic dishwasher, computer, swords sheathed in barnacles, coins turned to stone. The astounded gaze raced among these things; the population who had fled from their toppling houses to the maritime hills ran down. Where terrestrial crash and bellow had terrified them, there was naked silence. The saliva of the sea glistened upon these objects; it is given that time does not, never did, exist down here where the materiality of the past and the present as they lie has no chronological order, all is one, all is nothing – or all is possessible at once.

People rushed to take; take, take. This was – when, anytime, sometime – valuable, that might be useful, what was this, well someone will know, that must have belonged to the rich, it's mine now, if you don't grab what's over there someone else will, feet slipped and slithered on seaweed and sank in soggy sand, gasping sea-plants gaped at them, no one remarked there were no fish, the living inhabitants of this unearth had been swept up and away with the water. The ordinary opportunity of looting shops which was routine to people during the political uprisings was no comparison. Orgiastic joy gave men, women and their children strength to heave out of the slime and sand what they did not know they wanted, quickened their staggering gait as they ranged, and this was more than profiting by happenstance, it was robbing the power of nature before which they had fled helpless. Take, take; while grabbing they were able to forget the wreck of their houses and the loss of time-bound possessions there. They had tattered the silence with their shouts to one another and under these cries like the cries of the absent seagulls they did not hear a distant approach of sound rising as a great wind does. And then the sea came back, engulfed them to add to its treasury.

That is what is known; in television coverage that really had nothing to show but the pewter skin of the depths, in radio interviews with those few infirm, timid or prudent who had not come down from the hills, and in newspaper accounts of bodies that for some reason the sea rejected, washed up down the coast somewhere.

But the writer knows something no one else knows; the sea-change of the imagination.

Now listen, there's a man who has wanted a certain object (what) all his life. He has a lot of – things – some of which his eye falls upon often, so he must be fond of, some of which he doesn't notice, deliberately, that he probably shouldn't have acquired but cannot cast off, there's an art nouveau lamp he reads by, and above his bedhead a Japanese print, a Hokusai, *The Great Wave*, he doesn't really collect oriental stuff, although if it had been on the wall facing him it might have been more than part of the furnishings, it's been out of sight behind his head for years. All these – things – but not the one.

He's a retired man, long divorced, chosen an old but well-appointed villa in the maritime hills as the site from which to turn his back on the assault of the city. A woman from the village cooks and cleans and doesn't bother him with any other communication. It is a life blessedly freed of excitement, he's had enough of that kind of disturbance, pleasurable or not, but the sight from his lookout of what could never have happened, never ever have been vouchsafed, is a kind of command. He is one of those who are racing out over the glistening seabed, the past – detritus=treasure, one and the same – stripped bare.

Like all the other looters with whom he doesn't mix, has nothing in common, he races from object to object, turning over the shards of painted china, the sculptures created by destruction, abandonment and rust, the brine-vintaged wine casks, a plunged racing motorcycle, a dentist's chair, his stride landing on disintegrated human ribs and metatarsals he does not identify. But unlike the others, he takes nothing – until: there, ornate with tresses of orange-brown seaweed, stuck fast with nacreous shells and crenellations of red coral, is *the* object. (A mirror?) It's as if the impossible is true; he knew that was where it was, beneath the sea, that's why he didn't know what it was, could never find it before. It could be revealed only by something that had never happened, the greatest paroxysm of our earth ever measured on the Richter scale.

He takes it up, the object, the mirror, the sand pours off it, the water that was the only bright glance left to it streams from it, he is taking it back with him, taking possession at last.

And the great wave comes from behind his bedhead and takes him.

His name well known in the former regime circles in the capital is not among the survivors. Along with him among the skeletons of the latest victims, with the ancient pirates and fishermen, there are those dropped from planes during the dictatorship so that with the accomplice of the sea they would never be found. Who recognised them, that day, where they lie?

No carnation or rose floats.

Full fathom five.

The Generation Gap

He was the one told: James, the youngest of them. The father to the son – and it was Jamie, with whom he'd never got on since Jamie was a kid; Jamie who ran away when he was adolescent, was brought back resentful, nothing between them but a turned-aside head (the boy's) and the tight tolerant jaw of suppressed disapproval (the father's). Jamie who is doing – what was it now? Running a cybersurfers' restaurant with a friend, that's the latest, he's done so many things but the consensus in the family is that he's the one who's done nothing with his life. His brother and sisters love him but see it as a waste: of charm and some kind of ill-defined talent, sensed but not directed in any of the ways they recognise.

So it was from Jamie that they received the *announcement*. The father had it conveyed by Jamie to them – Virginia, Barbara, and Matthew called at some unearthly hour in Australia. The father has left the mother.

A husband leaves his wife. It is one of the most unexceptional of events. The father has left the mother: that is a completely different version, their version.

A husband leaves his wife for another woman. Of course. Their father, their affectionate, loyal, considerate father, *announces*, just like that: he has left their mother for another woman. Inconceivable.

And to have chosen, of all of them, the younger brother as confidant, confessor, messenger – whatever the reasoning was?

They talked to each other on the telephone, calls those first few days frustratingly blocked while numbers were being dialled simultaneously and the occupied whine sounded on and on. Matthew in Brisbane sent an email. They got together in Barbara's house – his Ba, his favourite. Even Jamie appeared, summoned – for an explanation he could not give.

Why should I ask why, how?

Or would not give. *He* must have said something beyond this announcement; but no. And Jamie had to get back to the bar nook and the espresso machine, leave them to it with his archaic smile of irresponsible comfort in any situation.

And suddenly, from the door – We're all grown up now. Even he.

It was established that no one had heard from the mother. Ginnie had called her and waited to see if she would say anything, but she chatted about the grandchildren and the progress of a friend she had been visiting in hospital. Not a word. Perhaps she doesn't know. But even if he kept the affair somehow secret from her until now, he would hardly 'inform' his children before telling his wife of a decision to abandon her.

Perhaps she thinks we don't know.

No, can't you see – she doesn't want us to know because she thinks he'll come back, and we don't need ever to know. A private thing. As Jamie said.

That's ridiculous, she's embarrassed, ashamed, I don't know what – humiliated at the idea of us . . .

Ginnie had to intervene as chairperson to restore clarity out of the spurting criss-cross of sibling voices. Now what do we do? What are we talking about: are we going to try and change his mind? Talk some sense into him. Are we going to go to her?

We must. First of all.

Then Ba should go.

One would have thought Ba was the child he would have turned to. She said nothing, stirred in her chair and took a gulp of gin and tonic with a pull of lip muscles at its kick. There was no need to ask, why me, because she's her Daddy's favourite, she's closest to him, the one best to understand if anyone can, what has led him to do what he has done – to himself, to their mother.

And the woman? The voices rise as a temperature of the room, what about the woman? Anybody have any idea of who she might be. None of those wives in their circle of friends – it's Alister, Ginnie's husband, considering – Just look at them. Your poor dad.

But where did he and she ever go that he'd meet anyone new?

Well, *she'll* know who it is. Ba will be told.

Nothing sure about that.

As the youngest of them said, they're all grown up, there are two among the three present (and that's not counting sports commentator Matthew in Brisbane) who know how affairs may be and are concealed; it's only if they take the place of the marriage that they have to be revealed.

Sick. That's what it is. He's sick.

Ba – all of them anticipating for Ba to deal with the mother – expected tears and heartbreak to burst the conventions that protect the intimacy of parents' marriage from their sons and daughters. But there are no tears.

Derision and scorn, from their mother become the discarded wife. Indeed she knows who the woman is. A pause. As if the daughter, not the mother, were the one who must prepare herself.

She's exactly your age, Ba.

And the effect is what the mother must have counted on as part of the kind of triumph she has set herself to make of the disaster, deflecting it to the father. The woman has a child, never been married. Do? Plays the fiddle in an orchestra. How and where he found her, God only knows – you know we never go to concerts, he has his CD collection here in this room. Everything's been just as usual, while it's been going on – he says, very exact – for eight months. So when he finally had the courage to come out with it, I told him, eight months after forty-two years, you've made your choice. May he survive it.

When I said (Ba is reporting), doesn't sound as if it will work for him, it's just an episode, something he's never tried, never done, a missing experience, he'll come back to his life (of course, that would be the way Ba would put it), *she* said – I won't give it back to him. I can't tell you what she's like. It's as if the place they were in together – not just the house – is barricaded. She's in there, guns cocked.

What can they do for her, their mother, who doesn't want sympathy, doesn't want reconciliation brokered even if it were to be possible, doesn't want the healing of their love, any kind of love, if the love of forty-two years doesn't exist.

His Ba offers to bring the three available of his sons and daughters together again to meet him at her house, but he tells her he would rather 'spend some time' with each separately. She is the last he comes to and his presence is strange, both to him and to her. How can it be otherwise? When he sleeps with the woman, she could have been his daughter. It's as if something forbidden has happened between him and his favourite child. Something unspeakable exists.

Ba has already heard it all before – all he will allow himself to tell – from the others. Same story to Ginnie, Jamie and according to an email from Matthew, much the same in a 'bloody awful' call to him. Yes, she is not married, yes, she plays second violin in a symphony orchestra, and yes – she is thirty-five years old. He looks up slowly and he gives his daughter this fact as if he must hold her gaze and she cannot let hers waver; a secret between them. So she feels able to ask him what the others didn't, perhaps because the enquiry might somehow imply acceptance of the validity of happenstance in a preposterous decision of a sixty-seven-year-old to overturn his life. How did he meet this woman?

He shapes that tight tolerant jaw, now not of disapproval (he has no right to that, in these circumstances) but of hurt resignation to probing: on a plane. On a plane! The daughter cannot show her doubtful surprise; when did he ever travel without the mother? While he continues, feeling himself pressed to it: he went to Cape Town for negotiations with principals from the American company who didn't have time to come to him up in Pretoria. The orchestra was going to the coast to open a music festival. He found her beside him. They got talking and she kindly offered to arrange a seat for him at the over-subscribed concert. And then? And then? But her poor father, she couldn't humiliate him, she couldn't follow him, naked, the outer-inner man she'd never seen, through the months in the woman's bed beside the violin case.

What are you going to do, she asked.

It's done.

That's what he said (the siblings compare notes). And he gave such explanation as he could. Practical. I've moved out – but Isabel must have told you. I've taken a furnished flat. I'll leave the number, I'd rather you didn't call at the office, at present.

And then? What will happen to you, my poor father – but all she spoke out was, So you want to marry this girl. For in comparison with his mate, his wife of forty-two years, his sixty-seven years, she is no more than that.

I'll never marry again.

Yes, he told the others that, too. Is the vehemence prudence (the huge age difference, for God's sake: Matthew, from Australia) or is it telling them something about the marriage that produced them, some parental sorrow they weren't aware of while in the family home, or ignored, too preoccupied with their own hived-off lives to bother with, after.

There's nothing wrong between Isabel and me, but for a very long time there's been nothing right, either.

Wishing you every happiness. The wedding gift maxim. Grown apart? Put together mistakenly in the first place – they're all of them too close to the surface marriage created for them, in self-defence and in protection of *them*, the children, no doubt, to be able to speculate.

And what is going to happen to our mother, your Isabel?

And then. And then. That concert, after the indigestion of a three-hour lunch and another three hours of business-speak wrangling I had with those jocular sharks from Seattle. Mahler's Symphony No. 1 following Respighi. I've forgotten there's no comparison between listening to recorded music in a room filled with all the same things – the photographs, the glass, the coffee cup in your hand, the chair that fits you – and hearing music, live. Seeing it, as well, that's the difference, because acoustically reproduction these days is perfect – I know I used to say it was better than the bother of driving to concerts. Watching the players, how they're creating what you're hearing, their movements, their breathing, the expressions of concentration, even the way they sit, sway in obedience to the conductor, he's a magician transforming their bodies into sound. I don't think I took particular notice of her. Maybe I did without knowing it, these things are a human mystery, I've realised. But that would have been that – she'd told me her name but I didn't know where she lived, so I wouldn't even have known where to thank her for the concert reservation – if it hadn't been that she was on the plane again next day when I was returning home. We were seated in the same row, both aisle seats, separated this time only by that narrow gap we naturally could talk across. About the concert, what it was like to be a musician, people like myself are always curious about artists – she was teasing, saying we regard theirs as a free, undisciplined life compared with being – myself – a businessman, but it was a much more disciplined life than ours – the rehearsals, the performance, the 'red-eye night-work, endless overtime' she called it, while we others have regular hours and leisure. We had the freebie drink together and a sort of mock argument about stress, hers, facing an audience and knowing she'd get hell afterwards if she played a wrong note, and mine with the example of the principals from Seattle the day before. The kind of exchange you hear strangers making on a plane, and that I always avoid.

I avoid now talking about her to my children – what can you call sons and daughters who are far from children. I know they think it's ridiculous – it's all ridiculous, to them – but I don't want anyone running around making 'enquiries' about her, her life, as if her 'suitability' is an issue that has anything to do with them. But of course everything about what I suppose must be called this affair has to do with them because it's their mother, someone they've always seen – will see – as the other half of me. They'll want to put me together again.

The children (he's right, what do you call a couple's grown-up children) often had found weeks go by without meeting one another or getting in touch. Ginnie is a lecturer in the maths department at the university and her husband is a lawyer, their friends are fellow academics and lawyers, with a satisfying link between the two in concerns over the need for a powerful civil society to protect human rights. Their elder son and daughters are almost adult, and they have a latecomer, a four-year-old boy. Ba – she's barren – Ginnie is the repository of this secret of her childlessness. Ba and her husband live in the city as week-long exiles: from the bush. Carl was manager of a wildlife reserve when she fell in love with him, he now manages a branch of clothing chain stores and she is personal secretary to a stockbroker; every weekend they are away, camping and walking, incommunicado to humans, animal-watching, bird-watching, insect-watching, plant-identifying, returned to the lover-arms of the veld. As Ginnie and Alister have remarked, if affectionately, her sister and brother-in-law are more interested in buck and beetles than in any endangered human species. Jamie – to catch up with him, except for Christmas! He was always all over the place other than where you would expect to find him. And Matthew: he was the childhood and adolescence photographs displayed in the parents' house, and a commentator's voice broadcasting a test cricket match from Australia in which recognisable quirks of home pronunciation came and went like the fading and return of an unclear line.

Now they are in touch again as they have not been since a time, times, they wouldn't remember or would remember differently, each according to a need that made this sibling then seek out that, while avoiding the others.

Ginnie and Ba even meet for lunch. It's in a piano bar-cum-bistro with deep armchairs and standing lamps which fan a sunset light to the ceiling beneath which you eat from the low table at your knees. A most unlikely place to be chosen by Ba, who picks at the spicy olives and peri-peri cashew nuts as if she were trying some unfamiliar seed come upon in the wild; but she has suggested the place because she and Carl don't go to restaurants and it's the one she knows of since her stockbroker asks her to make bookings there for him. When the sisters meet they don't know where to begin. The weeks go by, when the phone rings and (fairly regularly, duty bound) it's the father, or (rarely, she's in a mood when duty is seen to be a farce) it's the mother, the siblings have a high moment when it could be another announcement – that it is over, *he's* back, *she's* given his life back to him, the forty-two years. But no, no.

May he survive. That's the axiom the daughters and sons have, ironically, taken from her. Who is this woman who threatens it?

Her name is Alicia (affected choice on the part of whoever engendered her?), surname Parks (commonplace enough, which explains a certain level of origin, perhaps?). She was something of a prodigy for as long as childhood lasts, but has not fulfilled this promise and has ended up no further than second violinist in a second-best symphony orchestra – so rated by people who really know music. Which the father, poor man, doesn't, just his CD shelf in the living room, for relaxation with his wife on evenings at home.

The woman's career will have impressed him; those who can, play; those who can't, listen: he and Isabel.

What happened to the man, father of the child? Has their father a rival? Is he a hopeful sign? Or – indeed – is he a threat, a complication in the risk the darling crazy sixty-seven-year-old is taking, next thing he'll be mixed up in some *crime passionnel* – but Jamie, captured for drinks at Ginnie's house, laughs – Daddy-O, right on, the older man has appeal! And Jamie's the one who does what as youngsters they called 'picking up stompies' – cigarette butts of information and gossip. The child's father lives in London, he's a journalist and he's said to be a coloured. So the little boy to whom *he* must be playing surrogate father is a mixed-blood child, twice or thrice diluted, since the father might be heaven knows what concoction of human variety.

At least that shows this business has brought progress in some way. Ginnie is privately returning to something in her own experience of the parental home only one other sibling (Matthew) happens to know about. The parents always affirmed they were not racist and brought up their children that way. So far as they felt they could without conflict with the law of the time. Ginnie, as a student, had a long love affair with a young Indian who was admitted to study at the white university on a quota. She never could tell the parents. When it came to a daughter or son of their own . . .

The fact of the child obviously doesn't matter to *him*, now. Of course the mother, in her present mood, if she gets to hear . . .

Ginnie was at a door of the past, opening contiguous to the present. You never know about anything like that. Principles. Look at me. I wear a ribbon in support of no discrimination against Aids victims, but what if I found the woman who takes care of my kid was HIV positive – would I get rid of her?

Alister, merely a husband among them, had something to say to the siblings. The matter of the child might be an added attraction for him. The rainbow child. Many well-meaning people in the past now want some way to prove in practice the abstract positions they hid in, then. Of course I don't know your father as well as you do.

His wife had something to add.

Or as we think we do.

Ba did not speak at these family meetings.

She is in a house with her father. The house is something familiar to her but it isn't either the family home or her own. Or maybe it's both – dreams can do these things. Just she and her father; she wonders why he's there in the middle of the day. He says he's waiting for the arrival of the maid. There's the tring-tring of an old-fashioned bicycle bell, the kind they had on their bikes as children. She looks out the window, he's standing behind her, and she sees – they see, she's aware he knows she's looking – a young and pretty redhead/blonde dismount from a bicycle, smiling. But there are no whites who work as maids in this country.

Ginnie and Ba, not telling anyone else, go to a concert. Seats chosen neither too near nor too far back. Yes, she is there with the violin nestling between jaw and shoulder. Follow white hands doing different intricate things, some fingers depressing strings, those of the other hand folded around the bow. She wears the sort of informal evening dress the other women players in the orchestra wear, not quite a uniform; the equivalent of the not quite black-tie outfits the male players allow themselves – roll-collar shirts and coloured cummerbunds. There's some sort of fringed shawl slipped off the side of the bowing arm. Apparently the dress is quite sexily *décolleté*. They'll verify when the orchestra rises at interval. She is certainly very slim – the left leg stretched gracefully, and there's a lot of hair piled on top of her head. Not blonde, not redhead. It's the colour of every second woman's at present, an unidentifiable brown overlaid with a purplish shine of henna. She rests her bow, plays when summoned by the conductor, and the sisters are summoned to listen to her. They feel she knows they are there, although she doesn't know them. She's looking at them although blinded by the stage lights. She's playing to *them*.

* * *

The palm of the hand.

All that you go through your life (sixty-seven years, how long it's been) without knowing. Most of it you'll never suspect you lack and it's pure chance that you may come upon. An ordinary short flight between one familiar city and another in daily, yearly time. The palm of a hand: that it can be so erotic. Its pads and valleys and lines to trace and kiss; she laughs at me and says they're lines of fortune, that's why I'm here with her. The palm that holds enfolds the rod of the bow and it sings. Enfolds holds me.

Matthew mustn't think he can stay out of it! They send him email letters, dispatched by Ginnie but addressing him as from a collective 'we' – the sisters and their husbands, the younger brother – who expect him to take part in decisions: whatever there is to be done. Matthew writes, I suppose we gave them the general amount of trouble sons and daughters do. The parents, he means. And what is meant by that? What's that got to do with anything that can be done? What's he getting at? Is it that it's the parents' turn now – for God's sake, at their, at *his* age! Or is it that because of their past youth the sons and daughters ought to understand the parents better? All these irrelevances – relevances, who knows – come upon, brought up by the one nice and far away among the cricket bats and kangaroos. What is there for Matthew to disinter; he was always so uncomplicated – so far as they know, those who grew up close to him in the entanglements of a family; never ran away from anything – unless you count Australia, where he's made what is widely recognised as a success.

The general amount of trouble. Jamie. And for the parents he's unlikely ever to be regarded as anything other than troubling. *As long as they're happy*, parents say of their engendered adults, swallowing dismay and disappointment. What did the parents really know of what was happening to their young, back then. Ginnie's Indian; the irony, she sees it now, that it was his parents who found out about the affair and broke it off. Never mind falling in love, that kind of love was called miscegenation in those days, punishable by law, and would have put his studies at risk; his parents planned for him to be a doctor, not a lover – in prison. Ba's abortion. How *he* would have anguished over his favourite daughter if he had known. Only Ginnie knows that this botched back-room process is the reason why Ba is childless. No one else; not Carl. It belongs to a life before Ba found him, her rare and only elect mate, come upon in the bush. It's unlikely that Jamie has a passing thought (in the reminder of the general amount of trouble they've given) for what he arranged for his frantic sister, that time; even as a teenager he had precociously the kind of friends who were used to mutual efforts in getting one another out of all manner of youthful trouble. Yes, it was Jamie – Jamie of all of them – Ba turned to; as it was Jamie – of all of them – her father had turned to in his trouble, now.

It became possible to have *him* to eat a meal at one or other of their homes, without the mother. As if it were normal. And not easy to convey to him implicitly that it was not; that his place as a lover was not at this table, his place here was as a husband with his wife, mother-and-father. This displacement did not apply to their mother because she, as they saw it, was the victim of this invading lover in the family circle. She had accepted to come to them, in her own right (so to speak), now and then, her carefully erected composure forbidding any discussion of the situation at table, and now she had gone to spend a holiday with her cousin, a consular official in Mauritius.

After the meal with her at Ginnie's or Ba's house, one of them, her daughters or their husbands, insisted on a sense of reality by bringing up the subject; the only subject. How did things stand now? Was there any exchange of ideas, say, about the future, going on between *him* and her?

Her lawyer had met him and an allowance for her had been arranged; there were other matters to be cleared up. Possessions. These were not specified, as if it had nothing to do with anyone but herself. It was Carl who was able to say, out of his privileged innocence close to nature's organic cycles of change and renewal, Maybe your absence will be the right thing. For both of you. When you come back you may find you can work things out again together.

She looked at him half-pityingly, for his concern.

Things are worked out. It was his work.

And she turned away *as of her right* to grandmotherly talk with Ginnie's small boy, for whom she had brought a model jeep, and then to a low exchange in intimate tone with her favourite, the elder of the two teenage daughters, who happened to be at home in the family that evening. No boyfriends around tonight? Usually when I come at the weekend I hear a lot of music and laughing going on upstairs. Helen's friends, the girl says. And not yours, not your type – I understand. What's your type . . . all right, *the* one, then – I have a pretty good idea of what would interest you, you know.

And the girl lies, describing the non-existent one as she thinks an adult would wish him to be.

When the mother-grandmother had left, Ginnie's husband Alister told them: Isabel thinks we're on *his* side, that's the problem.

Why should we be.

Nobody takes up Ba's statement.

May he survive.

Best of all. Early in the morning some days to wake at the sound of the key turning in the lock; her key. Hear it but not sufficiently awake to open eyes; and there's a cold fresh cheek laid against the unshaven one. She's left her apartment before seven to deliver the child to nursery school and after, she's suddenly here. Yesterday. Heard her shoes drop and opened eyes to follow her clothes to the floor. She glides into bed, the cheek is still cold and the rest of her is her special warmth. Not today: waiting for the key to turn. Tomorrow. Again it will turn. Again and again.

They broach to one another the obligation – the usefulness, perhaps – of inviting him to bring her along some time. Sunday lunch? No, too familial a gesture, and Ba and Carl would not be there, why should Ginnie and Alister deal with this on their own, you can't count on Jamie. Come by for a drink sixish, that would do. What's she like – look like? The two men want to know in advance – after all, they are the father's fellow males – what to expect in order to put themselves in his place. But the splash of stage lights drops a mask on faces, there were cave-hollows of eyes, white cheeks, bright mouth. It was the hands in movement by which an identity was followed.

The man who brings her to Ginnie's house is another personage: their father? He who always listened, talks. Although this is not his home, he is not the host, he rises to refill glasses and offer snacks. He is courting her, in front of them, they see it! Their mother is much better-looking; still beautiful; this one has a long, thin, voracious face, the light did not exaggerate its hollows, and her intelligently narrowed eyes – hazel? greenish? doesn't matter – are iconised by make-up in the style of Egyptian statues. She's chosen a loose but clinging tunic and the sisters see that she has firm breasts. When they compare impressions afterwards it seems it was the women who noted this rather than, as they would have thought, the men. Her hands are unadorned (the mother has had gifts of beautiful rings from *him*, over the years) and lie half-curled, the palms half-open on chair-arm or lap; it's as if the hands' lack of tension is meant to put them at ease, these hands that make music. And pleasure their father. She has a voice with what the women suspect as an adopted huskiness they believe men find attractive. It turns out no one of the men – Jamie was present – noticed it either as an affectation or an attraction *he* might have responded to.

The talk was quite animated and completely artificial; they were *all* other people; chatting about nothing that mattered to whom and what they really were. There are so many harmless subjects, you can really get along in any situation by sticking to what has been in the newspapers and on television about the floods/drought, the times of day to avoid driving in traffic congestion (keep off wars and politics, both local and international, those are intimate subjects), and, of course about music. It is the lover who brings that up; Ginnie and Ba would have preferred to keep off that, too. She might somehow sense how their eyes had been upon her while she played . . . *He* even boasts about her: Alicia will go with the orchestra to an international music festival in Montreal in the winter, and it will be particularly enjoyable for her because Alicia also speaks fluent French. He might be – ought to be – boring someone with the achievements of his seventeen-year-old granddaughter, Ginnie's eldest child. Ginnie's biological afterthought, four-year-old Shaun, had been playing with his jeep around everyone's feet. When the father and his woman were leaving, she bent to the child: I've got a little boy like you, you know. He has a collection of cars but I don't think he has a jeep, yours's great.

They are not embarrassed about anything, these lovers.

The new father of some other man's progeny makes a pledge for the rainbow child. We'll have to find one for him. Where did you get it?

Shaun asserts the presence not admitted to the drinks party. My grandmother did bring it for me.

A curious – almost shaming – moment comes to the siblings and husbands when they suddenly laugh about the whole business – mother, father, the woman. It begins to happen when they get together – less and less frequently – dutifully to try and decide yet again what they ought to be doing about it. The outbreak's akin to the hysterical giggle that sometimes accompanies tearful frustration. What can you do about Papa in his bemused state, and oh my God, next thing is he'll get her pregnant, he'll be Daddy all over again. No no no – spare us that! What do you mean *no* – presumably that's what it's all about, his pride in an old man's intact male prowess! And Alister in an aside to Jamie – Apparently he's still able to get it up – right on, as you would say – and they all lose control again. What is there to do with the mother who is unapproachable, wants to be left alone like a sulky teenager, and a father who's broken loose like a youth sowing wild oats? Who could ever do anything with people in such conditions? Ah – but these are mature people! So nobody knows what maturity is, after all? Is that it? Not any longer, not any more, now that the mother and father have taken away that certainty from their sons and daughters. Matthew calls and sends email from his safe distance, reproaching, What is the matter with all of you? Why can't you get some reality into them, bring them together for what's left after their forty-two years? How else can this end?

Well, the mother seems to be making an extended holiday-of-a-lifetime out of the situation, and *he*, he's out of reach (spaced out: Jamie) dancing to a fiddle. Shaking their heads with laughter; that dies in exasperation. There's *nothing* you can do with the parents.

Only fear for them. Ba's tears are not of laughter.

At least adolescents grow up; that could have been counted on to solve most of the general trouble they'd given. In the circumstances of parents it seems there isn't anything to be counted on, least of all the much-vaunted wisdom of old age. The mother wrote a long round-robin letter (copy to each sibling, just a different name after 'Dearest') telling that she was going to Matthew in Australia. So Mauritius had been halfway there, halfway from her rightful home, all along, in more than its geographical position across the Indian Ocean between Africa and Australia. She would 'keep house' in Matthew's bachelor apartment while she looked for a new place of her own, with space enough for them to come and visit her. Send the grandchildren.

Alicia Parks, second violinist, did not return from Montreal. *He* continued to exchange letters and calls with her over many months. The family gathered this when he gave them news of her successes with the orchestra on tour, as if whether this was of interest or welcome to them or not, they must recognise her as an extension of his life – and therefore theirs. They, it obviously implied, could make up their minds about that.

What he did not tell them was that she had left the orchestra at the invitation to join a Montreal chamber group. As first violinist: an ambition he knew she had and he wanted to see fulfilled for her. But Canada. She had taken into consideration (that was her phrase) that there were not many such opportunities for her back in Africa.

With him. In his long late-night calls to her he completed, to himself, what she didn't say.

She sent for her child; told him only after the child had left the country. Then she did not tell him that she was with someone other than her child, a new man, but he knew from her voice.

Ginnie came out with it to their father. Is she coming back?

When she gets suitable engagements here, of course. She's made a position for herself in the world of music.

So he's waiting for her, they decided, poor man. Why can't he accept it's over, inevitably, put the whole thing behind him, come back to ageing as a *father*, there's a dignified alternative to this disastrous regression to adolescence.

May he survive.

Together and individually, they are determined in pursuit of him.

The best was the cold cheek. Just that. What alternative to that.

In the mirror in the bathroom, there was her body as she dried herself after the love-making bath together, towelling between her spread legs, and then across the back of her neck as beautifully as she bowed across the violin, steam sending trickles of her hair over her forehead. A mirror full of her. For me, old lover she knew how to love so well, so well, her old lover sixty-seven. What alternative.

Death is a blank mirror, emptied of all it has seen and shown.

Death waits, was waiting, but I took the plane to Cape Town, instead.

Look-Alikes

It was scarcely worth noticing at first; an out-of-work lying under one of the rare indigenous shrubs cultivated by the Botany Department on campus. Some of us remembered, afterwards, having passed him. And he – or another like him – was seen rummaging in the refuse bins behind the Student Union; one of us (a girl, of course) thrust out awkwardly to him a pitta she'd just bought for herself at the canteen, and she flushed with humiliation as he turned away mumbling. When there were more of them, the woman in charge of catering came out with a kitchen-hand in a blood-streaked apron to chase them off like a band of marauding monkeys.

We were accustomed to seeing them panhandling in the streets of the city near the university and gathered in this vacant lot or that, clandestine with only one secret mission, to beg enough to buy another bottle; moving on as the druids' circle of their boxes and bits of board spread on the ground round the ashes of their trash fires was cleared for the erection of postmodern office blocks. We all knew the one who waved cars into empty parking bays. We'd all been confronted, as we crossed the road or waited at the traffic lights, idling in our minds as the engine of the jalopy idles, by the one who held up a piece of cardboard with a message running out of space at the edges: NO JOB IM HUNGRY EVEYONE HELP PLeas.

At first; yes, there were already a few of them about. They must have drifted in by the old, unfrequented entrance down near the tennis courts, where the security fence was not yet completed. And if they were not come upon, there were the signs: trampled spaces in the bushes, empty bottles, a single split shoe with a sole like a lolling tongue. No doubt they had been chased out by a patrolling security guard. No student, at that stage, would have bothered to report the harmless presence; those of us who had cars might have been more careful than usual to leave no sweaters or radios visible through the locked windows. We followed our familiar rabbit-runs from the lecture rooms and laboratories back, forth and around campus, between residences, libraries, Student Union and swimming pool, through avenues of posters making announcements of debates and sports events, discos and rap sessions, the meetings of Muslim, Christian or Jewish brotherhoods, gay or feminist sisterhoods, with the same lack of attention to all but the ones we'd put up ourselves.

It was summer when it all started. We spend a lot of time on the lawns around the pool, in summer. We swot down there, we get a good preview of each other more or less nude, boys and girls, there's plenty of what you might call foreplay – happy necking. And the water to cool off in. The serious competitive swimmers come early in the morning when nobody else is up, and it was they who discovered these people washing clothes in the pool. When the swimmers warned them off they laughed and jeered. One left a dirt-stiff pair of pants that a swimmer balled and threw after him. There was argument among the swimmers; one felt the incident ought to be reported to Security, two were uncomfortable with the idea in view of the university's commitment to being available to the city community. They must have persuaded him that he would be exposed for elitism, because although the pool was referred to as The Wishee-Washee, among us, after that, there seemed to be no action taken.

Now you began to see them all over. Some greeted you smarmily (my baas, sir, according to their colour and culture), retreating humbly into the undergrowth, others, bold on wine or stoned on meths, sentimental on pot, or transformed in the wild hubris of all three, called out a claim (Hey man, *Ja boetie*) and even beckoned to you to join them where they had formed one of their circles, or huddled, just two, with the instinct for seclusion that only couples looking for a place to make love have, among us. The security fence down at the tennis courts was completed, reinforced with spikes and manned guardhouse, but somehow they got in. The guards with their Alsatian dogs patrolled the campus at night but every day there were more shambling figures disappearing into the trees, more of those thick and battered faces looking up from the wells between buildings, more supine bodies contoured like sacks of grass cuttings against the earth beneath the struts of the sports grandstands.

And they were no longer a silent presence. Their laughter and their quarrels broadcast over our student discussions, our tête-à-tête conversations and love-making, even our raucous fooling about. They had made a kind of encampment for themselves, there behind the sports fields where there was a stretch of ground whose use the university had not yet determined: it was for future expansion of some kind, and in the meantime equipment for maintenance of the campus was kept there – objects that might or might not be useful, an old tractor, barrels for indoor plants when the Vice-Chancellor requested a bower to decorate some hall for the reception of distinguished guests, and – of course – the compost heaps. The compost heaps were now being used as a repository for more than garden waste. If they had not been there with their odours of rot sharpened by the chemical agents for decay with which they were treated, the conclave living down there might have been sniffed out sooner. Perhaps they had calculated this in the secrets of living rough: perhaps they decided that the Alsatians' noses would be bamboozled.

So we knew about them – everybody knew about them, students, faculty, administrative staff, Vice-Chancellor – and yet nobody knew about them. Not officially. Security was supposed to deal with trespassers as a routine duty; but although Security was able to find and escort beyond the gates one or two individuals too befuddled or not wily enough to keep out of the way, they came back or were replaced by others. There was some kind of accommodation they had worked out within the order of the campus, some plan of interstices they had that the university didn't have; like the hours at which security patrols could be expected, there must have been other certainties we students and our learned teachers had relied on so long we did not realise that they had become useless as those red bomb-shaped fire extinguishers which, when a fire leaps out in a room, are found to have evaporated their content while hanging on the wall.

We came to recognise some of the bolder characters; or rather it was that they got to recognise us – with their streetwise judgement they knew who could be approached. For a cigarette. Not money – you obviously don't ask students for what they themselves are always short of. They would point to a wrist and ask the time, as an opener. And they must have recognised something else, too; those among us who come to a university because it's the cover where you think you can be safe from surveillance and the expectations others have of you – back to play-school days, only the sand pit and the finger-painting are substituted by other games. The dropouts, just cruising along until the end of the academic year, sometimes joined the group down behind the grandstands, taking a turn with the zol and maybe helping out with the donation of a bottle of wine now and then. Of course only we, their siblings, identified them; with their jeans bought ready-torn at the knees, and hair shaved up to a topknot, they would not have been distinguished from the younger men in the group by a passing professor dismayed at the sight of the intrusion of the campus by hobos and loafers. (An interesting point, for the English Department, that in popular terminology the whites are known as hobos and the blacks as loafers.) If student solidarity with the underdog was expressed in the wearing of ragged clothes, then the invaders' claim to be within society was made through adoption of acceptable fashionable unconventions. (I thought of putting that in my next essay for Sociology II.) There were topknots and single earrings among the younger invaders, dreadlocks, and one had long tangled blond hair snaking about his dark-stubbled face. He could even have passed for a certain junior lecturer in the Department of Political Science.

So nobody said a word about these recruits from among the students, down there. Not even the Society of Christian Students, who campaigned for moral regeneration on the campus. In the meantime, 'the general situation had been brought to the notice' of Administration. The implication was that the intruders were to be requested to leave, with semantic evasion of the terms 'squatter' or 'eviction'. SUJUS (Students For Justice) held a meeting in protest against forced removal under any euphemism. ASOCS (Association of Conservative Students) sent a delegation to the Vice-Chancellor to demand that the campus be cleared of degenerates.

Then it was discovered that there were several women living among the men down there. The white woman was the familiar one who worked along the cars parked in the streets, trudging in thonged rubber sandals on swollen feet. The faces of the two black women were darkened by drink as white faces are reddened by it. The three women were seen swaying together, keeping upright on the principle of a tripod. The Feminist Forum took them food, tampons, and condoms for their protection against pregnancy and Aids, although it was difficult to judge which was still young enough to be a sex object in need of protection; they might be merely prematurely aged by the engorged tissues puffing up their faces and the exposure of their skin to all weathers, just as, in a reverse process, pampered females look younger than they are through the effect of potions and plastic surgery.

From ASOCS came the rumour that one of the group had made obscene advances to a girl student – although she denied this in tears, *she* had offered *him* her pitta, which he had refused, mumbling 'I don't eat rubbish'. The Vice-Chancellor was importuned by parents who objected to their sons' and daughters' exposure to undesirables, and by Hope For The Homeless who wanted to put up tents on this territory of the overprivileged. The City Health authorities were driven off the campus by SUJUS and The Feminist Forum while the Jewish Student Congress discussed getting the Medical School to open a clinic down at the grandstands, the Islamic Student Association took a collection for the group while declaring that the area of their occupation was out of bounds to female students wearing the *chador*, and the Students Buddhist Society distributed tracts on meditation among men and women quietly sleeping in the sun with their half-jacks, discreet in brown paper packets up to the screw top, snug beside them as hot-water bottles.

These people could have been removed by the police, of course, on a charge of vagrancy or some such, but the Vice-Chancellor, the University Council and the Faculty Association had had too much experience of violence resulting from the presence of the police on campus to invite this again. The matter was referred back and forth. When we students returned after the Easter vacation the blond man known by his head of hair, the toothless ones, the black woman who always called out *Hello lovey how'you* and the neat queen who would buttonhole anyone to tell of his student days in Dublin, *You kids don't know what a real university is*, were still there. Like the stray cats students (girls again) stooped to scratch behind the ears.

And then something really happened. One afternoon I thought I saw Professor Jepson in a little huddle of four or five comfortably under a tree on their fruit-box seats. Someone who looked the image of him; one of the older men, having been around the campus some months, now, was taking on some form of mimesis better suited to him than the kid-stuff garb the younger ones and the students aped from each other. Then I saw him again, and there was Dr Heimrath from Philosophy just in the act of taking a draw, next to him – if any social reject wanted a model for look-alike it would be from that department. And I was not alone, either; the friend I was with that day saw what I did. We were the only ones who believed a student who said he had almost stepped on Bell, Senior Lecturer from Maths, in the bushes with one of the three women; Bell's bald head shone a warning signal just in time. Others said they'd seen Kort wrangling with one of the men, there were always fights when the gatherings ran out of wine and went on to meths. Of course Kort had every kind of pure alcohol available to him in his domain, the science laboratories; everybody saw him, again and again, down there, it was Kort, all right, no chance of simple resemblance, and the euphoria followed by aggression that a meths concoction produces markedly increased in the open-air coterie during the following weeks. The papers Maths students handed in were not returned when they were due; Bell's secretary did not connect calls to his office, day after day, telling callers he had stepped out for a moment. Jepson, Professor Jepson who not only had an international reputation as a nuclear physicist but also was revered by the student body as the one member of faculty who was always to be trusted to defend students' rights against authoritarianism, our old prof, everybody's enlightened grandfather – he walked down a corridor unbuttoned, stained, with dilated pupils that were unaware of the students who shrank back, silent, to make way.

There had been sniggers and jokes about the other faculty members, but nobody found anything to say over Professor Jepson; nothing, nothing at all. As if to smother any comment about him, rumours about others got wilder; or facts did. It was said that the Vice-Chancellor himself was seen down there, sitting round one of their trash fires; but it could have been that he was there to reason with the trespassers, to flatter them with the respect of placing himself in their company so that he could deal with the situation. Heimrath was supposed to have been with him, and Bester from Religious Studies with Franklin-Turner from English – but Franklin-Turner was hanging around there a lot, anyway, that snobbish closet drinker come out into the cold, no more fastidious ideas about race keeping him out of that mixed company, eh?

And it was no rumour that Professor Russo was going down there, now. Minerva Russo, of Classics, young, untouchable as one of those lovely creatures who can't be possessed by men, can be carried off only by a bull or penetrated only by the snowy penis-neck of a swan. We males all had understood, through her, what it means to feast with your eyes, but we never speculated about what we'd find under her clothes; further sexual awe, perhaps, a mother-of-pearl scaled tail. Russo was attracted. She sat down there and put their dirty bottle to her mouth and the black-rimmed fingernails of one of them fondled her neck. Russo heard their wheedling, brawling, booze-snagged voices calling and became a female along with the other unwashed three. We saw her scratching herself when she did still turn up – irregularly – to teach us Greek poetry. Did she share their body-lice too?

It was through her, perhaps, that real awareness of the people down there came. The revulsion and the pity; the old white woman with the suffering feet ganging up with the black ones when the men turned on the women in the paranoia of betrayal – by some mother, some string of wives or lovers half-drowned in the bottles of the past – and cursing her sisters when one of them took a last cigarette butt or hung on a man the white sister favoured; tended by the sisterhood or tending one of them when the horrors shook or a blow was received. The stink of the compost heaps they used drifted through the libraries with the reminder that higher functions might belong to us but we had to perform the lower ones just like the wretches who made us stop our noses. Shit wasn't a meaningless expletive, it was part of the hazards of the human condition. They were ugly, down there at the grandstands and under the bushes, barnacled and scaled with disease and rejection, no one knows how you may pick it up, how it is transmitted, turning blacks grey and firing whites' faces in a furnace of exposure, taking away shame so that you beg, but leaving painful pride so that you can still rebuff, *I don't eat rubbish*, relying on violence because peace has to have shelter, but sticking together with those who threaten you because that is the only bond that's left. The shudder at it, and the freedom of it – to let go of assignments, assessments, tests of knowledge, hopes of tenure, the joy and misery of responsibility for lovers and children, money, debts. No goals and no failures. It was enviable and frightening to see them down there – Bester, Franklin-Turner, Heimrath and the others, Russo pulling herself to rights to play the goddess when she caught sight of us but too bedraggled to bring it off. Jepson, our Jepson, all that we had to believe in of the Old Guard's world, passing and not recognising us.

And then one day, they had simply disappeared. Gone. The groundsmen had swept away the broken bottles and discarded rags. The compost was doused with chemicals and spread on the campus's floral display. The Vice-Chancellor had never joined the bent backs round the zol and the bottle down there and was in his panelled office. The lines caging Heimrath's mouth in silence did not release him to ask why students gazed at him. Minerva sat before us in her special way with matched pale narrow hands placed as if one were the reflection of the other, its fingertips raised against a mirror. Jepson's old bristly sow's ear sagged patiently towards the discourse of the seminar's show-off.

From under the bushes and behind the grandstands they had gone, or someone had found a way to get rid of them overnight. But they are always with us. Just somewhere else.

The Diamond Mine

I'll call her Tilla, you may call her by another name. You might think you knew her. You might have been the one: him. It's not by some simple colloquial habit we 'call' someone instead of naming: call them up.

It was during the war, your war, the forties, that has sunk as far away into the century as the grandfathers' nineteen-fourteen. He was blond, stocky in khaki, attractively short-sighted so that the eyes that were actually having difficulty with focus seemed to be concentrating attentively on her. The impression is emphasised by the lashes blond and curly as his hair. He is completely different from the men she knows in the life of films – the only men she knows apart from her father – and whom she expected to come along one day not too far off, Robert Taylor or even the foreigner, Charles Boyer. He is different because – at last – he is real; she is sixteen. He is no foreigner nor materialisation of projection from Hollywood. He's the son of friends of a maternal grandmother, detailed to a military training camp in the province where the girl and her parents live. Some people even take in strangers from the camp for the respite of weekend leave; with a young daughter in the house this family would not go so far as to risk that but when the man of the family is beyond call-up age an easy way to fulfil patriotic duty is to offer hospitality to a man vouched for by connections. He's almost to be thought of as an elective grandson of the old lady. In war these strangers, remember, are Our Boys.

When he comes on Friday nights and stays until Sunday his presence makes a nice change for the three, mother, father and young daughter who live a quiet life, not given to socialising. That presence is a pleasant element in the closeness between parents and daughter: he is old enough to be an adult along with them, and only eight years ahead of her, young enough to be her contemporary. The mother cooks a substantial lunch on the Sundays he's there; you can imagine what the food must be like in a military camp. The father at least suggests a game of golf – welcome to borrow clubs, but it turns out the soldier doesn't play. What's his game, then? He likes to fish. But this hospitality is four hundred miles from the sea; the soldier laughs along in a guest's concession of manly recognition that there must be a game. The daughter – for her, she could never tell anyone, his weekend presence is a pervasion that fills the house, displaces all its familiar odours of home, is fresh and pungent: he's here. It's the emanation of khaki washed with strong soap and fixed, as in perfume the essence of flowers is fixed by alcohol, by the pressure of a hot iron.

The parents are reluctant cinema-goers, so it is thoughtful of this visiting friend of the family that he invites the daughter of the house to choose a film she'd like to see on a Saturday night. She has no driving licence yet (seventeen the qualifying age in those days) and the father does not offer his car to the soldier. So the pair walk down the road from street light to street light, under the trees, all that autumn, to the small town's centre where only the cinema and the pub in the hotel are awake. She is aware of window dummies in the closed shops her mother's friends patronise, observing her as she walks past with a man. If she is invited to a party given by a schoolfriend, she must be home strictly by eleven, usually fetched by her father. But now she is with a responsible friend, a family connection, not among unknown youths on the loose; if the film is a nine o'clock showing the pair are not home before midnight, and the lights are already extinguished in the parents' bedroom. It is then that, schoolgirlish, knowing nothing else to offer, she makes cocoa in the kitchen and it is then that he tells her about fishing. The kitchen is locked up for the night, the windows are closed and it is amazing how strong that presence of a man can be, that stiff-clean clothing warmed – not a scent, not a breath, but, as he moves his arms graphically in description of playing a catch, coming from the inner crease of his bare elbows where the sun on manoeuvres hasn't got at the secret fold, coming from that centre of being, the pliant hollow that vibrates between collarbones as he speaks, the breast-plate rosy down to where a few brownish-blond hairs disappear into the open neck of the khaki shirt – he will never turn dark, his skin retains the sun, glows. Him.

Tilla has never gone fishing. Her father doesn't fish. Four hundred miles from the sea the boys at school kick and throw balls around – they know about, talk about, football and cricket. The father knows about, talks about, golf. Fishing. It opens the sea before her, the salt wind gets in the narrowed eyes conveying to her whole nights passed alone on the rocks. He walks from headland to headland on dawn-wet sand, the tide is out – sometimes in mid-sentence there's a check, half smile, half breath, because he's thinking of something this child couldn't know, this is his incantation that shuts out the smart parade-ground march towards killing and blinds the sights the gun trains on sawdust-stuffed figures where he is being drilled to see the face of the enemy to whom he, himself, is the enemy, with guts (he pulls the intricately perfect innards out of the fish he's caught, the fisherman's simple skill) in place of sawdust. Sleeping parents are right; he will not touch her innocence of what this century claims, commands from him.

Walking home where she used to race her bicycle up and down under the same trees, the clothing on their arms, the khaki sleeve, the sweater her mother has handed her as a condition of permission to be out in the chill night air, brushes by proximity, not intention. The strap of her sandal slips and as she pauses to right it, hopping on one leg, he steadies her by the forearm and then they walk on hand in hand. He's taking care of her. The next weekend they kiss in one of the tree-dark intervals between street lights. Boys have kissed her; it happened only to her mouth; the next Saturday her arms went around him, his around her, her face approached, was pressed, breathed in and breathed against the hollow of neck where the pendulum of heartbeat can be felt, the living place above the breast-plate from which the incense of his presence had come. She was there.

In the kitchen there was no talk. The cocoa rose to top of the pot, made ready. All the sources of the warmth that her palms had extended to, everywhere in the house, as a domestic animal senses the warmth of a fire to approach, were in this body against hers, in the current of arms, the contact of chest, belly muscles, the deep strange heat from between his thighs. But he took care of her. Gently loosened her while she was discovering that a man has breasts, too, even if made of muscle, and that to press her own against them was an urgent exchange, walking on the wet sands with the fisherman.

The next weekend leave – but the next weekend leave is cancelled. Instead there's a call from the public phone at the canteen bar. The mother happened to answer and there were expressions of bright and encouraging regret that the daughter tried to piece into what they were responding to. The family was at supper. The father's mouth bunched stoically – Marching orders. Embarkation.

The mother nodded round the table, confirming.

She – the one I call Tilla – stood up appalled at the strength to strike the receiver from her mother and the inability of a good girl to do so. Then her mother was saying, But of course we'll take a drive out on Sunday, say goodbye and Godspeed. Grandma'd never forgive me if she thought . . . now can you tell me how to get there, beyond Pretoria, I know . . . I didn't catch it, what mine? And after the turn-off at the main road? Oh don't bother, I suppose we can ask at a petrol station if we get lost, everyone must know where that camp is, is there something we can bring you, anything you'll need . . .

It seems there's to be an outing made of it. Out of her stun: that essence, ironed khaki and soap, has been swept from the house, from the kitchen, by something that's got nothing to do with a fisherman except that he is a man, and as her father has stated – Embarkation – men go to war. Her mother makes picnic preparations: do you think a chicken or pickled ox-tongue, hard-boiled eggs, don't know where one can sit to eat in a military camp, there must be somewhere for visitors. Her father selects from his stack of travel brochures a map of the local area to place on the shelf below the windscreen. Petrol is rationed but he has been frugal with coupons, there are enough to provide a full tank. Because of this, plans for the picnic are abandoned, no picnic, her mother thinks wouldn't it be a nice gesture to take the soldier out for a restaurant lunch in the nearest city? There won't be many such luxuries for the young man on his way to war in the North African desert.

They have never shown her the mine, the diamond mine, although since she was a small child they have taken their daughter to places of interest as part of her education. They must have talked about it – her father is a mining company official himself, but the exploitation is gold, not precious stones – or more likely it has been cited in a general knowledge text at school: some famous diamond was dug there.

The camp is on part of the vast mine property, commandeered by the Defence Force, over the veld there are tents to the horizon, roped and staked, dun as the scuffed and dried grass and the earth scoured by boots – boots tramping everywhere, khaki everywhere, the wearers replicating one another, him; where shall they find him? He did give a tent number. The numbers don't seem to be consecutive. Her father is called to a halt by a replica with a gun, slow-spoken and polite. The car follows given directions retained each differently by the mother and father, the car turns, backs up, take it slowly for heaven's sake.

She is the one: – There. There he is.

Of course, when you find him you see there is no one like him, no bewilderment. They are all laughing in the conventions of greeting but his eyes have their concentrated attention for her. It is his greeting of the intervals between street lights, and of the kitchen. This weekend which ends weekends seems also to be the first of winter; it's suddenly cold, wind bellies and whips at that tent where he must have slept, remote, between weekends. It's the weather for hot food, shelter. At the restaurant he chooses curry and rice for this last meal. He sprinkles grated coconut and she catches his eye and he smiles for her as he adds dollops of chutney. The smile is that of a greedy boy caught out and is also as if it were a hand squeezed under the table. No wine – the father has to drive, and young men oughtn't to be encouraged to drink, enough of that in the army – but there is ice cream with canned peaches, coffee served, and peppermints with the compliments of the management.

It was too warm in the restaurant. Outside, high-altitude winds carry the breath of what must be early snow on the mountains far away, unseen, as this drive in return to the camp carries the breath of war, far away, unseen, where all the replicas in khaki are going to be shipped. No heating in the family car of those days, the soldier has only his thin, well-pressed khaki and the daughter, of course, like all young girls has taken no precaution against a change in the weather, she is wearing the skimpy flounced cotton dress (secretly chosen although he, being older, and a disciple of the sea's mysteries, probably won't even notice) that she was wearing the first time they walked to the cinema. The mother, concealing – she believes – irritation at the fecklessness of the young, next thing she'll have bronchitis and miss school – fortunately keeps a rug handy and insists that the passengers in the back seat put it over their knees.

It was easy to chat in the preoccupations of food along with the budgerigar chitter of other patrons in the restaurant. In the car, headed back for that final place, the camp, the outing is over. The father feels an obligation: at least, he can tell something about the diamond mine, that's of interest, and soon they'll actually be passing again the site of operations though you can't see much from the road.

The rug is like the pelt of some dusty pet animal settled over them. The warmth of the meal inside them is bringing it to life; a life they share, one body. It's pleasant to put your hand beneath it; the hands, his right, her left, find one another.

you know what a diamond is, of course, although you look at it as something pretty a woman wears on her finger mmh? well actually it consists of pure carbon crystallised

He doesn't like to be interrupted, there's no need to make any response, even if you still hear him. The right hand and left hand become so tightly clasped that the pad of muscle at the base of each thumb is flattened against the bone and the interlaced fingers are jammed down between the joints. It isn't a clasp against imminent parting, it's got nothing to do with any future, it belongs in the urgent purity of this present.

the crystallisation in regular octahedrons that's to say eight-sided and in allied forms and the cut and polished ones you see in jewellery more or less follow

The hands lay together, simply happened, on the skirt over her left thigh, because that is where she had slipped her hand beneath the woolly comfort of the rug. Now he slowly released, first fingers, then palms – at once awareness signals between them that the rug is their tender accomplice, it must not be seen to be stirred by something – he released himself from her and for one bereft moment she thought he had left her behind, his eight-year advantage prevailed against such fusion of palms as it had done, so gently (oh but why) when they were in the dark between trees, when they were in the kitchen.

colourless or they may be tinted occasionally yellow pink even black

The hand had not emerged from the rug. She followed as if her eyes were closed or she was in the dark, it went as if it were playing, looking for a place to tickle as children do to make one another wriggle and laugh, where her skirt ended at her knee, going under her knee without displacing the skirt and touching the tendons and the hollow there. She didn't want to laugh (what would her father make of such a response to his knowledgeable commentary) so she glided her hand to his and put it back with hers where it had been before.

one of the biggest diamonds in the world after the Koh-i-noor's hundred-and-nine carats but that was found in India

The hand, his hand, pressed fingers into her thigh through the cotton flounce as if testing to see what was real about her; and stopped, and then out of the hesitation went down and, under the rug, up under the gauze of skirt, moved over her flesh. She did not look at him and he did not look at her.

and there are industrial gems you can cut glass with make bits for certain drills the hardest substance known

At the taut lip of her pants he hesitated again, no hurry, all something she was learning, he was teaching, the anticipation in his fingertips, he stroked along one of the veins in there in the delicate membrane-like skin that is at the crevice between leg and body (like the skin that the sun on manoeuvres couldn't reach in the crook of his elbow) just before the hair begins. And then he went under the elastic edge and his hand was soft on soft hair, his fingers like eyes attentive to her.

look at this veld nothing suggests one of the greatest ever, anywhere, down there, down in what we call Blue Earth the diamondiferous core

She has no clear idea of where his hand is now, what she feels is that they are kissing, they are in each other's mouths although they cannot look to one another.

Are you asleep back there? – the mother is remarking her own boredom with the mine – he is eight years older, able to speak: Just listening. His finger explores deep down in the dark, the hidden entrance to some sort of cave with its slippery walls and smooth stalagmite; she's found, he's found her.

The car is passing the mine processing plant.

product of the death and decay of forests millennia ago just as coal is but down there the ultimate alchemy you might say

Those others, the parents, they have no way of knowing. It has happened, it is happening under the old woolly rug that was all they can provide for her. She is free; of them. Found; and they don't know where she is.

At the camp, the father shakes the soldier's hand longer than in the usual grip. The mother for a moment looks as if she might give him a peck on the cheek, Godspeed, but it is not her way to be familiar.

Aren't you going to say goodbye? She's not a child, good heavens, a mother shouldn't have to remind of manners.

He's standing outside one of the tents with his hands hanging open at his sides as the car is driven away and the attention is upon her until, with his furry narrowed sight, he'll cease to be able to make her out while she still can see him, see him until he is made one with all the others in khaki, replicated, crossing and crowding, in preparation to embark.

If he had been killed in that war they would have heard, through the grandmother's connections.

Is it still you; somewhere, old?

Beethoven Was One-Sixteenth Black

Tape Measure

No one of any kind or shape or species can begin to imagine what it's like for me being swirled and twisted around all manner of filthy objects in a horrible current. I, who was used to, knew only, the calm processes of digestion as my milieu. How long will this chaos last (the digestion has its ordained programme) and where am I going? Helpless. All I can do is trace back along my length – it is considerable also in the measure of its time – how I began and lived and what has happened to me.

My beginning is ingestion – yes, sounds strange. But there it is. I might have been ingested on a scrap of lettuce or in a delicacy of raw minced meat known as, I believe, Beefsteak Tartare. Could have got in on a finger licked by my human host after he'd ignored he'd been caressing his dog or cat. Doesn't matter. Once I'd been ingested I knew what to do where I found myself, I gained consciousness; nature is a miracle in the know how it has provided, ready, in all its millions of varieties of eggs: I hatched from my minute containment that the human eye never could have detected on the lettuce, the raw meat, the finger, and began to grow myself. Segment by segment. Measuredly. That's how my species adapts and maintains itself, advances to feed along one of the most intricately designed passageways in the world. An organic one. Of course, that's connected with perhaps an even more intricate system, the whole business of veins and arteries – bloody; our species has nothing to do with that pulsing about all over in narrow tubes.

My place was warm and smooth-walled, rosy-dark, and down into its convolutions (around thirty coiled feet of it) came, sometimes more regularly than others, always ample, many different kinds of nourishment to feed on, silently, unknown and unobserved. An ideal existence! The many forms of life, in particular that of millions of the species of my host who go hungry in the cruel light and cold my darkness protected me from (with the nourishment comes not only what the host eats but intelligence of what he knows of his kind's being and environment) – they would envy one of my kind. No enemy, no predator after you, no rival. Just your own winding length, moving freely, resting sated. The nourishment that arrived so reliably – years and years in my case – was even already broken down for consumption, ready mashed, you might say, and mixed with sustaining liquids. Sometimes during my long habitation there would be a descent of some potent liquid that roused me pleasurably all my length – which, as I've remarked, had become considerable – so that I was lively, so to speak, right down to the last, most recently added segments of myself.

Come to think of it, there were a couple of attempts on my life before the present catastrophe. But they didn't succeed. No! I detected at once, infallibly, some substance *aggressive* towards me concealed in the nourishment coming down. Didn't touch that delivery. Let it slowly urge its way wherever it was going – in its usual pulsions, just as when I have had my fill; untouched! No thank you. I could wait until the next delivery came down: clean, I could tell. Whatever my host had in mind, then, I was my whole length aware, ahead of him. Yes! Oh and there was one occurrence that might or might not have had to do with whatever this aggression against my peaceful existence might mean. My home, my length, were suddenly irradiated with some weird seconds-long form of what I'd learnt second-hand from my host must have been light, as if some – Thing – was briefly enabled to look inside my host. All the wonderful secret storage that was my domain. But did those rays find me? See me? I didn't think so. All was undisturbed, for me, for a long time. I continued to grow myself, perfectly measured segment by segment. Didn't brood upon the brief invasion of my privacy; I have a calm nature, like all my kind. Perhaps I should have thought more about the incident's implication: that thereafter my host *knew I was there*; the act of ingestion conveys nothing about what's gone down with the scrap of lettuce or the meat: he wouldn't have been aware of my residency until then. But suspected something? How, I'd like to know; I was so discreet.

The gouts of that agreeable strong liquid began to reach me more frequently. No objection on my part! The stuff just made me more active for a while, I had grown to take up a lot of space in my domain, and I have to confess that I would find myself inclined to ripple and knock about a bit. Harmlessly, of course. We don't have voices so I couldn't sing. Then there would follow a really torpid interval of which I'd never remember much when it was over . . .

A contented, shared life; I knew that my host had always taken what he needed from the nourishment that came on down to me. A just and fair coexistence, I still maintain. And why should I have troubled myself with where the residue was bound for, when both of us had been satisfied?

O how I have come to know now! How I have come to know!

For what has just happened to me – I can only relive again, again, in all horror, as if it keeps recurring all along me. First there was that period, quite short, when no nourishment or liquid came down at all. My host must have been abstaining.

Then—

The assault of a terrible flood, bitter burning, whipping and pursuing all down and around into a pitch-black narrow passage filled with stinking filth. I've become part of what is pushing its path there – *that* was where the nourishment was bound for all the years, after the host and I had done with it, a suffocating putrefaction and unbearable effusions.

Jonah was spewed by the whale.

But I – the term for it, I believe – was shat out.

From that cess I've been ejected into what was only a more spacious one, round, hard-surfaced, my segments have never touched against anything like it, in my moist-padded soft home space, and I am tossed along with more and many, many kinds of rottenness, objects, sections of which I sense from my own completeness must be dismembered from organic wholes that one such as myself, who has never before known the outside, only the insides of existence, cannot name. Battered through this conduit by these forms, all ghastly, lifeless, I think I must somehow die among them – I have the knowledge how to grow but not how to die if, as it seems, that is necessary. And now! Now! The whole putrid torrent had somewhere it was bound for – it discharges (there is a moment's blinding that must be light) and disperses into a volume of liquid inconceivable in terms of the trickles and even gouts that had fed me. Unfathomable: I am swept up in something heady, frothy, exhilarating; down with something that flows me. And I am clean, clean the whole length of me! Ah to be cleansed of that filth I had never suspected was what the nourishment I shared with my host became when we'd taken our fill of it. Blessed ignorance, all those years I was safe inside . . .

My host. So *he* knew. This's how he planned to get rid of me. Why? What for? This's how he respected our coexistence, after even sharing with me those gouts of agreeable liquid whose happy effects we must have enjoyed together. It ends up, him driving me out mercilessly, hatefully, with every kind of ordure. Deadly.

But I'm adapting to this vastness! Can, at least, for a while, I believe. It's not what I was used to and there's no nourishment of my habitude but I find that my segments, the entire length of me still obeys; I can progress by my normal undulation. Undulating, I'm setting out in an element that also does, I'm setting out for what this powerful liquid vastness is bound for – nature's built into my knowledge that everything has to move somewhere – and maybe there, where this force lands, one of my eggs (we all have a store within us, although we are loners and our fertilisation is a secret) will find a housefly carrier and settle on a scrap of lettuce or a fine piece of meat in a Beefsteak Tartare. Ingestion. The whole process shall begin over again. Come to life.

Dreaming of the Dead

Did you come back last night?

I try to dream you into materialisation but you don't appear. I keep expecting you. Because dream has no place, time. The Empyrean – always liked that as my free-floating definition of Somenowhere – balloon without tether to earth. There is no past no present no future. All is occupied at once. Everyone there is without boundaries of probability.

I don't know why it was a Chinese restaurant – ah, no, the choice is going to come clear later when a particular one of the guests arrives! Guests? Whose invitation is it. Who hosts. Such causation doesn't apply; left behind. Look up and there's Edward, the coin-clear profile of Edward Said that is aware how masculinely beautiful it still exists in photographs, he's turning this way and that to find where the table is that expects him. It's his decision it's this one. He's always known what was meant for him, the placing of himself, by himself, through the path of any obstacles, Christian-Muslim, Palestinian-Cairene, American. He's his own usher, shining a torch of distinctive intellectual light and sensibility to guide him. It's not the place to remember this, here, but if you're the one still living in the flesh wired up by synapses and neurons you recall his wife Mariam told that on his last journey to the hospital he disputed the route taken by the driver.

Edward. He stands a moment, before the embrace of greeting. His familiar way of marking the event of a meeting brought about by the coordination of friends' commitments and lucky happenstance. It's reassuring he's wearing one of the coloured shirts and the flourished design of his tie is confirmed by the ear of a silk handkerchief showing above the breast pocket of the usual elegant jacket. Edward never needed to prove his mental superiority by professorial dowdiness and dandruff. We don't bother with how-are-yous, there's no point in that sort of banality, here. He says why don't we have a drink while we're waiting – he seems to know for whom although I don't (except, for you) any more than I knew he would come to this place hung with fringed paper lanterns. He beckons a waiter who doesn't pretend in customary assertion of dignity against servility that he hasn't noticed. Edward never had to command, I'd often noted that, there is something in those eyes fathomless black with ancient Middle Eastern ancestry, that has no need of demanding words. With the glance back to me, he orders what we've always drunk to being well-met. He apologises with humour 'I don't know how I managed to be late, it's quite an art' though he isn't late because he never was expected, and there can be no explanation I could understand of what could have kept him.

We plunge right away into our customary eager exchange of interpretations of political events, international power-mongering, national religious and secular conflicts, the obsessional scaffolding of human existence on earth, then ready to turn to personal preoccupations, for which, instinctively selected in each friendship, there is a different level of confidences. Before we get to ours, someone else arrives at our table; even I, who have known that face in its changes over many years and in relation to many scenes and circumstances, from treason trials in the country where I am still one of the living, to all-night parties in London, don't recognise his entry. Once standing at this table, the face creased in his British laugh of greeting: it's Anthony Sampson. Who? Because instead of the baggy pants unworthy of tweed jacket, he's wearing an African robe. Not just a dashiki shirt he might have picked up on his times in Africa, and donned for comfortable summer informality of whatever this gathering is, but a robe to the ankles – by the way, it can't be hot in the Chinese restaurant; there's no climate in dream. When he was editor of a black-staffed newspaper in South Africa and belonged, was an intimate of shebeen ghettos, never mind his pink British skin, this preceded the era when African garb became fashionable as a mark of the wearer's non-racism. Sampson had no interest in being fashionable within any convention. He showed no consciousness, now, of his flowing robe. So neither did I; nor did Edward though I suppose they had met in the Elsewhere. Edward rose while Anthony and I hugged, kissed on either cheek, he greeted Edward with recollected – it seemed – admiration and chose a chair, having to arrange the robe out of the way of his shoes, like a skirt.

We took up, three of us now, the interrupted talk of political conflict and scandals, policies and ideologies, corrupt governments, tyrant fundamentalists, homegrown in the Middle East and Eastern Europe, and those created by the hubris of the West. A waiter subserviently intruded with distributed menus but we all ignored him as if it were understood we were waiting for someone. I was waiting for you. Even in that Chinese restaurant though it was never your favourite cuisine.

Whom were we waiting for?

I wonder now, awakened in bed by a heavy cat settling on my feet, but I didn't then, no one asked me so I didn't have to give my answer: you. Edward opened a menu big and leather-bound as a book of world maps. Perhaps this meant he and Anthony knew no one was coming. No one else was available among the dead in their circle. Maybe the too newly dead cannot enter dreams. But no; Anthony was recent, and here he was, if strangely got up in the category of the childhood belief that when you die you grow wings, become angels in the Empyrean.

Suddenly she was there, sitting at the head of the table as if she had been with us all along or because there was no time we hadn't remarked when it was she'd joined us. Susan. Susan Sontag. How to have missed the doorway entrance of that presence always larger-than-life (stupid metaphor to have chosen in the circumstances, but this is a morning-after account) not only in sense of her height and size: a mythical goddess, Athena-Medea statue with that magnificent head of black hair asserting this doubling authority, at once inspiring, menacing, unveiling a sculptor's bold marble features, gouged by commanding eyes.

It seemed there had been greetings. Exclamations of pleasure, embraces and less intimate but just as sincere pressures of hands left animation, everyone talking at once across one another. Susan's deep beautiful voice interrupted itself in an aside to call a waiter by name – well of course, so this is the Chinese restaurant in New York's SoHo she used to take me to! The waiters know her, she's the habituée who judges what's particularly good to order, in fact she countermands with an affectionate gesture of a fine hand the hesitant choices of the others and questions, insists, laughs reprovingly at some of the waiter's suggestions; he surely is aware of what the cooks can't get away with, with her. She does let us decide on what to drink. Susan was never a drinker and this one among her favourite eating places probably doesn't have a cellar of the standard that holds the special French and Italian cultivars for which she makes an exception.

As if, non-smoker, she carries a box of matches, there strikes from her a flame flaring the Israeli-Palestinian situation. The light's turned on Edward, naturally, although this is not a group in which each sees personal identity and its supposed unquestioning loyalty cast by birth, faith, country, race, as the decisive and immutable sum of self. Edward is a Palestinian, he's also in his ethics of human being, a Jew, we know that from his writings, his exposure of the orientalism within us, the invention of the Other that's survived the end of the old-style colonialism into globalisation. If Susan's a Jew, she too has identity beyond that label, hers has been one with Vietnamese, Sarajevans, many others, to make up the sum of self.

They carry all this to the Somenowhere. In the Chinese restaurant, there between us.

Sampson doesn't interject much in that understated rapidity of half-audible upper-class English delivery, yet gives a new twist to what's emerging from the other two eloquently contesting one another from different points of view even on what they agree upon. A journalist who's achieved distinction of complete integrity in venturous success must have begun by being a good listener. And I – my opinions and judgements are way down in the confusion of living, I don't have the perspective the dead must have attained. But the distance with which Edward seems to regard Susan's insistent return to passionate views of opposing legitimacies between Palestinians and Israelis is puzzling. After all his clarity and commitment on that conflict-trampled ground of the earth he's left behind, searching the unambiguous words and taking the actions for a just resolution (on the premise there is one), putting his brilliant mind to it against every hostility, including the last – death: how this lack of response? Lassitude? Is that the peace of the dead that passeth all understanding the public relations spin doctors of religions advertise? The hype by one to counter that other, a gratis supply of virgins? Lassitude. But Edward Said: never an inactive cell in that unique brain.

'What did you leave unfinished?'

The favoured waiter had wheeled to the table a double-deck buffet almost the table's length, displaying a composition of glistening mounds, gardens of bristling greens. Susan with her never-sated search for truth rather than being fobbed off with information, dared to introduce as she turned to the food's array, a subject it perhaps isn't done to raise among the other guests.

She was helping herself with critical concentration, this, no, then that – and some more of that – filling to her satisfaction, aesthetic and anticipatory, the large plates the restaurant earned its reputation by providing.

Edward waited for her to reach this result. 'Everything is unfinished. Finality: that's the mistake. It's the claim of dictatorship. Hegemony. In our turn, always we'll be having to pick up the baggage taking from experience what's good, discarding what's conned us into prizing, if it's destructive.'

Dream has no sequence as we know it, this following that. This over, that beginning. You can be making love with someone unrecognised, picking up coins spilled in the street, giving a speech at a board meeting, pursued naked in a shopping mall, without the necessary displacements of sequence. Whether the guests were serving themselves – the others, Anthony and Edward – and whether they were talking between mouthfuls and those swallows of wine or water which precede what one's going to say at table, I was mistaken in my logic of one still living, that they were continuing their exchange of the responsibilities for 9/11, the Tsunami, famine in Darfur, elections in Iraq, the Ukraine, student riots against youth employment restrictions in Paris, a rape charge in court indicting a member of government in my country: preoccupations of my own living present or recent months, years; naturally all one to them. What was I doing there in Susan's Chinese restaurant, anyway?

It is news they're exchanging of what they're engaged in. Now. Edward's being urged to tell something that at least explains to me his certain distance from Susan's perceptions of the developments (at whatever stage these might have been when she left access to newspapers, television, inside informants) in the Middle East. He's just completed a piano concerto. I can't resist putting in with delight 'For two pianos'. The Said apartment on the Upper West Side in New York had what you'd never expect to walk in on, two grand pianos taking up one of the living rooms. Edward once remarked to me, if affectionately, 'You have the writing but I have the writing and the music.' An amateur pianist of concert performance level, he'd played with an orchestra under the baton of his friend Daniel Barenboim.

Here was his acknowledging smile of having once led me into that exotically furnished living room; maybe a brush of his hand. Touch isn't always felt, in dream. There was a scholar, a politico-philosophical intellect, an enquirer of international morality in the order of the world, a life whose driving motivation was not chosen but placed upon him: Palestinian. An existential destiny, among his worldly others. It's cast in the foundations, the academic chairs, honours endowed in the name. All that. But death's the discarder he didn't mention. Edward Said is a composer. There's also the baggage you do take. Two grand pianos. Among the living, it's Carlos Fuentes who asks if music is not the 'true fig leaf of our shames, the final sublimation – beyond death – of our mortal visibility: body of words'. Is only music 'free of visible ties, the purification and illusions of our bodily misery'?

Edward. A composer. What he always was, should have been; but there was too much demand upon him from the threatening outer world? It's a symphony Edward Said's working on now.

'What's the theme, what are you giving us?' Susan is never afraid to be insistent, her passion for all creation so strong this justifies intrusion.

'I don't have to tell you that the movements of a symphony are in sum just that, a resolution, symphonically.' Edward is paying an aside tribute to her non-performer's love and knowledge of music. 'It's still – what should I say—'

'You hear it, you play it? It's in your fingers?' Susan is relentless in pursuit of the process, from one who's been an eloquent man of words people haven't always wanted to hear.

He lifts his shoulders and considers. Doesn't she know that's the way, equivalent of scribbled phrases, jotted half-sentences, essential single words spoken into a recording gadget, which preceded the books she's written, the books he wrote. The symphony he's – hearing? playing? transposing to the art's hieroglyphics? – it's based on Jewish folk songs and Palestinian laments or chants.

Ours is a choir of enthusiasm. When will the work be completed. How far along realised. 'It's done,' Edward says. Ready. 'For the orchestra,' and spreads palms and forearms wide from elbows pressed at his sides. I read his mind as the dreamer can: just unfortunate Barenboim can't be ready to conduct the work; isn't here yet.

These are people who are accustomed to being engaged by the directions taken by one another, ideas, thought and action. No small table talk. Anthony Sampson takes the opportunity, simply because he hasn't before been able to acknowledge to Susan she shamed the complacent acceptance of suffering as no one else has done. Since Goya!

Susan gives her splendid congratulatory, deprecatory laugh, and in response quotes what confronts TV onlookers 'still in Time, the pictures will not go away: that is the nature of the digital world'. Not long dead, she hasn't quite vacated it: this comes from one of her last looks at the world, the book which Anthony is praising, *Regarding the Pain of Others*.

But that's for the memory museum left behind as if it were the phenomenon that, for a while, the hair of the dead continues to grow. Susan has brought with her the sword of words she has always flashed skilfully in defence of the disarmed. She's taken up the defence of men.

'You!' Edward appreciates what surely will be a new style of feminist foil. We're all laughing anticipation. But Susan Sontag is no Quixote, wearing a barber's basin as the helmet of battledress.

'What has made them powerless to live fully? Never mind Huntington and his clash of civilisations. The clash of the sexes has brought about subjection of the heterosexual male. We women have achieved the last result, surely, as emancipated beings, we wanted? A reversal of roles of oppressor and oppressed, the demeaning of fellow humans. Affirmative action has created a gender elite which behaves as the male one did, high positions for pals just as the men awarded whether the individual was or was not qualified except by what was between the legs.'

Someone – might have been I – said, 'Muslim women – still behind the black veil – men suffer from them.' It's taken as rhetorical.

I'm no match for Susan.

'See them trailing the wives and mothers grandmothers matriarchs aunts sisters along with endless children: that's the power behind the burka. *Their* men – don't forget the possessive – carry the whole female burden through entire male lives, bearing women who know that to come out and fend for yourself means competing economically, politically, psychologically in the reality of the world. The black rag's an iron curtain.'

'And gay men?' Anthony's a known lover of women but his sense of justice is alert and quizzical as anyone's.

Susan looks him over: maybe she's mistaken his obvious heterosexuality, his confidence that he's needed no defence in his relations with females. She's addressing us all.

'When the gay bar closes, it's the lesbians who get the jobs – open to their gender *as women*. Gay men aren't even acceptable for that last resort of traditional male *amour propre*, the army, in many countries. Unfit even to be slaughtered.'

Meanwhile Edward's found his appetite, he's considering this dish, then that, in choice of which promises the subtlety that appeals to him as (oh unworthy comparison I'm making) he might consider between the performance of one musician and another at the piano. As the left hand pronounces a chord and the right hand answers higher. But the discrimination of taste buds' pleasures does not temper his demand, 'What's happened to penis envy?'

Nevertheless, Susan gives him the advice he clearly needs, not duck, the prawns are better, no, no, that chicken concoction is for dull palates.

The waiter is already swaying servilely this way and that with a discreet offer of the dessert menu; some of us have done with the main spread. Maybe we're ready for what I remember comes next in this place which is just as it was, the trolleys of bounty will never empty. Fortune cookies. Sorbet with lychees; mangoes? Perhaps it's the names of tropical fruits that remind us of Anthony's form of dress.

'What are you up to?' It's Edward. 'Whose international corporate anatomy are you dissecting?' As if the African robe must be some kind of journalist surgeon's operating garb. Oracular Edward recalls, 'Who would have foreseen even the most powerful in the world come to fear of running dry – except you, of course, when you wrote your *Seven Sisters* . . . that was . . .' The readers of his book about the oil industry, the writer himself, ignore reference to the memory museum, its temporal documentation. 'Who foresaw it was those oilfields witches' brew that fuels the world which was going to be more pricey than gold, platinum, uranium, yes! Yes! – in terms of military strategy for power, the violent grab for spheres of supply, never mind political influence. Who saw it was going to be guns for oil, blood for oil. *You did!*'

I don't know at what stage the continuing oil crisis exists in the awareness of the Chinese restaurant Empyrean.

Anthony is shrugging and laughing embarrassedly under an accolade. Now – for ever – he's proved prophet but there's only the British tribe's understatement, coming from him. 'Anybody could have known it.'

Susan takes up with her flourish, Edward's imagery. 'Double, double, toil and trouble, the cauldron that received what gushed from earth and seabed? They didn't.'

Edward and Susan enjoy Sampson's modesty, urging him on.

'Well, if the book should – could – might have been somehow . . .' Dismissing bent tilt of head.

Of course, who knows if hindsight's seeing it reprinted, best-selling. There's no use for royalties anyway. No tariff for the Chinese lunch.

Now it's Susan who presses. 'So what're you up to?'

Maybe he's counting that Mandela will arrive soon, so he can add an afterword to his famous biography of the great man.

'Oh it'd be good to see you sometime at the tavern.'

Tavern?

Probably I'm the only one other than Sampson himself who knows that's the South African politically correct term for what used to be black ghetto shebeens (old term second-hand from the Irish).

Susan turns down her beautiful mouth generously shaped for disbelief and looks to Edward. The wells of his gaze send back from depths, reflection of shared intrigue.

Anthony Sampson has some sort of bar.

Did he add 'my place' – that attractive British secretive mumble always half-audible. So that would explain the African dress. And yet make it more of a mystery to us (if, the dreamer, I'm not one of those summoned up, can be included in the dream).

'How long has this place been going?' Susan again.

Where?

Where isn't relevant. There's no site, just as with the Chinese restaurant conjured up by Susan's expectation of her arrival. (Couldn't have been a place of my expectation of you.)

How long?

The African garment isn't merely a comfortable choice for what might have been anticipated as an overheated New York-style restaurant. It is a ritual accoutrement, a professional robe. Anthony Sampson has spent some special kind of attention, since there is no measure by time, in induction as a sangoma.

Sangoma. What. *What* is that.

I know it's what's commonly understood as a 'witch doctor', but that's an imperio-colonialist term neither of Anthony's companions would want to use, particularly not Edward, whose classic work *Orientalism* is certainly still running into many editions as evidence of the avatars of the old power phenomenon in guise under new names.

Sampson's 'place' is a shebeen which was part of his place in Africa that was never vacated by him when he went back to England, as the Chinese restaurant is part of her place, never vacated in Susan's New York. But the shebeen seems put to a different purpose; or rather carries in its transformation what really had existed there already. Sampson's not one in a crowd and huddle that always made itself heard above the music in 'The House of Truth' – ah, that was the name in the Sophiatown 'slum' of the white city, poetic in such claims for its venues. He's not just one of the swallowers of a Big Mama's concoction of beer-brandy-brake fluid, Godknowswhat, listening to, entering the joys, sorrows, moods defiant and despairing, brazenly alive, of men and women who made him a brother there.

He has returned to this, to something of the world, from isolation in the bush of Somenowhere with knowledge to offer instead of, as bar proprietor, free drinks. The knowledge of the traditional healer. He serves the sangoma's diagnoses of and alleviations of the sorrows, defiances and despairs that can't be drowned or danced, sung away together.

'Oh, a shrink!'

Who would have thought Susan, savant of many variations of cultures, could be so amazed. The impact throws back her splendid head in laughter.

At 'Tony's Place', his extraordinary gifts as a journalist elevated to another sphere of inquiry, he guides with the third eye his bar patrons – wait a minute; his patients – to go after what's behind their presented motives of other people, and what's harmful behind the patient's own. He dismisses: doesn't make love potions. Hate potions to sprinkle, deadly, round a rival's house? That's witch doctor magic, not healing. The patrons, beer in hand, talk to him, talk out the inner self. As he reluctantly continues to recount, he says that he observes their body language, he gathers what lies unconfessed between the words. No. He doesn't tell them what to do, dictate a solution to confound, destroy the enemy, he directs them to deal with themselves.

'A psychotherapist! Oh of course, that's it. Dear Anthony!' He's proved psychotherapy was first practised in ancient Africa, like so many Western 'discoveries' claimed by the rest of the world. Susan puts an arm round his shoulders to recognise him as an original.

And aren't they, all three. How shall we do without them? They're drifting away, they're leaving the table, I hear in the archive of my head broken lines from adolescent reading, an example that fits Edward's definition of Western orientalism, some European's version of the work of an ancient Persian poet. It's not the bit about the jug of wine and thou.

> . . . Some we loved, the loveliest and the best . . .
> Have drunk their cup a round or two before
> And one by one crept silently to rest.

Alone in the Chinese restaurant, it comes to me not as exotic romanticism but as the departure of the three guests.

I sat at the table, you didn't turn up, too late.

You will not come. Never.

Beethoven Was One-Sixteenth Black

Beethoven was one-sixteenth black . . .

. . . the presenter of a classical music programme on the radio announces along with the names of musicians who will be heard playing the String Quartets No. 13, op. 130, and No. 16, op. 135.

Does the presenter make the claim as restitution for Beethoven? Presenter's voice and cadence give him away as irremediably white. Is one-sixteenth an unspoken wish for himself?

Once there were blacks wanting to be white.
Now there are whites wanting to be black.
It's the same secret.

Frederick Morris (of course that's not his name, you'll soon catch on I'm writing about myself, a man with the same initials) is an academic who teaches biology and was an activist back in the apartheid time, among other illegal shenanigans an amateur cartoonist of some talent who made posters depicting the regime's leaders as the ghoulish murderers they were and, more boldly, joined groups to paste these on city walls. At the university, new millennium times, he's not one of the academics the student body (a high enrolment robustly black, he approves) singles out as among those particularly reprehensible, in protests against academe as the old white male crowd who inhibit transformation of the university from a white intellectuals' country club to a non-racial institution with a black majority (politically correct-speak). Neither do the students value much the support of whites, like himself, dissident from what's seen as the other, the gowned body. You can't be on somebody else's side. That's the reasoning? History's never over; any more than biology, functioning within every being.

One-sixteenth. The trickle seemed enough to be asserted out of context? What does the distant thread of blood matter in the genesis of a genius. Then there's Pushkin, if you like; his claim is substantial, look at his genuine frizz on the head – not some fashionable faked Afro haloing a white man or woman, but coming, it's said, from Ethiopia.

Perhaps because he's getting older – Morris doesn't know he's still young enough to think fifty-two is old – he reflects occasionally on what was lived in his lifeline before him. He's divorced, a second time; that's a past, as well, if rather immediate. His father was also not a particular success as a family man. Family: the great-grandfather, dead long before the boy was born: there's a handsome man, someone from an old oval-framed photograph, the strong looks not passed on. There are stories about this forefather, probably related at family gatherings but hardly listened to by a boy impatient to leave the grown-ups' table. Anecdotes not in the history book obliged to be learned by rote. What might call upon amused recognition to be adventures, circumstances taken head-on, good times enjoyed out of what others would submit to as bad times, characters – 'they don't make them like that any more' – as enemies up to no good, or joined forces with as real mates. No history-book events: tales of going about your own affairs within history's fall-out. He was some sort of frontiersman, not in the colonial military but in the fortune-hunters' motley.

A descendant in the male line, Frederick Morris bears his surname, of course. Walter Benjamin Morris apparently was always called Ben, perhaps because he was the Benjamin indeed of the brood of brothers who did not, like him, emigrate to Africa. No one seems to know why he did; just an adventurer, or maybe the ambition to be rich which didn't appear to be achievable anywhere other than a beckoning Elsewhere. He might have chosen the Yukon. At home in London he was in line to inherit the Hampstead delicatessen shop, see it full of cold cuts and pickles, he was managing for another one of the fathers in the family line, name lost. He was married for only a year when he left. Must have convinced his young bride that their future lay in his going off to prospect for the newly discovered diamonds in a far place called Kimberley, from where he would promptly return rich. As a kind of farewell surety for their love, he left inside her their son to be born.

Frederick surprises his mother by asking if she kept the old attaché case – a battered black bag, actually – where once his father had told him there was stuff about the family they should go through some time; both had forgotten this rendezvous, his father had died before that time came. He did not have much expectation that she still kept the case somewhere, she had moved from what had been the home of marriage and disposed of possessions for which there was no room, no place in her life in a garden complex of elegant contemporary-design cottages. There were some things in a communal storeroom tenants had use of. There he found the bag and squatting among the detritus of other people's pasts he blew away the silverfish moths from letters and scrap jottings, copied the facts recorded above. There are also photographs, mounted on board, too tough for whatever serves silverfish as jaws, which he took with him, didn't think his mother would be sufficiently interested in for him to inform her. There is one portrait in an elaborate frame.

The great-grandfather has the same stance in all the photographs whether he is alone beside a photographer's studio palm or among piles of magical dirt, the sieves that would sift from the earth the rough stones that were diamonds within their primitive forms, the expressionless blacks and half-coloured men leaning on spades. Prospectors from London and Paris and Berlin – anywhere where there are no diamonds – did not themselves race to stake their claims when the starter's gun went off, the hired men who belonged on the land they ran over were swifter than any white foreigner, they staked the foreigners' claims and wielded the picks and spades in the open-cast mining concessions these marked. Even when Ben Morris is photographed sitting in a makeshift overcrowded bar his body, neck tendons, head are upright as if he were standing so immovably confident – of what? (Jottings reveal that he unearthed only small stuff. Negligible carats.) Of virility. That's unmistakable, it's untouched by the fickleness of fortune. Others in the picture have become slumped and shabbied by poor luck. The aura of sexual virility in the composure, the dark, bright, on-the-lookout inviting eyes: a call to the other sex as well as elusive diamonds. Women must have heard, read him the way males didn't, weren't meant to. Dates on the scraps of paper made delicately lacy by insects show that he didn't return promptly, he prospected with obstinate faith in his quest, in himself, for five years.

He didn't go home to London, the young wife, he saw the son only once on a single visit when he impregnated the young wife and left her again. He did not make his fortune; but he must have gained some slowly accumulated profit from the small stones the black men dug for him from their earth, because after five years it appears he went back to London and used his acquired knowledge of the rough stones to establish himself in the gem business, with connections in Amsterdam.

The great-grandfather never returned to Africa. Frederick's mother can at least confirm this, since her son is interested. The later members of the old man's family – his fertility produced more sons, from one of whom Frederick is descended – came for other reasons, as doctors and lawyers, businessmen, conmen and entertainers, to a level of society created from profit of the hired fast-runners' unearthing of diamonds and gold for those who had come from beyond the seas, another kind of elsewhere.

And that's another story. You're not responsible for your ancestry, are you.

But if that's so, why have you marched under banned slogans, got yourself beaten up by the police, arrested a couple of times; plastered walls with subversive posters. That's also the past. The past is valid only in relation to whether the present recognises it.

How did that handsome man with the beckoning gaze, the characteristic slight flare of the nostrils as if picking up some tempting scent (in every photograph), the strong beringed hands (never touched a spade) splayed on tight-trousered thighs, live without his pretty London bedmate all the nights of prospecting? And the Sunday mornings when you wake, alone, and don't have to get up and get out to educate the students in the biological facts of life behind their condomed cavortings – even a diamond prospector must have lain a while longer in his camp bed, Sundays, known those surges of desire, and no woman to turn to. Five years. Impossible that a healthy male, as so evidently this one, went five years without making love except for the brief call on the conjugal bed. Never mind the physical implication; how sad. But of course it wasn't so. He obviously didn't have to write and confess to his young wife that he was having an affair – this is the past, not the sophisticated protocol of suburban sexual freedom – it's unimaginably makeshift, rough as the diamonds. There were those black girls who came to pick up prospectors' clothes for washing (two in the background of a photograph where, bare-chested, the man has fists up, bunched in a mock fight with a swinging-bellied mate at the diggings) and the half-black girls (two coffee one milk the description at the time) in confusion of a bar-tent caught smiling, passing him carrying high their trays of glasses. Did he have many of these girls over those years of deprived nights and days? Or was there maybe a special one, several special ones, there are no crude circumstances, Frederick himself has known, when there's not a possibility of tenderness coming uninvited to the straightforward need for a fuck. And the girls. What happened to the girls if in male urgencies there was conception? The foreigners come to find diamonds came and went, their real lives with women were Elsewhere, intact far away. What happened? Are there children's children of those conceptions on the side engendered by a handsome prospector who went home to his wife and sons and the gem business in London and Amsterdam – couldn't they be living where he propagated their predecessors?

Frederick knows as everyone in a country of many races does that from such incidents far back there survives proof in the appropriation, here and there, of the name that was all the progenitor left behind him, adopted without his knowledge or consent out of – sentiment, resentment, something owed? More historical fall-out. It was not in mind for a while, like the rendezvous with the stuff in the black bag, forgotten with his father. There was a period of renewed disturbances at the university, destruction of equipment within the buildings behind their neo-classical columns; not in the Department of Biology, fortunately.

The portrait of his great-grandfather in its oval frame under convex glass that had survived unbroken for so long stayed propped up where the desk moved to his new apartment was placed when he and his ex-wife divided possessions. Photographs give out less meaning than painted portraits. Open less contemplation. But *he* is there, he is – a statement.

One-sixteenth black.

In the telephone directory for what is now a city where the diamonds were first dug, are there any listings of the name Morris? Of course there will be, it's not uncommon and so has no relevance.

As if he has requested her to reserve cinema tickets with his credit card he asks his secretary to see if she can get hold of a telephone directory for a particular region. There are Morrises and Morrisons. In his apartment he calls up the name on the internet one late night, alone. There's a Morris who is a theatre director now living in Los Angeles and a Morris a champion bridge player in Cape Town. No one of that name in Kimberley worthy of being noted in this infallible source.

Now and then he and black survivors of the street marches of blacks and whites in the past get together for a drink. 'Survivors' because some of the black comrades (comrades because that form of address hadn't been exclusive to the communists among them) had moved on to high circles in cabinet posts and boardrooms. The talk turned to reform of the education system and student action to bring it about. Except for Frederick, in their shared seventies and eighties few of this group of survivors had the chance of a university education. They're not inhibited to be critical of the new regime their kind brought about or of responses to its promises unfulfilled. 'Trashing the campus isn't going to scrap tuition fees for our kids too poor to pay. Yelling freedom songs, toyi-toying at the Principal's door isn't going to reach the Minister of Education's big ears. Man! Aren't there other tactics now? They're supposed to be intelligent, getting educated, not so, and all they can think of is use what we had, throw stones, trash the facilities – but the buildings and the libraries and laboratories whatnot are *theirs* now, not whitey's only – they're rubbishing what we fought for, *for* them.'

Someone asks, your department OK, no damage?

Another punctuates with a laugh. 'They wouldn't touch you, no way.'

Frederick doesn't know whether to put the company right, the students don't know and if they do don't care about his actions in the past, why should they, they don't know who he *was*, the modest claim to be addressed as comrade. But that would bring another whole debate, one focused on himself.

When he got home rather late he was caught under another focus, seemed that of the eyes of the grandfatherly portrait. Or was it the mixture, first beer then whisky, unaccustomedly downed.

* * *

The Easter vacation is freedom from both work and the family kind of obligation it brought while there was marriage. Frederick did have children with the second wife but it was not his turn, in the legal conditions of access, to have the boy and girl with him for this school holiday. There were invitations from university colleagues and an attractive Italian woman he'd taken to dinner and a film recently, but he said he was going away for a break. The coast? The mountains? Kimberley.

What on earth would anyone take a break there for. If they asked, he offered, see the Big Hole, and if they didn't remember what that was he'd have reminded it was the great gouged-out mouth of the diamond pipe formation.

He had never been there and knew no one. No one, that was the point, the negative. The man whose eyes, whose energy of form remain open to you under glass from the generations since he lived five years here, staked his claim. One-sixteenth. There certainly are men and women, children related thicker than that in his descendant's bloodstream. The telephone directory didn't give much clue to where the cousins, collaterals, might be found living on the territory of diamonds; assuming the addresses given with the numbers are white suburban rather than indicating areas designated under the old segregation which everywhere still bear the kind of euphemistic flowery names that disguised them and where most black and colour-mixed people, around the cities, still live. And that assumption? An old colour/class one that the level of people from whom came the girls great-grandpapa used must still be out on the periphery in the new society? Why shouldn't 'Morris, Walter J.S.' of 'Golf Course Place' be a shades-of-black who had become a big businessman owning a house where he was forbidden before and playing the game at a club he was once barred from?

Scratch a white man, Frederick Morris, and find trace of the serum of induced superiority; history never over. But while he took a good look at himself, pragmatic reasoning set him leaving the chain hotel whose atmosphere confirmed the sense of anonymity of his presence and taking roads to what were the old townships of segregation. A public holiday, so the streets, some tarred and guttered, some unsurfaced dirt with puddles floating beer cans and plastic, were cheerful racetracks of cars, taxis and buses, avoiding skittering children and men and women taking their right and time to cross where they pleased.

No one took much notice of him. His car, on an academic's salary, was neither a newer model nor a more costly make than many of those alongside, and like them being ousted from lane to lane by the occasional Mercedes with darkened windows whose owner surely should have moved by now to somesuch Golf Course Place. And as a man who went climbing at weekends and swam in the university pool early every morning since the divorce, he was sun-pigmented, not much lighter than some of the men who faced him a moment, in passing, on the streets where he walked a while as if he had a destination.

Schools were closed for the holidays, as they were for his children; he found himself at a playground. The boys were clambering the structure of the slide instead of taking the ladder, and shouting triumph as they reached the top ahead of conventional users, one lost his toe-hold and fell, howling, while the others laughed. But who could say who could have been this one or that one, give or take a shade, his boy; there's simply the resemblance all boys have in their grimaces of emotion, boastful feats, agile bodies. The girls on the swings clutching younger siblings, even babies; most of them pretty but aren't all girls of the age of his daughter, pretty, though one couldn't imagine her being entrusted with a baby the way the mothers sitting by placidly allowed this. The mothers. The lucky ones (favoured by prospectors?) warm honey-coloured, the others dingy between black and white, as if determined by an under-exposed photograph. Genes the developing agent. Which of these could be a Morris, a long-descended sister-cousin, whatever, alive, we're together here in the present. Could you give me a strand of your hair (his own is lank and straight but that proves nothing after the Caucasian blood mixtures of so many following progenitors) to be matched with my toenail cutting or a shred of my skin in DNA tests. Imagine the reaction when I handed in these to the laboratories at the university. Faculty laughter to cover embarrassment, curiosity. Fred behaving oddly nowadays.

He ate a *boerewors* roll at a street barrow, asking for it in the language, Afrikaans, that was being spoken all around him. Their mother tongue, the girls who visited the old man spoke (not old then, no, all the vital juices flowing, showing); did he pick it up from them and promptly forget it in London and Amsterdam as he did them, never came back to Africa. He, the descendant, hung on in the township until late afternoon, hardly knowing the object of lingering, or leaving. Then there were bars filling up behind men talking at the entrances against kwaito music. He made his way into one and took a bar stool warm from the backside of the man who swivelled off it. After a beer the voices and laughter, the beat of the music made him feel strangely relaxed on this venture of his he didn't try to explain to himself that began before the convex glass of the oval-framed photograph. When his neighbour, whose elbow rose and fell in dramatic gestures to accompany a laughing bellowing argument, jolted and spilled the foam of the second beer, the interloper grinned, gave assurances of no offence taken and was drawn into friendly banter with the neighbour and his pals. The argument was about the referee's decision in a soccer game; he'd played when he was a student and could contribute a generalised opinion of the abilities, or lack of, among referees. In the pause when the others called for another round, including him without question, he was able to ask (it was suddenly remembered) did anyone know a Morris family living around? There were self-questioning raised foreheads, they looked to one another: one moved his head slowly side to side, down over the dregs in his glass; drew up from it, when I was a kid, another kid . . . his people moved to another section, they used to live here by the church.

Alternative townships were suggested. Might be people with that name there. So did he know them from somewhere? Wha'd'you want them for?

It came quite naturally. They're family we've lost touch with.

Oh that's how it is people go all over, you never hear what's with them, these days, it's let's try this place let's try that and you never know they's alive or dead, my brothers gone off to Cape Town they don't know who they are any more . . . so where you from?

From the science faculty of the university with the classical columns, the progeny of men and women in the professions, generations of privilege that have made them whatever it is they are. They don't know what they might have been.

Names, unrecorded on birth certificates – if there were any such for the issue of foreign prospectors' passing sexual relief – get lost, don't exist, maybe abandoned as worthless. These bar-room companions buddies comrades, could any one of them be men who should have my family name included in theirs?

So where am I from.

What was it all about.

Dubious. What kind of claim do you *need*? The standard of privilege changes with each regime. Isn't it a try at privilege. Yes? One up towards the ruling class whatever it may happen to be. One-sixteenth. A cousin how many times removed from the projection of your own male needs on to the handsome young buck preserved under glass. So what's happened to the ideal of the Struggle (the capitalised generic of something else that's never over, never mind history-book victories) for recognition, beginning in the self, that our kind, humankind, doesn't need any distinctions of blood percentage tincture. That fucked things up enough in the past. Once there were blacks, poor devils, wanting to claim white. Now there's a white, poor devil, wanting to claim black. It's the same secret.

His colleagues in the faculty coffee room at the university exchange Easter holiday pleasures, mountains climbed, animals in a game reserve, the theatre, concerts – and one wryly confessing: trying to catch up with reading for the planning of a new course, sustained by warm beer consumed in the sun.

'Oh and how was the Big Hole?'

'Deep.'

Everyone laughs at witty deadpan brevity.

Stories Since 2007

Parking Tax

Round the corner from the bank, a roofless two-sided enclosure on the pavement by sections usefully taken from a cardboard packing case bears a home-drawn sign: Shoe Soles. Within the demarcation a man of indeterminate age has his awl, his rags and pot of treacle-black potion, his small stack of thick plastic material curling up at the edges as if already treading the streets.

Between the supermarket and the intersection where taxi-buses swerve to answer the finger language of people signalling where they want to go, the client of a woman who braids hair with amplifying swathes of other people's hair sits on an upturned fruit box filched from supermarket trash.

At the patch of ground somehow overlooked when the freeway rose at the intersection in the area where panel-beating workshops are the beauty salons for luxury cars, a painted shed has been provided and there are set out oranges, peanuts, cigarettes, jars of Vaseline, packets of condoms and mobile phone batteries.

In the entrance to the enclave between the pharmacy and the liquor store, where there is an ATM dispensing cash, someone has been granted shelter to set up her one-woman craft accommodated on her ample lap. She sits threading necklaces and beading badges, safety-pin backed, which display the red twist emblem of support for people living with HIV Aids.

These are enterprises of the Informal Sector, now a category in the new theory of the economic structure of the country, which declares that the price of the privilege of recognition is a share of the responsibility in reducing unemployment. The unemployed must rouse – not arise, in protest against their condition – and do something for themselves. The shoe repairer's premises are a Small Business venture as defined within this initiative. The bank belongs to an international consortium which gives modest grants, get-started cash, to encourage such entrepreneurs. He was supplied with his awl, glue and plastic material. The hair artist, with a sum to purchase, as she must know where, from people who grow their hair as a crop. The man in his shed, its array spread on the ground before it, is aware from his own streetwise experience as a customer, what will sell and has had a one-off provision to begin his stock.

The men and women who sleep in the toilet block at the park nearby meant for people who walk their dogs and gays who cruise there, have made it disgustingly unusable, can't be regarded as part of the Informal Sector. Many are illegal immigrants, refugees from the civil wars in neighbouring countries, they're just an inflation of unemployment figures, uncounted, rivals for any work to be come upon.

There are other initiatives that if they may be minimally self-supporting don't seem to qualify for the Informal Sector standard. There's the man who attempts to sell greeting cards mostly for occasions already outdated, Christmas, Valentine's Day, from a tray suspended round his neck. Perhaps people might buy them and paste an Easter message over the greetings? The cards may be charity dumping from the stationer's. Anyway, he is at least in the class of economic activity above the one who has no set stand but hawks brooms made of dried grass-stalks up and down the street.

Beggars have no status whatsoever.

Responsibility, when you operate among others practising the same initiative, implies leadership if you mean to qualify for the collective challenge of the Sector's recognition; that first indication that you're going to be let in to the Formal Economy. Some time. But a leader must have an organisation, and here, coming up with a self-invented occupation, what high-ups call initiative, is the personal property of each one alone; to share it is to risk having it seized away from you. In place of leadership there can only be domination. And that's a matter of discovering something which is inside you. Politicians have it, or they couldn't win elections and recognise, at last, whether for their own purposes or something better, an Informal Sector.

The man who found the something in himself was one of those who wave in a car's path to a vacant parking space, arms wing-wide, and then perform a repertoire of gestures, warnings, encouragements to the driver successfully to occupy it. Some driver-clients dub the process Parking Tax along with all the other taxes of the Formal Sector they occupy. It's surely some sort of recognition above the patronage of a tip, when they give the Parking Tax man some coins as they drive away.

He is a little older and a little less black than other Parking Tax collectors fulfilling their inventive responsibilities. He probably came from a region of the country where the aboriginal inhabitants, wiped out by darker peoples descended upon them from the west of the African continent, and whites from Europe, have left ancient traces in the brew of DNA. The shopping street is in an old suburb, prosperous, not wealthy; not a mall in the suburbs where blacks of the new Formal Sector live in class solidarity with their white equals. The residents of the old suburb, some young, speak of their shopping street as the village.

He's a rather small man with limbs and body appearing to be strung taut on wire rather than bone. His voice and movements spark, as that of men of his morphology often do for the lack of the stodgy physical superiority of others, whether Parking Tax brothers or members of the bank's board. His manner of speaking, a personal mixture of the many languages of which one is his mother tongue, makes his communication easy, better than that of some others on the street. He's never bothered to take part in the angry rivalry between his fellow Parking Tax collectors for the right to command this or that vehicle into this or that space, although a youngster among them would always know to step back if the two hailed at the same time the hesitancy of a driver seeking a bay. It was he who decided that this random situation was nonsense, no good to anyone. The others accepted his capability instinctively, although not proven in any way. It was he who organised them; each man to have his own pitch, reserved in this block or that, so many bays this side or that. Brothers, not street people.

There was some grumbling among themselves after the allocation had been made mutually, but no violence the way things used to be settled. If there was resentment against his taking for himself the pitch he did, no one would challenge him. Not just because of authority; he was so popular.

He chose what he saw had a number of advantages. The pitch begins at a corner, so there are vehicles coming both from the shopping street and from the connecting one. It is close to the supermarket – better than directly in front, where there is a loading space kept clear for delivery trucks and vans. His pitch is before the church, and not only do the Sunday devout come from the service with a conscience towards the less fortunate than themselves that makes them generous, the departing entourages of wedding ceremonies are even more so. The minister allows certain privileges to one of the children of the Lord, not a member of the congregation, who watches over their material possessions – their cars.

The man has a wife along with him at his pitch. She sits not on a fruit box but a small sturdy crate from the liquor store. There is no purpose in her being there. She doesn't thread beads, sell cigarettes or plait hair, somehow incapacitated not by illness but by the natural haze of being at one level or another, drunk. No one objects to her presence, it is part of the privilege he took to himself. She has a kind of clientele of her own for her chaffing and laughter, mostly the homeless of the park, when her level is mild, which he tolerates, the Parking Tax brothers jeer at only privately, and even the white shoppers ignore as at a dinner party one didn't embarrass a man whose wife was a known lush. The church's compassion allows her, an invalid of sorts, to use the church lavatory in its grounds and her husband to draw water at the garden tap, which permission he has extended for himself to pull off his shirt and take a wash in hot weather. When her level is high and she sags from her seat, someone, usually a woman among her cronies, will support her a short way up the pavement where the grass has overgrown the paving, and she collapses there as if she's put to bed. He takes no part. On the other hand, he isn't seen to reproach her, beat her up. Simply keeps his busy professional front, as any corporate official must in the event of a problem with a woman. She lies, passing people taking suitable avoidance round her, until sobered enough to get herself up, smiling, and totter back to her crate.

Other Parking Tax men either pocket their dues silently or have obeisant gestures to go with thanks. He takes the right of starting up an exchange, based on his observation and memory of his clients. He'd given them his name (or rather a version of it, Lucas, because his African name was too complex) and while accepting they wouldn't be likely to offer theirs, addresses them personally the way he assesses them. An elderly white man will be greeted as 'Oupa' while he locks his car doors behind him – 'Old Papa' in one of the whites' languages – and a distinguished-looking woman with the widow's companion, groomed dog on a lead, is met with the feminine equivalent, 'Hi Ouma, so how's it going today?' Young white men are flattered with male bondage in tributes to their prowess: 'Cool, my man! Sharp! You look you dressed for a *big* night this weekend.' Every young woman, black or white, is indiscriminately 'Sweetie' – a driver as she hits the kerb or is nervous about reversing: 'No sweat, Sweetie, I'm looking out for you.' His evident sense of self makes any offence taken, outdated. The familiarity transposes what might have seemed charitable tolerance on these individuals' part, to an obligation of recognition; equality, even of gender as well as race, simply assuming colloquial intimacy of usage in mutual possession.

He's on particularly good terms – a calling-out exchange – with a young couple who happen to be white, like most of the shoppers. Of course he doesn't know that the husband is a junior partner in an advertising agency, TV and print media, and the wife a lawyer in a legal aid centre for people who can't afford paid representation in the courts, but he recognises the up-and-coming. Their car regularly bypasses other vacant bays to occupy one of their man's, under his surveillance, as he would expect. Later he uplifts a palm coaxing encouragement as he or she approaches with a burden of shopping achieved, and saunters over his territory to help load the stuff, questioning, commiserating along with them the robbery cost of everything.

While talking one Saturday he was looking at the young woman's shoes, gave the calculated observation: 'Same size as hers', jerked his head back to his wife and as if at a command, she waved to the couple. 'Haven't you got a pair for her you don't like to wear?' As naturally, in the winter: 'She ought to have a better coat – you can see. Maybe you can spare.' If the suggestion was forgotten or overlooked (he never accepted the offence that it was ignored), he gave a reminder: 'What happened to the shoes [coat, sweater] you had for her?'

The wife has never been seen wearing any of these items that were duly supplied. The young lawyer was too respectful of the privacy everyone was entitled to, to enquire: 'What happened to . . .' Everyone's lives are unpredictable. The predicaments and unheard-of resorts turned to, as related to her at her legal aid desk. How unexpected (he lets her lie drunk on the grass) that now, a Saturday morning, the wife has her lap spread and he's sitting there locked by her crossed arms, her drinking coterie prancing applause around them. The young couple come shopping are drawn in. Their man struggles up and puts an arm on the shoulder of each, sways them into laughter at him, with them: it's not that they're one with the people, the people are one with them.

They don't have to remark upon it to one another, that would be unconscious admittance of what they were before: bleeding heart syndrome, believing they didn't have any class, let alone race feelings of superiority. Now this freedom of spirit is coming in its validity, granted, from the most unlikely quarter, on the other side of the divides. Here was a man, Lucas, organising people who have no recognised place, told they're Informal, a definition without function – except, of course, expected to create – whatever – for themselves. In his self-appointed domain of the shopping street, there is – something? – in him that brings coherence.

'Without property, the principle of ownership?' The lawyer knows the sources of the economy. 'But isn't that just it: they don't have the incentives we have' – she tries again.

'Don't have the access.' That's her advertising man's response.

To herself, unspoken: They have found a way, and we haven't.

She sometimes bumped into him along the shops – literally, he would be in what was bantering argument or his tutoring advice with a few of his Parking Tax men in the middle of the pavement, assumed that people would step round them in recognition of their responsibility for the order of the street. He might follow beside her into the supermarket or the liquor store as if he also just happened to be shopping, talking about the new extended shopping hours, row over liquor on sale on Sundays, the church kicking up a fuss, local gossip (did she hear, that old man with the sports car – yes – the red one – bashed into a police patrol car) and loading her shopping cart for her, pushing it before her to her car that was his charge. In his chatter there were threads of reasoning and disciplined logic that made her think – no, shamed her that he had no real occupation to draw on what were probably his capabilities and provide remuneration earned, not handouts in small change.

Over Christmas he was seen helping out at the liquor store, on the pavement loading boxes of party supplies into delivery vans. When they exchanged the usual greeting, she called, congratulatory, 'You're working here now?' He grinned vociferously. After New Year he was back outside the church, where one of the residents of the park toilets had been standing in for him. He turned away his head as at an intrusion when she remarked, 'You're not at the bottle store?' (Local jargon on the shopping street.)

It seemed he forgave her, and closed the subject. 'They don't know how to treat people.'

She knew what he meant. He's not the proprietor's 'boy'. When she dashed to pick up food at the shops as an unwelcome distraction from her day's absorbed involvement in gaining redress for people whose ignorance of rights complicated their need, she was conscious – again, he really ought to have some proper employment. All the prevarication of authorities, and the frightened sycophantic obfuscation of victims she met with at Legal Aid – in this street man there's at last found something else; the only principle you can live by, now, another kind of respect. The something – can't define, within his presumption, crudity, that she can trust. He lets his woman lie drunk on the pavement. As if he'd just step over her. But drink is her only occupation; he's got nothing else to offer her but tolerance, her only freedom, to do what she's resorted to. He accepts people's laughter at this; it's his share of the informal situation. That's how one must recognise it.

Your Parking Tax pet, the young husband teases, over her concern. A colleague of his own trips from the Olympic level of drinking tolerated among the publicity fraternity, goes into rehab, loses his job and, incidentally, his wife.

One Saturday there is no encouraging beckon when she approaches a church bay and no saunter to help load the contents of her week's provisions into the car. The man's preoccupied with some other of his regular shoppers to whom he's pointing out the problem of a flat tyre leaning their station wagon against the kerb.

Meanwhile a tenant of the toilets in the park belays her insistently, desolately, old, unshaven, dirty in worn cast-offs those people beg from the church. He doesn't ask for money: 'Please, please just buy me tin of sardines. Please.' He sticks a forefinger down a toothless mouth. 'Just one tin. Sardines.' She has tuna in her trolley load. She's fumbling in a carrier bag when *he* breaks away from his other regular clientele and thrusts between her and the imploring man. Ignoring her, he's shouting at the bowed head, words are blows in a language she doesn't know. Battered to less than a man, the other cringes, presses arms to his body, bends with knees locked, disowning himself. The ruthless debasement sets a shudder through her, the tin she's found drops from her hand. He, more than a man, an elect, among the rulers of the world, swiftly bends to retrieve the tin and toss it back to the trolley.

'He's hungry, what are you doing!'

'Hungry? – don't give him anything. Nothing. He doesn't eat it, he takes it to the park and sells it to get money to buy drink.' A hand of dismissal gestured not as at anyone worth threatening, but chasing a dog out of the way. He takes a deep chest-raising breath, snorts to clear his head of the interruption, and smiles. He's there to protect her from exploitation by the Informal Sector.

In her car driving away she sees she's got it all wrong – there's no new way. Nothing's changed. He's fitting himself for the Formal Sector. Some day.

Second Coming

Christians await the return that will raise the dead from the grave as He was raised. They rehearse this each Easter. Kafka records in his diaries 'On Friday evening two angels accompany each pious man from the synagogue to his home; the master of the house stands while he greets them in the dining room.' Every Friday night Seder an extra place is laid at table. Maybe the one the Jews are expecting is not an angel but the Messiah, the lost son. Muslims don't anticipate the final physical presence of the Prophet Mohammed, they bless his name as if he were always among them.

He was clothed like any other man in the rough denim jeans that were the garb of men of any age in the era of the twenty-first millennium. No robes provided. And the return to the mortal state meant that the weals of nail-driven wounds came back, were there scarred under the shirt, and on the feet and hands. It's of no account where he arrived. Apparently no one was about to claim a vision, now that there was a reality. Many over centuries had been sanctified for declaring a manifestation of him or his mother, celebrated in more recent times graphically, digitally, by all the successive technological means of disseminating announcement of miracles, or were exposed as fraudulent hysterical girls and adults in a dubious mental condition of religious exaltation. The sandals that he wore in the carpenter's shop were the same as, himself ageless, he set out in now, the same as any young man might have been wearing if there were to have been any young men around. But no disciples appeared. No Romans manifest in their mutation as riot police with AK-47s, out to deal with suspicious immigrants of rebel reputation.

His sandalled feet took him along the ways he had to go, some of which had a surface hard and blue-black glinting, exploded, strange to the soles, and others receiving them sinking into familiar sand, the feel of the desert land come to be known as Holy, because of him. There were hulks of what must be some kind of chariot, unlike the ones the Romans used, but anyway too buckled and contorted to form a coherent image; a mass of sword-sharp glass shards, peeling colours, bent plates like some form of shielding, and hubs that must have held wheels as such objects have served since the power of the rolling circle was discovered, these in rounds of a black substance that had apparently disintegrated viscid, and set. He looked to someone to be regarding this – a consequence of *what* – as he did. But he was alone.

He found himself entering a city, recognisable as one because of the layout for human concourse that he had known, has existed in some design or another, in one era back behind another. Streets. Jerusalem. Streets; his way was barred by tumbles of rubble risen against great blocks of stone and brick conglomerates thrust about together. Lifted to his eyes he followed constructions that must have been the containments of this time he had come to in fulfilment of faith: fallen, half-fallen under some sort of quake (what evil power has challenged his Father's Creation). As once there had been a flood on earth. Disaster. Cosmic; or some unthinkable disintegration, brought about by human acts, attrition beyond the wars they had sinned against their own kind?

The Romans had constructions, palaces, barracks, great walls, temples of the gods, tall premises of power. Here were premises evidently once so aspiring as to be lost in the sky. Fallen into the shaft of such a ruin, its empty stagger to heaven, there was something part never-covered grave pit, part ordure heap. A confusion cast without respect. Scraps of unrecognisable coded script: Gordon's Dry, Dom Perignon: needles carrying no thread but pointing from small containers reduced to shapes of glass dust, from which, picked up, there is sensed a faint trace of something that was there, transporting essence, an agent of ecstasy not of the transports of the Faith. Where are the people to whom all this belongs, on whose possessions this disrespect was performed?

There are towers and steeples toppled, cast from what were his homes, each one his Father's house. The cross on which his First Coming ended in agony – yes, reproduced in dirt-smeared trinket gold, in rusted iron, and the sacrilege of the cruciform hideously distorted, the arms twisted, wrenched at the ends into an emblem of atrocities. Wherever they were, the people who awaited him, what desecrated heritage had they left as the detritus of their years?

Someone must have survived to bear witness. Surely he would come upon some of his Father's flock, hidden in the countryside.

There was the beginning of open spaces near the streets he had quit. No ruins but fallen icons flung supine or poking up, 7TH HOLE, 18TH HOLE; dead bushes, roots in the air, the condition of growth reversed, from under which he took a hard small object, a dimpled ball, it fits in his cupped palm on the scars. Dead trees, as beggar figures arrested against the line of sky, but then the fragile intricacy of beak-woven bird nests suggests there will be calls to be heard although there are no children playing whom he can tenderly summon.

The wind brings no cry, only stirs rasping branches in a movement he's alert to as that of a bird; no bird hiding from him. But on a measured stretch of open land there are what must be gigantic birds of inconceivable size, outside his Father's Creation, without bones, flesh and feathers, lying in the charred deformation of some self-consuming violent end, fires of hell. The broken skeletons of a kind of throne they evidently had inside them in place of the vital organs of birds and beasts lie within and spewed about them.

On and on. Where are fields of grain, terrace of vines?

The straps of the sandals curl worn, dragging between the toes, abrading the skin. No matter. There must be an encounter soon with the people of God who have waited so long. Everywhere animal and human bones – the feet stop, of their own volition, at the sight – the relics of life are indistinguishable except for the rise of hope that is faith, for here is a jaw that could only belong to one who could speak, and the wonder of a skull so magnificent it must testify to the continual resumption of life in that of a pachyderm mutated through the millennia, survived until – what? What catastrophe?

O Lord have you forsaken them? What have your people done to the beautiful earthly abode you gave them, that you have forsaken them?

Where are they, his Father's people to whom He has sent his son, come at last to save from the death sentence of Time itself; to save them from themselves? Always there have been some survivors. Receiving manna in the form of a plague of locusts become sustenance, consumed as food. Men, women, children, animals somehow clinging to a rock on Ararat. The Flood. Water: yes, he must direct himself to the waters, the sea, fishermen use an element of his Father's Creation other than earth, from which to take and sustain life. In this Coming as again a mortal, the paths he makes for himself, the mountain pass he climbs and descends are of a long duration, maybe more than two risings and fallings of the light and day ordained in the Beginning. Emptiness. Still no one, nothing walking, grazing, crawling, flying, scuttling from his footsteps, no one hearing his weary intake and release of breath, no face to meet with the sweat bleeding down his brow, the scars wakening under the sweat-soaked shirt. His thick-tongued thirst. The pools where he stumbled to quench it are so putrid they hold no reflected image of what bent to them and the swallows he took were vomited in rejection from his body. The pains the flesh is heir to that he took on for himself with human existence, the first Coming.

And here they are, the waters. The sea spread in peace down there. Certainly soon, the scent of it to pass a cool tongue over the sweat. The seas of the world, of Creation. The sandals slipped and slid taking him to fisherfolk, that steadfast flock who master the wild elements, land, wind and water as everyday circumstance; they would be there for him as they had been since he was among them and in what has been measured while awaiting him. Whatever had befallen, they would be there to begin again, with life netted from the sea.

There are no huts, no boats, no spread nets. Scatters and heaps of what once were these, half-buried by the smoothing hands of sand dunes, half-fumbled through by water along with bones of rotted men, sea creatures on a piled tideline.

He wades in, the sandals which have brought him so far from so long ago are hooked off his feet by the vast decay that clutches at him, thrusts at him. Breast heaves; no cleansing smell of salt to draw into it. Through the shallows, up to his waist, his armpits, and to rocks where mussel and sea urchin shells are fallen choking pools where fingerlings should find shelter from predators. The decomposed corpses of seals buffet against him. No salt scent but a suffocating charnelhouse stink of decay, putrescence.

This was where he achieved the miracle of loaves and fishes.

This water, the day of his Coming, has no properties of transfiguration.

He brings himself in desperate desolation even to consider the heresy (may he be forgiven), the possibilities of the theory which denies the Creation of human life formed divinely in the image of the Father; a belief that a fish struggled out of this element, the waters, to learn to breathe in another, and transform fins into legs that propelled, to walk on earth. But there is no life in the seas. No fish to come a second time, begin again evolution, become human, on one of the planets of the six-day Creation.

The sea is dead.

AVAILABLE FROM PENGUIN

BY NADINE GORDIMER

Beethoven Was One-Sixteenth Black
ISBN 978-0-14-311423-9

Get a Life
ISBN 978-0-14-303792-7

Loot and Other Stories
ISBN 978-0-14-200468-5

A Sport of Nature
ISBN 978-0-14-008470-2

The Conservationist
ISBN 978-0-14-004716-5

July's People
ISBN 978-0-14-006140-6

Burger's Daughter
ISBN 978-0-14-005593-1

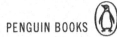

PENGUIN BOOKS